Each volume in The Viking Portable Library either presents a representative selection from the works of a single outstanding writer or offers a comprehensive anthology on a special subject. Averaging 700 pages in length and designed for compactness and readability, these books fill a need not met by other compilations. All are edited by distinguished authorities, who have written introductory essays and included much other helpful material.

"The Viking Portables have done more for good reading and good writers than anything that has come along since I can remember."
—Arthur Mizener

Gabriel Josipovici is a lecturer in the School of European Studies at Sussex University in England. He has published two novels and has written extensively on modern fiction.

The Portable

Saul Bellow

With a critical introduction by
Gabriel Josipovici

*Compiled under the supervision
of the author by* Edith Tarcov

PENGUIN BOOKS

Penguin Books Ltd, Harmondsworth,
Middlesex, England
Penguin Books, 40 West 23rd Street,
New York, New York 10010, U.S.A.
Penguin Books Australia Ltd, Ringwood,
Victoria, Australia
Penguin Books Canada Limited, 2801 John Street,
Markham, Ontario, Canada L3R 1B4
Penguin Books (N.Z.) Ltd, 182–190 Wairau Road,
Auckland 10, New Zealand

First published in the United States of America
by The Viking Press 1974
Published in Penguin Books 1977
Reprinted 1978, 1983

LIBRARY OF CONGRESS CATALOGING IN PUBLICATION DATA
Bellow, Saul.
The portable Saul Bellow.
Bibliography: p.
CONTENTS: Seize the day—From the Adventures of Augie
March: The Einhorns—Henderson the Rain King—From Her-
zog: A visit to Ramona. Herzog writes his last letters. [etc.]
I. Tarcov, Edith.   II. Title.
[PZ3.B41937Po5] [PS3503.E4488]   813'.5'2   77-7994
ISBN 0 14 015.079 X

Printed in the United States of America by
Kingsport Press, Inc., Kingsport, Tennessee
Set in Times Roman

Some of these novels, stories, and
excerpts from novels originally appeared in
somewhat different form in *Atlantic Monthly,
Botteghe Oscure, Esquire, Hudson Review,
The New Yorker, Partisan Review, Perspectives USA, Playboy*.

Contents

Introduction

by Gabriel Josipovici

> *When we think of Saul Bellow's work, we* think of a certain tone of voice, a tone of voice that combines the utmost formality with the utmost desperation. We think of Mr. Willis Mosby, diplomat and memoir writer, struggling for breath in the Mexican tombs and saying simply, "I must get out. Ladies, I find it very hard to breathe." Or of Herzog, one-time academic and historian of ideas, sitting alone with his thoughts in his crumbling country house and saying into the silence, "If I am out of my mind, it's all right with me." But "think" is the wrong word here. Such phrases are not called up consciously into the mind; they surge into our throats, begging to be spoken, to be released by us into the outside world. And to give way to this impulse (submit to this discipline) is to experience a peculiar pleasure.

Bellow has been described as a great realist; a follower of Dreiser and the American urban naturalist tradition; a great fantasist, especially in *Henderson the Rain King*; and as the last of the Yiddish storytellers. But these are ways of shrugging off the demands of that voice, of avoiding its implications by placing it safely in a literary or historical context. Bellow is too important a writer to have this done to him. His style, that tone of voice, emerges as an answer to his most pressing preoccupations, and what we need to do is to see how the two intertwine and reinforce each other, and how they are discovered and made manifest.

vii

Just as, according to Proust, all Dostoevsky's novels could well be called *Crime and Punishment* and all Flaubert's *L'Education sentimentale,* so all Bellow's could be called *Dangling Man.* In each one the protagonist is a dangler, someone who, either through inclination or through the force of circumstances, has drawn back from the rush of the world and hangs in a limbo, trying to make sense of things. But is this possible? We cannot simply step back into a room, a house, even a state of mind, and expect to be freed from the pressures of life. Time crowds us, the past no less than the present asserting its claims; and even space does not seem all that easy to find, especially in a big city. In fact, to step back from the rush of the world is to be made even more aware of the size and violence of what one is trying to avoid. Tommy Wilhelm, in *Seize the Day,* is overwhelmed by the sheer density of the crowd on Broadway, "the great, great crowd, the inexhaustible current of millions of every race and kind pouring out, pressing round, of every age, of every genius," and Asa Leventhal, in *The Victim,* speaks for all Bellow's protagonists when he remarks that "there was not a single part of him on which the whole world did not press with full weight."

From this seething mass characters emerge, relatives, friends, acquaintances, to argue with the hero, plead with him, or otherwise try to cajole him back into "the world." These fall into three types, though there is of course much overlapping. The first and least interesting, because offering the least temptation to the hero, are those Joseph, in the opening lines of the first novel, calls "the hard-boiled"; such characters as Simon, Augie March's brother, who, in his determination to get on, marries a bovine heiress and urges his brother to do likewise and "not to dissolve in bewilderment of choices" but to make himself hard "and learn how to stay with the necessary, undistracted by the trimmings." Then there are the soft sentimentalists, the believers in what Herzog calls "potato love," usually women and members of the family, using emotional blackmail to try to force the hero back into the world. Their power stems from the fact that they appear to stand for values he believes in, yet when they make their claims he can never respond. Is the fault his, then? Is he lacking in simple humanity as well as in the drive for worldly power and wealth?

However, the most typical representative of "the world" in Bellow's novels, its most appealing and dangerous product, is the fast talker, the Machiavel and autodidact, peddler of crisis ethics and solver of the riddles of the universe, the man driven by a violent energy of whose source he is scarcely conscious. His enormous appeal lies partly in this overwhelming energy and partly in the fact that, unlike the other two types, his response to the world is not instinctual but seems to be the result of a real effort to understand. He is thus much closer to the dangling hero, who is himself possessed of unusual energy but who seems unable to find a channel in which to direct it, and thus feels it eating into him and destroying him.

The close relationship between the hero and the fast talker is established as early as *The Victim,* Bellow's second novel. Kirby Allbee, once a casual acquaintance of Leventhal's, comes back years later to pester him with the insistence that Leventhal was responsible for Allbee's losing his job and for his eventual fall into the world of bums and outcasts. Allbee is a sort of Dostoevskian buffoon, ready to abase himself at any moment, bridling up with false pride the next, turning everything into a joke and every joke into an insult. Leventhal is baffled and enraged: " 'Well, you're a crazy, queer bastard,' he said. 'What's the matter with you? . . . One minute you're on the bottom, couldn't be any lower, and the next you're a regular Lord Byron.' " Allbee's strength, like that of Dostoevsky's buffoons, comes from the fact that he has utterly given in to despair and thus has absolutely nothing to lose. This despair leads not to silence but to feverish talk, and he showers Leventhal not only with hard-luck stories but with all sorts of metaphysical and religious theories of life:

> Now let me explain something to you. It's a Christian idea but I don't see why you shouldn't be able to understand it. "Repent!" That's John the Baptist coming out of the desert.

Change yourself, that's what he's saying, and be another man. . . . You see, you have to get yourself so that you can't stand to keep on in the old way. . . . It takes a long time before you're ready to quit dodging. Meanwhile, the pain is horrible. . . . We're mulish; that's why we have to take such a beating. When we can't stand another lick without dying of it, then we change.

Leventhal answers dryly, "We'll see what you are next year," and his skepticism is justified, for Allbee shortly afterward tries (unsuccessfully, of course) to commit suicide. But it would be wrong to imagine from this exchange that Allbee is incapable of hurting Leventhal. The fast talkers who fill Bellow's books press in on the hero, throwing him into confusion and waiting for him to make a false move so they can pounce and crush him. Augie may well say at the end of his adventures, "To tell the truth, I'm good and tired of all these big personalities, destiny molders and heavy-water brains, Machiavellis and wizard evil-doers, big wheels, imposers-upon, absolutists," but the fact is that he has spent most of his life struggling only half successfully to get free of such types. And Tommy Wilhelm, the large, pathetic, middle-aged hero of *Seize the Day,* finds himself reduced to helplessness when the fraudulent Dr. Tamkin fastens on him, draining him of his last few dollars even as he lectures him on how a man must live his life: "The past is no good to us. The future is full of anxiety. Only the present is real—the here-and-now. Seize the day." Tamkin hypnotizes Wilhelm with his patter, his crazy stories about lunatics, crooks, cancer patients, bigamists, Egyptian princesses. The more he talks the wilder his stories get, but just when credulity is strained to breaking point he comes up with a truth that cannot be denied:

"In telling you this," said Tamkin with one of his hypnotic subtleties, "I do have a motive. I want you to see how some people free themselves from morbid guilt feelings and follow their instincts. Innately, the female knows how to

cripple by sickening a man with guilt. It is a very special destruct, and she sends her curse to make a fellow impotent. . . . You're a halfway case. You want to follow your instinct, but you're too worried still. For instance, about your kids—"

Tamkin may only be saying all this to bewilder and confuse Wilhelm while he pockets his money, and the pseudomedical jargon and general air of authority may only be part of a professional patter, but he does touch on a partial truth. Like all the dangling heroes, Wilhelm *is* a halfway case, a partial believer in the value of instinct and with a sense that he has lost his way and needs to find it again. Yet he also believes in quite different instincts from the ones Tamkin is talking about, though these he is able to formulate only in negative terms, as when he interrupts Tamkin angrily: "One thing! Don't bring up my boys. Just lay off." But despite such outbursts both Wilhelm and Leventhal are easy prey for any determined assault on their confidence and values.

There are two reasons for the vulnerability of the dangling hero, and they are deeply interconnected. The first is that, however hard he tries, he is quite incapable of putting up anything positive against the views of life offered to him by those with whom he comes in contact. And these are not only the bums and villains, like Allbee and Tamkin; even someone like Ramona, Herzog's kind and beautiful mistress, is convinced that she understands his real needs better than he does himself:

> *She told Herzog that he was a better man than he knew—a deep man, beautiful . . . , but sad, unable to take what his heart really desired, a man tempted by God, longing for grace, but escaping headlong from his salvation. . . .*

And Dahfu, the noble king of the Wariri, a man for whom Henderson feels nothing but love and admiration, urges him down into the underground den where he keeps his pet lion, and, when Henderson draws back in instinctive terror at the sight and smell of the great beast, admonishes him:

"You ask, what can she do for you? Many things. First she is unavoidable. Test it, and you will find she is unavoidable. And this is what you need, as you are an avoider. Oh, you have accomplished momentous avoidances. But she will change that. She will make consciousness to shine. She will burnish you."

The difficulty Herzog and Henderson have in countering such arguments stems from the fact that for all they know they might well be true. In fact they are true: Herzog *is* sad, he *does* long for grace, Henderson *is* in some ways an avoider. Yet both are uneasy with the formulation of the problem; it is both true and not true. But their unease cannot be turned into an adequate basis for action, since, as Augie March says:

How does anybody form a decision to be against and persist against? When does he choose and when is he chosen instead? This one hears voices; that one is a saint, a chieftain, an orator, a Horatius, a kamikazi; one says Ich kann nicht anders—so help me God! And why is it I who cannot do otherwise?

The hero dangles because he won't fit into the world the way people seem to want him to, but he lacks the drive or egocentricity or madness of the Protestant hero or the Romantic rebel that would lead him to create an alternative world. He can't sit still, but he can't find the confidence in himself to make a move. In fact, as the hero stands back from the world, objects start to gain in clarity, but this, far from helping him to act, inhibits action more and more, for the multiplicity of detail assaulting his senses only bewilders and confuses him. Henderson feels memories piling into him from all sides till all turns into chaos; Herzog, reading the letter in which a friend reports how his wife and her lover are treating his child, finds the handwriting keeps getting in the way of the meaning and he has to struggle to grasp the sense of the words. It is as though he were too close to the world to make sense of it any more.

No wonder that in a situation like this the hero longs for something that will restore order and balance to his life. No wonder Joseph cries at the end of *Dangling Man*: "Hurray for regular hours! And for the supervision of the spirit! Long live regimentation!" But is this longing really very different from that of someone like Allbee? Is it not the desire to come in out of the limbo in which he finds himself, throw off the weight of a meaningless freedom, let the world take care of him for a change? "Marry me! Be my wife! End my troubles!" Herzog finds himself saying to Ramona under his breath, and though he is immediately "staggered by his rashness, his weakness, and by the characteristic nature of such an outburst," the longing from which it springs is not something he can simply eliminate.

The Victim, naturally enough, is the fullest exploration of the interconnection of the fast talker and the dangling hero. When we first meet Leventhal we discover that, though he is not particularly successful in public or private life, he at least thinks of himself as one of those "who got away with it." By this he means that

> *his bad start, his mistakes, the things that might have wrecked him, had somehow combined to establish him. He had almost fallen in with that part of humanity of which he was frequently mindful . . . , the part that did not get away with it—the lost, the outcast, the overcome, the effaced, the ruined.*

But to think in this way is already to have closed the gap between the two groups. Leventhal is like the man who says with relief that he doesn't have a headache, but only because somewhere at the edge of his consciousness there lurks the awareness of an incipient headache. Leventhal is a natural victim; Allbee calls out to something within him and which at the start of the book he is fighting to keep from himself. Thus on the ferryboat, going to visit his sister-in-law whose child is very ill, he sees a barge spraying paint over the hull of a freighter and the light there seems like "the yellow revealed in the slit of the eye of a wild animal, say a lion, something inhuman that didn't care about anything human and yet was implanted in every human being too." This animal quality of the city, corresponding to something animal in man, pulls at Leventhal's heart, unbalancing him; and when to it is added the horror of his little nephew's suffering and possible death, all those forces with which we normally protect ourselves are brushed aside and Leventhal is made to face memories he would rather do without, such as his mother dying insane, which drags with it the recurring fear that he too might one day go mad. Clearly if Allbee had not appeared Leventhal would have had to invent him, for Allbee seems to provide a way of forcing things to a crisis and releasing Leventhal from his tormenting thoughts. "He kept telling himself, 'The showdown is coming,'" and what he means by the term is "a crisis which would bring an end of his resistance to something he had no right to resist."

Yet in spite of everything he does resist. He doesn't let Allbee drag him down; he refuses to let the little boy's death present him with an excuse for some desperate action. He retains his sanity and his sense of responsibility, though not by growing hard-boiled and ceasing to care. And in this he is like Augie and Wilhelm and Henderson and Herzog. They all have reason, and more, to give up, break down, despair, or grow hard, callous, indifferent to the claims of others. Yet they do neither, but weather the blows and trust their initial instincts. In so doing they come to understand both their own motives and the nature of the forces that oppose them. The growth of this awareness is of course gradual, and varies in depth from novel to novel, but the picture that emerges for them is consistent in its broad outlines, from *Dangling Man* to *Mr. Sammler's Planet*. Since much of all the novels is taken up with a delineation of this picture, it is important to step back for a moment and consider its main features.

The first thing to grasp is that things are not what they seem. This is not to say that one thing hides another, or that men act hypocritically, as classical analyses of society and behavior would have us believe. Rather, Bellow's heroes come to see, with Marx and Nietzsche and Freud, that the facts and events of the history of man and the individual histories of men are in effect a mute attempt by human beings to express something which they do not quite know themselves. Mr. Sammler, miraculous survivor of the Nazi holocaust and one-time friend of H. G. Wells, recognizes this fact even in something as ordinary and trivial as his niece's obsession with potted plants in her flat:

> This botanical ugliness, the product of so much fork-digging, watering, so much breast and arm, heart and hope, told you something, didn't it? First of all, it told you that the individual facts were filled with messages and meanings, but you couldn't be sure what the messages meant. She wanted a bower in her living room, a screen of glossy leaves. . . . Humankind, crazy for symbols, trying to utter what it doesn't know itself.

In a short story dating from 1949, "A Sermon by Doctor Pep," we find Dr. Pep ready to provide an explanation of what it is that drives humanity in this fashion. Dr. Pep is not, of course, to be trusted too readily, for he is one of Bellow's fast-speaking cranks, but his contrast of man and animal makes a lot of sense:

> I marvel at the Guiana spider that takes the ant's disguise to perfection. But let me suggest to you, listeners, that he comes into the world instructed in mimicry and belongs to the cast of the giant creation that goes through a performance of days and ages without a falter and without a rehearsal. Whereas we, fallible and in need of instruction . . . being creatures and more . . . embracing everything with infinite desire . . .

Man is an animal *and* more, yet what that more consists of seems to be a deep longing to become creature and only creature again. All his energy, all his aggression, all his inventiveness seems to be taken up with removing that "and more" from the face of the earth:

> *The Walrus was sorry for the poor oysters. The Carpenter ate without caring. But both of them wept like anything to see such quantities of sand. Why did they? Because civilization is never complete enough? In dead earnest, it is profound. The sand remains in spite of the maids and mops. It creeps back . . . And were the fierce moppers of Auschwitz inspired by their square and polished home towns and the pleasant embroidery of the regulated Rhine?*

Dr. Pep's queer mode of expression makes vivid a truth we find it hard to acknowledge because it cannot be derived from empirical observation: human beings have a desperate need to mop up, enclose, control, bring order out of chaos. And this tendency has been exacerbated by the events of the last five hundred years, first the Renaissance and Reformation and then the French Revolution, which removed the limits within which men had previously lived and gave each man a freedom which he found difficult to bear. "We were important enough then for our souls to be fought over," Joseph noted in *Dangling Man.* "Now each of us is responsible for his own salvation, which is his greatness." So we all dream of greatness, all long to be great lovers, great warriors, even, like Raskolnikov, great criminals. We will do anything to be *something, someone,* and "the fear of lagging pursues and maddens us. The fear lies in us like a cloud. It makes an inner climate of darkness."

But what does this fear come from? And why do we find, since the time of the Romantics, this craze for originality allied to a desire to experience as much as possible and as deeply as possible? Why have we come to regard sheer experience as an unquestioned good? Henderson has an answer to these questions in a contrast he draws between man and child:

> *The world may be strange to a child, but he does not fear it the way a man fears. He marvels at it. But the grown man*

mainly dreads it. And why? Because of death. So he arranges to have himself abducted like a child. So what happens will not be his fault. And who is this kidnapper— this gypsy? It is the strangeness of life—a thing that makes death more remote, as in childhood.

In the end it all boils down to this: do we believe that the world owes us a living, or that it is we who are loaned a life? Behind all the wildness and striving, all the restlessness and anguish, this is the message a dumb mankind is striving to utter: that individuals do not want to die and relinquish their individuality. So they will do anything to silence the little voice of consciousness, the voice that tells them they are separate and distinct from other people and from the world and that one day they will cease to exist while the world just goes on and on. Schlossberg, the wise old Jew in *The Victim*, makes the point with extraordinary clarity:

> *Here I'm sitting here, and my mind can go around the world. Is there any limit to what I can think? But in another minute I can be dead, on this spot. There's a limit to me. But I have to be myself in full. Which is somebody who dies, isn't it? That's what I was from the beginning. I'm not three people, four people. I was born once and I will die once. You want to be two people? More than human? Maybe it's because you don't know how to be one.*

So death and the fact of death in life and the interconnection of death and responsibility are what the dangling hero comes to understand in each of the novels. But understanding alone is never enough. What is still required is for the hero to feel the meaning of these words, to grasp that death will come to him too, that not even he (as each of us persists in believing) will be exempt at the final count. Such an awareness can never come from himself alone; there must be an intrusion from the outside world into the world of imagination and desire we each of us construct for ourselves. This can take many forms. In *Herzog* it comes in the form of a minor car accident in which, taking his little daughter out for a drive, Herzog finds himself involved. The incident is both farcical and banal. No one is seriously hurt, but Herzog is shaken by it, and especially by its aftermath, a confrontation at the police station with his furious ex-wife. How could he act like this, he wonders, and show himself in this light to his daughter? The incident seems to bring him down to earth from "his strange spiraling flight of the last few days"; he can no longer run away from himself; he is at last up against the wall. For all his talk about the ordinariness of life being the important thing and how one must be what one is and ask no questions, Herzog, like the other dangling heroes, has really been engaged in whirlwind activity simply in order to escape from himself and from the way things are. Exactly like Allbee in *The Victim,* or like Ramona's ex-lover George Hoberly in this novel, who both try to awaken sympathy by acts of deliberate self-destruction, Herzog has been secretly trying to force from life an answer to the question: Who am I? Who am I *really*? The accident and its aftermath serve to free him from this compulsion. He literally bangs into reality. Not hard, but hard enough to remind him of what might have happened, and to make him see how difficult it is to eradicate the notions of crisis and salvation from our minds. We long all the time, however unconsciously, for some decisive event that will change things forever and show us how from then on we are to lead our lives.

Henderson too has to learn the hard way. When a wood chip flew up and hit him in the face as he was chopping logs, he felt for a moment that here was reality, but the moment passes and things slip away from him again, until, in despair at the chaos and lack of clarity in things, he decides to take the trip to Africa. There the lessons of the woman of Bittahness and of the noble King Dahfu touch on many truths about himself and the world, and Henderson feels at last that he is coming to an understanding of the central facts. But then instead of the Truth, an answer to life and its problems, something that will still the insistent voice within him that keeps pressing him forward with its *I want, I want, I want,* what does he find? Dahfu, having to catch a grown male lion single-handed (the laws of kingship require it), makes a false move and all Henderson's fears are borne out: in a second Dahfu is mauled by the beast and dies almost at once. So, instead of Truth, Henderson finds death, and where he expected an enrichment of life he is faced with loss. He raises his voice in a great cry of lament:

> *"Oh, the poor guy is dead. Oh, ho, ho, ho, ho! It kills me. It could be time we were blown off the earth. If only we didn't have hearts we wouldn't know how sad it was. But we carry around these hearts, these spotty damn mangoes in our breasts, which give us away. . . . There'll be nobody to talk to any more. I've gotten to that age where I need human voices and intelligence. That's all that's left. Kindness and love."*

Yet perhaps Truth and death, enrichment and loss, are more intimately bound up than we think. For it is indeed now that Henderson learns the lesson he had hoped Africa would teach him. Now he feels that "the sleep is burst and I've come to myself." You can't win against death, loss, separation. This is the reality he has been seeking all his life but never found with his wives, the lioness, his pigs. It resides neither in the world nor in ourselves, but is the paradox that the longing for a Truth, an answer, is human and natural, but that it will never be appeased, but only denied, again and again and again. So Henderson, on the plane back to civilization, suddenly sees the world and himself as they are and not as we imagine them or would like them to be:

> *Other passengers were reading. . . . But I, Henderson, with my glowering face, with corduroy and Bersagliere feathers . . . I couldn't get enough of the water, and of these upside-down sierras of the clouds. Like courts of eternal heaven. (Only they aren't eternal, that's the whole thing; they are seen once and never seen again, being figures and*

not abiding realities; Dahfu will never be seen again, and
presently I will never be seen again; but everyone is given
the components to see: the water, the sun, the air, the
earth.)

Soon this insight will no doubt slip away from him, but what
he has experienced, understood, is that we are fragments and
can only ever be fragments. In the other novels the hero is
often made aware of this by witnessing sudden death or
violence in the streets, in courtrooms, or in hospitals. Both
Seize the Day and *Mr. Sammler's Planet* move to a climax of
understanding as the hero confronts the reality of death. Even
Sammler, left for dead among the stinking corpses and
miraculously surviving the war to end his days in New York,
even he has to be re-awakened to the facts again, and again:

They went down in the elevator, the gray woman and Mr.
Sammler, and through lower passages paved in speckled
material, through tunnels, up and down ramps, past labora-
tories and supply rooms. Well, this famous truth for which
he was so keen, he had it now, or it had him.

He looks down at the corpse of his nephew, the man who had
made it possible for him to come to America, and as he utters
the words of lament that come unbidden to his lips, he holds
the truth for a moment:

Remember, God, the soul of Elya Gruner. . . . At his best
this man was much kinder than at my best I have ever been
or could ever be. He was aware that he must meet, and he
did meet . . .

The words, muttered under his breath, lose direction and
become in the end only a rhythmic repetition, an assertion of
what is: "For that is the truth of it—that we know, God, that
we know, that we know, we know, we know."

There are in Bellow's novels two views of man, or rather,
two different conclusions which can be drawn from the same
set of facts. The facts are that man is at odds with nature,

alien, inauthentic, forever striving to reach peace, wholeness, oneness with the rest of nature, but never getting there. One response to this is to insist that if man fails, then it is his fault, and that what he needs is to be flogged like a mule till he succeeds. Unfortunately the exaltation which usually accompanies such an attitude soon turns to despair when it becomes clear that man will not be saved once and for all; the flogging then starts to take the form of masochistic self-laceration. For those who hold such views, our imagination has allowed us hints of paradise, and what is needed is to turn imagination into reality. This they believe to be possible, given the right degree of fear and dedication on our part. Dahfu, the lovable king of the Wariri (he is lovable because he holds his ideas like a child, wanting to confer them on other people not in order to do them down or get something out of them but only to see them happy), maintains such a view in its extreme form:

> *What he was engrossed by was a belief in the transformation of human material . . . the flesh influencing the mind, the mind influencing the flesh, back again to the mind, back once more to the flesh. The process as he saw it was utterly dynamic.*

Henderson is impressed, but skeptical: "Thinking of mind and flesh as I knew them, I said: 'Are you really and truly sure it's like that, Your Highness?' " But Dahfu is more than sure:

> *"Although I do not wish to reduce the stature of our discussion," he said, "yet for the sake of example the pimple on a lady's nose may be her own idea, accomplished by a conversion at the solemn command of her psyche; even more fundamentally the nose itself, though part hereditary, is part also her own idea."*

There is, however, a second way of responding to the fact of man's alienated state. This is to accept it as an unalterable part of the human condition: this is how we are, divided, self-conscious, full of impossible longings, never free of the burden of daily care and responsibility, and this is how we will always be. It is hard to accept this as something that can never be altered, and, as we have seen, the dangling hero frequently longs to be finished with things once and for all. But because he never gives in to this longing he comes to see the imagination not as something to be transcended, willed into becoming reality, but as man's most valuable possession. For imagination, by allowing us to sense what others are feeling, is the springboard of sympathy and love. When Dahfu tries to convince Henderson that what he needs is to become like the lion, in effect to *become a lion*, Henderson is overwhelmed by the grandeur of the idea, but his common sense forces him to reply:

> *"If she doesn't try to be human, why should I try to act the lion? I'll never make it. If I have to copy someone, why can't it be you?"*

Henderson's fate is to be constantly associated with animals— a fairground bear, pigs, frogs, cattle, lions—and one of the themes of the novel, which it develops from a section of *Augie March,* is the dialectic of our imagination in our relation to animals. We recall the hint Leventhal had of the teeming city calling out to something animal in his nature, and his vision on the ferry of something like the yellow slit of a lion's eye. The lesson Leventhal, like the other dangling heroes, learns, is just this, that we must be sure not to misunderstand our natures. We must not crush our animal instincts, nor grant them covert satisfaction in the pursuit of wealth or power or women; nor, finally, must we commit the folly of trying to extirpate that part of ourselves which is *not* animal in any misguided attempt to turn ourselves entirely *into* animals. For that is not an enrichment of the instincts and the imagination but the guarantee of their final destruction.

Gooley MacDowell, in his "Address to the Hasbeens Club of Chicago" (another early Bellow story), uncovers this dialectic very well:

> *How is any man going to account for having closed up in his head, above his teeth and palate and below his hair,*

what there is? This folding! This isthmus! This finding!
That baroque pearl of an inmost thing! . . . And isn't it
maybe the curiosity over these internal discoveries that
leads us to have captive animals—eagles in the Park,
canaries at home? We keep pets within and without.
Imprisoned power. The heart in its cage of bone.

Allbee and Dahfu, though different in practically every
respect, come together on this point, that for them a man must
not hold back but must give in to the animal within, must turn
his dreams into reality. Only then will he be renewed, saved,
radiant. And this is the message of Thea Fenchel, the crazy
rich girl who falls in love with Augie March and takes him
with her to Mexico to hunt iguanas with an eagle. Augie
secretly rejoices when the eagle fails to live up to its fierce
looks, and though for Henderson the outcome of his experience with wild animals is not comic but tragic, he too is
confirmed in his feeling that there is something inherently
wrong in men trying to be animals. Like Herzog, Henderson
learns from his experiences that the power of the imagination
is linked to the power of sympathy and love, and that love
means the acceptance of responsibility for ourselves and for
those who are dependent on us, especially those who are
helpless like children and animals. And the last we see of him,
on his way back to America and his wife, he has a lion cub in
a basket and he holds a little lost Persian boy by the hand. "It
is our humanity that we are responsible for, our dignity, our
freedom," Joseph had written in the diary which forms the
substance of *Dangling Man,* and that is the truth which all the
novels fill out and give meaning to, so that we too, by the end,
are aware of and can feel what Joseph meant.

"It has only been in the last two centuries," Mr. Sammler
notes, "that the majority of people in civilized countries have
claimed the privilege of being individuals. Formerly they were
slave, peasant, laborer, even artisan, but not person." However, the revolution which occurred at the end of the

xxiv *Introduction*

eighteenth century, and which was a triumph for justice and reason in so many ways, brought huge problems in its wake: "Hearts that get no real wage, souls that find no nourishment . . . Desire unlimited. Possibility unlimited . . ." We have seen the answer to these problems arrived at by the dangling heroes, but there is one vital aspect of the situation we have not touched on, and that is how the writer himself is affected by this situation. For the writer too, liberated from a function as scribe or court poet, seems to have a burdensome freedom thrust upon him. He is free, it is true, to give rein to his imagination and originality, but what is the nature of this freedom? "Around our heads we have a dome of thought as thick as atmosphere to breathe," says Gooley MacDowell in his address to the Hasbeens Club of Chicago. "And what's it about? One thought leads to another as breath leads to breath. I find it barren just to breathe or only to have thoughts." Words swirl about, and because there are so many of them, and they can be had for the asking, they soon cease to have any meaning. The writer withdraws into his room, freeing himself from the immediate pressures of the world in order to give himself the time and the space to write. But once in his room, what is there except boredom and the merging of days into one meaningless continuity? Bellow's first novel may be about a young man waiting to be drafted, but it is also about any writer at any time, including the writer of *that* book at *that* time.

In response to the historical situation just outlined, writers have made determined efforts to dispense with "mere literature," to wring the neck of "mere rhetoric" and close with the real. And readers and critics have welcomed this, judging novels most often by how close to reality they get, criticizing them for being conventional and derivative and praising them for giving us "life itself" in all its rawness. Part of Hemingway's popularity was no doubt due to the fact that by dispensing with the formalities of a literary prose he gave the impression of actually getting reality down on the page. But this can, of course, never be done, and it is easy to see that a

writer like Hemingway has many of the characteristics of
Bellow's fast talkers and hardheaded salesmen of a home-
brewed reality. In fact in one of his rare reviews Bellow talks
of Hemingway in these very terms:

> *Hemingway has an intense desire to impose his version of
> the thing upon us, to create an image of manhood, to define
> the manner of baptism and communion. . . . When he
> dreams of a victory it is a total victory; one great battle, one
> great issue. Everyone wants to be the right man, and this is
> by no means a trivial desire. But Hemingway now appears
> to feel that he is winning and his own personality, always an
> important dramatic element in his writing, is, in* The Old
> Man and the Sea, *a kind of moral background. He tends to
> speak for Nature itself. Should Nature and Hemingway
> become identical one or the other will have won too total a
> victory.*

The writer in the modern age may insist: "Here I stand, I
cannot do otherwise," but for Bellow the nagging question
remains: "Why is it *I* who cannot do otherwise?" Like Augie
March, Bellow cannot find it in himself to assert the truth of
his vision and then impose it on other people. On the other
hand, the urge to write persists and, like Augie, the writer
finds himself faced "with this double poser"—"that if you
make a move you may lose, but if you sit still you will decay."

The problem, as always, is to channel one's energies
correctly, and, when one acts, to act responsibly. But what
does it *mean* for a writer to act responsibly? In *Dangling Man*
Joseph has an affair with another woman, but he soon realizes
that what he is doing is out of character and that "at the root
of it all was my unwillingness to miss anything. A compact
with one woman puts beyond reach what others might give us
to enjoy." He recognizes that "a man must accept limits and
cannot give in to the wild desire to be everything and
everyone to everything and everyone." But what of the writer?
He cannot make a comparable choice because for him there is
nothing to renounce. He really is an embodiment of Dahfu's

ideal in that whatever he imagines can instantly become reality—in a book. And the problem with this is that there is no pressure, nothing for the writer to press against, to define himself against, nothing except his whim to give a shape to his book. What Joseph does and how he acts depends entirely on Bellow's private decision; he has to make decisions, to get the book written, but his very freedom from constraint goes against the implications of the book. The sense of failure Joseph feels at the end must be very close to that felt by the author.

As though recognizing all this, Bellow, in his next novel, set out to make the limits as tight as possible, taking as his theme the romantic idea of the double. In Romantic literature, as in *The Victim*, the double who haunts the hero is his other, darker self, and when the two come together there are crisis and the destruction of the hero. Thus, since the story is synonymous with the consciousness of the hero, the story is itself haunted by the specter of its own annihilation. Bellow, however, deliberately keeps the context absolutely realistic; he is not going to indulge in Romantic mythology, since his covert theme is in effect a form of demythologizing. But as a result he, as the maker of the book, remains well outside it. Once again he is both too constrained and too free: too constrained by plot and chronology, but too free from any meaningful pressure in his construction of the book. Here, as in *Dangling Man*, we sense that great energy is not finding an outlet. As a result the frequent pain in the chest which afflicts all Bellow's heroes at one time or another is also what the reader is left with. There is a sense of tightness, of constriction, which comes of too much being left unsaid.

In the late forties, however, Bellow started experimenting with ways of loosening up without automatically going soft. The remarkable monologues of Dr. Pep and Gooley Mac-Dowell are the result. And in the novel he was then working on, *The Adventures of Augie March*, he came to the decision that the answer lay in letting the hero speak for himself and simply following his life from childhood to middle age. In this way he clearly hoped to make a break with moribund European forms of the novel and get to something more genuine, closer to the heart, perhaps more truly American. And this is certainly the impression the novel itself seems to want to give from its very opening:

> *I am an American, Chicago-born—Chicago, that somber city—and go at things as I have taught myself, free-style, and will make the record in my own way.*

But the freedom which the book flaunts is illusory. For Augie, as we have seen, lacks the Lutheran confidence in his own views which these lines imply. He is passive for all of the book's six hundred pages, giving in to this pressure or that for a while and only pulling out when it looks as though he would finally have to commit himself. His is the stubbornness of silent negation, not of confident self-assertion, so that lines like the above, or other remarks, such as "I have put in my time in the capitals of the world" or "I am a sort of Columbus of those near-at-hand," sound forced and unreal.

Yet something happens in the course of this book which could not have happened had Bellow not taken the plunge in the way he has. The novel occupies a place in Bellow's development curiously analogous to the one *Molloy* occupies in Beckett's. I say curiously because where Beckett turned to French with *Molloy* in order to escape from the too great freedom of his first two novels, Bellow plunged into *The Adventures of Augie March* to get away from the constrictions of plot and diction imposed on him by *his* first two novels. Both works, however, mark turning points in their authors' careers, and both exhibit that courage, that readiness to follow where instinct seems to lead, which is perhaps what distinguishes the major from the minor writer.

It is in *Augie March* that Bellow at last discovers his style, and he discovers it by accident, on the way, and where he probably least expected it. For the book comes to life when it focuses not on the banal hero but on those who set out to use him, on the grotesque Machiavels like Einhorn or Basteshaw

or Mintouchian. And the reason for this is that our focus here
is no longer single but double: we are made to see both the
absurdity of these men with their schemes for running the
world, *and* how human their wild energy is. Where Augie
remains shadowy because he is himself the source of light,
Einhorn and the other characters, because they are both
allowed to speak for themselves *and* looked at by Augie,
suddenly come alive:

> *I see before me next a fellow named Mintouchian, who is an
> Armenian, of course. We are sitting together in a Turkish
> bath having a conversation, except that Mintouchian is
> doing most of the talking, explaining various facts of
> existence to me. . . .*

Note the proximity of the two bodies, so that the physical
weight of Mintouchian presses in on the narrator, and the way
in which the narrative (this is the start of a chapter) seems
suddenly to be free of its dependence on time. Seeing
Mintouchian in his mind's eye, Augie can move freely from
this specific scene to others and back as the whim takes him.
But now the play of Augie's mind itself becomes an element of
the book, not something to be denied or disguised as was the
play of the author's mind in the earlier novels.

If one has to locate the place where the style seems
suddenly to find itself, one ought perhaps to turn to a scene in
an earlier part of the book:

> *Einhorn kept me with him that evening; he didn't want to
> be alone. While I sat by he wrote his father's obituary in the
> form of an editorial for the neighborhood paper. "The
> return of the hearse from the newly covered grave leaves a
> man to pass through the last changes of nature who found
> Chicago a swamp and left it a great city. He came after the
> Great Fire, said to be caused by Mrs. O'Leary's cow, in
> flight from the conscription of the Hapsburg tyrant, and in
> his life as a builder proved that great palaces do not have to
> be founded on the bones of slaves. . . . The lesson of an*

American life like my father's, in contrast to that of the murderer of the Strelitzes and of his own son, is that achievements are compatible with decency. My father was not familiar with the observation of Plato that philosophy is the study of death, but he died nevertheless like a philosopher, saying to the ancient man who watched by his bedside in the last moments . . ." This was the vein of it, and he composed it energetically in half an hour, printing on sheets of paper at his desk, the tip of his tongue forward, scrunched up in his bathrobe and wearing his stocking cap.*

Why is this both very funny and very moving? Old Einhorn, like Augie, represents the best of the American tradition of honesty, self-reliance, and fortitude. But he is not telling us this about himself. It is not even being *said* of him by someone else. In the forefront is the bereaved son, writing down the words quickly and elegantly as he leans over the desk, the tip of his tongue between his lips. That is one barrier between us and the dead man. But Einhorn's absurd style is a second barrier. The more he writes the wider grows the gap between the words going down on paper and the actuality of the dead man. We laugh, but neither at the pretentiousness of Einhorn nor at the pretensions of his father. We laugh at the recognition of the fact that there will always exist a gap between a man and anything that can be said of him, and we laugh too at the way human beings suffer and cope with their suffering and know so little about themselves and cling even at moments like this to their foolish pride in what they feel they can do well, and are nevertheless capable of deep love.

What Bellow has done here, as well as in Dr. Pep's sermon and Gooley MacDowell's address, is to force the *act* of expression into greater and greater prominence. He does this by placing highly idiosyncratic speakers in situations of great formality: the writing of an obituary, the delivering of an address, a sermon. *Seize the Day* is particularly interesting here. For how are we to take Wilhelm? He seems so sentimental, despairing, histrionic. He begs his wife:

"Margaret, go easy on me. You ought to. I'm at the end of my rope and feel that I'm suffocating. You don't want to be responsible for a person's destruction. You've got to let up. I feel I'm about to burst."

Are these not the sort of antics a man like Allbee would go in for? A conversation Wilhelm has with his father about Margaret would seem to confirm this:

"Strange, Father? I'll show you what she's like." Wilhelm took hold of his broad throat with brown-stained fingers and bitten nails and began to choke himself.
"What are you doing?" cried the old man.
"I'm showing you what she does to me."
"Stop that—stop it!" the old man said and tapped the table commandingly. . . . "Stop this bunk. Don't expect me to believe in all kinds of voodoo."

Dr. Adler seems to be responding with the same sort of horror as Leventhal felt before the antics of Allbee. But there is a vital difference between Wilhelm and Allbee. The latter acted as he did partly out of sheer despair and partly out of the desire to force the world to give him what he felt it owed him. Wilhelm, on the other hand, seems to be acting out some obscure piece of ritualization, as if by showing on his own body what is happening to his spirit he would reveal something important about what it is to be a man:

The spirit, the peculiar burden of his existence lay upon him like an accretion, a load, a hump. In any moment of quiet, when sheer fatigue prevented him from struggling, he was apt to feel this mysterious weight, this growth or collection of nameless things which it was the business of his life to carry about.

What does a man do with this burden, the weight of his own being? As the book moves to its climax, Wilhelm is swept into the funeral service of someone he doesn't know. Looking down at this dead stranger, Wilhelm feels the tears welling up, and he makes no effort to stop them:

Soon he was past words, past reason, coherence. He could
not stop. The source of all tears had suddenly sprung open
within him, black, deep, and hot, and they were pouring out
and convulsed his body, bending his stubborn head. . . .
The great knot of ill and grief in his throat swelled upward
and he gave in utterly and held his face and wept. He cried
with all his heart.

A man looks at him and utters the words that sum up the
whole book: "Oh my, oh my! To be mourned like that." For
now at last Wilhelm has found release for his great energy.
But what he has *done* is not any action designed to further
himself in the world; it is rather a gesture, a ritualized release
which is the act of mourning. He cries not for the dead man or
for himself, but for man, that creature of infinite potential who
turns his urges against himself and others and can find no way
of making good use of the rich desire that is in his heart. The
day is finally seized by Wilhelm because he has a sudden
overpowering sense that the day can never be seized, only its
passing *mourned*. In that public ritual action we touch what it
is that we are and how we are related to the world.

There is of course something primitive in such an open
exhibition of suffering that does not go down well in our
hard-boiled yet sentimental Western society. As Mr. Sammler
tells the Indian scientist, Dr. Lal, Jews are Asians too; despite
their Westernization they retain something of the primitive-
ness of the Eastern Mediterranean. But it would be wrong to
identify Bellow's new-found style with his cultural or ethnic
origins; before being a Jew or an American he is a man and a
writer. His style, as we have seen, emerged as the answer to
the problems of freedom and the nature of man with which
the novels had always been concerned. In the later novels and
stories the fast talker has moved into the center of the picture
and is now the hero. His histrionics, his peculiar way of
putting things, as though he always thought at an angle to the
English language, are the result of his own attempts to find a
way out of the crisis in which he finds himself without losing

hold of his humanity. Herzog's letters are a symptom of his illness, but it is they which help him through it. Like Hamlet, he deliberately exaggerates his condition, "as if by staggering he could recover his balance . . . or by admitting a bit of madness could recover his senses." Instead of trying to sort out the complications, Bellow lets his characters *express* them. He no longer needs the overt formality of an address or a sermon to give us the sense of the man speaking the words: the whole novel becomes a theater in which the hero struts and shouts, hoping to surprise himself into an understanding of the truth. Here is Henderson as we first see him:

> *The facts begin to crowd me and soon I get a pressure in the chest. A disorderly rush begins—my parents, my wives, my girls, my children, my farm, my animals, my habits, my money, my music lessons, my drunkenness, my prejudices, my brutality, my teeth, my face, my soul! I have to cry, "No, no, get back, curse you, let me alone!" But how can they let me alone? They belong to me. They are mine. And they pile into me from all sides. It turns into chaos.*

Here is the familiar pressure in the chest, but this time, for the reader, there is release. We laugh at Henderson: the amazing, ridiculous man! But we also sympathize. And a curious thing starts to happen: the words acquire weight, a tangible quality, and it is the weight of the words that removes the weight on the chest. Because Henderson is speaking these words and not writing them in a diary or having his thought paraphrased, and because he speaks them as they come, following out strands in his own fashion and coming back to the main business when he feels like it, *we too,* the readers, have to speak the words. Henderson goes to Africa to silence the voice within him, but what he learns is that we are saddled with speech as with our bodies, and that it is only through speech that understanding—a certain, limited understanding—eventually comes. And we too, as we turn the words over in our mouths, aware all the time of their histrionic absurdity, but aware too that what matters is that Henderson should not fall silent, we too live that experience.

What happens to us as we read this novel? The book itself provides the answer. The very title suggests a Romantic triumph of the imagination, for if human beings can bring about the rain, then Dahfu is right and there is no gap at all between our desires and the laws of the world. But the title is both true and untrue. In one sense Henderson is tricked into becoming rain king and the onset of rain has clearly nothing to do with his own efforts. At the same time there is clearly some link between the religious ceremony that precedes it and the opening of the skies. In the same way the title tells us that as the title of a book it is accurate (in this book Henderson does indeed become rain king), but that as a description of what can happen in the world it is a delusion to believe it can be accurate.

The crucial moment comes when Henderson has to lift the huge statue of the goddess of rain. She glitters before him, oiled and smooth. None of the members of the tribe has been able to lift her. He steps up close, puts his arms around her, presses his belly against her, and sinks his knees. To him she is alive, an opponent rather than a statue, an intimate and a friend rather than an enemy:

> *. . . with the close pleasure you experience in a dream or one of those warm beneficial floating idle days when every desire is satisfied, I laid my cheek against her wooden bosom. I cranked down my knees and said to her, "Up you go, dearest. No use trying to make yourself heavier; if you weighed twice as much I'd lift you anyway." The wood gave to my pressure and benevolent Mummah with her fixed smile yielded to me; I lifted her from the ground and carried her twenty feet to her new place among the other gods.*

There is something in this of every schoolboy adventure story. But there is something of the schoolboy adventure story in every novel, though normally it is heavily disguised. Bellow, however, is luminously honest here. He does not pretend that it requires a superhuman effort to lift the idol; it all comes as easily as a dream, as easily as imagining it, as easily as writing and reading. Yet we sense that a very great effort has also been made. It is the effort required to speak the truth, to convey the pleasurable ease of the imagination while refusing the delusion that the imagination and the world are one. And, strangely, it is we, the readers, who have made this effort.

Chronology

1915 Born on June 10 in Lachine, a suburb of Montreal, Canada, of parents who had immigrated from St. Petersburg, Russia, in 1913.

1924 The Bellow family moves to Chicago, which becomes their permanent home.

1933 Graduates from Tuley High School (on Chicago's Northwest Side). Enrolls at the University of Chicago.

1935 Transfers to Northwestern University.

1937 Graduates from Northwestern with honors in sociology and anthropology.
Does graduate work in anthropology at the University of Wisconsin in Madison. Leaves before the end of the year, realizing he wants to become a writer.

1938 Returns to Chicago. Works on the WPA Writers' Project.

1939 Supports himself for a number of years with teaching, odd jobs, work on the Index (*Syntopicon*) of the *Great Books* series (published by the Encyclopaedia Britannica, in collaboration with the University of Chicago) —and leads a bohemian life.

1941 "Two Morning Monologues," first published story.

1942 "The Mexican General."

1943 At work on *Dangling Man*.
"Notes of a Dangling Man," an early version of sections of the novel (see Bibliography).

1944 *Dangling Man*, first novel, is published.

1946–1948   Teaches at the University of Minnesota in Minneapolis.

1947   *The Victim.*

1948   Awarded a Guggenheim fellowship.

1948–1950   Writes and lives in Paris and travels in Europe. Begins work on *The Adventures of Augie March,* and over the next few years early versions of a number of sections of the novel appear in various magazines (see Bibliography).

1949   "Sermon of Doctor Pep."

1950   Returns home to the United States and, for most of the next decade, lives in New York City and Dutchess County, New York. Teaches evening courses at New York University, Washington Square (later on the faculty of other colleges and universities). Reviews books, writes articles. Continues work on his novels, writes stories.

1951   "Looking for Mr. Green"; "By the Rock Wall"; "Address by Gooley MacDowell to the Hasbeens Club of Chicago."

1952   Creative Writing Fellow, Princeton University.

1953   *The Adventures of Augie March.* Awarded the National Book Award for Fiction.
Translates, from the Yiddish, Isaac Bashevis Singer's story "Gimpel the Fool."

1955   "A Father-to-be."

1956   "The Gonzaga Manuscripts"; *Seize the Day* (first published in magazine, then in book form; see Bibliography).

1958   "Leaving the Yellow House."

1958–1960   Receives two-year Ford Foundation grant.
At work on *Henderson the Rain King*; early versions of two sections of the novel appear in magazines (see Bibliography).

1959   *Henderson the Rain King.*

1960–1962   Co-edits, with Keith Botsford and Aaron Asher, the periodical *The Noble Savage.*

1961–1964 Works, for the next three years, on *Herzog*. A number of sections of the novel, in early versions, appear in various magazines (see Bibliography).

1962 "Scenes from Humanitis," an early version of the play *The Last Analysis*.

1963 Edits *Great Jewish Short Stories* and writes introduction to the collection.
Returns to Chicago in the fall.

1963– present (1974) Professor, Committee on Social Thought, at the University of Chicago.

1964 *Herzog*. Bellow receives, for the second time, the National Book Award for Fiction.
The Last Analysis is produced in October, for a short run, on Broadway, directed by Joseph Anthony (producer, Stevens Productions), at the David Belasco Theatre.
Awarded the International Literary Prize (for *Herzog*).

1965 Writes three one-act plays:
"Out from Under"; "Orange Soufflé"; "A Wen."
"Orange Soufflé" and "A Wen" are staged in April off-off Broadway by Nancy Walker, for a private showing at the Loft.

1966 The three one-act plays are staged in May in London by the Traverse Company, directed by Charles Marowitz, at the Jeanette Cochrane Theatre, moving in June to the Fortune Theatre. Arthur Storch directs the plays in July at the Festival of Two Worlds in Spoleto, Italy, and presents them in October, under the title *Under the Weather*, for a short run (producer Theodore R. Brauer), at the Cort Theatre on Broadway.

1967 "The Old System."
In June Bellow covers the Six-Day War in Israel for *Newsday*, then published by Bill Moyers.

1968 "Mosby's Memoirs" (story); *Mosby's Memoirs and other Stories*.
Receives the Jewish Heritage Award from B'nai B'rith.

Receives the Croix de Chevalier des Arts et Lettres from the French government.

Begins work on *Mr. Sammler's Planet*.

1969   Early version of *Mr. Sammler's Planet* appears, in two parts, in magazine form (see Bibliography).

1970   *Mr. Sammler's Planet*. Awarded, for the third time, the National Book Award for Fiction. Untitled work in progress.

1970–present (1974)   At work on two (so far untitled) novels in progress.

1974   "Humboldt's Gift," excerpt from a (so far untitled) novel in progress, appears in magazine form (see Bibliography).

"Zetland: By a Character Witness," excerpt from another (so far untitled) novel in progress, appears in a collection (see Bibliography).

Bibliography

Books: Novels, Plays, Collected Stories

The Adventures of Augie March (novel). New York: Viking, 1953.
Dangling Man (novel). New York: Vanguard, 1944.
Henderson the Rain King (novel). New York: Viking, 1959.
Herzog (novel). New York: Viking, 1964.
The Last Analysis (play). New York: Viking, 1965.
Mosby's Memoirs and Other Stories (collection of six stories). New York: Viking, 1968.
Mr. Sammler's Planet (novel). New York: Viking, 1970.
Seize the Day (novel). New York: Viking, 1956.*
The Victim (novel). New York: Vanguard, 1947.

Stories, One-Act Plays

"Address by Gooley MacDowell to the Hasbeens Club of Chicago," *Hudson Review,* Summer 1951. Reprinted in *Algren's Book of Lonesome Monsters*, Nelson Algren, editor. New York: Geis, 1963. Also in *The Writer's Signature: Idea in Story and Essay*, Elaine Gottlieb Hemley and Jack Matthews, editors. Glenview, Ill.: Scott, Foresman, 1972.
"By the Rock Wall," *Harper's Bazaar,* April 1951.

* The first edition (out-of-print) included three stories—"A Father-to-Be," "The Gonzaga Manuscripts," "Looking for Mr. Green"—and a one-act play, "The Wrecker." The 1961 Viking Compass paperback edition contains the novel alone.

"Dora," *Harper's Bazaar,* November 1949.

"A Father-to-Be," *The New Yorker,* February 5, 1955.*

"The Gonzaga Manuscripts," *Discovery No. 4,* 1956.* Reprinted in *Prize Stories 1956: The O. Henry Awards,* P. Engle and H. Martin, editors. Garden City: Doubleday, 1956.

"Leaving the Yellow House," *Esquire,* January 1958.*

"Looking for Mr. Green," *Commentary,* March 1951.*

"The Mexican General," *Partisan Review,* May–June 1942. Reprinted in *More Stories in the Modern Manner,* from *Partisan Review,* Philip Rahv and William Phillips, editors. New York, Avon, 1955.

"Mosby's Memoirs," *The New Yorker,* July 20, 1968.*

"The Old System," *Playboy,* January 1967.*

"Orange Soufflé" (one-act play), *Esquire,* October 1965. Reprinted in *Traverse Plays,* Jim Haynes, editor. London: Penguin, 1966. Staged in 1965 and 1966 (see Chronology). Reprinted in *Best Short Plays of the World Theatre 1968–1973,* Stanley Richards, editor. New York: Crown, 1973.

"Out from Under" (unpublished one-act play). Staged in 1966 (see Chronology).

"Sermon by Doctor Pep," *Partisan Review,* May 1949. Reprinted in *Best American Short Stories, 1950,* Martha Foley, editor. Boston: Houghton Mifflin, 1950. Also in *The New Partisan Reader, 1945–1953,* William Phillips and Philip Rahv, editors. New York: Harcourt, Brace, 1953. Also in *Fiction of the Fifties,* Herbert Gold, editor. Garden City: Doubleday, 1959.

"Trip to Galena," *Partisan Review,* November–December 1950.

"Two Morning Monologues," *Partisan Review,* May–June 1941. Reprinted in *Partisan Reader,* William Phillips and Philip Rahv, editors. New York: Dial, 1946. Also in *The American Disinherited: A Profile in Fiction,* Abe C. Ravitz, editor. Encino, Calif.: Dickenson, 1970.

* Included in the collection *Mosby's Memoirs and Other Stories.*

"A Wen" (one-act play), *Esquire,* January 1965. Reprinted in *Traverse Plays,* Jim Haynes, editor. London: Penguin, no date. Staged in 1965 and 1966 (see Chronology).

"The Wrecker" (one-act play), *New World Writing,* 6, 1954. (Included, as a separate work, in the first edition of *Seize the Day* [New York: Viking, 1956]; in later editions the novel appears alone.)

Early Versions, Excerpts

These early versions of novels and excerpts from novels were published in magazine form. They underwent many changes.

The Adventures of Augie March (1953):

"From the Life of Augie March," *Partisan Review,* November 1949.

"The Coblins," *Sewanee Review,* Autumn 1951.

"The Einhorns," *Partisan Review,* November–December 1951. Reprinted in *Perspectives USA,* Winter 1953.

"Interval in a Lifeboat," *The New Yorker,* December 27, 1952.

"The Eagle," *Harper's Bazaar,* February 1953.

"Mintouchian," *Hudson Review,* Summer 1953.

Dangling Man (1944):

"Notes of a Dangling Man" (excerpt), *Partisan Review,* September–October 1943. Reprinted in *Best American Short Stories, 1944,* Martha Foley, editor. Boston: Houghton Mifflin, 1944.

Henderson the Rain King (1959):

"Henderson in Africa," *Botteghe Oscure,* 1958.

"Henderson the Rain King," *Hudson Review,* Spring 1958.

Herzog (1964):

"Herzog," *Esquire,* July 1961.

"Sono and Moso," *Location,* Spring 1963.

"Letter to Doctor Edvig," *Esquire,* July 1963.

"Napoleon Street," *Commentary,* July 1964.

"Herzog Visits Chicago," *The Saturday Evening Post*, August 8, 1964.

The Last Analysis (play) (1965):

"Scenes from Humanitis—A Farce" (play), *Partisan Review*, Summer 1962.

Mr. Sammler's Planet (1970):

"Mr. Sammler's Planet" (early version of whole novel), *Atlantic Monthly*, November 1969, December 1969.

Seize the Day (1956):

"Seize the Day" (early version of whole novel), *Partisan Review*, Summer 1956.

An unpublished dramatization was read in New York, May 8, 1966, by the HB Playwrights Foundation at the Hagen-Berghoff Studio.

From two (as yet untitled) novels in progress:

"Humboldt's Gift," *Playboy*, January 1974.

"Zetland: By a Character Witness," in *Modern Occasions*, Philip Rahv, editor. Port Washington, N.Y.: Kennikat, 1974.

Essays, Reviews, Translation

"Beatrice Webb's America," *The Nation*, September 7, 1963. (Review of *Beatrice Webb's American Diary* [1898], David A. Shannon, editor.)

"Broadway and the Book Shop," *The National Observer*, October 5, 1964.

"Cloister Culture," in *Page 2*, E. F. Brown, editor. New York: Holt, Rinehart & Winston, 1969.

"A Comment on 'Form and Despair,'" *Location*, Summer 1964.

"Culture Now: Some Animadversions, Some Laughs," *Modern Occasions*, Winter 1971. Reprinted in *Intellectual Digest*, September 1971. Also in *The Norton Reader*, 3rd edition, Arthur M. Eastman *et al.*, editors. New York: Norton, 1973.

"Deep Readers of the World, Beware!" *The New York Times Book Review*, February 15, 1959. Reprinted in *The Plain Style*, Robert Hogan and Herbert Bogart, editors. New York: Van Nostrand, 1967.

"Distractions of a Fiction Writer," *New World Writing* 12, 1957. Reprinted in *The Living Novel*, Granville Hicks, editor. New York: Macmillan, 1957.

"Dreiser and the Triumph of Art," *Commentary*, May 1951. (Review of F. O. Matthiessen, *Theodore Dreiser.*) Reprinted in *The Stature of Theodore Dreiser: A Critical Survey of the Man and His Work*, Alfred Kazin and Carl Shapiro, editors. Bloomington: Indiana University Press, 1955.

"Facts That Put Fancy to Flight," *The New York Times Book Review*, February 15, 1962.

"Foreword" to Fyodor M. Dostoevsky, *Winter Notes on Summer Impressions*, Richard Lee Renfield, translator. New York: Criterion, 1955; paper, McGraw-Hill, 1965. (See: "The French as Dostoevsky Saw Them.")

"Foreword" to Isaac Rosenfeld, *An Age of Enormity*, Theodore Solotaroff, editor. Cleveland and New York: World, 1962.

"The French as Dostoevsky Saw Them," *The New Republic*, May 23, 1955. Reprinted as "Foreword" to F. M. Dostoevsky, *Winter Notes on Summer Impressions*. (See above.)

"Gide as Autobiographer," *The New Leader*, June 4, 1951. (Review of André Gide, *The Counterfeiters.*)

Great Jewish Short Stories, Saul Bellow, editor. New York: Dell, 1963.

"Hemingway and the Image of Man," *Partisan Review*, May–June 1953. (Review of Philip Young, *Ernest Hemingway.*)

"How I Wrote Augie March's Story," *The New York Times Book Review*, January 31, 1954.

"Illinois Journey," *Holiday*, September 1959.

"Introduction" to *Great Jewish Short Stories*, Saul Bellow, editor. (See above.)

"Isaac Rosenfeld," *Partisan Review,* Fall 1956. (Written on the occasion of the death of this young writer, Bellow's friend.)

"Israel Diary," *Jewish Heritage Quarterly,* Winter 1967–1968. Reprinted from *Newsday.* (Reportage from Israel on the Six-Day War.)

"Italian Fiction: Without Hope," *The New Leader,* December 11, 1950. (Review of *The New Italian Writers: An Anthology from Botteghe Oscure,* Marguerite Caetani, editor.)

"The Jewish Writer and the English Literary Tradition," *Commentary,* October 1949.

"John Berryman," foreword to John Berryman, *Recovery.* New York: Farrar, Straus & Giroux, 1973. Reprinted as "John Berryman, Friend," in *The New York Times Book Review,* March 27, 1973.

"Laughter in the Ghetto," *The Saturday Review of Literature,* May 30, 1953. (Review of Sholom Aleichem, *The Adventures of Mottel the Cantor's Son.*)

"Literary Notes on Khrushchev," *Esquire,* March 1961. Reprinted in *First Person Singular,* Herbert Gold, editor. New York: Dial, 1963. Reprinted in *Esquire,* October 1973 (40th anniversary issue). Also in *The Plain Style*, Robert Hogan and Herbert Bogart, editors. New York: Van Nostrand, 1967.

"Literature," *The Great Ideas Today,* Mortimer Adler and Robert M. Hutchins, editors. Chicago: Encyclopaedia Britannica, 1963.

"Literature in the Age of Technology," lecture presented at the Smithsonian Institution's National Museum of History and Technology, November 14, 1972. Printed in *Frank K. Nelson Doubleday Lecture Series/Technology and the Frontiers of Knowledge*, Introduction, Daniel J. Boorstin. Garden City, N.Y.: Doubleday, 1974.

"Man Underground," *Commentary*, June 1952. (Review of Ralph Ellison, *The Invisible Man.*) Reprinted in *Ralph Ellison: A Collection of Critical Essays*, John Hersey, editor. Englewood Cliffs, N.J.: Prentice-Hall, 1973.

"Movies" (reviews and criticism), *Horizon, A Magazine of the*

Arts; "Movies: The Art of Going It Alone" (on the films of Morris Engel and Ruth Orkin), September 1962; "Movies: Buñuel's Unsparing Vision," November 1962; "Movies: The Mass-Produced Insight" (on the state of Hollywood movies), January 1963; "Movies: Adrift on a Sea of Gore" (on *Barabbas,* producer, D. de Laurentiis; director, R. Fleischer; based on P. Lagerkvist's novel, adapted by C. Fry), March 1963.

"My Man Bummidge," *The New York Times,* September 27, 1964, Section Two.

The Noble Savage, periodical. Five issues (1960–1962). Co-editor, with Keith Botsford and Aaron Asher. Contributed some unsigned editorial comments.

"On Jewish Storytelling," *Jewish Heritage Quarterly,* Winter 1964–1965.

"A Personal Record," *The New Republic,* February 22, 1954. (Review of Joyce Cary, *Except the Lord.*)

"Pleasures and Pains of Playgoing," *Partisan Review,* May–June 1954. (Critique of four plays, including T. S. Eliot's *The Confidential Clerk.*)

"Rabbi's Boy in Edinburgh," *The Saturday Review of Literature,* March 24, 1956. (Review of David Daiches, *Two Worlds.*)

"Recent American Fiction," Gertrude Clarke Whittal Poetry and Literature Fund lecture. Washington: Library of Congress, 1963. Reprinted in *Encounter,* November 1963, entitled "Some Notes on Recent American Fiction." (See below.)

"The Riddle of Shakespeare's Sonnets," *The Griffin,* June 1962. (Review of book of same title, containing the sonnets, and essays by R. P. Blackmur, Leslie A. Fiedler, Edward Hubler, Northrop Frye, and Stephen Spender.)

"The Sealed Treasure," London *Times Literary Supplement,* July 1, 1960. Reprinted in *The Open Form,* Alfred Kazin, editor. New York: Harcourt, Brace & World, 1965, 2nd edition.

"Skepticism and the Depth of Life," *The Arts and the Public,*

James E. Miller and Paul D. Herring, editors. Chicago: University of Chicago Press, 1967.

"Some Notes on Recent American Fiction," *Encounter*, November 1963. (See: "Recent American Fiction.")

"Spanish Letter," *Partisan Review*, February 1948.

"Solzhenitsyn's Truth," *The New York Times*, January 15, 1974, p. 36.

"The Swamp of Prosperity," *Commentary*, July 1959. (Review of Philip Roth, *Goodbye, Columbus.*)

"A Talk with the Yellow Kid," *The Reporter*, September 6, 1956. Also in *The Writer's Signature: Idea in Story and Essay*, Elaine Gottlieb Hemley and Jack Matthews, editors. Glenview, Ill.: Scott, Foresman, 1972.

"The Thinking Man's Wasteland" (excerpt from acceptance speech for the National Book Award for *Herzog*), *The Saturday Review of Literature*, April 3, 1965.

Translation of Isaac Bashevis Singer's "Gimpel the Fool," *Partisan Review*, May–June 1953. Reprinted in *A Treasury of Yiddish Stories*, Irving Howe and Eliezer Greenberg, editors. New York: Viking, 1954. Also in Isaac Bashevis Singer, *Gimpel the Fool and Other Stories.* New York: Noonday, 1957.

"Two Faces of a Hostile World," *The New York Times Book Review*, August 26, 1956. (Review of Jean Dutourd, *5 A.M.*)

"The University as Villain," *The Nation*, November 16, 1957.

"The Uses of Adversity," *The Reporter*, October 1, 1959. (Review of Oscar Lewis, *Five Families.*)

"Where Do We Go from Here: The Future of Fiction," *Michigan Quarterly Review*, Winter 1962. Reprinted in *To the Young Writer*, Hopwood Lectures, 2nd Series, A. L. Bader, editor. Ann Arbor: University of Michigan Press, 1965. Reprinted in Irving Malin, editor, *Saul Bellow and the Critics.* New York: New York University Press, 1967.

"A Word from Writer Directly to Reader," *Fiction of the Fifties*, Herbert Gold, editor. Garden City: Doubleday, 1959.

"The Writer and the Audience," *Perspectives USA*, Autumn 1954.

"The Writer as Moralist," *Atlantic Monthly*, March 1963.

Selected Books on
Saul Bellow's Work

A great deal has been written about Bellow's work. Two of the books below contain extensive bibliographies, and one is a comprehensive bibliography, listing reviews and essays on Bellow's writings that have appeared over the years in various periodicals and the press, and/or in book collections.

John J. Clayton, *Saul Bellow: In Defense of Man.* Bloomington: Indiana University Press, 1968.

Robert Detweiler, *Saul Bellow: A Critical Essay.* Grand Rapids, Michigan: Eerdmans, 1967.

Pierre Dommergues, *Saul Bellow.* Paris: Grasset, 1967.

Robert R. Dutton, *Saul Bellow.* New York: Twayne, 1971.

David D. Galloway, *The Absurd Hero in American Fiction: Updike, Styron, Bellow, Salinger.* Austin: University of Texas Press, 1966, revised edition 1970. Contains an extensive bibliography.

Irving Malin, *Saul Bellow's Fiction.* Carbondale: Southern Illinois University Press, 1969.

Irving Malin, editor, *Saul Bellow and the Critics.* New York: New York University Press, 1967.

Keith Opdahl, *The Novels of Saul Bellow: An Introduction.* University Park: Pennsylvania State University Press, 1967. Contains an extensive bibliography.

Earl Rovit, *Saul Bellow.* Minneapolis: University of Minnesota Press, 1967.

Brigitte Scheer-Schaetzler, *Saul Bellow.* New York: Ungar, 1972.

B. A. Sokoloff, *Saul Bellow: A Comprehensive Bibliography.* Folcroft, Pennsylvania: Folcroft Library Editions, 1972.

Tony Tanner, *Saul Bellow.* Edinburgh and London: Oliver & Boyd, 1965; New York: Barnes & Noble, 1965.

Novels

Seize the Day

Chapter I

       When it came to concealing his troubles, Tommy Wilhelm was not less capable than the next fellow. So at least he thought, and there was a certain amount of evidence to back him up. He had once been an actor—no, not quite, an extra—and he knew what acting should be. Also, he was smoking a cigar, and when a man is smoking a cigar, wearing a hat, he has an advantage; it is harder to find out how he feels. He came from the twenty-third floor down to the lobby on the mezzanine to collect his mail before breakfast, and he believed—he hoped—that he looked passably well: doing all right. It was a matter of sheer hope, because there was not much that he could add to his present effort. On the fourteenth floor he looked for his father to enter the elevator; they often met at this hour, on the way to breakfast. If he worried about his appearance it was mainly for his old father's sake. But there was no stop on the fourteenth, and the elevator sank and sank. Then the smooth door opened and the great dark-red uneven carpet that covered the lobby billowed toward Wilhelm's feet. In the foreground the lobby was dark, sleepy. French drapes like sails kept out the sun, but three high, narrow windows were open, and in the blue air Wilhelm saw a pigeon about to light on the great chain that supported the marquee of the movie house directly underneath

  Minor corrections in the text have been made by the author for this Portable.

3

the lobby. For one moment he heard the wings beating strongly.

Most of the guests at the Hotel Gloriana were past the age of retirement. Along Broadway in the Seventies, Eighties, and Nineties, a great part of New York's vast population of old men and women lives. Unless the weather is too cold or wet they fill the benches about the tiny railed parks and along the subway gratings from Verdi Square to Columbia University, they crowd the shops and cafeterias, the dime stores, the tearooms, the bakeries, the beauty parlors, the reading rooms and club rooms. Among these old people at the Gloriana, Wilhelm felt out of place. He was comparatively young, in his middle forties, large and blond, with big shoulders; his back was heavy and strong, if already a little stooped or thickened. After breakfast the old guests sat down on the green leather armchairs and sofas in the lobby and began to gossip and look into the papers; they had nothing to do but wait out the day. But Wilhelm was used to an active life and liked to go out energetically in the morning. And for several months, because he had no position, he had kept up his morale by rising early; he was shaved and in the lobby by eight o'clock. He bought the paper and some cigars and drank a Coca-Cola or two before he went in to breakfast with his father. After breakfast —out, out, out to attend to business. The getting out had in itself become the chief business. But he had realized that he could not keep this up much longer, and today he was afraid. He was aware that his routine was about to break up and he sensed that a huge trouble long presaged but till now formless was due. Before evening, he'd know.

Nevertheless he followed his daily course and crossed the lobby.

Rubin, the man at the newsstand, had poor eyes. They may not have been actually weak but they were poor in expression, with lacy lids that furled down at the corners. He dressed well. It didn't seem necessary—he was behind the counter most of the time—but he dressed very well. He had on a rich brown suit; the cuffs embarrassed the hairs on his small hands. He wore a Countess Mara painted necktie. As Wilhelm approached, Rubin did not see him; he was looking out dreamily at the Hotel Ansonia, which was visible from his corner, several blocks away. The Ansonia, the neighborhood's great landmark, was built by Stanford White. It looks like a baroque palace from Prague or Munich enlarged a hundred times, with towers, domes, huge swells and bubbles of metal gone green from exposure, iron fretwork and festoons. Black television antennae are densely planted on its round summits. Under the changes of weather it may look like marble or like sea water, black as slate in the fog, white as tufa in sunlight. This morning it looked like the image of itself reflected in deep water, white and cumulous above, with cavernous distortions underneath. Together, the two men gazed at it.

Then Rubin said, "Your dad is in to breakfast already, the old gentleman."

"Oh, yes? Ahead of me today?"

"That's a real knocked-out shirt you got on," said Rubin. "Where's it from, Saks?"

"No, it's a Jack Fagman—Chicago."

Even when his spirits were low, Wilhelm could still wrinkle his forehead in a pleasing way. Some of the slow, silent movements of his face were very attractive. He went back a step, as if to stand away from himself and get a better look at his shirt. His glance was comic, a comment upon his untidiness. He liked to wear good clothes, but once he had put it on each article appeared to go its own way. Wilhelm, laughing, panted a little; his teeth were small; his cheeks when he laughed and puffed grew round, and he looked much younger than his years. In the old days when he was a college freshman and wore a raccoon coat and a beanie on his large blond head his father used to say that, big as he was, he could charm a bird out of a tree. Wilhelm had great charm still.

"I like this dove-gray color," he said in his sociable, good-natured way. "It isn't washable. You have to send it to the cleaner. It never smells as good as washed. But it's a nice shirt. It cost sixteen, eighteen bucks."

This shirt had not been bought by Wilhelm; it was a present from his boss—his former boss, with whom he had had a falling-out. But there was no reason why he should tell Rubin the history of it. Although perhaps Rubin knew—Rubin was the kind of man who knew, and knew and knew. Wilhelm also knew many things about Rubin, for that matter, about Rubin's wife and Rubin's business, Rubin's health. None of these could be mentioned, and the great weight of the unspoken left them little to talk about.

"Well, y'lookin' pretty sharp today," Rubin said.

And Wilhelm said gladly, "Am I? Do you really think so?" He could not believe it. He saw his reflection in the glass cupboard full of cigar boxes, among the grand seals and paper damask and the gold-embossed portraits of famous men, García, Edward the Seventh, Cyrus the Great. You had to allow for the darkness and deformations of the glass, but he thought he didn't look too good. A wide wrinkle like a comprehensive bracket sign was written upon his forehead, the point between his brows, and there were patches of brown on his dark-blond skin. He began to be half amused at the shadow of his own marveling, troubled, desirous eyes, and his nostrils and his lips. Fair-haired hippopotamus!—that was how he looked to himself. He saw a big round face, a wide, flourishing red mouth, stump teeth. And the hat, too; and the cigar, too. I should have done hard labor all my life, he reflected. Hard honest labor that tires you out and makes you sleep. I'd have worked off my energy and felt better. Instead, I had to distinguish myself—yet.

He had put forth plenty of effort, but that was not the same as working hard, was it? And if as a young man he had got off to a bad start it was due to this very same face. Early in the nineteen-thirties, because of his striking looks, he had been very briefly considered star material, and he had gone to Hollywood. There for seven years, stubbornly, he had tried to become a screen artist. Long before that time his ambition or delusion had ended, but through pride and perhaps also through laziness he had remained in California. At last he turned to other things, but those seven years of persistence and defeat had unfitted him somehow for trades and businesses, and then it was too late to go into one of the professions. He had been slow to mature, and he had lost ground, and so he hadn't been able to get rid of his energy and he was convinced that this energy itself had done him the greatest harm.

"I didn't see you at the gin game last night," said Rubin.

"I had to miss it. How did it go?"

For the last few weeks Wilhelm had played gin almost nightly, but yesterday he had felt that he couldn't afford to lose any more. He had never won. Not once. And while the losses were small they weren't gains, were they? They were losses. He was tired of losing, and tired also of the company, and so he had gone by himself to the movies.

"Oh," said Rubin, "it went okay. Carl made a chump of himself yelling at the guys. This time Doctor Tamkin didn't let him get away with it. He told him the psychological reason why."

"What was the reason?"

Rubin said, "I can't quote him. Who could? You know the way Tamkin talks. Don't ask me. Do you want the *Trib*? Aren't you going to look at the closing quotations?"

"It won't help much to look. I know what they were yesterday at three," said Wilhelm. "But I suppose I better had get the paper." It seemed necessary for him to lift one shoulder in order to put his hand into his jacket pocket. There, among little packets of pills and crushed cigarette butts and strings of cellophane, the red tapes of packages which he sometimes used as dental floss, he recalled that he had dropped some pennies.

"That doesn't sound so good," said Rubin. He meant to be conversationally playful, but his voice had no tone and his eyes, slack and lid-blinded, turned elsewhere. He didn't want to hear. It was all the same to him. Maybe he already knew, being the sort of man who knew and knew.

No, it wasn't good. Wilhelm held three orders of lard in the commodities market. He and Dr. Tamkin had bought this lard together four days ago at 12.96, and the price at once began to fall and was still falling. In the mail this morning there was sure to be a call for additional margin payment. One came every day.

The psychologist, Dr. Tamkin, had got him into this. Tamkin lived at the Gloriana and attended the card game. He had explained to Wilhelm that you could speculate in commodities at one of the uptown branches of a good Wall Street house without making the full deposit of margin legally required. It was up to the branch manager. If he knew you—and all the branch managers knew Tamkin—he would allow you to make short-term purchases. You needed only to open a small account.

"The whole secret of this type of speculation," Tamkin had told him, "is in the alertness. You have to act fast—buy it and sell it; sell it and buy in again. But quick! Get to the window and have them wire Chicago at just the right second. Strike and strike again! Then get out the same day. In no time at all you turn over fifteen, twenty thousand dollars' worth of soy beans, coffee, corn, hides, wheat, cotton." Obviously the doctor understood the market well. Otherwise he could not make it sound so simple. "People lose because they are greedy and can't get out when it starts to go up. They gamble, but I do it scientifically. This is not guesswork. You must take a few points and get out. Why, ye gods!" said Dr. Tamkin with his bulging eyes, his bald head, and his drooping lip. "Have you stopped to think how much dough people are making in the market?"

Wilhelm with a quick shift from gloomy attention to the panting laugh which entirely changed his face had said, "Ho, have I ever! What do you think? Who doesn't know it's way beyond nineteen-twenty-eight–twenty-nine and still on the rise? Who hasn't read the Fulbright investigation? There's money everywhere. Everyone is shoveling it in. Money is—is—"

"And can you rest—can you sit still while this is going on?" said Dr. Tamkin. "I confess to you I can't. I think about people, just because they have a few bucks to invest, making fortunes. They have no sense, they have no talent, they just have the extra dough and it makes them more dough. I get so worked up and tormented and restless, so restless! I haven't even been able to practice my profession. With all this money around you don't want to be a fool while everyone else is making. I know guys who make five, ten thousand a week just by fooling around. I know a guy at the Hotel Pierre. There's nothing to him, but he has a whole case of Mumm's champagne at lunch. I know another guy on Central Park South— But what's the use of talking. They make millions. They have smart lawyers who get them out of taxes by a thousand schemes."

"Whereas I got taken," said Wilhelm. "My wife refused to sign a joint return. One fairly good year and I got into the thirty-two-per-cent bracket and was stripped bare. What of all my bad years?"

"It's a businessmen's government," said Dr. Tamkin. "You can be sure that these men making five thousand a week—"

"I don't need that sort of money," Wilhelm had said. "But oh! if I could only work out a little steady income from this. Not much. I don't ask much. But how badly I need—! I'd be so grateful if you'd show me how to work it."

"Sure I will. *I* do it regularly. I'll bring you my receipts if you like. And do you want to know something? I approve of your attitude very much. You want to avoid catching the money fever. This type of activity is filled with hostile feeling and lust. You should see what it does to some of these fellows. They go on the market with murder in their hearts."

"What's that I once heard a guy say?" Wilhelm remarked. "A man is only as good as what he loves."

"That's it—just it," Tamkin said. "You don't have to go about it their way. There's also a calm and rational, a psychological approach."

Wilhelm's father, old Dr. Adler, lived in an entirely different world from his son's, but he had warned him once against Dr. Tamkin. Rather casually—he was a very bland old man—he said, "Wilky, perhaps you listen too much to this Tamkin. He's interesting to talk to. I don't doubt it. I think he's pretty common but he's a persuasive man. However, I don't know how reliable he may be."

It made Wilhelm profoundly bitter that his father should speak to him with such detachment about his welfare. Dr. Adler liked to appear affable. Affable! His own son, his one and only son, could not speak his mind or ease his heart to him. I wouldn't turn to Tamkin, he thought, if I could turn to him. At least Tamkin sympathizes with me and tries to give me a hand, whereas Dad doesn't want to be disturbed.

Old Dr. Adler had retired from practice; he had a considerable fortune and could easily have helped his son. Recently Wilhelm had told him, "Father—it so happens that I'm in a bad way now. I hate to have to say it. You realize that I'd rather have good news to bring you. But it's true. And since it's true, Dad— What else am I supposed to say? It's true."

Another father might have appreciated how difficult this confession was—so much bad luck, weariness, weakness, and failure. Wilhelm had tried to copy the old man's tone and made himself sound gentlemanly, low-voiced, tasteful. He didn't allow his voice to tremble; he made no stupid gesture. But the doctor had no answer. He only nodded. You might have told him that Seattle was near Puget Sound, or that the Giants and Dodgers were playing a night game, so little was he moved from his expression of healthy, handsome, good-humored old age. He behaved toward his son as he had formerly done toward his patients, and it was a great grief to Wilhelm; it was almost too much to bear. Couldn't he see—couldn't he feel? Had he lost his family sense?

Greatly hurt, Wilhelm struggled, however, to be fair. Old people are bound to change, he said. They have hard things to think about. They must prepare for where they are going. They can't live by the old schedule any longer and all their perspectives change, and other people become alike, kin and acquaintances. Dad is no longer the same person, Wilhelm reflected. He was thirty-two when I was born, and now he's going on eighty. Furthermore, it's time I stopped feeling like a kid toward him, a small son.

The handsome old doctor stood well above the other old people in the hotel. He was idolized by everyone. This was what people said: "That's old Professor Adler, who used to teach internal medicine. He was a diagnostician, one of the best in New York, and had a tremendous practice. Isn't he a wonderful-looking old guy? It's a pleasure to see such a fine old scientist, clean and immaculate. He stands straight and understands every single thing you say. He still has all his buttons. You can discuss any subject with him." The clerks, the elevator operators, the telephone girls and waitresses and chambermaids, the management flattered and pampered him. That was what he wanted. He had always been a vain man. To see how his father loved himself sometimes made Wilhelm madly indignant.

He folded over the *Tribune* with its heavy, black, crashing sensational print and read without recognizing any of the words, for his mind was still on his father's vanity. The doctor had created his own praise. People were primed and did not know it. And what did he need praise for? In a hotel where everyone was busy and contacts were so brief and had such small weight, how could it satisfy him? He could be in people's thoughts here and there for a moment; in and then out. He could never matter much to them. Wilhelm let out a long, hard breath and raised the brows of his round and somewhat circular eyes. He stared beyond the thick borders of the paper.

. . . love that well which thou must leave ere long.

Involuntary memory brought him this line. At first he thought it referred to his father, but then he understood that it was for himself, rather. *He* should love that well. "This thou perceivest, which makes *thy* love more strong." Under Dr.

Tamkin's influence Wilhelm had recently begun to remember
the poems he used to read. Dr. Tamkin knew, or said he knew,
the great English poets and once in a while he mentioned a
poem of his own. It was a long time since anyone had spoken
to Wilhelm about this sort of thing. He didn't like to think
about his college days, but if there was one course that now
made sense it was Literature I. The textbook was Lieder and
Lovett's *British Poetry and Prose*, a black heavy book with thin
pages. Did I read that? he asked himself. Yes, he had read it
and there was one accomplishment at least he could recall
with pleasure. He had read "Yet once more, O ye laurels."
How pure this was to say! It was beautiful.

> Sunk though he be beneath the wat'ry floor . . .

Such things had always swayed him, and now the power of
such words was far, far greater.

Wilhelm respected the truth, but he could lie and one of the
things he lied often about was his education. He said he was
an alumnus of Penn State; in fact he had left school before his
sophomore year was finished. His sister Catherine had a B. S.
degree. Wilhelm's late mother was a graduate of Bryn Mawr.
He was the only member of the family who had no education.
This was another sore point. His father was ashamed of him.

But he had heard the old man bragging to another old man,
saying, "My son is a sales executive. He didn't have the
patience to finish school. But he does all right for himself. His
income is up in the five figures somewhere."

"What—thirty, forty thousand?" said his stooped old
friend.

"Well, he needs at least that much for his style of life. Yes,
he needs that."

Despite his troubles, Wilhelm almost laughed. Why, that
boasting old hypocrite. He knew the sales executive was no
more. For many weeks there had been no executive, no sales,
no income. But how we love looking fine in the eyes of the
world—how beautiful are the old when they are doing a snow

job! It's Dad, thought Wilhelm, who is the salesman. He's selling me. *He* should have gone on the road.

But what of the truth? Ah, the truth was that there were problems, and of these problems his father wanted no part. His father was ashamed of him. The truth, Wilhelm thought, was very awkward. He pressed his lips together, and his tongue went soft; it pained him far at the back, in the cords and throat, and a knot of ill formed in his chest. Dad never was a pal to me when I was young, he reflected. He was at the office or the hospital, or lecturing. He expected me to look out for myself and never gave me much thought. Now he looks down on me. And maybe in some respects he's right.

No wonder Wilhelm delayed the moment when he would have to go into the dining room. He had moved to the end of Rubin's counter. He had opened the *Tribune*; the fresh pages drooped from his hands; the cigar was smoked out and the hat did not defend him. He was wrong to suppose that he was more capable than the next fellow when it came to concealing his troubles. They were clearly written out upon his face. He wasn't even aware of it.

There was the matter of the different names, which, in the hotel, came up frequently. "Are you Doctor Adler's son?" "Yes, but my name is Tommy Wilhelm." And the doctor would say, "My son and I use different monickers. I uphold tradition. He's for the new." The Tommy was Wilhelm's own invention. He adopted it when he went to Hollywood, and dropped the Adler. Hollywood was his own idea, too. He used to pretend that it had all been the doing of a certain talent scout named Maurice Venice. But the scout had never made him a definite offer of a studio connection. He had approached him, but the results of the screen tests had not been good. After the test Wilhelm took the initiative and pressed Maurice Venice until he got him to say, "Well, I suppose you might make it out there." On the strength of this Wilhelm had left college and had gone to California.

Someone had said, and Wilhelm agreed with the saying, that in Los Angeles all the loose objects in the country were collected, as if America had been tilted and everything that wasn't tightly screwed down had slid into Southern California. He himself had been one of these loose objects. Sometimes he told people, "I was too mature for college. I was a big boy, you see. Well, I thought, when do you start to become a man?" After he had driven a painted flivver and had worn a yellow slicker with slogans on it, and played illegal poker, and gone out on Coke dates, he had *had* college. He wanted to try something new and quarreled with his parents about his career. And then a letter came from Maurice Venice.

The story of the scout was long and intricate and there were several versions of it. The truth about it was never told. Wilhelm had lied first boastfully and then out of charity to himself. But his memory was good, he could still separate what he had invented from the actual happenings, and this morning he found it necessary as he stood by Rubin's showcase with his *Tribune* to recall the crazy course of the true events.

I didn't seem even to realize that there was a depression. How could I have been such a jerk as not to prepare for anything and just go on luck and inspiration? With round gray eyes expanded and his large shapely lips closed in severity toward himself he forced open all that had been hidden. Dad I couldn't affect one way or another. Mama was the one who tried to stop me, and we carried on and yelled and pleaded. The more I lied the louder I raised my voice, and charged—like a hippopotamus. Poor Mother! How I disappointed her. Rubin heard Wilhelm give a broken sigh as he stood with the forgotten *Tribune* crushed under his arm.

When Wilhelm was aware that Rubin watched him, loitering and idle, apparently not knowing what to do with himself this morning, he turned to the Coca-Cola machine. He swallowed hard at the Coke bottle and coughed over it, but he ignored his coughing, for he was still thinking, his eyes upcast and his lips closed behind his hand. By a peculiar twist of habit he wore his coat collar turned up always, as though there were a wind. It never lay flat. But on his broad back, stooped with its own weight, its strength warped almost into deformity, the collar of his sports coat appeared anyway to be no wider than a ribbon.

He was listening to the sound of his own voice as he explained, twenty-five years ago in the living room on West End Avenue, "But Mother, if I don't pan out as an actor I can still go back to school."

But she was afraid he was going to destroy himself. She said, "Wilky, Dad could make it easy for you if you wanted to go into medicine." To remember this stifled him.

"I can't bear hospitals. Besides, I might make a mistake and hurt someone or even kill a patient. I couldn't stand that. Besides, I haven't got that sort of brains."

Then his mother had made the mistake of mentioning her nephew Artie, Wilhelm's cousin, who was an honor student at Columbia in math and languages. That dark little gloomy Artie with his disgusting narrow face, and his moles and self-sniffing ways and his unclean table manners, the boring habit he had of conjugating verbs when you went for a walk with him. "Roumanian is an easy language. You just add a *tl* to everything." He was now a professor, this same Artie with whom Wilhelm had played near the soldiers' and sailors' monument on Riverside Drive. Not that to be a professor was in itself so great. How could anyone bear to know so many languages? And Artie also had to remain Artie, which was a bad deal. But perhaps success had changed him. Now that he had a place in the world perhaps he was better. Did Artie love his languages, and live for them, or was he also, in his heart, cynical? So many people nowadays were. No one seemed satisfied, and Wilhelm was especially horrified by the cynicism of successful people. Cynicism was bread and meat to everyone. And irony, too. Maybe it couldn't be helped. It was probably even necessary. Wilhelm, however, feared it intensely. Whenever at the end of the day he was unusually fatigued he attributed it to cynicism. Too much of the world's business done. Too much falsity. He had various words to express the effect this had on him. Chicken! Unclean!

Congestion! he exclaimed in his heart. Rat race! Phony!
Murder! Play the Game! Buggers!

At first the letter from the talent scout was nothing but a
flattering sort of joke. Wilhelm's picture in the college paper
when he was running for class treasurer was seen by Maurice
Venice, who wrote to him about a screen test. Wilhelm at once
took the train to New York. He found the scout to be huge
and oxlike, so stout that his arms seemed caught from beneath
in a grip of flesh and fat; it looked as though it must be
positively painful. He had little hair. Yet he enjoyed a healthy
complexion. His breath was noisy and his voice rather difficult
and husky because of the fat in his throat. He had on a
double-breasted suit of the type then known as the pillbox; it.
was chalk-striped, pink on blue; the trousers hugged his
ankles.

They met and shook hands and sat down. Together these
two big men dwarfed the tiny Broadway office and made the
furnishings look like toys. Wilhelm had the color of a Golden
Grimes apple when he was well, and then his thick blond hair
had been vigorous and his wide shoulders unwarped; he was
leaner in the jaws, his eyes fresher and wider; his legs were
then still awkward but he was impressively handsome. And he
was about to make his first great mistake. Like, he sometimes
thought, I was going to pick up a weapon and strike myself a
blow with it.

Looming over the desk in the small office darkened by
overbuilt midtown—sheer walls, gray spaces, dry lagoons of
tar and pebbles—Maurice Venice proceeded to establish his
credentials. He said, "My letter was on the regular stationery,
but maybe you want to check on me?"

"Who, *me?*" said Wilhelm. "Why?"

"There's guys who think I'm in a racket and make a charge
for the test. I don't ask a cent. I'm no agent. There ain't no
commission."

"I never even thought of it," said Wilhelm. Was there
perhaps something fishy about this Maurice Venice? He
protested too much.

In his husky, fat-weakened voice he finally challenged Wilhelm, "If you're not sure, you can call the distributor and find out who I am, Maurice Venice."

Wilhelm wondered at him. "Why shouldn't I be sure? Of course I am."

"Because I can see the way you size me up, and because this is a dinky office. Like you don't believe me. Go ahead. Call. I won't care if you're cautious. I mean it. There's quite a few people who doubt me at first. They can't really believe that fame and fortune are going to hit 'em."

"But I tell you I do believe you," Wilhelm had said, and bent inward to accommodate the pressure of his warm, panting laugh. It was purely nervous. His neck was ruddy and neatly shaved about the ears—he was fresh from the barber-shop; his face anxiously glowed with his desire to make a pleasing impression. It was all wasted on Venice, who was just as concerned about the impression *he* was making.

"If you're surprised, I'll just show you what I mean," Venice had said. "It was about fifteen months ago right in this identical same office when I saw a beautiful thing in the paper. It wasn't even a photo but a drawing, a brassière ad, but I knew right away that this was star material. I called up the paper to ask who the girl was, they gave me the name of the advertising agency; I phoned the agency and they gave me the name of the artist; I got hold of the artist and he gave me the number of the model agency. Finally, finally I got her number and phoned her and said, 'This is Maurice Venice, scout for Kaskaskia Films.' So right away she says, 'Yah, so's your old lady.' Well, when I saw I wasn't getting nowhere with her I said to her, 'Well, miss. I don't blame you. You're a very beautiful thing and must have a dozen admirers after you all the time, boy friends who like to call and pull your leg and give a tease. But as I happen to be a very busy fellow and don't have the time to horse around or argue, I tell you what to do. Here's my number, and here's the number of the Kaskaskia Distributors, Inc. Ask them who am I, Maurice Venice. The scout.' She did it. A little while later she phoned me back, all apologies and excuses, but I didn't want to embarrass her and get off on the wrong foot with an artist. I know better than to do that. So I told her it was a natural precaution, never mind. I wanted to run a screen test right away. Because I seldom am wrong about talent. If I see it, it's there. Get that, please. And do you know who that little girl is today?"

"No," Wilhelm said eagerly. "Who is she?"

Venice said impressively, " 'Nita Christenberry."

Wilhelm sat utterly blank. This was failure. He didn't know the name, and Venice was waiting for his response and would be angry.

And in fact Venice had been offended. He said, "What's the matter with you! Don't you read a magazine? She's a starlet."

"I'm sorry," Wilhelm answered. "I'm at school and don't have time to keep up. If I don't know her, it doesn't mean a thing. She made a big hit, I'll bet."

"You can say that again. Here's a photo of her." He handed Wilhelm some pictures. She was a bathing beauty—short, the usual breasts, hips, and smooth thighs. Yes, quite good, as Wilhelm recalled. She stood on high heels and wore a Spanish comb and mantilla. In her hand was a fan.

He had said, "She looks awfully peppy."

"Isn't she a divine girl? And what personality! Not just another broad in the show business, believe me." He had a surprise for Wilhelm. "I found happiness with her," he said.

"You have?" said Wilhelm, slow to understand.

"Yes, boy, we're engaged."

Wilhelm saw another photograph, taken on the beach. Venice was dressed in a terry-cloth beach outfit, and he and the girl, cheek to cheek, were looking into the camera. Below, in white ink, was written "Love at Malibu Colony."

"I'm sure you'll be very happy. I wish you—"

"I *know*," said Venice firmly, "I'm going to be happy. When I saw that drawing, the breath of fate breathed on me. I felt it over my entire body."

"Say, it strikes a bell suddenly," Wilhelm had said. "Aren't you related to Martial Venice the producer?"

Venice was either a nephew of the producer or the son of a first cousin. Decidedly he had not made good. It was easy enough for Wilhelm to see this now. The office was so poor, and Venice bragged so nervously and identified himself so scrupulously—the poor guy. He was the obscure failure of an aggressive and powerful clan. As such he had the greatest sympathy from Wilhelm.

Venice had said, "Now I suppose you want to know where you come in. I saw your school paper, by accident. You take quite a remarkable picture."

"It can't be so much," said Wilhelm, more panting than laughing.

"You don't want to tell me my business," Venice said. "Leave it to me. I studied up on this."

"I never imagined— Well, what kind of roles do you think I'd fit?"

"All this time that we've been talking, I've been watching. Don't think I haven't. You remind me of someone. Let's see who it can be—one of the great old-timers. Is it Milton Sills? No, that's not the one. Conway Tearle, Jack Mulhall? George Bancroft? No, his face was ruggeder. One thing I can tell you, though, a George Raft type you're not—those tough, smooth, black little characters."

"No, I wouldn't seem to be."

"No, you're not that flyweight type, with the fists, from a nightclub, and the glamorous sideburns, doing the tango or the bolero. Not Edward G. Robinson, either—I'm thinking aloud. Or the Cagney fly-in-your-face role, a cabbie, with that mouth and those punches."

"I realize that."

"Not suave like William Powell, or a lyric juvenile like Buddy Rogers. I suppose you don't play the sax? No. But—"

"But what?"

"I have you placed as the type that loses the girl to the George Raft type or the William Powell type. You are steady, faithful, you get stood up. The older women would know better. The mothers are on your side. With what they been through, if it was up to them, they'd take you in a minute.

You're very sympathetic, even the young girls feel that. You'd make a good provider. But they go more for the other types. It's as clear as anything."

This was not how Wilhelm saw himself. And as he surveyed the old ground he recognized now that he had been not only confused but hurt. Why, he thought, he cast me even then for a loser.

Wilhelm had said, with half a mind to be defiant, "Is that your opinion?"

It never occurred to Venice that a man might object to stardom in such a role. "Here is your chance," he said. "Now you're just in college. What are you studying?" He snapped his fingers. "Stuff." Wilhelm himself felt this way about it. "You may plug along fifty years before you get anywheres. This way, in one jump, the world knows who you are. You become a name like Roosevelt, Swanson. From east to west, out to China, into South America. This is no bunk. You become a lover to the whole world. The world wants it, needs it. One fellow smiles, a billion people also smile. One fellow cries, the other billion sob with him. Listen, bud—" Venice had pulled himself together to make an effort. On his imagination there was some great weight which he could not discharge. He wanted Wilhelm, too, to feel it. He twisted his large, clean, well-meaning, rather foolish features as though he were their unwilling captive, and said in his choked, fat-obstructed voice, "Listen, everywhere there are people trying hard, miserable, in trouble, downcast, tired, trying and trying. They need a break, right? A break-through, a help, luck, or sympathy."

"That certainly is the truth," said Wilhelm. He had seized the feeling and he waited for Venice to go on. But Venice had no more to say; he had concluded. He gave Wilhelm several pages of blue hectographed script, stapled together, and told him to prepare for the screen test. "Study your lines in front of a mirror," he said. "Let yourself go. The part should take ahold of you. Don't be afraid to make faces and be emotional. Shoot the works. Because when you start to act you're no more an ordinary person, and those things don't apply to you. You don't behave the same way as the average."

And so Wilhelm had never returned to Penn State. His roommate sent his things to New York for him, and the school authorities had to write to Dr. Adler to find out what had happened.

Still, for three months Wilhelm delayed his trip to California. He wanted to start out with the blessings of his family, but they were never given. He quarreled with his parents and his sister. And then, when he was best aware of the risks and knew a hundred reasons against going and had made himself sick with fear, he left home. This was typical of Wilhelm. After much thought and hesitation and debate he invariably took the course he had rejected innumerable times. Ten such decisions made up the history of his life. He had decided that it would be a bad mistake to go to Hollywood, and then he went. He had made up his mind not to marry his wife, but ran off and got married. He had resolved not to invest money with Tamkin, and then had given him a check.

But Wilhelm had been eager for life to start. College was merely another delay. Venice had approached him and said that the world had named Wilhelm to shine before it. He was to be freed from the anxious and narrow life of the average. Moreover, Venice had claimed that he never made a mistake. His instinct for talent was infallible, he said.

But when Venice saw the results of the screen test he did a quick about-face. In those days Wilhelm had had a speech difficulty. It was not a true stammer, it was a thickness of speech which the sound track exaggerated. The film showed that he had many peculiarities, otherwise unnoticeable. When he shrugged, his hands drew up within his sleeves. The vault of his chest was huge, but he really didn't look strong under the lights. Though he called himself a hippopotamus, he more nearly resembled a bear. His walk was bearlike, quick and rather soft, toes turned inward, as though his shoes were an impediment. About one thing Venice had been right. Wilhelm was photogenic, and his wavy blond hair (now graying) came out well, but after the test Venice refused to encourage him. He tried to get rid of him. He couldn't afford to take a chance on him, he had made too many mistakes already and lived in fear of his powerful relatives.

Wilhelm had told his parents, "Venice says I owe it to myself to go." How ashamed he was now of this lie! He had begged Venice not to give him up. He had said, "Can't you help me out? It would kill me to go back to school now."

Then when he reached the Coast he learned that a recommendation from Maurice Venice was the kiss of death. Venice needed help and charity more than he, Wilhelm, ever had. A few years later when Wilhelm was down on his luck and working as an orderly in a Los Angeles hospital, he saw Venice's picture in the papers. He was under indictment for pandering. Closely following the trial, Wilhelm found out that Venice had indeed been employed by Kaskaskia Films but that he had evidently made use of the connection to organize a ring of call girls. Then what did he want with me? Wilhelm had cried to himself. He was unwilling to believe anything very bad about Venice. Perhaps he was foolish and unlucky, a fall guy, a dupe, a sucker. You didn't give a man fifteen years in prison for that. Wilhelm often thought that he might write him a letter to say how sorry he was. He remembered the breath of fate and Venice's certainty that he would be happy. 'Nita Christenberry was sentenced to three years. Wilhelm recognized her although she had changed her name.

By that time Wilhelm too had taken his new name. In California he became Tommy Wilhelm. Dr. Adler would not accept the change. Today he still called his son Wilky, as he had done for more than forty years. Well, now, Wilhelm was thinking, the paper crowded in disarray under his arm, there's really very little that a man can change at will. He can't change his lungs, or nerves, or constitution or temperament. They're not under his control. When he's young and strong and impulsive and dissatisfied with the way things are he wants to rearrange them to assert his freedom. He can't overthrow the government or be differently born; he only has a little scope and maybe a foreboding, too, that essentially you can't change. Nevertheless, he makes a gesture and becomes Tommy Wilhelm. Wilhelm had always had a great longing to be Tommy. He had never, however, succeeded in feeling like Tommy, and in his soul had always remained Wilky. When he was drunk he reproached himself horribly as Wilky. "You fool, you clunk, you Wilky!" he called himself. He thought that it was a good thing perhaps that he had not become a success as Tommy since that would not have been a genuine success. Wilhelm would have feared that not he but Tommy had brought it off, cheating Wilky of his birthright. Yes, it had been a stupid thing to do, but it was his imperfect judgment at the age of twenty which should be blamed. He had cast off his father's name, and with it his father's opinion of him. It was, he knew it was, his bid for liberty. Adler being in his mind the title of the species, Tommy the freedom of the person. But Wilky was his inescapable self.

In middle age you no longer thought such thoughts about free choice. Then it came over you that from one grandfather you had inherited such and such a head of hair which looked like honey when it whitens or sugars in the jar; from another, broad thick shoulders; an oddity of speech from one uncle, and small teeth from another, and the gray eyes with darkness diffused even into the whites, and a wide-lipped mouth like a statue from Peru. Wandering races have such looks, the bones of one tribe, the skin of another. From his mother he had gotten sensitive feelings, a soft heart, a brooding nature, a tendency to be confused under pressure.

The changed name was a mistake, and he would admit it as freely as you liked. But this mistake couldn't be undone now, so why must his father continually remind him how he had sinned? It was too late. He would have to go back to the pathetic day when the sin was committed. And where was that day? Past and dead. Whose humiliating memories were these? His and not his father's. What had he to think back on that he could call good? Very, very little. You had to forgive. First, to forgive yourself, and then, general forgiveness. Didn't he suffer from his mistakes far more than his father could?

"Oh, God," Wilhelm prayed. "Let me out of my trouble.

Let me out of my thoughts, and let me do something better
with myself. For all the time I have wasted I am very sorry.
Let me out of this clutch and into a different life. For I am all
balled up. Have mercy."

Chapter II

The mail.

The clerk who gave it to him did not care what sort of
appearance he made this morning. He only glanced at him
from under his brows, upward, as the letters changed hands.
Why should the hotel people waste courtesies on him? They
had his number. The clerk knew that he was handing him,
along with the letters, a bill for his rent. Wilhelm assumed a
look that removed him from all such things. But it was bad.
To pay the bill he would have to withdraw money from his
brokerage account, and the account was being watched
because of the drop in lard. According to the *Tribune*'s figures
lard was still twenty points below last year's level. There were
government price supports. Wilhelm didn't know how these
worked but he understood that the farmer was protected and
that the SEC kept an eye on the market and therefore he
believed that lard would rise again and he wasn't greatly
worried as yet. But in the meantime his father might have
offered to pick up his hotel tab. Why didn't he? What a selfish
old man he was! He saw his son's hardships; he could so
easily help him. How little it would mean to him, and how
much to Wilhelm! Where was the old man's heart? Maybe,
thought Wilhelm, I was sentimental in the past and exaggerated his kindliness—warm family life. It may never have been
there.

Not long ago his father had said to him in his usual affable,
pleasant way, "Well, Wilky, here we are under the same roof
again, after all these years."

Wilhelm was glad for an instant. At last they would talk over old times. But he was also on guard against insinuations. Wasn't his father saying, "Why are you here in a hotel with me and not at home in Brooklyn with your wife and two boys? You're neither a widower nor a bachelor. You have brought me all your confusions. What do you expect me to do with them?"

So Wilhelm studied the remark for a bit, then said, "The roof is twenty-six stories up. But how many years has it been?"

"That's what I was asking you."

"Gosh, Dad, I'm not sure. Wasn't it the year Mother died? What year was that?"

He asked this question with an innocent frown on his Golden Grimes, dark-blond face. *What year was it!* As though he didn't know the year, the month, the day, the very hour of his mother's death.

"Wasn't it nineteen-thirty-one?" said Dr. Adler.

"Oh, was it?" said Wilhelm. And in hiding the sadness and the overwhelming irony of the question he gave a nervous shiver and wagged his head and felt the ends of his collar rapidly.

"Do you know?" his father said. "You must realize, an old fellow's memory becomes unreliable. It was in winter, that I'm sure of. Nineteen-thirty-two?"

Yes, it was age. Don't make an issue of it, Wilhelm advised himself. If you were to ask the old doctor in what year he had interned, he'd tell you correctly. All the same, don't make an issue. Don't quarrel with your own father. Have pity on an old man's failings.

"I believe the year was closer to nineteen-thirty-four, Dad," he said.

But Dr. Adler was thinking, Why the devil can't he stand still when we're talking? He's either hoisting his pants up and down by the pockets or jittering with his feet. A regular mountain of tics he's getting to be. Wilhelm had a habit of moving his feet back and forth as though, hurrying into a house, he had to clean his shoes first on the doormat.

Then Wilhelm had said, "Yes, that was the beginning of the end, wasn't it, Father?"

Wilhelm often astonished Dr. Adler. Beginning of the end?

What could he mean—what was he fishing for? Whose end? The end of family life? The old man was puzzled but he would not give Wilhelm an opening to introduce his complaints. He had learned that it was better not to take up Wilhelm's strange challenges. So he merely agreed pleasantly, for he was a master of social behavior, and said, "It was an awful misfortune for us all."

He thought, What business has he to complain to *me* of his mother's death?

Face to face they had stood, each declaring himself silently after his own way. It was: it was not, the beginning of the end—*some* end.

Unaware of anything odd in his doing it, for he did it all the time, Wilhelm had pinched out the coal of his cigarette and dropped the butt in his pocket, where there were many more. And as he gazed at his father the little finger of his right hand began to twitch and tremble; of that he was unconscious, too.

And yet Wilhelm believed that when he put his mind to it he could have perfect and even distinguished manners, outdoing his father. Despite the slight thickness in his speech—it amounted almost to a stammer when he started the same phrase over several times in his effort to eliminate the thick sound—he could be fluent. Otherwise he would never have made a good salesman. He claimed also that he was a good listener. When he listened he made a tight mouth and rolled his eyes thoughtfully. He would soon tire and begin to utter short, loud, impatient breaths, and he would say, "Oh yes . . . yes . . . yes. I couldn't agree more." When he was forced to differ he would declare, "Well, I'm not sure. I don't really see it that way. I'm of two minds about it." He would never willingly hurt any man's feelings.

But in conversation with his father he was apt to lose control of himself. After any talk with Dr. Adler, Wilhelm generally felt dissatisfied, and his dissatisfaction reached its greatest intensity when they discussed family matters. Ostensibly he had been trying to help the old man to remember a date, but in reality he meant to tell him, "You were set free when Ma died. You wanted to forget her. You'd like to get rid of Catherine, too. Me, too. You're not kidding anyone"—Wilhelm striving to put this across, and the old man not having it. In the end he was left struggling, while his father seemed unmoved.

And then once more Wilhelm had said to himself, "But man! you're not a kid. Even then you weren't a kid!" He looked down over the front of his big, indecently big, spoiled body. He was beginning to lose his shape, his gut was fat, and he looked like a hippopotamus. His younger son called him "a hummuspotamus"; that was little Paul. And here he was still struggling with his old dad, filled with ancient grievances. Instead of saying, "Good-by, youth! Oh, good-by those marvelous, foolish wasted days. What a big clunk I was—I *am.*"

Wilhelm was still paying heavily for his mistakes. His wife Margaret would not give him a divorce, and he had to support her and the two children. She would regularly agree to divorce him, and then think things over again and set new and more difficult conditions. No court would have awarded her the amounts he paid. One of today's letters, as he had expected, was from her. For the first time he had sent her a postdated check, and she protested. She also enclosed bills for the boys' educational insurance policies, due next week. Wilhelm's mother-in-law had taken out these policies in Beverly Hills, and since her death two years ago he had to pay the premiums. Why couldn't she have minded her own business! They were his kids, and he took care of them and always would. He had planned to set up a trust fund. But that was on his former expectations. Now he had to rethink the future, because of the money problem. Meanwhile, here were the bills to be paid. When he saw the two sums punched out so neatly on the cards he cursed the company and its IBM equipment. His heart and his head were congested with anger. Everyone was supposed to have money. It was nothing to the company. It published pictures of funerals in the magazines and frightened the suckers, and then punched out little holes, and the customers would lie awake to think out ways to raise the dough. They'd be ashamed not to have it. They couldn't let a great company down, either, and they got the scratch. In the old days a man was put in prison for debt, but there were subtler things now. They made it a shame not to have money and set everybody to work.

Well, and what else had Margaret sent him? He tore the envelope open with his thumb, swearing that he would send any other bills back to her. There was, luckily, nothing more. He put the hole-punched cards in his pocket. Didn't Margaret know that he was nearly at the end of his rope? Of course. Her instinct told her that this was her opportunity, and she was giving him the works.

He went into the dining room, which was under Austro-Hungarian management at the Hotel Gloriana. It was run like a European establishment. The pastries were excellent, especially the strudel. He often had apple strudel and coffee in the afternoon.

As soon as he entered he saw his father's small head in the sunny bay at the farther end, and heard his precise voice. It was with an odd sort of perilous expression that Wilhelm crossed the dining room.

Dr. Adler liked to sit in a corner that looked across Broadway down to the Hudson and New Jersey. On the other side of the street was a supermodern cafeteria with gold and purple mosaic columns. On the second floor a private-eye school, a dental laboratory, a reducing parlor, a veteran's club, and a Hebrew school shared the space. The old man was sprinkling sugar on his strawberries. Small hoops of brilliance were cast by the water glasses on the white tablecloth, despite a faint murkiness in the sunshine. It was early summer, and the long window was turned inward; a moth was on the pane; the putty was broken and the white enamel on the frames was streaming with wrinkles.

"Ha, Wilky," said the old man to his tardy son. "You haven't met our neighbor Mr. Perls, have you? From the fifteenth floor."

"How d'do," Wilhelm said. He did not welcome this stranger; he began at once to find fault with him. Mr. Perls carried a heavy cane with a crutch tip. Dyed hair, a skinny forehead—these were not reasons for bias. Nor was it Mr. Perls's fault that Dr. Adler was using him, not wishing to have breakfast with his son alone. But a gruffer voice within Wilhelm spoke, asking, "Who is this damn frazzle-faced herring with his dyed hair and his fish teeth and this drippy mustache? Another one of Dad's German friends. Where does he collect all these guys? What is the stuff on his teeth? I never saw such pointed crowns. Are they stainless steel, or a kind of silver? How can a human face get into this condition. Uch!" Staring with his widely spaced gray eyes, Wilhelm sat, his broad back stooped under the sports jacket. He clasped his hands on the table with an implication of suppliance. Then he began to relent a little toward Mr. Perls, beginning at the teeth. Each of those crowns represented a tooth ground to the quick, and estimating a man's grief with his teeth as two per cent of the total, and adding to that his flight from Germany and the probable origin of his wincing wrinkles, not to be confused with the wrinkles of his smile, it came to a sizable load.

"Mr. Perls was a hosiery wholesaler," said Dr. Adler.

"Is this the son you told me was in the selling line?" said Mr. Perls.

Dr. Adler replied, "I have only this one son. One daughter. She was a medical technician before she got married—anesthetist. At one time she had an important position in Mount Sinai."

He couldn't mention his children without boasting. In Wilhelm's opinion, there was little to boast of. Catherine, like Wilhelm, was big and fair-haired. She had married a court reporter who had a pretty hard time of it. She had taken a professional name, too—Philippa. At forty she was still ambitious to become a painter. Wilhelm didn't venture to criticize her work. It didn't do much to him, he said, but then he was no critic. Anyway, he and his sister were generally on the outs and he didn't often see her paintings. She worked very hard, but there were fifty thousand people in New York with paints and brushes, each practically a law unto himself. It was the Tower of Babel in paint. *He* didn't want to go far into this. Things were chaotic all over.

Dr. Adler thought that Wilhelm looked particularly untidy this morning—unrested, too, his eyes red-rimmed from excessive smoking. He was breathing through his mouth and he was evidently much distracted and rolled his red-shot eyes barbarously. As usual, his coat collar was turned up as though he had had to go out in the rain. When he went to business he pulled himself together a little; otherwise he let himself go and looked like hell.

"What's the matter, Wilky, didn't you sleep last night?"

"Not very much."

"You take too many pills of every kind—first stimulants and then depressants, anodynes followed by analeptics, until the poor organism doesn't know what's happened. Then the luminal won't put people to sleep, and the Pervitin or Benzedrine won't wake them. God knows! These things get to be as serious as poisons, and yet everyone puts all their faith in them."

"No, Dad, it's not the pills. It's that I'm not used to New York any more. For a native, that's very peculiar, isn't it? It was never so noisy at night as now, and every little thing is a strain. Like the alternate parking. You have to run out at eight to move your car. And where can you put it? If you forget for a minute they tow you away. Then some fool puts advertising leaflets under your windshield wiper and you have heart failure a block away because you think you've got a ticket. When you do get stung with a ticket, you can't argue. You haven't got a chance in court and the city wants the revenue."

"But in your line you have to have a car, eh?" said Mr. Perls.

"Lord knows why any lunatic would want one in the city who didn't need it for his livelihood."

Wilhelm's old Pontiac was parked in the street. Formerly,

when on an expense account, he had always put it up in a garage. Now he was afraid to move the car from Riverside Drive lest he lose his space, and he used it only on Saturdays when the Dodgers were playing in Ebbets Field and he took his boys to the game. Last Sunday, when the Dodgers were out of town, he had gone out to visit his mother's grave.

Dr. Adler had refused to go along. He couldn't bear his son's driving. Forgetfully, Wilhelm traveled for miles in second gear; he was seldom in the right lane and he neither gave signals nor watched for lights. The upholstery of his Pontiac was filthy with grease and ashes. One cigarette burned in the ashtray, another in his hand, a third on the floor with maps and other waste paper and Coca-Cola bottles. He dreamed at the wheel or argued and gestured, and therefore the old doctor would not ride with him.

Then Wilhelm had come back from the cemetery angry because the stone bench between his mother's and his grandmother's graves had been overturned and broken by vandals. "Those damn teen-age hoodlums get worse and worse," he said. "Why, they must have used a sledge-hammer to break the seat smack in half like that. If I could catch one of them!" He wanted the doctor to pay for a new seat, but his father was cool to the idea. He said he was going to have himself cremated.

Mr. Perls said, "I don't blame you if you get no sleep up where you are." His voice was tuned somewhat sharp, as though he were slightly deaf. "Don't you have Parigi the singing teacher there? God, they have some queer elements in this hotel. On which floor is that Estonian woman with all her cats and dogs? They should have made her leave long ago."

"They've moved her down to twelve," said Dr. Adler.

Wilhelm ordered a large Coca-Cola with his breakfast. Working in secret at the small envelopes in his pocket, he found two pills by touch. Much fingering had worn and weakened the paper. Under cover of a napkin he swallowed a Phenaphen sedative and a Unicap, but the doctor was sharp-eyed and said, "Wilky, what are you taking now?"

"Just my vitamin pills." He put his cigar butt in an ashtray on the table behind him, for his father did not like the odor. Then he drank his Coca-Cola.

"That's what you drink for breakfast, and not orange juice?" said Mr. Perls. He seemed to sense that he would not lose Dr. Adler's favor by taking an ironic tone with his son.

"The caffeine stimulates brain activity," said the old doctor. "It does all kinds of things to the respiratory center."

"It's just a habit of the road, that's all," Wilhelm said. "If you drive around long enough it turns your brains, your stomach, and everything else."

His father explained, "Wilky used to be with the Rojax Corporation. He was their northeastern sales representative for a good many years but recently ended the connection."

"Yes," said Wilhelm, "I was with them from the end of the war." He sipped the Coca-Cola and chewed the ice, glancing at one and the other with his attitude of large, shaky, patient dignity. The waitress set two boiled eggs before him.

"What kind of line does this Rojax company manufacture?" said Mr. Perls.

"Kiddies' furniture. Little chairs, rockers, tables, jungle gyms, slides, swings, seesaws."

Wilhelm let his father do the explaining. Large and stiff-backed, he tried to sit patiently, but his feet were abnormally restless. All right! His father had to impress Mr. Perls? He would go along once more, and play his part. Fine! He would play along and help his father maintain his style. Style was the main consideration. That was just fine!

"I was with the Rojax Corporation for almost ten years," he said. "We parted ways because they wanted me to share my territory. They took a son-in-law into the business—a new fellow. It was his idea."

To himself, Wilhelm said, Now God alone can tell why I have to lay my whole life bare to this blasted herring here. I'm sure nobody else does it. Other people keep their business to themselves. Not me.

He continued, "But the rationalization was that it was too

big a territory for one man. I had a monopoly. That wasn't so. The real reason was that they had gotten to the place where they would have to make me an officer of the corporation. Vice presidency. I was in line for it, but instead this son-in-law got in, and—"

Dr. Adler thought Wilhelm was discussing his grievances much too openly and said, "My son's income was up in the five figures."

As soon as money was mentioned, Mr. Perls's voice grew eagerly sharper. "Yes? What, the thirty-two-per-cent bracket? Higher even, I guess?" He asked for a hint, and he named the figures not idly but with a sort of hugging relish. Uch! How they love money, thought Wilhelm. They adore money! Holy money! Beautiful money! It was getting so that people were feeble-minded about everything except money. While if you didn't have it you were a dummy, a dummy! You had to excuse yourself from the face of the earth. Chicken! that's what it was. The world's business. If only he could find a way out of it.

Such thinking brought on the usual congestion. It would grow into a fit of passion if he allowed it to continue. Therefore he stopped talking and began to eat.

Before he struck the egg with his spoon he dried the moisture with his napkin. Then he battered it (in his father's opinion) more than was necessary. A faint grime was left by his fingers on the white of the egg after he had picked away the shell. Dr. Adler saw it with silent repugnance. What a Wilky he had given to the world! Why, he didn't even wash his hands in the morning. He used an electric razor so that he didn't have to touch water. The doctor couldn't bear Wilky's dirty habits. Only once—and never again, he swore—had he visited his room. Wilhelm, in pajamas and stockings, had sat on his bed, drinking gin from a coffee mug and rooting for the Dodgers on television. "That's two and two on you, Duke. Come on—hit it, now." He came down on the mattress—bam! The bed looked kicked to pieces. Then he drank the gin as though it were tea, and urged his team on with his fist. The

smell of dirty clothes was outrageous. By the bedside lay a
quart bottle and foolish magazines and mystery stories for the
hours of insomnia. Wilhelm lived in worse filth than a savage.
When the doctor spoke to him about this he answered, "Well,
I have no wife to look after my things." And who—*who!*—had
done the leaving? Not Margaret. The doctor was certain that
she wanted him back.

Wilhelm drank his coffee with a trembling hand. In his full
face, his abused bloodshot gray eyes moved back and forth.
Jerkily he set his cup back and put half the length of a
cigarette into his mouth; he seemed to hold it with his teeth, as
though it were a cigar.

"I can't let them get away with it," he said. "It's also a
question of morale."

His father corrected him. "Don't you mean a moral
question, Wilky?"

"I mean that, too. I have to do something to protect myself.
I was promised executive standing." Correction before a
stranger mortified him, and his dark-blond face changed
color, more pale, and then more dark. He went on talking to
Perls but his eyes spied on his father. "I was the one who
opened the territory for them. I could go back for one of their
competitors and take away their customers. *My* customers.
Morale enters into it because they've tried to take away my
confidence."

"Would you offer a different line to the same people?" Mr.
Perls wondered.

"Why not? I know what's wrong with the Rojax product."

"Nonsense," said his father. "Just nonsense and kid's talk,
Wilky. You're only looking for trouble and embarrassment
that way. What would you gain by such a silly feud? You have
to think about making a living and meeting your obligations."

Hot and bitter, Wilhelm said with pride, while his feet
moved angrily under the table, "I don't have to be told about
my obligations. I've been meeting them for years. In more
than twenty years I've never had a penny of help from
anybody. I preferred to dig a ditch on the WPA but never
asked anyone to meet my obligations for me."

"Wilky has had all kinds of experiences," said Dr. Adler. The old doctor's face had a wholesome reddish and almost translucent color, like a ripe apricot. The wrinkles beside his ears were deep because the skin conformed so tightly to his bones. With all his might, he was a healthy and fine small old man. He wore a white vest of a light check pattern. His hearing-aid doodad was in the pocket. An unusual shirt of red and black stripes covered his chest. He bought his clothes in a college shop farther uptown. Wilhelm thought he had no business to get himself up like a jockey, out of respect for his profession.

"Well," said Mr. Perls. "I can understand how you feel. You want to fight it out. By a certain time of life, to have to start all over again can't be a pleasure, though a good man can always do it. But anyway you want to keep on with a business you know already, and not have to meet a whole lot of new contacts."

Wilhelm again thought, Why does it have to be me and my life that's discussed, and not him and his life? He would never allow it. But I am an idiot. I have no reserve. To me it can be done. I talk. I must ask for it. Everybody wants to have intimate conversations, but the smart fellows don't give out, only the fools. The smart fellows talk intimately about the fools, and examine them all over and give them advice. Why do I allow it? The hint about his age had hurt him. No, you can't admit it's as good as ever, he conceded. Things do give out.

"In the meantime," Dr. Adler said, "Wilky is taking it easy and considering various propositions. Isn't that so?"

"More or less," said Wilhelm. He suffered his father to increase Mr. Perls's respect for him. The WPA ditch had brought the family into contempt. He was a little tired. The spirit, the peculiar burden of his existence lay upon him like an accretion, a load, a hump. In any moment of quiet, when sheer fatigue prevented him from struggling, he was apt to feel this mysterious weight, this growth or collection of nameless things which it was the business of his life to carry about. That must be what a man was for. This large, odd, excited, fleshy, blond, abrupt personality named Wilhelm, or Tommy, was here, present, in the present—Dr. Tamkin had been putting into his mind many suggestions about the present moment, the here and now—this Wilky, or Tommy Wilhelm, forty-four years old, father of two sons, at present living in the Hotel Gloriana, was assigned to be the carrier of a load which was his own self, his characteristic self. There was no figure or estimate for the value of this load. But it is probably exaggerated by the subject, T. W. Who is a visionary sort of animal. Who has to believe that he can know why he exists. Though he has never seriously tried to find out why.

Mr. Perls said, "If he wants time to think things over and have a rest, why doesn't he run down to Florida for a while? Off season it's cheap and quiet. Fairyland. The mangoes are just coming in. I got two acres down there. You'd think you were in India."

Mr. Perls utterly astonished Wilhelm when he spoke of fairyland with a foreign accent. Mangoes—India? What did he mean, India?

"Once upon a time," said Wilhelm, "I did some public-relations work for a big hotel down in Cuba. If I could get them a notice in Leonard Lyons or one of the other columns it might be good for another holiday there, gratis. I haven't had a vacation for a long time, and I could stand a rest after going so hard. You know that's true, Father." He meant that his father knew how deep the crisis was becoming; how badly he was strapped for money; and that he could not rest but would be crushed if he stumbled; and that his obligations would destroy him. He couldn't falter. He thought, The money! When I had it, I flowed money. They bled it away from me. I hemorrhaged money. But now it's almost all gone, and where am I supposed to turn for more?

He said, "As a matter of fact, Father, I am tired as hell."

But Mr. Perls began to smile and said, "I understand from Doctor Tamkin that you're going into some kind of investment with him, partners."

"You know, he's a very ingenious fellow," said Dr. Adler. "I really enjoy hearing him go on. I wonder if he really is a medical doctor."

"Isn't he?" said Perls. "Everybody thinks he is. He talks about his patients. Doesn't he write prescriptions?"

"I don't really know what he does," said Dr. Adler. "He's a cunning man."

"He's a psychologist, I understand," said Wilhelm.

"I don't know what sort of psychologist or psychiatrist he may be," said his father. "He's a little vague. It's growing into a major industry, and a very expensive one. Fellows have to hold down very big jobs in order to pay those fees. Anyway, this Tamkin is clever. He never said he practiced here, but I believe he was a doctor in California. They don't seem to have much legislation out there to cover these things, and I hear a thousand dollars will get you a degree from a Los Angeles correspondence school. He gives the impression of knowing something about chemistry, and things like hypnotism. I wouldn't trust him, though."

"And why wouldn't you?" Wilhelm demanded.

"Because he's probably a liar. Do you believe he invented all the things he claims?"

Mr. Perls was grinning.

"He was written up in *Fortune*," said Wilhelm. "Yes, in *Fortune* magazine. He showed me the article. I've seen his clippings."

"That doesn't make him legitimate," said Dr. Adler. "It might have been another Tamkin. Make no mistake, he's an operator. Perhaps even crazy."

"Crazy, you say?"

Mr. Perls put in, "He could be both sane and crazy. In these days nobody can tell for sure which is which."

"An electrical device for truck drivers to wear in their caps," said Dr. Adler, describing one of Tamkin's proposed inventions. "To wake them with a shock when they begin to be drowsy at the wheel. It's triggered by the change in blood-pressure when they start to doze."

"It doesn't sound like such an impossible thing to me," said Wilhelm.

Mr. Perls said, "To me he described an underwater suit so a man could walk on the bed of the Hudson in case of an atomic attack. He said he could walk to Albany in it."

"Ha, ha, ha, ha, ha!" cried Dr. Adler in his old man's voice. "Tamkin's Folly. You could go on a camping trip under Niagara Falls."

"This is just his kind of fantasy," said Wilhelm. "It doesn't mean a thing. Inventors are supposed to be like that. I get funny ideas myself. Everybody wants to make something. Any American does."

But his father ignored this and said to Perls, "What other inventions did he describe?"

While the frazzle-faced Mr. Perls and his father in the unseemly, monkey-striped shirt were laughing, Wilhelm could not restrain himself and joined in with his own panting laugh. But he was in despair. They were laughing at the man to whom he had given a power of attorney over his last seven hundred dollars to speculate for him in the commodities market. They had bought all that lard. It had to rise today. By ten o'clock, or half-past ten, trading would be active, and he would see.

Chapter III

Between white tablecloths and glassware and glancing silverware, through overfull light, the long figure of Mr. Perls went away into the darkness of the lobby. He thrust with his cane, and dragged a large built-up shoe which Wilhelm had not included in his estimate of troubles. Dr. Adler wanted to talk about him. "There's a poor man," he said, "with a bone condition which is gradually breaking him up."

"One of those progressive diseases?" said Wilhelm.

"Very bad. I've learned," the doctor told him, "to keep my sympathy for the real ailments. This Perls is more to be pitied than any man I know."

Wilhelm understood he was being put on notice and did not express his opinion. He ate and ate. He did not hurry but kept putting food on his plate until he had gone through the muffins and his father's strawberries, and then some pieces of bacon that were left; he had several cups of coffee, and when he was finished he sat gigantically in a state of arrest and didn't seem to know what he should do next.

For a while father and son were uncommonly still. Wilhelm's preparations to please Dr. Adler had failed completely, for the old man kept thinking, You'd never guess he had a clean upbringing, and, What a dirty devil this son of mine is. Why can't he try to sweeten his appearance a little? Why does he want to drag himself like this? And he makes himself look so idealistic.

Wilhelm sat, mountainous. He was not really so slovenly as his father found him to be. In some aspects he even had a certain delicacy. His mouth, though broad, had a fine outline, and his brow and his gradually incurved nose, dignity, and in his blond hair there was white but there were also shades of gold and chestnut. When he was with the Rojax Corporation Wilhelm had kept a small apartment in Roxbury, two rooms in a large house with a small porch and garden, and on mornings of leisure, in late spring weather like this, he used to sit expanded in a wicker chair with the sunlight pouring through the weave, and sunlight through the slug-eaten holes of the young hollyhocks and as deeply as the grass allowed into small flowers. This peace (he forgot that that time had had its troubles, too), this peace was gone. It must not have belonged to him, really, for to be here in New York with his old father was more genuinely like his life. He was well aware that he didn't stand a chance of getting sympathy from his father, who said he kept his for real ailments. Moreover, he advised himself repeatedly not to discuss his vexatious problems with him, for his father, with some justice, wanted to be left in peace. Wilhelm also knew that when he began to talk about these things he made himself feel worse, he became congested with them and worked himself into a clutch.

Therefore he warned himself, Lay off, pal. It'll only be an aggravation. From a deeper source, however, came other promptings. If he didn't keep his troubles before him he risked losing them altogether, and he knew by experience that this was worse. And furthermore, he could not succeed in excusing his father on the ground of old age. No. No, he could not. I am his son, he thought. He is my father. He is as much father as I am son—old or not. Affirming this, though in complete silence, he sat, and, sitting, he kept his father at the table with him.

"Wilky," said the old man, "have you gone down to the baths here yet?"

"No, Dad, not yet."

"Well, you know the Gloriana has one of the finest pools in New York. Eighty feet, blue tile. It's a beauty."

Wilhelm had seen it. On the way to the gin game you passed the stairway to the pool. He did not care for the odor of the wall-locked and chlorinated water.

"You ought to investigate the Russian and Turkish baths, and the sunlamps and massage. I don't hold with sunlamps. But the massage does a world of good, and there's nothing better than hydrotherapy when you come right down to it. Simple water has a calming effect and would do you more good than all the barbiturates and alcohol in the world."

Wilhelm reflected that this advice was as far as his father's help and sympathy would extend.

"I thought," he said, "that the water cure was for lunatics."

The doctor received this as one of his son's jokes and said with a smile, "Well, it won't turn a sane man into a lunatic. It does a great deal for me. I couldn't live without my massages and steam."

"You're probably right. I ought to try it one of these days. Yesterday, late in the afternoon, my head was about to bust and I just had to have a little air, so I walked around the Reservoir, and I sat down for a while in a playground. It rests me to watch the kids play potsy and skiprope."

The doctor said with approval, "Well, now, that's more like the idea."

"It's the end of the lilacs," said Wilhelm. "When they burn it's the beginning of summer. At least, in the city. Around the time of year when the candy stores take down the windows and start to sell sodas on the sidewalk. But even though I was raised here, Dad, I can't take city life any more, and I miss the country. There's too much push here for me. It works me up too much. I take things too hard. I wonder why you never retired to a quieter place."

The doctor opened his small hand on the table in a gesture so old and so typical that Wilhelm felt it like an actual touch upon the foundations of his life. "I am a city boy myself, you must remember," Dr. Adler explained. "But if you find the city so hard on you, you ought to get out."

"I'll do that," said Wilhelm, "as soon as I can make the right connection. Meanwhile—"

His father interrupted, "Meanwhile I suggest you cut down on drugs."

"You exaggerate that, Dad. I don't really— I give myself a little boost against—" He almost pronounced the word "misery" but he kept his resolution not to complain.

The doctor, however, fell into the error of pushing his advice too hard. It was all he had to give his son and he gave it once more. "Water and exercise," he said.

He wants a young, smart, successful son, thought Wilhelm, and he said, "Oh, Father, it's nice of you to give me this medical advice, but steam isn't going to cure what ails me."

The doctor measurably drew back, warned by the sudden weak strain of Wilhelm's voice and all that the droop of his face, the swell of his belly against the restraint of his belt intimated.

"Some new business?" he asked unwillingly.

Wilhelm made a great preliminary summary which involved the whole of his body. He drew and held a long breath, and his color changed and his eyes swam. "New?" he said.

"You make too much of your problems," said the doctor. "They ought not to be turned into a career. Concentrate on real troubles—fatal sickness, accidents." The old man's whole manner said, Wilky, don't start this on me. I have a right to be spared.

Wilhelm himself prayed for restraint; he knew this weakness of his and fought it. He knew, also, his father's character. And he began mildly, "As far as the fatal part of it goes, everyone on this side of the grave is the same distance from death. No, I guess my trouble is not exactly new. I've got to pay premiums on two policies for the boys. Margaret sent them to me. She unloads everything on me. Her mother left her an income. She won't even file a joint tax return. I get stuck. Etcetera. But you've heard the whole story before."

"I certainly have," said the old man. "And I've told you to stop giving her so much money."

Wilhelm worked his lips in silence before he could speak. The congestion was growing. "Oh, but my kids, Father. My kids. I love them. I don't want them to lack anything."

The doctor said with a half-deaf benevolence, "Well, naturally. And she, I'll bet, is the beneficiary of that policy."

"Let her be. I'd sooner die myself before I collected a cent of such money."

"Ah yes." The old man sighed. He did not like the mention of death. "Did I tell you that your sister Catherine—Philippa —is after me again."

"What for?"

"She wants to rent a gallery for an exhibition."

Stiffly fair-minded, Wilhelm said, "Well, of course that's up to you, Father."

The round-headed old man with his fine, feather-white, ferny hair said, "No, Wilky. There's not a thing on those canvases. I don't believe it; it's a case of the emperor's clothes. I may be old enough for my second childhood, but at least the first is well behind me. I was glad enough to buy crayons for her when she was four. But now she's a woman of forty and too old to be encouraged in her delusions. She's no painter."

"I wouldn't go so far as to call her a born artist," said Wilhelm, "but you can't blame her for trying something worth while."

"Let her husband pamper her."

Wilhelm had done his best to be just to his sister, and he had sincerely meant to spare his father, but the old man's tight, benevolent deafness had its usual effect on him. He said, "When it comes to women and money, I'm completely in the dark. What makes Margaret act like this?"

"She's showing you that you can't make it without her," said the doctor. "She aims to bring you back by financial force."

"But if she ruins me, Dad, how can she expect me to come back? No, I have a sense of honor. What you don't see is that she's trying to put an end to me."

His father stared. To him this was absurd. And Wilhelm thought, Once a guy starts to slip, he figures he might as well be a clunk. A real big clunk. He even takes pride in it. But there's nothing to be proud of—hey, boy? Nothing. I don't blame Dad for his attitude. And it's no cause for pride.

"I don't understand that. But if you feel like this why don't you settle with her once and for all?"

"What do you mean, Dad?" said Wilhelm, surprised. "I thought I told you. Do you think I'm not willing to settle? Four years ago when we broke up I gave her everything— goods, furniture, savings. I tried to show good will, but I didn't get anywhere. Why when I wanted Scissors, the dog, because the animal and I were so attached to each other—it was bad enough to leave the kids—she absolutely refused me. Not that she cared a damn about the animal. I don't think you've seen him. He's an Australian sheep dog. They usually have one blank or whitish eye which gives a misleading look, but they're the gentlest dogs and have unusual delicacy about eating or talking. Let me at least have the companionship of this animal. Never." Wilhelm was greatly moved. He wiped his face at all corners with his napkin. Dr. Adler felt that his son was indulging himself too much in his emotions.

"Whenever she can hit me, she hits, and she seems to live for that alone. And she demands more and more, and still more. Two years ago she wanted to go back to college and get another degree. It increased my burden but I thought it would be wiser in the end if she got a better job through it. But still she takes as much from me as before. Next thing she'll want to be a doctor of philosophy. She says the women in her family live long, and I'll have to pay and pay for the rest of my life."

The doctor said impatiently, "Well, these are details, not principles. Just details which you can leave out. The dog! You're mixing up all kinds of irrelevant things. Go to a good lawyer."

"But I've already told you, Dad. I got a lawyer, and she got one, too, and both of them talk and send me bills, and I eat my heart out. Oh, Dad, Dad, what a hole I'm in!" said Wilhelm in utter misery. "The lawyers—see?—draw up an agreement, and she says okay on Monday and wants more money on Tuesday. And it begins again."

"I always thought she was a strange kind of woman," said Dr. Adler. He felt that by disliking Margaret from the first and disapproving of the marriage he had done all that he could be expected to do.

"Strange, Father? I'll show you what she's like." Wilhelm took hold of his broad throat with brown-stained fingers and bitten nails and began to choke himself.

"What are you doing?" cried the old man.

"I'm showing you what she does to me."

"Stop that—stop it!" the old man said and tapped the table commandingly.

"Well, Dad, she hates me. I feel that she's strangling me. I can't catch my breath. She just has fixed herself on me to kill me. She can do it at long distance. One of these days I'll be struck down by suffocation or apoplexy because of her. I just can't catch my breath."

"Take your hands off your throat, you foolish man," said his father. "Stop this bunk. Don't expect me to believe in all kinds of voodoo."

"If that's what you want to call it, all right." His face flamed and paled and swelled and his breath was laborious.

"But I'm telling you that from the time I met her I've been a slave. The Emancipation Proclamation was only for colored people. A husband like me is a slave, with an iron collar. The churches go up to Albany and supervise the law. They won't have divorces. The court says, 'You want to be free. Then you have to work twice as hard—twice, at least! Work! you bum.' So then guys kill each other for the buck, and they may be free of a wife who hates them but they are sold to the company. The company knows a guy has got to have his salary, and takes full advantage of him. Don't talk to me about being free. A rich man may be free on an income of a million net. A poor man may be free because nobody cares what he does. But a fellow in my position has to sweat it out until he drops dead."

His father replied to this, "Wilky, it's entirely your own fault. You don't have to allow it."

Stopped in his eloquence, Wilhelm could not speak for a while. Dumb and incompetent, he struggled for breath and frowned with effort into his father's face.

"I don't understand your problems," said the old man. "I never had any like them."

By now Wilhelm had lost his head and he waved his hands and said over and over, "Oh, Dad, don't give me that stuff, don't give me that. Please don't give me that sort of thing."

"It's true," said his father. "I come from a different world. Your mother and I led an entirely different life."

"Oh, how can you compare Mother," Wilhelm said. "Mother was a help to you. Did she harm you ever?"

"There's no need to carry on like an opera, Wilky," said the doctor. "This is only your side of things."

"What? It's the truth," said Wilhelm.

The old man could not be persuaded and shook his round head and drew his vest down over the gilded shirt, and leaned back with a completeness of style that made this look, to anyone out of hearing, like an ordinary conversation between a middle-aged man and his respected father. Wilhelm towered and swayed, big and sloven, with his gray eyes red-shot and his honey-colored hair twisted in flaming shapes upward. Injustice made him angry, made him beg. But he wanted an understanding with his father, and he tried to capitulate to him. He said, "You can't compare Mother and Margaret, and neither can you and I be compared, because you, Dad, were a success. And a success—is a success. I never made a success."

The doctor's old face lost all of its composure and became hard and angry. His small breast rose sharply under the red and black shirt and he said, "Yes. Because of hard work. I was not self-indulgent, not lazy. My old man sold dry goods in Williamsburg. We were nothing, do you understand? I knew I couldn't afford to waste my chances."

"I wouldn't admit for one minute that I was lazy," said Wilhelm. "If anything, I tried too hard. I admit I made many mistakes. Like I thought I shouldn't do things you had done already. Study chemistry. You had done it already. It was in the family."

His father continued, "I didn't run around with fifty women, either. I was not a Hollywood star. I didn't have time to go to Cuba for a vacation. I stayed at home and took care of my children."

Oh, thought Wilhelm, eyes turning upward. Why did I come here in the first place, to live near him? New York is like a gas. The colors are running. My head feels so tight I don't know what I'm doing. He thinks I want to take away his money or that I envy him. He doesn't see what I want.

"Dad," Wilhelm said aloud, "you're being very unfair. It's true the movies was a false step. But I love my boys. I didn't abandon them. I left Margaret because I had to."

"Why did you have to?"

"Well—" said Wilhelm, struggling to condense his many reasons into a few plain words. "I had to—I had to."

With sudden and surprising bluntness his father said, "Did you have bed-trouble with her? Then you should have stuck it out. Sooner or later everyone has it. Normal people stay with it. It passes. But you wouldn't, so now you pay for your stupid romantic notions. Have I made my view clear?"

It was very clear. Wilhelm seemed to hear it repeated from various sides and inclined his head different ways, and listened and thought. Finally he said, "I guess that's the medical standpoint. You may be right. I just couldn't live with Margaret. I wanted to stick it out, but I was getting very sick. She was one way and I was another. She wouldn't be like me, so I tried to be like her, and I couldn't do it."

"Are you sure she didn't tell *you* to go?" the doctor said.

"I wish she had. I'd be in a better position now. No, it was me. I didn't want to leave, but I couldn't stay. Somebody had to take the initiative. I did. Now I'm the fall guy too."

Pushing aside in advance all the objections that his son would make, the doctor said, "Why did you lose your job with Rojax?"

"I didn't, I've told you."

"You're lying. You wouldn't have ended the connection. You need the money too badly. But you must have got into trouble." The small old man spoke concisely and with great strength. "Since you have to talk and can't let it alone, tell the truth. Was there a scandal—a woman?"

Wilhelm fiercely defended himself. "No, Dad, there wasn't any woman. I told you how it was."

"Maybe it was a man, then," the old man said wickedly.

Shocked, Wilhelm stared at him with burning pallor and dry lips. His skin looked a little yellow. "I don't think you know what you're talking about," he answered after a moment. "You shouldn't let your imagination run so free. Since you've been living here on Broadway you must think you understand life, up-to-date. You ought to know your own son a little better. Let's drop that, now."

"All right, Wilky, I'll withdraw it. But something must have happened in Roxbury nevertheless. You'll never go back. You're just talking wildly about representing a rival company. You won't. You've done something to spoil your reputation, I think. But you've got girl friends who are expecting you back, isn't that so?"

"I take a lady out now and then while on the road," said Wilhelm. "I'm not a monk."

"No one special? Are you sure you haven't gotten into complications?"

He had tried to unburden himself and instead, Wilhelm

thought, he had to undergo an inquisition to prove himself worthy of a sympathetic word. Because his father believed that he did all kinds of gross things.

"There is a woman in Roxbury that I went with. We fell in love and wanted to marry, but she got tired of waiting for my divorce. Margaret figured that. On top of which the girl was a Catholic and I had to go with her to the priest and make an explanation."

Neither did this last confession touch Dr. Adler's sympathies or sway his calm old head or affect the color of his complexion.

"No, no, no, no; all wrong," he said.

Again Wilhelm cautioned himself. Remember his age. He is no longer the same person. He can't bear trouble. I'm so choked up and congested anyway I can't see straight. Will I ever get out of the woods, and recover my balance? You're never the same afterward. Trouble rusts out the system.

"You really *want* a divorce?" said the old man.

"For the price I pay I should be getting something."

"In that case," Dr. Adler said, "it seems to me no normal person would stand for such treatment from a woman."

"Ah, Father, Father!" said Wilhelm. "It's always the same thing with you. Look how you lead me on. You always start out to help me with my problems, and be sympathetic and so forth. It gets my hopes up and I begin to be grateful. But before we're through I'm a hundred times more depressed than before. Why is that? You have no sympathy. You want to shift all the blame on to me. Maybe you're wise to do it." Wilhelm was beginning to lose himself. "All you seem to think about is your death. Well, I'm sorry. But I'm going to die too. And I'm your son. It isn't my fault in the first place. There ought to be a right way to do this, and be fair to each other. But what I want to know is, why do you start up with me if you're not going to help me? What do you want to know about my problems for, Father? So you can lay the whole responsibility on me—so that you won't have to help me? D'you want me to comfort you for having such a son?"

Wilhelm had a great knot of wrong tied tight within his chest, and tears approached his eyes but he didn't let them out. He looked shabby enough as it was. His voice was thick and hazy, and he was stammering and could not bring his awful feelings forth.

"You have some purpose of your own," said the doctor, "in acting so unreasonable. What do you want from me? What do you expect?"

"What do I expect?" said Wilhelm. He felt as though he were unable to recover something. Like a ball in the surf, washed beyond reach, his self-control was going out. "I expect *help!*" The words escaped him in a loud, wild, frantic cry and startled the old man, and two or three breakfasters within hearing glanced their way. Wilhelm's hair, the color of whitened honey, rose dense and tall with the expansion of his face, and he said, "When I suffer—you aren't even sorry. That's because you have no affection for me, and you don't want any part of me."

"Why must I like the way you behave? No, I don't like it," said Dr. Adler.

"All right. You want me to change myself. But suppose I could do it—what would I become? What could I? Let's suppose that all my life I have had the wrong ideas about myself and wasn't what I thought I was. And wasn't even careful to take a few precautions, as most people do—like a woodchuck has a few exits to his tunnel. But what shall I do now? More than half my life is over. More than half. And now you tell me I'm not even normal."

The old man too had lost his calm. "You cry about being helped," he said. "When you thought you had to go into the service I sent a check to Margaret every month. As a family man you could have had an exemption. But no! The war couldn't be fought without you and you had to get yourself drafted and be an office-boy in the Pacific theater. Any clerk could have done what you did. You could find nothing better to become than a GI."

Wilhelm was going to reply, and half raised his bearish

figure from the chair, his fingers spread and whitened by their grip on the table, but the old man would not let him begin. He said, "I see other elderly people here with children who aren't much good, and they keep backing them and holding them up at a great sacrifice. But I'm not going to make that mistake. It doesn't enter your mind that when I die—a year, two years from now—you'll still be here. I do think of it."

He had intended to say that he had a right to be left in peace. Instead he gave Wilhelm the impression that he meant it was not fair for the better man of the two, and the more useful, the more admired, to leave the world first. Perhaps he meant that, too—a little; but he would not under other circumstances have come out with it so flatly.

"Father," said Wilhelm with an unusual openness of appeal. "Don't you think I know how you feel? I have pity. I want you to live on and on. If you outlive me, that's perfectly okay by me." As his father did not answer this avowal and turned away his glance, Wilhelm suddenly burst out, "No, but you hate me. And if I had money you wouldn't. By God, you have to admit it. The money makes the difference. Then we would be a fine father and son, if I was a credit to you—so you could boast and brag about me all over the hotel. But I'm not the right type of son. I'm too old, I'm too old and too unlucky."

His father said, "I can't give you any money. There would be no end to it if I started. You and your sister would take every last buck from me. I'm still alive, not dead. I am still here. Life isn't over yet. I am as much alive as you or anyone. And I want nobody on my back. Get off! And I give you the same advice, Wilky. Carry nobody on your back."

"Just keep your money," said Wilhelm miserably. "Keep it and enjoy it yourself. That's the ticket!"

Chapter IV

Ass! Idiot! Wild boar! Dumb mule! Slave! Lousy, wallowing hippopotamus! Wilhelm called himself as his bending legs carried him from the dining room. His pride! His inflamed feelings! His begging and feebleness! And trading insults with his old father—and spreading confusion over everything. Oh, how poor, contemptible, and ridiculous he was! When he remembered how he had said, with great reproof, "You ought to know your own son"—why, how corny and abominable it was.

He could not get out of the sharply brilliant dining room fast enough. He was horribly worked up; his neck and shoulders, his entire chest ached as though they had been tightly tied with ropes. He smelled the salt odor of tears in his nose.

But at the same time, since there were depths in Wilhelm not unsuspected by himself, he received a suggestion from some remote element in his thoughts that the business of life, the real business—to carry his peculiar burden, to feel shame and impotence, to taste these quelled tears—the only important business, the highest business was being done. Maybe the making of mistakes expressed the very purpose of his life and the essence of his being here. Maybe he was supposed to make them and suffer from them on this earth. And though he had raised himself above Mr. Perls and his father because they adored money, still they were called to act energetically and this was better than to yell and cry, pray and beg, poke and blunder and go by fits and starts and fall upon the thorns of life. And finally sink beneath that watery floor—would that be tough luck, or would it be good riddance?

But he raged once more against his father. Other people with money, while they're still alive, want to see it do some good. Granted, he shouldn't support me. But have I ever asked him to do that? Have I ever asked for dough at all, either for Margaret or for the kids or for myself? It isn't the money, but only the assistance; not even assistance, but just the feeling. But he may be trying to teach me that a grown man should be cured of such feeling. Feeling got me in dutch at Rojax. I had the *feeling* that I belonged to the firm, and my *feelings* were hurt when they put Gerber in over me. Dad thinks I'm too simple. But I'm not so simple as he thinks. What about his feelings? He doesn't forget death for one single second, and that's what makes him like this. And not only is death on his mind but through money he forces me to think about it, too. It gives him power over me. He forces me that way, he himself, and then he's sore. If he were poor, I could care for him and show it. The way I *could* care, too, if I only had a chance. He'd see how much love and respect I had in me. It would make him a different man, too. He'd put his hands on me and give me his blessing."

Someone in a gray straw hat with a wide cocoa-colored band spoke to Wilhelm in the lobby. The light was dusky, splotched with red underfoot; green, the leather furniture; yellow, the indirect lighting.

"Hey, Tommy. Say, there."

"Excuse me," said Wilhelm, trying to reach a house phone. But this was Dr. Tamkin, whom he was just about to call.

"You have a very obsessional look on your face," said Dr. Tamkin.

Wilhelm thought, Here he is, Here he is. If I could only figure this guy out.

"Oh," he said to Tamkin. "Have I got such a look? Well, whatever it is, you name it and I'm sure to have it."

The sight of Dr. Tamkin brought his quarrel with his father to a close. He found himself flowing into another channel.

"What are we doing?" he said. "What's going to happen to lard today?"

"Don't worry yourself about that. All we have to do is hold on to it and it's sure to go up. But what's made you so hot under the collar, Wilhelm?"

"Oh, one of those family situations." This was the moment to take a new look at Tamkin, and he viewed him closely but gained nothing by the new effort. It was conceivable that Tamkin was everything that he claimed to be, and all the gossip false. But was he a scientific man, or not? If he was not, this might be a case for the district attorney's office to investigate. Was he a liar? That was a delicate question. Even a liar might be trustworthy in some ways. Could he trust Tamkin—could he? He feverishly, fruitlessly sought an answer.

But the time for this question was past, and he had to trust him now. After a long struggle to come to a decision, he had given him the money. Practical judgment was in abeyance. He had worn himself out, and the decision was no decision. How had this happened? But how had his Hollywood career begun? It was not because of Maurice Venice, who turned out to be a pimp. It was because Wilhelm himself was ripe for the mistake. His marriage, too, had been like that. Through such decisions somehow his life had taken form. And so, from the moment when he tasted the peculiar flavor of fatality in Dr. Tamkin, he could no longer keep back the money.

Five days ago Tamkin had said, "Meet me tomorrow, and we'll go to the market." Wilhelm, therefore, had had to go. At eleven o'clock they had walked to the brokerage office. On the way, Tamkin broke the news to Wilhelm that though this was an equal partnership he couldn't put up his half of the money just yet; it was tied up for a week or so in one of his patents. Today he would be two hundred dollars short; next week, he'd make it up. But neither of them needed an income from the market, of course. This was only a sporting proposition anyhow, Tamkin said. Wilhelm had to answer, "Of course." It was too late to withdraw. What else could he do? Then came the formal part of the transaction, and it was frightening. The very shade of green of Tamkin's check looked wrong; it was a false, disheartening color. His handwriting was peculiar, even monstrous; the e's where like i's, the t's and l's the same, and the h's like wasps' bellies. He wrote like a fourth-grader. Scientists, however, dealt mostly in symbols; they printed. This was Wilhelm's explanation.

Dr. Tamkin had given him his check for three hundred dollars. Wilhelm, in a blinded and convulsed aberration, pressed and pressed to try to kill the trembling of his hand as he wrote out his check for a thousand. He set his lips tight, crouched with his huge back over the table, and wrote with crumbling, terrified fingers, knowing that if Tamkin's check bounced his own would not be honored either. His sole cleverness was to set the date ahead by one day to give the green check time to clear.

Next he had signed a power of attorney, allowing Tamkin to speculate with his money, and this was an even more frightening document. Tamkin had never said a word about it, but here they were and it had to be done.

After delivering his signatures, the only precaution Wilhelm took was to come back to the manager of the brokerage office and ask him privately, "Uh, about Doctor Tamkin. We were in here a few minutes ago, remember?"

That day had been a weeping, smoky one and Wilhelm had gotten away from Tamkin on the pretext of having to run to the post office. Tamkin had gone to lunch alone, and here was Wilhelm, back again, breathless, his hat dripping, needlessly asking the manager if he remembered.

"Yes, sir, I know," the manager had said. He was a cold, mild, lean German who dressed correctly and around his neck wore a pair of opera glasses with which he read the board. He was an extremely correct person except that he never shaved in the morning, not caring, probably, how he looked to the fumblers and the old people and the operators and the gamblers and the idlers of Broadway uptown. The market closed at three. Maybe, Wilhelm guessed, he had a thick beard and took a lady out to dinner later and wanted to look fresh-shaven.

"Just a question," said Wilhelm. "A few minutes ago I signed a power of attorney so Doctor Tamkin could invest for me. You gave me the blanks."

"Yes, sir, I remember."

"Now this is what I want to know," Wilhelm had said. "I'm no lawyer and I only gave the paper a glance. Does this give Doctor Tamkin power of attorney over any other assets of mine—money, or property?"

The rain had dribbled from Wilhelm's deformed, transparent raincoat; the buttons of his shirt, which always seemed tiny, were partly broken, in pearly quarters of the moon, and some of the dark, thick golden hairs that grew on his belly stood out. It was the manager's business to conceal his opinion of him; he was shrewd, gray, correct (although unshaven) and had little to say except on matters that came to his desk. He must have recognized in Wilhelm a man who reflected long and then made the decision he had rejected twenty separate times. Silvery, cool, level, long-profiled, experienced, indifferent, observant, with unshaven refinement, he scarcely looked at Wilhelm, who trembled with fearful awkwardness. The manager's face, low-colored, long-nostriled, acted as a unit of perception; his eyes merely did their reduced share. Here was a man, like Rubin, who knew and knew and knew. He, a foreigner, knew; Wilhelm, in the city of his birth, was ignorant.

The manager had said, "No, sir, it does not give him."

"Only over the funds I deposited with you?"

"Yes, that is right, sir."

"Thank you, that's what I wanted to find out," Wilhelm had said, grateful.

The answer comforted him. However, the question had no value. None at all. For Wilhelm had no other assets. He had given Tamkin his last money. There wasn't enough of it to cover his obligations anyway, and Wilhelm had reckoned that he might as well go bankrupt now as next month. "Either broke or rich," was how he had figured, and that formula had encouraged him to make the gamble. Well, not rich; he did not expect that, but perhaps Tamkin might really show him how to earn what he needed in the market. By now, however, he had forgotten his own reckoning and was aware only that he stood to lose his seven hundred dollars to the last cent.

Dr. Tamkin took the attitude that they were a pair of gentlemen experimenting with lard and grain futures. The money, a few hundred dollars, meant nothing much to either of them. He said to Wilhelm, "Watch. You'll get a big kick out of this and wonder why more people don't go into it. You think the Wall Street guys are so smart—geniuses? That's because most of us are psychologically afraid to think about the details. Tell me this. When you're on the road, and you don't understand what goes on under the hood of your car, you'll worry what'll happen if something goes wrong with the engine. Am I wrong?" No, he was right. "Well," said Dr. Tamkin with an expression of quiet triumph about his mouth, almost the suggestion of a jeer. "It's the same psychological principle, Wilhelm. They are rich because you don't understand what goes on. But it's no mystery, and by putting in a little money and applying certain principles of observation, you begin to grasp it. It can't be studied in the abstract. You have to take a specimen risk so that you feel the process, the money-flow, the whole complex. To know how it feels to be a seaweed you have to get in the water. In a very short time we'll take out a hundred-per-cent profit." Thus Wilhelm had had to pretend at the outset that his interest in the market was theoretical.

"Well," said Tamkin when he met him now in the lobby, "what's the problem, what is this family situation? Tell me." He put himself forward as the keen mental scientist. Whenever this happened Wilhelm didn't know what to reply. No matter what he said or did it seemed that Dr. Tamkin saw through him.

"I had some words with my dad."

Dr. Tamkin found nothing extraordinary in this. "It's the eternal same story," he said. "The elemental conflict of parent and child. It won't end, ever. Even with a fine old gentleman like your dad."

"I don't suppose it will. I've never been able to get anywhere with him. He objects to my feelings. He thinks they're sordid. I upset him and he gets mad at me. But maybe all old men are alike."

"Sons, too. Take it from one of them," said Dr. Tamkin. "All the same, you should be proud of such a fine old patriarch of a father. It should give you hope. The longer he lives, the longer your life expectancy becomes."

Wilhelm answered, brooding, "I guess so. But I think I

inherit more from my mother's side, and she died in her fifties."

"A problem arose between a young fellow I'm treating and his dad—I just had a consultation," said Dr. Tamkin as he removed his dark gray hat.

"So early in the morning?" said Wilhelm with suspicion.

"Over the telephone, of course."

What a creature Tamkin was when he took off his hat! The indirect light showed the many complexities of his bald skull, his gull's nose, his rather handsome eyebrows, his vain mustache, his deceiver's brown eyes. His figure was stocky, rigid, short in the neck, so that the large ball of the occiput touched his collar. His bones were peculiarly formed, as though twisted twice where the ordinary human bone was turned only once, and his shoulders rose in two pagodalike points. At mid-body he was thick. He stood pigeon-toed, a sign perhaps that he was devious or had much to hide. The skin of his hands was aging, and his nails were moonless, concave, clawlike, and they appeared loose. His eyes were as brown as beaver fur and full of strange lines. The two large brown naked balls looked thoughtful—but were they? And honest—but was Dr. Tamkin honest? There was a hypnotic power in his eyes, but this was not always of the same strength, nor was Wilhelm convinced that it was completely natural. He felt that Tamkin tried to make his eyes deliberately conspicuous, with studied art, and that he brought forth his hypnotic effect by an exertion. Occasionally it failed or drooped, and when this happened the sense of his face passed downward to his heavy (possibly foolish?) red underlip.

Wilhelm wanted to talk about the lard holdings, but Dr. Tamkin said, "This father-and-son case of mine would be instructive to you. It's a different psychological type completely than your dad. This man's father thinks that he isn't his son."

"Why not?"

"Because he has found out something about the mother carrying on with a friend of the family for twenty-five years."

"Well, what do you know!" said Wilhelm. His silent thought was, Pure bull. Nothing but bull!

"You must note how interesting the woman is, too. She has two husbands. Whose are the kids? The fellow detected her and she gave a signed confession that two of the four children were not the father's."

"It's amazing," said Wilhelm, but he said it in a rather distant way. He was always hearing such stories from Dr. Tamkin. If you were to believe Tamkin, most of the world was like this. Everybody in the hotel had a mental disorder, a secret history, a concealed disease. The wife of Rubin at the newsstand was supposed to be kept by Carl, the yelling, loud-mouthed gin-rummy player. The wife of Frank in the barbershop had disappeared with a GI while he was waiting for her to disembark at the French Lines pier. Everyone was like the faces on a playing card, upside down either way. Every public figure had a character neurosis. Maddest of all were the businessmen, the heartless, flaunting, boisterous business class who ruled this country with their hard manners and their bold lies and their absurd words that nobody could believe. They were crazier than anyone. They spread the plague. Wilhelm, thinking of the Rojax Corporation, was inclined to agree that many businessmen were insane. And he supposed that Tamkin, for all his peculiarities, spoke a kind of truth and did some people a sort of good. It confirmed Wilhelm's suspicions to hear that there was a plague, and he said, "I couldn't agree with you more. They trade on anything, they steal everything, they're cynical right to the bones."

"You have to realize," said Tamkin, speaking of his patient, or his client, "that the mother's confession isn't good. It's a confession of duress. I try to tell the young fellow he shouldn't worry about a phony confession. But what does it help him if I am rational with him?"

"No?" said Wilhelm, intensely nervous. "I think we ought to go over to the market. It'll be opening pretty soon."

"Oh, come on," said Tamkin. "It isn't even nine o'clock, and there isn't much trading the first hour anyway. Things don't get hot in Chicago until half-past ten, and they're an hour behind us, don't forget. Anyway, I say lard will go up, and it will. Take my word. I've made a study of the guilt-aggression cycle which is behind it. I ought to know *something* about that. Straighten your collar."

"But meantime," said Wilhelm, "we have taken a licking this week. Are you sure your insight is at its best? Maybe when it isn't we should lay off and wait."

"Don't you realize," Dr. Tamkin told him, "you can't march in a straight line to the victory? You fluctuate toward it. From Euclid to Newton there was straight lines. The modern age analyzes the wavers. On my own accounts, I took a licking in hides and coffee. But I have confidence. I'm sure I'll outguess them." He gave Wilhelm a narrow smile, friendly, calming, shrewd, and wizardlike, patronizing, secret, potent. He saw his fears and smiled at them. "It's something," he remarked, "to see how the competition-factor will manifest itself in different individuals."

"So? Let's go over."

"But I haven't had my breakfast yet."

"I've had mine."

"Come, have a cup of coffee."

"I wouldn't want to meet my dad." Looking through the glass doors, Wilhelm saw that his father had left by the other exit. Wilhelm thought, He didn't want to run into me, either. He said to Dr. Tamkin, "Okay, I'll sit with you, but let's hurry it up because I'd like to get to the market while there's still a place to sit. Everybody and his uncle gets in ahead of you."

"I want to tell you about this boy and his dad. It's highly absorbing. The father was a nudist. Everybody went naked in the house. Maybe the woman found men *with* clothes attractive. Her husband didn't believe in cutting his hair, either. He practiced dentistry. In his office he wore riding pants and a pair of boots, and he wore a green eyeshade."

"Oh, come off it," said Wilhelm.

"This is a true case history."

Without warning, Wilhelm began to laugh. He himself had

had no premonition of his change of humor. His face became
warm and pleasant, and he forgot his father, his anxieties; he
panted bearlike, happily, through his teeth. "This sounds like
a horse-dentist. He wouldn't have to put on pants to treat a
horse. Now what else are you going to tell me? Did the wife
play the mandolin? Does the boy join the cavalry? Oh,
Tamkin, you really are a killer-diller."

"Oh, you think I'm trying to amuse you," said Tamkin.
"That's because you aren't familiar with my outlook. I deal in
facts. Facts always are sensational. I'll say that a second time.
Facts *always!* are sensational."

Wilhelm was reluctant to part with his good mood. The
doctor had little sense of humor. He was looking at him
earnestly.

"I'd bet you any amount of money," said Tamkin, "that the
facts about you are sensational."

"Oh—ha, ha! You want them? You can sell them to a
true-confession magazine."

"People forget how sensational the things are that they do.
They don't see it on themselves. It blends into the background
of their daily life."

Wilhelm smiled. "Are you sure this boy tells you the truth?"

"Yes, because I've known the whole family for years."

"And you do psychological work with your own friends? I
didn't know that was allowed."

"Well, I'm a radical in the profession. I have to do good
wherever I can."

Wilhelm's face became ponderous again and pale. His
whitened gold hair lay heavy on his head, and he clasped
uneasy fingers on the table. Sensational, but oddly enough,
dull, too. Now how do you figure that out? It blends with the
background. Funny but unfunny. True but false. Casual but
laborious, Tamkin was. Wilhelm was most suspicious of him
when he took his driest tone.

"With me," said Dr. Tamkin, "I am at my most efficient
when I don't need the fee. When I only love. Without a
financial reward. I remove myself from the social influence.

Especially money. The spiritual compensation is what I look for. Bringing people into the here-and-now. The real universe. That's the present moment. The past is no good to us. The future is full of anxiety. Only the present is real—the here-and-now. Seize the day."

"Well," said Wilhelm, his earnestness returning. "I know you are a very unusual man. I like what you say about here-and-now. Are all the people who come to see you personal friends and patients too? Like that tall handsome girl, the one who always wears those beautiful broomstick skirts and belts?"

"She was an epileptic, and a most bad and serious pathology, too. I'm curing her successfully. She hasn't had a seizure in six months, and she used to have one every week."

"And that young cameraman, the one who showed us those movies from the jungles of Brazil, isn't he related to her?"

"Her brother. He's under my care, too. He has some terrible tendencies, which are to be expected when you have an epileptic sibling. I came into their lives when they needed help desperately, and took hold of them. A certain man forty years older than she had her in his control and used to give her fits by suggestion whenever she tried to leave him. If you only knew one per cent of what goes on in the city of New York! You see, I understand what it is when the lonely person begins to feel like an animal. When the night comes and he feels like howling from his window like a wolf. I'm taking complete care of that young fellow and his sister. I have to steady him down or he'll go from Brazil to Australia the next day. The way I keep him in the here-and-now is by teaching him Greek."

This was a complete surprise! "What, do you know Greek?"

"A friend of mine taught me when I was in Cairo. I studied Aristotle with him to keep from being idle."

Wilhelm tried to take in these new claims and examine them. Howling from the window like a wolf when night comes sounded genuine to him. That was something really to think about. But the Greek! He realized that Tamkin was watching to see how he took it. More elements were continually being

added. A few days ago Tamkin had hinted that he had once
been in the underworld, one of the Detroit Purple Gang. He
was once head of a mental clinic in Toledo. He had worked
with a Polish inventor on an unsinkable ship. He was a
technical consultant in the field of television. In the life of a
man of genius, all of these things might happen. But had they
happened to Tamkin? Was he a genius? He often said that he
had attended some of the Egyptian royal family as a
psychiatrist. "But everybody is alike, common or aristocrat,"
he told Wilhelm. "The aristocrat knows less about life."

An Egyptian princess whom he had treated in California,
for horrible disorders he had described to Wilhelm, retained
him to come back to the old country with her, and there he
had had many of her friends and relatives under his care.
They turned over a villa on the Nile to him. "For ethical
reasons, I can't tell you many of the details about them," he
said—but Wilhelm had already heard all these details, and
strange and shocking they were, if true. *If* true—he could not
be free from doubt. For instance, the general who had to wear
ladies' silk stockings and stand otherwise naked before the
mirror—and all the rest. Listening to the doctor when he was
so strangely factual, Wilhelm had to translate his words into
his own language, and he could not translate fast enough or
find terms to fit what he heard.

"Those Egyptian big shots invested in the market, too, for
the heck of it. What did they need extra money for? By
association, I almost became a millionaire myself, and if I had
played it smart there's no telling what might have happened. I
could have been the ambassador." The American? The
Egyptian ambassador? "A friend of mine tipped me off on the
cotton. I made a heavy purchase of it. I didn't have that kind
of money, but everybody there knew me. It never entered their
minds that a person of their social circle didn't have dough.
The sale was made on the phone. Then, while the cotton
shipment was at sea, the price tripled. When the stuff suddenly
became so valuable all hell broke loose on the world cotton
market, they looked to see who was the owner of this big

shipment. Me! They investigated my credit and found out I was a mere doctor, and they canceled. This was illegal. I sued them. But as I didn't have the money to fight them I sold the suit to a Wall Street lawyer for twenty thousand dollars. He fought it and was winning. They settled with him out of court for more than a million. But on the way back from Cairo, flying, there was a crash. All on board died. I have this guilt on my conscience, of being the murderer of that lawyer. Although he was a crook."

Wilhelm thought, I must be a real jerk to sit and listen to such impossible stories. I guess I am a sucker for people who talk about the deeper things of life, even the way he does.

"We scientific men speak of irrational guilt, Wilhelm," said Dr. Tamkin, as if Wilhelm were a pupil in his class. "But in such a situation, because of the money, I wished him harm. I realize it. This isn't the time to describe all the details, but the money made me guilty. *M*oney and *M*urder both begin with *M*. *M*achinery. *M*ischief."

Wilhelm, his mind thinking for him at random, said, "What about *M*ercy? *M*ilk-of-human-kindness?"

"One fact should be clear to you by now. Money-making is aggression. That's the whole thing. The functionalistic explanation is the only one. People come to the market to kill. They say, 'I'm going to make a killing.' It's not accidental. Only they haven't got the genuine courage to kill, and they erect a symbol of it. The money. They make a killing by a fantasy. Now, counting any number is always a sadistic activity. Like hitting. In the Bible, the Jews wouldn't allow you to count them. They knew it was sadistic."

"I don't understand what you mean," said Wilhelm. A strange uneasiness tore at him. The day was growing too warm and his head felt dim. "What makes them want to kill?"

"By and by, you'll get the drift," Dr. Tamkin assured him. His amazing eyes had some of the rich dryness of a brown fur. Innumerable crystalline hairs or spicules of light glittered in their bold surfaces. "You can't understand without first spending years on the study of the ultimates of human and

animal behavior, the deep chemical, organismic, and spiritual
secrets of life. I am a psychological poet."

"If you're this kind of poet," said Wilhelm, whose fingers in
his pocket were feeling in the little envelopes for the Phenaphen capsules, "what are you doing on the market?"

"That's a good question. Maybe I am better at speculation
because I don't care. Basically, I don't wish hard enough for
money, and therefore I come with a cool head to it."

Wilhelm thought, Oh, sure! That's an answer, is it? I bet
that if I took a strong attitude he'd back down on everything.
He'd grovel in front of me. The way he looks at me on the sly,
to see if I'm being taken in! He swallowed his Phenaphen pill
with a long gulp of water. The rims of his eyes grew red as it
went down. And then he felt calmer.

"Let me see if I can give you an answer that will satisfy
you," said Dr. Tamkin. His flapjacks were set before him. He
spread the butter on them, poured on brown maple syrup,
quartered them, and began to eat with hard, active, muscular
jaws which sometimes gave a creak at the hinges. He pressed
the handle of his knife against his chest and said, "In here, the
human bosom—mine, yours, everybody's—there isn't just one
soul. There's a lot of souls. But there are two main ones, the
real soul and a pretender soul. Now! Every man realizes that
he has to love something or somebody. He feels that he must
go outward. 'If thou canst not love, what art thou?' Are you
with me?"

"Yes, Doc, I think so," said Wilhelm, listening—a little
skeptically but nonetheless hard.

"'What art thou?' Nothing. That's the answer. Nothing. In
the heart of hearts—Nothing! So of course you can't stand
that and want to be Something, and you try. But instead of
being this Something, the man puts it over on everybody
instead. You can't be that strict to yourself. You love a *little*.
Like you have a dog" (*Scissors!*) "or give some money to a
charity drive. Now that isn't love, is it? What is it? Egotism,
pure and simple. It's a way to love the pretender soul. Vanity.
Only vanity is what it is. And social control. The interest of

the pretender soul is the same as the interest of the social life, the society mechanism. This is the main tragedy of human life. Oh, it is terrible! Terrible! You are not free. Your own betrayer is inside of you and sells you out. You have to obey him like a slave. He makes you work like a horse. And for what? For who?"

"Yes, for what?" The doctor's words caught Wilhelm's heart. "I couldn't agree more," he said. "When do we get free?"

"The purpose is to keep the whole thing going. The true soul is the one that pays the price. It suffers and gets sick, and it realizes that the pretender can't be loved. Because the pretender is a lie. The true soul loves the truth. And when the true soul feels like this, it wants to kill the pretender. The love has turned into hate. Then you become dangerous. A killer. You have to kill the deceiver."

"Does this happen to everybody?"

The doctor answered simply, "Yes, to everybody. Of course, for simplification purposes, I have spoken of the soul; it isn't a scientific term, but it helps you to understand it. Whenever the slayer slays, he wants to slay the soul in him which has gypped and deceived him. Who is his enemy? Him. And his lover? Also. Therefore, all suicide is murder, and all murder is suicide. It's the one and identical phenomenon. Biologically, the pretender soul takes away the energy of the true soul and makes it feeble, like a parasite. It happens unconsciously, unawaringly, in the depths of the organism. Ever take up parasitology?"

"No, it's my dad who's the doctor."

"You should read a book about it."

Wilhelm said, "But this means that the world is full of murderers. So it's not the world. It's a kind of hell."

"Sure," the doctor said. "At least a kind of purgiatory. You walk on the bodies. They are all around. I can hear them cry *de profundis* and wring their hands. I hear them, poor human beasts. I can't help hearing. And my eyes are open to it. I have to cry, too. This is the human tragedy-comedy."

Wilhelm tried to capture his vision. And again the doctor looked untrustworthy to him, and he doubted him. "Well," he said, "there are also kind, ordinary, helpful people. They're—out in the country. All over. What kind of morbid stuff do you read, anyway?" The doctor's room was full of books.

"I read the best of literature, science, and philosophy," Dr. Tamkin said. Wilhelm had observed that in his room even the TV aerial was set upon a pile of volumes. "Korzybski, Aristotle, Freud, W. H. Sheldon, and all the great poets. You answer me like a layman. You haven't applied your mind strictly to this."

"Very interesting," said Wilhelm. He was aware that he hadn't applied his mind strictly to anything. "You don't have to think I'm a dummy, though. I have ideas, too." A glance at the clock told him that the market would soon open. They could spare a few minutes yet. There were still more things he wanted to hear from Tamkin. He realized that Tamkin spoke faultily, but then scientific men were not always strictly literate. It was the description of the two souls that had awed him. In Tommy he saw the pretender. And even Wilky might not be himself. Might the name of his true soul be the one by which his old grandfather had called him—Velvel? The name of a soul, however, must be only that—soul. What did it look like? Does my soul look like me? Is there a soul that looks like Dad? Like Tamkin? Where does the true soul get its strength? Why does it have to love truth? Wilhelm was tormented, but tried to be oblivious to his torment. Secretly, he prayed the doctor would give him some useful advice and transform his life. "Yes, I understand you," he said. "It isn't lost on me."

"I never said you weren't intelligent, but only you just haven't made a study of it all. As a matter of fact you're a profound personality with very profound creative capacities but also disturbances. I've been concerned with you, and for some time I've been treating you."

"Without my knowing it? I haven't felt you doing anything. What do you mean? I don't think I like being treated without my knowledge. I'm of two minds. What's the matter, don't you think I'm normal?" And he really was divided in mind. That the doctor cared about him pleased him. This was what he craved, that someone should care about him, wish him well. Kindness, mercy, he wanted. But—and here he retracted his heavy shoulders in his peculiar way, drawing his hands up into his sleeves; his feet moved uneasily under the table—but he was worried, too, and even somewhat indignant. For what right had Tamkin to meddle without being asked? What kind of privileged life did this man lead? He took other people's money and speculated with it. Everybody came under his care. No one could have secrets from him.

The doctor looked at him with his deadly brown, heavy, impenetrable eyes, his naked shining head, his red hanging underlip, and said, "You have lots of guilt in you."

Wilhelm helplessly admitted, as he felt the heat rise to his wide face, "Yes, I think so too. But personally," he added, "I don't feel like a murderer. I always try to lay off. It's the others who get me. You know—make me feel oppressed. And if you don't mind, and it's all the same to you, I would rather know it when you start to treat me. And now, Tamkin, for Christ's sake, they're putting out the lunch menus already. Will you sign the check, and let's go!"

Tamkin did as he asked, and they rose. They were passing the bookkeeper's desk when he took out a substantial bundle of onionskin papers and said, "These are receipts of the transactions. Duplicates. You'd better keep them as the account is in your name and you'll need them for income taxes. And here is a copy of a poem I wrote yesterday."

"I have to leave something at the desk for my father," Wilhelm said, and he put his hotel bill in an envelope with a note. *Dear Dad, Please carry me this month, Yours, W.* He watched the clerk with his sullen pug's profile and his stiff-necked look push the envelope into his father's box.

"May I ask you really why you and your dad had words?" said Dr. Tamkin, who had hung back, waiting.

"It was about my future," said Wilhelm. He hurried down the stairs with swift steps, like a tower in motion, his hands in his trouser pockets. He was ashamed to discuss the matter. "He says there's a reason why I can't go back to my old territory, and there is. I told everybody I was going to be an officer of the corporation. And I was supposed to. It was promised. But then they welshed because of the son-in-law. I bragged and made myself look big."

"If you was humble enough, you could go back. But it doesn't make much difference. We'll make you a good living on the market."

They came into the sunshine of upper Broadway, not clear but throbbing through the dust and fumes, a false air of gas visible at eye level as it spurted from the bursting buses. From old habit, Wilhelm turned up the collar of his jacket.

"Just a technical question," Wilhelm said. "What happens if your losses are bigger than your deposit?"

"Don't worry. They have ultramodern electronic bookkeeping machinery, and it won't let you get in debt. It puts you out automatically. But I want you to read this poem. You haven't read it yet."

Light as a locust, a helicopter bringing mail from Newark Airport to La Guardia sprang over the city in a long leap.

The paper Wilhelm unfolded had ruled borders in red ink. He read:

MECHANISM VS FUNCTIONALISM
ISM VS HISM

If thee thyself couldst only see
Thy greatness that is and yet to be,
Thou would feel joy-beauty-what ecstasy.
They are at thy feet, earth-moon-sea, the trinity.

Why-forth then dost thou tarry
And partake thee only of the crust
And skim the earth's surface narry
When all creations art thy just?

Seek ye then that which art not there

In thine own glory let thyself rest.
Witness. Thy power is not bare.
Thou art King. Thou art at thy best.

Look then right before thee.
Open thine eyes and see.
At the foot of Mt. Serenity
Is thy cradle to eternity.

Utterly confused, Wilhelm said to himself explosively, What kind of mishmash, claptrap is this! What does he want from me? Damn him to hell, he might as well hit me on the head, and lay me out, kill me. What does he give me this for? What's the purpose? Is it a deliberate test? Does he want to mix me up? He's already got me mixed up completely. I was never good at riddles. Kiss those seven hundred bucks good-by, and call it one more mistake in a long line of mistakes— Oh, Mama, what a line! He stood near the shining window of a fancy fruit store, holding Tamkin's paper, rather dazed, as though a charge of photographer's flash powder had gone up in his eyes.

But he's waiting for my reaction. I have to say something to him about his poem. It really is no joke. What will I tell him? Who is this King? The poem is written *to* someone. But who? I can't even bring myself to talk. I feel too choked and strangled. With all the books he reads, how come the guy is so illiterate? And why do people just naturally assume that you'll know what they're talking about? No. I don't know, and nobody knows. The planets don't, the stars don't, infinite space doesn't. It doesn't square with Planck's Constant or anything else. So what's the good of it? Where's the need of it? What does he mean here by Mount Serenity? Could it be a figure of speech for Mount Everest? As he says people are all committing suicide, maybe those guys who climbed Everest were only trying to kill themselves, and if we want peace we should stay at the foot of the mountain. In the here-and-now. But it's also here-and-now on the slope, and on the top, where they climbed to seize the day. Surface narry is something he can't mean, I don't believe. I'm about to start foaming at the mouth. "Thy cradle . . ." *Who* is resting in his cradle—in his glory? My thoughts are at an end. I feel the wall. No more. So ——k it all! The money and everything. Take it away! When I have the money they eat me alive, like those piranha fish in the movie about the Brazilian jungle. It was hideous when they ate up that Brahma bull in the river. He turned pale, just like clay, and in five minutes nothing was left except the skeleton still in one piece, floating away. When I haven't got it any more, at least they'll let me alone.

"Well, what do you think of this?" said Dr. Tamkin. He gave a special sort of wise smile, as though Wilhelm must now see what kind of man he was dealing with.

"Nice. Very nice. Have you been writing long?"

"I've been developing this line of thought for years and years. You follow it all the way?"

"I'm trying to figure out who this Thou is."

"Thou? Thou is you."

"Me! Why? This applies to *me?*"

"Why shouldn't it apply to you. You were in my mind when I composed it. Of course, the hero of the poem is sick humanity. If it would open its eyes it would be great."

"Yes, but how do I get into this?"

"The main idea of the poem is *con*struct or *de*struct. There is no ground in between. Mechanism is *de*struct. Money of course is *de*struct. When the last grave is dug, the gravedigger will have to be paid. If you could have confidence in nature you would not have to fear. It would keep you up. Creative is nature. Rapid. Lavish. Inspirational. It shapes leaves. It rolls the waters of the earth. Man is the chief of this. All creations are his just inheritance. You don't know what you've got within you. A person either creates or he destroys. There is no neutrality . . ."

"I realized you were no beginner," said Wilhelm with propriety. "I have only one criticism to make. I think 'why-forth' is wrong. You should write 'Wherefore then dost

thou . . .'" And he reflected, So? I took a gamble. It'll have
to be a miracle, though, to save me. My money will be gone,
then it won't be able to destruct me. He can't just take and
lose it, though. He's in it, too. I think he's in a bad way
himself. He must be. I'm sure because, come to think of it, he
sweated blood when he signed that check. But what have I let
myself in for? The waters of the earth are going to roll over
me.

Chapter V

Patiently, in the window of the fruit store, a man with a
scoop spread crushed ice between his rows of vegetables.
There were also Persian melons, lilacs, tulips with radiant
black at the middle. The many street noises came back after a
little while from the caves of the sky. Crossing the tide of
Broadway traffic, Wilhelm was saying to himself, The reason
Tamkin lectures me is that somebody has lectured him, and
the reason for the poem is that he wants to give me good
advice. Everybody seems to know something. Even fellows
like Tamkin. Many people know what to do, but how many
can do it?

He believed that he must, that he could and would recover
the good things, the happy things, the easy tranquil things of
life. He had made mistakes, but he could overlook these. He
had been a fool, but that could be forgiven. The time
wasted—must be relinquished. What else could one do about
it? Things were too complex, but they might be reduced to
simplicity again. Recovery was possible. First he had to get
out of the city. No, first he had to pull out his money. . . .

From the carnival of the street—pushcarts, accordion and
fiddle, shoeshine, begging, the dust going round like a woman
on stilts—they entered the narrow crowded theater of the
brokerage office. From front to back it was filled with the
Broadway crowd. But how was lard doing this morning? From
the rear of the hall Wilhelm tried to read the tiny figures. The
German manager was looking through his binoculars. Tamkin

placed himself on Wilhelm's left and covered his conspicuous bald head. "The guy'll ask me about the margin," he muttered. They passed, however, unobserved. "Look, the lard has held its place," he said.

Tamkin's eyes must be very sharp to read the figures over so many heads and at this distance—another respect in which he was unusual.

The room was always crowded. Everyone talked. Only at the front could you hear the flutter of the wheels within the board. Teletyped news items crossed the illuminated screen above.

"Lard. Now what about rye?" said Tamkin, rising on his toes. Here he was a different man, active and impatient. He parted people who stood in his way. His face turned resolute, and on either side of his mouth odd bulges formed under his mustache. Already he was pointing out to Wilhelm the appearance of a new pattern on the board. "There's something up today," he said.

"Then why'd you take so long with breakfast?" said Wilhelm.

There were no reserved seats in the room, only customary ones. Tamkin always sat in the second row, on the commodities side of the aisle. Some of his acquaintances kept their hats on the chairs for him.

"Thanks. Thanks," said Tamkin, and he told Wilhelm, "I fixed it up yesterday."

"That was a smart thought," said Wilhelm. They sat down.

With folded hands, by the wall, sat an old Chinese businessman in a seersucker coat. Smooth and fat, he wore a white Vandyke. One day Wilhelm had seen him on Riverside Drive pushing two little girls along in a baby carriage—his grandchildren. Then there were two women in their fifties, supposed to be sisters, shrewd and able money-makers, according to Tamkin. They had never a word to say to Wilhelm. But they would chat with Tamkin. Tamkin talked to everyone.

Wilhelm sat between Mr. Rowland, who was elderly, and

Mr. Rappaport, who was very old. Yesterday Rowland had told him that in the year 1908, when he was a junior at Harvard, his mother had given him twenty shares of steel for his birthday, and then he had started to read the financial news and had never practiced law but instead followed the market for the rest of his life. Now he speculated only in soy beans, of which he had made a specialty. By his conservative method, said Tamkin, he cleared two hundred a week. Small potatoes, but then he was a bachelor, retired, and didn't need money.

"Without dependents," said Tamkin. "He doesn't have the problems that you and I do."

Did Tamkin have dependents? He had everything that it was possible for a man to have—science, Greek, chemistry, poetry, and now dependents too. That beautiful girl with epilepsy, perhaps. He often said that she was a pure, marvelous, spiritual child who had no knowledge of the world. He protected her, and, if he was not lying, adored her. And if you encouraged Tamkin by believing him, or even if you refrained from questioning him, his hints became more daring. Sometimes he said that he paid for her music lessons. Sometimes he seemed to have footed the bill for the brother's camera expedition to Brazil. And he spoke of paying for the support of the orphaned child of a dead sweetheart. These hints, made dully as asides, grew by repetition into sensational claims.

"For myself, I don't need much," said Tamkin. "But a man can't live for himself and I need the money for certain important things. What do you figure you have to have, to get by?"

"Not less than fifteen grand, after taxes. That's for my wife and the two boys."

"Isn't there anybody else?" said Tamkin with a shrewdness almost cruel. But his look grew more sympathetic as Wilhelm stumbled, not willing to recall another grief.

"Well—there was. But it wasn't a money matter."

"I should hope!" said Tamkin. "If love is love, it's free.

Fifteen grand, though, isn't too much for a man of your intelligence to ask out of life. Fools, hard-hearted criminals, and murderers have millions to squander. They burn up the world—oil, coal, wood, metal, and soil, and suck even the air and the sky. They consume, and they give back no benefit. A man like you, humble for life, who wants to feel and live, has trouble—not wanting," said Tamkin in his parenthetical fashion, "to exchange an ounce of soul for a pound of social power—he'll never make it without help in a world like this. But don't you worry." Wilhelm grasped at this assurance. "Just you never mind. We'll go easily beyond your figure."

Dr. Tamkin gave Wilhelm comfort. He often said that he had made as much as a thousand a week in commodities. Wilhelm had examined the receipts, but until this moment it had never occurred to him that there must be debit slips too; he had been shown only the credits.

"But fifteen grand is not an ambitious figure," Tamkin was telling him. "For that you don't have to wear yourself out on the road, dealing with narrow-minded people. A lot of them don't like Jews, either, I suppose?"

"I can't afford to notice. I'm lucky when I have my occupation. Tamkin, do you mean you can save our money?"

"Oh, did I forget to mention what I did before closing yesterday? You see, I closed out one of the lard contracts and bought a hedge of December rye. The rye is up three points already and takes some of the sting out. But lard will go up, too."

"Where? God, yes, you're right," said Wilhelm, eager, and got to his feet to look. New hope freshened his heart. "Why didn't you tell me before?"

And Tamkin, smiling like a benevolent magician, said, "You must learn to have trust. The slump in lard can't last. And just take a look at eggs. Didn't I predict they couldn't go any lower? They're rising and rising. If we had taken eggs we'd be far ahead."

"Then why didn't we take them?"

"We were just about to. I had a buying order in at .24, but

the tide turned at .26¼ and we barely missed. Never mind. Lard will go back to last year's levels."

Maybe. But when? Wilhelm could not allow his hopes to grow too strong. However, for a little while he could breathe more easily. Late-morning trading was getting active. The shining numbers whirred on the board, which sounded like a huge cage of artificial birds. Lard fluctuated between two points, but rye slowly climbed.

He closed his strained, greatly earnest eyes briefly and nodded his Buddha's head, too large to suffer such uncertainties. For several moments of peace he was removed to his small yard in Roxbury.

He breathed in the sugar of the pure morning.

He heard the long phrases of the birds.

No enemy wanted his life.

Wilhelm thought, I will get out of here. I don't belong in New York any more. And he sighed like a sleeper.

Tamkin said, "Excuse me," and left his seat. He could not sit still in the room but passed back and forth between the stocks and commodities sections. He knew dozens of people and was continually engaging in discussions. Was he giving advice, gathering information, or giving it, or practicing— whatever mysterious profession he practiced? Hypnotism? Perhaps he could put people in a trance while he talked to them. What a rare, peculiar bird he was, with those pointed shoulders, that bare head, his loose nails, almost claws, and those brown, soft, deadly, heavy eyes.

He spoke of things that mattered, and as very few people did this he could take you by surprise, excite you, move you. Maybe he wished to do good, maybe give himself a lift to a higher level, maybe believe his own prophecies, maybe touch his own heart. Who could tell? He had picked up a lot of strange ideas; Wilhelm could only suspect, he could not say with certainty, that Tamkin hadn't made them his own.

Now Tamkin and he were equal partners, but Tamkin had put up only three hundred dollars. Suppose he did this not only once but five times; then an investment of fifteen

hundred dollars gave him five thousand to speculate with. If
he had power of attorney in every case, he could shift the
money from one account to another. No, the German
probably kept an eye on him. Nevertheless, it was possible.
Calculations like this made Wilhelm feel ill. Obviously Tamkin was a plunger. But how did he get by? He must be in his
fifties. How did he support himself? Five years in Egypt;
Hollywood before that; Michigan; Ohio; Chicago. A man of
fifty has supported himself for at least thirty years. You could
be sure that Tamkin had never worked in a factory or in an
office. How did he make it? His taste in clothes was horrible,
but he didn't buy cheap things. He wore corduroy or velvet
shirts from Clyde's, painted neckties, striped socks. There was
a slightly acid or pasty smell about his person; for a doctor, he
didn't bathe much. Also, Dr. Tamkin had a good room at the
Gloriana and had had it for about a year. But so was Wilhelm
himself a guest, with an unpaid bill at present in his father's
box. Did the beautiful girl with the skirts and belts pay him?
Was he defrauding his so-called patients? So many questions
impossible to answer could not be asked about an honest
man. Nor perhaps about a sane man. Was Tamkin a lunatic,
then? That sick Mr. Perls at breakfast had said that there was
no easy way to tell the sane from the mad, and he was right
about that in any big city and especially in New York—the
end of the world, with its complexity and machinery, bricks
and tubes, wires and stones, holes and heights. And was
everybody crazy here? What sort of people did you see? Every
other man spoke a language entirely his own, which he had
figured out by private thinking; he had his own ideas and
peculiar ways. If you wanted to talk about a glass of water,
you had to start back with God creating the heavens and
earth; the apple; Abraham; Moses and Jesus; Rome; the
Middle Ages; gunpowder; the Revolution; back to Newton;
up to Einstein; then war and Lenin and Hitler. After
reviewing this and getting it all straight again you could
proceed to talk about a glass of water. "I'm fainting, please get
me a little water." You were lucky even then to make yourself

understood. And this happened over and over and over with everyone you met. You had to translate and translate, explain and explain, back and forth, and it was the punishment of hell itself not to understand or be understood, not to know the crazy from the sane, the wise from the fools, the young from the old or the sick from the well. The fathers were no fathers and the sons no sons. You had to talk with yourself in the daytime and reason with yourself at night. Who else was there to talk to in a city like New York?

A queer look came over Wilhelm's face with its eyes turned up and his silent mouth with its high upper lip. He went several degrees further—when you are like this, dreaming that everybody is outcast, you realize that this must be one of the small matters. There is a larger body, and from this you cannot be separated. The glass of water fades out. You do not go from simple a and simple b to the great x and y, nor does it matter whether you agree about the glass but, far beneath such details, what Tamkin would call the real soul says plain and understandable things to everyone. There sons and fathers are themselves, and a glass of water is only an ornament; it makes a hoop of brightness on the cloth; it is an angel's mouth. There truth for everybody may be found, and confusion is only—only temporary, thought Wilhelm.

The idea of this larger body had been planted in him a few days ago beneath Times Square, when he had gone downtown to pick up tickets for the baseball game on Saturday (a double-header at the Polo Grounds). He was going through an underground corridor, a place he had always hated and hated more than ever now. On the walls between the advertisements were words in chalk: "Sin No More," and "Do Not Eat the Pig," he had particularly noticed. And in the dark tunnel, in the haste, heat, and darkness which disfigure and make freaks and fragments of nose and eyes and teeth, all of a sudden, unsought, a general love for all these imperfect and lurid-looking people burst out in Wilhelm's breast. He loved them. One and all, he passionately loved them. They were his brothers and his sisters. He was imperfect and disfigured himself, but what difference did that make if he was united with them by this blaze of love? And as he walked he began to say, "Oh my brothers—my brothers and my sisters," blessing them all as well as himself.

So what did it matter how many languages there were, or how hard it was to describe a glass of water? Or matter that a few minutes later he didn't feel anything like a brother toward the man who sold him the tickets?

On that very same afternoon he didn't hold so high an opinion of this same onrush of loving-kindness. What did it come to? As they had the capacity and must use it once in a while, people were bound to have such involuntary feelings. It was only another one of those subway things. Like having a hard-on at random. But today, his day of reckoning, he consulted his memory again and thought, I must go back to that. That's the right clue and may do me the most good. Something very big. Truth, like.

The old fellow on the right, Mr. Rappaport, was nearly blind and kept asking Wilhelm, "What's the new figure on November wheat? Give me July soy beans too." When you told him he didn't say thank you. He said, "Okay," instead, or, "Check," and turned away until he needed you again. He was very old, older even than Dr. Adler, and if you believed Tamkin he had once been the Rockefeller of the chicken business and had retired with a large fortune.

Wilhelm had a queer feeling about the chicken industry, that it was sinister. On the road, he frequently passed chicken farms. Those big, rambling, wooden buildings out in the neglected fields; they were like prisons. The lights burned all night in them to cheat the poor hens into laying. Then the slaughter. Pile all the coops of the slaughtered on end, and in one week they'd go higher than Mount Everest or Mount Serenity. The blood filling the Gulf of Mexico. The chicken shit, acid, burning the earth.

How old—old this Mr. Rappaport was! Purple stains were buried in the flesh of his nose, and the cartilage of his ear was twisted like a cabbage heart. Beyond remedy by glasses, his eyes were smoky and faded.

"Read me that soy-bean figure now, boy," he said, and Wilhelm did. He thought perhaps the old man might give him a tip, or some useful advice or information about Tamkin. But no. He only wrote memoranda on a pad, and put the pad in his pocket. He let no one see what he had written. And Wilhelm thought this was the way a man who had grown rich by the murder of millions of animals, little chickens, would act. If there was a life to come he might have to answer for the killing of all those chickens. What if they all were waiting? But if there was a life to come, everybody would have to answer. But if there was a life to come, the chickens themselves would be all right.

Well! What stupid ideas he was having this morning. Phooey!

Finally old Rappaport did address a few remarks to Wilhelm. He asked him whether he had reserved his seat in the synagogue for Yom Kippur.

"No," said Wilhelm.

"Well, you better hurry up if you expect to say *Yiskor* for your parents. I never miss."

And Wilhelm thought, Yes, I suppose I should say a prayer for Mother once in a while. His mother had belonged to the Reform congregation. His father had no religion. At the cemetery Wilhelm had paid a man to say a prayer for her. He was among the tombs and he wanted to be tipped for the *El molai rachamin.* "Thou God of Mercy," Wilhelm thought that meant. *B'gan Aden*—"in Paradise." Singing, they drew it out. *B'gan Ay–den.* The broken bench beside the grave made him wish to do something. Wilhelm often prayed in his own manner. He did not go to the synagogue but he would occasionally perform certain devotions, according to his feelings. Now he reflected, In Dad's eyes I am the wrong kind of Jew. He doesn't like the way I act. Only he is the right kind of Jew. Whatever you are, it always turns out to be the wrong kind.

Mr. Rappaport grumbled and whiffed at his long cigar, and the board, like a swarm of electrical bees, whirred.

"Since you were in the chicken business, I thought you'd speculate in eggs, Mr. Rappaport." Wilhelm, with his warm, panting laugh, sought to charm the old man.

"Oh. Yeah. Loyalty, hey?" said old Rappaport. "I should stick to them. I spent a lot of time amongst chickens. I got to be an expert chicken-sexer. When the chick hatches you have to tell the boys from the girls. It's not easy. You need long, long experience. What do you think, it's a joke? A whole industry depends on it. Yes, now and then I buy a contract eggs. What have you got today?"

Wilhelm said anxiously, "Lard. Rye."

"Buy? Sell?"

"Bought."

"Uh," said the old man. Wilhelm could not determine what he meant by this. But of course you couldn't expect him to make himself any clearer. It was not in the code to give information to anyone. Sick with desire, Wilhelm waited for Mr. Rappaport to make an exception in his case. Just this once! Because it was critical. Silently, by a sort of telepathic concentration, he begged the old man to speak the single word that would save him, give him the merest sign. "Oh, please— please help," he nearly said. If Rappaport would close one eye, or lay his head to one side, or raise his finger and point to a column in the paper or to a figure on his pad. A hint! A hint!

A long perfect ash formed on the end of the cigar, the white ghost of the leaf with all its veins and its fainter pungency. It was ignored, in its beauty, by the old man. For it was beautiful. Wilhelm he ignored as well.

Then Tamkin said to him, "Wilhelm, look at the jump our rye just took."

December rye climbed three points as they tensely watched; the tumblers raced and the machine's lights buzzed.

"A point and a half more, and we can cover the lard losses," said Tamkin. He showed him his calculations on the margin of the *Times*.

"I think you should put in the selling order now. Let's get out with a small loss."

"Get out now? Nothing doing."

"Why not? Why should we wait?"

"Because," said Tamkin with a smiling, almost openly scoffing look, "you've got to keep your nerve when the market starts to go places. Now's when you can make something."

"I'd get out while the getting's good."

"No, you shouldn't lose your head like this. It's obvious to me what the mechanism is, back in the Chicago market. There's a short supply of December rye. Look, it's just gone up another quarter. We should ride it."

"I'm losing my taste for the gamble," said Wilhelm. "You can't feel safe when it goes up so fast. It's liable to come down just as quick."

Dryly, as though he were dealing with a child, Tamkin told him in a tone of tiring patience, "Now listen, Tommy. I have it diagnosed right. If you wish I should sell I can give the sell order. But this is the difference between healthiness and pathology. One is objective, doesn't change his mind every minute, enjoys the risk element. But that's not the neurotic character. The neurotic character—"

"Damn it, Tamkin!" said Wilhelm roughly. "Cut that out. I don't like it. Leave my character out of consideration. Don't pull any more of that stuff on me. I tell you I don't like it."

Tamkin therefore went no further; he backed down. "I meant," he said, softer, "that as a salesman you are basically an artist type. The seller is in the visionary sphere of the business function. And then you're an actor, too."

"No matter what type I am—" An angry and yet weak sweetness rose into Wilhelm's throat. He coughed as though he had the flu. It was twenty years since he had appeared on the screen as an extra. He blew the bagpipes in a film called *Annie Laurie*. Annie had come to warn the young Laird; he would not believe her and called the bagpipers to drown her out. He made fun of her while she wrung her hands. Wilhelm, in a kilt, barelegged, blew and blew and blew and not a sound came out. Of course all the music was recorded. He fell sick with the flu after that and still suffered sometimes from chest weakness.

"Something stuck in your throat?" said Tamkin. "I think

maybe you are too disturbed to think clearly. You should try some of my 'here-and-now' mental exercises. It stops you from thinking so much about the future and the past and cuts down confusion."

"Yes, yes, yes, yes," said Wilhelm, his eyes fixed on December rye.

"Nature only knows one thing, and that's the present. Present, present, eternal present, like a big, huge, giant wave—colossal, bright and beautiful, full of life and death, climbing into the sky, standing in the seas. You must go along with the actual, the Here-and-Now, the glory—"

. . . chest weakness, Wilhelm's recollection went on. Margaret nursed him. They had had two rooms of furniture, which was later seized. She sat on the bed and read to him. He made her read for days, and she read stories, poetry, everything in the house. He felt dizzy, stifled when he tried to smoke. They had him wear a flannel vest.

> Come then, Sorrow!
> Sweetest Sorrow!
> Like an own babe I nurse thee on my breast!

Why did he remember that? Why?

"You have to pick out something that's in the actual, immediate present moment," said Tamkin. "And say to yourself here-and-now, here-and-now, here-and-now. 'Where am I?' 'Here.' 'When is it?' 'Now.' Take an object or a person. Anybody. 'Here and now I see a person.' 'Here and now I see a man.' 'Here and now I see a man sitting on a chair.' Take me, for instance. Don't let your mind wander. 'Here and now I see a man in a brown suit. Here and now I see a corduroy shirt.' You have to narrow it down, one item at a time, and not let your imagination shoot ahead. Be in the present. Grasp the hour, the moment, the instant."

Is he trying to hypnotize or con me? Wilhelm wondered. To take my mind off selling? But even if I'm back at seven hundred bucks, then where am I?

As if in prayer, his lids coming down with raised veins, frayed out, on his significant eyes, Tamkin said, " 'Here and now I see a button. Here and now I see the thread that sews the button. Here and now I see the green thread.' " Inch by inch he contemplated himself in order to show Wilhelm how calm it would make him. But Wilhelm was hearing Margaret's voice as she read, somewhat unwillingly,

> Come then, Sorrow!
>
> .   .   .   .
>
> I thought to leave thee,
> And deceive thee,
> But now of all the world I love thee best.

Then Mr. Rappaport's old hand pressed his thigh, and he said, "What's my wheat? Those damn guys are blocking the way. I can't see."

Chapter VI

Rye was still ahead when they went out to lunch, and lard was holding its own.

They ate in the cafeteria with the gilded front. There was the same art inside as outside. The food looked sumptuous. Whole fishes were framed like pictures with carrots, and the salads were like terraced landscapes or like Mexican pyramids; slices of lemon and onion and radishes were like sun and moon and stars; the cream pies were about a foot thick and the cakes swollen as if sleepers had baked them in their dreams.

"What'll you have?" said Tamkin.

"Not much. I ate a big breakfast. I'll find a table. Bring me some yogurt and crackers and a cup of tea. I don't want to spend much time over lunch."

Tamkin said, "You've got to eat."

Finding an empty place at this hour was not easy. The old

people idled and gossiped over their coffee. The elderly ladies were rouged and mascaraed and hennaed and used blue hair rinse and eye shadow and wore costume jewelry, and many of them were proud and stared at you with expressions that did not belong to their age. Were there no longer any respectable old ladies who knitted and cooked and looked after their grandchildren? Wilhelm's grandmother had dressed him in a sailor suit and danced him on her knee, blew on the porridge for him and said, "Admiral, you must eat." But what was the use of remembering this so late in the day?

He managed to find a table, and Dr. Tamkin came along with a tray piled with plates and cups. He had Yankee pot roast, purple cabbage, potatoes, a big slice of watermelon, and two cups of coffee. Wilhelm could not even swallow his yogurt. His chest pained him still.

At once Tamkin involved him in a lengthy discussion. Did he do it to stall Wilhelm and prevent him from selling out the rye—or to recover the ground lost when he had made Wilhelm angry by hints about the neurotic character? Or did he have no purpose except to talk?

"I think you worry a lot too much about what your wife and your father will say. Do they matter so much?"

Wilhelm replied, "A person can become tired of looking himself over and trying to fix himself up. You can spend the entire second half of your life recovering from the mistakes of the first half."

"I believe your dad told me he had some money to leave you."

"He probably does have something."

"A lot?"

"Who can tell," said Wilhelm guardedly.

"You ought to think over what you'll do with it."

"I may be too feeble to do anything by the time I get it. If I get anything."

"A thing like this you ought to plan out carefully. Invest it properly." He began to unfold schemes whereby you bought bonds, and used the bonds as security to buy something else and thereby earned twelve per cent safely on your money. Wilhelm failed to follow the details. Tamkin said, "If he made you a gift now, you wouldn't have to pay the inheritance taxes."

Bitterly, Wilhelm told him, "My father's death blots out all other considerations from his mind. He forces me to think about it, too. Then he hates me because he succeeds. When I get desperate—of course I think about money. But I don't want anything to happen to him. I certainly don't want him to die." Tamkin's brown eyes glittered shrewdly at him. "You don't believe it. Maybe it's not psychological. But on my word of honor. A joke is a joke, but I don't want to joke about stuff like this. When he dies, I'll be robbed, like. I'll have no more father."

"You love your old man?"

Wilhelm grasped at this. "Of course, of course I love him. My father. My mother—" As he said this there was a great pull at the very center of his soul. When a fish strikes the line you feel the live force in your hand. A mysterious being beneath the water, driven by hunger, has taken the hook and rushes away and fights, writhing. Wilhelm never identified what struck within him. It did not reveal itself. It got away.

And Tamkin, the confuser of the imagination, began to tell, or to fabricate, the strange history of *his* father. "He was a great singer," he said. "He left us five kids because he fell in love with an opera soprano. I never held it against him, but admired the way he followed the life-principle. I wanted to do the same. Because of unhappiness, at a certain age, the brain starts to die back." (True, true! thought Wilhelm.) "Twenty years later I was doing experiments in Eastman Kodak, Rochester, and I found the old fellow. He had five more children." (False, false!) "He wept; he was ashamed. I had nothing against him. I naturally felt strange."

"My dad is something of a stranger to me, too," said Wilhelm, and he began to muse. Where is the familiar person he used to be? Or I used to be? Catherine—she won't even talk to me any more, my own sister. It may not be so much my trouble that Papa turns his back on as my confusion. It's too much. The ruins of life, and on top of that confusion—chaos and old night. Is it an easier farewell for Dad if we don't part friends? He should maybe do it angrily— "Blast you with my curse!" And why, Wilhelm further asked, should he or anybody else pity me; or why should I be pitied sooner than another fellow? It is my childish mind that thinks people are ready to give it just because you need it.

Then Wilhelm began to think about his own two sons and to wonder how he appeared to them, and what they would think of him. Right now he had an advantage through baseball. When he went to fetch them, to go to Ebbets Field, though, he was not himself. He put on a front but he felt as if he had swallowed a fistful of sand. The strange, familiar house, horribly awkward; the dog, Scissors, rolled over on his back and barked and whined. Wilhelm acted as if there were nothing irregular, but a weary heaviness came over him. On the way to Flatbush he would think up anecdotes about old Pigtown and Charlie Ebbets for the boys and reminiscences of the old stars, but it was very heavy going. They did not know how much he cared for them. No. It hurt him greatly and he blamed Margaret for turning them against him. She wanted to ruin him, while she wore the mask of kindness. Up in Roxbury he had to go and explain to the priest, who was not sympathetic. They don't care about individuals, their rules come first. Olive said she would marry him outside the Church when he was divorced. But Margaret would not let go. Olive's father was a pretty decent old guy, an osteopath, and he understood what it was all about. Finally he said, "See here, I have to advise Olive. She is asking me. I am mostly a freethinker myself, but the girl has to live in this town." And by now Wilhelm and Olive had had a great many troubles and she was beginning to dread his days in Roxbury, she said. He trembled at offending this small, pretty, dark girl whom he adored. When she would get up late on Sunday morning she would wake him almost in tears at being late for Mass. He would try to help her hitch her garters and smooth out her slip and dress and even put on her hat with shaky hands; then he would rush her to church and drive in second gear in his forgetful way, trying to apologize and to calm her. She got out a block from church to avoid gossip. Even so she loved him, and she would have married him if he had obtained the divorce. But Margaret must have sensed this. Margaret would tell him he did not really want a divorce; he was afraid of it. He cried, "Take everything I've got, Margaret. Let me go to Reno. Don't you want to marry again?" No. She went out with other men, but took his money. She lived in order to punish him.

Dr. Tamkin told Wilhelm, "Your dad is jealous of you."

Wilhelm smiled. "Of *me?* That's rich."

"Sure. People are always jealous of a man who leaves his wife."

"Oh," said Wilhelm scornfully. "When it comes to wives he wouldn't have to envy me."

"Yes, and your wife envies you, too. She thinks, He's free and goes with young women. Is she getting old?"

"Not exactly old," said Wilhelm, whom the mention of his wife made sad. Twenty years ago, in a neat blue wool suit, in a soft hat made of the same cloth—he could plainly see her. He stooped his yellow head and looked under the hat at her clear, simple face, her living eyes moving, her straight small nose, her jaw beautifully, painfully clear in its form. It was a cool day, but he smelled the odor of pines in the sun, in the granite canyon. Just south of Santa Barbara, this was.

"She's forty-some years old," he said.

"I was married to a lush," said Tamkin. "A painful alcoholic. I couldn't take her out to dinner because she'd say she was going to the ladies' toilet and disappear into the bar. I'd ask the bartenders they shouldn't serve her. But I loved her deeply. She was the most spiritual woman of my entire experience."

"Where is she now?"

"Drowned," said Tamkin. "At Provincetown, Cape Cod. It must have been a suicide. She was that way—suicidal. I tried everything in my power to cure her. Because," said Tamkin, "my real calling is to be a healer. I get wounded. I suffer from it. I would like to escape from the sicknesses of others, but I can't. I am only on loan to myself, so to speak. I belong to humanity."

Liar! Wilhelm inwardly called him. Nasty lies. He invented a woman and killed her off and then called himself a healer, and made himself so earnest he looked like a bad-natured sheep. He's a puffed-up little bogus and humbug with smelly feet. A doctor! A doctor would wash himself. He believes he's making a terrific impression, and he practically invites you to take off your hat when he talks about himself; and he thinks he has an imagination, but he hasn't, neither is he smart.

Then what am I doing with him here, and why did I give him the seven hundred dollars? thought Wilhelm.

Oh, this was a day of reckoning. It was a day, he thought, on which, willing or not, he would take a good close look at the truth. He breathed hard and his misshapen hat came low upon his congested dark-blond face. A rude look. Tamkin was a charlatan, and furthermore he was desperate. And furthermore, Wilhelm had always known this about him. But he appeared to have worked it out at the back of his mind that Tamkin for thirty or forty years had gotten through many a tight place, that he would get through this crisis too and bring him, Wilhelm, to safety also. And Wilhelm realized that he was on Tamkin's back. It made him feel that he had virtually left the ground and was riding upon the other man. He was in the air. It was for Tamkin to take the steps.

The doctor, if he was a doctor, did not look anxious. But then his face did not have much variety. Talking always about spontaneous emotion and open receptors and free impulses, he was about as expressive as a pincushion. When his hypnotic spell failed, his big underlip made him look weak-minded. Fear stared from his eyes, sometimes, so humble as to make you sorry for him. Once or twice Wilhelm had seen that look. Like a dog, he thought. Perhaps he didn't look it now, but he was very nervous. Wilhelm knew, but he could not afford to recognize this too openly. The doctor needed a little room, a little time. He should not be pressed now. So Tamkin went on, telling his tales.

Wilhelm said to himself, I am on his back—his back. I gambled seven hundred bucks, so I must take this ride. I have to go along with him. It's too late. I can't get off.

"You know," Tamkin said, "that blind old man Rappaport —he's pretty close to totally blind—is one of the most interesting personalities around here. If you could only get him to tell his true story. It's fascinating. This is what he told me. You often hear about bigamists with a secret life. But this old man never hid anything from anybody. He's a regular patriarch. Now, I'll tell you what he did. He had two whole families, separate and apart, one in Williamsburg and the other in the Bronx. The two wives knew about each other. The wife in the Bronx was younger; she's close to seventy now. When he got sore at one wife he went to live with the other one. Meanwhile he ran his chicken business in New Jersey. By one wife he had four kids, and by the other six. They're all grown, but they never have met their half-brothers and sisters and don't want to. The whole bunch of them are listed in the telephone book."

"I can't believe it," said Wilhelm.

"He told me this himself. And do you know what else? While he had his eyesight he used to read a lot, but the only books he would read were by Theodore Roosevelt. He had a set in each of the places where he lived, and he brought his kids up on those books."

"Please," said Wilhelm, "don't feed me any more of this stuff, will you? Kindly do not—"

"In telling you this," said Tamkin with one of his hypnotic subtleties, "I do have a motive. I want you to see how some people free themselves from morbid guilt feelings and follow their instincts. Innately, the female knows how to cripple by sickening a man with guilt. It is a very special *de*struct, and she sends her curse to make a fellow impotent. As if she says, 'Unless I allow it, you will never more be a man.' But men like

my old dad or Mr. Rappaport answer, 'Woman, what art thou
to me?' You can't do that yet. You're a halfway case. You
want to follow your instinct, but you're too worried still. For
instance, about your kids—"

"Now look here," said Wilhelm, stamping his feet. "One
thing! Don't bring up my boys. Just lay off."

"I was only going to say that they are better off than with
conflicts in the home."

"I'm deprived of my children." Wilhelm bit his lip. It was
too late to turn away. The anguish struck him. "I pay and pay.
I never see them. They grow up without me. She makes them
like herself. She'll bring them up to be my enemies. Please let's
not talk about this."

But Tamkin said, "Why do you let her make you suffer so?
It defeats the original object in leaving her. Don't play her
game. Now, Wilhelm, I'm trying to do you some good. I want
to tell you, don't marry suffering. Some people do. They get
married to it, and sleep and eat together, just as husband and
wife. If they go with joy they think it's adultery."

When Wilhelm heard this he had, in spite of himself, to
admit that there was a great deal in Tamkin's words. Yes,
thought Wilhelm, suffering is the only kind of life they are
sure they can have, and if they quit suffering they're afraid
they'll have nothing. He knows it. This time the faker knows
what he's talking about.

Looking at Tamkin, he believed he saw all this confessed
from his usually barren face. Yes, yes, he too. One hundred
falsehoods, but at last one truth. Howling like a wolf from the
city window. No one can bear it any more. Everyone is so full
of it that at last everybody must proclaim it. It! It!

Then suddenly Wilhelm rose and said, "That's enough of
this. Tamkin, let's go back to the market."

"I haven't finished my melon."

"Never mind that. You've had enough to eat. I want to go
back."

Dr. Tamkin slid the two checks across the table. "Who paid
yesterday? It's your turn, I think."

It was not until they were leaving the cafeteria that Wilhelm remembered definitely that he had paid yesterday too. But it wasn't worth arguing about.

Tamkin kept repeating as they walked down the street that there were many who were dedicated to suffering. But he told Wilhelm, "I'm optimistic in your case, and I have seen a world of maladjustment. There's hope for you. You don't really want to destroy yourself. You're trying hard to keep your feelings open, Wilhelm. I can see it. Seven per cent of this country is committing suicide by alcohol. Another three, maybe, narcotics. Another sixty just fading away into dust by boredom. Twenty more who have sold their souls to the Devil. Then there's a small percentage of those who want to live. That's the only significant thing in the whole world of today. Those are the only two classes of people there are. Some want to live, but the great majority don't." This fantastic Tamkin began to surpass himself. "They don't. Or else, why these wars? I'll tell you more," he said. "The love of the dying amounts to one thing; they want you to die with them. It's because they love you. Make no mistake."

True, true! thought Wilhelm, profoundly moved by these revelations. How does he know these things? How can he be such a jerk, and even perhaps an operator, a swindler, and understand so well what gives? I believe what he says. It simplifies much—everything. People are dropping like flies. I am trying to stay alive and work too hard at it. That's what's turning my brains. This working hard defeats its own end. At what point should I start over? Let me go back a ways and try once more.

Only a few hundred yards separated the cafeteria from the broker's, and within that short space Wilhelm turned again, in measurable degrees, from these wide considerations to the problems of the moment. The closer he approached to the market, the more Wilhelm had to think about money.

They passed the newsreel theater where the ragged shoe-shine kids called after them. The same old bearded man with his bandaged beggar face and his tiny ragged feet and the old press clipping on his fiddle case to prove he had once been a concert violinist, pointed his bow at Wilhelm, saying, "You!" Wilhelm went by with worried eyes, bent on crossing Seventy-second Street. In full tumult the great afternoon current raced for Columbus Circle, where the mouth of midtown stood open and the skyscrapers gave back the yellow fire of the sun.

As they approached the polished stone front of the new office building, Dr. Tamkin said, "Well, isn't that old Rappaport by the door? I think he should carry a white cane, but he will never admit there's a single thing the matter with his eyes."

Mr. Rappaport did not stand well; his knees were sunk, while his pelvis only half filled his trousers. His suspenders held them, gaping.

He stopped Wilhelm with an extended hand, having somehow recognized him. In his deep voice he commanded him, "Take me to the cigar store."

"You want me—? Tamkin!" Wilhelm whispered, "You take him."

Tamkin shook his head. "He wants you. Don't refuse the old gentleman." Significantly he said in a lower voice. "This minute is another instance of the 'here-and-now.' You have to live in this very minute, and you don't want to. A man asks you for help. Don't think of the market. It won't run away. Show your respect to the old boy. Go ahead. That may be more valuable."

"Take me," said the old chicken merchant again.

Greatly annoyed, Wilhelm wrinkled his face at Tamkin. He took the old man's big but light elbow at the bone. "Well, let's step on it," he said. "Or wait—I want to have a look at the board first to see how we're doing."

But Tamkin had already started Mr. Rappaport forward. He was walking, and he scolded Wilhelm, saying, "Don't leave me standing in the middle of the sidewalk. I'm afraid to get knocked over."

"Let's get a move on. Come." Wilhelm urged him as Tamkin went into the broker's.

The traffic seemed to come down Broadway out of the sky, where the hot spokes of the sun rolled from the south. Hot, stony odors rose from the subway grating in the street.

"These teen-age hoodlums worry me. I'm ascared of these Puerto Rican kids, and these young characters who take dope," said Mr. Rappaport. "They go around all hopped up."

"Hoodlums?" said Wilhelm. "I went to the cemetery and my mother's stone bench was split. I could have broken somebody's neck for that. Which store do you go to?"

"Across Broadway. That La Magnita sign next door to the Automat."

"What's the matter with this store here on this side?"

"They don't carry my brand, that's what's the matter."

Wilhelm cursed, but checked the words.

"What are you talking?"

"Those damn taxis," said Wilhelm. "They want to run everybody down."

They entered the cool, odorous shop. Mr. Rappaport put away his large cigars with great care in various pockets while Wilhelm muttered, "Come on, you old creeper. What a poky old character! The whole world waits on him." Rappaport did not offer Wilhelm a cigar, but, holding one up, he asked, "What do you say at the size of these, huh? They're Churchill-type cigars."

He barely crawls along, thought Wilhelm. His pants are dropping off because he hasn't got enough flesh for them to stick to. He's almost blind, and covered with spots, but this old man still makes money in the market. Is loaded with dough, probably. And I bet he doesn't give his children any. Some of them must be in their fifties. This is what keeps middle-aged men as children. He's master over the dough. Think—just think! Who controls everything? Old men of this type. Without needs. They don't need, therefore they have. I need, therefore I don't have. That would be too easy.

"I'm older even than Churchill," said Rappaport.

Now he wanted to talk! But if you asked him a question in the market, he couldn't be bothered to answer.

"I bet you are," said Wilhelm. "Come, let's get going."

"I was a fighter, too, like Churchill," said the old man. "When we licked Spain I went into the Navy. Yes, I was a gob that time. What did I have to lose? Nothing. After the battle of San Juan Hill, Teddy Roosevelt kicked me off the beach."

"Come, watch the curb," said Wilhelm.

"I was curious and wanted to see what went on. I didn't have no business there, but I took a boat and rowed myself to the beach. Two of our guys was dead, layin' under the American flag to keep the flies off. So I says to the guy on duty, there, who was the sentry, 'Let's have a look at these guys. I want to see what went on here,' and he says, 'Naw,' but I talked him into it. So he took off the flag and there were these two tall guys, both gentlemen, lying in their boots. They was very tall. The two of them had long mustaches. They were high-society boys. I think one of them was called Fish, from up the Hudson, a big-shot family. When I looked up, there was Teddy Roosevelt, with his hat off, and he was looking at these fellows, the only ones who got killed there. Then he says to me, 'What's the Navy want here? Have you got orders?' 'No, sir,' I says to him. 'Well, get the hell off the beach, then.'"

Old Rappaport was very proud of this memory. "Everything he said had such snap, such class. Man! I love that Teddy Roosevelt," he said, "I love him!"

Ah, what people are! He is almost not with us, and his life is nearly gone, but T. R. once yelled at him, so he loves him. I guess it is love, too. Wilhelm smiled. So maybe the rest of Tamkin's story was true, about the ten children and the wives and the telephone directory.

He said, "Come on, come on, Mr. Rappaport," and hurried the old man back by the large hollow elbow; he gripped it through the thin cotton cloth. Re-entering the brokerage office where under the lights the tumblers were speeding with the clack of drumsticks upon wooden blocks, more than ever resembling a Chinese theater, Wilhelm strained his eyes to see the board.

The lard figures were unfamiliar. That amount couldn't be lard! They must have put the figures in the wrong slot. He traced the line back to the margin. It was down to .19, and had dropped twenty points since noon. And what about the contract of rye? It had sunk back to its earlier position, and they had lost their chance to sell.

Old Mr. Rappaport said to Wilhelm, "Read me my wheat figure."

"Oh, leave me alone for a minute," he said, and positively hid his face from the old man behind one hand. He looked for Tamkin, Tamkin's bald head, or Tamkin with his gray straw and the cocoa-colored band. He couldn't see him. Where was he? The seats next to Rowland were taken by strangers. He thrust himself over the one on the aisle, Mr. Rappaport's former place, and pushed at the back of the chair until the new occupant, a red-headed man with a thin, determined face, leaned forward to get out of his way but would not surrender the seat. "Where's Tamkin?" Wilhelm asked Rowland.

"Gee, I don't know. Is anything wrong?"

"You must have seen him. He came in a while back."

"No, but I didn't."

Wilhelm fumbled out a pencil from the top pocket of his coat and began to make calculations. His very fingers were numb, and in his agitation he was afraid he made mistakes with the decimal points and went over the subtraction and multiplication like a schoolboy at an exam. His heart, accustomed to many sorts of crisis, was now in a new panic. And, as he had dreaded, he was wiped out. It was unnecessary to ask the German manager. He could see for himself that the electronic bookkeeping device must have closed him out. The manager probably had known that Tamkin wasn't to be trusted, and on that first day he might have warned him. But you couldn't expect him to interfere.

"You get hit?" said Mr. Rowland.

And Wilhelm, quite coolly, said, "Oh, it could have been worse, I guess." He put the piece of paper into his pocket with its cigarette butts and packets of pills. The lie helped him out—although, for a moment, he was afraid he would cry. But he hardened himself. The hardening effort made a violent, vertical pain go through his chest, like that caused by a pocket of air under the collarbones. To the old chicken millionaire, who by this time had become acquainted with the drop in rye and lard, he also denied that anything serious had happened. "It's just one of those temporary slumps. Nothing to be scared about," he said, and remained in possession of himself. His need to cry, like someone in a crowd, pushed and jostled and abused him from behind, and Wilhelm did not dare turn. He said to himself, I will not cry in front of these people. I'll be damned if I'll break down in front of them like a kid, even though I never expect to see them again. No! No! And yet his unshed tears rose and rose and he looked like a man about to drown. But when they talked to him, he answered very distinctly. He tried to speak proudly.

". . . going away?" he heard Rowland ask.

"What?"

"I thought you might be going away too. Tamkin said he was going to Maine this summer for his vacation."

"Oh, going away?"

Wilhelm broke off and went to look for Tamkin in the men's toilet. Across the corridor was the room where the machinery of the board was housed. It hummed and whirred like mechanical birds, and the tubes glittered in the dark. A couple of businessmen with cigarettes in their fingers were having a conversation in the lavatory. At the top of the closet door sat a gray straw hat with a cocoa-colored band. "Tamkin," said Wilhelm. He tried to identify the feet below the door. "Are you in there, Doctor Tamkin?" he said with stifled anger. "Answer me. It's Wilhelm."

The hat was taken down, the latch lifted, and a stranger came out who looked at him with annoyance.

"You waiting?" said one of the businessmen. He was warning Wilhelm that he was out of turn.

"Me? Not me," said Wilhelm. "I'm looking for a fellow."

Bitterly angry, he said to himself that Tamkin would pay

him the two hundred dollars at least, his share of the original deposit. "And before he takes the train to Maine, too. Before he spends a penny on vacation—that liar! We went into this as equal partners."

Chapter VII

I was the man beneath; Tamkin was on my back, and I thought I was on his. He made me carry him, too, besides Margaret. Like this they ride on me with hoofs and claws. Tear me to pieces, stamp on me and break my bones.

Once more the hoary old fiddler pointed his bow at Wilhelm as he hurried by. Wilhelm rejected his begging and denied the omen. He dodged heavily through traffic and with his quick, small steps ran up the lower stairway of the Gloriana Hotel with its dark-tinted mirrors, kind to people's defects. From the lobby he phoned Tamkin's room, and when no one answered he took the elevator up. A rouged woman in her fifties with a mink stole led three tiny dogs on a leash, high-strung creatures with prominent black eyes, like dwarf deer, and legs like twigs. This was the eccentric Estonian lady who had been moved with her pets to the twelfth floor.

She identified Wilhelm. "You are Doctor Adler's son," she said.

Formally, he nodded.

"I am a dear friend of your father."

He stood in the corner and would not meet her glance, and she thought he was snubbing her and made a mental note to speak of it to the doctor.

The linen wagon stood at Tamkin's door, and the chambermaid's key with its big brass tongue was in the lock.

"Has Doctor Tamkin been here?" he asked her.

"No, I haven't seen him."

Wilhelm came in, however, to look around. He examined the photos on the desk, trying to connect the faces with the strange people in Tamkin's stories. Big, heavy volumes were stacked under the double-pronged TV aerial. *Science and Sanity*, he read, and there were several books of poetry. The *Wall Street Journal* hung in separate sheets from the bed-table under the weight of the silver water jug. A bathrobe with lightning streaks of red and white was laid across the foot of the bed with a pair of expensive batik pajamas. It was a box of a room, but from the windows you saw the river as far uptown as the bridge, as far downtown as Hoboken. What lay between was deep, ázure, dirty, complex, crystal, rusty, with the red bones of new apartments rising on the bluffs of New Jersey, and huge liners in their berths, the tugs with matted beards of cordage. Even the brackish tidal river smell rose this high, like the smell of mop water. From every side he heard pianos, and the voices of men and women singing scales and opera, all mixed, and the sounds of pigeons on the ledges.

Again Wilhelm took the phone. "Can you locate Doctor Tamkin in the lobby for me?" he asked. And when the operator reported that she could not, Wilhelm gave the number of his father's room, but Dr. Adler was not in either. "Well, please give me the masseur. I say the massage room. Don't you understand me? The men's health club. Yes, Max Schilper's—how am I supposed to know the name of it?"

There a strange voice said, "Toktor Adler?" It was the old Czech prizefighter with the deformed nose and ears who was attendant down there and gave out soap, sheets, and sandals. He went away. A hollow endless silence followed. Wilhelm flickered the receiver with his nails, whistled into it, but could not summon either the attendant or the operator.

The maid saw him examining the bottles of pills on Tamkin's table and seemed suspicious of him. He was running low on Phenaphen pills and was looking for something else. But he swallowed one of his own tablets and went out and rang again for the elevator. He went down to the health club. Through the steamy windows, when he emerged, he saw the reflection of the swimming pool swirling green at the bottom of the lowest stairway. He went through the locker-room curtains. Two men wrapped in towels were playing Ping-pong.

They were awkward and the ball bounded high. The Negro in
the toilet was shining shoes. He did not know Dr. Adler by
name, and Wilhelm descended to the massage room. On the
tables naked men were lying. It was not a brightly lighted
place, and it was very hot, and under the white faint moons of
the ceiling shone pale skins. Calendar pictures of pretty girls
dressed in tiny fringes were pinned on the wall. On the first
table, eyes deeply shut in heavy silent luxury lay a man with a
full square beard and short legs, stocky and black-haired. He
might have been an orthodox Russian. Wrapped in a sheet,
waiting, the man beside him was newly shaved and red from
the steambath. He had a big happy face and was dreaming.
And after him was an athlete, strikingly muscled, powerful
and young, with a strong white curve to his genital and a
half-angry smile on his mouth. Dr. Adler was on the fourth
table, and Wilhelm stood over his father's pale, slight body.
His ribs were narrow and small, his belly round, white, and
high. It had its own being, like something separate. His thighs
were weak, the muscles of his arms had fallen, his throat was
creased.

The masseur in his undershirt bent and whispered in his ear,
"It's your son," and Dr. Adler opened his eyes into Wilhelm's
face. At once he saw the trouble in it, and by an instantaneous reflex he removed himself from the danger of contagion,
and he said serenely, "Well, have you taken my advice,
Wilky?"

"Oh, Dad," said Wilhelm.

"To take a swim and get a massage?"

"Did you get my note?" said Wilhelm.

"Yes, but I'm afraid you'll have to ask somebody else,
because I can't. I had no idea you were so low on funds. How
did you let it happen? Didn't you lay anything aside?"

"Oh, please, Dad," said Wilhelm, almost bringing his hands
together in a clasp.

"I'm sorry," said the doctor. "I really am. But I have set up
a rule. I've thought about it, I believe it is a good rule, and I
don't want to change it. You haven't acted wisely. What's the
matter?"

"Everything. Just everything. What isn't? I did have a little, but I haven't been very smart."

"You took some gamble? You lost it? Was it Tamkin? I told you, Wilky, not to build on that Tamkin. Did you? I suspect—"

"Yes, Dad, I'm afraid I trusted him."

Dr. Adler surrendered his arm to the masseur, who was using wintergreen oil.

"Trusted! And got taken?"

"I'm afraid I kind of—" Wilhelm glanced at the masseur but he was absorbed in his work. He probably did not listen to conversations. "I did. I might as well say it. I should have listened to you."

"Well, I won't remind you how often I warned you. It must be very painful."

"Yes, Father, it is."

"I don't know how many times you have to be burned in order to learn something. The same mistakes, over and over."

"I couldn't agree with you more," said Wilhelm with a face of despair. "You're so right, Father. It's the same mistakes, and I get burned again and again. I can't seem to—I'm stupid, Dad, I just can't breathe. My chest is all up—I feel choked. I just simply can't catch my breath."

He stared at his father's nakedness. Presently he became aware that Dr. Adler was making an effort to keep his temper. He was on the verge of an explosion. Wilhelm hung his face and said, "Nobody likes bad luck, eh Dad?"

"So! It's bad luck, now. A minute ago it was stupidity."

"It is stupidity—it's some of both. It's true that I can't learn. But I—"

"I don't want to listen to the details," said his father. "And I want you to understand that I'm too old to take on new burdens. I'm just too old to do it. And people who will just wait for help—must *wait* for help. They have got to stop waiting."

"It isn't all a question of money—there are other things a father can give to a son." He lifted up his gray eyes and his nostrils grew wide with a look of suffering appeal that stirred his father even more deeply against him.

He warningly said to him, "Look out, Wilky, you're tiring my patience very much."

"I try not to. But one word from you, just a word, would go a long way. I've never asked you for very much. But you are not a kind man, Father. You don't give the little bit I beg you for."

He recognized that his father was now furiously angry. Dr. Adler started to say something, and then raised himself and gathered the sheet over him as he did so. His mouth opened, wide, dark, twisted, and he said to Wilhelm, "You want to make yourself into my cross. But I am not going to pick up a cross. I'll see you dead, Wilky, by Christ, before I let you do that to me."

"Father, listen! Listen!"

"Go away from me now. It's torture for me to look at you, you slob!" cried Dr. Adler.

Wilhelm's blood rose up madly, in anger equal to his father's, but then it sank down and left him helplessly captive to misery. He said stiffly, and with a strange sort of formality, "Okay, Dad. That'll be enough. That's about all we should say." And he stalked out heavily by the door adjacent to the swimming pool and the steam room, and labored up two long flights from the basement. Once more he took the elevator to the lobby on the mezzanine.

He inquired at the desk for Dr. Tamkin.

The clerk said, "No, I haven't seen him. But I think there's something in the box for you."

"Me? Give it here," said Wilhelm and opened a telephone message from his wife. It read, "Please phone Mrs. Wilhelm on return. Urgent."

Whenever he received an urgent message from his wife he was always thrown into a great fear for the children. He ran to the phone booth, spilled out the change from his pockets onto the little curved steel shelf under the telephone, and dialed the Digby number.

"Yes?" said his wife. Scissors barked in the parlor.

"Margaret?"

"Yes, hello." They never exchanged any other greeting. She instantly knew his voice.

"The boys all right?"

"They're out on their bicycles. Why shouldn't they be all right? Scissors, quiet!"

"Your message scared me," he said. "I wish you wouldn't make 'urgent' so common."

"I had something to tell you."

Her familiar unbending voice awakened in him a kind of hungry longing, not for Margaret but for the peace he had once known.

"You sent me a postdated check," she said. "I can't allow that. It's already five days past the first. You dated your check for the twelfth."

"Well, I have no money. I haven't got it. You can't send me to prison for that. I'll be lucky if I can raise it by the twelfth."

She answered, "You better get it, Tommy."

"Yes? What for?" he said. "Tell me. For the sake of what? To tell lies about me to everyone? You—"

She cut him off. "You know what for. I've got the boys to bring up."

Wilhelm in the narrow booth broke into a heavy sweat. He dropped his head and shrugged while with his fingers he arranged nickels, dimes, and quarters in rows. "I'm doing my best," he said. "I've had some bad luck. As a matter of fact, it's been so bad that I don't know where I am. I couldn't tell you what day of the week this is. I can't think straight. I'd better not even try. This has been one of those days, Margaret. May I never live to go through another like it. I mean that with all my heart. So I'm not going to try to do any thinking today. Tomorrow I'm going to see some guys. One is a sales manager. The other is in television. But not to act," he hastily added. "On the business end."

"That's just some more of your talk, Tommy," she said. "You ought to patch things up with Rojax Corporation.

They'd take you back. You've got to stop thinking like a youngster."

"What do you mean?"

"Well," she said, measured and unbending, remorselessly unbending, "you still think like a youngster. But you can't do that any more. Every other day you want to make a new start. But in eighteen years you'll be eligible for retirement. Nobody wants to hire a new man of your age."

"I know. But listen, you don't have to sound so hard. I can't get on my knees to them. And really you don't have to sound so hard. I haven't done you so much harm."

"Tommy, I have to chase you and ask you for money that you owe us, and I hate it."

She hated also to be told that her voice was hard.

"I'm making an effort to control myself," she told him.

He could picture her, her graying bangs cut with strict fixity above her pretty, decisive face. She prided herself on being fair-minded. We could not bear, he thought, to know what we do. Even though blood is spilled. Even though the breath of life is taken from someone's nostrils. This is the way of the weak; quiet and fair. And then smash! They smash!

"Rojax take me back? I'd have to crawl back. They don't need me. After so many years I should have got stock in the firm. How can I support the three of you, and live myself, on half the territory? And why should I even try when you won't lift a finger to help? I sent you back to school, didn't I? At that time you said—"

His voice was rising. She did not like that and intercepted him. "You misunderstood me," she said.

"You must realize you're killing me. You can't be as blind as all that. Thou shalt not kill! Don't you remember that?"

She said, "You're just raving now. When you calm down it'll be different. I have great confidence in your earning ability."

"Margaret, you don't grasp the situation. You'll have to get a job."

"Absolutely not. I'm not going to have two young children running loose."

"They're not babies," Wilhelm said. "Tommy is fourteen. Paulie is going to be ten."

"Look," Margaret said in her deliberate manner. "We can't continue this conversation if you're going to yell so, Tommy. They're at a dangerous age. There are teen-aged gangs—the parents working, or the families broken up."

Once again she was reminding him that it was he who had left her. She had the bringing up of the children as her burden, while he must expect to pay the price of his freedom.

Freedom! he thought with consuming bitterness. Ashes in his mouth, not freedom. Give me my children. For they are mine too.

Can you be the woman I lived with? he started to say. Have you forgotten that we slept so long together? Must you now deal with me like this, and have no mercy?

He would be better off with Margaret again than he was today. This was what she wanted to make him feel, and she drove it home. "Are you in misery?" she was saying. "But you have deserved it." And he could not return to her any more than he could beg Rojax to take him back. If it cost him his life, he could not. Margaret had ruined him with Olive. She hit him and hit him, beat him, battered him, wanted to beat the very life out of him.

"Margaret, I want you please to reconsider about work. You have that degree now. Why did I pay your tuition?"

"Because it seemed practical. But it isn't. Growing boys need parental authority and a home."

He begged her, "Margaret, go easy on me. You ought to. I'm at the end of my rope and feel that I'm suffocating. You don't want to be responsible for a person's destruction. You've got to let up. I feel I'm about to burst." His face had expanded. He struck a blow upon the tin and wood and nails of the wall of the booth. "You've got to let me breathe. If I should keel over, what then? And it's something I can never understand about you. How you can treat someone like this whom you lived with so long. Who gave you the best of himself. Who tried. Who loved you." Merely to pronounce the word "love" made him tremble.

"Ah," she said with a sharp breath. "Now we're coming to it. How did you imagine it was going to be—big shot? Everything made smooth for you? I thought you were leading up to this."

She had not, perhaps, intended to reply as harshly as she did, but she brooded a great deal and now she could not forbear to punish him and make him feel pains like those she had to undergo.

He struck the wall again, this time with his knuckles, and he had scarcely enough air in his lungs to speak in a whisper, because his heart pushed upward with a frightful pressure. He got up and stamped his feet in the narrow enclosure.

"Haven't I always done my best?" he yelled, though his voice sounded weak and thin to his own ears. "Everything comes from me and nothing back again to me. There's no law that'll punish this, but you are committing a crime against me. Before God—and that's no joke. I mean that. Before God! Sooner or later the boys will know it."

In a firm tone, levelly, Margaret said to him, "I won't stand to be howled at. When you can speak normally and have something sensible to say I'll listen. But not to this." She hung up.

Wilhelm tried to tear the apparatus from the wall. He ground his teeth and seized the black box with insane digging fingers and made a stifled cry and pulled. Then he saw an elderly lady staring through the glass door, utterly appalled by him, and he ran from the booth, leaving a large amount of change on the shelf. He hurried down the stairs and into the street.

On Broadway it was still bright afternoon and the gassy air was almost motionless under the leaden spokes of sunlight, and sawdust footprints lay about the doorways of butcher shops and fruit stores. And the great, great crowd, the inexhaustible current of millions of every race and kind pouring out, pressing round, of every age, of every genius, possessors of every human secret, antique and future, in every face the refinement of one particular motive or essence—*I labor, I spend, I strive, I design, I love, I cling, I uphold, I give*

way, I envy, I long, I scorn, I die, I hide, I want. Faster, much
faster than any man could make the tally. The sidewalks were
wider than any causeway; the street itself was immense, and it
quaked and gleamed and it seemed to Wilhelm to throb at the
last limit of endurance. And although the sunlight appeared
like a broad tissue, its actual weight made him feel like a
drunkard.

"I'll get a divorce if it's the last thing I do," he swore. "As
for Dad— As for Dad— I'll have to sell the car for junk and
pay the hotel. I'll have to go on my knees to Olive and say,
'Stand by me a while. Don't let her win. Olive!'" And he
thought, I'll try to start again with Olive. In fact, I must. Olive
loves me. Olive—

Beside a row of limousines near the curb he thought he saw
Dr. Tamkin. Of course he had been mistaken before about the
hat with the cocoa-colored band and didn't want to make the
same mistake twice. But wasn't that Tamkin who was
speaking so earnestly, with pointed shoulders, to someone
under the canopy of the funeral parlor? For this was a huge
funeral. He looked for the singular face under the dark gray,
fashionable hatbrim. There were two open cars filled with
flowers, and a policeman tried to keep a path open to
pedestrians. Right at the canopy-pole, now wasn't that that
damned Tamkin talking away with a solemn face, gesticu-
lating with an open hand?

"Tamkin!" shouted Wilhelm, going forward. But he was
pushed to the side by a policeman clutching his nightstick at
both ends, like a rolling pin. Wilhelm was even farther from
Tamkin now, and swore under his breath at the cop who
continued to press him back, back, belly and ribs, saying,
"Keep it moving there, please," his face red with impatient
sweat, his brows like red fur. Wilhelm said to him haughtily,
"You shouldn't push people like this."

The policeman, however, was not really to blame. He had
been ordered to keep a way clear. Wilhelm was moved
forward by the pressure of the crowd.

He cried, "Tamkin!"

But Tamkin was gone. Or rather, it was he himself who was carried from the street into the chapel. The pressure ended inside, where it was dark and cool. The flow of fan-driven air dried his face, which he wiped hard with his handkerchief to stop the slight salt itch. He gave a sigh when he heard the organ notes that stirred and breathed from the pipes and he saw people in the pews. Men in formal clothes and black homburgs strode softly back and forth on the cork floor, up and down the center aisle. The white of the stained glass was like mother-of-pearl, with the blue of a great star fluid, like velvet ribbon.

Well, thought Wilhelm, if that was Tamkin outside I might as well wait for him here where it's cool. Funny, he never mentioned he had a funeral to go to today. But that's just like the guy.

But within a few minutes he had forgotten Tamkin. He stood along the wall with others and looked toward the coffin and the slow line that was moving past it, gazing at the face of the dead. Presently he too was in this line, and slowly, slowly, foot by foot, the beating of his heart anxious, thick, frightening, but somehow also rich, he neared the coffin and paused for his turn, and gazed down. He caught his breath when he looked at the corpse, and his face swelled, his eyes shone hugely with instant tears.

The dead man was gray-haired. He had two large waves of gray hair at the front. But he was not old. His face was long, and he had a bony nose, slightly, delicately twisted. His brows were raised as though he had sunk into the final thought. Now at last he was with it, after the end of all distractions, and when his flesh was no longer flesh. And by this meditative look Wilhelm was so struck that he could not go away. In spite of the tinge of horror, and then the splash of heartsickness that he felt, he could not go. He stepped out of line and remained beside the coffin; his eyes filled silently and through his still tears he studied the man as the line of visitors moved with veiled looks past the satin coffin toward the standing bank of lilies, lilacs, roses. With great stifling sorrow, almost

admiration, Wilhelm nodded and nodded. On the surface, the
dead man with his formal shirt and his tie and silk lapels and
his powdered skin looked so proper; only a little beneath
so—black, Wilhelm thought, so fallen in the eyes.

Standing a little apart, Wilhelm began to cry. He cried at
first softly and from sentiment, but soon from deeper feeling.
He sobbed loudly and his face grew distorted and hot, and the
tears stung his skin. A man—another human creature, was
what first went through his thoughts, but other and different
things were torn from him. "What'll I do? I'm stripped and
kicked out. . . . Oh, Father, what do I ask of you? What'll I
do about the kids—Tommy, Paul? My children. And Olive?
My dear! Why, why, why—you must protect me against that
devil who wants my life. If you want it, then kill me. Take,
take it, take it from me."

Soon he was past words, past reason, coherence. He could
not stop. The source of all tears had suddenly sprung open
within him, black, deep, and hot, and they were pouring out
and convulsed his body, bending his stubborn head, bowing
his shoulders, twisting his face, crippling the very hands with
which he held the handkerchief. His efforts to collect himself
were useless. The great knot of ill and grief in his throat
swelled upward and he gave in utterly and held his face and
wept. He cried with all his heart.

He, alone of all the people in the chapel, was sobbing. No
one knew who he was.

One woman said, "Is that perhaps the cousin from New
Orleans they were expecting?"

"It must be somebody real close to carry on so."

"Oh my, oh my! To be mourned like that," said one man
and looked at Wilhelm's heavy shaken shoulders, his clutched
face and whitened fair hair, with wide, glinting, jealous eyes.

"The man's brother, maybe?"

"Oh, I doubt that very much," said another bystander.
"They're not alike at all. Night and day."

The flowers and lights fused ecstatically in Wilhelm's blind,
wet eyes; the heavy sea-like music came up to his ears. It

poured into him where he had hidden himself in the center of a crowd by the great and happy oblivion of tears. He heard it and sank deeper than sorrow, through torn sobs and cries toward the consummation of his heart's ultimate need.

From

The Adventures of Augie March:

The Einhorns

William Einhorn was the first superior man I knew. He had a brain and many enterprises, real directing power, philosophical capacity, and if I were methodical enough to take thought before an important and practical decision and also (*N.B.**) if I were really his disciple and not what I am, I'd ask myself, "What would Caesar suffer in this case? What would Machiavelli advise or Ulysses do? What would Einhorn think?" I'm not kidding when I enter Einhorn in this eminent list. It was him that I knew, and what I understand of them in him. Unless you want to say that we're at the dwarf end of all times and mere children whose only share in grandeur is like a boy's share in fairy-tale kings, beings of a different kind from times better and stronger than ours. But if we're comparing men and men, not men and children or men and demigods, which is just what would please Caesar among us teeming democrats, and if we don't have any special wish to abdicate into some different, lower form of existence out of shame for our defects before the golden faces of these and other old-time men, then I have the right to praise Einhorn and not care about smiles of derogation from those who think the race no longer has in any important degree the traits we honor in these fabulous names.

This chapter has been slightly revised by the author for this volume.
* FDR, in one of his Fireside Chats, made a deep impression on the nation by saying "*N.B.*—which means *nota bene*." —S. B.

But I don't want to be pushed into exaggeration by such opinion, which is the opinion of students who, at all ages, feel their boyishness when they confront the past.

I went to work for Einhorn while I was a high-school junior, not long before the great crash, during the Hoover administration, when Einhorn was still a wealthy man, though I don't believe he was ever so rich as he later claimed, and I stayed on with him after he had lost most of his property. Then, actually, I became essential to him, not just metaphorical right hand but virtually arms and legs. Einhorn was a cripple who didn't have the use of either, not even partial; only his hands still functioned, and they weren't strong enough to drive a wheel chair. He had to be rolled and drawn around the house by his wife, brother, relations, or one of the people he usually had on call, either employed by or connected with him. Whether they worked for him or were merely around his house or office, he had a talent for making supernumeraries of them, and there were always plenty of people hoping to become rich, or more rich if already well-to-do, through the Einhorns. They were the most important real-estate brokers in the district and owned and controlled much property, including the enormous forty-flat building where they lived. The poolroom in the corner store of it was owned outright by them and called Einhorn's Billiards. There were six other stores—hardware, fruit, a tin shop, a restaurant, barbershop, and a funeral parlor belonging to Kinsman, whose son it was that ran away with my cousin Howard Coblin to join the Marines against Sandino. The restaurant was the one in which Tambow, the Republican vote-getter, played cards. The Einhorns were his ex-wife's relatives; they, however, had never taken sides in the divorce. It wouldn't have become Einhorn Senior, the old Commissioner, who had had four wives himself, two getting alimony still, to be strict with somebody on that account. The Commissioner had never held office, that was just people's fun. He was still an old galliard, with white Buffalo Bill vandyke, and he swanked around, still healthy and fleshy in white suits, looking things over with big sex-amused eyes. He had a lot of respect from everyone for his shrewdness, and when he opened his grand old mouth to say something about a chattel mortgage or the location of a lot, in his laconic, single-syllabled way, the whole hefty, serious crowd of businessmen in the office stopped their talk. He gave out considerable advice, and Coblin and Five Properties got him to invest some of their money. Kreindl, who did a job for him once in a while, thought he was as wise as a god. "The son is smart," he said, "but the Commissioner—that's really a man you have to give way to on earth." I disagreed then and do still, though when the Commissioner was up to something he stole the show. One of my responsibilities in summer was to go with him to the beach, where he swam daily until the second week in September. I was supposed to see that he didn't go out too far, and also to hand him lighted cigarettes while he floated near the pier in the pillow striping of his suit with large belly, large old man's sex, and yellow, bald knees; his white back-hair spread on the water, yellowish, like polar bear's pelt, his vigorous foreskull, tanned and red, turned up; while his big lips uttered and his nose drove out smoke, clever and pleasurable in the warm, heavy blue of Michigan; while wood-bracketed trawlers, tarred on the sides, chuffed and vapored outside the water reserved for the bawling, splashing, many-actioned, brilliant-colored crowd; waterside structures and towers, and skyscrapers beyond in a vast right angle to the evading bend of the shore.

Einhorn was the Commissioner's son by his first wife. By the second or third he had another son who was called Shep or, by his poolroom friends, Dingbat, for John Dingbat O'Berta, the candy kid of city politics and friend of Polack Sam Zincowicz. Since he didn't either know or resemble O'Berta and wasn't connected with Thirteenth Ward politics or any other, I couldn't exactly say how he came by the name. But without being a hoodlum himself he was taken up with gang events and crime, a kind of amateur of the lore and done up in the gangster taste so you might take him for somebody tied in with the dangerous Druccis or Big Hayes Hubacek:

sharp financial hat, body-clasping suit, the shirt Andalusian style buttoned up to the collar and worn without a necktie, trick shoes, pointed and pimpy, polished like a tango dancer's; he clumped hard on the leather heels. Dingbat's hair was violent, brilliant, black, treated, ripple-marked. Bantam, thin-muscled, swift, almost frail, he had an absolutely unreasonable face. To be distinguished from brutal—it wasn't that, there was all kind of sentiment in it. But wild, down-twisting, squint-eyed, unchangeably firm and wrong in thoughts, with the prickles coming black through his unmethodical after-shave talcum: the puss of an executioner's subject, provided we understand the prototype not as a murderer (he attacked with his fists and had a killer's swing but not the real intention) but as somebody intractable. As far as that goes, he was beaten all the time and wore a mishealed scar where his cheek had been caught between his teeth by a ring, but he went on springing and boxing, rushing out from the poolroom on a fresh challenge to spin around on his tango shoes and throw his tense, weightless punches. The beatings didn't squelch him. I was by one Sunday when he picked a fight with that huge Five Properties and thrust him on the chest with his hands, failing to move him; Five Properties picked him up and threw him down on the floor. When Dingbat came back punching, Five Properties grinned but was frightened and shied back against the cue rack. Somebody in the crowd began to shout that Five Properties was yellow, and it was thought the right thing to hold Dingbat back, by the arms, struggling with a blinded, drawn face of rage. A pal of his said what a shame that a veteran of Château Thierry should be shoved around by a greenhorn. Five Properties took it to heart and thereafter stayed away from the poolroom.

Dingbat had had charge of the poolroom at one time, but he was unreliable and the Commissioner had replaced him with a manager. Now he was around as the owner's son—racked up balls, once in a while changed color like a coal when a green table felt was ripped—and in the capacity of key-man and bravo, referee, bet-holder, sports expert, and gang-war historian, on the watch for a small deal, a fighter to manage, or a game of rotation at ten cents a ball. Between times he was his father's chauffeur. The Commissioner couldn't drive the big red Blackhawk-Stutz he owned—the Einhorns never could see anything in a small car—and Dingbat took him to the beach when it was too hot to walk. After all, the old man was pushing seventy-five and couldn't be allowed to risk a stroke. I'd ride with him in the back seat while Dingbat sat with mauled, crazy neck and a short grip on the wheel, ukelele and bathing suit on the cushion beside him; he was particularly sex-goaded when he drove, shouting, whistling, and honking after quiff, to the entertainment of his father. Sometimes we had the company of Clem or Jimmy, or of Sylvester, the movie bankrupt, who was now flunking out of his engineer's course at Armour Tech and talking about moving away to New York altogether. On the beach Dingbat, athletically braced up with belt and wristbands, a bandanna to keep the sand out of his hair when he stood on his head, streaked down with suntan oil, was with a crowd of girls and other beach athletes, dancing and striking into his ukelele with:

> Ani-ka, hula wicki-wicki
> Sweet brown maiden said to me,
> And she taught me hula-hula
> On the beach at Waikiki . . .

Kindled enough, he made it suggestive, his black voice cracking, and his little roosterish flame licked up clear, queer, and crabbed. His old sire, gruff and mocking, deeply tickled, lay like the Buffalo Bill of the Etruscans in the beach chair and bath towel drawn up burnoose-wise to keep the dazzle from his eyes—additionally shaded by his soft, flesh-heavy arm—his bushy mouth open with laughter.

"Ee-*dyot!*" he said to his son.

If the party began after the main heat of the day William Einhorn might come down too, wheel chair brought on the baggage rack of the Stutz, and his wife carrying an umbrella to shade them both. He was taken pick-a-back by his brother, or by me, from the office into the car, from the car to the right site on the lakeshore; all as distinguished, observing, white, untouched and nobiliary as a margrave. Quickeyes. Originally a big man, of the Commissioner's stature, well-formed, well-favored, he had more delicacy of spirit than the Commissioner, and of course Dingbat wasn't a patch on him. Einhorn was very pale, a little flabby in the face; considerable curvature of the nose, small lips, and graying hair let grow thickly so that it touched on the ears; and continually watchful, his look going forward uninterruptedly to fasten on subject matters. His heavy, attractive wife sat by him with the parasol, languorous, partly in smiles, with her free, soft, brown fist on her lap and strong hair bobbed with that declivity that you see in pictures of the Egyptian coif, the flat base forming a black brush about the back of the neck. Entertained by the summer breeziness and the little boats on the waves and the cavorting and minstrelsy.

If you want to know what she thought, it was that back home was locked. There were two pounds of hotdogs on the shelf of the gas range, two pounds of cold potatoes for salad, mustard, a rye bread already sliced. If she ran out, she could send me for more. Mrs. Einhorn liked to feel that things were ready. The old man would want tea. He needed to be pleased, and she was willing, asking only in return that he stop spitting on the floor, and that not of him directly, being too shy, but through her husband, to him it was merely a joking matter. The rest of us would have Coca-Cola, Einhorn's favorite drink. One of my daily chores was to fetch him Cokes, in bottles from the poolroom or glasses from the drugstore, depending on which he judged to have the better mixture that day.

My brother Simon, seeing me carry a glass on a tray through the gathering on the sidewalk—there was always an overflow of businessmen in front of Einhorn's, mixing with the mourners from Kinsman's chapel and the poolroom characters—gave a big laugh of surprise and said, "So this is your job! You're the butler."

But it was only one function of hundreds, some even more menial, more personal, others calling for cleverness and training—secretary, deputy, agent, companion. He was a man who needed someone beside him continually; the things that had to be done for him made him autocratic. At Versailles or in Paris the Sun King had one nobleman to hand him his stockings, another his shirt, in his morning levee. Einhorn had to be lifted up in bed and dressed. Now and then it was I who had to do it. The room was dark and unfresh, for he and his wife slept with the windows shut. So it was sleep rank from nights of both bodies. I see I had no sense of criticism about such things; I got used to it quickly. Einhorn slept in his underwear because changing to pajamas was a task, and he and his wife kept late hours. Thus, the light switched on, there was Einhorn in his BVDs, wasted arms freckled, grizzled hair afly from his face that was inclined to flatness, the shrewd curved nose and clipped mustache. If peevish, and sometimes he was, my cue was to be quiet until he got back his spirits. It was against policy to be out of temper in the morning. He preferred to be jocular. Birdy, teasing, often corny or lewd, he guyed his wife about the noise and bother she made getting breakfast. In dressing him, my experience with George came in handy, but there was more style about Einhorn than I was used to. His socks were of grand silk, trousers with a banker's stripe; he had several pairs of shoes, fine Walkovers that of course never wrinkled below the instep, much less wore out, a belt with a gothic monogram. Dressed to the waist, he was lifted into his black leather chair and pulled on quaky wheels to the bathroom. At times the first settling in the chair drew a frown from him, sometimes a more oblique look of empoisoned acceptance; but mostly it was a stoical operation. I eased him down and took him, traveling backwards, to the toilet, a sunny room with an east window to the yard. The Commissioner and Einhorn, both rather careless in their habits, made this a difficult place to keep clean. But for people of some nobility allowances have always been made in this regard. I understand that British aristocrats are still legally entitled to piss, if they should care to, on the hind wheels of carriages.

There wasn't anything Mrs. Einhorn could do about the wet floor. Once in a while when Bavatsky the handyman was gone too long in Polack Town or drunk in the cellar, she asked me to clean up. She said she didn't like to impose on me because I was a student. Nevertheless I was getting paid. For unspecified work of a mixed character. I accepted it as such; the mixed character of it was one of the things I liked. I was just as varietistic and unfit for discipline and regularity as my friend Clem Tambow; only I differed from Clem in being a beaver, once my heart was attached to a work or a cause. Naturally, when Einhorn found this out, and he quickly did, he kept me going steadily; it suited him perfectly because of the great number of things he had to be done. Should he run out, my standing by made him invent more. So I didn't often get the toilet detail; he had too many important tasks for me. And when I did get it, why, what I had had under Grandma Lausch made an inconsiderable thing of it to be porter for an hour.

But now in the toilet with Einhorn: he kept me by him to read the morning headlines from the *Examiner*, the financial news, closing quotations from Wall Street and La Salle Street. Local news next, something about Big Bill Thompson, that he had hired the Cort Theatre, for instance, and presented himself on the stage with two caged giant rats from the stockyards whom he addressed by the names of Republican renegades—I came to know what items Einhorn would want first. "Yes, it's just as Thompson says. He's a big gasbag, but this time it's true. He rushed back from Honolulu to save what's-his-name from the penitentiary." He was long and well-nigh perfect of memory, a close and detailed reader of the news, and kept a file on matters of interest to him, for he was highly systematic, and one of my jobs was to keep his files in order in the long steel and wood cases he surrounded himself with, being masterful, often fussy for reasons hard to understand when I placed something before him, proposing to throw it away. The stuff had to be where he could lay his hands on it at once, his clippings and pieces of paper, in folders labeled Commerce, Invention, Major Local Transactions, Crime and Gang, Democrats, Republicans, Archaeology, Literature, League of Nations. Search me, why the League of Nations, but he lived by Baconian ideas of what makes the man this and that, and had a weakness for complete information. Everything was going to be properly done, with Einhorn, and was thoroughly organized on his desk and around it—Shakespeare, Bible, Plutarch, dictionary and thesaurus, *Commercial Law for Laymen*, real-estate and insurance guides, almanacs and directories; then typewriter in black hood, dictaphone, telephones on bracket arms, and a little screwdriver to hand for touching off the part of the telephone mechanism that registered the drop of the nickel—for even at his most prosperous Einhorn was not going to pay for every call he made; the company was raking in a fortune from the coinboxes used by the other businessmen who came to the office—wire trays labeled Incoming and Outgoing, molten Aetna weights, notary's seal on a chain, staplers, flap-moistening sponges, keys to money, confidential papers, notes, condoms, personal correspondence and poems and essays. When all this was arranged and in place, all proper, he could begin to operate, back of his polished barrier approached by two office gates, where he was one of the chiefs of life, a white-faced executive, much aware of himself and even of the freakish, willful shrewdness that sometimes spoiled his dignity and proud, plaquelike good looks.

He had his father to keep up with, whose business ideas were perhaps less imaginative but broader, based on his connections with his rich old-time cronies. The old Commissioner had made the Einhorn money and still kept the greater part of the titles in his name, not because he didn't trust his son, but only for the reason that to the business community he was *the* Einhorn, the one who was approached first with offers.

William was the heir and was also to be trustee of the shares of his son Arthur, who was a sophomore at the University of Illinois, and of Dingbat. Sometimes Einhorn was unhappy about the Commissioner's habit of making private loans, some of them sizable, from the bankroll he carried pinned inside the pocket of his Mark Twain suit. More often he bragged about him as a pioneer builder on the Northwest Side and had dynastic ideas about the Einhorns—the organizer coming after the conqueror, the poet and philosopher succeeding the organizer, and the whole development typically American, the work of intelligence and strength in an open field, a world of possibilities. But really, with all respect for the Commissioner, Einhorn, while still fresh and palmy, had his father's over-riding powers plus something else, statesmanship, fineness of line, Parsee sense, deep-dug intrigue, the scorn of Pope Alexander VI for custom. One morning while I was reading from a column on the misconduct of an American heiress with an Italian prince at Cannes, he stopped me to quote, " 'Dear Kate, you and I cannot be confined within the weak list of a country's fashion. We are the makers of manners, Kate, and the liberty that follows our places stops the mouth of all find-faults. . . .' That's Henry Fifth for you. Meaning that there's one way for people at large and another for those that have something special to do. Which those at large have to have in front of them. It braces them up that there's a privilege they can't enjoy, as long as they know it's there. Besides, there's law, and then there's Nature. There's opinion, and then there's Nature. Somebody has to get outside of law and opinion and speak for Nature. It's even a public duty, so customs won't have us all by the windpipe." Einhorn had a teaching turn similar to Grandma Lausch's, both believing they could show what could be done with the world, where it gave or resisted, where you could be confident and run or where you could only feel your way and were forced to blunder. And with his son at the university I was the only student he had at hand.

He put on a judicious head, and things, no matter how they

ran, had to be collared and brought to a standstill when he
was ready to give out. He raised his unusable arms to the desk
by a neat trick that went through several stages, tugging the
sleeve of the right with the fingers of the left, helping on the
left with the right. There wasn't any appeal to feelings as he
accomplished this; it was only an operation. But it had
immense importance. As a robust, full-blooded man might
mount up to a pulpit and then confess his weakness before
God, Einhorn, with his feebleness demonstrated for a preliminary, got himself situated to speak of strength, with strength.
It was plenty queer to hear him on this note, especially in view
of the daily drift of life here.

But let's take it back to the toilet, where Einhorn got himself
ready in the morning. At one time he used to have the barber
in to shave him. But this reminded him too much of the
hospital, he said, where he had put in a total of two and
one-half years. Besides, he preferred to do things for himself
as much as possible; he had to rely on too many people as it
was. So now he used a safety razor stropped in a gadget a
Czech inventor had personally sold him; he swore by it. To
shave took better than half an hour, chin on the edge of the
sink and hands in the water, working round his face. He fished
out the washrag, muffled himself in it; I could hear him
breathe through its papillae. He soaped, he rubbed and
played, scraped, explored with fingers for patches of bristle,
and I sat on the cover of the pot and read. The vapor woke up
old smells, and there was something astringent in the shaving
cream he used that cut into my breath. Then he pomaded his
wet hair and slipped on a little cap made of an end of
woman's hose. Dried and powdered, he had to be helped into
his shirt, his tie put on, the knot inspected many times by his
fingers and warped exactly into place with some nervousness
about the top button. The jacket next, finished off with the dry
noise of the whiskbroom. Fly re-examined, shoes wiped of
water drops, we were all set and I got the nod to draw him
into the kitchen for breakfast.

His appetite was sharp and he crowded his food. A stranger

with a head on him, unaware that Einhorn was paralyzed, would have guessed he was not a well man from seeing him suck a pierced egg, for it was something humanly foxy, paw-handled, hungry above average need. Then he had this cap of a woman's stocking, like a trophy from another field of appetites, if you'll excuse a sporting reference, or martial one, on his head. He was conscious of this himself, for pretty much everything was thought of, and his mind in its way performed admirable work with many of the things he did; or did not care to stop himself from doing; or was not able to stop; or thought it only creaturely human nature to do; or enjoyed, indulged; was proud his disease had not killed his capacity for but rather left him with more capacity than many normal men. Much that's nameless to many people through disgust or shame he didn't mind naming to himself or to a full confidant (or pretty nearly so) like me, and caught, used, and worked all feelings freely. There was plenty to be in on; he was a very busy man.

There was a short executive period, after coffee, when Einhorn threw his weight around about household matters. Wrinkled, gloomy Tiny Bavatsky, string-muscled, was fetched up from the basement and told what he must do, warned to lay off the bottle till night. He went away, hitch-gaited, talking to himself in words of menace, to start his tasks. Mrs. Einhorn was not really a good housekeeper even though she complained about the floor of the toilet and the old man's spitting. But Einhorn was a thoughtful proprietor and saw to it that everything was kept humming, running, flushing, and constantly improved—rats killed, cement laid in the backyard, machines cleaned and oiled, porches retimbered, tenants sanitary, garbage cans covered, screens patched, flies sprayed. He was able to tell you how fast pests multiplied, how much putty to buy for a piece of glazing, the right prices of nails or clothesline or fuses and many such things; as much as any ancient Roman senator knew of husbandry before such concerns came to be thought wrong. Then, when everything was under control, he had himself taken into his office on the

specially constructed chair with cackly casters. I had to dust
the desk and get him a Coke to drink with his second
cigarette, and he was already on his mail when I got back with
it. His mail was large—he had to have it so, and from many
kinds of correspondents in all parts of the country.

Let it be hot—for I'm reporting on summers, during
vacations, when I spent full time with him—and he was
wearing his vest in the office. The morning, this early, was
often gentle prairie weather, long before the rugged grind—
like the naïveté you get to expect in the hardest and
toughest-used when you've been with them long enough—I
refer to business and heat of a Chicago summer afternoon.
But it was breathing time. The Commissioner wasn't finished
dressing yet; he went into the mild sun of the street in his
slippers, his galluses hung down, and the smoke of his Claro
passed up and back above his white hair, while his hand was
sunk comfortable and deep below his waistband. And Einhorn, away back, the length of the office, slit open his letters,
made notes for replies, dipped into his files or passed things on
for me to check on—me, the often stumped aide, trying to get
straight what he was up to in his numerous small swindles. In
this respect there was hardly anything he didn't get into, like
ordering things on approval he didn't intend to pay for—
stamps, little tubes of lilac perfume, packages of linen sachet,
Japanese paper roses that opened in water, and all the sort of
items advertised in the back pages of the Sunday supplement.
He had me write for them in my hand and give fictitious
names, and he threw away the dunning letters, of course, and
said all of these people calculated losses into what they
chargedn He sent away for everything that was free: samples
of food, soaps, medicine, the literature of all causes, reports of
the Bureau of American Ethnology and publications of the
Smithsonian Institution, the Bishop Museum in Hawaii, the
Congressional Record, laws, pamphlets, prospectuses, college
catalogues, quack hygiene books, advice on bust-develop-
ment, on getting rid of pimples, on longevity and Couéism,
pamphlets on Fletcherism, Yoga, spirit-rapping, antivivisec-

tion; he was on the mailing list of the Henry George Institute and the Rudolf Steiner Foundation in London, the local bar association, the American Legion. He had to be in touch with everything. And all this material he kept; the overflow went down to the basement. Bavatsky or I or Lollie Fewter, who came in three days a week to do the ironing, carried it below. Some of it, when it went out of print, he sold to bookstores or libraries, and some he remailed to his clients with the Einhorn stamp on it, for good will. He had much to do also with contests and entered every competition he got wind of, suggesting names for new products, slogans; he made up bright sayings and most embarrassing moments, most delightful dreams, omens he should have heeded, telepathic experiences, and jingles:

> When radio first appeared, I did rave,
> And all my pennies I did save,
> Even neglected to shave.
> I'll take my dear Dynamic to the grave.

He won the *Evening American*'s first prize of five dollars with this, and one of my jobs was to see that what was sent out to contests, anagrams on the names of presidents or on the capitals of states, or elephants composed of tiny numbers (making what sum?), that these entries were neat, mounted right, inside ruled borders, accompanied by the necessary coupons, boxtops, and labels. Furthermore, I had to do reference work for him in his study or at the library downtown, one of his projects being to put out an edition of Shakespeare indexed as the Gideon Bible was: Slack Business, Bad Weather, Difficult Customers, Stuck with Big Inventory of Last Year's Models, Woman, Marriage, Partners. One thousand and one catchpenny deals, no order too big, no sum too small. And, all the time, talkative, clowning, classical, philosophical, homiletic, corny, passing around French poses and imitation turds from the Clark Street novelty stores, pornographic Katzenjammers and Somebody's Stenog; teas-

ing with young Lollie Fewter who was fresh up from the coal
fields, that girl with her green eyes from which she didn't try to
keep the hotness, and her freckled bust presented to the
gathering of men she came among with her waxing rags and
the soft shake of her gait. Yea, Einhorn, careful of his perch,
with dead legs, and yet denying in your teeth he was different
from other men. He never minded talking about his paralysis;
on the contrary, sometimes he would boast of it as a thing he
had overcome, in the manner of a successful businessman who
tells you of the farm poverty of his boyhood. Nor did he
overlook any chance to exploit it. To a mailing list he got
together from houses that sold wheel chairs, braces, and
appliances, he sent out a mimeographed paper called "The
Shut-In." Two pages of notices and essays, sentimental bits
cribbed from *Elbert Hubbard's Scrapbook*, tags from "Thanatopsis." "Not like the slave scourged to his quarry" but like a
noble, stoical Greek; or from Whittier: "Prince thou art, the
grown up man/Only is Republican," and other such sources.
"Build thee more stately mansions, O my soul!" The third
page was reserved for readers' letters. This thing—I put it out
on the mimeograph and stapled and carried it to the post
office—gave me the creeps once in a while, uneasy flesh
around the neck. But he spoke of it as a service to shut-ins. It
was a help to him as well; it brought in considerable insurance
business, for he signed himself, "William Einhorn, a neighborhood broker," and various companies paid the costs. Like
Grandma Lausch again, he knew how to use large institutions.
He had an important bearing with their representatives—clab-
ber-faced, with his intelligent bit of mustache and shrewd
action of his dark eyes, chicken-winged arms at rest. He wore
sleeve garters—another piece of feminine apparel. He tried to
maneuver various insurance companies into competitive bid-
ding to increase his commissions.

Many repeated pressures with the same effect as one strong
blow, that was his method, he said, and it was his special pride
that he knew how to use the means contributed by the age to
connive as ably as anyone else; when in a not-so-advanced

time he'd have been mummy-handled in a hut or somebody might have had to help him be a beggar in front of a church, the next thing to a *memento mori* or, more awful, a reminder of what difficulties there were before you could even become dead. Whereas now—well, it was probably no accident that it was the cripple Hephaestus who made ingenious machines; a normal man didn't have to hoist or jack himself over hindrances by means of cranks, chains, and metal parts. Then it was in the line of human advance that Einhorn could do so much; especially since the whole race was so hepped-up about appliances, he was not a hell of a lot more dependent than others who couldn't make do without this or that commodity, engine, gizmo, sliding door, public service, and this being relieved of small toils made mind the chief center of trial. Find Einhorn in a serious mood when his fatty, beaky, noble Bourbon face was thoughtful, and he'd give you the lowdown on the mechanical age, and on strength and frailty, and piece it out with little digressions on the history of cripples—the dumbness of the Spartans, the fact that Oedipus was lame, that gods were often maimed, that Moses had faltering speech and Dmitri the Sorcerer a withered arm, Caesar and Mahomet epilepsy, Lord Nelson a pinned sleeve—but especially on the machine age and the kind of advantage that had to be taken of it; with me like a man-at-arms receiving a lecture from the learned *signor* who felt like passing out discourse.

I was a listener by upbringing. And Einhorn with his graces, learning, oratory, and register of effects was not out to influence me practically. He was not like Grandma, with her educational seventy-fives trained on us. He wanted to flow along, be admirable and eloquent. Not fatherly. I wasn't ever to get it into my head that I was part of the family. There was small chance that I would, the way Arthur, the only son, figured in their references, and I was sent out when any big family deal began to throb around. To make absolutely sure I wouldn't get any such notions, Einhorn would now and then ask me some question about my people, as if he hadn't informed himself through Coblin, Kreindl, Clem, and Jimmy.

Pretty clever, he was, to place me this way. If Grandma had
ideas about a wealthy man who might take a fancy to us and
make our fortune, Simon's and mine, Einhorn had the reverse.
I wasn't to think because we were intimately connected and
because he liked me that I was going to get into the will. The
things that had to be done for him were such that anybody
who worked for him was necessarily intimate with him. It
sometimes got my goat, he and Mrs. Einhorn made so sure I
knew my place. But maybe they were right; the old woman
had implanted the thought, though I never entertained it in
earnest. However, there was such a thought, and it bulged
somewhat into my indignation. Einhorn and his wife were
selfish. They weren't mean, I admitted in fairness, and
generally I could be fair about it; merely selfish, like two
people enjoying their lunch on the grass and not asking you to
join them. If you weren't dying for a sandwich yourself it
could even make a pleasant picture, smacking on the mustard,
cutting cake, peeling eggs and cucumbers. Selfish Einhorn
was, nevertheless; his nose in constant action smelled, and
smelled out everything, sometimes austerely, or again without
manners, covert, half an eye out for observers but not to be
deterred if there were any, either.

I don't think I would have considered myself even remotely
as a legatee of the Commissioner if they hadn't, for one thing,
underlined my remoteness from inheritance, and, for another,
discussed inheritances all the time.

Well, they were steeped and soaked necessarily in insurance
and property, lawsuits and legal miscarriages, sour partner-
ships and welshings and contested wills. This was what you
heard when the connoisseurs' club of weighty cronies met,
who all showed by established marks—rings, cigars, quality of
socks, newness of panamas—where they were situated; they
were classified, too, in grades of luck and wisdom, darkness by
birth or vexations, power over or subjection to wives, women,
sons and daughters, grades of disfigurement; or by the roles
they played in comedies, tragedies, sex farces; whether they
screwed or were screwed, whether they themselves did the

manipulating or were roughly handled, tugged, and bobbled by their fates; their frauds, their smart bankruptcies, the fires they had set; what were their prospects of life, how far death stood from them. Also their merits: which heavy character of fifty was a good boy, a donor, a friend, a compassionate man, a man of balls, a lucid percentage calculator, a fellow willing to make a loan of charity though he couldn't sign his name, a giver of scrolls to the synagogue, a protector of Polish relatives. It was known; Einhorn had it all noted. And apparently everybody knew everything. There was a good circulation of frankness and a lot of respect going back and forth. Also a lot of despicable things. Be this as it might, the topic inside the railed space of benches or at the pinochle game in the side-office annex was mostly business—receiverships, amortizations, wills, and practically nothing else. As rigor is the theme of Labrador, breathing of the summits of the Andes, space to the Cornish miner who lies in a seam under the sea. And, on the walls, insurance posters of people in the despair of firetraps and the undermining of rats in the beams, housewives bringing down the pantry shelves in their fall. Which all goes to show how you couldn't avoid the question of inheritance. Was the old Commissioner fond of me? While Mrs. Einhorn was a kindly woman ordinarily, now and again she gave me a glance that suggested Sarah and the son of Hagar. Notwithstanding that there was nothing to worry about. Nothing. I wasn't of the blood, and the old man had dynastic ideas too. And I wasn't trying to worm my way into any legacy and get any part of what was coming to her elegant and cultivated son Arthur. Sure the Commissioner was fond of me, stroked my shoulder, gave me tips; and he thought of me no further.

But he and Einhorn were an enigma to Tillie. Her pharaoh-bobbed hair grew out of a head mostly physically endowed; she couldn't ever tell what they might take it into their minds to do. And especially her husband, he was so supple, fertile, and changeable. She worshipfully obeyed him and did his biddings and errands just as the rest of us did. He'd send her to City Hall with requests for information from the Recorder's Office or the License Bureau; he wrote notes, because she could never explain what he wanted, and she brought back the information written out by a clerk. To get her out of the way when he was up to something he sent her to visit her cousin on the South Side, an all-day junket on the streetcars. To be sure she'd be good and gone; and what's more, she knew it.

But now suppose we're at lunchtime, in Einhorn's specimen day. Mrs. Einhorn didn't like to bother in the kitchen and favored ready-made or easy meals, delicatessen, canned salmon with onion and vinegar, or hamburger and fried potatoes. And these hamburgers weren't the flat lunch-wagon jobs, eked out with cornmeal, but big pieces of meat souped up with plenty of garlic and fried to blackness. Covered with horseradish and chili sauce, they didn't go down so hard. This was the food of the house, in the system of its normalcy like its odors and furnishings, and if you were the visiting albatross come to light, you'd eat the food you ne'er had eat and offer no gripe. The Commissioner, Einhorn, and Dingbat asked no questions about it but ate a great deal, with tea or Coca-Cola as usual. Then Einhorn took a white spoonful of Bisodol and a glass of Waukesha water for his gas. He made a joke of it, but he never forgot to take them and heeded all his processes with much seriousness, careful that his tongue was not too coated and his machinery smooth. Very grave he was sometimes, when he acted as his own physician. He liked to say that he was fatal to doctors, especially to those who had never given him much hope. "I buried two of them," he said. "Each one told me I'd be gone in a year, and before the year was out he croaked." It made him feel good to tell other doctors of this. Still, he was zealous about taking care of himself; and with this zeal he had a brat's self-mockery about the object of his cares, bottomless self-ribbing; he let his tongue droop over his lip, comic and stupid, and made dizzy crosses with his eyes. Nevertheless he was always thinking about his health and took his powders and iron and liver pills. You might almost say he followed assimilation with his thoughts; all through his body that death had already moved in on, to the Washington of his brain, to his sex and to his studying eyes. Ah, sure, he was still a going concern, very much so, but he had to take thought more than others did about himself, since if *he* went wrong he was a total loss, nowise justified, a dead account, a basket case, an encumbrance, zero. I knew this because he expressed everything, and though he wouldn't talk openly about the money he had in the bank or the property he owned, he was absolutely outspoken about vital things, and he'd open his mind to me, especially when we were together in his study and busy with one of his projects that got more fanciful and muddled the more notions he had about being systematic, so that in the end there'd be a super-monstrous apparatus you couldn't set in motion either by push or crank.

"Augie, you know another man in my position might be out of life for good. There's a view of man anyhow that he's only a sack of craving guts; you find it in *Hamlet*, as much as you want of it. What a piece of work is a man, and the firmament frotted with gold—but the whole *gescheft* bores him. Look at me, I'm not even express and admirable in action. You could say a man like me ought to be expected to lie down and quit the picture. Instead, I'm running a big business today"—that was not the pure truth; it was the Commissioner who was still the main wheel, but it wasn't uninteresting all the same— "while nobody would blame me for rotting in the back room under a blanket or for crabbing and blabbing my bitter heart out, with fresh and healthy people going around me, so as not to look. A kid like you, for instance, strong as a bronco and rosy as an apple. An Alcibiades beloved-of-man, by Jesus. I don't know what brain power you've got; you're too frisky yet, and even if you turn out to be smart you'll never be in the class of my son Arthur. You shouldn't be angry for hearing the truth, if you're lucky enough to find somebody to hear it from. Anyhow, you're not bad off, being an Alcibiades. That's already way and above your fellow creatures. And don't think they didn't hate the original either. All but Socrates himself, ugly as an old dog, they tell us. Nor just because that the young fellow knocked the dongs of the holy figures off, either, before he shipped for Sicily. But to get back to the subject, it's one thing to be buried with all your pleasures, like Sardanapalus; it's another to be buried right plunk in front of them, where you can see them. Ain't it so? You need a genius to raise you above it . . ."

Quiet, quiet, quiet afternoon in the back-room study, with an oil-cloth on the library table, busts on the wall, invisible cars snoring and trembling toward the park, the sun shining into the yard outside the window barred against house-breakers, billiard balls kissing and bounding on the felt and sponge rubber, and the undertaker's back door still and stiller, cats sitting on the paths in the Lutheran gardens over the alley that were swept and garnished and scarcely ever trod by the chin-tied Danish deaconesses who'd come out on the cradle-ribbed and always fresh-painted porches of their home.

Somewhat it stung me, the way in which he compared me with his son. But I didn't mind being Alcibiades, and let him be in the same bracket with Socrates in the bargain, since that was what he was driving at. We had title just as good as the chain-mail English kings had to Brutus. If you want to pick your own ideal creature in the mirror coastal air and sharp leaves of ancient perfections and be at home where a great mankind was at home, I've never seen any reason why not. Though unable to go along one hundred per cent with a man like the Reverend Beecher telling his congregation, "Ye are Gods, you are crystalline, your faces are radiant!" I'm not an optimist of that degree, from the actual faces, congregated or separate, that I've seen; always admitting that the true vision of things is a gift, particularly in times of special disfigurement and world-wide Babylonishness, when plug-ugly macadam and volcanic peperino look commoner than crystal—to eyes with an ordinary amount of grace, anyhow—and when it appears like a good sensible policy to settle for medium-grade quartz. I wonder where in the creation there would be much of a double-take at the cry *"Homo sum!"* But I was and have always been ready to venture as far as possible; even though I

was never as much imposed on by Einhorn as he wanted me
to be in his big moments, with his banker's trousers and
chancellor's cravat, and his unemployable squiggle feet on the
barber-chairlike mount of his wheeled contraption made to his
specifications. And I never could decide whether he meant
that he was a genius or had one, and I suppose he wanted
there should be some doubt about the meaning. He wasn't the
man to come out and declare that he wasn't a genius while
there was the chance he might be one, a thing like that coming
about *nolens volens*. To some, like his half-brother Dingbat, he
was one. Dingbat swore up and down, "Willie is a wizard.
Give him two bits' worth of telephone slugs and he'll parlay it
into big dough." His wife agreed too, without reservations,
that Einhorn was a wizard. Anything he did—and that covers
a lot of territory—was all right with her. There wasn't any
higher authority, not even her cousin Karas, who ran the
Holloway Enterprises and Management Co. and was a demon
money-maker himself. Karas, that bad, rank character, cin-
der-crawed, wise to all angles, dressed to kill, with a kitty-cor-
nered little smile and extortionist's eyes, she was in awe of him
also, but he wasn't presumed to be in Einhorn's class.

But Einhorn wasn't exactly buried in front of his pleasures.
He carried on with one woman or another, and in particular
he had a great need of girls like Lollie Fewter. His explanation
was that he took after his father. The Commissioner, in a
kindly, sleepy, warm-aired, fascinated way, petted and admired all women and put his hands wherever he liked. I
imagine women weren't very angry when he saluted them in
this style because he picked out whatever each of them herself
prized most—color, breasts, hair, hips, and all the little secrets
and connivances with which she emphasized her own good
things. You couldn't rightly say it was a common letch he
had; it was a sort of Solomonic regard of an old chief or aged
sea lion. With his spotty big old male hands, he felt up the
married and the unmarried ones, and even the little girls for
what they promised, and nobody ever was offended by it or by
the names he invented, names like "the Tangerines," or "the

Little Sled," "Madame Yesteryear," "the Six-Foot Dove." The
grand old gentleman. Satisfied and gratified. You could feel
from the net pleasantness he carried what there had been
between him and women now old or dead, whom he
recognized, probably, and greeted in this nose or that bosom.

His sons didn't share this quality. Of course you don't
expect younger men to have this kind of evening-Mississippi
serenity, but there wasn't much disinterestedness or contem-
plation in either of them. There was more romantic feeling in
Dingbat than in his brother. There scarcely was a time when
Dingbat wasn't engaged to a nice girl. He scrubbed himself
and dressed himself to go to see her in a desperate, cracked
rage of earnest respect. Sometimes he would look ready to cry
from devotion, and in his preparations he ran out of the
perfumed bathroom, clean starched shirt open on his skinny
hairiness, to remind me to fetch the corsage from Bluegren's.
He could never do enough for these girls and never thought
himself good enough for them. And the more he respected
them the more he ran with tramps between times, whom he
picked up at Guyon's Paradise and took to the Forest
Preserves in the Stutz, or to a little Wilson Avenue hotel that
Karas-Holloway owned. But Friday evenings, at family dinner, there was often a fiancée, now a piano teacher, now a
dress designer or bookkeeper, or simply a home girl, wearing
an engagement ring and other presents; and Dingbat with a
necktie, tense and daffy, homagefully calling her "Honey,"
"Isabel, hon," "Janice dear," in his hoarse, thin black voice.

Einhorn, however, didn't have such sentiments at all,
whatever sentiments he entertained on other scores. He took
the joking liberties his father did, but his jokes didn't have the
same ring; which isn't to say that they weren't funny but that
he cast himself forward on them toward a goal—seduction.
What the laugh was about was his disability; he was after a
fashion laughing about it, and he was not so secretly saying to
women that if they'd look further they'd find to their surprise
that there was the real thing, not disabled. He promised. So
that when he worked his wicked, lustful charm, apparently so

safe, like a worldly priest or elderly gentleman from whom it's safe to accept a little complimentary badinage or tickle, he was really single-mindedly and grimly fixed on the one thing, ultimately *the* thing, for which men and women came together. And he was the same with them all; not, of course, foreseeing any great success, but hoping all the same that one of them—beautiful, forward, intrigued with him, wishing to play a secret game, maybe a trifle perverse (he suggested), would see, would grasp, would crave, would burn for him. He looked and hoped for this in every woman.

He wouldn't stay a cripple, Einhorn; he couldn't hold his soul in crippledom. Sometimes it was dreadful, this; he'd lose everything he'd thought through uncountable times to reconcile himself to it, and be like the wolf in the pit in the zoo who keeps putting his muzzle to the corners of the walls, back and forth, back and forth. It didn't happen often; probably not oftener than ordinary people get a shove of the demon. But it happened. Touch him when he was off his feed, or had a cold and a little fever, or when there was a rift in the organization, or his position didn't feel so eminent and he wasn't getting the volume of homage and mail he needed—or when it was the turn of a feared truth to come up unseen through the multitude of elements out of which he composed his life, and then he'd say, "I used to think I'd either walk again or else swallow iodine. I'd have massages and exercises, and drills, and I'd concentrate on a single muscle and think I was building it up by my will. And it was all the bunk, Augie, the Coué theory, etcetera. For the birds. And *It Can Be Done* and the sort of stuff that bigshot Teddy Roosevelt wrote in his books. Nobody'll ever know all the things I tried before I finally decided it was no go. I couldn't take it, and I took it. And I *can't* take it, yet I do take it. But how! You can get along twenty-nine days with your trouble, but there's always that thirtieth day when goddammit you can't, when you feel like the stinking fly in the first cold snap, when you look about and think you're the Old Man of the Sea on Sinbad's neck; and why should anybody carry an envious piece of human junk? If society had any sense they'd give me euthanasia. They'd leave me the way the Eskimos do their old folks in an igloo with food for two days. Don't you look so miserable. Go on away. See if Tillie wants you for something."

But this was on the thirtieth day, or more seldom, because in general he enjoyed good health and looked on himself as a useful citizen and even an extraordinary one, and he bragged that there was hardly anything he couldn't bring off if he put his mind to it. And he certainly did some bang-up things. He'd clear us all out of the way to be alone with Lollie Fewter; he'd arrange for the whole lot of us to drive out to Niles Center and show the Commissioner a piece of property. Ostensibly getting ready to occupy himself with a piece of work while we were away—the files and information were laid out for him—he was unhurried, engaging, and smooth-tempered in his tortoise-shell specs, answering every last question in full and even detaining the excursion to have some last words with his father about frontages or improvements. "Wait till I show you on the map just where the feeder-bus comes through. Bring the map, Augie." He'd have me fetch it and kept the Commissioner till he became impatient, with Dingbat grinding the klaxon and Mrs. Einhorn already settled with bags of fruit in the back seat, calling, "Come, it's hot. I'm fainting here." And Lollie in the passage between the flat and the offices sauntered up and down with the dustmop in the polished dimness, big and soft, comfortable for the heat in a thin blouse and straw sandals, like an overgrown girl walking a doll and keeping a smile to herself about this maternal, matrimonial game, lazy and careless and, you could say, saving force for the game to follow. Clem Tambow had tried to tell me what the score was but hadn't convinced me, not just because of the oddness of the idea, and that I had a boyish respect for Einhorn, but also because I had made a start with Lollie myself. I found excuses to be with her in the kitchen while she was ironing. She told me of her family in the Franklin County coal fields, and then about the men there, and what they tried and did. She rolled me in feelings. From suggestion alone, I didn't have the strength to keep my feet. We soon were kissing and feeling; she now held off my hands and now led them inside her dress, alleging instruction, boisterous that I was still cherry, and at last, from kindness, she one day said that if I'd come back in the evening I could take her home. She left me so horny I was scarcely able to walk. I hid out in the poolroom, dreading that Einhorn would send for me. But Clem came with a message from her that she had changed her mind. I was bitter about that but I reckon I felt freed, too, from a crisis. "Didn't I tell you?" said Clem, "You both work for the same boss, and she's his little nooky. His and a couple of other guys'. But not for you. You don't know anything and you don't have any money."

"Why, damn her soul!"

"Well, Einhorn would give her anything. He's nuts about her."

I couldn't conceive that. It wouldn't be like Einhorn to settle his important feelings on a tramp. But that exactly was what he had done. He was mad for her. Einhorn knew, too, that he shared her with a few hoodlums from the poolroom. Of course he knew. It wasn't in his life to be without information; he had the stowage of an anthill for it, with weaving black lines of provisioners creeping into the crest from every direction. They told him what would be the next turn in the Lingle case, or what the public-auction schedule would be, or about appellate court decisions before they were in print, or where there were hot goods, from furs to school supplies; so he had a line on Lollie from the beginning to the end.

Eleanor Klein asked me sentimental questions. Did I have a sweetheart yet? It was a thing I appeared ripe for. Our old neighbor, Kreindl, asked me too, but in a different way, on the q.t. He judged I was no longer a kid and he could reveal himself, his cockeyes turning fierce and gay. "*Schmeist du schon*, Augie? You've got friends? Not my son. He comes home from the store and reads the paper. *S'interesiert ihm nicht*. You're not too young, are you? I was younger than you and *gefährlich*. I couldn't get enough. Kotzie doesn't take after me." He much needed to pronounce himself the better, and in fact the only, man in his house; and he did look very sturdy when he massed up his teeth and creased his out-of-doors, rugged face into a smile. He saw a lot of weather, for he went through the entire West Side on foot with his satchel of samples. Because he had to count every nickel. And he had the patience and hardness of steady pavement going, passing the same lead-whited windows of a factory twenty times a month and knowing to the last weed every empty lot between him and his destination. Arriving, he could hang around hours for a six-bit commission or a piece of information. "Kotzie takes after my missis: He is *kaltblutig*." Sure I knew it was he himself that did all the trumpeting, screaming, and stamping down in his flat, throwing things on the floor.

"And how is your brother?" he said intriguingly. "I understand the little *maidelech* wet their pants for him. What is he doing?"

As a matter of fact I didn't know what Simon was up to these days. He didn't tell me, nor did he seem curious as to what was happening to me, having decided in his mind that I was nothing but a handyman at Einhorn's.

Once I went with Dingbat to a party one of his fiancées was giving, and I met my brother with a Polish girl in a fur-trimmed orange dress; he wore a big, smooth, check suit and looked handsome and sufficient to himself. He didn't stay long, and I had a feeling that he didn't want to spend his evenings where I did. Or maybe it was the kind of evening Dingbat made of it that didn't please him, Dingbat's recitations and hoarse parodies, his turkey girding and obscene cackles that made the girls scream. For several months Dingbat and I were very thick. At parties I horsed around with him, goofy, his straight man; or I hugged girls on porches and in backyards, exactly as he did. He took me under his protection in the poolroom, and we did some friendly boxing, at which I was never much good, and played snooker—a little better—and hung about there with the hoods and loud-mouths. So that Grandma Lausch would have thought that the very worst she had ever said about me let me off too lightly seeing me in the shoeshine seat above the green tables, in a hat with diamond airholes cut in it and decorated with brass kiss-me pins and Al Smith buttons, in sneakers and Mohawk sweatshirt, there in the frying jazz and the buzz of baseball broadcasts, the click of markers, butt thumping of cues, spat-out pollyseed shells and blue chalk crushed underfoot and dust of hand-slickening talcum hanging in the air. Along with the blood-smelling swaggeroos, recruits for mobs, automobile thieves, stick-up men, sluggers and bouncers, punks with ambition to become torpedoes, neighborhood cowboys with Jack Holt sideburns down to the jawbone, collegiates, tinhorns and small-time racketeers and pugs, ex-servicemen, home-evading husbands, hackies, truckers, and bush-league athletes. Whenever someone had a notion to work out on me—and there were plenty of touchy characters here to catch your eye in a misconstrued way—Dingbat flew around to protect me.

"This kid is a buddy of mine and he works for my bro. Monkey with him and you'll get something broke on your head. What's the matter, you tough or hungry!"

He was never anything but through-and-through earnest when the subject was loyalty or honor; his bony dukes were ready and his Cuban heels dug down sharply; his furrowed chin was already seeking its fighting position on the shoulder of his starched shirt. Then he was prepared to go into his stamping dance and start slugging.

But there weren't any fights over me. If there was one doctrine of Grandma Lausch's that went home, it was the one of the soft answer, though with her this was of tactical not merciful origin, the dust-off for heathen, stupes, and brute-heads. So I don't claim it was a trained spirit turning aside wrath, or *integer vitae* (how could I?) making the wolves respect me; but I didn't have any taste for the perpetual danger-sign, eye-narrowing, tricky Tybalt all coiled up to stab, for that code, and was without curiosity for what it was like to

hit or to be hit, and so I refused all bids to outface or be
outfaced.

On this I had Einhorn's views also, whose favorite example
was his sitting in the driver's seat of the Stutz—as he
sometimes did, having been moved over to watch tennis
matches or sandlot games—and a coal heaver running up with
a tire tool because he had honked once or twice for the Stutz
to move and Dingbat wasn't there to move it. "What could I
do," said Einhorn, "if he asked me no questions but started to
swing or punch me in the face? With my hands on the wheel,
he'd think I was the driver. I'd have to talk fast. Could I talk
fast enough? What could make an impression on an animal
like that? Would I pretend to faint or play dead? Oh my God!
Even before I was sick, and I was a pretty husky young fellow,
I'd do anything possible before I started to trade punches with
any sonofabitch, muscle-minded ape or bad character looking
for trouble. This city is one place where a person who goes out
for a peaceful walk is liable to come home with a shiner or
bloody nose, and he's almost as likely to get it from a cop's
nightstick as from a couple of squareheads who haven't got
the few dimes to chase pussy on the high rides in Riverview
and so hang around the alley and plot to jump someone.
Because you know it's not the city salary the cops live on now,
not with all the syndicate money there is to pick up. There
isn't a single bootleg alky truck that goes a mile without being
convoyed by a squad car. So they don't care what they do.
I've heard of them almost killing guys who didn't know
enough English to answer questions."

And now, with eager shrewdness of nose and baggy eyes, he
began to increase his range. Sometimes, with that white hair
bunched over his ears and his head lifted back, he looked
grand, suffering more *for* than *from* something, relaxing his
self-protective tension. "But there is some kind of advantage
in the roughness of a place like Chicago, of not having any
illusions either. Whereas in all the great capitals of the world
there's some reason to think humanity is very different. All
that ancient culture and those beautiful works of art right out

in public, by Michelangelo and Christopher Wren, and those ceremonies, like trooping the color at the Horse Guards' parade or burying a great man in the Pantheon over in Paris. You see those marvelous things and you think that everything savage belongs to the past. So you think. And then you have another think, and you see that after they rescued women from the coal mines, or pulled down the Bastille and got rid of Star Chambers and *lettres de cachet,* ran out the Jesuits, increased education, and built hospitals and spread courtesy and politeness, they have five or six years of war and revolutions and kill off twenty million people. And do they think there's less danger to life than here? That's a riot. Let them say rather that they blast better specimens, but not try to put it over that the only human beings who live by blood are away down on the Orinoco where they hunt heads, or out in Cicero with Al Capone. But the best specimens always have been maltreated or killed. I've seen a picture of Aristotle mounted and ridden like a horse by some nasty whore. There was Pythagoras who got killed over a diagram; there was Seneca who had to cut his wrists; there were the teachers and the saints who became martyrs.

"But I sometimes think," he said, "what if a guy came in here with a gun and saw me at this desk? If he said 'Stick 'em up!' do you think he'd wait until I explained that my arms were paralyzed? He'd let me have it. He'd think I was reaching in a drawer or pushing a signal button, and that would be the finish of Einhorn. Just have a look at the holdup statistics and then tell me I'm dreaming up trouble. What I ought to do is have a sign up above my head saying 'Cripple.' But I wouldn't like to be seeing that on the wall all the time. I just hope the Brink's Express and Pinkerton Protective labels all over the place will keep them away."

He often abandoned himself to ideas of death, and notwithstanding that he was advanced in so many ways, his Death was still the old one in shriveled mummy longjohns; the same Death that beautiful maidens failed to see in their mirrors because the mirrors were filled with their white breasts, with

the blue light of old German rivers, with cities beyond the
window checkered like their own floors. This Death was a
cheating old rascal with bones showing, in buckskin fringes,
not a gentle Sir Cedric Hardwicke greeting young boys from
the branches of an apple tree (in a play I once saw). Einhorn
had no kind familiar thoughts about *him,* but was superstitious about him, superstitious about this frightful snatcher,
and he only played the Thanatopsis stoic but always maneuvered to beat this other—Death!—who had already gained so
much on him.

Who maybe was the only real god he had.

Often I thought that in his heart Einhorn had completely
surrendered to this fear. But when you believed you had
tracked Einhorn through his acts and doings and were about
to capture him, you found yourself not in the center of a
labyrinth but on a wide boulevard; and here he came from a
new direction—a governor in a limousine, with state troopers
around him, dominant and necessary, everybody's lover,
whose death was only one element, and a remote one, of his
privacy.

Henderson the
Rain King

Chapter I

What made me take this trip to Africa? There is no quick explanation. Things got worse and worse and worse and pretty soon they were too complicated.

When I think of my condition at the age of fifty-five when I bought the ticket, all is grief. The facts begin to crowd me and soon I get a pressure in the chest. A disorderly rush begins—my parents, my wives, my girls, my children, my farm, my animals, my habits, my money, my music lessons, my drunkenness, my prejudices, my brutality, my teeth, my face, my soul! I have to cry, "No, no, get back, curse you, let me alone!" But how can they let me alone? They belong to me. They are mine. And they pile into me from all sides. It turns into chaos.

However, the world which I thought so mighty an oppressor has removed its wrath from me. But if I am to make sense to you people and explain why I went to Africa I must face up to the facts. I might as well start with the money. I am rich. From my old man I inherited three million dollars after taxes, but I thought myself a bum and had my reasons, the main reason being that I behaved like a bum. But privately when things got very bad I often looked into books to see whether I could find some helpful words, and one day I read, "The forgiveness of

Minor corrections in the text have been made by the author for this Portable.

sins is perpetual and righteousness first is not required." This impressed me so deeply that I went around saying it to myself. But then I forgot which book it was. It was one of thousands left by my father, who had also written a number of them. And I searched through dozens of volumes but all that turned up was money, for my father had used currency for bookmarks—whatever he happened to have in his pockets—fives, tens, or twenties. Some of the discontinued bills of thirty years ago turned up, the big yellowbacks. For old times' sake I was glad to see them and locking the library door to keep out the children I spent the afternoon on a ladder shaking out books and the money spun to the floor. But I never found that statement about forgiveness.

Next order of business: I am a graduate of an Ivy League university—I see no reason to embarrass my alma mater by naming her. If I hadn't been a Henderson and my father's son, they would have thrown me out. At birth I weighed fourteen pounds, and it was a tough delivery. Then I grew up. Six feet four inches tall. Two hundred and thirty pounds. An enormous head, rugged, with hair like Persian lambs' fur. Suspicious eyes, usually narrowed. Blustering ways. A great nose. I was one of three children and the only survivor. It took all my father's charity to forgive me and I don't think he ever made it altogether. When it came time to marry I tried to please him and chose a girl of our own social class. A remarkable person, handsome, tall, elegant, sinewy, with long arms and golden hair, private, fertile, and quiet. None of her family can quarrel with me if I add that she is a schizophrenic, for she certainly is that. I, too, am considered crazy, and with good reason—moody, rough, tyrannical, and probably mad. To go by the ages of the kids, we were married for about twenty years. There are Edward, Ricey, Alice, and two more—Christ, I've got plenty of children. God bless the whole bunch of them.

In my own way I worked very hard. Violent suffering is labor, and often I was drunk before lunch. Soon after I came back from the war (I was too old for combat duty but nothing could keep me from it; I went down to Washington and pressured people until I was allowed to join the fight), Frances and I were divorced. This happened after V-E Day. Or was it so soon? No, it must have been in 1948. Anyway, she's now in Switzerland and has one of our kids with her. What she wants with a child I can't tell you, but she has one, and that's all right. I wish her well.

I was delighted with the divorce. It offered me a new start in life. I had a new wife already picked out and we were soon married. My second wife is called Lily (maiden name, Simmons). We have twin boys.

Now I feel the disorderly rush—I gave Lily a terrible time, worse than Frances. Frances was withdrawn, which protected her, but Lily caught it. Maybe a change for the better threw me; I was adjusted to a bad life. Whenever Frances didn't like what I was doing, and that was often, she turned away from me. She was like Shelley's moon, wandering companionless. Not so Lily; and I raved at her in public and swore at her in private. I got into brawls in the country saloons near my farm and the troopers locked me up. I offered to take them all on, and they would have worked me over if I hadn't been so prominent in the county. Lily came and bailed me out. Then I had a fight with the vet over one of my pigs, and another with the driver of a snowplow on US 7 when he tried to force me off the road. Then about two years ago I fell off a tractor while drunk and ran myself over and broke my leg. For months I was on crutches, hitting everyone who crossed my path, man or beast, and giving Lily hell. With the bulk of a football player and the color of a gipsy, swearing and crying out and showing my teeth and shaking my head—no wonder people got out of my way. But this wasn't all.

Lily is, for instance, entertaining ladies and I come in with my filthy plaster cast, in sweat socks; I am wearing a red velvet dressing gown which I bought at Sulka's in Paris in a mood of celebration when Frances said she wanted a divorce. In addition I have on a red wool hunting cap. And I wipe my nose and mustache on my fingers and then shake hands with the guests, saying, "I'm Mr. Henderson, how do you do?" And I go to Lily and shake her hand, too, as if she were merely another lady guest, a stranger like the rest. And I say, "How do you do?" I imagine the ladies are telling themselves, "He doesn't know her. In his mind he's still married to the first. Isn't that awful?" This imaginary fidelity thrills them.

But they are all wrong. As Lily knows, it was done on purpose, and when we're alone she cries out to me, "Gene, what's the big idea? What are you trying to do?"

All belted up with the red braid cord, I stand up to her in my velvet bathrobe, sticking out behind, and the foot-shaped cast scraping hard on the floor, and I wag my head and say, "Tchu-tchu-tchu!"

Because when I was brought home from the hospital in this same bloody heavy cast, I heard her saying on the telephone, "It was just another one of his accidents. He has them all the time but oh, he's so strong. He's unkillable." Unkillable! How do you like that! It made me very bitter.

Now maybe Lily said this jokingly. She loves to joke on the telephone. She is a large, lively woman. Her face is sweet, and her character mostly is consistent with it. We've had some pretty good times, too. And, come to think of it, some of the very best occurred during her pregnancy, when it was far advanced. Before we went to sleep, I would rub her belly with baby oil to counteract the stretch marks. Her nipples had turned from pink to glowing brown, and the children moved inside her belly and changed the round shape.

I rubbed lightly and with greatest care lest my big thick fingers do the slightest harm. And then before I put out the light I wiped my fingers on my hair and Lily and I kissed good night, and in the scent of the baby oil we went to sleep.

But later we were at war again, and when I heard her say I was unkillable I put an antagonistic interpretation on it, even though I knew better. No, I treated her like a stranger before the guests because I didn't like to see her behave and carry on like the lady of the house; because I, the sole heir of this famous name and estate, am a bum, and she is not a lady but merely my wife—merely my wife.

As the winters seemed to make me worse, she decided that we should go to a resort hotel on the Gulf, where I could do some fishing. A thoughtful friend had given each of the little twins a slingshot made of plywood, and one of these slingshots I found in my suitcase as I was unpacking, and I took to shooting with it. I gave up fishing and sat on the beach shooting stones at bottles. So that people might say, "Do you see that great big fellow with the enormous nose and the mustache? Well, his great-grandfather was Secretary of State, his great-uncles were ambassadors to England and France, and his father was the famous scholar Willard Henderson who wrote that book on the Albigensians, a friend of William James and Henry Adams." Didn't they say this? You bet they did. There I was at that resort with my sweet-faced anxious second wife who was only a little under six feet herself, and our twin boys. In the dining room I was putting bourbon in my morning coffee from a big flask and on the beach I was smashing bottles. The guests complained to the manager about the broken glass and the manager took it up with Lily; me they weren't willing to confront. An elegant establishment, they accept no Jews, and then they get me, E. H. Henderson. The other kids stopped playing with our twins, while the wives avoided Lily.

Lily tried to reason with me. We were in our suite, and I was in swimming trunks, and she opened the discussion on the slingshot and the broken glass and my attitude toward the other guests. Now Lily is a very intelligent woman. She doesn't scold, but she does moralize; she is very much given to this, and when it happens she turns white and starts to speak under her breath. The reason is not that she is afraid of me, but that it starts some crisis in her own mind.

But as it got her nowhere to discuss it with me she started to cry, and when I saw tears I lost my head and yelled, "I'm going to blow my brains out! I'm shooting myself. I didn't forget to pack the pistol. I've got it on me now."

"Oh, Gene!" she cried, and covered up her face and ran away.

I'll tell you why.

Chapter II

Because her father had committed suicide in that same way, with a pistol.

One of the bonds between Lily and me is that we both suffer with our teeth. She is twenty years my junior but we wear bridges, each of us. Mine are at the sides, hers are in front. She has lost the four upper incisors. It happened while she was still in high school, out playing golf with her father, whom she adored. The poor old guy was a lush and far too drunk to be out on a golf course that day. Without looking or giving warning, he drove from the first tee and on the backswing struck his daughter. It always kills me to think of that cursed hot July golf course, and this drunk from the plumbing supply business, and the girl of fifteen bleeding. Damn these weak drunks! Damn these unsteady men! I can't stand these clowns who go out in public as soon as they get swacked to show how broken-hearted they are. But Lily would never hear a single word against him and wept for him sooner than for herself. She carries his photo in her wallet.

Personally I never knew the old guy. When we met he had already been dead for ten or twelve years. Soon after he died she married a man from Baltimore, of pretty good standing, I have been told—though come to think of it it was Lily herself who told me. However, they could not become adjusted and during the war she got her divorce (I was then fighting in Italy). Anyway, when we met she was at home again, living with her mother. The family is from Danbury, the hatters' capital. It happened that Frances and I went to a party in Danbury one winter night, and Frances was only half willing because she was in correspondence with some intellectual or other over in Europe. Frances is a very deep reader and an intense letter-writer and a heavy smoker, and when she got on one of her kicks of philosophy or something I would see very little of her. I'd know she was up in her room smoking Sobranie cigarettes and coughing and making notes, working things out. Well, she was in one of these mental crises when we went to that party, and in the middle of it she recalled something she had to do at once and so she took the car and left, forgetting all about me. That night I had gotten mixed up too, and was the only man there in black tie. Midnight blue. I must have been the first fellow in that part of the state with a blue tuxedo. It felt as though I were wearing a whole acre of this blue cloth, while Lily, to whom I had been introduced about ten minutes before, had on a red and green Christmas-striped dress and we were talking.

When she saw what had happened, Lily offered me a ride, and I said, "Okay." We trod the snow out to her car.

It was a sparkling night and the snow was ringing. She was parked on a hill about three hundred yards long and smooth as iron. As soon as she drove away from the curb the car went into a skid and she lost her head and screamed, "Eugene!" She threw her arms about me. There was no other soul on that hill or on the shoveled walks, nor, so far as I could see, in the entire neighborhood. The car turned completely around. Her bare arms came out of the short fur sleeves and held my head while her large eyes watched through the windshield and the car went over the ice and hoarfrost. It was not even in gear and I reached the key and switched off the ignition. We slid into a snowdrift, but not far, and I took the wheel from her. The moonlight was very keen.

"How did you know my name?" I said, and she said, "Why, everybody knows you are Eugene Henderson."

After we had spoken some more she said to me, "You ought to divorce your wife."

I said to her, "What are you talking about? Is that a thing to say? Besides, I'm old enough to be your father."

We didn't meet again until the summer. This time she was shopping and was wearing a hat and a white piqué dress, with white shoes. It looked like rain and she didn't want to be caught in those clothes (which I noticed were soiled already) and she asked me for a lift. I had been in Danbury buying some lumber for the barn and the station wagon was loaded with it. Lily started to direct me to her house and lost the way

in her nervousness; she was very beautiful, but wildly nervous.
It was sultry and then it began to rain. She told me to take a
right turn and that brought us to a gray cyclone fence around
the quarry filled with water—a dead-end street. The air had
grown so dark that the mesh of the fence looked white.
Lily began to cry out, "Oh, turn around, please! Oh, quick,
turn around! I can't remember the streets and I have to go
home."

Finally we got there, a small house filled with the odor of
closed rooms in hot weather, just as the storm was beginning.
"My mother is playing bridge," said Lily. "I have to phone
her and tell her not to come home. There is a phone in my
bedroom." So we went up. There was nothing loose or
promiscuous about Lily, I assure you. When she took off her
clothes she started to speak out in a trembling voice, "I love
you! I love you!" And I said to myself as we embraced, "Oh,
how can she love you—you—you!" There was a huge knot of
thunder, and then a burst of rain on the streets, trees, roofs,
screens, and lightning as well. Everything got filled and
blinded. But a warm odor like fresh baking arose from her as
we lay in her sheets which were darkened by the warm
darkness of the storm. From start to finish she had not
stopped saying "I love you!" Thus we lay quietly, and the
early hours of the evening began without the sun's returning.

Her mother was waiting in the living room. I didn't care too
much for that. Lily had phoned her and said, "Don't come
home for a while," and therefore her mother had immediately
left the bridge party through one of the worst summer storms
in many years. No, I didn't like it. Not that the old lady scared
me, but I read the signs. Lily had made sure she would be
found out. I was the first down the stairs and saw a light
beside the chesterfield. And when I got to the foot of the
stairs, face to face with her, I said, "Henderson's the name."
Her mother was a stout pretty woman, made up for the bridge
party in a china-doll face. She wore a hat, and had a
patent-leather pocketbook on her stout knees when she sat
down. I realized that she was mentally listing accounts against

Lily. "In my own house. With a married man." And so on. Indifferent, I sat in the living room, unshaved, my lumber in the station wagon outside. Lily's odor, that baking odor, must have been noticeable about me. And Lily, extremely beautiful, came down the stairs to show her mama what she had accomplished. Acting oblivious, I kept my big boots apart on the carpet and frisked my mustache once in a while. Between them I sensed the important presence of Simmons, Lily's papa, the plumbing supply wholesaler who had committed suicide. In fact he had killed himself in the bedroom adjoining Lily's, the master bedroom. Lily blamed her mother for her father's death. And what was I, the instrument of her anger? "Oh no, pal," I said to myself, "this is not for you. Be no party to this."

It looked as though the mother had decided to behave well. She was going to be big about it and beat Lily at this game. Perhaps it was natural. Anyway, she was highly ladylike to me, but there came a moment when she couldn't check herself, and she said, "I have met your son."

"Oh yes, a slender fellow? Edward? He drives a red M G. You see him around Danbury sometimes."

Presently I left, saying to Lily, "You're a fine-looking big girl, but you oughtn't to have done that to your mother."

The stout old lady was sitting there on the sofa with her hands clasped and her eyes making a continuous line under her brows from tears or vexation.

"Good-by, Eugene," said Lily.

"So long, Miss Simmons," I said.

We didn't part friends exactly.

Nevertheless we soon met again, but in New York City, for Lily had separated from her mother, quitted Danbury, and had a cold-water flat on Hudson Street where the drunks hid from the weather on the staircase. I came, a great weight, a huge shadow on those stairs, with my face full of country color and booze, and yellow pigskin gloves on my hands, and a ceaseless voice in my heart that said, *I want, I want, I want, oh, I want—yes, go on,* I said to myself, *Strike, strike, strike,*

strike! And I kept going on the staircase in my thick padded coat, in pigskin gloves and pigskin shoes, a pigskin wallet in my pocket, seething with lust and seething with trouble, and realizing how my gaze glittered up to the top banister where Lily had opened the door and was waiting. Her face was round, white, and full, her eyes clear and narrowed.

"Hell! How can you live in this stinking joint? It stinks here," I said. The building had hall toilets; the chain pulls had turned green and there were panes of plum-colored glass in the doors.

She was a friend of the slum people, the old and the mothers in particular. She said she understood why they had television sets though on relief, and she let them keep their milk and butter in her refrigerator and filled out their social-security forms for them. I think she felt she did them good and showed these immigrants and Italians how nice an American could be. However, she genuinely tried to help them and ran around with her impulsive looks and said a lot of disconnected things.

The odors of this building clutched at your face, and I was coming up the stairs and said, "Whew, I am out of condition!"

We went into her apartment on the top floor. It was dirty, too, but there was light in it at least. We sat down to talk and Lily said to me, "Are you going to waste the rest of your life?"

With Frances the case was hopeless. Only once after I came back from the Army did anything of a personal nature take place between us, and after that it was no soap, so I let her be, more or less. Except that one morning in the kitchen we had a conversation that set us apart for good and all. Just a few words. They went like this:

"And what would you like to do now?"

(I was then losing interest in the farm.)

"I wonder," I said, "if it's too late for me to become a doctor—if I could enter medical school."

Frances opened her mouth, usually so sober, not to say dismal and straight, and laughed at me; and as she laughed I saw nothing but her dark open mouth, and not even teeth, which is certainly strange, for she has teeth, white ones. What had happened to them?

"Okay, okay, okay," I said.

Thus I realized that Lily was perfectly right about Frances. Nevertheless the rest did not follow.

"I need to have a child. I can't wait much longer," said Lily. "In a few years I'll be thirty."

"Am I responsible?" I said. "What's the matter with you?"

"You and I have got to be together," she said.

"Who says so?"

"We'll die if we're not," she said.

A year or so went by, and she failed to convince me. I didn't believe the thing could be so simple. So she suddenly married a man from New Jersey, a fellow named Hazard, a broker. Come to think of it she had spoken of him a few times, but I thought it was only more of her blackmail. Because she was a blackmailer. Anyway, she married him. This was her second marriage. Then I took Frances and the two girls and went to Europe, to France, for a year.

Several years of my boyhood were spent in the south of the country, near the town of Albi, where my old man was busy with his research. Fifty years ago I used to taunt a kid across the way, "François, oh François, ta soeur est constipée." My father was a big man, solid and clean. His long underwear was made of Irish linen and his hatboxes were lined with red velvet and he ordered his shoes from England and his gloves from Vitale Milano, Rome. He played pretty well on the violin. My mother used to write poems in the brick cathedral of Albi. She had a favorite story about a lady from Paris who was very affected. They met in a narrow doorway of the church and the lady said, "Voulez-vous que je passasse?" So my mother said, "Passassassez, Madame." She told everyone this joke and for many years would sometimes laugh and say in a whisper, "Passassassez." Gone, those times. Closed, sealed, and gone.

But Frances and I didn't go to Albi with the children. She

was attending the Collège de France, where all the philosophers were. Apartments were hard to get but I rented a good
one from a Russian prince. De Vogüé mentions his grandfather, who was minister under Nicolas I. He was a tall, gentle
creature; his wife was Spanish and his Spanish mother-in-law,
Señora Guirlandes, rode him continually. The guy was
suffering from her. His wife and kids lived with the old woman
while he moved into the maid's room in the attic. About three
million bucks, I have. I suppose I might have done something
to help him. But at this time my heart was consumed with the
demand I have mentioned—*I want, I want!* Poor prince,
upstairs! His children were sick, and he said to me that if his
condition didn't improve he would throw himself out of the
window.

I said, "Don't be nuts, Prince."

Guiltily, I lived in his apartment, slept in his bed, and
bathed in his bath twice a day. Instead of helping, those two
hot baths only aggravated my melancholy. After Frances
laughed at my dream of a medical career I never discussed
another thing with her. Around and around the city of Paris I
walked every day; all the way to the Gobelin factories and the
Père Lachaise Cemetery and St. Cloud I went on foot. The
only person who considered what my life was like was Lily,
now Lily Hazard. At the American Express I received a note
from her written on one of the wedding announcements long
after the date of the marriage. I was bursting with trouble, and
as there are a lot of whores who cruise that neighborhood near
the Madeleine, I looked some of them over, but this terrible
repetition within—*I want, I want!*—was not stopped by any
face I saw. I saw quite some faces.

"Lily may arrive," I thought. And she did. She cruised the
city in a taxi looking for me and caught up with me near
the Metro Vavin. Big and shining, she cried out to me from
the cab. She opened the antique door and tried to stand on the
runningboard. Yes, she was beautiful—a good face, a clear,
pure face, hot and white. Her neck as she stretched forward
from the door of the cab was big and shapely. Her upper lip

was trembling with joy. But, stirred as she was, she remembered those front teeth and kept them covered. What did I care then about new porcelain teeth! Blessed be God for the mercies He continually sends me!

"Lily! How are you, kid? Where did you come from?"

I was terribly pleased. She thought I was a big slob but of substantial value just the same, and that I should live and not die (one more year like this one in Paris and something in me would have rusted forever), and that something good might even come of me. She loved me.

"What have you done with your husband?" I said.

On the way back to her hotel, down Boulevard Raspail, she told me, "I thought I should have children. I was getting old." (Lily was then twenty-seven.) "But on the way to the wedding I saw it was a mistake. I tried to get out of the car at a stoplight in my wedding dress, but he caught me and pulled me back. He punched me in the eye," she said, "and it was a good thing I had a veil because the eye turned black, and I cried all the way through the ceremony. Also, my mother is dead."

"What! He gave you a shiner?" I said, furious. "If I ever come across him again I will break him in pieces. Say, I'm sorry about your mother."

I kissed her on the eyes, and then we arrived at her hotel on the Quai Voltaire and were on top of the world, in each other's arms. A happy week followed; we went everywhere, and Hazard's private detective followed us. Therefore I rented a car and we began a tour of the cathedral towns. And Lily in her marvelous way—always marvelously—began to make me suffer. "You think you can live without me, but you can't," she said, "any more than I can live without you. The sadness just drowns me. Why do you think I left Hazard? Because of the sadness. When he kissed me I felt saddest of all. I felt all alone. And when he—"

"That's enough. Don't tell me," I said.

"It was better when he punched me in the eye. There was some truth in that. Then I didn't feel like drowning."

And I began to drink, harder than ever, and was drunk in every one of the great cathedrals—Amiens, Chartres, Vézelay, and so on. She often had to do the driving. The car was a little one (a Deux Cent Deux décapotable or convertible) and the two of us, of grand size, towered out of the seats, fair and dark, beautiful and drunk. Because of me she had come all the way from America, and I wouldn't let her accomplish her mission. Thus we traveled all the way up to Belgium and back again to the Massif, and if you loved France that would have been fine, but I didn't love it. From start to finish Lily had just this one topic, moralizing: one can't live for this but has to live for that; not evil but good; not death but life; not illusion but reality. Lily does not speak clearly; I guess she was taught in boarding school that a lady speaks softly, and consequently she mumbles, and I am hard of hearing on the right side, and the wind and the tires and the little engine also joined their noise. All the same, from the joyous excitement of her great pure white face I knew she was still at it. With lighted face and joyous eyes she persecuted me. I learned she had many negligent and even dirty habits. She forgot to wash her underthings until, drunk as I was, I ordered her to. This may have been because she was such a moralist and thinker, for when I said, "Wash out your things," she began to argue with me. "The pigs on my farm are cleaner than you are," I told her; and this led to a debate. The earth itself is like that, corrupt. Yes, but it transforms itself. "A single individual can't do the nitrogen cycle all by herself," I said to her; and she said, Yes, but did I know what love *could* do? I yelled at her, "Shut up." It didn't make her angry. She was sorry for me.

The tour continued and I was a double captive—one, of the religion and beauty of the churches which I was not too drunk to see, and two, of Lily, and her glowing and mumbling and her embraces. She said a hundred times if she said it once, "Come back to the States with me. I've come to take you back."

"No," I said finally. "If there was any heart in you at all you wouldn't torture me, Lily. Damn you, don't forget I'm a

Purple Heart veteran. I've served my country. I'm over fifty, and I've had my bellyful of trouble."

"All the more reason why you should do something now," she said.

Finally I told her at Chartres, "If you don't quit it I'm going to blow my brains out."

This was cruel of me, as I knew what her father had done. Drunk as I was, I could hardly bear the cruelty myself. The old man had shot himself after a family quarrel. He was a charming man, weak, heartbroken, affectionate, and senti-mental. He came home full of whisky and would sing old-time songs for Lily and the cook; he told jokes and tap-danced and did corny vaudeville routines in the kitchen, joking with a catch in his throat—a dirty thing to do to your child. Lily told me all about it until her father became so actual to me that I loved and detested the old bastard myself. "Here, you old clog-dancer, you old heart-breaker, you pitiful joker—you cornball!" I said to his ghost. "What do you mean by doing this to your daughter and then leaving her on my hands?" And when I threatened suicide in Chartres cathedral, in the very face of this holy beauty, Lily caught her breath. The light in her face turned fine as pearl. She silently forgave me.

"It's all the same to me whether you forgive me or not," I told her.

We broke up at Vézelay. From the start our visit there was a strange one. The décapotable Deux Cent Deux had a flat when we came down in the morning. It being fine June weather, I had refused to put the car in a garage and in my opinion the management had let out the air. I accused the hotel and stood shouting until the office closed its iron shutter. I changed the tire quickly, using no jack but in my anger heaving up the little car and pushing a rock under the axle. After fighting with the hotel manager (both of us saying, "Pneu, pneu"), my mood was better, and we walked around the cathedral, bought a kilo of strawberries in a paper funnel, and went out on the ramparts to lie in the sun. Yellow dust was dropping from the lime trees, and wild roses grew on the trunks of the apple trees. Pale red, gorged red, fiery, aching, harsh as anger, sweet as drugs. Lily took off her blouse to get the sun on her shoulders. Presently she took off her slip, too, and after a time her brassière, and she lay in my lap. Annoyed, I said to her, "How do you know what I want?" And then more gently, because of the roses on all the tree trunks, piercing and twining and flaming, I said, "Can't you just enjoy this beautiful churchyard?"

"It isn't a churchyard, it's an orchard," she said.

I said, "Your period just began yesterday. So what are you after?"

She said I had never objected before, and that was true. "But I do object now," I said, and we began to quarrel and the quarrel got so fierce I told her she was going back to Paris alone on the next train.

She was silent. I had her, I thought. But no, it only seemed to prove how much I loved her. Her crazy face darkened with the intensity of love and joy.

"You'll never kill me, I'm too rugged!" I cried at her. And then I began to weep from all the unbearable complications in my heart. I cried and sobbed.

"Get in there, you mad bitch," I said, weeping. And I rolled back the roof of the décapotable. It has rods which come out, and then you reef back the canvas.

Under her breath, pale with terror but consumed also with her damned exalted glory, she mumbled as I was sobbing at the wheel about pride and strength and soul and love, and all of that.

I told her, "Curse you, you're nuts!"

"Without you, maybe it's true. Maybe I'm not all there and I don't understand," she said. "But when we're together, I *know*."

"Hell you know. How come I don't know anything! Stay the hell away from me. You tear me to pieces."

I dumped her foolish suitcase with the unwashed clothes in it on the platform. Still sobbing, I turned around in the station, which was twenty kilometers or so from Vézelay, and

I headed for the south of France. I drove to a place on the Vermilion Coast called Banyules. They keep a marine station there, and I had a strange experience in the aquarium. It was twilight. I looked in at an octopus, and the creature seemed also to look at me and press its soft head to the glass, flat, the flesh becoming pale and granular—blanched, speckled. The eyes spoke to me coldly. But even more speaking, even more cold, was the soft head with its speckles, and the Brownian motion in those speckles, a cosmic coldness in which I felt I was dying. The tentacles throbbed and motioned through the glass, the bubbles sped upward, and I thought, "This is my last day. Death is giving me notice."

So much for my suicide threat to Lily.

Chapter III

And now a few words about my reasons for going to Africa.

When I came back from the war it was with the thought of becoming a pig farmer, which maybe illustrates what I thought of life in general.

Monte Cassino should never have been bombed; some blame it on the dumbness of the generals. But after that bloody murder, where so many Texans were wiped out, and my outfit also took a shellacking later, there were only Nicky Goldstein and myself left out of the original bunch, and this was odd because we were the two largest men in the outfit and offered the best targets. Later I was wounded too, by a land mine. But at that time, Goldstein and I were lying down under the olive trees—some of those gnarls open out like lace and let the light through—and I asked him what he aimed to do after the war. He said, "Why, me and my brother, if we live and be well, we're going to have a mink ranch in the Catskills." So I said, or my demon said for me, "I'm going to start breeding pigs." And after these words were spoken I knew that if Goldstein had not been a Jew I might have said cattle and not pigs. So then it was too late to retract. So for all I know Goldstein and his brother have a mink business while I have—something else. I took all the handsome old farm buildings, the carriage house with paneled stalls—in the old days a rich man's horses were handled like opera singers—and the fine old barn with the belvedere above the hayloft, a beautiful piece of architecture, and I filled them up with pigs, a pig kingdom, with pig houses on the lawn and in the flower garden. The greenhouse, too—I let them root out the old bulbs. Statues from Florence and Salzburg were turned over. The place stank of swill and pigs and the mashes cooking, and dung. Furious, my neighbors got the health officer after me. I dared him to take me to law. "Hendersons have been on this property over two hundred years," I said to this man, a certain Dr. Bullock.

By my then wife, Frances, no word was said except, "Please keep them off the driveway."

"You'd better not hurt any of them," I said to her. "Those animals have become a part of me." And I told this Dr. Bullock, "All those civilians and 4Fs have put you up to this. Those twerps. Don't they ever eat pork?"

Have you seen, coming from New Jersey to New York, the gabled pens and runways that look like models of German villages from the Black Forest? Have you smelled them (before the train enters the tunnel to go under the Hudson)? These are pig-fattening stations. Lean and bony after their trip from Iowa and Nebraska, the swine are fed here. Anyway, I was a pig man. And as the prophet Daniel warned King Nebuchadnezzar, "They shall drive thee from among men, and thy dwelling shall be with the beasts of the field." Sows eat their young because they need the phosphorus. Goiter attacks them as it does women. Oh, I made a considerable study of these clever doomed animals. For all pig breeders know how clever they are. The discovery that they were so intelligent gave me a kind of trauma. But if I had not lied to Frances and those animals had actually become a part of me, then it was curious that I lost interest in them.

But I see I haven't got any closer to giving my reasons for going to Africa, and I'd better begin somewhere else.

Shall I start with my father? He was a well-known man. He had a beard and played the violin, and he . . .

No, not that.

Well, then, here: My ancestors stole land from the Indians. They got more from the government and cheated other settlers too, so I became heir to a great estate.

No, that won't do either. What has that got to do with it?

Still, an explanation is necessary, for living proof of something of the highest importance has been presented to me so I am obliged to communicate it. And not the least of the difficulties is that it happened as in a dream.

Well, then, it must have been about eight years after the war ended. I was divorced from Frances and married to Lily, and I felt that something had to be done. I went to Africa with a friend of mine, Charlie Albert. He, too, is a millionaire.

I have always had a soldierly rather than a civilian temperament. When I was in the Army and caught the crabs, I went to get some powder. But when I reported what I had, four medics grabbed me, right at the crossroads, in the open they stripped me naked and they soaped and lathered me and shaved every hair from my body, back and front, armpits, pubic hair, mustache, eyebrows, and all. This was right near the waterfront at Salerno. Trucks filled with troops were passing, and fishermen and paisanos and kids and girls and women were looking on. The GIs were cheering and laughing and the paisans laughed, the whole coast laughed, and even I was laughing as I tried to kill all four. They ran away and left me bald and shivering, ugly, naked, prickling between the legs and under the arms, raging, laughing, and swearing revenge. These are things a man never forgets and afterward truly values. That beautiful sky, and the mad itch and the razors; and the Mediterranean, which is the cradle of mankind; the towering softness of the air; the sinking softness of the water, where Ulysses got lost, where he, too, was naked as the sirens sang.

In passing—the crabs found refuge in a crevice; I had dealings afterward with these cunning animals.

The war meant much to me. I was wounded when I stepped on that land mine and got the Purple Heart, and I was in the hospital in Naples quite a while. Believe me, I was grateful that my life was spared. The whole experience gave my heart a large and real emotion. Which I continually require.

Beside my cellar door last winter I was chopping wood for the fire—the tree surgeon had left some pine limbs for me—and a chunk of wood flew up from the block and hit me in the nose. Owing to the extreme cold I didn't realize what had happened until I saw the blood on my mackinaw. Lily cried out, "You broke your nose." No, it wasn't broken. I have a lot of protective flesh over it but I carried a bruise there for some time. However as I felt the blow my only thought was *truth*. Does truth come in blows? That's a military idea if there ever was one. I tried to say something about it to Lily; she, too, had felt the force of truth when her second husband, Hazard, punched her in the eye.

Well, I've always been like this, strong and healthy, rude and aggressive, and something of a bully in boyhood; at college I wore gold earrings to provoke fights, and while I got an M.A. to please my father I always behaved like an ignorant man and a bum. When engaged to Frances I went to Coney Island and had her name tattooed on my ribs in purple letters. Not that this cut any ice with her. Already forty-six or forty-seven when I got back from Europe after V-E Day (Thursday, May 8) I went in for pigs, and then I confided to Frances that I was drawn to medicine; and she laughed at me; she remembered how enthusiastic I had been at eighteen over Sir Wilfred Grenfell and afterward over Albert Schweitzer.

What do you do with yourself if you have a temperament like mine? A student of the mind once explained to me that if you inflict your anger on inanimate things, you not only spare the living, as a civilized man ought to do, but you get rid of the bad stuff in you. This seemed to make good sense, and I tried it out. I tried with all my heart, chopping wood, lifting, plowing, laying cement blocks, pouring concrete, and cooking mash for the pigs. On my own place, stripped to the waist like a convict, I broke stones with a sledgehammer. It helped, but not enough. Rude begets rude, and blows, blows; at least in my case; it not only begot but it increased. Wrath increased with wrath. So what do you do with yourself? More than three million bucks. After taxes, after alimony and all expenses I still have one hundred and ten thousand dollars in income absolutely clear. What do I need it for, a soldierly character like me! Taxwise, even the pigs were profitable. I couldn't lose money. But they were killed and they were eaten. They made ham and gloves and gelatin and fertilizer. What did I make? Why, I made a sort of trophy, I suppose. A man like me may become something like a trophy. Washed, clean, and dressed in expensive garments. Under the roof is insulation; on the windows thermopane; on the floors carpeting; and on the carpets furniture, and on the furniture covers, and on the cloth covers plastic covers; and wallpaper and drapes! All is swept and garnished. And who is in the midst of this? Who is sitting there? Man! That's who it is, man!

But there comes a day, there always comes a day of tears and madness.

Now I have already mentioned that there was a disturbance in my heart, a voice that spoke there and said, *I want, I want, I want!* It happened every afternoon, and when I tried to suppress it it got even stronger. It only said one thing, *I want, I want!*

And I would ask, "What do you want?"

But this was all it would ever tell me. It never said a thing except *I want, I want, I want!*

At times I would treat it like an ailing child whom you offer rhymes or candy. I would walk it, I would trot it. I would sing to it or read to it. No use. I would change into overalls and go up on the ladder and spackle cracks in the ceiling; I would chop wood, go out and drive a tractor, work in the barn among the pigs. No, no! Through fights and drunkenness and labor it went right on, in the country, in the city. No purchase, no matter how expensive, would lessen it. Then I would say, "Come on, tell me. What's the complaint, is it Lily herself? Do you want some nasty whore? It has to be some lust?" But this was no better a guess than the others. The demand came louder, *I want, I want, I want, I want, I want!* And I would cry, begging at last, "Oh, tell me then. Tell me what you want!" And finally I'd say, "Okay, then. One of these days, stupid. You wait!"

This was what made me behave as I did. By three o'clock I was in despair. Only toward sunset the voice would let up. And sometimes I thought maybe this was my occupation because it would knock off at five o'clock of itself. America is so big, and everybody is working, making, digging, bulldozing, trucking, loading, and so on, and I guess the sufferers suffer at the same rate. Everybody wanting to pull together. I tried every cure you can think of. Of course, in an age of madness, to expect to be untouched by madness is a form of madness. But the pursuit of sanity can be a form of madness, too.

Among other remedies I took up the violin. One day as I was poking around in a storeroom I found the dusty case and I opened it, and there lay the instrument my father used to play, inside that little sarcophagus, with its narrow scrolled neck and incurved waist and the hair of the bow undone and loose all around it. I tightened the bow screw and scrubbed on the strings. Harsh cries awoke. It was like a feeling creature that had been neglected too long. Then I began to recall my old man. Maybe he would deny it with anger, but we are much alike. He could not settle into a quiet life either. Sometimes he was very hard on Mama; once he made her lie prostrate in her nightgown at the door of his room for two weeks before he would forgive her some silly words, perhaps like Lily's on the telephone when she said I was unkillable. He was a very strong man, too, but as he declined in strength, especially after the death of my brother Dick (which made me the heir), he shut himself away and fiddled more and more. So I began to recall his bent back and the flatness or lameness of his hips, and his beard like a protest that gushed from his very soul—washed white by the trembling weak blood of old age. Powerful once, his whiskers lost their curl and were pushed back on his collarbone by the instrument while he sighted with the left eye along the fingerboard and his big hollow elbow came and went, and the fiddle trembled and cried.

So right then I decided, "I'll try it too." I banged down the cover and shut the clasps and drove straight to New York to a repair shop on Fifty-seventh Street to have the violin reconditioned. As soon as it was ready I started to take lessons from an old Hungarian fellow named Haponyi who lived near the Barbizon-Plaza.

At this time I was alone in the country, divorced. An old lady, Miss Lenox from across the way, came in and fixed my breakfast and this was my only need at the time. Frances had stayed behind in Europe. And so one day as I was rushing to my lesson on Fifty-seventh Street with the case under my arm, I met Lily. "Well!" I said. I hadn't seen her in more than a year, not since I put her on that train for Paris, but we were immediately on the old terms of familiarity just as before. Her large, pure face was the same as ever. It would never be steady, but it was beautiful. Only she had dyed her hair. It was now orange, which was not necessary, and it was parted from the middle of her forehead like the two panels of a curtain. It's the curse of these big beauties sometimes that they are short on taste. Also she had done something with mascara to her eyes so that they were no longer of equal length. What are you supposed to do if such a person is "the same as ever"? And what are you supposed to think when this tall woman, nearly six feet, in a kind of green plush suit like the stuff they used to have in Pullman cars and high heels, sways; sturdy as her legs are, great as her knees are, she sways; and in one look she throws away all the principles of behavior observed on Fifty-seventh Street—as if throwing off the plush suit and hat and blouse and stockings and girdle to the winds and crying, "Gene! My life is misery without you"?

However, the first thing she actually said was, "I am engaged."

"What, again?" I said.

"Well, I could use your advice. We *are* friends. You *are* my friend, you know. I think we're each other's only friends in the world, after all. Are you studying music?"

"Well, if it isn't music then I'm in a gang war," I said. "Because this case holds either a fiddle or a tommy gun." I guess I must have felt embarrassed. Then she began to tell me about the new fiancé, mumbling. "Don't talk like that," I said. "What's the matter with you? Blow your nose. Why do you give me this Ivy League jive? This soft-spoken stuff? It's just done to take advantage of common people and make them bend over so as to hear you. You know I'm a little deaf," I said. "Raise your voice. Don't be such a snob. So tell me, did your fiancé go to Choate or St. Paul's? Your last husband went to President Roosevelt's prep school—whatchuma-jigger."

Lily now spoke more clearly and said, "My mother is dead."

"Dead?" I said. "Hey, that's terrible. But wait just one minute, didn't you tell me in France that she was dead?"

"Yes," she said.

"Then when did she die?"

"Just two months ago. It wasn't true then."

"Then why did you say it? That's a hell of a way. You can't do that. Are you playing chicken-funeral with your own mother? You were trying to con me."

"Oh, that was very bad of me, Gene. I didn't mean any harm. But this time it is true." And I saw the warm shadows of tears in her eyes. "She is gone now. I had to hire a plane to scatter her ashes over Lake George as she wanted."

"Did you? God, I'm sorry about it," I said.

"I fought her too much," said Lily. "Like that time I brought you home. But *she* was a fighter, and I am one, too. You were right about my fiancé. He did go to Groton."

"Ha, ha, I hit it, didn't I?"

"He's a nice man. He's not what you think. He's very decent and he supports his parents. But when I ask myself whether I could live without him, I guess the answer is yes.

But I am learning to get along alone. There's always the universe. A woman doesn't have to marry, and there are perfectly good reasons why people should be lonely."

You know, compassion is useless, too, sometimes I feel. It just lasts long enough to get you in dutch. My heart ached for Lily, and then she tried to con me.

"All right, kid, what are you going to do now?"

"I sold the house in Danbury. I'm living in an apartment. But there was one thing I wanted you to have, and I sent it to you."

"I don't want anything."

"It's a rug," she said. "Hasn't it come yet?"

"Hell, what do I want with your Christly rug! Was it from your room?"

"No."

"You're a liar. It's the rug from your bedroom."

She denied it, and when it arrived at the farm I accepted it from the delivery man; I felt I should. It was creepy-looking and faded, a Baghdad mustard color, the threads surrendering to time and sprigs of blue all over it. It was so ugly I had to laugh. This crummy rug! It tickled me. So I put it on the floor of my violin studio, which was down in the basement. I had poured the concrete there myself but not thick enough, for the damp comes through. Anyway, I thought this rug might improve the acoustics.

All right, then, I'd come into the city for my lessons with that fat Hungarian Haponyi, and I'd see Lily too. We courted for about eighteen months, and then we got married, and then the children were born. As for the violin, I was no Heifetz but I kept at it. Presently the daily voice, *I want, I want,* arose again. Family life with Lily was not all that might have been predicted by an optimist; but I'm sure that she got more than she had bargained for, too. One of the first decisions she made after looking over the whole place as lady of the house was to get her portrait painted and hung with the rest of the family. This portrait business was very important to her and it went on until about six months before I took off for Africa.

So let's look at a typical morning of my married life with

Lily. Not inside the house but outside, for inside it is filthy.
Let's say it's one of those velvety days of early autumn when
the sun is shining on the pines and the air has a spice of cold
and stings your lungs with pleasure. I see a large pine tree on
my property, and in the green darkness underneath, which
somehow the pigs never got into, red tuberous begonias grow,
and a broken stone inscription put in by my mother says,
"Goe happy rose . . ." That's all it says. There must be more
fragments beneath the needles. The sun is like a great roller
and flattens the grass. Beneath this grass the earth may be
filled with carcasses, yet that detracts nothing from a day like
this, for they have become humus and the grass is thriving.
When the air moves the brilliant flowers move too in the dark
green beneath the trees. They brush against my open spirit
because I am in the midst of this in the red velvet dressing
gown from the Rue de Rivoli bought on the day that Frances
spoke the word divorce. I am there and am looking for
trouble. The crimson begonias, and the dark green and the
radiant green and the spice that pierces and the sweet gold
and the dead transformed, the brushing of the flowers on my
undersurface are just misery to me. They make me crazy with
misery. To somebody these things may have been given, but
that somebody is not me in the red velvet robe. So what am I
doing here?

Then Lily comes up with the two kids, our twins, twenty-six
months old, tender, in their short pants and neat green jerseys,
the dark hair brushed down on their foreheads. And here
comes Lily with that pure face of hers going to sit for the
portrait. And I am standing on one foot in the red velvet robe,
heavy, wearing dirty farm boots, those Wellingtons which I
favor when at home because they are so easy to put on and
take off.

She starts to get into the station wagon and I say, "Use the
convertible. I am going to Danbury later to look for some
stuff, and I need this." My face is black and angry. My gums
are aching. The joint is in disorder, but she is going and the
kids will be playing indoors at the studio while she sits for the

portrait. So she puts them in the back seat of the convertible and drives away.

Then I go down to the basement studio and take the fiddle and start warming up on my Sevcik exercises. Ottokar Sevcik invented a technique for the quick and accurate change of position on the violin. The student learns by dragging or sliding his fingers along the strings from first position to third and from third to fifth and from fifth to second, on and on, until the ear and fingers are trained and find the notes with precision. You don't even start with scales, but with phrases, and go up and down the strings, crawling. It is frightful: but Haponyi says it is the only way, this fat Hungarian. He knows about fifty words of English, the main one being "dear." He says, "Dear, take de bow like dis vun, not like dis vun, so. Und so, so, so. Not to kill vid de bow. Make nice. Do not stick. Yo, yo, yo. Seret lek! Nice."

And after all, I am a commando, you know. And with these hands I've pushed around the pigs; I've thrown down boars and pinned them and gelded them. So now these same fingers are courting the music of the violin and gripping its neck and toiling up and down on the Sevcik. The noise is like smashing egg crates. Nevertheless, I thought, if I discipline myself eventually the voice of angels may come out. But anyway I didn't hope to perfect myself as an artist. My main purpose was to reach my father by playing on his violin.

Down in the basement of the house, I worked very hard as I do at everything. I had felt I was pursuing my father's spirit, whispering, "Oh, Father, Pa. Do you recognize the sounds? This is me, Gene, on your violin, trying to reach you." For it so happens that I have never been able to convince myself the dead are utterly dead. I admire rational people and envy their clear heads, but what's the use of kidding? I played in the basement to my father and my mother, and when I learned a few pieces I would whisper, "Ma, this is 'Humoresque' for you." Or, "Pa, listen—'Meditation' from *Thaïs*." I played with dedication, with feeling, with longing, love—played to the point of emotional collapse. Also down there in my studio I sang as I played, "Rispondi! Anima bella" (Mozart). "He was despised and rejected, a man of sorrows and acquainted with grief" (Handel). Clutching the neck of the little instrument as if there were strangulation in my heart, I got cramps in my neck and shoulders.

Over the years I had fixed up the little basement for myself, paneled it with chestnut and put in a dehumidifier. There I keep my little safe and my files and war souvenirs; and there also I have a pistol range. Under foot was now Lily's rug. At her insistence I had got rid of most of the pigs. But she herself was not very cleanly, and for one reason or another we couldn't get anyone from the neighborhood to do the cleaning. Yes, she swept up once in a while, but toward the door and not out of it, so there were mounds of dust in the doorway. Then she went to sit for her portrait, running away from the house altogether while I was playing Sevcik and pieces of opera and oratorio, keeping time with the voice within.

Chapter IV

Is it any wonder I had to go to Africa?

But I have told you there always comes a day of tears and madness.

I had fights, I had trouble with the troopers, I made suicide threats, and then last Xmas my daughter Ricey came home from boarding school. She has some of the family difficulty. To be blunt, I do not want to lose this child in outer space, and I said to Lily, "Keep an eye on her, will you?"

Lily was very pale. She said, "Oh, I want to help her. I will. But I've got to win her confidence."

Leaving the matter to her, I went down the kitchen back stairs to my studio and picked up the violin, which sparkled with rosin dust, and began to practice Sevcik under the fluorescent light of the music stand. I bent down in my robe

and frowned, as well I might, at the screaming and grating of
those terrible slides. Oh, thou God and judge of life and
death! The ends of my fingers were wounded, indented
especially by the steel E string, and my collarbone ached and
a flaming patch, like the hives, came out on my jowl. But the
voice within me continued, *I want, I want!*

But soon there was another voice in the house. Perhaps the
music drove Ricey out. Lily and Spohr, the painter, were
working hard to get the portrait finished by my birthday. She
went away and Ricey, alone, took a trip to Danbury to visit a
school chum, but didn't find her way to this girl's house.
Instead, as she wandered through the back streets of Danbury
she passed a parked car and heard the cries of a newborn
infant in the back seat of this old Buick. It was in a shoebox.
The day was terribly cold; therefore she brought the foundling
back with her and hid it in the clothes closet of her room. On
the twenty-first of December, at lunch, I was saying, "Children, this is the winter solstice," and then the infant's cry
came out by way of the heating ducts from the register under
the buffet. I pulled down the thick, woolly bill of my hunting
cap, which, it so happens, I was wearing at the lunch table,
and to suppress my surprise I began to talk about something
else. For Lily was laughing toward me significantly with the
upper lip drawn down over her front teeth, and her white
color very warm. Looking at Ricey, I saw that silent happiness
had come up into her eyes. At fifteen this girl is something of a
beauty, though usually in a listless way. But she was not
listless now; she was absorbed in the baby. As I did not know
then who the kid was or how it had got into the house, I was
startled, thrown, and I said to the twins, "So, there is a little
pussy cat upstairs, eh?" They weren't fooled. Try and fool
them! Ricey and Lily had baby bottles on the kitchen stove to
sterilize. I took note of this caldron full of bottles as I was
returning to the basement to practice, but made no comment.
All afternoon, by way of the air ducts, I heard the infant
squalling, and I went for a walk but couldn't bear the
December ruins of my frozen estate and one-time pig king-

dom. There were a few prize animals whom I hadn't sold. I wasn't ready to part with them yet.

I had arranged to play "The First Noël" on Xmas Eve, and so I was rehearsing it when Lily came downstairs to talk to me.

"I don't want to hear anything," I said.

"But, Gene," said Lily.

"You're in charge," I shouted, "you are in charge and it's your show."

"Gene, when you suffer you suffer harder than any person I ever saw." She had to smile, and not at my suffering, of course, but at the way I went about suffering. "Nobody expects it. Least of all God," she said.

"As you're in a position to speak for God," I said, "what does He think of your leaving this house every day to go and have your picture painted?"

"Oh, I don't think you need to be ashamed of me," said Lily.

Upstairs was the child, its every breath a cry, but it was no longer the topic. Lily thought I had a prejudice about her social origins, which are German and lace-curtain Irish. But damn it, I had no such prejudice. It was something else that bothered me.

Nobody truly occupies a station in life any more. There are mostly people who feel that they occupy the place that belongs to another by rights. There are displaced persons everywhere.

"For who shall abide the day of His (the rightful one's) coming?"

"And who shall stand when He (the rightful one) appeareth?"

When the rightful one appeareth we shall all stand and file out, glad at heart and greatly relieved, and saying, "Welcome back, Bud. It's all yours. Barns and houses are yours. Autumn beauty is yours. Take it, take it, take it!"

Maybe Lily was fighting along this line and the picture was going to be her proof that she and I were the rightful ones. But there is already a painting of me among the others. They have hard collars and whiskers, while I am at the end of a line in my National Guard uniform and hold a bayonet. And what good has this picture ever done me? So I couldn't be serious about Lily's proposed solution to our problem.

Now listen, I loved my older brother, Dick. He was the sanest of us, with a splendid record in the First World War, a regular lion. But for one moment he resembled me, his kid brother, and that was the end of him. He was on vacation, sitting at the counter of a Greek diner, the Acropolis Diner, near Plattsburg, New York, having a cup of coffee with a buddy and writing a post card home. But his fountain pen was balky, and he cursed it, and said to his friend, "Here. Hold this pen up." The young fellow did it and Dick took out his pistol and shot the pen from his hand. No one was injured. The roar was terrible. Then it was discovered that the bullet which had smashed the pen to bits had also pierced the coffee urn and made a fountain of the urn, which gushed straight across the diner in a hot stream to the window opposite. The Greek phoned for the state troopers, and during the chase Dick smashed his car into an embankment. He and his pal then tried to swim the river, and the pal had the presence of mind to strip his clothes, but Dick had on cavalry boots and they filled up and drowned him. This left my father alone in the world with me, my sister having died in 1901. I was working that summer for Wilbur, a fellow in our neighborhood, cutting up old cars.

But now it is Xmas week. Lily is standing on the basement stairs. Paris and Chartres and Vézelay and Fifty-seventh Street are far behind us. I have the violin in my hands, and the fatal rug from Danbury under my feet. The red robe is on my back. And the hunting cap? I sometimes think it keeps my head in one piece. The gray wind of December is sweeping down the overhang of the roof and playing bassoons on the loose rain pipes. Notwithstanding this noise I hear the baby cry. And Lily says, "Can you hear it?"

"I can't hear a thing, you know I'm a little deaf," I said, which is true.

"Then how can you hear the violin?"

"Well, I'm standing right next to it, I should be able to hear it," I said. "Stop me if I'm wrong," I said, "but I seem to remember that you told me once I was your only friend in all the world."

"But—" said Lily.

"I can't understand you," I said. "Go away."

At two o'clock there were some callers, and they heard the cries from upstairs but were too well bred to mention them. I'd banked on that. To break up the tension, however, I said, "Would anybody like to visit my pistol range downstairs?" There were no takers and I went below myself and fired a few rounds. The bullets made a tremendous noise among the hot-air ducts. Soon I heard the visitors saying good-by.

Later, when the baby was asleep, Lily talked Ricey into going skating on the pond. I had bought skates for everyone, and Ricey is still young enough to be appealed to in this way. When they were gone, Lily having given me this opportunity, I laid down the fiddle and stole upstairs to Ricey's room. Quietly I opened the closet door and saw the infant sleeping on the chemises and stockings in Ricey's valise, for she had not finished unpacking. It was a colored child, and made a solemn impression on me. The little fists were drawn up on either side of its broad head. About the middle was a fat diaper made of a Turkish towel. And I stooped over it in the red robe and the Wellingtons, my face flaming so that my head itched under the wool cap. Should I close up the valise and take the child to the authorities? As I studied the little baby, this child of sorrow, I felt like the Pharaoh at the sight of little Moses. Then I turned aside and I went and took a walk in the woods. On the pond the cold runners clinked over the ice. It was an early sunset and I thought, "Well, anyway, God bless you, children."

That night in bed I said to Lily, "Well now, I'm ready to talk this thing over."

Lily said, "Oh, Gene, I'm very glad." She gave me a high mark for this, and told me, "It's good that you are more able to accept reality."

"What?" I said. "I know more about reality than you'll ever know. I am on damned good terms with reality, and don't you forget it."

After a while I began to shout, and Ricey, hearing me carrying on and perhaps seeing me through the door, threatening and shaking my fist, standing on the bed in my jockey shorts, probably became frightened for her baby. On the twenty-seventh of December she ran away with the child. I didn't want the police in on this and phoned Bonzini, a private dick who has done some jobs for me, but before he could get on the case the headmistress called from Ricey's boarding school and said she had arrived and was hiding the infant in the dormitory. "You go up there," I said to Lily.

"Gene, but how can I?"

"How do I know how you can?"

"I can't leave the twins," she said.

"I guess it will interfere with your portrait, eh? Well, I'm just about ready to burn down the house and every picture in it."

"That's not what it is," said Lily, muttering and flushing white. "I have got used to your misunderstanding. I used to want to be understood, but I guess a person must try to live without being understood. Maybe it's a sin to want to be understood."

So it was I who went and the headmistress said that Ricey would have to leave her institution as she had already been on probation for quite a while. She said, "We have the psychological welfare of the other girls to consider."

"What's the matter with you? Those kids can learn noble feelings from my Ricey," I said, "and that's better than psychology." I was pretty drunk that day. "Ricey has an impulsive nature. She is one of those rapturous girls," I said. "Just because she doesn't talk much . . ."

"Where does the child come from?"

"She told my wife she found it in Danbury in a parked car."

"That's not what she says. She claims to be the mother."

"Why, I'm surprised at you," I said. "You ought to know

something about that. She didn't even get her breasts till last year. The girl is a virgin. She is fifty million times more pure than you or I."

I had to withdraw my daughter from the school.

I said to her, "Ricey, we have to give the little boy back. It isn't time yet for you to have your own little boy. His mama wants him back. She has changed her mind, dear." Now I feel I committed an offense against my daughter by parting her from this infant. After it was taken by the authorities from Danbury, Ricey acted very listless. "You know you are not the baby's mama, don't you?" I said. The girl never opened her lips and she made no answer.

As we were on our way to Providence, Rhode Island, where Ricey was going to stay with her aunt, Frances' sister, I said, "Sweetheart, your daddy did what any other daddy would do." Still no answer, and it was vain to try, because the silent happiness of the twenty-first of December was gone from her eyes.

So bound home from Providence alone, I was groaning to myself on the train, and in the club car I took out a deck of cards and played a game of solitaire. A bunch of people waited to sit down but I kept the table to myself, and I was fuddled, but no man in his right mind would have dared to bother me. I was talking aloud and groaning and the cards kept falling on the floor. At Danbury the conductor and another fellow had to help me off the train and I lay on a bench in the station swearing, "There is a curse on this land. There is something bad going on. Something is wrong. There is a curse on this land!"

I had known the stationmaster for a long time; he is a good old guy and kept the cops from taking me away. He phoned Lily to come for me, and she arrived in the station wagon.

But as for the actual day of tears and madness, it came about like this: It is a winter morning and I am fighting with my wife at the breakfast table about our tenants. She has remodeled a building on the property, one of the few I didn't take for the pigs because it was old and out of the way. I told her to go ahead, but then I held back on the dough, and instead of wood, wallboard was put in, with other economies on down the line. She made the place over with a new toilet and had it painted inside and out. But it had no insulation. Came November and the tenants began to feel cool. Well, they were bookish people; they didn't move around enough to keep their body heat up. After several complaints they told Lily they wanted to leave. "Okay, let them," I said. Naturally I wouldn't refund the deposit, but told them to get out.

So the converted building was empty, and the money put into masonite and new toilet and sink and all the rest was lost. The tenants had also left a cat behind. And I was sore and yelling at the breakfast table, hammering with my fist until the coffee pot turned over.

Then all at once Lily, badly scared, paused long and listened, and I listened with her. She said, "Have you seen Miss Lenox in the last fifteen minutes? She was supposed to bring the eggs."

Miss Lenox was the old woman who lived across the road and came in to fix our breakfast. A queer, wacky little spinster, she wore a tam and her cheeks were red and mumpy. She would tickle around in the corners like a mouse and take home empty bottles and cartons and similar junk.

I went into the kitchen and saw this old creature lying dead on the floor. During my rage, her heart had stopped. The eggs were still boiling; they bumped the sides of the pot as eggs will do when the water is seething. I turned off the gas. Dead! Her small, toothless face, to which I laid my knuckles, was growing cold. The soul, like a current of air, like a draft, like a bubble, sucked out of the window. I stared at her. So this is it, the end—farewell? And all this while, these days and weeks, the wintry garden had been speaking to me of this fact and no other; and till this moment I had not understood what this gray and white and brown, the bark, the snow, the twigs, had been telling me. I said nothing to Lily. Not knowing what else to do, I wrote a note DO NOT DISTURB and pinned it to the old lady's skirt, and I went through the frozen winter garden and across the road to her cottage.

In her yard she had an old catalpa tree of which the trunk

and lower limbs were painted light blue. She had fixed little mirrors up there, and old bicycle lights which shone in the dark, and in summer she liked to climb up there and sit with her cats, drinking a can of beer. And now one of these cats was looking at me from the tree, and as I passed beneath I denied any blame that the creature's look might have tried to lay upon me. How could I be blamed—because my voice was loud, and my anger was so great?

In the cottage I had to climb from room to room over the boxes and baby buggies and crates she had collected. The buggies went back to the last century, so that mine might have been there too, for she got her rubbish all over the country-side. Bottles, lamps, old butter dishes, and chandeliers were on the floor, shopping bags filled with string and rags, and pronged openers that the dairies used to give away to lift the paper tops from milk bottles; and bushel baskets full of buttons and china door knobs. And on the walls, calendars and pennants and ancient photographs.

And I thought, "Oh, shame, shame! Oh, crying shame! How can we? Why do we allow ourselves? What are we doing? The last little room of dirt is waiting. Without windows. So for God's sake make a move, Henderson, put forth effort. You, too, will die of this pestilence. Death will annihilate you and nothing will remain, and there will be nothing left but junk. Because nothing will have been and so nothing will be left. While something still *is—now!* For the sake of all, get out."

Lily wept over the poor old woman.

"Why did you leave such a note?" she said.

"So nobody should move her until the coroner came," I said. "That's what the law is. I barely felt her myself." I then offered Lily a drink, which she refused, and I filled the water tumbler with bourbon and drank it down. Its only effect was a heartburn. Whisky could not coat the terrible fact. The old lady had fallen under my violence as people keel over during heat waves or while climbing the subway stairs. Lily was aware of this and started to mutter something about it. She was very thoughtful, and became silent, and her pure white color began to darken toward the eyes.

The undertaker in our town has bought the house where I used to take dancing lessons. Forty years ago I used to go there in my patent-leather shoes. When the hearse backed up the drive, I said, "You know, Lily, that trip that Charlie Albert is going to make to Africa? He'll be leaving in a couple of weeks, and I think I'll go along with him and his wife. Let's put the Buick in storage. You won't need two cars."

For once she didn't object to one of my ideas. "Maybe you ought to go," she said.

"I should do something."

So Miss Lenox went to the cemetery, and I went to Idlewild and took a plane.

Chapter V

I guess I hadn't taken two steps out into the world as a small boy when there was Charlie, a person in several ways like myself. In 1915 we attended dancing school together (in the house out of which Miss Lenox was buried), and such attachments last. In age he is only a year my junior and in wealth he goes me a little better, for when his old mother dies he will have another fortune. It was with Charlie that I took off for Africa, hoping to find a remedy for my situation. I guess it was a mistake to go with him, but I wouldn't have known how to go right straight into Africa by myself. You have to have a specific job to do. The excuse was that Charlie and his wife were going to film the Africans and the animals, for during the war Charlie was a cameraman with Patton's army—he could no more stay at home than I could—and so he learned the trade. Photography is not one of my interests.

Anyway, last year I asked Charlie to come out and photograph some of my pigs. This opportunity to show how good he was at his work pleased him, and he made some first-rate studies. Then we came back from the barn and he said he was engaged. So I told him, "Well, Charlie, I guess you know a lot about whores, but what do you know about girls—anything?"

"Oh," he said, "it's true that I don't know much, but I do know she is unique."

"Yes, I know all about this unique business," I said. (I had heard all about it from Lily but now she was never even at home.)

Nevertheless we went down to the studio to have a drink on his engagement, and he asked me to be his best man. He has almost no friends. We drank and kidded and reminisced about the dancing class, and made tears of nostalgia come to each other's eyes. It was then when we were both melted down that he invited me to come along to Africa where he and his wife would be going for their honeymoon.

I attended the wedding and stood up for him. However, because I forgot to kiss the bride after the ceremony, there developed a coolness on her side and eventually she became my enemy. The expedition that Charlie organized had all new equipment and was modern in every respect. We had a portable generator, a shower, and hot water, and from the beginning I was critical of this. I said, "Charlie, this wasn't the way we fought the war. Hell, we're a couple of old soldiers. What is this?" It wounded me to travel in Africa in this way.

But I had come to this continent to stay. When buying my ticket in New York I went through a silent struggle there at the airlines office (near Battery Park) as to whether or not to get a round-trip ticket. And as a sign of my earnestness, I decided to take it one way. So we flew from Idlewild to Cairo. I went on a bus to visit the Sphinx and the pyramids, and then we flew off again to the interior. Africa reached my feelings right away even in the air, from which it looked like the ancient bed of mankind. And at a height of three miles, sitting above the clouds, I felt like an airborne seed. From the cracks in the earth the rivers pinched back at the sun. They shone out like smelters' puddles, and then they took a crust and were covered over. As for the vegetable kingdom, it hardly existed from the air; it looked to me no more than an inch in height. And I dreamed down at the clouds, and thought that when I was a kid I had dreamed up at them, and having dreamed at the clouds from both sides as no other generation of men has done, one should be able to accept his death very easily. However, we made safe landings every time. Anyway, since I had come to this place under the circumstances described, it was natural to greet it with a certain emotion. Yes, I brought a sizable charge with me and I kept thinking, "Bountiful life! Oh, how bountiful life is." I felt I might have a chance here. To begin with, the heat was just what I craved, much hotter than the Gulf of Mexico, and then the colors themselves did me a world of good. I didn't feel the pressure in the chest, nor hear any voice within. At that time it was silent. Charlie and his wife and I, together with natives and trucks and equipment, were camped near some lake or other. The water here was very soft, with reeds and roots rotted, and there were crabs in the sand. The crocodiles boated around in the lilies, and when they opened their mouths they made me realize how hot a damp creature can be inside. The birds went into their jaws and cleaned their teeth. However, the people in this district were very sad, not lively. On the trees grew a featherlike bloom and the papyrus reeds began to remind me of funeral plumes, and after about three weeks of cooperating with Charlie, helping him with the camera equipment and trying to interest myself in his photographic problems, my discontent returned and one afternoon I heard the familiar old voice within. It began to say, *I want, I want, I want!*

I said to Charlie, "I don't want you to get sore, now, but I don't think this is working out, the three of us together in Africa."

Stolid, he looked me over through his sunglasses. We were beside the water. Was this the kid I used to know in dancing class? How time had changed us both. But we were now, as then, in short pants. His development is broad through the chest. And as I am much the taller, he was looking up, but he was angry, not intimidated. The flesh around his mouth became very lumpy as he deliberated, and then he said, "No? Why not?"

"Well," I said, "I took this chance to get here, Charlie, and

I'm very grateful because I've always been a sort of Africa buff, but now I realize that I didn't come to take pictures of it. Sell me one of the jeeps and I'll take off."

"Where do you want to go?"

"All I know is that this isn't the place for me," I said.

"Well, if you want to, shove off. I won't stop you, Gene."

It was all because I had forgotten to kiss his wife after the ceremony, and she couldn't forgive me. What would she want a kiss from me for? Some people don't know when they're well off. I can't say why I didn't kiss her; I was thinking of something else, I guess. But I think she concluded that I was jealous of Charlie, and anyway I was spoiling her African honeymoon.

"So, no hard feelings, eh, Charlie? But it does me no good to travel this way."

"That's okay. I'm not trying to stop you. Just blow."

And that was what I did. I organized a separate expedition that suited my soldierly temperament better. I hired two of Charlie's natives and when we drove away in the jeep I felt better at once. And after a few days, anxious to simplify more and more, I laid off one of the men and had a long conversation with the remaining African, Romilayu. We arrived at an understanding. He said that if I wanted to see some places off the beaten track, he could guide me to them.

"That's it," I said. "Now you've got the idea. I didn't come here to carry on a quarrel with a broad over a kiss."

"Me tek you far, far," he said.

"Oh, man! The farther the better. Why, let's go, let's go," I said. I had found the fellow I wanted, just the right man. We got rid of more baggage and, knowing how attached he was to the jeep, I told him I would give it to him if he would take me far enough. He said the place he was going to guide me to was so remote we could reach it only on foot. "So?" I said. "Let's walk. We'll put the jeep up on blocks, and she's yours when we get back." This pleased him deeply, and when we got to a town called Talusi we left the machine in dead storage in a grass hut. From here we took a plane to Baventai, an old

Bellanca, the wings looked ready to drop off, and the pilot was an Arab and flew with bare feet. It was an exceptional flight and ended on a field of hard clay beyond the mountain. Tall Negro cowherds came up to us with their greased curls and their deep lips. I had never seen men who looked so wild and I said to Romilayu, my guide, "This isn't the place you promised to bring me to, is it?"

"Wo, no sah," he said.

We were to travel for another week, afoot, afoot.

Geographically speaking I didn't have the remotest idea where we were, and I didn't care too much. It was not for me to ask, since my object in coming here was to leave certain things behind. Anyway, I had great trust in Romilayu, the old fellow. So for days and days he led me through villages, over mountain trails, and into deserts, far, far out. He himself couldn't have told me much about our destination in his limited English. He said only that we were going to see a tribe he called the Arnewi.

"You know these people?" I asked him.

A long time ago, before he was full grown, Romilayu had visited the Arnewi together with his father or his uncle—he told me many times but I couldn't make out which.

"Anyway, you want to go back to the scenes of your youth," I said. "I get the picture."

I was having a great time out here in the desert among the stones, and continually congratulated myself on having quit Charlie and his wife and on having kept the right native. To have found a man like Romilayu, who sensed what I was looking for, was a great piece of luck. He was in his late thirties, he told me, but looked much older because of premature wrinkles. His skin did not fit tightly. This happens to many black men of certain breeds and they say it has something to do with the distribution of the fat on the body. He had a bush of dusty hair which he tried sometimes, but vainly, to smooth flat. It was unbrushable and spread out at the sides of his head like a dwarf pine. Old tribal scars were cut into his cheeks and his ears had been mutilated to look like hackles so that the points stuck into his hair. His nose was fine-looking and Abyssinian, not flat. The scars and mutilations showed that he had been born a pagan, but somewhere along the way he had been converted, and now he said his prayers every evening. On his knees, he pressed his purple hands together under his chin, which receded, and with his lips pushed forward and the powerful though short muscles jumping under the skin of his arms, he'd pray. He fetched up deep sounds from his chest, like confiding groans of his soul. This would happen when we stopped to camp at twilight when the swallows were dipping back and forth. Then I would sit on the ground and encourage him; I'd say, "Go on. Tell 'em. And put in a word for me too."

I got clean away from everything, and we came into a region like a floor surrounded by mountains. It was hot, clear, and arid and after several days we saw no human footprints. Nor were there many plants; for that matter there was not much of anything here; it was all simplified and splendid, and I felt I was entering the past—the real past, no history or junk like that. The prehuman past. And I believe that there was something between the stones and me. The mountains were naked, and often snakelike in their forms, without trees, and you could see the clouds being born on the slopes. From this rock came vapor, but it was not like ordinary vapor, it cast a brilliant shadow. Anyway I was in tremendous shape those first long days, hot as they were. At night, after Romilayu had prayed, and we lay on the ground, the face of the air breathed back on us, breath for breath. And then there were the calm stars, turning around and singing, and the birds of the night with heavy bodies, fanning by. I couldn't have asked for anything better. When I laid my ear to the ground I thought I could hear hoofs. It was like lying on the skin of a drum. Those were wild asses maybe, or zebras flying around in herds. And this was how Romilayu traveled, and I lost count of the days. As, probably, the world was glad to lose track of me too for a while.

The rainy season had been very short; the streams were all

dry and the bushes would burn if you touched a match to
them. At night I would start a fire with my lighter, which was
the type in common use in Austria with a long trailing wick.
By the dozen they come to about fourteen cents apiece; you
can't beat that for a bargain. Well, we were now on a plateau
which Romilayu called the Hinchagara—this territory has
never been well mapped. As we marched over that hot and (it
felt so to me) slightly concave plateau, a kind of olive-colored
heat mist, like smoke, formed under the trees, which were
short and brittle, like aloes or junipers (but then I'm no
botanist) and Romilayu, who came behind me through the
strangeness of his shadow, made me think of a long wooden
baker's shovel darting into the oven. The place was certainly
at baking heat.

Finally one morning we found ourselves in the bed of a
good-sized river, the Arnewi, and we walked downstream in it,
for it was dry. The mud had turned to clay, and the boulders
sat like lumps of gold in the dusty glitter. Then we sighted the
Arnewi village and saw the circular roofs which rose to a
point. I knew they were just thatch and must be brittle,
porous, and light; they seemed like feathers, and yet heavy—
like heavy feathers. From these coverings smoke went up into
the silent radiance. Also an inanimate glitter came off the
ancient thatch. "Romilayu," I said, stopping him, "isn't that a
picture? Where are we? How old is this place, anyway?"

Surprised at my question, he said, "I no know, sah."

"I have a funny feeling from it. Hell, it looks like the
original place. It must be older than the city of Ur." Even the
dust had a flavor of great age, I thought, and I said, "I have a
hunch this spot is going to be very good for me."

The Arnewi were cattle raisers. We startled some of the
skinny animals on the banks, and they started to buck and
gallop, and soon we found ourselves amid a band of African
kids, naked boys and girls, yelling at the sight of us. Even the
tiniest of them, with the big bellies, wrinkled their faces and
screeched with the rest, above the bellowing of the cattle, and
flocks of birds who had been sitting in trees took off through

the withered leaves. Before I saw them it sounded like stones pelting at us and I thought we were under attack. Under the mistaken impression that we were being stoned, I laughed and swore. It amused me that they might be shying rocks at me, and I said, "Jesus, is this the way they meet travelers?" But then I saw the birds beating it through the sky.

Romilayu explained to me that the Arnewi were very sensitive to the condition of their cattle, whom they regarded as their relatives, more or less, and not as domestic animals. No beef was eaten here. And instead of one kid's being sent out with the herd, each cow had two or three child companions; and when the animals were upset, the children ran after them to soothe them. The adults were even more peculiarly attached to their beasts, which it took me some time to understand. But at the time I remember wishing that I had brought some treats for the children. When fighting in Italy I always carried Hershey bars and peanuts from the PX for the bambini. So now, coming down the river bed and approaching the wall of the town, which was made of thorns with some manure and reinforced by mud, we saw some of the kids waiting up for us, the rest having gone on to spread the news of our arrival. "Aren't they something?" I said to Romilayu. "Christ, look at the little pots on them, and those tight curls. Most of them haven't got their second teeth in yet." They jumped up and down, screaming, and I said, "I certainly wish I had a treat for them, but I haven't got anything. How do you think they'd like it if I set fire to a bush with this lighter?" And without waiting for Romilayu's advice I took out the Austrian lighter with the drooping wick, spun the tiny wheel with my thumb, and immediately a bush went flaming, almost invisible in the strong sunlight. It roared; it made a brilliant manifestation; it stretched to its limits and became extinct in the sand. I was left holding the lighter with the wick coming out of my fist like a slender white whisker. The kids were unanimously silent; they only looked, and I looked at them. That's what they call reality's dark dream? Then suddenly everyone scattered again, and the cows galloped. The embers of the bush had fallen by my boots.

"How do you think that went over?" I asked Romilayu. "I meant well." But before we could discuss the matter we were met by a party of naked people. In front of them all was a young woman, a girl not much older, I believe, than my daughter Ricey. As soon as she saw me she burst into loud tears.

I would never have expected this to wound me as it did. It wouldn't have been realistic to go into the world without being prepared for trials, ordeals, and suffering, but the sight of this young woman hit me very hard. Though of course the tears of women always affect me deeply, and not so long before, when Lily had started to cry in our hotel suite on the Gulf, I made my worst threat. But this young woman being a stranger, it's less easy to explain why her weeping loosed such a terrible emotion in me. What I thought immediately was "What have I done?"

"Shall I run back into the desert," I thought, "and stay there until the devil has passed out of me and I am fit to meet humankind again without driving it to despair at the first look? I haven't had enough desert yet. Let me throw away my gun and my helmet and the lighter and all this stuff and maybe I can get rid of my fierceness too and live out there on worms. On locusts. Until all the bad is burned out of me. Oh, the bad! Oh, the wrong, the wrong! What can I do about it? What can I do about all the damage? My character! God help me, I've made a mess of everything, and there's no getting away from the results. One look at me must tell the whole story."

You see, I had begun to convince myself that those few days of lightheartedness, tramping over the Hinchagara plateau with Romilayu, had already made a great change in me. But it seemed that I was still not ready for society. Society is what beats me. Alone I can be pretty good, but let me go among people and there's the devil to pay. Confronted with this weeping girl I was by this time ready to start bawling myself, thinking of Lily and the children and my father and the violin and the foundling and all the sorrows of my life. I felt that my nose was swelling, becoming very red.

Behind the weeping girl other natives were crying along softly. I said to Romilayu, "What the blast is going on?"

"Him shame," said Romilayu, very grave, with that upstanding bush of hair.

Thus this sturdy, virginal-looking girl was crying—simply crying—without gestures; her arms were meekly hanging by her sides and all the facts about her (speaking physically) were shown to the world. The tears fell from her wide cheekbones onto her breasts.

I said, "What's eating this kid? What do you mean, shame? This is very bad, if you ask me, Romilayu. I think we've walked into a bad situation and I don't like the looks of it. Why don't we cut around this town and go back into the desert? I felt a damned sight better out there."

Apparently Romilayu sensed that I was rattled by this delegation shedding tears and he said, "No, no sah. You no be blame."

"Maybe it was a mistake with that bush?"

"No, no, sah. You no mek him cry."

At this I struck myself in the head with my open hand and said, "Why sure! I *would*." (Meaning, "I *would* think first of myself.") "The poor soul is in trouble? Is there something I can do for her? She's coming to me for help. I feel it. Maybe a lion has eaten her family? Are there man-eaters around here? Ask her, Romilayu. Say that I've come to help, and if there are killers in the neighborhood I'll shoot them." I picked up my H and H Magnum with the scope sights and showed it to the crowd. With enormous relief it dawned on me that the crying was not due to any fault of mine, and that something could be done, that I did not have to stand and bear the sight of those tears boiling out. "Everybody! Leave it to me," I said. "Look! Look!" And I started to go through the manual of arms for them, saying, "Hut, hut, hut," as the drill instructors always did.

Everyone, however, went on crying. Only the very little kids with their jack-o'-lantern faces seemed happy at my entertainment. The rest were not done mourning, and covered their faces with their hands while their naked bodies shook.

"Well, Romilayu," I said, "I'm not getting anywhere, and our presence is very hard on them, that's for sure."

"Dem cry for dead cow," he said. And he explained the thing very clearly, that they were mourning for cattle which had died in the drought, and that they took responsibility for the drought upon themselves—the gods were offended, or something like that; a curse was mentioned. Anyway, as we were strangers they were obliged to come forward and confess everything to us, and ask whether we knew the reason for their trouble.

"How should I know—except the drought? A drought is drought," I said, "but my heart goes out to them, because I know what it is to lose a beloved animal." And I began to say, almost to shout, "Okay, okay, okay. All right, ladies—all right, you guys, break it up. That's enough, please. I get it." And this did have some effect on them, as I suppose they heard in the tone of my voice that I felt a certain amount of distress also, and I said to Romilayu, "So ask them what they want me to do. I intend to do something, and I really mean it."

"What you do, sah?"

"Never mind. There must be something that only I can do. I want you to start asking."

So he spoke to them, and the smooth-skinned, humped cattle kept grunting in their gentle bass voices (the African cows do not low like our own). But the weeping died down. And now I began to observe that the coloring of these people was very original and that the dark was more deeply burnt in about the eyes whereas the palms of their hands were the color of freshly washed granite. As if, you know, they had played catch with the light and some of it had come off. These peculiarities of color were altogether new to me. Romilayu had gone aside to speak with someone and left me among the natives, whose sobbing had almost stopped. Just then I deeply felt my physical discrepancies. My face is like some sort of terminal; it's like Grand Central, I mean—the big horse nose and the wide mouth that opens into the nostrils, and eyes like tunnels. So I stood there waiting, surrounded by this black humanity in the aromatic dust, with that inanimate brilliance coming off the thatch of the huts nearby.

Then the man with whom Romilayu had been speaking came up and talked to me in English, which astonished me, for I would never have thought that people who spoke English would have been capable of carrying on so emotionally. However, he was not one of those who had carried on. From his size alone I felt he must be an important person, for he was built very heavily and had an inch or two on me in stature. But he was not ponderous, as I am, he was muscular; nor was he naked like the others, but wore a piece of white cloth tied on his thighs rather than on his hips proper, and around his belly was a green silk scarf, and he had a short loose middy type of blouse, which he wore very free to give his arms lots of play, which, owing to the big muscles, they needed. At first he was rather heavy of expression and I thought he might be looking for trouble, sizing me up as if I were some kind of human mushroom, imposing in size but not hard to knock over. I was very upset, but what upset me was not his expression, which soon changed for the better; it was, among other things, the fact that he spoke to me in English. I don't know why I should have been so surprised—disappointed is the word. It's the great imperial language of today, taking its turn after Greek and Latin and so on. The Romans weren't surprised, I don't think, when some Parthian or Numidian started to speak to them in Latin; they probably took it for granted. But when this fellow, built like a champion, in his white drooping cloth and his scarf and middy, addressed me in English, I was both shaken up and grieved. Preparing to speak, he put his pale, slightly freckled lips into position, moving them forward, and said, "I am Itelo. I am here to introduce. Welcome. And how do you do?"

"What? What?" I said, holding my ear.

"Itelo." He bowed.

Quickly, I too bent and bowed in the short pants and corky white helmet with my overheated face and great nose. My face can be like the clang of a bell, and because I am hard of hearing on the right side I have a way of swinging the left into position, listening in profile and fixing my eyes on some object to help my concentration. So I did. I waited for him to say more, sweating boisterously, for I was confounded down to the ground. I couldn't believe it; I was so sure that I had left the world. And who could blame me, after that trip across the mountain floor on which there was no footprint, the stars flaming like oranges, those multimillion tons of exploding gas looking so mild and fresh in the dark of the sky; and altogether, that freshness, you know, that is like autumn freshness when you go out of the house in the morning and find the flowers have waked in the frost with piercing life? When I experienced this in the desert, night and morning, feeling everything to be so simplified, I was quite sure that I had gone clean out of the world, for, as is common knowledge, the world is complex. And besides, the antiquity of the place had struck me so, I was sure I had got into someplace new. And the weeping delegation; but here was someone who obviously had been around, as he spoke English, and I had been boasting, "Show me your enemies and I'll kill them. Where is the man-eater, lead me to him." And setting bushes on fire, and performing the manual of arms, and making like a regular clown. I felt extremely ridiculous, and I gave Romilayu a dark, angry look, as though it were his fault for not having briefed me properly.

But this native, Itelo, did not mean to work me over because of my behavior on arrival. It never seemed to enter his mind, even. He took my hand and placed it flat against his breast saying, "Itelo."

I did likewise, saying, "Henderson." I didn't want to be a shit about it, you see, but I am not good at suppressing my feelings. Whole crowds of them, especially the bad ones, wave to the world from the galleries of my face. I can't prevent them. "How do you do?" I said. "And say, what's going on around here—everybody crying to beat the band? My man says it's because of the cows. This isn't a good time for a visit, eh? Maybe I should go and come back some other time?"

"No, you be guest," said Itelo, and made me welcome. But he had observed that I was disappointed and that my offer to depart was not one hundred per cent gallantry and generosity, and he said, "You thought first footstep? Something new? I am very sorry. We are discovered."

"If I did expect it," I said, "then it's my own damn fault. I know the world has been covered. Hell, I'd have to be out of my mind. I'm no explorer, and anyway that's not what I came for." So, recalling to mind what I had come for, I started to look at this fellow more closely to see what he might know about the greater or deeper facts of life. And first of all I recognized that his heaviness of expression was misleading and that he was basically a good-humored fellow. Only he was very dignified. Two large curves starting above his nostrils came down beside his mouth and gave him the look I had misinterpreted. He had a backed-up posture which empha-sized the great strength of his legs and knees, and in the corners of his eyes, which had the same frame of darkness as the others in the tribe, there was a glitter which made me think of gold leaf.

"Well," I said, "I see you have been out in the world anyway. Or is English everybody's second language here?"

"Sir," he said, "oh, no, just only me." Perhaps because of the breadth of his nose he had a tone which was ever so slightly nasal. "Malindi school. I went, and also my late brother. Lot of young fellows sent from all over to Malindi school. After that, Beirut school. I have traveled all over. So I alone speak. And for miles and miles around nobody else, but only Wariri king, Dahfu."

I had completely forgotten to find out, and now I said, "Oh, excuse me, do you happen to be royalty yourself?"

"Queen is my auntie," he said, "Willatale. And you will stay with other auntie, Mtalba. Sir, she lend you her house."

"Oh, that's great," I said. "That's hospitable. And so you're a prince?"

"Oh, yes."

That was better. Owing to his size and appearance I thought

from the beginning that he must be distinguished. And then to console me he said that I was the first white visitor here in more than thirty years, so far as he knew. "Well, Your Highness," I said, "you're just as well off not to attract many outsiders. I think you've got a good thing here. I don't know what it is about the place, but I've visited some of the oldest ruins in Europe and they don't feel half as ancient as your village. If it worries you that I'm going to run and broadcast your whereabouts or that I want to take pictures, you can just forget about it. That's not my line at all." For this he thanked me but said there wasn't much of value to attract travelers here. And I'm still not convinced that I didn't penetrate beyond geography. Not that I care too much about geography; it's one of those bossy ideas according to which, if you locate a place, there's nothing more to be said about it.

"Mr. Henderson, sir. Please come in and enter the town," he said.

And I said, "I suppose you want me to meet everyone."

It was gorgeous weather, though far too dry, radiance everywhere, and the very dust of the place aromatic and stimulating. Waiting for us was a company of women, Itelo's wives, naked, and with the dark color worked in deeply around the eyes as if by special action of the sun. The lighter skin of their hands reminded me continually of pink stone. It made both hands and fingers seem larger than ordinary. Later I saw some of these younger women stand by the hour with a piece of string and play cat's cradle, and each pair of players usually had several spectators and they cried, "Awho!" when one of them took over a complicated figure. The women bystanders now laid their wrists together and flapped their hands, which was their form of applause. The men put their fingers in their mouths and whistled, sometimes in chorus. Now that the weeping had ended entirely, I stood laughing under the big soiled helmet, my mouth expanded greatly.

"Well," said Itelo, "we will go to see the queen, my aunt, Willatale, and afterward or maybe the same time the other one, Mtalba." By now a pair of umbrellas had come up,

carried by two women. The sun was very rich, and I was
sweating, and these two state umbrellas, about eight feet tall
and shaped like squash flowers, gave very little shade from
such a height. Everybody was extremely good-looking here;
some of them would have satisfied the standards of Michelangelo himself. So we went along by twos with considerable
ceremony, Itelo leading. I was grinning but pretended that it
was a grimace because of the sun. Thus we proceeded toward
the queen's compound.

And now I began to understand what the trouble here was
all about, the cause of all the tears. Coming to a corral, we saw
a fellow with a big clumsy comb of wood standing over a
cow—a humped cow like all the rest, but that's not the point;
the point is that he was grooming and petting her in a manner
I never saw before. With the comb he was doing her forelock,
which was thick over the bulge of the horns. He stroked and
hugged her, and she was not well; you didn't have to be
country bred, as I happen to be, to see at once that something
was wrong with this animal. She didn't even give him a knock
with her head as a cow in her condition will when she feels
affectionate, and the fellow himself was lost in sadness,
gloomily combing her. There was an atmosphere of hopeless-
ness around them both. It took a while for me to put all the
elements together. You have to understand that these people
love their cattle like brothers and sisters, like children; they
have more than fifty terms just to describe the various shapes
of the horns, and Itelo explained to me that there were
hundreds of words for the facial expressions of cattle and a
whole language of cow behavior. To a limited extent I could
appreciate this. I have had great affection for certain pigs
myself. But a pig is basically a career animal; he responds
very sensitively to human ambitions or drives and therefore
doesn't require a separate vocabulary.

The procession had stopped with Itelo and me, and
everyone was looking at the fellow and his cow. But seeing
how much emotional hardship there was in this sight I started
to move on; but the next thing I saw was even sadder. A man
of about fifty, white-haired, was kneeling, weeping and

shuddering, throwing dust on his head, because his cow was passing away. All watched with grief, while the fellow took her by the horns, which were lyre-shaped, begging her not to leave him. But she was already in the state of indifference and the skin over her eyes wrinkled as if he were only just keeping her awake. At this I myself was swayed; I felt compassion, and I said, "Prince, for Christ's sake, can't anything be done?"

Itelo's large chest lifted under the short, loose middy and he pulled a great sigh as if he did not want to spoil my visit with all this grief and mourning. "I do not think," said Itelo.

Just then the least expected of things happened, which was that I caught a glimpse of water in considerable amounts, and at first I was inclined to interpret this as the glitter of sheet metal coming and going before my eyes keenly. But there is something unmistakable about the closeness of water. I smelled it too and I stopped the prince and said to him, "Check me out on this, will you, Prince? But here is this guy killing himself with lamentation and if I'm not mistaken I actually see some water shining over there to the left. Is that a fact?"

He admitted that it was water.

"And the cows are dying of thirst?" I said. "So there must be something wrong with it? It's polluted? But look," I said, "there must be something you can do with it, strain it or something. You could make big pots—vats. You could boil out the impurities. Hey, maybe it doesn't sound practical, but you'd be surprised, if you mobilized the whole place and everybody pitched in—gung-ho! I know how paralyzing a situation like this can become."

But all the while the prince, though shaking his head up and down as though he agreed, in reality disagreed with me. His heavy arms were folded across his middy blouse, while a tattered shade came down from the squash-flower parasol held aloft by the naked women with their four hands as if they might be carried away by the wind. Only there was no wind. The air was as still as if it were knotted to the zenith and stuck there, parched and blue, a masterpiece of midday beauty.

"Oh . . . thank you," he said, "for good intention."

"But I should mind my own business? You may be right. I don't want to bust into your customs. But it's hard to see all this going on and not even make a suggestion. Can I have a look at your water supply at least?"

With a certain reluctance he said, "Okay. I suppose." And Itelo and I, the two of us almost of a size, left his wives and the other villagers behind and went to see the water. I inspected it, and except for some slime or algae it looked all right, and was certainly copious. A thick wall of dark green stone retained it, half cistern and half dam. I figured that there must be a spring beneath; a dry watercourse coming from the mountain showed what the main source of supply was normally. To prevent evaporation a big roof of thatch was pitched over this cistern, measuring at least fifty by seventy feet. After my long hike I would have been grateful to pull off my clothes and leap into this shady, warm, albeit slightly scummy water to swim and float. I would have liked nothing better than to lie floating under this roof of delicate-looking straw.

"Now, Prince, what's the complaint? Why can't you use this stuff?" I said.

Only the prince had come up with me to this sunken tank; the rest of them stood about twenty yards off, obviously unsettled and in a state of agitation, and I said, "What's eating your people? Is there something in this water?" And I stared in and realized for myself that there was considerable activity just below the surface. Through the webbing of the light I saw first polliwogs with huge heads, at all stages of development, with full tails like giant sperm, and with budding feet. And then great powerful frogs, spotted, swimming by with their neckless thick heads and long white legs, the short forepaws expressive of astonishment. And of all the creatures in the vicinity, bar none, it seemed to me they had it best, and I envied them myself. "So don't tell me! It's the frogs?" I said to Itelo. "They keep you from watering the cattle?"

He shook his head with melancholy. Yes, it was the frogs.

"How did they ever get in here? Where do they come from?"

These questions Itelo couldn't answer. The whole thing was a mystery. All he could tell me was that these creatures, never before seen, had appeared in the cistern about a month ago and prevented the cattle from being watered. This was the curse mentioned before.

"You call this a curse?" I said. "But you've been out in the world. Didn't they ever show you a frog at school—at least a picture of one? These are just harmless."

"Oh, yes, sure," said the prince.

"So you know you don't have to let your animals die because a few of these beasts are in the water."

But about this he could do nothing. He put up his large hands and said, "Mus' be no ahnimal in drink wattah."

"Then why don't you get rid of them?"

"Oh, no, no. Nevah touch ahnimal in drink wattah."

"Oh, come on, Prince, pish-posh," I said. "We could filter them out. We could poison them. There are a hundred things we could do."

He took his lip in his teeth and shut his eyes, meanwhile making loud exhalations to show how impossible my suggestions were. He blew the air through his nostrils and shook his head.

"Prince," I said, "let's you and I talk this over." I grew very intense. "Before long if this keeps up the town is going to be one continuous cow funeral. Rain isn't likely. The season is over. You need water. You've got this reserve of it." I lowered my voice. "Look here, I'm kind of an irrational person myself, but survival is survival."

"Oh, sir," said the prince, "the people is frightened. Nobody have evah see such a ahnimal."

"Well," I said, "the last plague of frogs I ever heard about was in Egypt." This reinforced the feeling of antiquity the place had given me from the very first. Anyway it was due to this curse that the people, led by that maiden, had greeted me with tears by the wall of the town. It was nothing if not extraordinary. So now, when everything fitted together, the tranquil water of the cistern became as black to my eyes as the lake of darkness. There really was a vast number of these creatures woggling and crowding, stroking along with the water slipping over their backs and their mottles, as if they owned the medium. And also they crawled out and thrummed on the wet stone with congested, emotional throats, and blinked with their peculiarly marbled eyes, red and green and white, and I shook my head much more at myself than at them, thinking that a damned fool going out into the world is bound and fated to encounter damned fool phenomena. Nevertheless, I told those creatures, just wait, you little sons of bitches, you'll croak in hell before I'm done.

Chapter VI

The gnats were spinning over the sun-warmed cistern, which was green and yellow and dark by turns. I said to Itelo, "You're not allowed to molest these animals, but what if a stranger came along—me for instance—and took them on for you?" I realized that I would never rest until I had dealt with these creatures and lifted the plague.

From his attitude I could tell that under some unwritten law he was not allowed to encourage me in my purpose, but that he and all the rest of the Arnewi would consider me their very greatest benefactor. For Itelo would not answer directly but kept sighing and repeating, "Oh, a very sad time. 'Strodinary bad time." And I then gave him a deep look and said, "Itelo, you leave this to me," and drew in a sharp breath between my teeth, feeling that I had it in me to be the doom of those frogs. You understand, the Arnewi are milk-drinkers exclusively and the cows are their entire livelihood; they never eat meat except ceremonially whenever a cow meets a natural death, and even this they consider a form of cannibalism and they eat in tears. Therefore the death of some of the animals was sheer disaster, and the families of the deceased every day were performing last rites and crying and eating flesh, so it was no wonder they were in this condition. As we turned away I felt as though that cistern of problem water with its algae and its frogs had entered me, occupying a square space in my interior, and sloshing around as I moved.

We went toward my hut (Itelo's and Mtalba's hut), for I wanted to clean up a little before my introduction to the queen, and on the way I read the prince a short lecture. I said, "Do you know why the Jews were defeated by the Romans? Because they wouldn't fight back on Saturday. And that's how it is with your water situation. Should you preserve yourself, or the cows, or preserve the custom? I would say, yourself. Live," I said, "to make another custom. Why should you be ruined by frogs?" The prince listened and said only, "Hm, very interestin'. Is that a fact? 'Strodinary."

We came to the house where Romilayu and I were to stay; it was within a courtyard and, like all the rest of the houses, round, made of clay, and with a conical roof. All inside seemed very brittle and light and empty. Smoke-browned poles were laid across the ceiling at intervals of about three feet, and beyond them the long ribs of the palm leaves resembled whalebone. Here I sat down, and Itelo, who had entered with me and left his followers outside in the sunlight, sat opposite me while Romilayu began to unpack. The heat of the day was now at the peak and the air was perfectly quiet; only in the canes above us, that light amber cone of thatch from which a dry vegetable odor descended, I heard small creatures, beetles and perhaps birds or mice, which stirred and batted and bristled. At this moment I was too tired even for a drink (we carried a few canteens filled with bourbon) and was thinking only of the crisis, and how to destroy the frogs in the cistern. But the prince wanted to talk; and at first I took this for sociability, but presently it appeared that he was leading up to something and I became watchful.

"I go to school in Malindi," he said. "Wondaful, beautiful town." This town of Malindi I later checked into; it was an old dhow port on the east coast famous in the Arab slave trade. Itelo spoke of his wanderings. He and his friend Dahfu, who was now king of the Wariri, had traveled together, taking off from the south. They shipped on the Red Sea in some old tubs and worked on the railroad built by the Turks to the Al Medinah before the Great War. With this I was slightly familiar, for my mother had been wrapped up in the Armenian cause, and from reading about Lawrence of Arabia I had long ago realized how much American education was spread through the Middle East. The Young Turks, and Enver Pasha himself, if I am not mistaken, studied in American schools—though how they got from "The Village Blacksmith" and "sweet Alice and laughing Allegra" to wars and plots and massacres would make an interesting topic. But this Prince Itelo of the obscure cattle tribe on the Hinchagara plateau had attended a mission school in Syria, and so had his Wariri friend. Both had returned to their remote home. "Well," I said, "I guess it was great for you to go and find out what things are like."

The prince was smiling, but his posture had become very tense at the same time; his knees had spread wide apart and he pressed the ground with the thumb and knuckle of one hand. Yet he continued to smile and I realized that we were on the verge of something. We were seated face to face on a pair of low stools within the thatched hut, which gave the effect of a big sewing basket; and everything that had happened to me—the long trek, hearing zebras at night, the sun moving up and down daily like a musical note, the color of Africa, and the cattle and the mourners, and the yellow cistern water and the frogs, had worked so on my mind and feelings that everything was balanced very delicately inside. Not to say precariously.

"Prince," I said, "what's coming off here?"

"When stranger guest comes we allways make acquaintance by wrestle. Invariable."

"That seems like quite a rule," I said, very hesitant. "Well, I wonder, can't you waive it once, or wait a while, as I am completely tuckered out?"

"Oh, no," he said. "New arrival, got to wrestle. Allways."

"I see," I said, "and I reckon you must be the champion here." This was a question I could answer for myself. Naturally, he was the champion, and this was why he had come to meet me and why he had entered the hut. It explained also the excitement of the kids back in the river bed, who knew there would be a wrestling match. "Well, Prince," I said, "I am almost willing to concede without a contest. After all, you have a tremendous build and, as you see, I am an older fellow."

· This however he disregarded, and he put his hand to the back of my neck and began to pull me to the ground. Surprised, but still respectful, I said, "Don't, Prince. Don't do that. I think I have the weight advantage on you." As a matter of fact, I didn't know how to take this. Romilayu was standing by but revealed no opinion in answer to the look I shot him. My white helmet, with passport, money, and papers taped into it, fell off and the long-unbarbered karakul hair sprang up at the back of my neck as Itelo tugged me down with him. All the while I was trying—trying, trying, to classify this event. This Itelo was terribly strong, and he got astride me, in his roomy white pants and the short middy, and worked me down on the floor of the hut. But I kept my arms rigid as if they were tied to the sides and let him push and pull me at will. Now I lay on my belly, face in the dust and my legs dragging on the ground.

"Come, come," he kept saying, "you mus' fight me, sir."

"Prince," I said, "with respect, I am fighting."

You couldn't blame him for not believing me, and he climbed over me in the low-hung white pants with his huge legs and bare feet of the same light color as his hands, and dropping onto his side he worked a leg under me as a fulcrum and caught me around the throat. Breathing very hard and saying (closer to my face than I liked), "Fight. Fight, you Henderson. What is the mattah?"

"Your Highness," I said, "I am a kind of commando. I was in the War, and they had a terrific program at Camp Blanding. They taught us to kill, not just wrestle. Consequently, I don't know how to wrestle. But in man-to-man combat I am pretty ugly to tangle with. I know all kinds of stuff, like how to rip open a person's cheek by hooking a finger in his mouth, and how to snap bones and gouge the eyes. Naturally I don't care for that kind of conflict. It so happens I am trying to stay off violence. Why, the last time I just raised my voice it had very bad consequences. You understand," I panted, as the dust had worked up into my nose, "they taught us all this dangerous know-how and I tell you I shrink from it. So let's not fight. We're too high," I said, "on the scale of civilization—we should be giving all our energy to the question of the frogs instead."

As he still continued to pull me by the throat with his arm, I indicated that I wanted to say something really serious. And I told him, "Your Highness, I am really kind of on a quest."

He released me. I think I was not so impulsive or lively—responsive, you see—as he would have liked. I could read all this in his expression as I cleaned the dust from my face with a piece of indigo cloth belonging to the lady of the house. I had pulled it from the rafter. As far as he was concerned, we were now acquainted. Having seen something of the world, at least from Malindi in Africa all the way up into Asia Minor, he must have known what sad sacks were, and as of this moment, to judge by his looks, I belonged in that category. Of course it was true I had been very downcast, what with the voice that said *I want* and all the rest of it. I had come to look upon the phenomena of life as so many medicines which would either cure my condition or aggravate it. But the condition! Oh, my condition! First and last that condition! It made me go around with my hand on my breast like the old picture of Montcalm passing away on the plains of Abraham. And I'll tell you something, excessive sadness has made me physically heavy, whereas I was once light and fast, for my weight. Until I was forty or so I played tennis, and one season hung up a record of five thousand sets, practically eating and sleeping out of doors. I covered the court like a regular centaur and smashed everything in sight, tearing holes in the clay and wrecking the rackets and bringing down the nets with my volleys. I cite this as proof that I was not always so sad and slow.

"I suppose you are the unbeaten champion here?" I said. And he said, "That is so. I allways win."

"It doesn't surprise me one single bit."

He answered me carelessly with a glint from the corners of his eyes, for as I had submitted to being rolled in the dust on my face, he thought we had already made acquaintance thoroughly, concluding that I was huge but helpless, formidable in looks, but of one piece like a totem pole, or a kind of human Galápagos turtle. Therefore I saw that to regain his respect I must activate myself, and I decided to wrestle him after all. So I put aside my helmet and stripped off my T-shirt, saying, "Let's give it a try for real, Your Highness." Romilayu was no more pleased by this than he had been by Itelo's challenge, but he was not the type to interfere, and merely looked forward with his Abyssinian nose, his hair making a substantial shadow over it. As for the prince, who had been sitting with a loose, indifferent expression, he livened up and began to laugh when I slipped off the T-shirt. He stood up and crouched, and fenced with his hands, and I did likewise. We revolved around the small hut. Next we began to try grips, and the muscles started into play all over his shoulders. At which I decided that I should make quick use of my weight advantage before my temper could be aroused, for if he punished me, and with those muscles it was very possible, I might lose my head and fall into those commando tricks at that. So I did a very simple thing; I gave him a butt with my belly (on which the name of Frances once tattooed had suffered some expansion) while putting my leg behind him and pushing him in the face, and by this elementary surprise I threw the man over. I was astonished myself that it had worked so easily, though I had hit him pretty brutally with both hands and abdomen, and thought he might be going to the ground only to pull some trick on me; thus I took no chances but followed through with all my bulk, while both my

hands covered his face. In this way I shut off sight and breath
and gave his head a good bang on the ground, knocking the
wind out of him, big as he was. When he slammed to the
ground under this assault, I threw myself with my knees on his
arms and so pinned him.

Thankful that it had not been necessary to call on my
murder technique, I let him up at once. I admit the element of
surprise (or luck) was overwhelmingly on my side, and that it
wasn't a fair test. That he was angry I could see from the
change in his color, though the frame of darkness about his
eyes showed no change, and he never said a word, but took off
his middy and green handkerchief and drew deep breaths
which made his belly muscles work inward toward his
backbone. We began once more to revolve and several times
circled the hut. I concentrated on my footwork, for that's
where I am weakest and tend to pull forward like a plow horse
with all the power in the neck, chest, belly, and, yes, face. As
he now seemed to realize, his best chance was to get me on the
mat, where I couldn't use my bulk against him, and as I was
stooping toward him, cautious, and with my elbows out
crabwise, he ducked under with great speed and caught me
beneath the chin, closing in fast behind me and trapping my
head. Which he began to squeeze. It wasn't a true headlock
but more what your old-timers used to call the chancery grip.
He had one arm free and could have used it to bang me across
the face, but this didn't seem to be in the rules. Instead he
carried me toward the ground and tried to make me fall on my
back, but I fell on my front, and very painfully, too, so that I
thought I had split myself upward from the navel. Also I got a
bad blow on the nose and was afraid the root of it had been
parted; I could almost feel the air enter between the separated
bones. But somehow I managed to keep a space clear in my
brain for counsels of moderation, which was no small
achievement in itself. Since that day of zero weather when I
was chopping wood and was struck by the flying log and
thought, "Truth comes with blows," I had evidently discovered how to take advantage of such experiences, and this was

useful to me now, only it took a different form; not "Truth comes with blows" but other words, and these words could not easily have been stranger. They went like this: "I do remember well the hour which burst my spirit's sleep."

Prince Itelo now took a grip high up on my chest with his legs; owing to my girth he could never have closed them about me lower down. As he tightened them, I felt my blood stop and my lips puffed out while my tongue panted and my eyes began to run. But my own hands were at work, and by applying pressure with both thumbs on his thigh near the knee, digging into the muscle (called the adductor, I believe), I was able to bend his leg straight and break his hold. Heaving upward, I snatched at his head; his hair was very short but gave all the grip I needed. Turning him by the hair I caught him at the back and spun him. I had him by the waistband of those loose drawers, my fingers inside, then I lifted him up high. I didn't whirl him at all, as that would have knocked the roof off the place. I threw him on the ground and followed up again, knocking the breath out of him doubly.

I suppose he had been very confident when he saw me, big but old, bulging out and sweating turbulently, heavy and sad. You couldn't blame him for thinking he was the fitter man. And now I almost wish that he had been the winner, for as he was going down, head first, I saw, as you can sometimes glimpse a lone object like a bottle dashing over Niagara Falls, how much bitterness was in his face. He could not believe that a gross old human trunk like myself was taking his championship from him. And when I landed on him for the second time his eyes rolled upward, and this intensity was not caused altogether by the weight I flung upon him.

It certainly did not behoove me to gloat or to act in any way like a proud winner, I can tell you. I felt almost as bad as he did. The whole straw case had almost come down about us when the prince's back struck the floor. Romilayu was standing out of the way against the wall. Though it made my breast ache to win, and my heart winced when I did it, I knelt nevertheless on the prince to make sure he was pinned, for if I

had let him up without pinning him squarely he would have
been deeply offended.

If the contest had taken place within nature he would have
won, I am willing to bet, but he was not matched against mere
bone and muscle. It was a question of spirit, too, for when it
comes to struggling I am in a special class. From earliest times
I have struggled without rest. But I said, "Your Highness,
don't take it so hard." He had covered his face with his hands,
the color of washed stone, and didn't even try to rise from the
ground. When I tried to comfort him I could think only of
things such as Lily would have said. I know damned well that
she would have flushed white and looked straight ahead and
started to speak under her breath, fairly incoherent. She would
have said that any man was only flesh and bone, and that
everyone who took pride in his strength would be humbled by
and by, and so on. I can tell you by the yard all that Lily
would have said, but I myself could only feel for him, dumbly.
It wasn't enough that they should be suffering from drought
and the plague of frogs, but on top of it all I had to appear
from the desert—to manifest myself in the dry bed of the
Arnewi River with my Austrian lighter—and come into town
and throw him twice in succession. The prince now got on his
knees, scooping dust on his head, and then he took my foot in
the suede, rubber-soled desert boot and put it on his head. In
this position he cried much harder than the maiden and the
delegation who had greeted us by the mud-and-thorn wall of
the town. But I have to tell you that it wasn't the defeat alone
that made him cry like this. He was in the midst of a great and
mingled emotional experience. I tried to get my foot off the
top of his head, but he held it there persistently, saying, "Oh,
Mistah Henderson! Henderson, I know you now. Oh, sir, I
know you now."

I couldn't say what I felt, which was: "No, you don't. You
never could. Grief has kept me in condition and that's why
this body is so tough. Lifting stones and pouring concrete and
chopping wood and toiling with the pigs—my strength isn't
happy strength. It wasn't a fair match. Take it from me, you
are a better man."

Somehow I could never make myself lose any contest, no matter how hard I tried. Even playing checkers with my little children, regardless how I maneuvered to let them win and even while their lips trembled with disappointment (oh, the little kids would be sure to hate me), I would jump all over the board and say rudely, "King me!" though all the while I would be saying to myself, "Oh, you fool, you fool, you fool!"

But I didn't really understand how the prince felt until he rose and wrapped his arms about me and laid his dusty head on my shoulder, saying we were friends now. This hit me where I lived, right in the vital centers, both with suffering and with gratification. I said, "Your Highness, I'm proud. I'm glad." He took my hand, and if this was awkward it was stirring also. I was covered with a strong flush which is the radiance an older fellow may allowably feel after such a victory. But I tried to deprecate the whole thing and said to him, "I have experience on my side. You'll never know how much and what kind."

He answered, "I know you now, sir. I do know you."

Chapter VII

The news of my victory was given out as we left the hut by the dust on Itelo's head and by his manner in walking beside me, so that the people applauded as I came into the sunshine, pulling on my T-shirt and setting the helmet back into place. The women flapped their hands at me from the wrist while opening their mouths to almost the same degree. The men made whistling noises on their fingers, spreading their cheeks wide apart. Far from looking hangdog or grudging, the prince himself participated in the ovation, pointing at me and smiling, and I said to Romilayu, "You know something? This is really a sweet bunch of Africans. I love them."

Queen Willatale and her sister Mtalba were waiting for me under a thatched shed in the queen's courtyard. The queen

was seated on a bench made of poles with a red blanket
displayed flagwise behind her, and as we came forward,
Romilayu with the bag of presents on his back, the old lady
opened her lips and smiled at me. To me she was typical of a
certain class of elderly lady. You will understand what I mean,
perhaps, if I say that the flesh of her arm overlapped the
elbow. As far as I am concerned this is the golden seal of
character. With not many teeth, she smiled warmly and held
out her hand, a relatively small one. Good nature emanated
from her; it seemed to puff out on her breath as she sat smiling
with many small tremors of benevolence and congratulation
and welcome. Itelo indicated that I should give the old woman
a hand, and I was astonished when she took it and buried it
between her breasts. This is the normal form of greeting
here—Itelo had put my hand against his breast—but from a
woman I didn't anticipate the same. On top of everything else,
I mean the radiant heat and the monumental weight which my
hand received, there was the calm pulsation of her heart
participating in the introduction. This was as regular as the
rotation of the earth, and it was a surprise to me; my mouth
came open and my eyes grew fixed as if I were touching the
secrets of life; but I couldn't keep my hand there forever and I
came to myself and drew it out. Then I returned the courtesy,
I held her hand on my chest and said, "Me Henderson.
Henderson." The whole court applauded to see how fast I
caught on. So I thought, "Hurray for me!" and drew an
endless breath into my lungs.

The queen expressed stability in every part of her body. Her
head was white and her face broad and solid and she was
wrapped in a lion's skin. Had I known then what I know now
about lions, this would have told me much about her. Even so,
it impressed me. It was the skin of a maned lion, with the wide
part not on the front where you would have expected it, but
on her back. The tail came down over her shoulder while the
paw was drawn up from beneath, and these two ends were tied
in a knot over her belly. I can't even begin to tell you how it
pleased me. The mane with its plunging hair she wore as a

collar, and on this grizzly and probably itching hair she rested her chin. But there was a happy light in her face. And then I observed that she had a defective eye, with a cataract, bluish white. I made the old lady a deep bow, and she began to laugh and her lion-bound belly shook and she wagged her head with its dry white hair at the picture I made bowing in those short pants while I presented my inflamed features, for the blood rushed into my face as I bent.

I expressed regret at the trouble they were having, the drought and the cattle and the frogs, and I said I thought I knew what it was to suffer from a plague and sympathized. I realized that they had to feed on the bread of tears and I hoped I wasn't going to be a bother here. This was translated by Itelo and I think it was well received by the old lady but when I spoke of troubles she smiled right along, as steady as the moonlight at the bottom of a stream. Meanwhile my heart was all stirred and I swore to myself every other minute that I would do something, I would make a contribution here. "I hope I may die," I said to myself, "if I don't drive out, exterminate, and crush those frogs."

I then told Romilayu to start with the presents. And first of all he brought out a plastic raincoat in a plastic envelope. I scowled at him, ashamed to offer this cheap stuff to the old queen, but as a matter of fact I had a perfectly good excuse, which was that I was traveling light. Moreover, I meant to render them a service here that would make the biggest present look silly. But the queen put her hands together at the wrists and flapped them at me more deliberately than the other ladies did, and smiled with marvelous constitutional gaiety. Some of the other women in attendance did the same and those who were holding infants lifted them up as if to impress the phenomenal visitor on their memories. The men drew their mouths wide, whistling on their fingers harmoniously. Years ago the chauffeur's son, Vince, tried to teach me how to do this and I held my fingers in my mouth until the skin wrinkled, but could never bring out those shrieking noises. Therefore I decided that as my reward for ridding them of the vermin, I would ask them to teach me to whistle. I thought it would be thrilling to pipe on my own fingers like that.

I said to Itelo, "Prince, please forgive this shabby present. I hate like hell to bring a raincoat during a drought. It's like a mockery, if you know what I mean?"

However, he said the present gave her happiness, and it evidently did. I had stocked up on trinkets and gimmicks through the back page of the _Times_ Sunday sports section and along Third Avenue, in the hock shops and army-navy stores. To the prince I gave a compass with small binoculars attached, not much good even for bird watchers. For the queen's fat sister, Mtalba, noticing that she smoked, I brought out one of those Austrian lighters with the long white wick. In some places, especially in the bust, Mtalba was so heavy that her skin had turned pink from the expansion. Women are bred like that in parts of Africa where you have to be obese to be considered a real beauty. She was all gussied up, for at such a weight a woman can't go without the support of clothes. Her hands were dyed with henna and her hair stood up stiffly with indigo; she looked like a very happy and pampered person, the baby of the family perhaps, and she shone and sparkled with fat and moisture and her flesh was puckered or flowered like a regular brocade. At the hips under the flowing gown she was as broad as a sofa, and she too took my hand and placed it on her breast, saying, "Mtalba. Mtalba awhonto." I am Mtalba. Mtalba admires you.

"I admire her, too," I told the prince.

I tried to get him to explain to the queen that the coat which she had now put on was waterproof, and, as he seemed unable to find a word for waterproof, I took hold of the sleeve and licked it. Misinterpreting this she caught and licked me as well. I started to let out a shout.

"No yell, sah," said Romilayu, and made it sound urgent. Whereupon I submitted, and she licked me on the ear and on the bristled cheek and then pressed my head toward her middle.

"All right, now, so what's this?" I said, and Romilayu

nodded his bush of hair, saying, "Kay, sah. Okay." In short,
this was a special mark of the old lady's favor. Itelo protruded
his lips to show that I was expected to kiss her on the belly. To
dry my mouth first, I swallowed. The fall I had taken while
wrestling had split my underlip. Then I kissed, giving a shiver
at the heat I encountered. The knot of the lion's skin was
pushed aside by my face, which sank inward. I was aware of
the old lady's navel and her internal organs as they made
sounds of submergence. I felt as though I were riding in a
balloon above the Spice Islands, soaring in hot clouds while
exotic odors arose from below. My own whiskers pierced me
inward, in the lip. When I drew back from this significant
experience (having made contact with a certain power—unmistakable!—which emanated from the woman's middle),
Mtalba also reached for my head, wishing to do the same, as
indicated by her gentle gestures, but I pretended I didn't
understand and said to Itelo, "How come when everybody
else is in mourning, your aunts are both so gay?"

He said, "Two women o' Bittahness."

"Bitter? I don't set up to be a judge of bitter and sweet," I
said, "but if this isn't a pair of happy sisters, my mind is
completely out of order. Why, they're having one hell of a
time."

"Oh, happy! Yes, happy—Bittah. Most Bittah," said Itelo.
And he began to explain. A Bittah was a person of real
substance. You couldn't be any higher or better. A Bittah was
not only a woman but a man at the same time. As the elder
Willatale had seniority in Bittahness, too. Some of these
people in the courtyard were her husbands and others her
wives. She had plenty of both. The wives called her husband,
and the children called her both father and mother. She had
risen above ordinary human limitations and did whatever she
liked because of her proven superiority in all departments.
Mtalba was Bittah too and was on her way up. "Both my
aunts like you. It is very good for you, Henderson," said
Itelo.

"Do they have a good opinion of me, Itelo? Is that a fact?" I
said.

"Very good. Primo. Class A. They admire how you look, and also they know you beat me."

"Boy, am I glad my physical strength is good for something," I said, "instead of being a burden, as it mostly has been throughout life. Only, tell me this: can't women of Bittahness do anything about frogs?"

At this he was solemn, and he said no.

Next it was the turn of the queen to ask questions, and first of all she said she was glad I had come. She could not hold still as she spoke, but her head was moved by many small tremors of benevolence, while her breath puffed from her lips and her open hand made passing motions before her face, and then she stopped and smiled, but without parting her mouth, while the live eye opened brightly toward me and the dry white hair rose and fell owing to the supple movement of her forehead.

I had two interpreters, for Romilayu couldn't be left out of things. He had a sense of dignity and position, and was a model of correctness in an African manner as though bred to court life, speaking in a high-pitched drawl and tucking in his chin while he pointed upward ceremoniously with a single finger.

After the queen had welcomed me she wanted to know who I was and where I came from. And as soon as I heard this question a shadow fell on all the pleasure and lightheartedness of the occasion and I began to suffer. I wish I could explain why it oppressed me to tell about myself, but so it was, and I didn't know what to say. Should I tell her that I was a rich man from America? Maybe she didn't even know where America was, as even civilized women are not keen on geography, preferring a world of their own. Lily might tell you a tremendous amount about life's goals, or what a person should or should not expect or do, but I don't believe she could say whether the Nile flows north or south. Thus I was sure that a woman like Willatale didn't ask such a question merely to be answered with the name of a continent. So I stood and considered what I should say, moody, thinking,

with my belly hanging forth (scratched under the shirt by the
contest with Itelo), my eyes wrinkling almost shut. And my
face, I have to repeat, is no common face, but like an
unfinished church. I was aware that women were tugging
nursing infants from the nipple to hold them up and show
them this memorable object. Nature going to extremes in
Africa, I think they genuinely appreciated my peculiarities.
And so the little kids were crying at the loss of the breast,
reminding me of the baby from Danbury brought home by
my unfortunate daughter Ricey. This again smote me straight
on the spirit, and I had all the old difficulty, thinking of my
condition. A crowd of facts came upon me with accompanying pressure in the chest. Who—who was I? A millionaire
wanderer and wayfarer. A brutal and violent man driven into
the world. A man who fled his own country, settled by his
forefathers. A fellow whose heart said, *I want, I want.* Who
played the violin in despair, seeking the voice of angels. Who
had to burst the spirit's sleep, or else. So what could I tell this
old queen in a lion skin and raincoat (for she had buttoned
herself up in it)? That I had ruined the original piece of goods
issued to me and was traveling to find a remedy? Or that I had
read somewhere that the forgiveness of sin was perpetual but
with typical carelessness had lost the book? I said to myself,
"You must answer the woman, Henderson. She is waiting. But
how?" And the process started over again. Once more it was,
Who are you? And I had to confess that I didn't know where
to begin.

But she saw that I was standing oppressed and, in spite of
my capable appearance and rude looks, was dumb, and she
changed the subject. By now she understood that the coat was
waterproof, so she called over one of the long-necked wives
and had her spit on the material and rub in the spittle, then
feel inside. She was astonished and told everybody, wetting
her finger and laying it against her arm, and again they started
to chant, "Awho," and whistle on the fingers and flap their
hands, and Willatale embraced me again. A second time my
face sank in her belly, that great saffron swelling with the knot

of lion skin sinking also, and I felt the power emanating again. I was not mistaken. And one thing I kept thinking as before, which was *the hour that burst the spirit's sleep.* Meanwhile the athletic-looking men continued piping musically, spreading their mouths like satyrs (not that they otherwise suggested satyrs). And the hand-flapping went on, exactly as when ladies are playing catch (they also bend their knees just as the ball comes in). So that at that first sight of the town I felt that living among such people might change a man for the better. It had done me some good already, I could tell. And I wanted to do something for them—my desire for this was something fierce. "At least," I thought, "if I were a doctor I would operate on Willatale's eye." Oh, yes, I know what cataract operations are, and I had no intention of trying. But I felt singularly ashamed of not being a doctor—or maybe it was shame at coming all this way and then having so little to contribute. All the ingenuity and development and coordination that it takes to bring a fellow so quickly and so deep into the African interior! And then—he is the wrong fellow! Thus I had once again the conviction that I filled a place in existence which should be filled properly by someone else. And I suppose it was ridiculous that it should trouble me not to be a doctor, as after all some doctors are pretty puny characters, and not a few I have met are in a racket, but I was thinking mostly about my childhood idol, Sir Wilfred Grenfell of Labrador. Forty years ago, when I read his books on the back porch, I swore I'd be a medical missionary. It's too bad, but suffering is about the only reliable burster of the spirit's sleep. There is a rumor of long standing that love also does it. Anyway, I was thinking that a more useful person might have arrived at this time among the Arnewi, as, for all the charm of the two women of Bittahness, the crisis was really acute. And I remembered a conversation with Lily. I asked her, "Dear, would you say it was too late for me to study medicine?" (Not that she's the ideal woman to answer a practical question like that.) But she said, "Why, no, darling. It's never too late. You may live to be a hundred"—a corollary to her belief I was unkillable. So I said to her, "I'd have to live that long to make it worth-while. I'd be starting internship at sixty-three, when other men are retiring. But also I am not like other men in this respect because I have nothing to retire from. However, I can't expect to live five or six lives, Lily. Why, more than half the people I knew as a young fellow have passed on and here am I, still planning for the future. And the animals I used to have, too. I mean a man in his lifetime has six or seven dogs and then it's time for him to go also. So how can I think about my textbooks and instruments and enrolling in courses and studying a cadaver? Where would I find the patience to learn anatomy now and chemistry and obstetrics?" But at least Lily didn't laugh at me as Frances had. "If I knew science," I was thinking now, "I could probably think of a simple way to eliminate those frogs."

But anyhow, I felt pretty good, and it was now my turn to receive presents. I got a bolster covered with leopard skin from the sisters, and a basketful of cold baked yams was brought, covered with a piece of straw matting. Mtalba's eyes grew bigger, while her brow rolled up softly and she appeared to suffer about the nose—all signs that she was gone on me. She licked my hand with her small tongue, and I withdrew it and wiped it on my shorts.

But I thought myself very lucky. This was a beautiful, strange, special place, and I was moved by it. I believed the queen could straighten me out if she wanted to; as if, any minute now, she might open her hand and show me the thing, the source, the germ—the cipher. The mystery, you know. I was absolutely convinced she must have it. The earth is a huge ball which nothing holds up in space except its own motion and magnetism, and we conscious things who occupy it believe we have to move too, in our own space. We can't allow ourselves to lie down and not do our share and imitate the greater entity. You see, this is our attitude. But now look at Willatale, the Bittah woman; she had given up such notions, there was no anxious care in her, and she was sustained. Why, nothing bad happened! On the contrary, it all seemed good!

Look how happy she was, grinning with her flat nose and gap teeth, the mother-of-pearl eye and the good eye, and look at her white head! It comforted me just to see her, and I felt that I might learn to be sustained too if I followed her example. And altogether I felt my hour of liberation was drawing near when the sleep of the spirit was liable to burst.

There was this happy agitation in me, which made me fix my teeth together. Certain emotions make my teeth itch. Esthetic appreciation especially does it to me. Yes, when I admire beauty I get these tooth pangs, and my gums are on edge. Like that autumn morning when the tuberous flowers were so red, when I was standing in my velvet bathrobe under the green blackness of the pine tree, when the sun was like the coat of a fox, and the animals were barking, when the crows were harsh on that golden decay of the stubble—my gums were hurting sharply then, and now similarly; and with this all my difficult, worried, threatening arrogance appeared to fade from me, and even the hardness of my belly kind of relented and sank down. I said to Prince Itelo, "Look, Your Highness, could you arrange it for me to have a real talk with the queen?"

"You don't talk?" he said, somewhat surprised. "You do talk, Mistah Henderson."

"Oh, a real talk, I mean. Not sociable fiddle-faddle. In earnest," I said. "About the wisdom of life. Because I know she's got it and I wouldn't leave without a sample of it. I'd be crazy to."

"Oh, yes. Very good, very good," he said. "Oh, all right. As you have won me I do not refuse you a difficult interpretation."

"So you know what I mean?" I said. "This is great. This is wonderful. I'll be grateful till my dying day, Prince. You have no idea how this fills my cup." The younger sister of Bittahness, Mtalba, meanwhile was holding my hand, and I said, "What does she want?"

"Oh, she have a strong affection for you. Don' you see she is the most beautiful woman and you the strongest of strong men. You have won her heart."

"Hell with her heart," I said. Then I began to think how to open a discussion with Willatale. What should I concentrate on? Marriage and happiness? Children and family? Duty? Death? The voice that said *I want?* (How could I explain this to her and to Itelo?) I had to find the simplest, most essential points, and all my thinking happens to be complicated. Here is a sample of such thinking, which happens to be precisely what I had on my mind as I stood in that parched courtyard under the mild shade of the thatch; Lily, my after-all dear wife, and she is the irreplaceable woman, wanted us to end each other's solitude. Now she was no longer alone, but I still was, and how did that figure? Next step: help may come either from other human beings or—from a different quarter. And between human beings there are only two alternatives, either brotherhood or crime. And what makes the good such liars? Why, they lie like fish. Evidently they believe there have to be crimes, and lying is the most useful crime, as at least it is on behalf of good. Well, when push comes to shove, I am for the good, all right, but I am very suspicious of them. So, in short, what's the best way to live?

However, I couldn't start at such an advanced point of my thought with the woman of Bittahness. I would have to work my way forward slowly so as to be sure of my ground. Therefore I said to Itelo, "Now please tell the queen for me, friend, that it does wonderful things for me simply to see her. I don't know whether it's her general appearance or the lion skin or what I feel emanating from her—anyway, it puts my soul at rest."

This was transmitted by Itelo and then the queen leaned forward with a tiny falter of her stout body, smiling, and spoke.

"She say she like to see you, too."

"Oh, really." I was beaming. "This is simply great. This is a big moment for me. The skies are opening up. It's a great privilege to be here." Taking away my hand from Mtalba, I put my arm around the prince and I shook my head, for I was utterly inspired and my heart was starting to brim over. "You know, you are really a stronger fellow than I am," I said. "I am strong all right, but it's the wrong kind of strength; it's coarse; because I'm desperate. Whereas you really are strong —just strong." The prince was affected by this and started to deny it, but I said, "Look, take it from me. If I tried to explain in detail it would be months and months before you even got a glimmer of what gives. My soul is like a pawn shop. I mean it's filled with unredeemed pleasures, old clarinets, and cameras, and moth-eaten fur. But," I said, "let's not get into a debate over it. I am only trying to tell you how you make me feel out here in this tribe. You're great, Itelo. I love you. I love the old lady, too. In fact you're all pretty damned swell, and I'll get rid of those frogs for you if I have to lay down my life to do it." They all saw that I was moved, and the men began to make the hollow whistle on their fingers and spread their mouths so like satyrs and yet sweetly, softly.

"My aunt says what do you request, sir?"

"Oh, does she? Well, that's wonderful. For a starter ask her what she sees in me since I find it so hard to tell her who I am."

Itelo delivered the question and Willatale furrowed up her brow in that flexible way peculiar to the Arnewi as a whole, which let the hemisphere of the eye be seen, purely, glistening with human intention; while the other, the white one, though blind, communicated humor as if she were giving me a wink to last me a lifetime. This closed white shutter also signified her inwardness to me. She spoke slowly without removing her gaze, and her fingers moved on her old thigh, shortened by her stoutness, as if taking an impression from Braille. Itelo transmitted her words. "You have, sir, a large personallity. Strong. (I add agreement to her.) Your mind is full of thought. Possess some fundamentall of Bittahness, also." (Good, good!) "You love send . . ." (It took him several seconds to find the word while I was standing, consumed—in this colorful court, on the gold soil, surroundings tinged by crimson, by black; the twigs of the bushes brown and smelling like cinnamon—consumed by desire to hear the judgment of her wisdom on me.)

"Send-sations." I nodded, and Willatale proceeded. "Says
. . . you are very sore, oh, sir! Mistah Henderson. You heart
is barking." "That's correct," I said, "with all three heads, like
Cerberus the watch dog. But why is it barking?" He, however,
was listening to her and leaning from the balls of his feet, as if
appalled to hear with what kind of fellow he had gone to the
mat in the customary ceremony of acquaintance. "Frenezy,"
he said. "Yes, yes, I'll confirm that," I said. "The woman has a
real gift." And I encouraged her. "Tell me, tell me, Queen
Willatale! I want the truth. I don't want you to spare me."
"Suffah," said Itelo, and Mtalba picked up my hand in
sympathy. "Yes, I certainly do." "She say now, Mistah
Henderson, that you have a great copacity, indicated by your
largeness, and especially your nose." My eyes were big and
sad as I touched my face. Beauty certainly vanishes. "I was
once a good-looking fellow," I said, "but it certainly is a nose
I can smell the whole world with. It comes down to me from
the founder of my family. He was a Dutch sausage-maker and
became the most unscrupulous capitalist in America."

"You excuse queen. She is fond on you and say she do not
wish to make you trouble."

"Because I have enough already. But look, Your Highness,
I didn't come to shilly-shally, so don't say anything to inhibit
her. I want it straight."

The woman of Bittahness began to speak again, slowly,
dwelling on my appearance with her one-eyed dreamy look.

"What does she say—what does she say?"

"She say she wish you tell her, sir, why you come. She know
you have to come across mountain and walk a very long time.
You not young, Mistah Henderson. You weight maybe a
hundred-fifty kilogram; your face have many colors. You are
built like a old locomotif. Very strong, yes, I know. Sir, I
concede. But so much flesh as a big monument . . ."

I listened, smarting at his words, my eyes wincing into their
surrounding wrinkles. And then I sighed and said, "Thank
you for your frankness. I know it's peculiar that I came all this
way with my guide over the desert. Please tell the queen that I

did it for my health." This surprised Itelo, so that he gave a
startled laugh. "I know," I said, "superficially I don't look
sick. And it sounds monstrous that anybody with my appearance should still care about himself, his health or anything
else. But that's how it is. Oh, it's miserable to be human. You
get such queer diseases. Just because you're human and for no
other reason. Before you know it, as the years go by, you're
just like other people you have seen, with all those peculiar
human ailments. Just another vehicle for temper and vanity
and rashness and all the rest. Who wants it? Who needs it?
These things occupy the place where a man's soul should be.
But as long as she has started I want her to read me the whole
indictment. I can fill her in on a lot of counts, though I don't
think I would have to. She seems to know. Lust, rage, and all
the rest of it. A regular bargain basement of deformities . . ."

Itelo hesitated, then transmitted as much of this as he could
to the queen. She nodded with sympathetic earnestness, slowly
opening and closing her hand on the knot of lion skin, and
gazing at the roof of the shed—those pipes of amber bamboo
and the peaceful, symmetrical palm leaves of the thatch. Her
hair floated like a million spider lines, while the fat of her arms
hung down over her elbows. "She say," Itelo translated
carefully, "world is strange to a child. You not a child, sir?"

"Oh, how wonderful she is," I said. "True, all too true. I
have never been at home in life. All my decay has taken place
upon a child." I clasped my hands, and staring at the ground I
started to reflect with this inspiration. And when it comes to
reflection I am like the third man in a relay race. I can hardly
wait to get the baton, but when I do get it I rarely take off in
the necessary direction. So what I thought was something like
this: The world may be strange to a child, but he does not fear
it the way a man fears. He marvels at it. But the grown man
mainly dreads it. And why? Because of death. So he arranges
to have himself abducted like a child. So what happens will
not be his fault. And who is this kidnaper—this gipsy? It is the
strangeness of life—a thing that makes death more remote, as
in childhood. I was pretty proud of myself, I tell you. And I

said to Itelo, "Please say to the old lady for me that most people hate to meet up with a man's trouble. Trouble stinks. So I won't forget your generosity. Now listen—listen," I said to Willatale and Mtalba and Itelo and the members of the court. I started to sing from Handel's *Messiah*: "He was despised and rejected, a man of sorrows and acquainted with grief," and from this I took up another part of the same oratorio, "For who shall abide the day of His coming, and who shall stand when He appeareth?" Thus I sang while Willatale, the woman of Bittahness, queen of the Arnewi, softly shook her head; perhaps admiringly. Mtalba's face gleamed with a similar expression and her forehead began to fold softly upward toward the stiffly standing indigo hair, while the ladies flapped and the men whistled in chorus. "Oh, good show, sir. My friend," Itelo said. Only Romilayu, stocky, muscular, short, and wrinkled, seemed disapproving, but due to his wrinkles he had an ingrained expression of that type, and he may have felt no disapproval at all.

"Grun-tu-molani," the old queen said.

"What's that? What does she say?"

"Say, you want to live. Grun-tu-molani. Man want to live."

"Yes, yes, yes! Molani. Me molani. She sees that? God will reward her, tell her, for saying it to me. I'll reward her myself. I'll annihilate and blast those frogs clear out of that cistern, sky-high, they'll wish they had never come down from the mountains to bother you. Not only I molani for myself, but for everybody. I could not bear how sad things have become in the world and so I set out because of this molani. Grun-tu-molani, old lady—old queen. Grun-tu-molani, everybody!" I raised my helmet to all the family and members of the court. "Grun-tu-molani. God does not shoot dice with our souls, and therefore grun-tu-molani." They muttered back, smiling at me, "Tu-molani." Mtalba, with her lips shut, but the rest of her face expanded to a remarkable extent with happiness and her little henna-dipped hands with puckered wrists at rest on her hips, was looking into my eyes meltingly.

Chapter VIII

Now, I come from a stock that has been damned and derided for more than a hundred years, and when I sat smashing bottles beside the eternal sea it wasn't only my great ancestors, the ambassadors and statesmen, that people were recalling, but the loony ones as well. One got himself mixed up in the Boxer Rebellion, believing he was an Oriental; one was taken for $300,000 by an Italian actress; one was carried away in a balloon while publicizing the suffrage movement. There have been plenty of impulsive or imbecile parties in our family (in French Am-Bay-Seel is a stronger term). A generation ago one of the Henderson cousins got the Corona Italia medal for rescue work during the earthquake at Messina, Sicily. He was tired of rotting from idleness at Rome. He was bored, and would ride his horse inside the Palazzo down from his bedroom and into the salon. After the earthquake he reached Messina by the first train and it is said that he didn't sleep for two entire weeks, but pulled apart hundreds of ruins and rescued countless families. This indicates that a service ideal exists in our family, though sometimes in a setting of mad habit. One of the old Hendersons, although far from being a minister, used to preach to his neighbors, and he would call them by hitting a bell in his yard with a crowbar. They all had to come.

They say that I resemble him. We have the same neck size, twenty-two. I might cite the fact that I held up a mined bridge in Italy and kept it from collapsing until the engineers arrived. But this is in the line of military duty, and a better instance was provided by my behavior in the hospital when I broke my leg. I spent all my time in the children's wards, entertaining and cheering the kids. On my crutches I hopped around the entire place in a hospital gown; I couldn't be bothered to tie the tapes and was open behind, and the old nurses ran after me to cover me, but I wouldn't hold still.

Here we were in the farthest African mountains—damn it,

they couldn't be much farther!—and it was a shame that these
good people should suffer so from frogs. But it was natural for
me to want to relieve them. It so happened that this was
something I could probably do, and it was the least that I
could undertake under the circumstances. Look what this
Queen Willatale had done for me—read my character,
revealed the grun-tu-molani to me. I figured that these
Arnewi, no exception to the rules, had developed unevenly;
they might have the wisdom of life, but when it came to frogs
they were helpless. This I already had explained to my own
satisfaction. The Jews had Jehovah, but wouldn't defend
themselves on the Sabbath. And the Eskimos would perish of
hunger with plenty of caribou around because it was forbidden to eat caribou in fish season, or fish in caribou season.
Everything depends on the values—the values. And where's
reality? I ask you, where is it? I myself, dying of misery and
boredom, had happiness, and objective happiness, too, all
around me, as abundant as the water in that cistern which
cattle were forbidden to drink. And therefore I thought, this
will be one of those mutual-aid deals; where the Arnewi are
irrational I'll help them, and where I'm irrational they'll help
me.

The moon had already come forward with her long face
toward the east and a fleece of clouds behind. It gave me
something to gauge the steepness of the mountains by, and I
believe they approached the ten-thousand-foot mark. The
evening air turned very green and yet the beams of the moon
kept their whiteness intact. The thatch became more than ever
like feathers, dark, heavy, and plumy. I said to Prince Itelo as
we were standing beside one of these iridescent heaps—his
company of wives and relatives were still in attendance with
the squash-flower parasols—"Prince, I'm going to have a shot
at those animals in the cistern. Because I'm sure I can handle
them. You aren't involved at all, and don't even have to give
an opinion one way or another. I'm doing this on my own
responsibility."

"Oh, Mistah Henderson—you 'strodinary man. But sir. Do
not be carry away."

"Ha, ha, Prince—pardon me, but this is where you happen to be wrong. If I don't get carried away I never accomplish anything. But that's okay," I said. "Just forget about it."

So then he left us at our hut and Romilayu and I had supper, which consisted mainly of cold yams and hardtack, to which I added a supplement of vitamin pills. On top of this I had a slug of whisky and then I said, "Come on, Romilayu, we'll go over to that cistern and case it by moonlight." I took along a flashlight to use under the thatch, for, as previously noted, a shed was built over it.

These frogs really had it better than anyone else. Here, due to the moisture, grew the only weeds in the village, and this odd variety of mountain frog, mottled green and white, was hopping and splashing, swimming. They say the air is the final home of the soul, but I think that as far as the senses go you probably can't find a sweeter medium than water. So the life of those frogs must have been beautiful, and they fulfilled their ideal, it seemed to me, as they coasted by our feet with those bright wet skins and their white legs and the emotional throats, their eyes like bubbles. While the rest of us, represented by Romilayu and me, were hot and sweaty, burning. In the thatch-intensified shadow of evening my face felt as if it were on fire, as if it were the opening of a volcano. My jaws were all swelled out and I half believed that if I had turned off the flashlight we could have seen those frogs in the cistern by the glare emanating from me.

"They've got it very good, these creatures," I said to Romilayu, "while it lasts." And I swung the big flashlight to and fro over the water in which they were massed. Under other circumstances I might have taken a tolerant or even affectionate attitude toward them. Basically, I had nothing against them.

"What fo' you laugh, sah?"

"Am I laughing? I didn't realize," I said. "These are really great singers. Back in Connecticut we have mostly cheepers, but these have bass voices. Listen," I said, "I can make out all kinds of things. Ta dam-dam-dum. Agnus Dei—Agnus Dei qui tollis peccata mundi, miserere no-ho-bis! It's Mozart.

Mozart, I swear! They've got a right to sing miserere, poor little bastards, as the hinge of fate is about to swing back on them."

"Poor little bastards" was what I said, but in actual fact I was gloating—yuck-yuck-yuck! My heart was already fattening in anticipation of their death. We hate death, we fear death, but when you get right down to cases, there's nothing like it. I was sorry for the cows, yes, and on the humane side I was fine. I checked out one hundred per cent. But still I hungered to let fall the ultimate violence on these creatures in the cistern.

At the same time I couldn't help being aware of the discrepancies between us. On the one side these fundamentally harmless little semi-fishes who were not to blame for the fear they were held in by the Arnewi. On the other side, a millionaire several times over, six feet four in height, weighing two hundred and thirty pounds, socially prominent, and a combat officer holding the Purple Heart and other decorations. But I wasn't responsible for this, was I? However, it remains to be recorded that I was once more fatally embroiled with animals, according to the prophecy of Daniel which I had never been able to shake off—"They shall drive you from among men, and thy dwelling shall be with the beasts of the field." Not counting the pigs, to whom I related myself legitimately as a breeder, there was an involvement with an animal very recently which weighed heavily on my mind and conscience. On the eve of my assault on the frogs it was this creature, a cat, I was thinking of, and I had better tell why.

I have told about the building remodeled by Lily on our property. She rented it to a mathematics teacher and his wife. The house had no insulation and the tenants complained and I evicted them. It was over them and their cat that Lily and I were having our row when Miss Lenox dropped dead. This cat was a young male with brown and gray smoky fur.

Twice these tenants came over to the house to discuss the heating. Pretending to know nothing about it, I followed the matter with interest, spying on them from upstairs when they arrived. I listened to their voices in the parlor and knew Lily was trying to conciliate them. I was lurking in the second-floor hall in my red bathrobe and the Wellingtons from the barnyard. Subsequently when Lily tried to discuss it with me I said to her, "It's your headache. I never wanted strangers around anyway." I believed that she had brought them on the place to make friends of them and I was opposed. "What bothers them? Is it the pigs?" "No," Lily said, "they haven't said a word against the pigs." "Hah! I have seen their faces when the mash was cooking," I said, "and I can't understand why you have to have a second house fixed up when you won't even take care of the first."

The second and last time they came much more determined to make their complaint, and I watched from the bedroom, brushing my hair with a pair of brushes; I saw the smoky tom cat following them, bounding through the broken stalks of the frozen vegetable garden. Broccoli looks spectacular when the frost hits it. The conference began below, and I couldn't stand it any more and started to stamp my feet on the floor above the parlor. Finally I yelled down the stairs, "Get the hell out of here, and move off my property!"

The tenant said, "We will, but we want our deposit and you ought to foot the moving bill too."

"Good," I said, "you come up and collect the money from me," and I pounded in the stairwell with my Wellingtons and yelled, "Get out!"

And so they did, but the point is they abandoned their cat, and I didn't want a cat going wild on my place. Cats gone wild are bad business, and this was a very powerful animal. I had watched him hunting and playing with a chipmunk. For five years once we had suffered with such a cat who lived in an old woodchuck burrow near the pond. He fought all the barn toms and gave them septic scratches and tore out their eyes. I tried to kill him with poisoned fish and smoke bombs and spent whole days in the woods on my knees near his burrow, waiting to get him. Therefore I said to Lily, "If this animal goes wild like the other one, you'll regret it."

"The people are coming back for him," she said.

"I don't believe it for a minute. They've dumped him. And you don't know what wild cats can be like. Why, I'd rather have a lynx around the place."

We had a hired man named Hannock, and I went to the barn and said to him, "Where's the tom those damned civilians left behind?" It was then late in the fall and he was storing apples, tossing aside windfalls for what pigs there were left. Hannock was very much opposed to the pigs, which had ruined the grass and the garden.

"He's no trouble, Mr. Henderson. He's a good little cat," said Hannock.

"Did they pay you to take care of him?" I said, and he was afraid to say yes and lied to me. In actuality they had given him two bottles of whisky and a case of dried milk (Starlac).

He said, "Naw, they didn't, but I will. He ain't no trouble to me."

"There's going to be no animal abandoned on my property," I said, and I went over the farm calling, "Minnie-Minnie." Finally the cat came into my hands and didn't fight when I lifted him by the scruff and carried him to a room in the attic and locked him in. I sent a registered letter special delivery to the owners and gave them until four o'clock next day to come for him. Otherwise, I threatened, I'd have him put away.

I showed Lily the receipt of the registered letter and told her the cat was in my possession. She tried to prevail on me and even got all dressed at dinner time, with powder on her face. At the table I could feel her tremble and knew she was about to reason with me. "What's the matter? You're not eating," I said, for she normally eats a great deal and I have had restaurant people tell me they never saw a woman who could put away the food like that. Two plank steaks and six bottles of beer are not too much for her when she's in condition. As a matter of fact, I am very proud of Lily's capacity.

"You're not eating, either," was Lily's answer.

"That's because I've got something on my mind. I'm extremely sore," I said. "I'm in a state."

"Baby, don't be like that," she said.

But the emotion, whatever it was, filled me so that my very flesh disagreed with the bones. I felt terrible.

I didn't tell Lily what I was planning to do, but at 3:59 next day, no answer having come from the ex-tenants, I went upstairs to carry out my threat. I carried a shopping bag from Grusan's market and in it was the pistol. There was plenty of light in the small wall-papered attic room. I said to the tom cat, "They've cast you away, kitty." He flattened himself to the wall, arched and bristling. I tried to aim at him from above and finally had to sit on the floor, sighting between the legs of a bridge table which was there. In this small space, I didn't want to fire more than a single shot. From reading about Pancho Villa I had picked up the Mexican method of marksmanship, which is to aim with the forefinger on the barrel and press the trigger with the middle finger, because the forefinger is the most accurate pointer at our disposal. Thus I got the center of his head under my (somewhat twisted) forefinger, and fired, but my will was not truly bent on his death, and I missed. That is the only explanation for missing at a distance of eight feet. I opened the door and he bolted. On the staircase, with her beautiful neck stretched forth and her face white with fear, was Lily. To her a pistol fired in a house meant only one thing—it recalled the death of her father. The shock of the shot was still upon me, the empty shopping bag hung by my side.

"What did you do?" said Lily.

"I tried to do what I said I would. Hell!"

The phone began to ring and I went past her to answer it. It was the tenant's wife, and I said, "What did you wait so long for? Now it's almost too late."

She burst into tears and I myself felt very bad. And I yelled, "Come and take your bloody damned cat away. You city people don't care about animals. Why, you can't just abandon a cat."

The confusing thing is that I always have some real basic motivation, and how I go so wrong, I can never understand.

And so, on the brink of the cistern, the problem of how to

eliminate the frogs touched off this other memory. "But this is different," I thought. "Here it is clear, and besides, it will show what I meant by going after that cat." So I hoped, for my heart was wrung by the memory, and I felt tremendous sorrow. It had been a very close thing—almost a deadly sin.

Facing the practical situation, however, I considered various alternatives, like dredging, or poisons, and none of them seemed advisable. I told Romilayu, "The only method that figures is a bomb. One blast will kill all these little buggers, and when they're floating dead on top all we have to do is come and skim them off, and the Arnewi can water their cattle again. It's simple.".

When my idea did get across to him at last, he said, "Oh, no, no, sah."

"What, 'No, no, sah!' Don't be a jerk, I'm an old soldier and I know what I'm talking about." But it was no use arguing with him; the idea of an explosion frightened him and I said, "Okay, Romilayu, let's go to our shack then and get some sleep. It's been a big day and we've got lots to do tomorrow."

So we went back to the hut, and he began to say his prayers. Romilayu had begun to get my number; I believe he liked me, but it was dawning on him that I was rash and unlucky and acted without sufficient reflection. So he sank on his knees and his haunches pressed on the muscles of his calves and spread them; his big heels were visible beneath. He pressed his hands together, palm to palm, with the fingers spread wide apart under his chin. Often I would say to him, or mutter, "Put in a good word for me," and I half meant it.

When Romilayu was done praying he lay on his side and tucked one hand between his knees, which were drawn up. The other hand he slipped under his cheek. In this position he always slept. I, too, lay down on my blanket in the dark hut, out of range of the moonbeams. I don't often suffer from insomnia but tonight I had a lot of things on my mind, the prophecy of Daniel, the cat, the frogs, the ancient-looking place, the weeping delegation, the wrestling match with Itelo, and the queen having looked into my heart and telling me of the grun-tu-molani. All this was mixed up in my head and excited me greatly, and I kept thinking of the best way to blow up those frogs. Naturally I know a little something about explosives, and I thought I could take out the two batteries and manufacture a pretty good bomb in my flashlight case by filling it with powder from the shells of my .375 H and H Magnum. They carry quite a charge, believe me, and could be used on an elephant. I had bought the .375 especially for this trip to Africa after reading about it in *Life* or *Look*. A fellow from Michigan who had one went to Alaska as soon as his vacation started; he flew to Alaska and hired a guide to track a Kodiak bear; they found the bear and chased him over cliffs and marshes and shot him at four hundred yards. Myself, I used to have a certain interest in hunting, but as I grew older it seemed a strange way to relate to nature. What I mean is, a man goes into the external world, and all he can do with it is to shoot it? It doesn't make sense. So in October when the season starts and the gunsmoke pours out of the bushes and the animals panic and run back and forth, I go out and pinch the hunters for shooting on my posted property. I take them to the Justice of the Peace and he fines them.

Thus having decided in the hut to take the shells and use them in my bomb, I lay grinning at the surprise those frogs had coming, and also somewhat at myself, because I was anticipating the gratitude of Willatale and Mtalba and Itelo and all the people; and I went so far as to imagine that the queen would elevate me to a position equal to her own. But I would say, "No, no. I didn't leave home to achieve power or glory, and any little favor I do you is free."

With all this going on within me I couldn't sleep, and if I were going to prepare the bomb tomorrow I needed my rest badly. I am something of a crank about sleep, for somehow if I get seven and a quarter hours instead of eight I feel afflicted and drag myself around, although there's nothing really wrong with me. It's just another *idea*. That's how it is with my ideas; they seem to get strong while I weaken.

While I was lying awake I had a visit from Mtalba. Coming

in, she shut off the moonlight in the doorway and then sat down near me on the floor, sighing, and took my hand, and talked softly and made me touch her skin, which was certainly wonderfully soft; she had a right to be vain of it. Though I felt it, I acted oblivious and refused to respond, but my bulk lay extended on the blanket and I fixed my gaze on the thatch while I tried to concentrate on putting together the bomb. I unscrewed the top of the flashlight (in thought) and dumped the batteries in the front end; I cut open the shells and let the powder trickle into the flashlight case. But how would I ignite it? The water presented me with a special problem. What would I use for a fuse, and how would I keep it from getting wet? I might take some strands from the wick of my Austrian lighter and soak them for a long time in the fluid. Or else a shoelace; a wax shoelace might be perfect. Such was my line of thought, and all the while Princess Mtalba sat beside me licking me and smooching my fingers. I felt very guilty about that and thought, if she knew what offenses I had committed with those same hands, she might think twice before lifting them to her lips. Now she was on the very finger with which I had aimed the revolver at the cat and a pang shot through it and into my arm and so on through the rest of the nervous system. If she had been able to understand I would have said, "Beautiful lady" (for she was considered a great beauty and I could see why)—"Beautiful lady, I am not the man you think I am. I have incredible things on my conscience and am very fierce in character. Even my pigs were afraid of me."

And yet it isn't always easy to deter women. They do take such types of men upon themselves—drunkards, fools, criminals. Love is what gives them the power to do it, I guess, canceling all those terrible things. I am not dumb and blind, and I have observed a connection between women's love and the great principles of life. If I hadn't picked this up by myself, surely Lily would have pointed it out to me.

Romilayu didn't wake but slept on with one hand slipped under his scarred cheek and the hair swelled out from his head to one side. Glassy rainbows from the moon passed across the doorway, and there were fires outside made with dried dung and thorn branches. The Arnewi were sitting up with their dying cattle. As Mtalba continued to sigh and caress and smooch me and lead my fingertips over her skin and between her lips, I realized she had come for a purpose, this mountainous woman with the indigo hair, and I lifted my arm and let it fall on Romilayu's face. He opened his eyes then but didn't remove the hand from under his cheek or otherwise change his position.

"Romilayu."

"Whut you want, sah?" said he, still lying there.

"Sit up, sit up. We have a visitor." He was unsurprised by this and he rose. Moonlight came in by way of the wickerwork and the door, the moon growing more clean and pure, as if perfuming the air, not only lighting it. Mtalba sat with her arms at rest upon the slopes of her body. "Find out what is the purpose of this visit," I said.

And so he began to talk to her, and addressed her formally, for he was a great stickler, Romilayu, for correctness, African style, and was on his court manners even in the middle of the night. Then Mtalba started to speak. She had a sweet voice, sometimes rapid and sometimes drawling in her throat. From this conversation the fact came out that she wanted me to buy her, and, realizing that I didn't have the bride price, she had brought it to me tonight. "Got to pay, sah, fo' womans."

"That I know, pal."

"You don' pay, womans no respect himself, sah."

Then I started to say that I was a rich man and could afford any kind of price, but I realized that money had nothing to do with it and I said, "Hah, that's very handsome of her. She is built like Mount Everest but has a lot of delicacy. Tell her I thank her and send her home. What time is it, I wonder. Christ, if I don't get my sleep I'll be in no condition to take on those frogs tomorrow. Don't you see, Romilayu, the thing is up to me alone?"

But he said all the stuff she had brought was lying outside, and she wanted me to see it, and so I rose, highly unwilling,

and we went out of the hut. She had come with an escort, and
when they saw me in the moonlight with my sun helmet they
began to cheer as if I were the groom already—they did it
softly as the hour was late. The gifts were lying on a big mat,
and they made a large mound—robes, ornaments, drums,
paints, and dyes: she gave Romilayu an inventory of the
contents and he was transmitting it.

"She's a grand person. A great human being," I said.
"Hasn't she got a husband already?" To this there could be no
definite answer, as she was a woman of Bittahness and it
didn't matter how many times she married. It would do no
good, I knew, to tell her that I already had a wife. It hadn't
stopped Lily, and it certainly would cut no ice with Mtalba.

To display the greatness of the dowry, Mtalba began to put
on some of the robes to the accompaniment of a xylophone
made of bones played by one of her party, a fellow with a big
knobby ring on his knuckle. He smiled as if he were giving the
woman of Bittahness away, and she meantime was showing
off the gowns and wrappers, gathering them around her
shoulders, and winding them about her hips, which required a
separate and broader movement. Sometimes she wore a
half-veil across the bridge of her nose, Arab style, which set
off her loving eyes and occasionally as she jingled with her
hennaed hands she took off, huge but gay, looking back at me
over her shoulder with those signs of suffering about her nose
and lips which come from love only. She would saunter, she
would teeter, depending on the rhythm given by the little
xylophone of hollow bones—the feet of a rhinoceros perhaps
emptied by the ants. All this was performed by a bluish
moonlight, while great white blotches of fire burned at
irregular points around the horizon.

"I want you to tell her, Romilayu," I said, "that she's a
damned attractive woman and that she certainly has an
impressive trousseau."

I'm sure Romilayu translated this into some conventional
African compliment.

"However," I added, "I have unfinished business with those

frogs. They and I have a rendezvous tomorrow, and I can't give my full consideration to any important matter until I have settled with them once and for all."

I thought this would send her away but she went on modeling her clothes and dancing, heavy but beautiful—those colossal thighs and hips—and furling her brow at me and sending glances from her eyes. Thus I realized as the night and the dancing wore on that this was enchantment. This was poetry, which I should allow to reach me, to penetrate the practical task of demolishing the frogs in the cistern. And what I had felt when I first laid eyes on the thatched roofs while descending the bed of the river, that they were so ancient, amounted to this same thing—poetry, enchantment. Somehow I am a sucker for beauty and can trust only it, but I keep passing through and out of it again. It never has enough duration. I know it is near because my gums begin to ache; I grow confused, my breast melts, and then bang, the thing is gone. Once more I am on the wrong side of it. However, this tribe of people, the Arnewi, seemed to have it in steady supply. And my idea was that when I had performed my great deed against the frogs, then the Arnewi would take me to their hearts. Already I had won Itelo, and the queen had a lot of affection for me, and Mtalba wanted to marry me, and so what was left was only to prove (and the opportunity was made to order; it couldn't have suited my capacities better) that I was deserving.

And so, Mtalba having touched my hands happily one final time with her tongue, giving me herself and all her goods— after all, it was a fine occasion—I said, "Thank you, and good night, good night all."

They said, "Awho."

"Awho, awho. Grun-tu-molani."

They answered, "Tu-molani."

My heart was expanded with happy emotion and now instead of wanting to sleep I was afraid when they left that if I shut my eyes tonight the feeling of enchantment would disappear. Therefore, when Romilayu after another short prayer—once more on his knees, and hand pressed to hand like a fellow about to dive into eternity—when Romilayu went to sleep, I lay with eyes open, bathed in high feeling.

Chapter IX

And this was still with me at daybreak when I got up. It was a fiery dawn, which made the interior of our hut as dark as a root-cellar. I took a baked yam from the basket and stripped it like a banana for my breakfast. Sitting on the ground I ate in the cool air and through the door I could see Romilayu, wrinkled, asleep, lying on his side like an effigy.

I thought, "This is going to be one of my greatest days." For not only was the high feeling of the night still with me, which set a kind of record, but I became convinced (and still am convinced) that things, the object-world itself, gave me a kind of go-ahead sign. This did not come about as I had expected it to with Willatale. I thought that she could open her hand and show me the germ, the true cipher, maybe you recall—if not, I'm telling you again. No, what happened was like nothing previously conceived; it took the form merely of the light at daybreak against the white clay of the wall beside me and had an extraordinary effect, for right away I began to feel the sensation in my gums warning of something lovely, and with it a close or painful feeling in the chest. People allergic to feathers or pollen will know what I'm talking about; they become aware of their presence with the most gradual subtlety. In my case the cause that morning was the color of the wall with the sunrise on it, and when it became deeper I had to put down the baked yam I was chewing and support myself with my hands on the ground, for I felt the world sway under me and I would have reached, if I were on a horse, for the horn of the saddle. Some powerful magnificence not human, in other words, seemed under me. And it was this same mild pink color, like the water of watermelon, that did it.

At once I recognized the importance of this, as throughout my life I had known these moments when the dumb begins to speak, when I hear the voices of objects and colors; then the physical universe starts to wrinkle and change and heave and rise and smooth, so it seems that even the dogs have to lean against a tree, shivering. Thus on this white wall with its prickles, like the gooseflesh of matter, was the pink light, and it was similar to flying over the white points of the sea at ten thousand feet as the sun begins to rise. It must have been at least fifty years since I had encountered such a color, and I thought I could remember waking as a tiny boy, alone in a double bed, a black bed, and looking at the ceiling where there was a big oval of plaster in the old style, with pears, fiddles, sheaves of wheat, and angel faces; and outside, a white shutter, twelve feet long and covered with the same pink color.

Did I say a tiny boy? I suppose I was never tiny, but at age five was like a twelve-year-old, and already a very rough child. In the town in the Adirondacks where we used to stay in summer, in the place where my brother Dick was drowned, there was a water mill, and I used to run in with a stick and pound the flour sacks and escape in the dust with the miller cursing. My old man would carry Dick and me into the mill pond and stand with us under the waterfall, one on each arm. With the beard he looked like a Triton; with his clear muscles and the smiling beard. In the green cold water I could see the long fish lounging a few yards away. Black, with spots of fire; with water embers. Like guys loafing on the pavement. Well then, I tell you, it was evening, and I ran into the mill with my stick and clubbed the flour sacks, almost choking with the white powder. The miller started to yell, "You crazy little sonofabitch. I'll break your bones like a chicken." Laughing, I rushed out and into this same pink color, far from the ordinary color of evening. I saw it on the floury side of the mill as the water dropped in the wheel. A clear thin red rose in the sky.

I never expected to see such a color in Africa, I swear. And I was worried lest it pass before I could get everything I should out of it. So I put my face, my nose, to the surface of this wall. I pressed my nose to it as though it were a precious rose, and knelt there on those old knees, lined and grieved-looking; like carrots; and I inhaled, I snuckered through my nose and caressed the wall with my cheek. My soul was in quite a condition, but not hectically excited; it was a state as mild as the color itself. I said to myself, "*I knew* that this place was of old." Meaning, I had sensed from the first that I might find things here which were of old, which I saw when I was still innocent and have longed for ever since, for all my life—and without which *I could not make it.* My spirit was not sleeping then, I can tell you, but was saying, Oh, ho, ho, ho, ho, ho, ho!

Gradually the light changed, as it was bound to do, but at least I had seen it again, like the fringe of the Nirvana, and I let it go without a struggle, hoping it would come again before another fifty years had passed. As otherwise I would be condemned to die a mere old rioter or dumbsock with three million dollars, a slave to low-grade fear and turbulence.

So now when I turned my thoughts to the relief of the Arnewi, I was a different person, or thought I was. I had passed through something, a vital experience. It was exactly the opposite at Banyules-sur-Mer with the octopus in the tank. That had spoken to me of death and I would never have tackled any big project after seeing that cold head pressed against the glass and growing paler and paler. After the good omen of the light I approached the making of a bomb with confidence, although it presented me with no small amount of problems. It would require all the know-how I had. Especially the fuse, and the whole question of timing. I'd have to wait until the last possible moment before throwing my device into the water. Now, I had followed with great interest the story in the papers of the bomb-scare man in New York, the fellow who had quarreled with the electric company and was bent on revenge. Diagrams of his bombs taken from a locker in Grand Central Station had appeared in the *News* or *Mirror,* and I was so absorbed in them I missed my subway stop (the violin case

being between my knees). For I had some pretty accurate
ideas about the design of a bomb and always found them of
great interest. He had used gas pipes, I believe. I thought then
I could have made a better bomb at home but of course I had
the advantage on my side of officers' training in the infantry
school where there had been a certain amount of guerrilla
instruction. However, even a factory-made grenade might
have failed in that cistern and the whole thing presented a
considerable challenge.

And sitting on the ground with my materials between my
legs and my helmet pushed back, I concentrated on the job
before me, breaking open the shells and emptying the powder
into the flashlight case. I have a positive ability to lose myself
in practical tasks. God knows that in the country where I have
had so many fights it has become harder and harder for me to
find help and I have of necessity turned into my own handy
man. I am best at rough carpentry, roofing, and painting, and
not so hot as an electrician or plumber. It may not be correct
to say that I have an ability to lose myself in practical work;
rather what happens is that I become painfully intense, and
this is true even when I lay out a game of solitaire. I took out
the glass end of the flashlight with the little bulb and fitted it
tightly with a circle of wood whittled to shape. Through this I
made a hole for the fuse. Now came the tricky part, for the
functioning of the apparatus depended on the rate at which
the fuse would burn. With this I experimented now and I did
not look at Romilayu often, but when I did I saw him shake
his head in doubt. To this I tried to pay no attention, but I
said at last, "Hell, don't throw gloom. Can't you see that I
know what I'm doing?" However, I could see I didn't have his
confidence, and so I cursed him in my heart and went on with
my lighter, setting fire to lengths of various materials to see
how they would burn. But if I could get no support from
Romilayu there was at least Mtalba, who returned at an early
hour of the morning. She was now wearing a pair of
transparent violet trousers and one of those veils over her
nose, and she took my hand and pressed it on her breast with

great liveliness, as if we had reached an understanding last night. She was full of pep. Serenaded by the rhinoceros-foot xylophone and occasionally a chorus of finger whistles, she began to stride—if that is the word (to wade?)—to do her dance, shaking and jolting her rich flesh, her face ornamented with a smile of coquetry and love. She recited to the court what she was doing and what I was doing (Romilayu translating). "The woman of Bittahness who loves the great wrestler, the man who is like two men who have grown together, came to him in the night." "She came to him," said the others. "She brought him the bride price"—here followed an inventory which included about twenty head of cattle who were all named and their genealogy given—"and the bride price was very noble. For she is Bittah and very beautiful. And the bridegroom's face has many colors." "Colors, colors." "And it has hair upon it, the cheeks hang and he is stronger than many bulls. The bride's heart is ready, its doors are standing open. The groom is making a thing." "A thing." "With fire." "Fire." And sometimes Mtalba kissed her hand in token of my own, and held it out to me, and her face in the lines about the nose exhibited those signs of love-suffering, the pains of love. Meanwhile I was burning a shoelace dipped in lighter fluid, watching closely, my head stooped between my knees, to see how it took the spark. Not bad, I thought. It was promising. A little coal descended. As for Mtalba, time was when I would have felt differently about the love she offered me. It would have seemed much more serious a matter. But, ah! The deep creases have begun to set in beside my ears and once in a while when I raise my head in front of the mirror a white hair appears in my nose, and therefore I told myself it was an imaginary Henderson, a Henderson of her mind she had fallen in love with. Thinking of this, I dropped my lids and nodded my head. But all the while I continued to burn scraps of wick and shoelace and even wisps of paper, and it turned out that a section of shoelace, held for about two minutes in the lighter fluid, served better than any other material. Accordingly I prepared a section of the lace taken from one of my desert boots and threaded it through the hole prepared in the wood block and then I said to Romilayu, "I think she's ready to go."

From stooping over the work I had a dizzy thickness at the back of the head, but it was all right. Owing to the vision of the pink light I was firm of purpose and believed in myself, and I couldn't allow Romilayu to show his doubts and forebodings so openly. I said, "Now, you've got to quit this, Romilayu. I am entitled to your trust, this once. I tell you it is going to work."

"Yes, sah," he said.

"I don't want you to think I'm not capable of doing a good job."

He said again, "Yes, sah."

"There is that poem about the nightingale singing that humankind cannot stand too much reality. But how much unreality can it stand? Do you follow? You understand me?"

"Me unnastand, sah."

"I fired that question right back at the nightingale. So what if reality may be terrible? It's better than what we've got."

"Kay, sah. Okay."

"All right, I let you out of it. It's better than what I've got. But every man feels from his soul that he has got to carry his life to a certain depth. Well, I have to go on because I haven't reached that depth yet. You get it?"

"Yes, sah."

"Hah! Life may think it has got me written off in its records. Henderson: type so and so, with the auk and the platypus and other experiments illustrating such-and-such a principle, and laid aside. But life may find itself surprised, for after all, we are men. I am Man—I myself, singular as it may look. Man. And man has many times tricked life when life thought it had him taped."

"Okay." He shrugged away from me, and offered his thick black hands in resignation.

Speaking so much had worn me out, and I stood clutching the bomb in its aluminum case, ready to carry out the promise

I had made to Itelo and his two aunts. The villagers knew this was a big event and were turning out in numbers, chattering or clapping their hands and singing out. Mtalba, who had gone away, came back in a changed costume of red stuff that looked like baize and her indigo-dyed hair freshly buttered, large brass rings in her ears, and a brass collar about her neck. Her people were swirling around in colored rags, and there were cows led on gay halters and tethers; they looked somewhat weak and people came up to give them a kiss and inquire about their health, practically as if they were cousins. Some of the maidens carried pet hens in their arms or perched on their shoulders. The heat was deadening, and the sky steep and barren.

"There is Itelo," I said. I thought that he, too, looked apprehensive. "Neither of these guys has any faith in me," I said to myself, and even though I realized why I didn't especially inspire confidence, my feelings, nevertheless, were stung. "Hi, Prince," I said. He was solemn and he took my hand as they all did here and led it to his chest so that I felt the heat of his body through the white middy, for he was dressed as yesterday in his loose whites with the green silk scarf. "Well, this is the day," I said, "and this is the hour." I showed the aluminum case with its shoelace fuse to his highness and I told Romilayu, "We ought to make arrangements to gather the dead frogs and bury them. We will do the graves-registration detail. Prince, how do your fellow tribesmen feel about these animals in death? Still taboo?"

"Mistah Henderson. Sir. Wattah is . . ." Itelo could not find the words to describe how precious this element was, and he rubbed his fingers with his thumb as if feeling velvet.

"I know. I know just exactly what the situation is. But there's one thing I can tell you, just as I told you yesterday, I love these folks. I have to do something to show my friendship. And I am aware that coming from the great outside it is up to me to take this on myself."

Under the heavy white shell of the pith helmet, the flies were beginning to bite; the cattle brought them along, as cattle will invariably, and so I said, "It is time to start." We set off for the cistern, myself in the lead holding the bomb. I checked to see whether the lighter was in the pocket of my shorts. One shoe dragged, as I had taken out the lace, nevertheless I set a good pace toward the reservoir while I held the bomb above my head like the torch of liberty in New York harbor, saying to myself, "Okay, Henderson. This is it. You'd better deliver on your promise. No horsing around," and so on. You can imagine my feelings!

In the dead of the heat we reached the cistern and I went forward alone into the weeds on the edge. All the rest remained behind, and not even Romilayu came up with me. That was all right, too. In a crisis a man must be prepared to stand alone, and actually standing alone is the kind of thing I'm good at. I was thinking, "By Judas, I should be good, considering how experienced I am in going it by myself." And with the bomb in my left hand and the lighter with the slender white wick in the other—this patriarchal-looking wick—I looked into the water. There in their home medium were the creatures, the polliwogs with fat heads and skinny tails and their budding little scratchers, and the mature animals with eyes like ripe gooseberries, submerged in their slums of ooze. While I myself, Henderson, like a great pine whose roots have crossed and choked one another—but never mind about me now. The figure of their doom, I stood over them and the frogs didn't—of course they couldn't—know what I augured. And meanwhile, all the chemistry of anxious fear, which I know so well and hate so much, was taking place in me—the light wavering before my eyes, the saliva drying, my parts retracting, and the cables of my neck hardening. I heard the chatter of the expectant Arnewi, who held their cattle on ornamented tethers, as a drowning man will hear the bathers on the beach, and I saw Mtalba, who stood between them and me in her red baize like a poppy, the black at the center of the blazing red. Then I blew on the wick of my device, to free it from dust (or for good luck), and spun the wheel of the lighter, and when it responded with a flame, I lit the fuse, formerly my shoelace. It started to burn and first the metal tip dropped off. The spark sank pretty steadily toward the case. There was nothing for me to do but clutch the thing, and fix my eyes upon it; my legs, bare to the heat, were numb. The burning took quite a space of time and even when the point of the spark descended through the hole in the wood, I held on because I couldn't risk quenching it. After this I had to call on intuition plus luck, and as there now was nothing I especially wanted to see in the external world I closed my eyes and waited for the spirit to move me. It was not yet time, and still not time, and I pressed the case and thought I heard the spark as it ate the lace and fussed toward the powder. At the last moment I took a Band-Aid which I had prepared for this moment and fastened it over the hole. Then I lobbed the bomb, giving it an underhand toss. It touched the thatch and turned on itself only once before it fell into the yellow water. The frogs fled from it and the surface closed again; the ripples traveled outward and that was all. But then a new motion began; the water swelled at the middle and I realized that the thing was working. Damned if my soul didn't rise with the water even before it began to spout, following the same motion, and I cried to myself, "Hallelujah! Henderson, you dumb brute, this time you've done it!" Then the water came shooting upward. It might not have been Hiroshima, but it was enough of a gush for me, and it started raining frogs' bodies upward. They leaped for the roof with the blast, and globs of mud and stones and polliwogs struck the thatch. I wouldn't have thought a dozen or so shells from the .375 had such a charge in them, and from the periphery of my intelligence the most irrelevant thoughts, which are fastest and lightest, rushed to the middle as I congratulated myself, the first thought being, "They'd be proud of old Henderson at school." (The infantry school. I didn't get high marks when I was there.) The long legs and white bellies and the thicker shapes of the infant frogs filled the column of water. I myself was spattered with the mud, but I started to yell, "Hey, Itelo—Romilayu! How do you like that? Boom! You wouldn't believe me!"

I had gotten more of a result than I could have known in the first instants, and instead of an answering cry I heard shrieks from the natives, and looking to see what was the matter I found that the dead frogs were pouring out of the cistern together with the water. The explosion had blasted out the retaining wall at the front end. The big stone blocks had fallen and the yellow reservoir was emptying fast. "Oh! Hell!" I grabbed my head, immediately dizzy with the nausea of disaster, seeing the water spill like a regular mill race with the remains of those frogs. "Hurry, hurry!" I started to yell. "Romilayu! Itelo! Oh, Judas priest, what's happening! Give a hand. Help, you guys, help!" I threw myself down against the escaping water and tried to breast it back and lift the stones into place. The frogs charged into me like so many prunes and fell into my pants and into the open shoe, the lace gone. The cattle started to riot, pulling at their tethers and straining toward the water. But it was polluted and nobody would allow them to drink. It was a moment of horror, with the cows of course obeying nature and the natives begging them and weeping, and the whole reservoir going into the ground. The sand got it all. Romilayu waded up beside me and did his best, but these blocks of stone were beyond our strength and because of the cistern's being also a dam we were downstream, or however the hell it was. Anyway, the water was lost—lost! In a matter of minutes I saw (sickening!) the yellow mud of the bottom and the dead frogs settling there. For them death was instantaneous by shock and it was all over. But the natives, the cows leaving under protest, moaning for the water! Soon everyone was gone except for Itelo and Mtalba.

"Oh, God, what's happened?" I said to them. "This is ruination. I have made a disaster." And I pulled up my wet and stained T-shirt and hid my face in it. Thus exposed, I said through the cloth, "Itelo, kill me! All I've got to offer is my life. So take it. Go ahead, I'm waiting."

I listened for his approach but all I could hear, instead of footsteps, were the sounds of heartbreak that escaped from Mtalba. My belly hung forth and I was braced for the blow of the knife.

"Mistah Henderson. Sir! What has happened?"

"Stab me," I said, "don't ask me. Stab, I say. Use my knife if you haven't got your own. It's all the same," I said, "and don't forgive me. I couldn't stand it. I'd rather be dead."

This was nothing but God's own truth, as with the cistern I had blown up everything else, it seemed. And so I held my face in the bagging, sopping shirt with the unbearable complications at heart. I waited for Itelo to cut me open, my naked middle with all its fevers and its suffering prepared for execution. Under me the water of the cistern was turning to hot vapor and the sun was already beginning to corrupt the bodies of the frog dead.

Chapter X

I heard Mtalba crying, "Aii, yelli, yelli."

"What is she saying?" I asked Romilayu.

"She say, goo'by. Fo' evah."

And Itelo in a trembling voice said to me, "You please, Mistah Henderson, covah down you face."

I asked, "What's the matter? You're not going to take my life?"

"No, no, you won me. You want to die, you got to die you'self. You are a friend."

"Some friend," I said.

I could hear that he was speaking against a great pressure in his throat; the lump in it must have been enormous. "I would have laid down my life to help you," I said. "You saw how long I held that bomb. I wish it had gone off in my hands and blown me to smashes. It's the same old story with me; as soon as I come amongst people I screw something up—I goof. They were right to cry when I showed up. They must have smelled trouble and knew that I would cause a disaster."

Under cover of the shirt, I gave in to my emotions, the emotion of gratitude included. I demanded, "Why for once, just once!, couldn't I get my heart's desire? I have to be doomed always to bungle." And I thought my life-pattern stood revealed, and after such a revelation death might as well ensue as not.

But as Itelo would not stab me, I pulled down the cistern-stained shirt and said, "Okay, Prince, if you don't want my blood on your hands."

"No, no," he said.

And I said, "Then thanks, Itelo. I'll just have to try to carry on from here."

Then Romilayu muttered, "Whut we do, sah?"

"We will leave, Romilayu. It's the best contribution I can make now to the welfare of my friends. Good-by, Prince. Good-by, dear lady, and tell the queen good-by. I hoped to learn the wisdom of life from her but I guess I am just too rash. I am not fit for such companionship. But I love that old woman. I love all you folks. God bless you all. I'd stay," I said, "and at least repair your cistern for you . . ."

"Bettah you not, sir," said Itelo.

I took his word for it; after all, he knew the situation best. And moreover I was too heartbroken to differ with him. Romilayu went back to the hut to collect our stuff while I walked out of the deserted town. There was not a soul in any of the lanes, and even the cattle had been pulled indoors so that they would not have to see me again. I waited by the wall of the town and when Romilayu showed up we went back into the desert together. This was how I left in disgrace and humiliation, having demolished both their water and my hopes. For now I'd never learn more about the grun-tu-mo-lani.

Naturally Romilayu wanted to go back to Baventai and I said to him that I knew he had fulfilled his contract. The jeep was his whenever he wanted it. "However," I asked, "how can I go back to the States now? Itelo wouldn't kill me. He's a noble character and friendship means something to him. But I might as well take this .375 and blow my brains out on the spot as go home."

"Whut you mean, sah?" said Romilayu, much puzzled.

"I mean, Romilayu, that I went into the world one last time to accomplish certain purposes, and you saw for yourself what has happened. So if I quit at this time I'll probably turn into a zombie. My face will become as white as paraffin, and I'll lie on my bed until I croak. Which is maybe no more than I deserve. So it's your choice. I can't give any orders now and I leave it up to you. If you are going to Baventai it will be by yourself."

"You go alone, sah?" he said, surprised at me.

"If I have to, yes, pal," I said. "For I can't turn back. It's okay. I have a few rations and four one-thousand-dollar bills in my hat, and I guess I can find food and water on the way. I can eat locusts. If you want my gun you can have that too."

"No," said Romilayu, after thinking briefly about it. "You no go alone, sah."

"You're a pretty regular guy. You're a good man, Romilayu. I may be nothing but an old failure, having muffed just about everything I ever put my hand to; I seem to have the Midas touch in reverse, so my opinion may not be worth having, but that's what I think. So," I said, "what's ahead of us? Where'll we go?"

"I no know," said Romilayu. "Maybe Wariri?" he said.

"Oh, the Wariri. Prince Itelo went to school with their king—what's his name?"

"Dahfu."

"That's it, Dahfu. Well, then, shall we go in that direction?"

Reluctantly Romilayu said, "Okay, sah." He seemed to have his doubts about his own suggestion.

I picked up more than my share of the burden and said, "Let's go. We may not decide to enter their town. We'll see how we feel about that later. But let's go. I haven't got much hope, but all I know is that at home I'd be a dead man."

Thus we started off toward the Wariri while I was thinking about the burial of Oedipus at Colonus—but he at least brought people luck after he was dead. At that time I might almost have been willing to settle for this.

We traveled eight or ten days more, through country very like the Hinchagara plateau. After the fifth or sixth day the character of the ground changed somewhat. There was more wood on the mountains, although mostly the slopes were still sterile. Mesas and hot granites and towers and acropolises held on to the earth; I mean they gripped it and refused to depart with the clouds which seemed to be trying to absorb them. Or maybe in my melancholy everything looked cocksyworsy to me. This marching over difficult terrain didn't bother Romilayu, who was as much meant for such travel as a deckhand is meant to be on the water. Cargo or registry or destination makes little difference in the end. With those skinny feet he covered ground and to him this activity was self-explanatory. He was very skillful at finding water and knew where he could stick a straw into the soil and get a drink, and he would pick up gourds and other stuff I would never even have noticed and chew them for moisture and nourishment. At night we sometimes talked. Romilayu was of the opinion that with their cistern empty the Arnewi would probably undertake a trek for water. And remembering the frogs and many things besides, I sat beside the fire and glowered at the coals, thinking of my shame and ruin, but a man goes on living and, living, things are either better or worse to a fellow. This will never stop, and all survivors know it. And when you don't die of a trouble somehow you begin to convert it—make use of it, I mean.

Giant spiders we saw, and nets set up like radar stations among the cactuses. There were ants in these parts whose bodies were shaped like diabolos and their nests made large gray humps on the landscape. How ostriches could bear to run so hard in this heat I never succeeded in understanding. I got close enough to one to see how round his eyes were and then he beat the earth with his feet and took off with a hot wind in his feathers, a rusty white foam behind.

Sometimes after Romilayu had prayed at night and lain down I would keep him awake telling him the story of my life, to see whether this strange background, the desert, the ostriches and ants, the night birds, and the roaring of lions occasionally, would take off some of the curse, but I came out still more exotic and fantastic always than any ants, ostriches, mountains. And I said, "What would the Wariri say if they knew who was traveling in their direction?"

"I no know, sah. Dem no so good people like Arnewi."

"Oh they're not, eh? But you won't say anything about the frogs and the cistern, now will you, Romilayu?"

"No, no, sah."

"Thanks, friend," I said. "I don't deserve credit for much, but when all is said and done I had only good intentions. Really and truly it kills me to think how the cattle must be suffering back there without water. No bunk. But then suppose I had satisfied my greatest ambition and become a doctor like Doctor Grenfell or Doctor Schweitzer—or a surgeon? Is there a surgeon anywhere who doesn't lose a patient once in a while? Why, some of those guys must tow a whole fleet of souls behind them."

Romilayu lay on the ground with his hand slipped under his cheek. His straight Abyssinian nose expressed great patience.

"The king of the Wariri, Dahfu, was Itelo's school chum. But you say they aren't good people, the Wariri. What's the matter with them?"

"Dem chillen dahkness."

"Well, Romilayu, you really are a very Christian fellow," I said. "You mean they are wiser in their generation and all the rest. But as between these people and myself, who do you think has got more to worry about?"

Without changing his position, a glitter of grim humor playing in his big soft eye, he said, "Oh, maybe dem, sah."

As you see, I had changed my mind about by-passing the Wariri, and it was partly because of what Romilayu had told me about them. For I felt I was less likely to do any damage amongst them if they were such tough or worldly savages.

So for nine or ten days we walked, and toward the end of this time the character of the mountains changed greatly. There were domelike white rocks which here and there

crumpled into huge heaps, and among these white circles of
stone on, I think, the tenth day, we finally encountered a
person. It happened while we were climbing, late in the
afternoon under a reddening sun. Behind us the high mountains we had emerged from showed their crumbled peaks and
prehistoric spines. Ahead shrubs were growing between these
rock domes, which were as white as chinaware. Then this
Wariri herdsman arose before us in a leather apron, holding a
twisted stick, and although he did nothing else he looked
dangerous. Something about his figure struck me as Biblical,
and in particular he made me think of the man whom Joseph
met when he went to look for his brothers, and who directed
him along toward Dothan. My belief is that this man in the
Bible must have been an angel and certainly knew the
brothers were going to throw Joseph into the pit. But he sent
him on nevertheless. Our black man not only wore a leather
apron but seemed leathery all over, and if he had had wings
those would have been of leather, too. His features were
pressed deep into his face, which was small, secret, and, even
in the direct rays of the red sun, very black. We had a talk
with him. I said, "Hello, hello," loudly as if assuming that his
hearing was sunk as deeply as his eyes. Romilayu asked him
for directions and with his stick the man showed us the way to
go. Thus old-time travelers must have been directed. I made
him a salute but he didn't appear to think much of it and his
leather face answered nothing. So we toiled upward among
the rocks along the way he had pointed.

"Far?" I said to Romilayu.

"No, sah. Him say not far."

I now thought we might pass the evening in a town, and
after ten days of toilsome wandering I had begun to look
forward to a bed and cooked food and some busy sights and
even to a thatch over me.

The way grew more and more stony and this made me
suspicious. If we were approaching a town we ought by now to
have found a path. Instead there were these jumbled white
stones that looked as if they had been combed out by an

ignorant hand from the elements that make least sense. There must be stupid portions of heaven, too, and these had rolled straight down from it. I am no geologist but the word calcareous seemed to fit them. They were composed of lime and my guess was that they must have originated in a body of water. Now they were ultra-dry but filled with little caves from which cooler air was exhaled—ideal places for a siesta in the heat of noon, provided no snakes came. But the sun was in decline, trumpeting downward. The cave mouths were open and there was this coarse and clumsy gnarled white stone.

We had just turned the corner of a boulder to continue our climb when Romilayu astonished me. He had set his foot up to take a long stride but to my bewilderment he began to slide forward on his hands, and, instead of mounting, lay down on the stones of the slope. When I saw him prostrate, I said, "What the hell is with you? What are you doing? Is this a place to lie down? Get up." But his extended body, pack and all, hugged the slope while his frizzled hair settled motionless among the stones. He didn't answer, and now no answer was necessary, because when I looked up I saw, in front of us and about twenty yards above, a military group. Three tribesmen knelt with guns aimed at us while eight or ten more standing behind them were crowding their rifle barrels together, so that we might have been blown off the hillside; they had the fire power to do it. A dozen guns massed at you is bad business, and therefore I dropped my .375 and raised my hands. Yet I was pleased just the same, due to my military temperament. Also that leathery small man had sent us into an ambush and for some reason this elementary cunning gave me satisfaction, too. There are some things the human soul doesn't need to be tutored in. Ha, ha! You know I was kind of pleased and I imitated Romilayu. Brought to the dust I put my face down among the pebbles and waited, grinning. Romilayu was stretched will-less, in an African manner. Finally one of the men came down, covered by the rest, and without speech but stoically, as soldiers usually do, he took the .375 and ammunition and knives and other weapons, and ordered us to

get up. When we did so he frisked us again. The squad above
us lowered their guns, which were old weapons, either the
Berber type with long barrels and inlaid butts, or old
European arms which might have been taken away from
General Gordon at Khartoum and distributed all over Africa.
Yes, I thought, old Chinese Gordon, poor guy, with his Bible
studies. But it was better to die like that than in smelly old
England. I have very little affection for the iron age of
technology. I feel sympathy for a man like Gordon because he
was brave and confused.

To be disarmed in ambush was a joke to me for the first few
minutes, but when we were told to pick up our packs and
move ahead I began to change my mind. These men were
smaller, darker, and shorter than the Arnewi but very tough.
They wore gaudy loincloths and marched energetically and
after we had gone on for an hour or more I was less merry at
heart than before. I began to feel atrocious toward those
fellows, and for a small inducement I would have swept them
up in my arms, the whole dozen or so of them, and run them
over the cliff. It took the recollection of the frogs to restrain
me. I suppressed my rash feeling and followed a policy of
waiting and patience. Romilayu looked very poorly and I put
my arm about him. His face because of the dust of surrender
was utterly in wrinkles, and his poodle hair was filled with
gray powder and even his mutilated ear was whitened like a
cruller.

I spoke to him, but he was so worried he scarcely seemed to
hear. I said, "Man, don't be in such a funk, what can they do?
Jail us? Deport us? Hold us for ransom? Crucify us?" But my
confidence did not reach him. I then told him, "Why don't
you ask if they're taking us to the king? He's Itelo's friend. I'm
positive he speaks English." In a discouraged voice Romilayu
tried to inquire of one of these troopers, but he only said,
"Harrrff!" And the muscles of his cheek had that familiar
tightness which belongs to the soldier's trade. I identified it
right away.

After two or three miles of this quick march upward,

scrambling, crawling, and trotting, we came in sight of the town. Unlike the Arnewi village, it had bigger buildings, some of them wooden, and much expanded under the red light of that time of day, which was between sunset and blackness. On one side night had already come in and the evening star had begun to spin and throb. The white stone of the vicinity had a tendency to fall from the domes in round shapes, in bowls or circles, and these bowls were in use in the town for ornamental purposes. Flowers were growing in them in front of the palace, the largest of the red buildings. Before it were several fences of thorn and these rocks, about the size of Pacific man-eating clams, held fierce flowers, of a very red color. As we passed, two sentries screwed themselves into a brace, but we were not marched between them. To my surprise we went by and were taken through the center of town and out among the huts. People left their evening meal to come and have a look, laughing and making high-pitched exclamations. The huts were pretty ordinary, hive-shaped and thatched. There were cattle, and I dimly saw gardens in the last of the light, so I supposed they were better supplied with water here, and on that score they were safe from my help. I didn't take it hard that they laughed at me, but adopted an attitude of humoring them and waved my hand and tipped my helmet. However, I didn't care one bit for this. It annoyed me not to have been given an immediate audience with King Dahfu.

They led us into a yard and ordered us to sit on the ground near the wall of a house somewhat larger than the rest. A white band was painted over the door, indicating an official residence. Here the patrol that had captured us went away, leaving only one fellow to guard us. I could have grabbed his gun and made scrap metal of it in one single twist, but what was the use of that? I let him stand at my back and waited. Five or six hens in this enclosed yard were pecking at an hour when they should have gone to roost, and a few naked kids played a game resembling skip rope and chanted with thick tongues. Unlike the Arnewi children, they didn't come near us. The sky was like terra cotta and then like pink gum, unfamiliar to my nostrils. Then final darkness. The hens and the kids disappeared, and this left us by the feet of the armed fellow, alone.

We waited, and for a violent person waiting is often a bed of troubles. I believed that the man who kept us waiting, the black Wariri magistrate or J.P. or examiner, was just letting us cool our bottoms. Maybe he had taken a look through the rushes of the door while there was still light enough to see my face. This might well have astonished him and so he was reflecting on it, trying to figure out what line to take with me. Or perhaps he was merely curled up in there like an ant to wear out my patience.

And I was certainly affected; I was badly upset. I am probably the worst waiter in the world. I don't know what it is but I am no good at it, it does something to my spirit. Thus I sat, tired and worried, on the ground, and my thoughts were mainly fears. Meanwhile the beautiful night crawled on as a continuum of dark and warmth, drawing the main star with it; and then the moon came along, incomplete and spotted. The unknown examiner was sitting within, and he exulted prob- ably over the indignity of the grand white traveler whose weapons had been taken away and who had to wait without supper.

And now one of those things occurred which life has not been willing to spare me. As I was sitting waiting here on this exotic night I bit into a hard biscuit and I broke one of my bridges. I had worried about that—what would I do in the wilds of Africa if I damaged my dental work? Fear of this has often kept me out of fights and at the time I was wrestling with Itelo and was thrown so heavily on my face I had thought about the effect on my teeth. Back home, unthinkingly eating a caramel in the movies or biting a chicken bone in a restaurant, I don't know how many times I felt a pulling or a grinding and quickly investigated with my tongue, while my heart almost stopped. This time the dreaded thing really happened and I chewed broken teeth together with the hardtack. I felt the jagged shank of the bridge and was furious, disgusted, frightened; damn! I was in despair and there were tears in my eyes.

"Whut so mattah?" said Romilayu.

I took out the lighter and fired it up and I showed him fragments of tooth in my hand, and pulled open my lip, raising the flame so that he could look inside. "I have broken some teeth," I said.

"Oh! Bad! You got lot so pain, sah?"

"No, no pain. Just anguish of spirit," I said. "It couldn't have happened at a worse time." Then I realized that he was horrified to see these molars in the palm of my hand and I blew out the light.

After this I was compelled to recall the history of my dental work.

The first major job was undertaken after the war, in Paris, by Mlle. Montecuccoli. The original bridge was put in by her. You see, there was a girl named Berthe, who was hired to take care of our two daughters, who recommended her. A General Montecuccoli was the last opponent of the great Marshal Turenne. Enemies used to attend each other's funerals in the old days, and Montecuccoli went to Turenne's and beat his breast and sobbed. I appreciated this connection. However, there were many things wrong. Mlle. Montecuccoli had a large bust, and when she forgot herself in the work she pressed down on my face and smothered me, and there were so many drains and dams and blocks of wood in my mouth that I couldn't even holler. Mlle. Montecuccoli with fearfully roused black eyes was meanwhile staring in. She had her office in the Rue du Colisée. There was a stone court, all yellow and gray, with shrunken poubelles, cats tugging garbage out, brooms, pails, and a latrine with slots for your shoes. The elevator was like a sedan chair and went so slowly you could ask the time of day from people on the staircase which wound around it. I had on a tweed suit and pigskin shoes. While waiting in the courtyard before the hut with the official stripe above the door, Romilayu beside me, and the guard standing over us both, I was forced to remember all this. . . . Rising in the

elevator. My heart is beating fast, and here is Mlle. Montecuccoli whose fifty-year-old face is heart-shaped, and who has a
slender long smile of French, Italian, and Romanian (from her
mother) pathos; and the large bust. And I sit down, dreading,
and she starts to stifle me as she extracts the nerve from a
tooth in order to anchor the bridge. And while fitting the same
she puts a stick in my mouth and says, "Grincez! Grincez les
dents! Fâchez-vous." And so I grince and fâche for all I'm
worth and eat the wood. She grinds her own teeth to show me
how.

The mademoiselle thought that on artistic grounds American dentistry was inexcusable and she wanted to give me a
new crown in front like the ones she had given Berthe, the
children's governess. When Berthe had her appendix out there
was nobody but myself to visit her in the hospital. My wife
was too busy at the Collège de France. Therefore I went,
wearing a derby and carrying gloves. Then this Berthe
pretended to be delirious and rolling in the bed with fever. She
took my hand and bit it, and thus I knew that the teeth Mlle.
Montecuccoli had given her were good and strong. Berthe had
broad, shapely nostrils, too, and a pair of kicking legs. I went
through a couple of troubled weeks over this same Berthe.

To stick to the subject, however, the bridge Mlle. Montecuccoli gave me was terrible. It felt like a water faucet in my
mouth and my tongue was cramped over to one side. Even my
throat ached from it, and I went up the little elevator
moaning. Yes, she admitted it was a little swollen, but said I'd
get used to it soon, and appealed to me to show a soldier's
endurance. So I did. But when I got back to New York,
everything had to come out.

All this information is essential. The second bridge, the one
I had just broken with the hardtack, was made in New York
by a certain Dr. Spohr, who was first cousin to Klaus Spohr,
the painter who was doing Lily's portrait. While I was in the
dentist's chair, Lily was sitting for the artist up in the country.
Dentist and violin lessons kept me in the city two days a week
and I would arrive in Dr. Spohr's office, panting, with my

violin case, after two subways and a few stops at bars along the way, my soul in strife and my heart saying that same old thing. Turning into the street I would sometimes wish that I could seize the whole building in my mouth and bite it in two, as Moby Dick had done to the boats. I tumbled down to the basement of the office where Dr. Spohr had a laboratory and a Puerto Rican technician was making casts and grinding plates on his little wheel.

Reaching behind some smocks to the switch, I turned on the light in the toilet and went in, and after flushing the john made faces at myself and looked into my own eyes saying, "Well?" "And when?" "And wo bist du, soldat?" "Toothless! Mon capitaine. Your own soul is killing you." And "It's you who makes the world what it is. Reality is *you*."

The receptionist would say, "Been for your violin lesson, Mr. Henderson?"

"Yah."

Waiting for the dentist as I waited now with the fragments of his work in my hand, I'd get to brooding over the children and my past and Lily and my prospects with her. I knew that at this moment with her lighted face, barely able to keep her chin still from intensity of feeling, she was in Spohr's studio. The picture of her was a cause of trouble between me and my eldest son, Edward. The one with the red MG. He is like his mother and thinks himself better than me. Well, he's wrong. Great things are done by Americans but not by the likes of either of us. They are done by people like that man Slocum who builds the great dams. Day and night, thousands of tons of concrete, machinery that moves the earth, lays mountains flat and fills the Punjab Valley with cement grout. That's the type that gets things done. On this my class, Edward's class, the class Lily was so eager to marry into, gets zero. Edward has always gone with the crowd. The most independent thing he ever did was to dress up a chimpanzee in a cowboy suit and drive it around New York in his open car. After the animal caught cold and died, he played the clarinet in a jazz band and lived on Bleecker Street. His income was $20,000 at least, and he was living next door to the Mills Hotel flophouse where the drunks are piled in tiers.

But a father is a father after all, and I had gone as far as California to try to talk to Edward. I found him living in a bathing cabin beside the Pacific in Malibu, so there we were on the sand trying to have a conversation. The water was ghostly, lazy, slow, stupefying, with a vast dull shine. Coppery. A womb of white. Pallor; smoke; vacancy; dull gold; vastness; dimness; fulgor; ghostly flashing. "Edward, where are we?" I said. "We are at the edge of the earth. Why here?" Then I told him, "This looks like a hell of a place to meet. It's got no foundation except smoke. Boy, I must talk to you about things. It's true I'm rough. It may be true I am nuts, but there is a reason for it all. 'The good that I would that I do not.'"

"Well, I don't get it, Dad."

"You should become a doctor. Why don't you go to medical school? Please go to medical school, Edward."

"Why should I?"

"There are lots of good reasons. I happen to know that you worry about your health. You take Queen Bee tablets. Now I *know* that . . ."

"You came all this way to tell me something—is that what it is?"

"You may believe that your father is not a thinking person, only your mother. Well, don't kid yourself, I have made some clear observations. First of all, few people are sane. That may surprise you, Edward, but it really is so. Next, slavery has never really been abolished. More people are enslaved to different things than you can shake a stick at. But it's no use trying to give you a résumé of my thinking. It's true I'm often confused but at the same time I am a fighter. Oh, I am a fighter. I fight very hard."

"What do you fight for, Dad?" said Edward.

"Why," I said, "what do I fight for? Hell, for the truth. Yes, that's it, the truth. Against falsehood. But most of the fighting is against myself."

I understood very well that Edward wanted me to tell him

what he should live for and this is what was wrong. This was what caused me pain. For every son expects and every father wishes to provide clear principles. And moreover a man wants to protect his children from the bitterness of things if he can.

A baby seal was weeping on the sand and I was very much absorbed by his situation, imagining that the herd had abandoned him, and I sent Edward to get a can of tunafish at the store while I stood guard against the roving dogs, but one of the beachcombers told me that this seal was a beggar, and if I fed him I would encourage him to be a parasite on the beach. Then he whacked him on the behind and without resentment the creature hobbled to the water on his flippers, where the pelican patrols were flying slowly back and forth, and entered the white foam. "Don't you get cold at night, Eddy, on the beach?" I said.

"I don't mind it much."

I felt love for my son and couldn't bear to see him like this. "Go on and be a doctor, Eddy," I said. "If you don't like blood you can be an internist or if you don't like adults you can be a pediatrician, or if you don't like kids perhaps you can specialize in women. You should have read those books by Doctor Grenfell I used to give you for Christmas. I know damned well you never even opened the packages. For Christ's sake, we should commune with people."

I went back alone to Connecticut, shortly after which the boy returned with a girl from Central America somewhere and said he was going to marry her, an Indian with dark blood, a narrow face, and close-set eyes.

"Dad, I'm in love," he tells me.

"What's the matter? Is she in trouble?"

"No. I tell you I love her."

"Edward, don't give me that," I say. "I can't believe it."

"If it's family background that worries you, then how about Lily?" he says.

"Don't let me hear a single word against your stepmother. Lily is a fine woman. Who is this Indian? I'm going to have her investigated," I say.

"Then I don't understand," he says, "why you don't allow

Lily to hang up her portrait with the others. You leave Maria Felucca alone." (If that was her name.) "I love her," he says, with an inflamed face.

I look at this significant son, Edward, with his crew-cut hair, his hipless trunk, his button-down collar and Princeton tie, his white shoes—his practically faceless face. "Gods!" I think. "Can this be the son of my loins? What the hell goes on around here? If I leave him with this girl she will eat him in three bites."

But even then, strangely enough, I felt a shock of love in my heart for this boy. My son! Unrest has made me like this, grief has made me like this. So never mind. Sauve qui peut! Marry a dozen Maria Feluccas, and if it will do any good, let her go and get her picture painted, too.

So Edward went back to New York with his Maria Felucca from Honduras.

I had taken down my own portrait in the National Guard uniform. Neither Lily nor I would hang in the main hall.

Nor was this all I was compelled to remember as Romilayu and I waited in the Wariri village. For I several times said to Lily, "Every morning you leave to get yourself painted, and you're just as dirty as you ever were. I find kids' diapers under the bed and in the cigar humidor. The sink is full of garbage and grease, and the joint looks as if a poltergeist lived here. You are running from me. I know damned well that you go seventy miles an hour in the Buick with the children in the back seat. Don't look impatient when I bring these subjects up. They may belong to what you consider the lower world, but I have to spend quite a bit of time there."

She looked very white at this and averted her face and smiled as if it would be a long time before I could understand how much good it was doing me to have this portrait painted.

"I know," I said. "The ladies around here gave you the business during the Milk Fund drive. They wouldn't let you on the committee. I know all about it."

But most of all what I recalled with those broken teeth in my hand on this evening in the African mountains was how I

had disgraced myself with the painter's wife and dentist's
cousin, Mrs. K. Spohr. Before the First World War (she's in
her sixties) she was supposed to have been a famous beauty
and has never recovered from the collapse of this, but dresses
like a young girl with flounces and flowers. She may have been
a hot lay once, as she claims, though among great beauties
that is rare. But time and nature had blown the whistle on her
and she was badly ravaged. However, her sex power was still
there and hid in her eyes, like a Sicilian bandit, like a
Giuliano. Her hair is red as chili powder and some of this
same red is sprinkled on her face in freckles.

One winter afternoon, Clara Spohr and I met in Grand
Central Station. I had had my sessions with Spohr the dentist
and Haponyi the violin teacher, and I was disgruntled,
hastening to the lower level so that my shoes and pants could
scarcely keep up with me—hastening through the dark brown
down-tilted passage with its lights aswoon and its pavement
trampled by billions of shoes, with amoeba figures of chewing
gum spread flat. And I saw Clara Spohr coming from the
Oyster Bar or being washed forth into this sea, dismasted,
clinging to her soul in the shipwreck of her beauty. But she
seemed to be sinking. As I passed she flagged me down and
took my arm, the one not engaged by my violin, and we went
to the club car and started, or continued, to drink. At this
same winter hour, Lily was posing for her husband, so she
said, "Why don't you get off with me and drive home with
your wife?" What she wanted me to say was, "Baby, why go to
Connecticut? Let's jump off the train and paint the town red."
But the train pulled out and soon we were running along Long
Island Sound, with snow, with sunset, and the atmosphere
corrupting the shape of the late sun, and the black boats
saying, "Foo!" and spilling their smoke on the waves. And
Clara was burning and she talked and talked and worked on
me with her eyes and her turned-up nose. You could see the
old mischief working, the life-craving, which wouldn't quit.
She was telling me how she had visited Samoa and Tonga in
her youth and had experienced passionate love on the

beaches, on the rafts, in the flowers. It was like Churchill's
blood, sweat, and tears, swearing to fight on the beaches, and
so on. I couldn't help feeling sympathetic, partly. But my
attitude is that if people are going to undo themselves before
you, you shouldn't do them up again. You should let them
retie their own parcels. Toward the last, as we got into the
station, she was weeping, this old crook, and I felt terrible. I've
told you how I feel when women cry. I was also incensed. We
got out in the snow, and I supported her and found a taxi.

When we entered her house, I tried to help her take off her
galoshes, but with a cry she lifted me up by the face and began
to kiss me. Whereupon, like a fool, instead of pushing her
away I kissed back. Yes, I returned the kisses. With the
bridgework, new then, in my mouth. It was certainly a
peculiar moment. Her shoes had come off with the galoshes.
We embraced in the overheated lamp-lighted entry which was
filled with souvenirs of Samoa and of the South Seas, and
kissed as if the next moment we were going to be separated by
the stroke of death. I have never understood this foolish thing,
for I was not passive. I tell you, I kissed back.

Oh, ho! Mr. Henderson. What? Sorrow? Lust? Kissing
has-been beauties? Drunk? In tears? Mad as a horsefly on the
window pane?

Furthermore Lily and Klaus Spohr saw it all. The studio
door was open. Within was a coal fire in the grate.

"Why are you kissing each other like that?" said Lily.

Klaus Spohr never said a word. Whatever Clara saw fit to
do was okay by him.

Chapter XI

And now I have told you the history of these teeth, which
were made of a material called acrylic that's supposed to be
unbreakable—fort comme la mort. But my striving wore them
out. I have been told (by Lily, by Frances, or by Berthe? I

can't remember which) that I grind my jaws in my sleep, and undoubtedly this has had a bad effect. Or maybe I have kissed life too hard and weakened the whole structure. Anyway my whole body was trembling when I spat out those molars, and I thought, "Maybe you've lived too long, Henderson." And I took a drink of bourbon from the canteen, which stung the cut in my tongue. Then I rinsed the fragments in whisky and buttoned them into my pocket on the chance that even out here I might run into someone who would know how to glue them into place.

"Why are they keeping us waiting like this, Romilayu?" I said. Then I lowered my voice, asking, "You don't think they've heard about the frogs, do you?"

"Wo, no, I no t'ink so, sah."

From the direction of the palace we then heard a deep roar, and I said, "Would that be a lion?"

Romilayu replied that he believed it was.

"Yes, I thought so too," I said. "But the animal must be inside the town. Do they keep a lion in the palace?"

He said uncertainly, "Dem mus' be."

The smell of animals was certainly very noticeable in the town.

At last the fellow who was guarding us received a sign in the dark which I didn't see, for he told us to get up and we entered the hut. Inside we were told to sit, and we sat on a pair of low stools. Torchlight was held over us by a couple of women both of whom were shaven. The shape of their heads thus revealed was delicate though large. They parted their large lips and smiled at us and there was some relief for me in those smiles. After we were seated, the women choking their laughter so that the torches wagged and the light was fitful and smoky, in came a man from the back of the house and my relief vanished. It dried right out when he looked at me, and I thought, "He has certainly heard something about me, either about those damned frogs or something else." The clutch of conscience gripped me to the bone. Totally against reason.

Was it a wig he wore? Some sort of official headdress, a

hempy-looking business. He took his place on a smooth bench between the torches. On his knees he held a stick or rod of ivory, looking very official; over his wrists were long tufts of leopard skin.

I said to Romilayu, "I don't like the way this man looks at us. He made us wait a long time, and I'm worried. What's your thinking on this?"

"I no know," he said.

I unbuckled the pack and took out a few articles—the usual cigarette lighters and a magnifying glass which I happened to have along. These articles, laid on the ground, were ignored. A huge book was brought forth, a sign of literacy which astonished and worried me. What was it, a guest register or something? Strange guesses leaped up in my mind, completely abandoned to fantasies by now. However, the book turned out to be an atlas, and he opened it toward me with skill in turning large pages, moistening two fingers on his tongue. Romilayu told me, "Him say you show home."

"That's a reasonable request," I said, and got on my knees, and with the lighter and magnifying glass, poring over North America, I found Danbury, Connecticut. Then I showed my passport, the women with those curious tender bald heads meanwhile laughing at my cumbersome kneeling and standing, my fleshiness, and the nervous, fierce, yet appeasing contortions or glowers of my face. This face, which sometimes appears to me to be as big as the entire body of a child, is always undergoing transformations making it as busy, as strange and changeful, as a creature of the tropical sea lying under a reef, now the color of carnations and now the color of a sweet potato, challenging, acting, harkening, pondering, with all the human passions at the point of doubt—I mean the humanity of them lying in doubt. A great variety of expressions was thus hurdling my nose from eye to eye and twisting my brows. I had good cause to hold my temper and try to behave moderately, my record in Africa being not so brilliant thus far.

"Where is the king?" I said. "This gentleman is not the king, is he? I could speak to him. The king knows English. What's all this about? Tell him I want to go straight to his royal highness."

"Wo, no, sah," said Romilayu. "We no tell him. Him police."

"Ha, ha, you're kidding."

But actually the fellow did examine me like a police official, and if you recall my conflict with the state troopers (they came that time to quell me in Kowinsky's tavern near Route 7, and Lily had to bail me out), you may guess how as a man of wealth and an aristocrat, and impatient as I am, I react to police questioning. Especially as an American citizen. In this primitive place. It made my hackles go up. However, I had a great many things lying on my mind and conscience, and I tried to be as politic and cautious as it was in me to be. So I endured this small fellow's interrogation. He was very grim and businesslike. We had come from Baventai how long ago? How long had we stayed with the Arnewi and what were we doing? I held my good ear listening for anything resembling the words cistern, water, or frog, though by this time I was aware that I could trust Romilayu, and that he would stand up for me. That's how it is, you bump into people casually by a tropical lake with crocodiles as part of a film-making expedition and you discover the good in them to be almost unlimited. However, Romilayu must have reported the severe drought back there on the Arnewi River, for this man, the examiner, declared positively that the Wariri were going to have a ceremony very soon and make all the rain they needed. "Wak-ta!" he said, and described a downpour by plunging the fingers of both hands downward. A skeptical expression came over my mouth, which I had the presence of mind to conceal. But I was very much handicapped in this interview, as the events of last week had undermined me. I was infinitely undermined.

"Ask him," I said, "why our guns were taken away and when we'll get them back."

The answer was that the Wariri did not permit outsiders to

carry arms in their territory. "That's a damned good rule," I said. "I don't blame these guys. They're very smart. It would have been better for all concerned if I had never laid eyes on a firearm. Ask him anyhow to be careful of those scope sights. I doubt whether these characters know much about such high-grade equipment."

The examiner showed a row of unusually mutilated teeth. Was he laughing? Then he spoke, Romilayu translating. What was the purpose of my trip, and why was I traveling like this?

Again that question! Again! It was like the question asked by Tennyson about the flower in the crannied wall. That is, to answer it might involve the history of the universe. I knew no more how to reply than when Willatale had put it to me. What was I going to tell this character? That existence had become odious to me? It was just not the kind of reply to offer under these circumstances. Could I say that the world, the world as a whole, the entire world, had set itself against life and was opposed to it—just down on life, that's all—but that I was alive nevertheless and somehow found it impossible to go along with it? That something in me, my grun-tu-molani, balked and made it impossible to agree? No, I couldn't say that either.

Nor: "You see, Mr. Examiner, everything has become so tremendous and involved, why, we're nothing but instruments of this world's processes."

Nor: "I am this kind of guy, rest is painful to me, and I have to have motion."

Nor: "I'm trying to learn something, before it all gets away from me."

As you can see for yourselves, these are all impossible answers. Having passed them in review, I concluded that the best thing would be to try to snow him a little, so I said that I had heard many marvelous reports about the Wariri. As I couldn't think of any details just then, I was just as glad that he didn't ask me to be specific.

"Could we see the king? I know a friend of his and I am dying to meet him," I said.

My request was ignored.

"Well, at least let me send him a message. I am a friend of his friend Itelo."

To this no reply was made either. The torch-bearing women giggled over Romilayu and me.

We were then conducted to a hut and left alone. They set no guard over us, but neither did they give us anything to eat. There was neither meat nor milk nor fruit nor fire. This was a strange sort of hospitality. We had been held since nightfall and I figured the time now would be half-past ten or eleven. Although what did this velvet night have to do with clocks? You understand me? But my stomach was growling, and the armed fellow, having brought us to our hut, went away and left us. The village was asleep. There were only small stirrings of the kind made by creatures in the night. We were left beside this foul hovel of stale, hairy-seeming old grass, and I am very sensitive about where I sleep, and I wanted supper. My stomach was not so much empty, perhaps, as it was anxious. I touched the shank of the broken bridge with my tongue and resolved that I wouldn't eat dry rations. I rebelled at the thought. So I said to Romilayu, "We'll build a little fire." He did not take to this suggestion but, dark as it was, he saw or sensed what a mood was growing on me and tried to caution me against making any disturbance. But I told him, "Rustle up some kindling, I tell you, and make it snappy."

Therefore he went out timidly to gather some sticks and dry manure. He may have thought I would burn down the town in revenge for the slight. By the fistful, rudely, I pulled out wisps from the thatch, after which I opened the package of dehydrated chicken noodle soup, mixing it with a little water and a stiffener of bourbon to help me sleep. I poured this in the aluminum cooking kit and Romilayu made a small blaze near the door. On account of the odors we did not dare to venture inside too far. The hut appeared to be a storehouse for odds and ends, worn-out mats and baskets with holes in them, old horns and bones, knives, nets, ropes, and the like. We drank the soup tepid, as it seemed it would never come to a boil, owing to the poverty of the fire. The noodles went down almost unwillingly. After which Romilayu, on his shinbones, said his usual prayers. And my sympathy went out to him, as this did not seem a good place in which we were about to lay our heads. He pressed his collected fingertips close under the chin, groaning from his chest and bending down his credulous head with the mutilated cheeks. He was very worried, and I said, "Tonight you want to make an especially good job, Romilayu." I spoke largely to myself.

But all at once I said, "Ah!" and the entire right side of me grew stiff as if paralyzed, and I could not even bring my lips together. As if the strange medicine of fear had been poured down my nose crookedly and I began to cough and choke. For by a momentary twisting upward of some of the larger chips from the flame I thought I saw a big smooth black body lying behind me within the hut against the wall.

"Romilayu!"

He stopped praying.

"There's somebody in the hut."

"No," he said, "dem nobody here. Jus' me—you."

"I tell you, somebody's in there. Sleeping. Maybe this house belongs to somebody. They should have told us we were going to share it with another party."

Dread and some of the related emotions will often approach me by way of the nose. As when you are given an injection of novocaine and feel the cold liquid inside the membranes and the tiny bones of that region.

"Wait until I find my lighter," I said. And I ground the little wheel of the Austrian lighter with my thumb harshly. There was a flare, and when I advanced into the hut, holding it above me to spread light over the ground, I saw the body of a man. I was then afraid my nose would burst under the pressure of terror. My face and throat and shoulders were all involved in the swelling and trembling that possessed me, and my legs spindled under me, feeling very feeble.

"Is he sleeping?" I said.

"No. Him dead," said Romilayu.

I knew that very well, better than I wished to.

"They have put us in here with a corpse. What can this be about? What are they trying to pull?"

"Wo! Sah, sah!"

I spread my arms before Romilayu, trying to communicate firmness to him and I said, "Man, hold on to yourself."

But I myself experienced a wrinkling inside the belly which made me very weak and faint. Not that the dead are strangers to me. I've seen my share of them and more. Nevertheless it took several moments for me to recover from this swamping by fear, and I thought (under my brows) what could be the meaning of this? Why was I lately being shown corpses—first the old lady on my kitchen floor and only a couple of months later this fellow lying in the dusty litter? He was pressed against the canes and raffia of which this old house was built. I directed Romilayu to turn him over. He wouldn't; he wasn't able to obey and so I handed him the lighter, which was growing hot, and did the job myself. I saw a tall person no longer young but still powerful. Something in his expression suggested that there had been an odor he didn't wish to smell and had averted his head, but the poor guy had to smell it at last. There may be something like that about it; till the moment comes we won't know. But he was scowling and had a wrinkle on his forehead somewhat like a high-water mark or a tidal line to show that life had reached the last flood and then receded. Cause of death not evident.

"He hasn't been gone long," I said, "because the poor sucker isn't hard yet. Examine him, Romilayu. Can you tell anything about him?"

Romilayu could not as the body was naked, and so revealed little. I tried to consult with myself as to what I should do, but I could not make sense, the reason being that I was becoming offended and angry.

"They've done this on purpose, Romilayu," I said. "This is why they made us wait so long and why those broads with the torches were laughing. All the time they were working on this frame-up. If that little crook with the twisted stick was capable of sending us into an ambush, then I don't put it past them to rig up this, either. Boy, they're the children of darkness, all right, just as you said. Maybe this is their idea of a hot practical joke. At daybreak we were supposed to wake up and see that we had spent the night with a corpse. But listen, you go and tell them, Romilayu, that I refuse to sleep in a morgue. I have waked up next to the dead all right, but that was on the battlefield."

"Who I tell?" said Romilayu.

And I started to storm at him, "Go on," I said. "I've given you an order. Go, wake somebody. Judas! This is what I call brass."

Romilayu cried, "Mistah Henderson, sah, whut I do?"

"Do what I tell you," I yelled, and the loathing of the dead I felt and all the rage of a tired man who had broken his bridgework filled me.

And so, unwillingly, Romilayu went out and probably sat down on a stone somewhere and prayed or wept that he had ever come with me or had been tempted by the jeep, and probably he repented of not having turned back to Baventai alone after the explosion of frogs. Certainly he was too timid to wake anyone with my complaint. And perhaps the thought had come to him, as it now did to me, that we were liable to be accused of a murder. I hurried to the door and leaned out into the thick night, which now smelled malodorous to me, and I said, as loud as I dared, and brokenly, "Come back, Romilayu, where are you? I've changed my mind. Come back, old fellow." For I was thinking that I shouldn't drive him from me, as tomorrow we might have to defend our lives. When he came back we squatted down, the two of us, beside the dead man to deliberate and what I felt was not so much fear now as sadness, a regular drawing pain of sadness. I felt my mouth become very wide with the sorrow of it and the two of us, looking at the body, suffered silently for a while, the dead man in his silence sending a message to me such as, "Here, man, is your being, which you think so terrific." And just as silently I replied, "Oh, be quiet, dead man, for Christ's sake."

Of one thing I presently became convinced, that the presence of this corpse was a challenge which had to be answered, and I said to Romilayu, "They aren't going to put this over on me." I told him what I thought we should do.

"No, sah," he said intensely.

"I have decided."

"No, no, we sleep outside."

"Never," I said. "It will make me look soft. They've unloaded this man on us and the thing for us to do is to give him right back to them."

Romilayu began to moan again, "Wo, wo! Whut we do, sah?"

"We'll do as I said. Now pay attention to me. I tell you I see through the whole thing. They may try to hang this on us. How would you like to stand trial?"

Again I spun the lighter with my thumb, and Romilayu and I saw each other under the small pointed orange flame as I held it up. He suffered from terror of the dead, whereas it was the affront, the challenge, that got me most. It seemed to me absolutely necessary to exert myself, as I was horribly stirred. And my mind was resolute; I had decided to drag him out of the hut.

"Okay, let's pull him out," I said.

And Romilayu insisted, "No, no. Us go out. I mek you bed on the ground."

"You'll do no such thing. I'm going to take him and stick him right in front of the palace. I can hardly believe that Itelo's friend the king could be involved in any such plot against a visitor."

Romilayu began to moan again, "Wo, no, no, no! Them catch you."

"Well, unloading him in front of the palace probably is too chancy," I conceded. "We'll lay him down somewhere else. But I can't bear not to do anything about it."

"Why you mus'?"

"Because I just must. It's practically constitutional with me. I can never take such things lying down. They just aren't going to do this to us," I said. I was too outraged to be reasoned with. Romilayu put his hands, which, with their shadows, looked like lobsters, to his wrinkled face.

"Wo, dem be trouble."

The provocation of this corpse to me thrust me to the spirit. I was maddened by his presence. The lighter had grown hot again and I blew it out and said to Romilayu, "This body goes, and right now."

I myself, this time, went out to reconnoiter.

Up in the heavens it was like a blue forest—so tranquil! Such a tapestry! The moon itself was yellow, an African moon in its peaceful blue forest, not only beautiful but hungering or craving to become even more beautiful. New ideas as to its beauty were coming back continually from the white heads of the mountain. Again I thought I could hear lions, but as though they were muffled in a cellar. However, everyone seemed asleep. I crept by the sleeping doors and about a hundred yards from the house the lane came to an end and I looked down into a ravine. "Good," I thought. "I'll dump him in here. Then let them blame me for his death." In the far end of the ravine burned a herdsman's fire; otherwise the place was empty. No doubt rats and other scavenging creatures came and went; they always did but I couldn't try to bury the fellow. It was not for me to worry about what might happen to him in the darkness of this gully.

The moonlight was a big handicap, but a still greater danger came from the dogs. One sniffed me as I was returning to the hut. When I stood still he went away. Dogs are peculiar, though, about the dead. This is a subject which should be studied. Darwin proved that dogs could reason. He had one who watched a parasol float across the lawn and thought about it. But these African village hounds were reminiscent of hyenas. You might reason with an English dog, especially a family pet, but what would I do if these near-wild dogs came running as I carried the corpse to the ravine? How would I deal with them? It came into my head how Dr. Wilfred Grenfell, when he was adrift on an ice floe with his team of huskies, had to butcher some and wrap himself in the skins to save his life. He raised a sort of mast with the frozen legs and paws. This was irrelevant, however. But I thought, what if the dead man's own dog were to appear?

Moreover, it was possible we were being watched. If it was no accident that we had been billeted with this corpse, perhaps the whole tribe was in on the joke; they might even now be spying, holding their mouths and killing themselves with laughter. While Romilayu wept and groaned and I was boiling with indignation.

I sat down at the door of my hut and waited for the blue-white trailing clouds to dim the piecemeal moon, and for the sleep of the villagers, if they were asleep, to deepen.

At last, not because the time was ripe, but because I couldn't bear waiting, I rose and tied a blanket under my chin, a precaution against stains. I had decided to carry the man on my back in case we had to run for it. Romilayu was not strong enough to shoulder the main burden. First I pulled the body away from the wall. Then I took it by the wrists and with a quick turn, bending, hauled it on my back. I was afraid lest the arms begin to exert a grip on my neck from behind. Tears of anger and repugnance began to hang from my eyes. I fought to stifle these feelings back into my chest. And I thought, what if this man should turn out to be a Lazarus? I believe in Lazarus. I believe in the awakening of the dead. I am sure that for some, at least, there is a resurrection. I was never better aware of my belief than when I stooped there with my heavy belly, my face far forward and tears of fear and sorrowful perplexity coming from my eyes.

But this dead man on my back was no Lazarus. He was cold and the skin in my hands was dead. His chin had settled on my shoulder. Determined as only a man can be who is saving his life, I made huge muscles in my jaw and shut my teeth to hold my entrails back, as they seemed to be rising on me. I suspected that if the dead man had been planted on me and the tribe was awake and watching, when I was halfway to the ravine they might burst out and yell, "Dead stealer! Ghoul!

Give back our dead man!" and they would hit me on the head
and lay me out for my sacrilege. Thus I would end—I,
Henderson, with all my striving and earnestness.

"You damned fool," I said to Romilayu, who stood off
half-concealed. "Pick up this guy's feet, and help me carry. If
we see anybody you can just drop them and beat it. I'll run for
it alone."

He obeyed me, and, as if dressed in a second man and
groaning, my head filled with flashes and thick noises, I went
into the lane. And a voice within me rose and said, "Do you
love death so much? Then here, have some."

"I do not love it," I said. "Who told you that? That's a
mistake."

Near me I then heard the snarl of a dog and I became more
dangerous to him than he could possibly be to me. I vowed
that if he made trouble I would drop the corpse and tear the
animal to pieces with my hands. When he came out bristling
and I saw his scruff by moonlight, I made a threatening noise
in my throat, and the animal was aghast and shrank from me.
Giving a long whine, he beat it. His whining was so unnatural
that it should have waked someone, but no, everyone went on
sleeping. The huts gaped like open haystacks. Still, however
like a heap of hay it may have looked, each was a careful
construction, and inside the families of sleepers lay breathing.
The air was more than ever like a blue forest, with the moon
releasing soft currents of yellow. As I ran, the mountains were
all turned over hugely, and the body was shaken, and
Romilayu, his head averted, twisted aside, still obeyed me and
carried the legs. The ravine was near but the added weight of
the corpse sank my feet in the soft soil and the sand poured
over my boot tops. I was wearing the type of shoe adopted by
the British Infantry in North Africa, and I had improvised
myself a new lace with a strip of canvas and it wasn't holding
up well. I struggled hard on the short slope that rose to the
edge of the ravine, and I said to Romilayu, "Come on. Can't
you take just a little more of the weight?" Instead of raising,
he pushed, and I stumbled and went down under the burden

of the corpse. This was a hard fall and I lay caught in the dusty sand. To my wet eyes the stars appeared elongated, each like a yardstick.

Then Romilayu said hoarsely, "Dem come, dem come."

I got out from under and, when I had freed myself, pushed the body from me into the gully. Something within me begged the dead man for his forgiveness—like, "Oh, you stranger, don't be sore. We have met and parted. I did you no harm. Now go your way and don't hold this against me." Closing my eyes I gave him a heave and he fell on the flat of his back, as it seemed from the thump I heard.

Then on my knees I turned around to see who was coming. Near our hut were several torches and it appeared that someone was looking either for us or for the body. Should we jump into the ravine, too? This would have made fugitives of us, and it was lucky for me that I didn't have the strength to take this leap. I was too bushed, and I suffered pangs in the glands of my mouth. So we remained in the same place until we were discovered by moonlight and a fellow with a gun came running toward us. But his behavior was not hostile, and unless my imagination misled me it was even respectful. He told Romilayu that the examiner wanted to see us again and he did not even look over the edge of the ravine, and no mention of any corpse was made.

We were marched back to the courtyard and without delay were brought before the examiner. Looking about for the two women, I discovered them asleep on some skins at either side of their husband's couch. The messengers he had sent for us entered with their torches.

If they wanted to hang a rap of sacrilege on me, I was guilty all right, having disturbed the rest of their dead. I had some points on my side too, though I had no intention of defending myself. So I waited, one eye almost closed, to hear what this lean fellow in the hemp wig, the examiner, with his leopard-skin cuffs, would say. I was told to sit down and I did so, stooping onto the low stool with my hands on my knees and putting my face forward very attentively.

Now the examiner made no mention of any corpse, but instead asked me a series of curious questions, such as my age and general health and was I a married man and did I have children. To all my answers, translated by poor Romilayu, whose voice showed the strain of terror, the examiner gave deep bows and he frowned, but favorably, and seemed to approve of what he heard. Because he didn't mention the dead man I felt gracious and obliging, if you please, and thought with a certain amount of satisfaction, and maybe even jubilation, that I had passed the ordeal they had set me. It had sickened me, it had wrung me, but in the end my boldness had paid off.

Would I sign my name? For comparison with the passport signature, I supposed. Willingly I dashed the signature down with my liberated and light fingers, saying to myself within, "Ha, ha! Oh, ha, ha, ha, ha, ha, ha! That's okay. You may have my autograph." Where were the ladies? Sleeping with those big contented horizontal mouths and round, shaved, delicate heads. And the torch bearers? Holding up the sizzling lights from which a hairy smoke was departing.

"Well, is everything in order now? I guess it's okay." I was really highly pleased and felt I had accomplished something.

Now the examiner made a curious request. Would I please take off my shirt? At this I balked a little and wanted to know what for. Romilayu couldn't tell me. I was somewhat worried and I said to him in low tones, "Listen, what's all this about?"

"I no know."

"Well, ask the guy."

Romilayu did as I had bid him but only got a repetition of the request.

"Ask him," I said, "if then he'll let us go to sleep peacefully."

As if he understood my terms, the examiner nodded, and I stripped off my T-shirt, which was greatly in need of a wash. The examiner then came up to me and looked me over very closely, which made me feel awkward. I wondered whether I might be asked to wrestle among the Wariri as I had been by Itelo; I thought perhaps I had strayed into a wrestling part of

Africa, where it was the customary mode of introduction. However, this did not seem to be the case.

"Well, Romilayu," I said, "it could be that they want to sell us into slavery. There are reports that they still keep slaves in Saudi Arabia. God! What a slave I'd make. Ha, ha!" I was still in a jesting frame of mind, you see. "Or do they want to put me into a pit and cover me with coals and bake me? The pygmies do that with elephants. It takes about a week's time."

While I was still kidding like this the examiner continued to size me up. I pointed to the name Frances, tattooed at Coney Island so many years ago, and explained that this was the name of my first wife. He did not seem much interested.

I put on my sweaty shirt again and said, "Ask him if we can see the king." This time the examiner was willing to reply. The king, Romilayu translated, wanted to see me tomorrow and to talk to me in my own language.

"That's wonderful," I said. "I have a thing or two to ask him."

Tomorrow, Romilayu repeated, King Dahfu wanted to see me. Yes, yes. In the morning before the day-long ceremonies to end the drought were begun.

"Oh, is that so?" I said. "In that case let's have a little sleep."

So we were allowed at last to rest, not that much of the night remained. All too soon the roosters were screaming and I awoke and grew aware first of foaming red clouds and the huge channel of the approaching sunrise. I then sat up, remembering that the king wished to see us early. Just inside the doorway, against the wall, sitting in very much my own posture, was the dead man. Someone had fetched him back from the ravine.

Chapter XII

I swore. "This is brain-washing." And I resolved that they would never drive me out of my mind. I had seen dead men before this, plenty of them. In the last year of the war I shared the European continent with about fifteen million of them, though it's always the individual case that's the worst. The corpse was sadly covered with the dust into which I had thrown it, and now that they had fetched him back, my relations with him were no secret, and I decided to sit tight and await the outcome of events. There was nothing more for me to do. Romilayu was still asleep, his hand pressed between his knees, the other under his wrinkled cheek. I saw no reason to wake him. And leaving him in the hut with the dead man, I went into the open air. I was aware of a great peculiarity either in myself or in the day, or in both. I must have been getting the fever from which I was to suffer for a while. It was accompanied by a scratchy sensation in my bosom, a little like eagerness or longing. In the nerves between my ribs this was especially noticeable. It was one of those mixed sensations, comparable to what one feels when smelling the fumes of gasoline. The air was warm and swooning about my face; the colors were all high. Those colors were extraordinary. No doubt my impressions were a consequence of stress and of lack of sleep.

As this was a day of festival the town was already beginning to jump, people were running about, and whether or not they knew whom Romilayu and I had in our hut was never revealed to me. A sweet, spicy smell of native beer burst from the straw walls. The drinking here began apparently at sunrise; there was also a certain amount of what seemed to be drunken noise. I took a cautious walk around and no one paid any particular attention to me, which I interpreted as a good sign. There appeared to be quite a few family quarrels, and some of the older people were particularly abusive and waspish. At which I marveled. A small stone struck me in the helmet, but I assumed it was not aimed at me, for kids were throwing pebbles at one another and tussling, rolling in the dust. A woman ran from her hut and swept them away, screaming and cuffing them. She did not seem particularly astonished to find herself face to face with me, but turned around and re-entered her house. I peeked in and saw an old

fellow lying there on a straw mat. She trod on his back with
her bare feet in a kind of massage calculated to straighten out
his spinal column, after which she poured liquid fat on him
and she skillfully rubbed him, ribs and belly. His forehead
wrinkled and his grizzled beard parted. Baring his great old
teeth he smiled at me, rolling his eyes toward the doorway
where I was standing. "What gives here?" I was thinking, and
I went about the small, narrow lanes and looked into the
yards and over fences, cautiously, of course, and mindful of
the sleeping Romilayu and the dead man sitting against the
wall. Several young women were gilding the horns of cattle
and painting and ornamenting one another too, putting on
ostrich feathers, vulture feathers, and ornaments. Some of the
men wore human jaw bones as neckpieces under their chins.
The idols and fetishes were being dressed up and whitewashed, receiving sacrifices. An ancient woman with hair in
small and rigid braids had dumped yellow meal over one of
these figures and was swinging a freshly killed chicken over it.
Meanwhile the noise grew in volume, every minute something
new added, a rattle, a snare drum, a deeper drum, a horn
blast, or a gunshot.

I saw Romilayu come from the door of our hut, and you
didn't have to be a fine observer to see what a state he was in.
I went toward him, and when he caught sight of me above the
gathering crowd, probably spotting that white shell on my
head, the helmet, before any other portion, he put his hand to
his cheek wincingly.

"Yes, yes, yes," I said, "but what can we do? We'll just have
to wait. It may not mean a thing. Anyway, the king—what's
his name, Itelo's friend, we're supposed to see him this
morning. Any minute now he'll send for us and I'll take it up
with him. Don't you worry, Romilayu, I'll soon find out what
gives. Don't you let on to a thing. Bring our stuff out of the
hut and keep an eye on it."

Then with a sort of fast march which was played on the
drums, deep drums carried by women of unusual stature, the
female soldiers or amazons of the king, Dahfu, there came

into the street a company of people carrying large state umbrellas. Under one of these, a large fuchsia-colored business of silk, marched a burly man. One of the other umbrellas had no user and I reckoned, correctly, that it must have been sent for me. "See," I said to Romilayu, "they wouldn't send that luxurious-looking article for a man they were going to frame up. That's a lightning deduction. Just an intuition, but I think we have nothing to worry about, Romilayu."

The drummers marched forward rapidly, the umbrellas twirling and dancing roundly and heavily, keeping time. As these huge fringed and furled silk canopies advanced the Wariri got out of the way. The heavily built man, smiling, had already seen me and extended his burly arms toward me, holding his head and smiling in such a way as to show that he was welcoming me affectionately. He was Horko, who turned out to be the king's uncle. The dress he wore, of scarlet broadcloth, was banded about from his ankles over his chest and up to the armpits. This wrapping was so tight as to make the fat swell upward under his chin and into his shoulders. Two rubies (garnets, maybe?) dragged down the soft flesh of his ears. He had a powerful, low-featured face. As he stepped out of the shade of his state umbrella, the sun flared richly into his eyes and made them seem as much red as black. When he raised his brows the whole of his scalp also moved backward and made a dozen furrows all the way up to the occiput. His hair grew tight and small, peppercorn style, in tiny droplike curls.

Genial, he gave me his hand to shake, in civilized manner, and laughed. He showed a broad, happy-looking, swollen tongue, dyed red as though he had been sucking candy. Adapting my mood to his, I laughed too, corpse or no corpse, and I poked Romilayu in the ribs and said, "See? See? What did I tell you?" Cautious, Romilayu refused to be reassured on such slight evidence. Villagers came about us, laughing with us, although more wildly than Horko, shrugging their shoulders and making pantomimes about me. Many were drunk on pombo, the native beer. The amazons, dressed in sleeveless leather vests, pushed them away. They weren't to get too close to Horko and myself. Corsetlike vests were the only garments worn by these large women, who were rather heavy or bunchy in build, and unusually expanded behind.

"Shake, shake," I said to Horko, and he invited me to take my place under the vacant umbrella. It was a real luxury article, a million-dollar umbrella if I ever saw one.

"The sun's hot," I said, "though it can't be eight o'clock in the morning. I appreciate the courtesy." I wiped my face, making looks of friendship, in other words exploiting the situation as much as possible and trying to put the greatest possible distance between us and the corpse.

"Me Horko," he said. "Dahfu uncle."

"Oh, you speak my language," I said, "how lucky for me. And King Dahfu is your nephew, is he? Hey, what do you know? And are we going to visit him now? The gentleman who questioned us last night said so."

"Me uncle, yes," he said. Then he gave a command to the amazons, who at once made an about-face which would have been noisy had they worn boots, and began to pummel out the same march rhythm on the bass drums. The great umbrellas began again to flash and sway and the light played beautifully on the watered silk as they wheeled. Even the sun seemed to lie down greedily on them. "Go to palace," said Horko.

"Let's," I said. "Yes, I am eager. We passed it yesterday coming into town."

Why shouldn't I admit it, I was worried still. Itelo seemed to think the world and all of his old school friend, Dahfu, and had spoken of him as though he were one in a million, but on the basis of my experience thus far with the Wariri I had little reason to feel comfortable.

I said, above the drums, "Romilayu, where is my man Romilayu?" I was worried, you see, lest they decide to hold him in connection with the body. I wanted him by my side. He was allowed to walk behind me in the procession, carrying all the gear. Tried in strength and patience, he bent under his double burden; it was out of the question for me to carry anything. We marched. Considering the size of the umbrellas and the drums, it was marvelous what speed we made. We flew forward, the drumming amazons before us and behind. And how different the town was today. Our route was lined with spectators, some of them bending over to spy out my face under the combined cover of umbrella and helmet. Thousands of hands, of restless feet, I saw, and faces glaring with heat and curiosity or intensity or holiday feeling. Chickens and pigs rushed across the route of the march. Shrill noises, squeals, and monkey shrieks swirled over the pounding of drums.

"This is certainly a contrast," I said, "to yesterday when everything was so quiet. Why was that, Mr. Horko?"

"Yestahday, sad day. All people fast."

"Executions?" I suddenly said. From a scaffold at some distance to the left of the palace I saw, or thought I saw, bodies hanging upside down. Through a peculiarity of the light they were small, like dolls. The atmosphere sometimes will act as a reducing and not only as a magnifying glass. "I certainly hope those are effigies," I said. But my misgiving heart said otherwise. It was no wonder they hadn't made any inquiry about their corpse. What was one corpse to them? They appeared to deal in them wholesale. With this my feverishness increased, plus the scratchiness in my breast, and within my face itself a curious overripe sensation developed. Fear. I don't hesitate to admit it. I turned my eyes backward toward Romilayu, but he was lagging under the weight of the equipment and we were separated by a rank of drumming amazons.

So I said to Horko, and was compelled to yell because of the drums, "Seem to be a lot of dead people." We had left the narrow lanes and were in a large thoroughfare approaching the palace.

He shook his big head, smiling with his red-stained tongue, and touched one of his ears, from the lobe of which there dragged a red jewel. He did not hear me.

"Dead people!" I said. And then I told myself, "Don't ask for information with such despair." My face was indeed hot and huge and anxious.

Laughing, he could not admit that he had understood me, not even when I made a pantomime of hanging at the end of a rope. I would have paid four thousand dollars in spot cash for Lily to have been brought here for one single instant, to see how she would square such things with her ideas of goodness. And reality. We had had that terrific argument about reality as a consequence of which Ricey had run away and returned to school with the child from Danbury. I have always argued that Lily neither knows nor likes reality. Me? I love the old bitch just the way she is and I like to think I am always prepared for even the very worst she has to show me. I am a true adorer of life, and if I can't reach as high as the face of it, I plant my kiss somewhere lower down. Those who understand will require no further explanation.

It consoled me for my fears to imagine that Lily would be unable to reply. Though at the present moment I can't for one instant believe that anything would stump her. She'd have an answer all right. But meanwhile we had crossed the parade ground and the sentries had opened the red gate. Here were the hollow stone bowls of yesterday with their hot flowers resembling geraniums, and here was the interior of the palace; it was three stories high with open staircases and galleries, quadrangular and barnlike. At ground level the rooms were doorless, like narrow stalls, open and bare. Here there could be no mistake about it—I heard the roar of a wild beast underneath. No creature but a lion could possibly make such a noise. Otherwise, relative to the streets of the town, the palace was quiet. In the yard were two small huts like doll-houses, each occupied by a horned idol, newly whitewashed this morning. Between these two was a trail of fresh calcimine. A rusty flag which had had too much sun was hung from the turret. It was diagonally divided by a meandering white line.

"Which way to the king?" I said.

But Horko was bound by the rules of etiquette to entertain me and visit with me before my audience with Dahfu. His quarters were on the ground floor. With high ceremony the umbrellas were planted and an old bridge table was brought

out by the amazons. It was laid with a cloth of the type that
Syrian peddlers used to deal in, red and yellow with fancy
Arabic embroideries. Then a silver service was brought,
teapot, jelly dishes, covered dishes, and the like. There was hot
water, and a drink made of milk mixed with the fresh blood of
cattle, which I declined, dates and pineapple, pombo, cold
sweet potatoes, and other dishes—mouse paws eaten with a
kind of syrup, which I also took a rain check on. I ate some
sweet potatoes and drank the pombo, a powerful beverage
which immediately acted on my legs and knees. In my
excitement and fever I swallowed several cups of this, since
nothing external gave me support, the bridge table being
highly rickety; I needed something inside, at least. Half
hopefully I thought I was going to be sick. I cannot endure
such excitement as I then felt. I did my best to perform the
social rigmarole with Horko. He wished me to admire his
bridge table, and to oblige him I made him several compliments on it, and said I had one just like it at home. As indeed
I do, in the attic. I sat under it when attempting to shoot the
cat. I told him it wasn't as nice as his. Ah, it was too bad we
couldn't sit as two gentlemen of about the same age, enjoying
the fine warm blur of a peaceful morning in Africa. But I was
a fugitive and multiple wrong-doer and greatly worried
because of the events of the night before. I anticipated that I
could clear myself with the king, and several times I thought it
was time to rise, and I stirred my large weight and made a
start, but the protocol didn't yet allow it. I tried to be patient,
cursing the vain waste of fear. Horko, puffing, bent across the
frail table, his knuckles like tree boles, clasping the handle of
the silver pot. He poured a hot drink that tasted like steamed
hay. Bound by a thousand restraints, I lifted the cup and
sipped with utmost politeness.

At last my reception by Horko was completed and he
indicated that we should rise. The amazons, in record time,
moved away the table and the things, and lined up in
formation ready to escort us to the king. Their behinds were
pitted like colanders. I set my helmet straight and hiked up my

short pants and wiped my hands on my T-shirt, for they were damp and I wanted to give the king a dry warm handshake. It means a lot. We started to march toward one of the staircases. Where was Romilayu? I asked Horko. He smiled and said, "Oh, fine. Oh, oh, fine." We were mounting the staircase, and I saw Romilayu below, waiting, dejected, his hands, discouraged, hanging over his knees, and his bent spine sticking out. Poor guy! I thought. I've got to do something for him. Just as soon as this is cleared up I will. I absolutely will. After the catastrophes I've led him into I owe him a real reward.

The outdoor staircase, wide, leisurely, and rambling, took a turn and brought us to the other side of the building. A tree was there and it was shaking and creaking because several men were engaged in a curious task, raising large rocks into the branches with ropes and crude wooden pulleys. They yelled at the ground crew who were pushing these boulders upward and their faces shone with the light of hard work. Horko said to me, and I didn't quite understand how he meant it, that these stones were connected with clouds for the rain they expected to make in the ceremony soon to come. They all seemed very confident that rain would be made today. The examiner last night with his expression, "Wak-ta," had described the downpour with his fingers. But there was nothing in the sky. It was bare of all but the sun itself. There were only, so far, these round boulders in the branches, apparently intended to represent rain clouds.

We came to the third floor, where King Dahfu had his quarters. Horko led me through several wide but low-pitched rooms which seemed to be obscurely supported from beneath; I wouldn't have answered for the beams. There were hangings and curtains. But the windows were narrow, and little could be seen except when a ray of sun would break in here and there and show a rack of spears, a low seat, or the skin of an animal. At the door of the king's apartment, Horko withdrew. I had not expected that and I said, "Hey, where're you going?" But one of the amazons took me by the bare arm and passed me through the door. Before I saw Dahfu himself, I

was aware of numbers of women—twenty or thirty was my
first estimate—and the density of naked women, their volupté
(only a French word would do the job here) pressed upon me
from all sides. The heat was great and the predominant odor
was feminine. The only thing I could compare it to in
temperature and closeness was a hatchery—the low ceiling
also is responsible for this association. Seated by the door on a
high stool, a stool that resembled an old-fashioned bookkeeper's, was a gray, heavy old woman in the amazon's vest plus a
garrison cap of the sort which went out of date with the Italian
army at the turn of the century. On behalf of the king she
shook my hand.

"How do you do?" I said.

The king! His women cleared a path for me, moving slowly
from my way, and I saw him at the opposite end of the room,
extended on a green sofa about ten feet in length, crescent-
shaped, with heavy upholstery, deeply pocketed and bulging.
On this luxurious article he was fully at rest, so that his
well-developed athletic body, in knee-length purple drawers of
a sort of silk crepe, seemed to float, and about his neck was
wrapped a white scarf embroidered in gold. Matching slippers
of white satin were on his feet. For all my worry and fever I
felt admiration as I sized him up. Like myself, he was a big
man, six feet or better by my estimate, and sumptuously at
rest. Women attended to his every need. Now and then one
wiped his face with a piece of flannel, and another stroked his
chest, and one kept his pipe filled and lit and puffed at it for
him to keep it going.

I approached or blundered forward. Before I could come
too close a hand checked me and a stool was placed for me
about five feet from this green sofa. I sat. Between us in a large
wooden bowl lay a couple of human skulls, tilted cheek to
cheek. Their foreheads shone jointly at me in the yellow way
skulls have, and I was confronted by the united eye sockets
and nose holes and the double rows of teeth.

The king observed how warily I looked at him and
appeared to smile. His lips were large and tumid, the most

negroid features of his face, and he said, "Do not feel alarm. These are for employment in the ceremony of this afternoon."

Some voices once heard will never stop resounding in your head, and such a voice I recognized in his from the first words. I leaned forward to get a better look. The king was much amused by my spreading my hands over my chest and belly as if to retain something, and raised himself to examine me. A woman slipped a cushion behind his head, but he knocked it to the floor and lay back again. My thought was, "I haven't run out of luck yet." For I saw that our ambush and capture and interrogation and all the business of billeting us with the dead man could not have originated with the king. He was not that sort, and although I did not know yet precisely what sort he might be, I was already beginning to rejoice in our meeting.

"Yesterday afternoon, I have receive report of your arrival. I have been so excited. I have scarcely slept last night, thinking about our meeting. . . . Oh, ha, ha. It positively was not good for me," he said.

"That's funny, I didn't get too much sleep myself," I said. "I've had to make do with only a few hours. But I am glad to meet you, King."

"Oh, I am very please. Tremendous. I am sorry over your sleep. But on my own I am please. For me this is a high occasion. Most significant. I welcome you."

"I bring you regards from your friend Itelo," I said.

"Oh, you have encountered with the Arnewi? I see it is your idea to visit some of the remotest places. How is my very dear friend? I miss him. Did you wrestle?"

"We certainly did," I said.

"And who won?"

"We came out about even."

"Well," he said, "you seem a mos' interesting person. Especially in point of physique. Exceptional," he said. "I am not sure I have ever encountered your category. Well, he is very strong. I could not throw him, which gave him very high pleasure. Invariably did."

"I'm beginning to feel my age," I said.

The king said, "Oh, why, nonsense. I think you are like a monument. Believe me, I have never seen a person of your particular endowment."

"I hope you and I do not have to go to the mat, Your Highness," I said.

"Oh, no, no. We have not that custom. It is not local with us. I must request forgiveness from you," he said, "for not arising to a handshake. I ask my generaless, Tatu, to act for me because I am so reluctant to rise. In principle."

"Is that so? Is that so?" I said.

"The less motion I expend, and the more I repose myself, the easier it is for me to attend to my duties. All my duties. Including also the prerogatives of these many wives. You may not think so on first glance, but it is a most complex existence requiring that I husband myself. Sir, tell me frankly—"

"Henderson is the name," I said. Because of the way he lolled, and the way he drew on his pipe, I somehow felt that I was being particularly tested.

"Mr. Henderson. Yes, I should have asked you. I am very sorry for neglecting the civility. But I could hardly contain myself that you were here, sir, a chance for conversation in English. Many things since my return I have felt lacking which I would not have suspected while at school. You are my first civilized visitor."

"Not many people come here?"

"It is by our preference. We have preferred a seclusion, for many generations now, and we are beautifully well hidden in these mountains. You are surprised that I speak English? I assume no. Our friend Itelo must have told you. I adore that man's character. We were steadfastly together through many experiences. It is an intense disappointment to me not to have surprise you more," he said.

"Don't worry, I'm plenty surprised. Prince Itelo told me all about that school that he and you attended in Malindi." As I have emphasized, I was in a peculiar condition, I had an anxious fever, and I was perplexed by the events of last night. But there was something about this man that gave me the conviction that we could approach ultimates together. I went only by his appearance and the tone of his voice, for thus far it seemed to me that there was a touch of frivolousness in his attitude, and that he was trying me out. As for the remoteness of the Wariri, this morning, owing to the peculiarity of my mental condition, the world was not itself; it took on the aspect of an organism, a mental thing, amid whose cells I had been wandering. From mind the impetus came and through mind my course was set, and therefore nothing on earth could really surprise me, utterly.

"Mr. Henderson, I would appreciate if you would return a candid answer to the question I am about to put. None of these women can understand, therefore no hesitancy is required. Do you envy me?"

This was not the moment to tell lies.

"Do you mean would I change places with you? Well, hell, Your Highness—no disrespect intended—you seem to me to be in a very attractive position. But then, I couldn't be at more of a disadvantage," I said. "Almost anyone would win a comparison with me."

His black face had a cocked nose, but it was not lacking in bridge. The reddened darkness of his eyes must have been a family trait, as I had observed it also in his Uncle Horko. But in the king there was a higher quality or degree of light. And now he wanted to know, pursuing the same line of inquiry, "Is it because of all these women?"

"Well, I have known quite a few myself, Your Highness," I said, "though not all at the same time. That seems to be your case. But at present I happen to be very happily married. My wife's a grand person, and we have a very spiritual union. I am not blind to her faults; I sometimes tell her she is the altar of my ego. She is a good woman, but something of a blackmailer. There is such a thing as scolding nature too much. Ha, ha." I have told you I was feeling a little displaced in my mind. And now I said, "Why do I envy you? You are in the bosom of your people. They need you. Look how they stick around and attend to your every need. It's obvious how much they value you."

"While I am in possession of my original youthfulness and

strength," he said, "but have you any conception of what will take place when I weaken?"

"What will . . . ?"

"These same ladies, so inordinate of attention, will report me and then the Bunam who is chief priest here, with other priests of the association, will convey me out into the bush and there I will be strangled."

"Oh, no, Christ!" I said.

"Indeed so. I am telling you with utmost faithfulness what a king of us, the Wariri, may look forward to. The priest will attend until a maggot is seen upon my dead person and he will wrap it in a slice of silk and bring it to the people. He will show it in public pronouncing and declaring it to be the king's soul, my soul. Then he will re-enter the bush and, a given time elapsing, he will carry to town a lion's cub, explaining that the maggot has now experienced a conversion into a lion. And after another interval, they will announce to the people the fact that the lion has converted into the next king. This will be my successor."

"Strangled? You? That's ferocious. What sort of an outfit is this?"

"Do you still envy me?" said the king, making the words softly with his large, warm, swollen-seeming mouth.

I hesitated, and he observed, "My deduction from brief observation I give you as follows—that you are probably prone to such a passion."

"What passion? You mean I'm envious?" I said touchily, and forgot myself with the king. Hearing a note of anger, the amazons of the guard who were arrayed behind the wives along the walls of the room began to stir and grew alert. One syllable from the king quieted them. He then cleared his throat, raising himself upon his sofa, and one of the naked beauties held a salver so that he might spit. Having drawn some tobacco juice from his pipe, he was displeased and threw the thing away. Another lady retrieved it and cleaned the stem with a rag.

I smiled, but I am certain my smile looked like a grievance. The hairs about my mouth were twisted by it. I was aware, however, that I could not demand an explanation of that remark. So I said, "Your Highness, something very irregular happened last night. I don't complain of having fallen into a trap on arrival or my weapons being swiped, but in my hut last night there was a dead body. This is not exactly in the nature of a complaint, as I can handle myself with the dead. Nevertheless I thought you ought to know about it."

The king looked really put out over this; there wasn't the least flaw of insincerity in his indignation and he said, "What? I am sure it is a confusion of arrangements. If intentional, I will be very put out. This is a matter I must have looked into."

"I'm obliged to confess, Your Highness, I felt a certain amount of inhospitality and *I* was put out. My man was reduced to hysterics. And I might as well make a clean breast. Though I didn't want to tamper with your dead, I took it upon myself to remove the body. Only what does it signify?"

"What can it?" he said. "As far as I am aware, nothing."

"Oh, then I am relieved," I said. "My man and I had a very bad hour or two with it. And during the night it was brought back."

"Apologies," said the king. "My most sincere. Genuine. I can see it was horrible and also discommoding."

He didn't ask me for any particulars. He did not say, "Who was it? What was the man like?" Nor did he even seem to care whether it was a man, a woman, or a child. I was so glad to escape the anxiety of the thing that at the time I didn't note this peculiar lack of interest.

"There must be quite a number of deaths among you at this time," I said. "On the way over to the palace I could have sworn I saw some fellows hanging."

He did not answer directly, but only said, "We must get you out of the undesirable lodging. So please be my guest in the palace."

"Thank you."

"Your things will be sent for."

"My man, Romilayu, has already brought them, but he hasn't had breakfast."

"Be assured, he will be taken care of."

"And my gun . . ."

"Whenever you have occasion to shoot, it will be in your hands."

"I keep hearing a lion," I said. "Does this have anything to do with the information you gave me about the death of . . ." I did not complete the question.

"What brings you here to us, Mr. Henderson?"

I had an impulse to confide in him—that was how he made me feel, trusting—but as he had steered away the subject from the roaring of the lions, which I clearly heard beneath, I couldn't very well start, just like that, to speak openly and so I said, "I am just a traveler." My position on the three-legged stool suggested that I was crouching there in order to avoid questioning. The situation required an amount of equipoise or calm of mind which I lacked. And I kept wiping or rubbing my nose with my Woolworth bandanna. I tried to figure, "Which of these women might be the queen?" Then, as it might not be polite to stare at the different members of the harem, most of them so soft, supple, and black, I turned my eyes to the floor, aware that the king was watching me. He seemed all ease, and I all limitation. He was extended, floating; I was contracted and cramped. The undersides of my knees were sweating. Yes, he was soaring like a spirit while I sank like a stone, and from my fatigued eyes I could not help looking at him grudgingly (thus becoming actually guilty of the passion he had seen in me), in his colors surrounded by cherishing attention. Suppose there was ultimately such a price to pay? To me it seemed that he was getting full value.

"Do you mind a further inquiry, Mr. Henderson? What kind of traveler are you?"

"Oh . . . that depends. I don't know yet. It remains to be seen. You know," I said, "you have to be very rich to take a trip like this." I might have added, as it entered my mind to do, that some people found satisfaction in *being* (Walt Whitman: "Enough to merely be! Enough to breathe! Joy! Joy! All over joy!"). *Being*. Others were taken up with *becoming*. Being people have all the breaks. Becoming people are very unlucky, always in a tizzy. The Becoming people are always having to make explanations or offer justifications to the Being people. While the Being people provoke these explanations. I sincerely feel that this is something everyone should understand about me. Now Willatale, the queen of the Arnewi, and principal woman of Bittahness, was a Be-er if there ever was one. And at present King Dahfu. And if I had really been capable of the alert consciousness which it required I would have confessed that Becoming was beginning to come out of my ears. Enough! Enough! Time to have Become. Time to Be! Burst the spirit's sleep. Wake up, America! Stump the experts. Instead I told this savage king, "I seem to be kind of a tourist."

"Or a wanderer," he said. "I already am fond of a diffident way which I see you to exhibit."

I tried to make a bow when he said this, but was prevented by a combination of factors, the main one being my crouching position with my belly against my bare knees (incidentally, I badly needed a bath, as sitting in this posture made me aware). "You do me too much credit," I said. "There are a lot of folks at home who have me down for nothing but a bum."

At this stage of our interview I tried to make out, I tried to feel as if with my fingers, the chief characteristics of the situation. Things seemed to be smooth, but how smooth could they really be? According to Itelo, this king, Dahfu, was one hell of a guy. He had gotten a blue-ribbon recommendation. Class A, as Itelo himself would have said. Primo. Actually, I was already greatly taken with him, but it was necessary to remember what I had seen that morning, that I was among savages and that I had been quartered with a corpse and had seen guys hanging upside down by the feet and that the king had made at least one dubious insinuation. Besides, my fever was increasing, and I had to make a special effort to remain alert. From this I developed a great strain at the back of the neck and in my eyes. I was glaring crudely at everything about me, including these women who should have elicited quite another kind of attitude. But my purpose was to see essentials, only essentials, nothing but essentials, and to guard against hallucinations. Things are not what they seem, anyway.

As for the king, his interest in me appeared to increase continually. Half smiling, he scrutinized me with growing closeness. How was I ever to guess the aims and purposes hidden in his heart? God has not given me half as much intuition as I constantly require. As I couldn't trust him, I had to understand him. Understand him? How was I going to understand him? Hell! It would be like extracting an eel from the chowder after it has been cooked to pieces. This planet has billions of passengers on it, and those were preceded by infinite billions and there are vaster billions to come, and none of these, no, not one, can I hope ever to understand. Never! And when I think how much confidence I used to have in understanding—you know?—it's enough to make a man weep. Of course, you may ask, what have numbers got to do with it? And that's right, too. We get too depressed by them, and should be more accepting of multitudes than we are. Being in point of size precisely halfway between the suns and the atoms, living among astronomical conceptions, with every thumb and fingerprint a mystery, we should get used to living with huge numbers. In the history of the world many souls have been, are, and will be, and with a little reflection this is marvelous and not depressing. Many jerks are made gloomy by it, for they think quantity buries them alive. That's just crazy. Numbers are very dangerous, but the main thing about them is that they humble your pride. And that's good. But I used to have great confidence in understanding. Now take a phrase like "Father forgive them; they know not what they do." This may be interpreted as a promise that in time we would be delivered from blindness and understand. On the other hand, it may also mean that with time we will understand our own enormities and crimes, and that sounds to me like a threat.

Thus I was sitting there with my pondering expression. Or maybe it would be more factual and descriptive to say that I was listening to the growling of my mind. Then the king observed, to my surprise, "You do not show too much wear and tear of the journey. I esteem you to be very strong. Oh, vastly. I see at a glance. You tell me you were able to hold your own with Itelo? Perhaps you were practicing mere courtesy. At a snap judgment you do not seem so very courteous. But I will not conceal you are a specimen of development I cannot claim ever to have seen."

First the examiner in the middle of the night, waiving the question of the corpse, had asked me to take off my shirt so he could study my physique, and now the king expressed a similar interest. I could have boasted, "I'm strong enough to run up a hill about a hundred yards with one of your bodies on my back." For I do have a certain pride in my strength (compensatory mechanism). But my feelings had been undergoing a considerable fluctuation. First I was reassured by the person and attitude of the king, and his tone of voice. I had rejoiced. My heart proclaimed a holiday. Then again suspicions supervened, and now the peculiar inquiry about my physique made me sweat anew with anxiety. I remembered, if they were thinking of using me as a sacrifice, that an ideal sacrifice has no blemishes. And so I said that I actually had not been in the best of health and that I felt feverish today.

"You cannot have a fever, as manifestly you are perspiring," said Dahfu.

"That's just another one of my peculiarities," I said. "I can run a high temperature while pouring sweat." He brushed this aside. "And a terrible thing happened to me just last night as I was eating a piece of hardtack," I said. "A real calamity. I broke my bridge." I widened my mouth with my fingers and threw back my head, inviting him to look at the gap. Also I unbuttoned my pocket and showed him the teeth, which I had put there for safekeeping. The king looked into that enormous moat, my mouth. Exactly what his impression was, I can't undertake to relate, but he said, "It does look exceedingly troublesome. Where did this happen?"

"Oh, just before that fellow grilled me," I said. "What do you call him?"

"The Bunam," he said. "Do you find him very dignified? He is top official of all the priests. It is no trouble to conceive how annoyed you were to break the teeth."

"I was fit to be tied," I said. "I could have kicked myself in the head for being so stupid. Of course I can chew on the stumps. But what if the shank should come out? I don't know how familiar you may be with dentistry, Your Highness, but underneath, everything has been ground down to the pulp and if I feel a draft on those stumps, believe me, there's no torment comparable. I have had very bad luck with teeth, as has my wife. Naturally you can't expect teeth to last forever. They wear down. But that's not all. . . ."

"Can there be other things that ail you?" he said. "You do present an appearance of utmost and solid physical organization."

I flushed, and answered, "I have a pretty bad case of hemorrhoids, Your Highness. Moreover I am subject to fainting fits."

Sympathetically he asked, "Not the falling sickness—petit mal or grand mal?"

"No," I said, "what I have defies classification. I've been to the biggest men in New York with this, and they say it isn't epilepsy. But a few years ago I started to have fits of fainting, very unpredictable, without warning. They may come over me while I am reading the paper, or on a stepladder, fixing a window shade. And I have blacked out while playing the violin. Then about a year ago, in the express elevator, going up in the Chrysler Building, it happened to me. It must have been the speed of overcoming gravity that did it. There was a lady in a mink coat next to me. I put my head on her shoulder and she gave a loud scream, and I fell down."

Having been a stoic for so many years I am not skillful in making my ailments sound convincing. Also, from much reading of medical literature I am aware how much mind, just mind itself, we needn't speak of drink or anything like that, lies at the root of my complaints. It was perversity of character that was making me faint. Moreover my heart so often repeated, *I want,* that I felt entitled to a little reprieve, and I found it very restful to pass out once in a while. Nevertheless I began to realize that the king would certainly use me if he could, for, nice as he was, he was also in a certain position with respect to the wives. As he would never make old bones, there was no reason why he should be particularly considerate of me.

I said in a loud voice, "Your Majesty, this has been a wonderful and interesting visit. Who'd ever think! In the middle of Africa! Itelo praised Your Majesty very highly to me. He said you were terrific, and I see you really are. All this couldn't be more memorable, but I don't want to outstay my welcome. I know you are planning to make rain today and probably I will only be in the way. So thanks for the hospitality of the palace, and I wish you all kinds of luck with the ceremony, but I think after lunch my man and I had better blow."

As soon as he saw my intention and while I still spoke, he began to shake his head, and when he did so, the women looked at me with expressions devoid of friendliness, as though I were crossing or exciting the king and costing him strength which might be better employed.

"Oh, no, Mr. Henderson," he said. "It is not even conceivable that we should relinquish you so immediately upon arrival. You have vast social charm, my dear guest. You must believe I should suffer a privation positively gruesome to lose your company. Anyways, I think Fate have intended we should be more intimate. I told you how excited I have been since the announcement of your appearance from the outside world. And so, as the time has come for the ceremonies to begin, I invite you to be my guest."

He put on a generous large-brimmed hat of the same purple color as his drawers, but in velvet. Human teeth, to protect him from the evil eye, were sewed to the crown. He arose from his green sofa but only to lie down again in a hammock. Amazons dressed in their short leather waistcoats were the bearers. Four on either side put their shoulders to the poles, and these shoulders, although they were amazons, were soft. Physical capacity always stirs me, especially in women. I love to watch movies in Times Square of the Olympic Games, in particular those vital Atalantas running and throwing the javelin. I always say, "Look at that! Ladies and gentlemen—look what women can be like!" It appeals to the soldier in me as well as the lover of beauty. I tried to replace those eight amazons with eight women of my acquaintance—Frances, Mlle. Montecuccoli, Berthe, Lily, Clara Spohr, and others—but of them all it was only Lily who had the right stature. I could not think of a matched team. Berthe, though strong, was too broad and Mlle. Montecuccoli had a large bust but lacked the shoulders. These friends, acquaintances, and loved ones could not have carried the king.

At his majesty's request, I walked beside him down the stairs and into the courtyard. He did not lie lazily in his hammock; his figure had real elegance; it showed his breeding. None of this might have been manifest if I had met him and Itelo during their student days in Beirut. We have all encountered students from Africa, and usually they wear baggy suits and their collars are wrinkled because knotting a tie is foreign to their habits.

In the courtyard the procession was joined by Horko with his umbrellas, amazons, wives, children carrying long sheaves of Indian corn, warriors holding idols and fetishes in their arms which were freshly smeared with ochre and calcimine and were as ugly as human conception could make them. Some were all teeth, and others all nostrils, while several had tools bigger than their bodies. The yard suddenly became very crowded. The sun blasted and blazed. Acetylene does not peel paint more than this sun did the doors of my heart. Foolishly, I told myself that I was feeling faint. (It was owing to my size and strength that this appeared foolish.) And I thought that this was like a summer's day in New York. I had taken the wrong subway and instead of reaching upper Broadway I had gone to Lenox Avenue and 125th Street, struggling up to the sidewalk.

The king said to me, "The Arnewi too have a difficulty of water, Mr. Henderson?"

I thought, "All is lost. The guy has heard about the cistern." But this did not actually appear to be the case. No hint was contained in his manner; he was only looking from the hammock into the windless and cloudless blue.

"Well, I'll tell you, King," I said. "They didn't have much luck in that particular department."

"Oh?" he said thoughtfully. "It is a peculiarity about luck with them, do you know that? A legend exists that we were once the same and one, a single tribe, but separated over the luck question. The word for them in our language is nibai. This may be translated 'unlucky.' Definitely, this is the equivalent in our tongue."

"Is that so? The Wariri feel lucky, eh?"

"Oh yes. In numerous instances. We claim ourselves to be the contrary. The saying is, Wariri ibai. Put in other words, Lucky Wariri."

"You don't say? Well, well. And what's your own opinion of that? Is the saying right?"

"Are we Wariri lucky?" he asked. Unmistakably he was setting me straight, for I had challenged him by the question. I tell you! It was an experience. It was a lesson to me. He pulled his majesty on me so lightly it was hardly noticeable. "We have luck," he said. "Incontrovertibly, it is a fact about the luck. You wouldn't dream how consistent it is."

"So do you think you will have rain today?" I said, grimly grinning.

He answered very mildly, "I have seen rain on days that began like this." And then he added, "I believe I can understand your attitude. It derives from the kindliness of the Arnewi. They have made the impression on you which so commonly they make. Do not forget that Itelo is my special chum and was my side-kick in situations making for great intimacy. Ah, yes, I know the qualities. Generous. Meek. Good. No substitutes should be accepted. On this my agreement is total and complete, Mr. Henderson."

I put my fist to my face and looked at the sky, giving a short laugh and thinking, Christ! What a person to meet at this distance from home. Yes, travel is advisable. And believe me, the world is a mind. Travel is mental travel. I had always suspected this. What we call reality is nothing but pedantry. I need not have had that quarrel with Lily, standing over her in our matrimonial bed and shouting until Ricey took fright and escaped with the child. I proclaimed I was on better terms with the real than she. Yes, yes, yes. The world of facts is real, all right, and not to be altered. The physical is all there, and it belongs to science. But then there is the noumenal department, and there we create and create and create. As we tread our overanxious ways, we think we know what is real. And I was telling the truth to Lily after a fashion. I knew it better, all right, but I knew it because it was mine—filled, flowing, and floating with my own resemblances; as hers was with *her* resemblances. Oh, what a revelation! Truth spoke to me. To *me,* Henderson!

The king's eyes gleamed into mine with such a power of significance that I felt he could, if he wanted to, pass right straight into my soul. He could invest it. I felt this. But because I am ignorant and untutored in higher things—in higher things I am a coarse beginner, because of my abused nature—I didn't know what to expect. However, under the light of King Dahfu's eyes I comprehended that in bombing the cistern I had not lost my last chance. No sir. By no means.

Horko, the king's uncle, was still marshaling the procession. Over the palace walls came howls and sounds surpassing anything I ever heard from mortal throats or lungs. But as soon as there was a lull the king said to me, "I easily gather, Mr. Traveler, that you have set forth to accomplish a very important matter."

"Right, Your Majesty. One hundred per cent right," I said, and bowed. "Otherwise I could have stayed in bed and looked at a picture atlas or slides of Angkor Wat. I have a box full of them, in color."

"Deuce. That is what I meant," he said. "And you have left

your heart with our Arnewi friends. We agree, they are excellent. I even have conjectured if it is environment or nature. Frequently I have inclined to the innate and not the nurture side. Sometimes I would like to see my friend Itelo. I would give away a very dear treasure to hear his voice. Unfortunately I cannot go. My office . . . official capacity. Good impresses you, eh, Mr. Henderson?"

In the flash of the sun, tiny gold platelets within my eyes blinding me, I nodded. I said, "Yes, Your Highness. No bunk. The true good. The honest-to-God good."

"Yes, I know how you feel over it," he said, and spoke with a weird softness or longing. I could never have believed that I could take this from anybody, or would ever have to, and least of all from this person in the royal hammock, with the purple large-brimmed hat, and the teeth sewed onto it, the huge, soft, eccentric eyes tinged very slightly with red, and his pink swelling mouth. "They say," he went on, "that bad can easily be spectacular, has dash or bravado and impresses the mind quicker than good. Oh, that is a mistake in my opinion. Perhaps of common good it is true. Many, many nice people. Oh yes. Their will tells them to perform good, and they do. How ordinary! Mere arithmetic. 'I have left undone the etceteras I should have done, and done the etceteras I ought not to have.' This does not even amount to a life. Oh, how sordid it is to bookkeep. My whole view is opposite or contrary, that good cannot be labor or conflict. When it is high and great, it is too superior. Oh, Mr. Henderson, it is far more spectacular. It is associated with inspiration, and not conflict, for where a man conflicts there he will fall, and if taking the sword also perishes by the sword. A dull will produces a very dull good, of no interest. Where a fellow draws a battle line there he is apt to be found, dead, a testimonial of the great strength of effort, and only effort."

I said eagerly, "Oh, King Dahfu—oh, Your Majesty!" He had stirred me so much. By just these few words spoken as he reclined in the hammock. "Do you know the queen over there, that woman of Bittahness, Willatale? She's Itelo's aunt, you

know. She was going to instruct me in grun-tu-molani, but one
thing and another came up, and—"

But the amazons had put their backs to the poles and the
hammock rose and moved forward. And the screams, the
excitement! The roars, the deep drum noises, as if the animals
were speaking again by means of the skins that had once
covered their bodies! It was a great release of sound, like
Coney Island or Atlantic City or Times Square on New Year's
Eve; at the king's exit from the gate the great cacophony left
all the previous noises in my experience far behind.

Shouting, I asked the king, "Where . . . ?"

I bent very close for the reply. ". . . possess a special . . . a
place . . . arena," he said.

I heard no more. The frenzy was so great it was metropoli-
tan. There was such a whirl of men and women and fetishes,
and snarls like dog-beating and whines like sickles sharpening,
and horns blasting and blazing into the air, that the scale
could not be recorded. The bonds of sound were about to be
torn to pieces. I tried to protect my good ear by plugging it
with my thumb, and even the defective one had more than it
could take. At least a thousand villagers must have been in
this mob, most of them naked, many painted and gaudy, all
using noisemakers and uttering screams. The weather was
heavy, sultry, so that my body itched. It was an ugly, dusty
heat, and there were times when my face felt as if wrapped up
in serge. But I had no time to take note of discomfort, being
carried forward beside the king. The procession entered a
stadium—I stretch the term—a big enclosure fenced with
wood. Within was a quadruple row of benches cut from the
white calcareous stone aforementioned. For the king there was
a royal box in which I sat, too, under a canopy with floating
ribbons, with wives, officials, and other royalty. The amazons
in their corsetlike vests and large smooth bodies and delicate,
shaved, immense heads, round like melons, oval like canta-
loupes, long like squashes, were posted all around. Accompanied by his retinue and umbrellas, Horko bowed and sa-
laamed before the king. The family resemblance between

these two suggested that they could communicate thoughts merely by looking at each other; sometimes it is like that. The same noses, the same eyes, the same implied message of the race. So, in a silent manner, Horko appeared to me to urge his royal nephew to do something previously discussed. But by the look of him the king wouldn't promise a thing. He was in command here; there could never be any question about that.

Carried aloft by four amazons, one at each leg, came the bridge table. On it was the bowl containing two skulls I had seen a short while ago in the royal apartment. But now they had ribbons tied through the eye sockets, very long and gleaming, of a dark blue color. They were set down before the king, who took note of them with one roll of his eyes and looked no more at them. Meantime this huge Horko, all rolled up so that he stood heel to heel in his crimson sheath, the fat crowded upward to his chin and shoulders, took the liberty of mocking my expression. At least I thought I recognized my own scowl on his face. I didn't mind. I made a short bow to acknowledge that he had taken me off pretty well. And, like the politician he was, he gave me a glad, impudent wave. The colored umbrella wheeled over him and he went back to his box on the king's left and sat down with the examiner who had kept me waiting last night, the character whom Dahfu called the Bunam, and the wrinkled old black-leather fellow who had sent us into the ambush. The one who had arisen out of the white rocks like the man met by Joseph. Who sent Joseph over to Dothan. Then the brothers saw Joseph and said, "Behold, the dreamer cometh." Everybody should study the Bible.

Believe me, I felt like a dreamer, and that's no lie.

"Who is that man all wrinkled like a Greek olive?" I said.

"Beg pardon?" said the king.

"With the Bunam and your uncle."

"Oh, of course. A senior priest. Diviner of a sort."

"Yesterday we met him with a twisted stick," I was saying, when several squads of amazons lined up with muskets and started to aim at the sky. I could not see the .375 anywhere.

These large women began to fire salutes, first in honor of the king and the king's late father, Gmilo, and for various others. Then, so the king told me, there was a salute for me.

"For me? You're kidding, Your Highness," I said. But he was not, so I asked him, "Should I stand up?"

"I think it would be widely appreciated," he said.

And I got to my feet, and there were loud shrieks and screams. I thought, "The word has got around how I dealt with that corpse. They know I'm no Caspar Milquetoast but a person of strength and courage. Plenty of moxie." I was beginning to feel the spirit of the occasion—pervaded by barbaric emotions—the scratchiness in my bosom was greatly aggravated. I had no words to speak, no mortar or bazooka to fire, replying to the guns of the amazons. But I was impelled to make a sound, and therefore I uttered a roar like the great Assyrian bull. You know, to be the center of attention in a crowd always stirs and disturbs me. It had done so when the Arnewi wept and when they gathered near the cistern. Also when shaved in Italy near the stronghold of the ancient Guiscardos that time in Salerno. In a big gathering my father also had a tendency to become excited. He once lifted up the speaker's stand and threw it down into the orchestra pit.

However, I roared. And the acclaim was magnificent. For I was heard. I was seen gripping my chest as I bellowed. The crowd went wild over this, and its yells were, I have to admit it, just like nourishment to me. I reflected, So this is what guys in public life get out of it? Well, well. I no longer wondered that this Dahfu had come back from civilization to be king of his tribe. Hell, who wouldn't be a king, even a small king? It was not a privilege to be missed. (The time of payment to a strong young fellow was remote; the wives couldn't invent enough attentions and expressions of gratitude; he was the darling of their hearts.)

I stood as long as was feasible and luxuriated in this applause, laughing, and I sat down when I had to.

Now, horrified, I saw a grinning face with a mouth like a big open loop and a forehead infinitely wrinkled. It was the sort of vision you might have in a shop window on Fifth Avenue, and, when you turned to see what fantastic apparition New York had thrown up behind you, there would be no one. This face, however, stood its ground and held steady while it grinned at the party in the king's box. Deep bloody cuts were being made meanwhile on the chest that belonged to this face. A green old knife—a cruel clutch. Oh, the man is being slashed and stabbed. Stop, stop! Holy God! Why, this is murder being committed, said I. Through my depths as in a tunnel went a shock like the ones big buildings get from trains which pass beneath.

But the cutting wasn't deep, it was lateral and superficial, and despite the speed of the painted priest who wielded the knife it was done according to plan, and with skill. Ochre was rubbed into the wounds, which must have stung like frenzy, but the fellow grinned and the king said, "This proceeding is about semiusual, Mr. Henderson. The worry is not necessary. He is thus advanced in his priesthood career and so is very pleased. As to the blood, that is supposed to induce the heavens also to flow, or prime the pumps of the firmament."

"Ha, ha!" I laughed and cried. "Say, King! What's that? Oh, Jesus—come again? The pumps of the firmament? Isn't that the dandiest!"

However, the king had no time for me. At a signal from Horko's box there was an all-out, slam-bang, grand salute of the guns and with it a pounding of the deep liquid bass drums. The king arose. Wild hosannas! Fountains of praise! Faces screaming fiercely with pride and twisted with diverse inspirations. From the basic blackness of the flesh of the tribe there broke or erupted a wave of red color, and the people all arose on the white stone of the grandstands and waved red objects, waved or flaunted. Crimson was the holy-day color of the Wariri. The amazons saluted with purple banners, the king's colors. His purple umbrella was raised, and its taut head swayed.

The king himself was no longer beside me. He had gone down from the box to take a position in the arena. At the other side of the circle, which was no bigger than the infield of a ball park, there arose a tall woman. To the waist she was naked and her head had woolly ringlets. When she came closer I saw that her face was covered with a beautiful design of scars that looked like Braille. Two peaks of this came down beside each ear, and a third descended to the bridge of her nose. As far as the belly she was painted a russet or dull gold color. She was young, for her breasts were small and didn't waver when she walked, as is the case with more adult females, and her arms were long and thin. They manifested the three major bones; I mean the tapered humerus and the radius and ulna. Her face was small and sloping, and when I first saw her from across the field she had no more features than the ball of a flagpole; at a distance she had a face like a gilded apple. She wore a pair of purple trousers, mates to the king's, and was his partner in a game they now began to play. For the first time, I realized that there was a group of shrouded figures in the center of the arena—roughly, let's say, where the pitcher's mound would have been. I figured correctly that these were the gods. Around them and over them the king and this gilded woman began to play a game with the two skulls. Whirling them by the long ribbons, each took a short run and threw them high in the air, above the figures of wood which stood under the tarpaulins—the biggest of these idols about as tall as an old upright Steinway piano. The two skulls flew up high, and then the king and the girl each made the catch. It was very neat. All the noise had died, had gone like the wrinkles of a cloth under the hot iron. A perfectly smooth silence followed the first throws, so you could even hear how hollow the catch sounded. Soon even the whiff the skulls made as they were being whirled around came to my unhandicapped ear. The woman threw her skull. The thick purple and blue ribbons made it look like a flower in the air. I swear before God, it appeared just like a gentian. In midair it passed the skull coming from the hand of the king. Both came streaming down with the blue satin ribbons following, as though they were a couple of ocean polyps. Soon

I understood that this wasn't only a game, but a contest, and naturally I rooted for the king. I didn't know but what the penalty for dropping one of those skulls might have been death. Now I myself have become ultrafamiliar with death, not only owing to my age, but for a lot of reasons unnecessary to cite at this time. Death and I are just about kissing cousins. But the thought of anything happening to the king was horrible to me. Though his confidence seemed great, and his bounding and his quick turns and his sureness made beautiful watching as he warmed to the game like a fine tennis player or a great rider, and he—well, he was virile to a degree that made all worry superfluous; such a man takes all he does upon himself; nevertheless I trembled and shook for him. I worried for the girl, too. Should either one of them stumble or let the ribbons slip or the skulls collide they might have to pay the ultimate price, like the poor guy I found in my hut. He certainly had not died of natural causes. You can't kid me; I would have made a terrific coroner. But the king and the woman were in top form, from which I judged that he didn't spend all his time on his back, pampered by those dolls of his, for he ran and jumped like a lion, full of power, and he looked magnificent. He hadn't even taken off the purple velvet hat with its adornment of human teeth. And he was equal to the woman, for in my mind she shaped up as the challenger. She behaved like a priestess, seeing to it that he came up to the mark. Because of the gold paint and Braille marks on her face she looked somewhat inhuman. As she sprang, dancing, her breasts were fixed, as if really made of gold, and because of her length and thinness, when she leaped it was something supernatural, like a giant locust.

Then the last pair of throws, and the catch was completed. Each tucked the skull under his arm, like a fencer's mask; each bowed. A tremendous noise followed, and again the crimson flags and rags erupted.

The king was breathing hard as he returned, with that Francis I hat, as Titian might have painted it. He sat down. When he did so, the wives surrounded him with a sheet so that he might not be seen drinking in public. This was taboo. Then they dried his sweat and massaged the muscles of his great legs and his panting belly, loosening the golden drawstring of his purple trousers. I wished to tell him how great he had been. I was dying to say what I felt. Like, "Oh, King, that was royally done. Like a true artist. God-dammit, an artist! King, I love nobility and beautiful behavior." But I couldn't say a thing. I have this brutal reticence of character. Such is the slavery of the times. We are supposed to be cool-mouthed. As I told my son Edward—slavery! And he thought I was a square when I said I loved the truth. Oh, that hurt! Anyway, I often want to say things and they stay in my mind. Therefore they don't actually exist; you can't take credit for them if they never emerge. By mentioning the firmament, the king himself had shown me the way, and I might have told him a lot, right then and there. What? Well, for instance, that chaos doesn't run the whole show. That this is not a sick and hasty ride, helpless, through a dream into oblivion. No, sir! It can be arrested by a thing or two. By art, for instance. The speed is checked, the time is redivided. Measure! That great thought. Mystery! The voices of angels! Why the hell else did I play the fiddle? And why were my bones molten in those great cathedrals of France so that I couldn't stand it and had to booze up and swear at Lily? And I was thinking that if I spoke of this to the king and told him what was in my heart he might become my friend. But the wives were between us with their naked thighs, and their behinds turned toward me, which would have been the height of discourtesy except that they were wild savages. So I had no chance to speak to the king under those inspired conditions. A few minutes later, when I was able again to talk to him, I said, "King, I had a feeling that if either of you missed, the consequences would not be pretty."

Before he answered he moistened his lips, and his chest still moved quickly. "I can explain to you, Mr. Henderson, why the factor of missing is negligible." His teeth shone toward me and the panting made him seem to smile, though there was nothing to smile about. "Some day the ribbons will be tied through here." With two fingers he pointed to his eyes. "My own skull will get the air." He made a gesture of soaring, and said, "Flying."

I said, "Were those the skulls of kings? Relatives of yours?" I didn't have the nerve to ask a direct question about his kinship with those heads. At the thought of making a similar catch, the flesh of my hands pricked and tingled.

But there was no time to go into this. Too much was happening. Now the cattle sacrifices were made, and they were done pretty much without ceremony. A priest with ostrich feathers that sprayed out in every direction threw his arm about the neck of a cow, caught the muzzle, raised her head, and slit her throat as if striking a match on the seat of his pants. She fell to the ground and died. Nobody took much notice.

Chapter XIII

After this came tribal dances and routines that were strictly like vaudeville. An old woman wrestled with a dwarf, only the dwarf lost his temper and tried to hurt her, and she stopped and scolded. One of the amazons entered the field and picked up the tiny man; with a swinging stride she carried him away under her arm. Cheers and handclapping came from the grandstands. Next there was another performance of an unserious nature. Two guys swung at each other's legs with whips, skipping into the air. Such Roman holiday high jinks were not reassuring to me. I was very nervous. I billowed with nervous feeling and a foreboding of coming abominations. Naturally I couldn't ask Dahfu for a preview. He was breathing deeply and watched with impervious calm.

Finally I said, "In spite of all these operations, the sun is still shining, and there aren't any clouds. I even doubt whether the humidity has increased, though it feels very close."

The king answered me, "Your observation is true, to all appearance. I do not contest you, Mr. Henderson. Nevertheless, I have seen all expectation defied and rain come on days like this. Yes, precisely."

I gave him a squinting, intense look. There was much meaning condensed into this, and I will not try to dilute it for you now. Maybe a certain amount of overweening crept in. But what it mostly expressed was, "Let us not kid each other, Your Royal H. Do you think it's so easy to get what you want from Nature? Ha, ha! I never have got what I asked for." Actually what I said was, "I would almost be willing to make you a bet, King."

I didn't expect the king to take me up so quickly on this. "Oh? Nice. Do you want to propose me a wager, Mr. Henderson?"

I found that my heart was hungry after provocation on this issue. I got involved. Something fierce. And naturally against reason. And I said, "Oh, sure, if you want to bet, I'll bet."

"I agree," said the king, with a smiling look, but stubbornly, too.

"Why, King Dahfu, Prince Itelo said you were interested in science."

"Did he tell you," said the guy with evident pleasure, "did he say that I was in attendance at medical school?"

"No!"

"A true fact. I did two years of the course."

"You didn't! You don't know how relevant that is, as a piece of information. But in that case, what sort of a bet are we making? You are just humoring me. You know, Your Highness, my wife Lily subscribes to the *Scientific American*, and so I am in on the rain problem. The technique of seeding the clouds with dry ice hasn't worked out well. Some recent ideas are that, first of all, the rain comes from showers of dust which arrive from outer space. When that dust hits the atmosphere it does something. The other theory which appeals more to me is that the salt spray of the ocean, the sea foam in other words, is one of the main ingredients of rain. Moisture takes and condenses on these crystals carried in the air, as it has to have something to condense on. So, it's a real wowzer, Your Highness. If there were no sea foam, there would be no rain, and if there were no rain there would be no life. How would all the wise guys like that? If the ocean didn't have this peculiar form of beauty the land would be bare." With increasing intimacy, as if confidentially, I laughed and said, "Your Majesty, you have no idea how the whole thing tickles me. Life comes from the cream of the seas. We used to sing a song in school, 'O Marianina. Come O come and turn us into foam.' " I sang for him a little, sotto voce, almost. He liked it; I could tell.

"You do not have a common run of a voice," he said, smiling and gay. I was beginning to feel that the fellow liked me. "And the information is fascinating indeed."

"Ha, I'm glad you see it that way. Boy! That's something, isn't it? But I guess this puts an end to our bet."

"Not of the very least. Just the same, we shall bet."

"Well, King Dahfu, I have opened my big mouth. Allow me to take back what I said about the rain. I am prepared to eat crow. Naturally, as the king you have to back the rain ceremony. So I apologize. So why don't you just say, 'Nuts to you, Henderson,' and forget it?"

"Oh, by no means. No basis for that. We shall bet, and why not?" He spoke with such finality that I had no out to take.

"Okay, Your Highness, have it your way."

"Word of honor. What shall we bet?" he said.

"Anything you want."

"Very good. Whatever I want."

"This is unfair of me. I have to give you good odds," I said. He waved his hand, on which there was a large red jewel. His body had sunk back into the hammock, for he sat and lay by turns. I could see that it pleased him to gamble; he had the character of a betting man. Anyway, my eyes were on this ring of his, a huge garnet set in thick gold and encircled by smaller stones, and he said, "Does the ring appeal?"

"It's pretty nice," I said, meaning that I was reluctant to specify any object.

"What are you betting?"

"I've got cash money on me, but I don't suppose that would interest you. I have a pretty good Rolleiflex in my kit. Not that I've taken any pictures except by accident. I've been too busy out here in Africa. Then there is my gun, an H and H Magnum .375 with telescopic sights."

"I do not foresee how it would be usable if won."

"At home I've got some objects I would be glad to put up," I said. "I've got some beautiful Tamworth pigs left."

"Oh, indeed?"

"I can see you're not interested."

"It would be fitting to bet something personal," he said.

"Oh, yes. The ring is personal. I get it. If I could detach my troubles I'd put them up. They're personal. Ho, ho. Only I wouldn't wish them on my worst enemy. Well, let's see, what do I have that you might use; what have I got that would go with being a king? Carpets? I've got a nice one in my studio. Then there's a velvet dressing gown that might look good on you. There's even a Guarnerius violin. But hey! I've got it—paintings. There's one of me and one of my wife. They're oils."

At this moment I wasn't sure that he heard me, but he said, "You should not assume at all that you have a sure thing."

Then I said, "So? What if I lose?"

"It will be interesting."

This made me begin to worry.

"Well, it is settled. We may match ring against oil portraits. Or let us say that if I win you will remain a guest of mine, a length of time."

"Okay. But how long?"

"Oh, it is too theoretical," he said, looking away. "Let us leave it an open consideration for the moment."

This arrangement made, we both looked upward. The sky was a bald, pale blue and rested on the mountains, windless. I figured that this king must have a lot of delicacy. He wanted to make it up to me for the corpse last night and also to indicate that he would appreciate it if I would visit with him for a while. The discussion ended with the king making a florid African gesture, as if peeling off his gloves or rehearsing the surrender of the ring. I sweated hugely, but my body was not cooled. To try to assuage the heat, I held my mouth open.

Then I said, "Haw, haw! Your Majesty, this is a screwy bet."

At this moment came furious or quarrelsome shouts, and I thought, "Ha, the light part of the ceremony is over." Several men in black plumes, like beggarly bird men—the rusty feathers hung to their shoulders—began to lift the covers from the gods. Disrespectfully, they pulled them away. This irreverence was no accident, if you get what I mean. It was done to raise a laugh, and it did exactly that. These bird or plume characters, encouraged by the laughter, started to perform burlesque antics; they stepped on the feet of the statues, and bowled some of the smaller ones over and made passes at them, mockeries, and so on. The dwarf was set on the knees of one goddess and he rocked the crowd with laughter by pulling his lower lids down and sticking out his tongue, making like a wrinkled lunatic. The family of gods, all quite short in the legs and long in the trunk, was very tolerant about these abuses. Most of them had disproportionate, small faces set on tall necks. All in all, they didn't look like a stern bunch. Just the same they had dignity—mystery; they were after all the gods, and they made the awards of fate. They ruled the air, the mountains, fire, plants, cattle, luck, sickness, clouds, birth, death. Damn it, even the squattest, kicked over onto his belly, ruled over something. The attitude of the tribe seemed to be that it was necessary to come to the gods with their vices on display, as nothing could be concealed from them anyway by ephemeral men. I grasped the idea, but basically I thought it was a big mistake. I wanted to say to the king, "You mean to tell me all this bad blood is necessary?" Also I marveled that such a man should be king over a gang like this. He took it all pretty calmly, however.

By and by they began to move the whole pantheon. Bodily. They started with the smaller gods, whom they handled very roughly and with a lot of wickedness. They let them fall or rolled them around, scolding them as if they were clumsy. Hell! I thought. To me it seemed like a pretty cheap way to behave, although I could see, to be objective about it, plenty of grounds for resentment against the gods. But anyway I didn't care one bit for this. Grumbling, I sat under the shell of my helmet and tried to appear as if it was none of my business.

When this crew of ravens came to the larger statues, they tugged and pulled but couldn't manage, and had to call for help from the crowd. One strong man after another jumped into the arena to pick up an idol, toting it from the original position to, let's say, short center field, while cheers and rooting came from the stands. From the stature and muscular development of the champions who moved the larger idols I gathered that this display of strength was a traditional part of the ceremony. Some approached the bigger gods from behind and clasped arms about their middles, some backed up to them like men unloading flour from the tailgate of a truck and hauled them on their shoulders. One gave a twist to the arms of a figure as I had done to the corpse last night. Seeing my own technique applied, I gave a gasp.

"What is it, Mr. Henderson?" said the king.

"Nothing, nothing, nothing," I said.

The group of gods remaining grew small. The strong men had carted them away, almost all of them. The last of these fellows were superb specimens, and I have a good eye for the points of strong men. During a certain period of my life I took quite an interest in weight-lifting and used to train on the barbells. As everyone knows, the development of the thighs counts heavily. I tried to get my son Edward interested; there might have been no Maria Felucca if I had been able to influence him to build his muscles. Although, when all that is said and done, I have grown this portly front and the other strange distortions that attend all the larger individuals of a species. (Like those mammoth Alaska strawberries.) Oh, my body, my body! Why have we never really got together as friends? I have loaded it with my vices, like a raft, like a barge.

Oh, who shall deliver me from the body of this death? Anyway, from these distortions owing to my scale and the work performed by my psyche. And sometimes a voice has counseled me, crazily, "Scorch the earth. Why should a good man die? Let it be some blasted fool who is dumped in the grave." What wickedness! What perversity! Alas, what things go on within a person!

However—I was more and more intensely a spectator— when there were only two gods left, the two biggest (Hummat the mountain god and Mummah the goddess of clouds) there were several strong men who came out and failed. Yes, they flunked. They couldn't stir this Hummat, who had whiskers like a catfish and spines all over his forehead, plus a pair of boulder-like shoulders. After several of them had quit on the job and been hooted and jeered, a fellow came forward wearing a red fez and a kind of jaunty jockstrap of oilcloth. He walked quickly, swinging his open hands, this man who was going to pick up Hummat, and prostrated himself before the god—the first devotional attitude yet shown. Then he went round to the back of the statue and inserted his head under one of its arms. A small taut beard glittered about his round face. He spread his legs, feeling for position with sensitive feet, patting the dust. After this he wiped his hands on his own knees and took hold of Hummat, grasping him by the arm and from beneath in the fork. With huge, set eyes, which became humid from the static effort, he began to lift the great Hummat. From his mouth, distended until the jaws blended with the collar bones, the sinews set in like the thin spokes of a bicycle, and his hip muscles formed large knots at the groin, swelling beside the soiled pants of oilcloth. This was a good man, and I appreciated him. He was my own type. You put a burden in front of him and he clasped it, he threw his chest into it, he lifted, he went to the limit of his strength. "That's the ticket," I said. "Get your back muscles going." As everyone else was cheering, except Dahfu, I got up also and began to yell, "Yay, yaay for you! You got him. You'll do it. You're husky enough. Push—that's it! Now up! Yay, he's doing it. He's going to crack it. Oh, God bless the guy. What a sweetheart! That's a real man—that's the type I love. Go on. Heave-ho. Wow! There he goes. He did it. Ah, thank God!" Then I realized how I had been shouting and I sat down again beside the king, wondering at my own fervor.

The champion tipped Hummat back on his shoulder, and carried the mountain god twenty feet. Among the rest, he set him down on his base. Winded, the man now turned and looked back at Mummah, alone in the middle of the ring. She was even bigger than Hummat. Amid the applause the champion looked her over. And she awaited him. She was very obese, not to say hideous, this female power. They had made her very ponderous, and the strong man facing her seemed already daunted. Not that she forbade you to try. No, in spite of her hideousness she seemed pretty tolerant, even happy-go-lucky like most of the gods. However, she appeared to express confidence in her immovability. The crowd was egging him on, everyone standing; even Horko and his friends in their own box were on foot. His umbrella now threw a shadow of old rose, and in his tight red robe he held out his stout arm and pointed at Mummah with his thumb—that great, wooden, happy Mummah, whose knees gave a little under the weight of her breasts and belly so that she had to spread her fingers on her thighs for support. And, as gross women sometimes do, she had elegant, graceful hands. She awaited the man who would move her.

"You can do her, guy," I too shouted. I asked the king, "What is this fellow's name?"

"The strong man? Oh, that is Turombo."

"What's the matter, doesn't he think he can move her?"

"Evidently he lacks confidence. Every year he can move Hummat, but not Mummah."

"Oh, he must be able to."

"Just the contrary, I fear," said the king, in his curious, singsong, nasal, African English. His large, swelled lips were more red than was the case with others of his tribe. Consequently his mouth was more visible than mouths usually are.

"This man, as you see, is powerful, and a good man, as I believe I overheard you to exclaim. But when he has moved Hummat, he is worn out, and this is annual. Do you see, Hummat has to be moved first, as otherwise he would not permit the clouds passage over the mountains."

Benevolent Mummah, her fat face shone to the sun with splendor. Her tresses of wood were like a stork's nest and broadened upward—a homely, happy, stupid, patient figure, she invited Turombo or any other champion to try his strength.

"You know what it is?" I said to the king. "It's the memory of past defeats—past defeats, you can ask *me* about this problem of past defeats. Brother, I could really tell you. But that's what got him. I just know it."

Turombo, a very short man for his girth and strength, really seemed to be bucking a whole lot of trouble. Those eyes of his, which had grown large and humid with strain when he took a grip on Hummat, now wore a duller light. He was prepared for failure, and the motion of his eyes, rolling at us and at the crowd, showed it. This, I want to tell you, I hated to see. Anyway, he tipped his fez to the king with a gesture of dedication that already acknowledged defeat. He had no illusions about Mummah. Nevertheless, he was going to try. He gave his short beard a rub with his knuckles, walking toward her slowly and sizing her up with a view to doing business.

Ambition must have played a very small role in Turombo's life. Whereas in my breast there was a flow—no, that's too limited—there opened up an estuary, a huge bay of hope and ambition. For here was my chance. I knew I could do this. Ye gods! I was shivering and cold. I simply knew that I could lift up Mummah, and I flowed, I burned to go out there and do it. Craving to show what was in me, burning like that bush I had set afire with my Austrian lighter for the Arnewi children. Stronger than Turombo I certainly was. And in the process of proving it, should my heart be ruptured, should the old sack split, okay, then let me die. I didn't care any more. I had

longed to do some good to the Arnewi when I arrived and saw
their distress. Instead of accomplishing which, I had rashly
brought down the full weight of my blind will and ambition
upon those frogs. I arrived clothed in light, or thinking so, and
I departed draped in shadow and darkness, humiliated, so that
perhaps it would have been better to obey my first impulse on
arrival, when the young woman burst into tears and I said to
myself maybe I should cast away my gun and my fierceness
and go into the wilderness until I was fit to meet humankind
again. My longing to perform a benefit there, because I was so
taken with the Arnewi, and especially old blind-eye Willatale,
was sincere and intense, but it was not even a ripple on the
desire I felt now in the royal box beside the semibarbarous
king in his trousers and purple velvet hat. So inflamed was my
wish to *do* something. For I saw something I could do. Let
these Wariri whom so far (with the corpse in the night and all
in all) I didn't care for—let them be worse than the sons of
Sodom and Gomorrah combined, I still couldn't pass up this
opportunity to *do,* and to distinguish myself. To work the right
stitch into the design of my destiny before it was too late. So I
was glad that Turombo was so meek. I thought he'd better be
meek. Even before he had touched Mummah he had implicitly
confessed he would never be able to budge her. And that was
the way I wanted it. She was mine! And I wanted to say to the
king, "I can do it. Let me in there." However, these words
found no utterance, for Turombo had already come upon the
goddess from behind. He took a lifting stance, crouching,
while he folded his thick arms about her belly. Then beside
her hip there appeared his face. It was filled with effort,
preparation for strain, fear and suffering, as if Mummah,
toppling, might crush him beneath her weight. However, she
now began to move in his embrace. The stork's nest, her
wooden tresses, tipped and swayed like a horizon at sea in
rough weather when you stand in the bow of the ship. I put it
like that as I felt this motion in my stomach. Turombo heaved
from the base like a man trying to uproot an old tree. This was
how he labored. But though he shook the old girl he couldn't
raise her base from the ground.

The crowd razzed him as he acknowledged at last that this was beyond his strength. He simply couldn't do it. And I rejoiced at the guy's failure. Which is a hell of a thing to admit, but it happens to have been the case. "Good man," I thought to myself. "You are strong but it so happens I am stronger. It's not a personal matter at all. It's only the fates—they willed it. As in the case of Itelo. This is a job for me. Yield, yield! Cede! Because here comes Henderson! Just let me get my hands on that Mummah, and by God . . . !"

I said to Dahfu, "I'm real sorry he didn't make it. It must be tough on him."

"Oh, it was foregone he could not," said King Dahfu. "I was certain."

Then I began in deepest, grimmest earnest, as only I can be grim, "Your Majesty—" I was excited to the bursting point. I swelled, I was sick, and my blood circulated peculiarly through my body—it was turbid and ecstatic both. It prickled within my face, especially in the nose, as if it might begin to discharge itself there. And as though a crown of gas were burning from my head, so I was tormented. And I said, "Sir, sire, I mean . . . let me! I must."

If the king made any answer I couldn't have heard it just then, because I saw only one face in this hot and dry air, off to my left and deaf to the raging cries made by the crowd against Turombo. A face concentrated exclusively upon me, so that it was detached from all the world. This was the face of the examiner, the guy I had dealt with last night, the man Dahfu called the Bunam. That face! A stare of wrinkled and everlasting human experience was formed on it. I could feel myself how charged those veins of his must be. Ah, holy God! The guy was speaking to me, inexorable. By the furrows of his face and the pressure of his brows and the fullness of his veins he was conveying a message to me. And what he was saying I knew. I heard it. The silent speech of the world to which my most secret soul listened continually now came to me with spectacular clarity. Within—within I heard. Oh, what I heard! The first stern word was *Dummy!* I was greatly shaken by this. And yet there was something there. It was true. And I was obliged, it was my bounden duty to hear. *And nevertheless you are a man. Listen! Harken unto me, you shmohawk! You are blind. The footsteps were accidental and yet the destiny could be no other. So now do not soften, oh, no, brother, intensify rather what you are. This is the one and only ticket—intensify. Should you be overcome, you slob, should you lie in your own fat blood senseless, unconscious of nature whose gift you have betrayed, the world will soon take back what the world unsuccessfully sent forth. Each peculiarity is only one impulse of a series from the very heart of things—that old heart of things. The purpose will appear at last though maybe not to you.* The voice did not sink away. It just stopped. Just like that, it finished what it had to say.

But I understood now why the corpse had been quartered with me. The Bunam was behind it. He sized me up right. He had wanted to see whether I was strong enough to move the idol. And I had met the ordeal. Damn! I had met it at all costs. When I gripped the dead man, his weight had felt to me like the weight of my own limbs fallen asleep and ponderous, but I had fought this revulsion and overcome it, I had lifted up the man. And here was the examiner's grim, exalted, vein-full, knotted, silent face, announcing the results. I had passed. With highest marks. One hundred per cent.

And I said, loudly, "This I must try."

"What is that?" said Dahfu.

"Your Highness," I said, "if it wouldn't be regarded as interference by a foreigner, I think that I could move the statue—the goddess Mummah. I would genuinely like to be of service, as I have certain capacities which ought to be put to definite use. I want to tell you that I didn't make out too well with the Arnewi, where I had a similar feeling. King, I had a great desire to do a disinterested and pure thing—to express my belief in something higher. Instead I landed in a lot of trouble. It's only right that I should make a clean breast."

I was not in control of myself, and thus I wasn't sure how clear my words might be, though my purpose in the comprehensive sense must have been very plain. On the king's face I saw a very mingled look of curiosity and sympathy.

"Do you not rush through the world too hard, Mr. Henderson?"

"Oh, yes, King, I am very restless. But the fact of the matter is I just couldn't continue as I was, where I was. Something had to be done. If I hadn't come to Africa my only other choice would have been to stay in bed. Ideally—"

"Yes, as to the ideal, I have the utmost fascination. What would it have been?"

"Well, King, I can't really say. It's all a puzzle. There is some kind of service motivation which keeps on after me. I have always admired Doctor Wilfred Grenfell. You know I was just crazy for that man. I would have liked to go on errands of mercy. Not necessarily with a dog team. But that's just a detail."

"Oh, I sensed," he said, "I should rather say, I intuited some such tendency."

"Well, I'd be happy to talk about that afterward," I said. "Right now I am asking what is the situation? Could I try my strength against Mummah? I don't know what it is, but I just have a feeling that I could move her."

He said, "I am obliged to tell you, Mr. Henderson, there may be consequences."

I should have taken him up on this and asked him what he meant by that, but I trusted the guy and could not foresee any really bad consequences. But anyway, that burning, that craving, that flowing estuary—you see what I mean?—a powerful ambition had me and I was a goner. Moreover, the king smiled and thus half retracted his warning.

"Do you really have conviction you can do it?" he said.

"All I can say to you, King, is just let me at her. All I want to do is get my arms around her."

I was in no state to identify the subtleties of the king's attitude. Now he had satisfied the requirements of his conscience, if any, and caught me, too. No man can do better than that, hey? But I had got caught up in the thing, and it had regard only to the unfinished business of years—*I want, I want,* and Lily, and the grun-tu-molani and the little colored kid brought home by my daughter from Danbury and the cat I had tried to destroy and the fate of Miss Lenox and the teeth and the fiddle and the frogs in the cistern and all the rest of it.

However, the king had not yet given his consent.

In his leopard mantle, walking with tense feet in a narrow-hipped gait, the Bunam came down from the box where he had been sitting with Horko. He was followed by the two wives with their large, shaved, delicate-looking heads and their gay short teeth. They were bigger than their husband and came along sauntering behind him and taking it easy.

The examiner, or Bunam, stopped before the king and bowed. The women, too, bowed. Small signs passed between them and the king's wives and concubines, or whatever their classification was, while the examiner addressed Dahfu. He pointed his index finger upward near his ear like a starter's pistol, bending often and stiffly from the waist. He spoke rapidly but with regularity, and seemed to know his mind very well, and when he had finished he bowed his head again and bent his eyes on me sternly as before, with a world of significance. The veins in his forehead were very heavy.

Dahfu turned to me in his gaudy hammock. In his fingers he still held the ribbons tied to the skull.

"The view of the Bunam is that you have been expected. Also you came in time. . . ."

"Your Highness, as to that . . . who can say? If you think the omens are good, I'll go along with you. Listen, Your Highness, I look like a bruiser, and I am gifted in strange ways, mostly physical; but also I am very sensitive. A while back you said something to me about envy and I must admit you kind of hurt my feelings. That's like a poem I once read called, 'Written in Prison.' I can't remember it all, but part of it goes, 'I envy e'en the fly its gleams of joy, in the green woods' and it ends, 'The fly I envy settling in the sun On the green leaf and wish my goal was won.' Now, King, you know as well as I do what goal I'm talking about. Now, Your Highness, I really do not wish to live by any law of decay. Just tell me, how long has the world got to be like this? Why should there be no hope for suffering? It so happens that I believe something can be done, and this is why I rushed out into the world as you have noted. All kinds of motives behind this. There's my wife, Lily, and then there are the children—you must have quite a few of them yourself, so maybe you'll understand how I feel. . . ."

I read sympathy in his face, and I wiped myself with my Woolworth bandanna. My nose, independently, itched within, and seemingly there was nothing I could do for it.

"Truly I regret if I wounded you," he said.

"Well, that's all right. I'm a pretty good judge of men and you are a fine one. And from you I can take it. Besides, truth is truth. Confidentially, I *have* envied flies, too. All the more reason to crash out of prison. Right? If I had the mental constitution to live inside the nutshell and think myself the king of infinite space, that would be just fine. But that's not how I am. King, I am a Becomer. Now you see your situation is different. You are a Be-er. I've just got to stop Becoming. Jesus Christ, when am I going to Be? I have waited a hell of a long time. I suppose I should be more patient, but for God's sake, Your Highness, you've got to understand what it's like with me. So I am asking you. You've got to let me out there. Why it is, I can't say, but I feel called upon to do it, and this may be my main chance." And I spoke to the examiner, who stood in his leopard mantle and cuffs, holding up the bone rod, and said, "Excuse me, sir." I held out a few fingers to him and said, "I will be with you soon." In the heat of my body and fever of mind I couldn't speak with any restraint whatever and I said, "King, I'm going to give you the straight poop about myself, as straight as I can make it. Every man born has to carry his life to a certain depth—or else! Well, King, I'm beginning to see my depth. You wouldn't expect me to back away now, would you?"

He said, "No, Mr. Henderson. In sincerity, I would not."

"Well, this is just one of those moments," I said.

He lay there, having listened with a kind of soft and even musing appreciation. "Well, whatever may come of it, I do grant the permission. As far as I am concerned I do not see why not."

"Thank you, Your Majesty. Thank you."

"Everybody is expectant."

I stood up at once and pulled my shirt over my head and hoisted up my chest broadly and passed my hands over it and over my face, and, with my shorts conforming awkwardly to my trunk, and feeling tall and huge, branded by the sun on the top of my head, I went down into the arena. I kneeled in front of the goddess—one knee. And I sized her up while drying my damp hands with dust and wiping them on my suntan pants. The yells of the Wariri, even the deep drums, came very lightly to my hearing. They occurred on a small, infinitely reduced scale, way out on the circumference of a great circle. The savagery and stridency of these Africans who mauled the gods and strung up the dead by their feet had nothing to do with the emotion of my heart. This was distinct and altogether separate, a thing unto itself. My heart desired only one great object. I had to put my arms about this huge Mummah and raise her up.

As I came closer I saw how huge she was, how overspilling and formless. She had been oiled, and glittered before my eyes. On her surface walked flies. One of these little sphinxes of the air who sat on her lip was washing himself. How fast a threatened fly departs! The decision is instantaneous and there seems to be no inertia to overcome and there is no superfluity in the way flies take off. As I began, all the flies fled with a tearing noise into the heat. Never hesitating, I encircled Mummah with my arms. I wasn't going to take no for an answer. I pressed my belly upon her and sank my knees somewhat. She smelled like a living old woman. Indeed, to me she was a living personality, not an idol. We met as challenged and challenger, but also as intimates. And with the close pleasure you experience in a dream or on one of those warm beneficial floating idle days when every desire is satisfied, I laid my cheek against her wooden bosom. I cranked down my knees and said to her, "Up you go, dearest. No use trying to make yourself heavier; if you weighed twice as much I'd lift you anyway." The wood gave to my pressure and benevolent Mummah with her fixed smile yielded to me; I lifted her from the ground and carried her twenty feet to her new place among the other gods. The Wariri jumped up and down in the white stone of their stands, screaming, singing, raving, hugging themselves and one another and praising me.

I stood still. There beside Mummah in her new situation I myself was filled with happiness. I was so gladdened by what I had done that my whole body was filled with soft heat, with soft and sacred light. The sensations of illness I had experienced since morning were all converted into their opposites. These same unhappy feelings were changed into warmth and personal luxury. You know, this kind of thing has happened to me before. I have had a bad headache change into a pain in the gums which is nothing but the signal of approaching beauty. I have known this, then, to pass down from the gums and appear again in my breast as a throb of pleasure. I have also known a stomach complaint to melt from my belly and turn into a delightful heat and go down into the genitals. This is the way I am. And so my fever was transformed into jubilation. My spirit was awake and it welcomed life anew. Damn the whole thing! Life anew! I was still alive and kicking and I had the old grun-tu-molani.

Beaming and laughing to myself, yes, sir, shining with contentment, I went back to sit beside Dahfu's hammock and wiped my face with a handkerchief, for I was anointed with sweat.

"Mr. Henderson," said the king in his African English voice, "you are indeed a person of extraordinary strength. I could not have more admiration."

"Thanks to you," I said, "for giving me such a wonderful chance. Not just hoisting up the old woman, but to get into my depth. That real depth. I mean that depth where I have always belonged."

I was grateful to him. I was his friend then. In fact, at this moment, I loved the guy.

Chapter XIV

After this feat of strength, when the sky began to fill with clouds, I was not so surprised as I might have been. From under my brows I noted their arrival. I was inclined to take it as my due.

"Ah, this shade is just what the doctor ordered," I said to King Dahfu as the first cloud passed across. For the canopy of his box was made only of ribbons, blue and purple, and there were of course the silk umbrellas but these did not really interrupt the brassy glare. However, the large cloud sailing in from eastward not only shaded us, it gave relief from the gaudy color. After my great effort, I sat quiet. My violent feelings seemed to have passed off or to have been transformed. The Wariri, however, were still demonstrating in my honor, flaunting the flags and clattering rattles and ringing hand bells while they climbed over one another with joy. That was all right. I didn't want such special credit for my achievement, especially considering how much I was the gainer personally. So I sat there and sweltered, and I pretended not to notice how the tribe was carrying on.

"But look who's here again," I said. For it was the Bunam. He stood before the box and he had his arms full of leaves and wreaths and grasses and pines. Next to him, proud and smart in her peculiar Italian-style garrison cap, was the stout woman whom Dahfu had had shake my hand when we were introduced, the generaless, as he called her, the leader of all the amazons. Accompanying her were more of these military women in their waistcoats of leather. And the tall woman who had played the skull game with the king appeared in the background, gilded and shining. She was not one of the amazons, no; but she was a personage, very high-ranking, and no great occasion was complete without her. It didn't give me much pleasure to see the Bunam, or examiner, smile, and I wondered whether he had come to express thanks or wanted something further, as the vines and leaves and wreaths and all that fodder led me to expect. Also, the women were strangely equipped. Two of them carried skulls on long rusty iron standards while others held odd-looking fly whisks which were made of strips of leather. But then from the way they grasped these instruments I suspected that they were not meant for flies. These were small whips. Now the drummers joined the group in front of the royal box and I figured they were about to begin a new rigmarole and were waiting for the king to give a signal.

"What do they want?" I asked Dahfu, for his look was directed at me rather than at the Bunam and those huge swelled nude women and the generaless in her antiquated garrison cap. The rest of them were looking at me, too. They had not come to the king, but to me. The black-leather angel-fellow, the man who had risen out of the ground with his crooked stick and sent Romilayu and me into ambush, was especially there, standing beside the Bunam. And these people had turned on me all the darkness, all the expectancy, all the wildness, all the power, of their eyes. Myself, I had remained stripped, half naked, cooling off after the labor I had performed and still panting. And under all this scrutiny of black eyes I began to worry. The king had tried to warn me that there might be consequences to my tangling with Mummah. But I had not failed. No, I was brilliant, a success.

"What do they want of me?" I said to Dahfu.

When you got right down to it he was a savage, too. He still dangled a skull (of perhaps his father) by the long smooth ribbon and wore human teeth sewed to his large-brimmed hat. Why should I expect any mercy from him when he himself, the moment he should weaken, would be doomed? I mean, if he didn't happen to be inspired by good motives, there was no reason to think that he wouldn't let evil happen to an intruding stranger. No, he might allow all hell to break loose over me. But under the velvet shade of this softly folded crownlike hat he parted his high swelled lips and said, "Now, Mr. Henderson. We have news for you. The man who moves Mummah occupies, in consequence, a position of rain king of the Wariri. The title of this post is the Sungo. You are now the Sungo, Mr. Henderson, and that is why they are here."

So I said, vigilant and mistrustful, "Give it to me in plain English. What does it mean?" And I began to say to myself, "This is a fine way to repay me for moving their goddess."

"Today you are the Sungo."

"Well, that may or may not be okay. Frankly, there's something about it that begins to make me uneasy. These guys look as if they meant business. What business? Now listen, Your Highness, don't sell me down the river. You know what I mean? I thought you liked me."

He moved a little closer to me from his swaying position in the hammock, pushing from the ground with his fingers, and said, "I do like you. Every circumstance thus far have increased my fond feeling. Why do you worry? You are the Sungo for them. They require you to go along."

I don't know why it was, but I couldn't at this moment wholly bring myself to trust the guy. "Just promise me one thing," I said, "if anything bad is going to happen, I would like a chance to send a message to my wife. Just along general lines saying good-by with love, and she has been a good woman to me basically. That's all. And don't hurt Romilayu. He hasn't done anything." I could just hear people back home saying, as at a party for instance, *"That big Henderson finally got his. What, didn't you hear? He went to Africa and disappeared in the interior. He probably bullied some natives and they stabbed him. Good riddance to bad rubbish. They say the estate is worth three million bucks. I guess he knew he was a lunatic and despised people for letting him get away with murder. Well, he was rotten to the heart."* "Rotten to the heart yourselves, you bastards." *"He was full of excess."* "Listen, you guys, my great excess was I wanted to live. Maybe I did treat everything in the world as though it was a medicine—okay! What's the matter with you guys? Don't you understand anything? Don't you believe in regeneration? You think a fellow is just supposed to go down the drain?"

"Oh, Henderson," said the king, "such suspicion. What

have made you think harm is imminent for you or your man?"

"Then why are they looking at me like that?"

The Bunam and the leathery-looking herdsman and the barbarous Negro women.

"You do not have a solitary item to fear," said Dahfu. "It is innocuous. No, no," said this strange prince of Africa, "they require your attendance to cleanse ponds and wells. They say you were sent for this purpose. Ha, ha, Mr. Henderson, you indicated earlier it was enviable to be in the bosom of the people. But that is where you now are, too."

"Yes, but I don't know the first thing about it. Anyway, you were born that way."

"Well, do not be ungrateful, Henderson. It is evident you too must have been born for something."

Well, I stood up on that one. This strange, many-figured, calcareous white stone was under my feet. That stone, too, was a world of its own, or more than a single world, world within world, in a dreaming series. I stepped down amid buzzing and cries which sounded like the interval between plays in a baseball broadcast. The examiner came up from behind and lifted off my helmet, while the stiff and stout old generaless, bending with some trouble, removed my shoes. And after this, useless to resist, she took off my Bermuda shorts. This left me in my jockey underpants, which were notably travel-stained. Nor was that the end, for as the Bunam dressed me in the vines and leaves, the generaless began to strip me of even the last covering of cotton. "No, no," I said, but by that time the underpants were already down around my knees. The worst had happened, and I was naked. The air was my only garment now. I tried to cover up with the leaves. I was dry, I was numb, I was burning, and my mouth worked silently; I tried to shield my nakedness with hands and leaves, but Tatu, the amazon generaless, pulled away my fingers and put one of those many-thonged whips into them. My clothes being taken away, I thought I would give a cry and fall and perish of shame. But I was supported by the hand of the old amazon on my back, and then urged forward. Everybody

began to yell, "Sungo, Sungo, Sungolay." Yes, that was me,
Henderson, the Sungo. We ran. We left the Bunam and the
king behind, and the arena too, and entered the crooked lanes
of the town. With feet lacerated by the stones, dazed, running
with terror in my bowels, a priest of the rain. No, the king, the
rain king. The amazons were crying and chanting in short,
loud, bold syllables. The big, bald, sensitive heads and the
open mouths and the force and power of those words—these
women with the tightly buttoned short leather garments and
swelling figures! They ran. And I amidst those naked companions, naked myself, bare fore and aft in the streamers of grass
and vine, I was dancing on burnt and cut feet over the hot
stones. I had to yell, too. Instructed by the generaless, Tatu,
who brought her face near mine with open mouth, shrieking, I
too cried, "Ya—na—bu—ni—ho—no—mum—mah!" A few
stray men, mostly old, who happened to be in the way were
beaten by the women and scrambled for their lives, and I
myself hopping naked in the flimsy leaves appeared to strike
terror into these stragglers. The skulls on the iron standards
were carried along as we ran. They were fixed on sconces. We
made a circle of the town way out as far as the gallows. Those
were dead men that hung there, each entertaining a crowd of
vultures. I passed beneath the swinging heads, having no time
to look, for we were running hard now, a hard course; panting
and sobbing I was, and saying to myself, Where the hell are
we going? We had a destination; it was a big cattle pond; the
women drew up here, leaping and chanting, and then about
ten of them threw themselves upon me. They picked me up
and gave me a heave that landed me in the super-heated sour
water in which some long-horned cattle were standing. This
water was only about six inches deep; the soft mud was far
deeper, and into this I sank. I thought they might mean me to
lie there sucked into the bottom of the pond, but now the skull
carriers offered me their iron standards, and I latched on to
these and was drawn forth. I might almost have preferred to
remain there in the mud, so low was my will. Anger was
useless. Nor was any humor intended. All was done in the

greatest earnestness. I came, dripping stale mud, out of the pond. I hoped at least this would cover my shame, for the flimsy grasses, flying, had left everything open. Not that these big fierce women subjected me to any scrutiny. No, no, they didn't care. But with the whips and skulls and guns I was whirled with them, their rain king, crying in my filth and frenzy, "Ya—na—bu—ni—ho—no—mum—mah!" as before. Yes, here he is, the mover of Mummah, the champion, the Sungo. Here comes Henderson of the U.S.A.—Captain Henderson, Purple Heart, veteran of North Africa, Sicily, Monte Cassino, etc., a giant shadow, a man of flesh and blood, a restless seeker, pitiful and rude, a stubborn old lush with broken bridgework, threatening death and suicide. Oh, you rulers of heaven! Oh, you dooming powers! Oh, I will black out! I will crash into death, and they will throw me on the dung heap, and the vultures will play house in my paunch. And with all my heart I yelled, "Mercy, have mercy!" And after that I yelled, "No, justice!" And after that I changed my mind and cried, "No, no, truth, truth!" And then, "Thy will be done! Not my will, but Thy will!" This pitiful rude man, this poor stumbling bully, lifting up his call to heaven for truth. Do you hear that?

We were yelling and jumping and whirling through terrified lanes, feet pounding, drums and skulls keeping pace. And meanwhile the sky was filling with hot, gray, long shadows, rain clouds, but to my eyes of an abnormal form, pressed together like organ pipes or like the ocean ammonites of Paleozoic times. With swollen throats the amazons cried and howled, and I, lumbering with them, tried to remember who I was. *Me.* With the slime-plastered leaves drying on my skin. The king of the rain. It came to me that still and all there must be some distinction in this, but of what kind I couldn't say.

Under the thickened rain clouds, a heated, darkened breeze sprang up. It had a smoky odor. This was something oppressive, insinuating, choky, sultry, icky. Desirous, the air was, and it felt tumescent, heavy. It was very heavy. It yearned for discharge, like a living thing. Covered with sweat,

the generaless with her arm urged me, rolling great eyes and
panting. The mud dried stiffly and made a kind of earth
costume for me. Inside it I felt like Vesuvius, all the upper part
flame and the blood banging upward like the pitch or magma.
The whips were hissing and gave a dry, mean sound, and I
wondered what in hell are they doing. After the gust of breeze
came deeper darkness, like the pungent heat of the trains
when they pass into Grand Central tunnel on a devastated
day of August, which is like darkness eternal. At that moment
I have always closed my eyes.

But I couldn't close them now. We ran back to the arena,
where the tribesmen of the Wariri were waiting. As the rain
was still held back, so were their voices from my hearing, by a
very thin dam, one of the thinnest. I heard Dahfu saying to
me, "After all, Mr. Henderson, you may lose the wager." For
we were again in front of his box. He gave an order to Tatu,
the generaless, and we all turned and rushed into the arena—I
with the rest, spinning around inspired, in spite of my great
weight, in spite of the angry cuts on my feet. My heart rioting,
my head dazed, and filled with something like the fulgor of
that vacant Pacific scene beside which I had walked with
Edward. Nothing but white, seething, and the birds arguing
over the herrings, with great clouds about. On the many-
figured white stones I saw the people standing, leaping,
frantic, under the oppression of Mummah's great clouds,
those colossal tuberous forms almost breaking. There was a
great delirium. They were shrieking, shrieking. And of all
these shrieks, my head, the rain king's head, was the hive. All
were flying toward me, entering my brain. Above all this I
heard the roaring of lions, while the dust was shivering under
my feet.

The women about me were dancing, if you want to call it
that. They were bounding and screaming and banging their
bodies into me. All together we were nearing the gods who
stood in their group, with Hummat and Mummah looking
over the heads of the rest. And now I wanted to fall on the
ground to avoid any share in what seemed to me a terrible

thing, for these women, the amazons, were rushing upon the figures of the gods with those short whips of theirs and striking them. "Stop!" I yelled. "Quit it! What's the matter? Are you crazy?" It would have been different, perhaps, if this had been a token whipping and the gods were merely touched with the thick leather straps. But great violence was loosed on these figures, so that the smaller ones rocked as they were beaten while the bigger without any change of face bore it defenseless. Those children of darkness, the tribe, rose and screamed like gulls on stormy water. And then I did fall to the ground. Naked, I threw myself down, roaring, "No, no, no!" But Tatu grasped me by the arm and with an effort raised me to my knees. So that, on my knees, I was pulled forward into this, crawling on the ground. My hand, which had the whip still in it, was lifted once or twice and brought down so that against my will I was made to perform the duty of the rain king. "Oh, I can't do this. You'll never make me," I was saying. "Oh, batter me and kill me. Run a spit up me and bake me over the fire." I tried to hide against the earth and in this posture was struck on the back of the head with a whip and afterward on the face as well, as the women were swinging in all directions now and struck one another as well as me and the gods. Caught up in this madness, I fended off blows from my position on my knees, for it seemed to me that I was fighting for my life, and I yelled. Until a thunder clap was heard.

And then, after a great, neighing, cold blast of wind, the clouds opened and the rain began to fall. Gouts of water like hand grenades burst all about and on me. The face of Mummah, which had been streaked by the whips, was now covered with silver bubbles, and the ground began to foam. The amazons with their wet bodies began to embrace me. I was too stunned to push them off. I have never seen such water. It was like the Dutch flood that swept over Alva's men when the sea walls were opened. In this torrent the people were hidden from me. I looked for Dahfu's box concealed in the storm and I worked my way around the arena, following the white stone with my hand. Then I met Romilayu, who recoiled from me as if I were dangerous to him. His hair was hugely flattened by the storm and his face showed great fear. "Romilayu," I said, "please, man, you've got to help me. Look at the condition I'm in. Find my clothes. Where is the king? Where are they all? Pick up my clothes—my helmet," I said. "I've got to have my helmet."

Naked, I held on to him and bent over, my feet slipping as he led me to the king's box. Four women were holding a cover over Dahfu to keep off the rain and his hammock had been raised. They were carrying him away.

"King, King," I cried.

He drew aside the edge of the cover they had thrown over him. Under it I saw him there in his broad-brimmed hat. I cried out to him, "What has struck us?"

He said simply, "It is rain."

"Rain? What rain? It's the deluge. It feels like the end. . . ."

"Mr. Henderson," he said, "it is a great thing you have performed for us, after which pains we must give you some pleasure, too." And seeing the look on my face he said, "Do you see, Mr. Henderson, the gods know us." And as he was carried from me in his hammock, the eight women supporting the poles, he said, "You have lost the wager."

I was left standing in my coat of earth, like a giant turnip.

Chapter XV

This is how I became the rain king. I guess it served me right for mixing into matters that were none of my damned business. But the thing had been irresistible, one of those drives which there was no question of fighting. And what had I got myself into? What were the consequences? On the ground floor of the palace, filthy, naked, and bruised, I lay in a little room. The rain was falling, drowning the town, dropping from the roof in heavy fringes, witchlike and gloomy. Shivering, I covered myself with hides and stared with circular eyes, wrapped to the chin in the skins of unknown animals, I kept saying, "Oh, Romilayu, don't be down on me. How was I supposed to know what I was getting myself into?" My upper lip grew long and my nose was distorted; it was aching with the whiplashes and I felt my eyes had grown black and huge. "Oh, I'm in a bad way. I lost the bet and am at the guy's mercy."

But as before Romilayu came through for me. He tried to hearten me a little and said he didn't think that worse was to be expected, and indicated that it was premature for me to feel trapped. He made very good sense. Then he said, "You sleep, sah. T'ink tomorrow."

And I said, "Romilayu, I'm learning more about your good points all the time. You're right, I've got to wait. I'm in a position and don't have a glimmer as to what it is."

Then he, too, prepared for sleep and got down on his shinbones, clasping his hands with the muscles beginning to jump under his skin and the groans of prayer arising from his chest. I must admit I took some comfort from this.

I said to him, "Pray, pray. Oh, pray, pal, pray like anything. Pray about the situation."

So when he was done he wound himself into the blanket and drew up his knees, slipping his hand under his cheek as usual. But before closing his eyes he said, "Whut fo' you did it, sah?"

"Oh, Romilayu," I said, "if I could explain that I wouldn't be where I am today. Why did I have to blast those holy frogs without looking left or right? I don't know why it is I have such extreme intensity. The whole thing is so peculiar the explanation will have to be peculiar too. Figuring will get me nowhere, it's only illumination that I have to wait for." And thinking of how black things were and how absent any illumination was I sighed and moaned again.

Instead of troubling himself that I hadn't been able to give a satisfactory answer, Romilayu fell asleep, and presently I passed out too while the rain whirled and the lion or lions roared beneath the palace. Mind and body went to rest. It was like a swoon. I had a ten-days' growth of beard on my face. Dreams and visions came to me but I don't need to speak of them; all that is necessary to say is that nature was kind to me and I must have slept twelve hours without stirring, sore in body as I was, with cut feet and a bruised face.

When I awoke the sky was clear and warm, and Romilayu was up and about. Two women, amazons, were in the small room with me. I washed myself and shaved and did my business in a large basin placed in the corner, I assumed, for that purpose. Then the women, whom I had ordered out, came back with some articles of clothing which Romilayu said were the Sungo's, or rain king's, outfit. He insisted that I had better wear them as it might make trouble to refuse. For I was now the Sungo. Therefore I examined these garments. They were green and made of silk, and cut to the same pattern as King Dahfu's—the drawers were, I mean.

"Belong Sungo," said Romilayu. "Now you Sungo."

"Why, these damned pants are transparent," I said, "but I suppose I'd better wear them." I was wearing my stained jockey shorts above-mentioned, and I slipped on the green trousers over them. In spite of my rest I was not in top condition. I still had fever. I suppose it is natural for white men to be ill in Africa. Sir Richard Burton was as close to iron as the flesh can be, and he was taken badly with fever. Speke was even sicker. Mungo Park was sick and staggered around. Dr. Livingstone day in, day out was sick. Hell! Who was I to be immune? One of the amazons, Tamba, who had ugly whiskers growing from her chin, got behind me, lifted my helmet, and combed at my head with a primitive wooden instrument. These women were supposed to render me service.

She said to me, "Joxi, joxi?"

"What does she want? What is this joxi? Breakfast? I have no appetite. I feel too emotional to swallow anything." I drank a little whisky instead from one of the canteens, merely to keep my digestive tract open; I thought it might help my fever as well.

"Dem show you joxi," said Romilayu.

Face downward, Tamba stretched herself on the ground and the other woman, whose name was Bebu, stood upon her back and with her feet she kneaded and massaged her and cracked her vertebrae into place. After she had plied her with those ugly feet—and to judge from the face of Tamba, the process was bliss—they changed positions. Afterward they tried to show me how beneficial it was and how it set them up. Together they tapped their chests with their knuckles.

"Tell them thanks for their good intentions," I said. "It's probably wonderful therapy, but I think I'll pass it by today."

After this Tamba and Bebu lay on the ground and took turns in saluting me formally. Each took my foot and placed it on her head as Itelo had done to acknowledge my supremacy. The women moistened their lips so that the dust should stick to them. When they were done Tatu the generaless came to conduct me to King Dahfu and she went through the identical abasement, with the garrison cap on her head. After this the two women brought me a pineapple on a wooden platter and I forced myself to swallow a slice of it.

Then I went up the stairs with Tatu, who today allowed me to take the lead. Grins, cries, blessings, handclapping, and chanting met me; the older people were especially earnest in speaking to me. I wasn't as yet used to the green costume; it felt both wide and loose about the legs. From the upper gallery I looked out and saw the mountains. The air was exceptionally clear and the mountains were gathered together lap over lap, brown and soft as the coat of a Brahma bull. Also the green looked as fine as fur today. The trees were clear and green, too, and the blossoms underneath were fresh and red in the bowls of white rock. I saw the Bunam's wives pass below us with their short teeth, turning their dainty big shaven heads. I guess I must have caused them to smile in those billowing, swelling, green drawers of the Sungo and the pith helmet and my rubber-soled desert boots.

Indoors, we passed through the anterooms and entered the king's apartment. His big tufted couch was empty, but the wives lay on their cushions and mats gossiping and combing their hair and trimming their fingernails and toes. The atmosphere was very social and talkative. Most of the women lay resting, and their form of relaxation was peculiar; they folded their legs as we might our arms and lay back, perfectly boneless. Amazing. I stared at them. The odor of the room was tropical, like certain parts of the botanical garden, or like charcoal fumes and honey, like hot buckwheat. No one looked at me, they pretended I was nonexistent. To me this appeared kind of impossible, like refusing to see the *Titanic*. Besides, I was the sensation of the place, the white Sungo who had picked up Mummah. But I figured it was improper for me to visit their quarters, and they had no alternative but to ignore me.

We left the apartment by a low door and I found myself then in the king's private chamber. He was sitting on a low backless seat, a square of red leather stretched over a broad frame. A similar seat was brought forward for me, and then Tatu withdrew and sat obscurely near the wall. Once more he and I were face to face. There was no tooth-bordered hat, there were no skulls. He had on the close-fitting trousers and the embroidered slippers. Beside him on the floor was a whole stack of books; he had been reading when I entered, and he folded down the corner of his page, pressed it several times with his knuckle, and put the volume on top of the pile. What sort of reading would interest such a mind? But then what sort of mind was it? I didn't have a clue.

"Oh," he said, "now you have shaved and rested you make a very good appearance."

"I feel like a holy show, that's what I feel like, King. But I understand that you want me to wear this rig, and I wouldn't like to welsh on a bet. I can only say that if you'd let me out I'd be grateful as anything."

"I understand," he said. "I would very much like to do so, but the clothing of the Sungo really is requisite. Except for the helmet."

"I have to be on my guard against sunstroke," I said.

"Anyway, I always have some headpiece or other. In Italy during the war I slept in my helmet, too. And it was a metal helmet."

"But surely a headcover indoors is not necessary," he said.

However, I refused to take the hint. I sat before him in my white pith hat.

Of course the king's extreme blackness of color made him fabulously strange to me. He was as black as—as wealth. By contrast his lips were red, and they swelled; and on his head the hair lived (to say that it grew wouldn't be sufficient). Like Horko's, his eyes revealed a red tinge. And even seated on the backless leather chair he was still, as on the sofa or in the hammock, sumptuously at rest.

"King," I said.

From the determination with which I began he understood me and he said, "Mr. Henderson, you are entitled to any explanation within my means to make. You see, the Bunam felt sure you would be strong enough to move our Mummah. I, when I saw what a construction you had, agreed with him. At once."

"Well," I said, "okay, so I'm strong. But how did it all happen? It seems to me that you were sure it would. You bet me."

"That was in a spirit of wager and nothing else," he said. "I knew as little about it as you do."

"Does it always happen like that?"

"Very far from always. Exceedingly seldom."

I looked my canniest, greatly lifting up my brows because I wanted him to see that the phenomenon was not yet explained to my satisfaction. Meanwhile I was trying also to make him out. And there were no airs or ostentations about the man. He was thoughtful in his replies but without making thinker's faces. And when he spoke of himself the facts he told me matched what I had heard from Prince Itelo. At the age of thirteen he had been sent to the town of Lamu and afterward he had gone to Malindi. "All preceding kings for several generations," he said, "have had to be acquainted with the

world and have been sent at that same time of life to the
school. You show up from nowhere, attend school, then go
back. One son in each generation is sent out to Lamu. An
uncle goes with him and waits for him there."

"Your Uncle Horko?"

"Yes, it is Horko. He was the link. He waited in Lamu nine
years for me. I had moved on with Itelo. I didn't care for that
life in the south. The young men at school were spoiled. Kohl
on their eyes. Rouge. Chitter-chatter. I wanted more than
that."

"Well, you are very serious," I said. "It's obvious. That was
how I sized you up from the first."

"After Malindi, Zanzibar. From there Itelo and I shipped as
deckhands. Once to India and Java. Then up the Red
Sea—Suez. Five years in Syria at denominational school. The
treatment was most generous. From my point of view the
science instruction was most especially worth while. I was
going for an M.D. degree, and would have done it except for
the death of my father."

"That's just remarkable," I said. "I'm only trying to put it
together with yesterday. With the skulls, and that fellow, the
Bunam, and the amazons and the rest of it."

"It is interesting, I do admit. But also it is not up to me,
Henderson—Henderson-Sungo—to make the world consistent."

"Maybe you were tempted not to come back?" I asked.

We sat close together, and, as I have noted, his blackness
made him fabulously strange to me. Like all people who have
a strong gift of life, he gave off almost an extra shadow—I
swear. It was a smoky something, a charge. I used to notice it
sometimes with Lily and was aware of it particularly that day
of the storm in Danbury when she misdirected me to the
water-filled quarry and then telephoned her mother from bed.
She had it noticeably then. It is something brilliant and yet
overcast; it is smoky, bluish, trembling, shining like jewel
water. It was similar to what I had felt also arising from
Willatale on the occasion of kissing her belly. But this King

Dahfu was more strongly supplied with it than any person I ever met.

In answer to my last question he said, "For more reasons than one I could have wished my father to live longer."

As I conceived, the old fellow must have been strangled.

I guess I looked remorseful at having reminded him of his father, for he laughed to put me at ease again, and said, "Do not worry, Mr. Henderson—I must call you Sungo, for you are the Sungo now. Don't worry, I say. It is a subject which could not be avoided. You do not necessarily refresh it. His time came, he died, and I was king. I had to recover the lion."

"What lion are you talking about?" I said.

"Why, I have told you yesterday. Possibly you have forgot—the king's body, the maggot that breeds in it, the king's soul, the lion cub?" I recalled it now. Sure, he had told me this. "Well, then," he said, "this very young animal, set free by the Bunam, the successor king has to capture it within a year or two when it is grown."

"What? You have to hunt it?"

He smiled. "Hunt it? I have another function. To capture it alive and keep it with me."

"So that's the animal I hear below? I could swear I was hearing a lion down there. Jupiter, so that's what it is," I said.

"No, no, no," he said, in that soft way of his. "That is not it, Mr. Henderson-Sungo. You have heard a quite other animal. I have not yet captured Gmilo. Accordingly I am not yet fully confirmed in the rule of king. You find me at a midpoint. To borrow your manner of speaking, I too must complete Becoming."

Despite all the shocks of yesterday I was beginning to comprehend why I felt reassured at first sight of the king. It comforted me to sit with him; it comforted me unusually. His large legs were stretched out as he sat, his back was curved, and his arms were folded on his chest, and on his face there was a brooding but pleasant expression. Through his high-swelled lips a low hum occasionally came. It reminded me of the sound you sometimes hear from a power station when you

pass one in New York on a summer night; the doors are open;
all the brass and steel is going, lustrous under one little light,
and some old character in dungarees and carpet slippers is
smoking a pipe with all the greatness of the electricity behind
him. Probably I am one of the most spell-prone people who
ever lived. Appearances to the contrary, I am highly mediumistic and attuned. "Henderson," I said to myself, and not for
the first time, "it's one of those *luth suspendu* deals, *sitôt qu'on
le touche il résonne.* And you saw yesterday what savagery can
be if you never saw it before, throwing passes with his own
father's skull. And now with the lions. Lions! And the man
almost a graduate physician. The whole thing is crazy." Thus I
reflected. But then I also had to take into account the fact that
I have a voice within me repeating, *I want,* raving and
demanding, making a chaos, desiring, desiring, and disappointed continually, which drove me forth as beaters drive
game. So I had no business to make terms with life, but had to
accept such conditions as it would let me have. But at
moments I would have been glad to find that my fever alone
had originated all that had happened since I left Charlie and
his bride and took off on my own expedition—the Arnewi, the
frogs, Mtalba, and the corpse and the gallop in vine leaves
with those giant women. And now this powerful black
personage who soothed me—but was he trustworthy? How
about trustworthy? And I, myself, hulking in the green silk
pants that went with the office of rain king. I was smarting,
harkening, straining my ears, my suspicious eyes. Oh, hell!
How shall a man be broken for whom reality has no fixed
dwelling! How he shall be broken! So I was sitting in this
palace with its raw red walls, and the white rocks amid which
the flowers flourished. By the door were amazons, and, more
particularly, this fierce old Tatu with big nostrils. She sat
dreaming on the floor in her garrison cap.

All the same, as we sat there talking I felt we were men of
unusual dimensions. Trustworthiness was a separate issue.

At this time there began a conversation which could never
be duplicated anywhere in the world. I hitched up the green

pants a little. My head was swayed by the fever but I demanded firmness of myself and I said, speaking steadily, "Your Majesty, I don't intend to back down on the bet. I have certain principles. But I still don't know what this is all about, being dressed up as the rain king."

"It is not merely dress," said Dahfu. "You are the Sungo. It is literal, Mr. Henderson. I could not have made Sungo of you if you had not had the strength to move Mummah."

"Well, that's okay then—but the rest, with the gods? I felt very bad, Your Highness, I don't mind telling you. I could never claim that I led a very good life. I'm sure it's written all over me. . . ." The king nodded. "I've done a hell of a lot of things, too, both as a soldier and a civilian. I'll say it straight out, I don't even deserve to be chronicled on toilet paper. But when I saw them start to beat Mummah and Hummat and all the others, I fell to the ground. It got to be pretty dark out there and I don't know whether you saw that or not."

"I saw you. It is not my idea, Henderson, of how to be." The king spoke softly. "I have far other ideas. You will see. But shall we speak only to each other?"

"You want to do me a favor, Your Highness, a big favor? The biggest favor possible?"

"Assuredly. Why certainly."

"All right, then, this is it: will you expect the truth from me? That's my only hope. Without it everything else might as well go bust."

He began to smile. "Why, how could I refuse you this? I am glad, Henderson-Sungo, but you must let me make the same request, otherwise it will be worthless if not mutual. But do you have expectation as to the form the truth is to take? Are you prepared if it comes in another shape, unanticipated?"

"Your Majesty, it's a deal. This is a pact between us. Oh, you don't understand how great a favor you're doing me. When I left the Arnewi (and I may as well tell you that I goofed there—maybe you know it) I thought that I had lost my last chance. I was just about to find out about the grun-tu-molani when this terrible thing happened, which was

all my fault, and I left under a cloud. Christ, I was humiliated.
You see, Your Highness, I keep thinking about the spirit's
sleep and when the hell is it ever going to burst. So yesterday,
when I became the rain king—oh, what an experience! How
will I ever communicate it to Lily (my wife)?"

"I do appreciate this, Mr. Henderson-Sungo. I intentionally
wished to keep you with me a while hoping that exchanges of
importance would be possible. For I do not find it easy to
express myself to my own people. Only Horko has been in the
world at all and with him I cannot freely exchange, either.
They are against me here. . . ."

This he said almost secretly, and after he spoke his broad
lips closed and the room became still. The amazons lay on the
floor as if asleep—Tatu in her hat and the other two naked
save for the leather jerkin articles they wore. Their black eyes
were only just open, but watchful. I could hear the wives
behind the thick door of our inner room, stirring there.

"You are right," I said. "It's not just a question of expecting
the truth. There's another question, too, of solitude. As if a
guy were his own grave. When he comes forth from this burial
he doesn't know good from bad. So for instance it has been
going through my mind for some time that there is a
connection between truth and blows."

"How is that again? You thought what?"

"Well, it's this way. Last winter as I was chopping wood a
piece flew up from the block and broke my nose. So the first
thing I thought was *truth!*"

"Ah," said the king, and then he began to speak, intimate
and low, of a variety of things I had never heard before, and I
stared toward him with my eyes grown big. "As things are," he
said, "such may appear to be related to the case. I do not
believe actually it is so. But I feel there is a law of human
nature in which force is concerned. Man is a creature who
cannot stand still under blows. Now take the horse—he never
needs a revenge. Nor the ox. But man is a creature of
revenges. If he is punished he will contrive to get rid of the
punishment. When he cannot get rid of punishment, his heart

is apt to rot from it. This may be—don't you think so, Mr. Henderson-Sungo? Brother raises a hand against brother and son against father (how terrible!) and the father also against son. And moreover it is a continuity-matter, for if the father did not strike the son, they would not be alike. It is done to perpetuate similarity. Oh, Henderson, man cannot keep still under the blows. If he must, for the time, he will cast down his eyes and think in silence of the ways to clear himself of them. Those prime-eval blows everybody still feels. The first was supposed to be struck by Cain, but how could that be? In the beginning of time there was a hand raised which struck. So the people are flinching yet. All wish to rid themselves and free themselves and cast the blow upon the others. And this I conceive of as the earthly dominion. But as for the truth content of the force, that is a separate matter."

The room was all shadow, but the heat with its odor of vegetable combustion pervaded the air.

"Wait a minute, now, sire," I said, having frowned and bitten on my lips. "Let me see if I have got you straight. You say the soul will die if it can't make somebody else suffer what it suffers?"

"For a while, I am sorry to say, it then feels peace and joy."

I lifted up my brows, and with difficulty, as the whiplashes all over the unprotected parts of my face were atrocious. I gave him one of my high looks, from one eye, "You are sorry to say, Your Highness? Is this why me and the gods had to be beaten?"

"Well, Henderson, I should have notified you better when you wished to move Mummah. To that extent you are right."

"But you thought I would be the fellow to do the job, and thought so before I laid eyes on them." Then I cut out the reproaches. I said to him, "You want to know something, Your Highness, there are some guys who can return good for evil. Even I understand that. Crazy as I am," I said. I began to tremble in all my length and breadth as I realized on which side of the issue I stood, and had stood all the time.

Curiously, I saw that he agreed with me. He was glad I had

said this. "Every brave man will think so," he told me. "He will not want to live by passing on the wrath. A hit B? B hit C?—we have not enough alphabet to cover the condition. A brave man will try to make the evil stop with him. He shall keep the blow. No man shall get it from him, and that is a sublime ambition. So, a fellow throws himself in the sea of blows saying he do not believe it is infinite. In this way many courageous people have died. But an even larger number who had more of impatience than bravery. Who have said, 'Enough of the burden of wrath. I cannot bear my neck should be unfree. I cannot eat more of this mess of fear-pottage.' "

I wish to say at this place that the beauty of King Dahfu's person prevailed with me as much as his words, if not more. His black skin shone as if with the moisture that gathers on plants when they reach their prime. His back was long and muscular. His high-rising lips were a strong red. Human perfections are short-lived, and we love them more than we should, maybe. But I couldn't help it. The thing was involuntary. I felt a pang in my gums, where such things register themselves without my will and then I knew how I was affected by him.

"Yet you are right for the long run, and good exchanged for evil truly is the answer. I also subscribe, but it appears a long way off, for the human specie as a whole. Perhaps I am not the one to make a prediction, Sungo, but I think the noble will have its turn in the world."

I was swayed; I thrilled when I heard this. Christ! I would have given anything I had to hear another man say this to me. My heart was moved to such an extent that I felt my face stretch until it must have been as long as a city block. I was blazing with fever and mental excitement because of the loftiness of our conversation and I saw things not double or triple merely, but in countless outlines of wavering color, gold, red, green, umber, and so on, all flowing concentrically around each object. Sometimes Dahfu seemed to be three times his size, with the spectrum around him. Larger than life, he loomed over me and spoke with more than one voice. I gripped my legs through the green silk trousers of the Sungo and I am sure I must have been demented at that time. Slightly. I was really sent, and I mean it. The king treated me with classic African dignity, and this is one of the summits of human behavior. I don't know where else people can be so dignified. Here, in the midst of darkness, in a small room in a hidden fold near the equator, in this same town where I had struggled along with the corpse on my back under the moon and the blue forests of heaven. Why, if a spider should get a stroke and suddenly begin to do a treatise on botany or something—a transfigured vermin, do you follow me? This is how I embraced the king's words about nobility's having its turn in the world.

"King Dahfu," I said, "I hope you will consider me your friend. I am deeply affected by what you say. Though I am a little woozy from all the novelty—the strangeness. Nevertheless I feel lucky here. Yesterday I took a beating. Well, all right. Since I am a suffering type of man anyhow, I am glad at least it served a purpose for a change. But let me ask you, when the noble gets its turn—how is that ever going to take place?"

"You would like to know what gives me such a confidence that my prediction will ultimately come?"

"Well, sure," I said, "of course. I am curious as all get-out. I mean what practical approach do you recommend?"

"I do not conceal, Mr. Henderson-Sungo, that I have a conception about it. As a matter of fact I do not wish it to be a secret with me. I am most eager to advance it to you. I am glad you want to consider me as a friend. Without reserve, I am developing a similar attitude toward you. Your coming has made me joyful. About the Sungo trouble I am genuinely very sorry. We could not refrain from making use of you. It was because of the circumstances. You will pardon me." This was practically an order, but I was only too glad to obey it, and I pardoned the guy, all right. I was not too corrupted or beat on the head by life to identify the extraordinary. I saw

that he was some kind of genius. Much more than that. I
realized that he was a genius of my own mental type.

"Well, sure, Your Highness. No question about that. I
wanted you to make use of me yesterday. I said so myself."

"Well, thank you, Mr. Henderson-Sungo. So that is over.
Do you know from the flesh standpoint you are something of
a figure? You are rather monumental. I am speaking somat-
ically."

At this I became somewhat stiff, as it had a dubious sound,
and I said, "Is that so?"

The king exclaimed, "Do not let us go backward on our
truth agreement, Mr. Henderson."

At this I got off my high horse. "Oh, no, Your Highness.
That stands," I said. "Come what may. That was no bull. I
meant every word and I want you to hold me to it."

This pleased him, and he told me, "I observed before, as to
truth, a person may be unready to receive except what he has
anticipated as true. However, I was referring to your outer
man as a formation. It speaks for itself in many ways."

With his eyes he referred to the pile of books beside his seat
as though they had a bearing on the matter. I turned my head
to read the titles but the room was too obscurely lighted for
that.

He said, "You are very fierce-looking."

This is no news to me; nevertheless, from him, this
observation hurt me. "Well, what do you want?" I said. "I am
the type of guy who couldn't survive without disfigurement.
Life has worked me over. It wasn't just the war, either. . . . I
got a bad wound, you know. But the shots of life . . ." I gave
myself a bang on the breast. "Right here! You know what I
mean, King? But naturally I don't want even such a life as
mine to be thrown away, the fact that I have sometimes
threatened suicide to the contrary notwithstanding. If I can't
make an active contribution at least I should illustrate
something. Even that I don't know anything about. I don't
seem to illustrate a thing."

"Oh, this is erroneous of you. You illustrate volumes," he

said. "To me you are a treasure of illustrations. I do not condemn your looks. Only I see the world in your constitution. In my medical study this became the greatest of fascinations to me and independently I have made a thorough study of the types, resulting in an entire classification system, as: The agony. The appetite. The obstinate. The immune elephant. The shrewd pig. The fateful hysterical. The death-accepting. The phallic-proud or hollow genital. The fast asleep. The narcissus intoxicated. The mad laughers. The pedantics. The fighting Lazaruses. Oh, Henderson-Sungo, how many shapes and forms! Numberless!"

"I see. This is quite a subject."

"Oh, yes, indeed. I have devoted years, and observed all the way from Lamu to Istanbul and Athens."

"A big chunk of the world," I said. "So tell me, what do I illustrate most?"

"Why," he said, "everything about you, Henderson-Sungo, cries out, 'Salvation, salvation! What shall I do? What must I do? At once! What will become of me?' And so on. That is bad."

At this moment I could not have concealed how astonished I was even if I had taken a Ph.D. degree in concealment, and I mused, "Yes. This was what Willatale was beginning to tell me, I guess. Grun-tu-molani was just a starter."

"I know that Arnewi expression," said the king. "Yes, I have been there, too, with Itelo. I understand what this grun-tu-molani implies. Indeed I do. And I know the lady also, a great success, a human gem, a triumph of the type—I refer to my system of classification. Granted, grun-tu-molani is much, but it is not alone sufficient. Mr. Henderson, more is required. I can show you something now—something without which you will never understand thoroughly my special aim nor my point of view. Will you come with me?"

"Where to?"

"I cannot say. You must trust me."

"Well, sure. Okay. I guess. . . ."

My consent was all he wanted and he rose, and Tatu, who

had been sitting by the wall with the garrison cap over her
eyes, got up too.

Chapter XVI

From this small room the door opened into a long gallery
screened with thatch. Tatu, the amazon, let us out and then
followed us. The king was already far ahead of me down this
private gallery of his. I tried to keep up with him, and the
necessity of walking faster made me feel how yesterday's cuts
had crippled my feet. So I hobbled and shambled while Tatu
in her sturdy military stride came behind me. She had bolted
the door of the small room from outside so that nobody could
follow, and after we had crossed the gallery, which was about
fifty feet long, she lifted another heavy wood bolt from the
door at that end. This must have weighed like iron, for her
knees sank, but the old woman had a powerful build and
knew her job. The king went through, and I saw a staircase
descending. It was wide enough, but dark—black ahead. A
corrupt moldering smell rose from this darkness, which made
me choke a little. But the king went right through into the
moldering darkness and I thought, "What this calls for is a
miner's lamp or a cage of canaries," trying to josh the fears
out of my heart. "But okay," I thought, "if I've got to go,
down I go. One, two, three, and on your way, Captain
Henderson." You see, at such a moment, I would call on my
military self. Thus I mastered my anxious feelings, chiefly by
making my legs go, and entered this darkness. "King?" I said,
when I was in. But there was no answer. My voice had a
quaver, I heard it myself, and then I caught the rapid
pounding of steps below. I extended both arms, but found no
rail or wall. However, by the cautious use of my feet I
discovered that the stairs were broad and even. All light from
above was cut off when Tatu slammed the door. Next moment
I heard a heavy bolt bump into place. Now I had no

alternative except to follow downward or to sit down and wait until the king turned back to me. With which alternative I risked the loss of his respect and all the rest that I had gained yesterday by overcoming Mummah. Therefore I continued, while I told myself what a rare and probably great man that king was, how he must be nothing less than a genius, and how astonishing his personal beauty was, how the hum he made reminded me of that power station on 16th Street in New York on a hot night, how we were friends, and bound by a truth-telling agreement; finally, how he predicted that nobility had a greater future than ever. Of all the elements in the catalogue, this last had most appeal to me. Thus I groped with sore feet after him and kept saying to myself, "Have faith, Henderson, it's about time you had some faith." Presently there was some light and the end of the staircase came in view. The width of the stairs was due to the architectural crudeness of the palace. I was now beneath the building. Daylight came from a narrow opening above my head; this light was originally yellow but became gray by contact with stones. In the opening two iron spikes were set to keep even a child from creeping through. Examining my situation I found a small passage cut from the granite which led downward to another flight of stairs, which were of stone too. These were narrower and ran to a great depth, and soon I found them broken, with grass springing and soil leaking out through the cracks. "King," I called, "King, hey, are you down there, Your Highness?"

But nothing came from below except drafts of warm air that lifted up the spider webs. "What's the guy's hurry?" I thought, and my cheeks twitched and I continued to go down. Instead of cooling, the air appeared warmer, the light filled up the stony space like a gray and yellow fluid, the surfaces of the wall acting as a filter, for the atmosphere was distributed as evenly as water. I came to the bottom, the last few steps being of earth and the bases of the walls themselves mixed with soil. Which recalled to me the speckled vision of twilight at Banyules-sur-Mer in that aquarium, where I saw that creature,

the octopus, pressing its head against the glass. But where I
had felt coldness there, here I felt very warm. I proceeded,
feeling my apparel—the helmet, of course, but even the green
silk pants of the rain king, which were light and flimsy—as
excessive, a drag on me. By and by the walls became more
spacious and widened into a sort of cave. To the left the
tunnel went off into darkness. This I certainly had no
intention of entering. The other way, there stood a semicircu-
lar wall in which there was a large door barred with wood. It
was partly open and on the edge of this door I saw Dahfu's
hand. For about the count of twenty, this was as much of him
as I saw, but it wasn't necessary now to ask myself where he
had been leading me. A low ripping sound behind the door
was self-explanatory. It was the lion's den. And because the
door was ajar I thought it advisable not to budge. I froze
where I was, as there was only the king between me and the
animal, of which I now began to see glimpses. This beast was
not the one he had to capture. I didn't yet understand exactly
what his relations with it were, but I did realize that he himself
had no hesitation about entering, but had to prepare the
animal for me. I was expected to go into the den with him.
There was no question about that. And now when I heard that
ripping, soft, dangerous sound the creature made, I felt as if I
had got astride a rope. Seemingly it passed between my knees.
I was under strict orders to myself to have faith, but as a
soldier I had to think of my line of retreat, and here I was in a
bad way. If I went up the stairs, at the top I would encounter a
bolted door. It would do no good to knock or cry. Tatu would
never open, and I could see myself chased all the way up and
lying there with the animal washing its face in my blood. I
expected the liver to go first, as with beasts of prey it is like
that, they eat the most nutritious and valuable organ immediately. My other course lay into that dark tunnel, and this I
speculated led to another closed door, probably. So I stood in
those sad green pants with the stained jockey shorts under
them, trying to steel myself. Meanwhile the snarling and
ripping rose and fell and I became also aware of the voice of

the king; he was talking to the animal, sometimes in Wariri, and sometimes in English, perhaps for my benefit, in order to reassure me. "Easy, easy, sweetheart. Here, here, my dolly." Thus it was a female, and he spoke low and steadily, calming her, and without raising his voice he said to me, "Henderson-Sungo, she now knows you are there. Gradually you must advance closer—little by little."

"Should I, Your Highness?"

He raised his hand toward me from the door, and his fingers moved. I came forward one step and I cannot deny that there lay over my consciousness the shadow of the cat I had attempted to shoot under the bridge table. There was little besides the king's arm that I could see. He kept beckoning and I took extremely small steps in my rubber-soled shoes. The snarls of the animal were now as sharp as thorns to me, and blind patches as big as silver dollars came and went before my eyes. Between these opaque interruptions I could see the body of the animal as it flowed back and forth before the opening—the calm, murderous face and clear eyes and the heavy feet. The king reached backward and touched me; he gathered my arm in his fingers and drew me to his side. He now held me in his arm. "King, what do you need me here for?" I said in a whisper. The lioness, in turning, then bumped into me and when I felt her I gave a sigh.

The king said, "Make no sign," and he began again to speak to the lioness, saying, "Oh, my sweetheart, dolly girl, this is Henderson." She rubbed herself against him so that I felt the stress of her weight through the medium of his body. She stood well above our hips in height. When he touched her her whiskered mouth wrinkled so that the root of each hair showed black. She then moved off, returned behind us, came back again, and this time began to investigate me. I felt her muzzle touch upward first at my armpits, and then between my legs, which naturally made the member there shrink into the shelter of my paunch. Clasping me and holding me up, the king still talked softly and calmingly to her while her breath blew out the green silk of the Sungo trousers. I was gripping the inside of my cheek with my teeth, including the broken bridgework, while my eyes shut, slowly, and my face became, as I was highly aware, one huge mass of acceptance directed toward fate. Suffering. (Here is all that remains of a certain life—take it away! was implied by my expression.) But the lioness withdrew her head from my crotch and began once more to walk back and forth, the king saying to me (my comforter), "Henderson-Sungo, it is all right. She is going to accept you easily."

"How do you know?" I said, dry in the throat.

"How do I know!" He spoke with a peculiar stress of confidence. "How do *I* know?" He gave a low laugh, saying, "Why, I know her—this is Atti."

"That's swell. It may seem obvious to you," I said, "but me . . ." My words ended, for she was making her swing back and I caught a glance from her eyes. They were so great, so clear, like circles of wrath. Then she passed me, rubbing against Dahfu's side; her belly swung softly, and she turned again and plunged her head under his hand, taking a caress from it. She went again to the far side of the den, this large, stone-walled room which filtered the gray and yellow light. She walked back along the walls, and when she snarled the freckles at the base of her whiskers were velvet and dark. The king, in a delighted, playful voice, nasal, African, and songlike, would call out after her, "Atti, Atti." And he said, "Ain't she the most beautiful?" Then he instructed me, "You will stand still, Mr. Henderson-Sungo."

I said, whispering fiercely, "No, no, don't move," but he didn't heed me. "King, for Christ's sake," I said. He tried to indicate that I should not worry, but was so taken up with his lioness, showing me how happy relations were between them, that in moving from me his step resembled the bounds he had made in the arena yesterday throwing the skulls. Yes, as he had done yesterday he danced and jumped, in his gold-embroidered white slippers, with powerful legs. There was something so proud and, seemingly, lucky about those legs in the neat, close trousers. Even through intensest fear it reached

my mind that a man with such legs must be lucky. I wished
that he would not push his luck, however, or demonstrate his
relationship with her in just that way, since so much confidence may often be the prelude to a crash, or my experience
isn't worth a nickel. Still the lioness trotted near him, keeping
her head under his fingers. He led her from me to the far side
of the den, where a wooden platform or bench was raised
against the wall on heavy posts. Here he sat down, taking her
head on his knee, scratching and stroking, while she pretended
to box at him. She sat on her haunches while her paws struck.
I saw the action of her shoulders while he pulled her ears,
which were small and round. Not an inch did I stir from the
position I was left in, not even to reset my helmet when it sank
over my brows with the wrinkling of my forehead that resulted
from the intensity of my concentration. No, I stood there half
deaf, half blind, with my throat closing and all the sphincters
shut. Meanwhile the king had taken one of those easy
positions of his, and was resting on his elbow. He had such a
relaxed way about him, and every moment of his earthly life
the extra shadow of brilliance was with him—the sign of an
intenser gift of being. Atti stood with forepaws on the edge of
the trestle, licking his breastbone; her tongue rasped and
flexed against his skin and he raised one of his legs and laid it
playfully over her back. At which I felt so smothered I almost
passed out, and I don't know whether the cause of this was
fear for his safety or something else. I don't know what—rap-
ture, maybe. Admiration. He stretched himself out at full
length on this platform, and lying down isn't worth speaking
of except as this king did it. It was a thing of art with him, and
maybe he had not been joking when he said he kept strong by
lying down, since it really seemed to add to his vitality. The
animal with a soft, deep, ripping noise got set on her great,
claw-hiding, hind paws and bounded up beside him. On the
trestle she walked up and down, now and then glancing at me
as if she were guarding him. When she looked at me it was
with that round, clear stare out of the vast background of
natural severity. There was no direct threat in this, it lacked

anything personal; nevertheless it made my hair, though cramped by the helmet, stir all over my head. I continued to entertain the obscure worry that my intended crime against the cat world might somehow be known here. Also I was anxious about the hour that burst the spirit's sleep. I might have misapprehended the nature of it completely. How did I know that it might not be the judgment hour for me?

However, there were no practical alternatives present. I could do nothing but stand. Which I did. Finally the king extended his hand from behind the lioness, who at that time was striding back and forth over him. He pointed to the door, calling, "Please shut it, Mr. Henderson." And he added, "Open door makes her very uneasy."

So I asked him, "Is it okay to move?" My throat sounded badly rusted.

"Very slow," he said, "but do not worry, as she does what I tell her, precisely."

I stole to the door, stepping backward, and when I had reached it in very slow motion I wanted to continue through it and sit down outside to wait. But under no circumstances, come hell or high water, could I afford to weaken my connection with the king. Therefore I leaned against the door and closed it with my weight, sighing inwardly as I sank against it. I was all broken up. I couldn't take crisis after crisis after crisis, like this.

"Now move forward, Henderson-Sungo," he said. "So far it is admirable. Just a little quicker, only not abrupt. You will be better on closer approach. Lion is far-sighted. Her eyes are meant for viewing at a distance. Come closer."

I approached, cursing under my breath, him and his lion both, trembling and watching the tip of her tail as it swiped back and forth as regular as a metronome. In the middle of the floor I had no more support in all of God's world than a stone.

"More, more. Nearer," he said, and gestured with two fingers. "She will get used to you."

"If I don't die of it," I said.

"Oh, no, Henderson, she will have an influence upon you as she has had upon me."

When I was within reach he pulled me to him, meanwhile thrusting away the face of the animal with his left hand. With great difficulty I clambered up beside him. Then I wiped my face. Needlessly, for owing to the fever it was entirely dry. Atti paced to the end of the platform and swung back. The king fended her off from the back of my head which bristled like a sea urchin when she approached. She sniffed at my back. The king was smiling and thought we were getting on famously. I cried a little. Then she went away and the king said, "Do not be so exceedingly troubled, Henderson-Sungo."

"Oh, Your Highness, I can't help myself. It's what I feel. It's not only that I'm scared of her, and I'm scared all right, but it isn't that alone. It's the richness of the mixture. That's what's getting me. The richness of the mixture. And what I can't understand is why, when fear has taken me on and licked me so many times, I still am not able to stand it." And I went on sobbing, but not too loud, as I didn't want to provoke anything.

"Try, better, to appreciate the beauty of this animal," he said. "Do not think I am attempting to submit you to any ordeal for ordeal's sake. Do you think it is a nerve test? Wash your brain? Honor bright, such is not the case. If I were not positive of my control I would not lead you into such a situation. That would truly be scandalous." He had his hand with the garnet ring on the beast's neck, and he said, "If you will remain where you are, I will give you the fullest confidence."

He jumped down from the platform, and the abruptness of this gave me a bad shock. I felt a burst of terror go off in my chest. The lioness leaped as soon as he did and the two of them together walked to the center of the den. He stopped and gave her an order. She sat. He spoke again and she stretched out on her back, opening her mouth, and then he crouched and pushed his arm into her jaws, bearing down against the wrinkled lips while her tail as she sprawled made a big arc on the stone, sweeping it with utmost power. Withdrawing the arm he made her stand again, and then he crept underneath her and put his legs about her back; his white-slippered feet crossed upon her haunches and his arms about her neck. Face to face she carried him up and down while he talked to her. She snarled, but not at him, seemingly. Together they went clear around the den and back to the platform, where she stood making her soft ripping noise and wrinkling her lips back. He hung on in his purple trousers, looking up at me. Till then I had only thought that I had seen the strangeness of the world. Obviously I had never even begun to see a thing! As he hung from her, smiling upside down into my face, with his high-swelled lips, I realized I had never even had a clue. Brother, this was what you call mastery—genius, that's all. The animal herself was aware of it. On her own animal level it was clear beyond any need of interpretation that she loved the guy. Loved him! With animal love. I loved him too. Who could have helped it?

I said, "That beats anything I ever saw."

He dropped from the animal and pushed her aside with his knee, then vaulted to the platform again. At the same moment Atti also returned and shook the trestle.

"Now is your opinion different, Mr. Henderson?"

"King, it's different. It's as different as can be."

"However, I note," he said, "you still are in fear."

I tried to say I wasn't but my face began to work and I couldn't get those words out. Then I began to cough, with my fist placed, thumb in, before my mouth, and my eyes watered. I finally said, "It's a reflex."

The animal was pacing by and the king irresistibly took me by the wrist and pressed my hand on her flank. Slowly her fur passed under my fingertips and the nails became like five burning tapers. The bones of the hand became incandescent. After this a frightful shock passed right up the arm into the chest.

"Now you have touched her, and what do you think?"

"What I think?" I tried to get my lower lip under control by means of my teeth. "Oh, Your Majesty, please. Not everything in one day. I am doing my best."

He admitted to me, "It is true I am attempting rapid progress. But I wish to overcome your preliminary difficulties in quick time."

I smelled my fingers, which had taken a peculiar odor from the lioness. "Listen," I said, "I suffer a lot from impatience myself. But I have to say that there is just so much I can take at one time. I still have wounds on my face from yesterday, and I'm afraid she'll smell fresh blood. I understand nobody can control these animals once they scent it."

This marvelous man laughed at me and said, "Oh, Henderson-Sungo, you are exquisite." (*That* I never suspected of myself.) "You are real precious to me, and do you know," he said, "not many persons have touched lions."

"I could have lived without it," was the answer I might have made. But as he thought so highly of lions I kept it to myself, mostly. I merely muttered.

"And how you are afraid! Really! In the highest degree. I am really delighted by it. I have never seen such a fear manifestation. It resembled anxious pleasure to me. Do you know, many strong people love this blended fear and satisfaction the most? I think you must be of that type. In addition, I love when your brows move. They are really ex-traordnary. And your chin gets like a peach stone, and you have a very strangulation color and facial swelling, and your mouth spread very wide. And when you cried! I adored when you began to cry."

I knew that this was not really personal but came from his scientific or medical absorption in these manifestations. "What happens to your labium inferiorum?" he said, still interested in my chin. "How do you get so innumerable puckers in the flesh?" (This was extremely revealing to me.) He was so superior to me and overwhelmed me so with his presence, with the extra shadow or smoky brilliancy that he had, and with his lion-riding, that I let him say everything without challenge. When the king had made several more

marveling observations about my nose and my paunch and
the lines in my knees, he told me, "Atti and I influence each
other. I wish you to become a party to this."

"Me?" I didn't know what he was talking about.

"You must not feel because I make observations of your
constitution that I do not appreciate how remarkable you are
in other levels."

"Do I understand you to say, Your Highness, that you have
plans for me with this animal?"

"Yes, and shall explain them."

"Well, I think we should proceed carefully," I said. "I don't
know how much strain my heart can take. As my fainting fits
indicate I can't take too much. Moreover, how do you think
she would behave if I keeled over?"

Then he said, "Perhaps you have had enough exposure to
Atti for the first day." He left the platform again, the animal
following. There was a heavy gate raised by a rope that passed
over a grooved wheel about eighteen feet above the ground by
means of which the king let the lioness out of the den into a
separate enclosure. I have never seen any member of the cat
species pass through a door except on its own terms, and she
was no exception. She needed to loiter in and out while the
king hung on to the rope by which the gate was suspended. As
she was in exit I wanted to suggest that he should give her a
boot in the tail to help her with the decision, since obviously
he was her master, but under those conditions I couldn't really
presume. At last, in that soft, narrow stride, so easy, so
deliberate, so vigilant, she entered the next room. Releasing
the hawser, the king let the great panel slide. It hit the stone
with a loud noise and he rejoined me on the trestle looking
very pleasant. Peaceful. He leaned backward and his lids,
large-veined, sank a little and he breathed calmly, resting.
Sitting close to him in my barbaric trousers with the jockey
shorts visible under them, it seemed to me that something
more than the planks beneath sustained him. For after all, I
was on them, and I was not similarly sustained. At any rate
I sat and waited for him to complete his rest. Once again I

brought to mind that old prophecy Daniel made to Nebuchadnezzar. *They shall drive thee from among men, and thy dwelling shall be with the beasts of the field.* The lion odor was still very keen on my fingers. I smelled it repeatedly and there returned to my thoughts the frogs of the Arnewi, the cattle whom they venerated, the tenants' cat I had tried to murder, to say nothing of the pigs I had bred. Sure enough, this prophecy had a peculiar relevance to me, implying perhaps that I was not entirely fit for human companionship.

The king, having completed a short rest, was ready to speak.

"Now, then, Mr. Henderson," he began to say in his exotic and specially accented way.

"Well, King, you were going to explain to me why it was desirable to associate with this lion. So far I haven't got a clue. Oh, am I confused!"

"I am to make the matter clear," he said, "so first of all I shall tell you how and what about the lions. A year ago or more I captured Atti. There is a traditionary way among the Wariri for obtaining a lion if you need him. Beaters go forth and the animal is driven into what we call a hopo, and this is a very large affair embracing several miles out in the bush. The animals are aroused by noises with drums and horns and pursued into the wide end of the hopo and toward the narrow. At that narrow end is the trap, and I myself as king am obliged to make the capture. In this way Atti was obtained. I have to tell you that any lion except my father, Gmilo, is forbidden and illicit. Atti was brought here in a condition of severest disapproval and opposition, causing a great anxiety and partisanship. Especially the Bunam."

"Say, what's the matter with those guys?" I said. "They don't deserve a king like you. With a personality like yours, you could rule a big country."

The king was glad, I think, to hear this from me. "Notwithstanding," he said, "there is considerable trouble with the Bunam and my Uncle Horko and others, to say nothing of the queen mother and some of the wives. For, Mr. Henderson, there is only one tolerable lion, who is the late king. It is conceived the rest are mischief-makers and evildoers. Do you see? The main reason why the late king has to be recaptured by his successor is that he cannot be left out there in company with such evildoers. The witches of the Wariri are said to hold an illicit intercourse with bad lions. Even some children assumed to come of such a union are dangerous. I add if a man can prove his wife has been unfaithful with a lion, he demands an extreme penalty."

"This is very peculiar," I said.

"Summarizing," the king went on, "I am the object of a double criticism. Firstly I have not yet succeeded in obtaining Gmilo, my father-lion. Secondly it is said that because I keep Atti I am up to no good. Before all opposition, however, I am determined to keep her."

"What do they want?" I said. "You should abdicate, like the Duke of Windsor?"

He answered with a soft laugh, then said, in the deeply founded stillness of the room—with the yellow-gray air weighing on us, deepening, darkening slowly—"I have no such intention."

"Well," I said, "if your back is up about it, that I understand perfectly."

"Henderson-Sungo," he said, "I see I must tell you more about this. From a very early age the king will bring his successor here. Thus I used to visit my lion-grandfather. His name was Suffo. Thus from my small childhood I have been on familiar or intimate terms with lions, and the world did not offer me any replacement. And I so missed the lion connection that when Gmilo my father died and I was notified at school of the tragic occurrence, despite my love of the medical course I was not one hundred per cent reluctant. I may go so far as to assert that I was weak from a continuing lack of such a relationship and went home to be replenished. Naturally it would have been the best of fortune to capture Gmilo at once. But as instead I caught Atti, I could not give her up."

I took a fold of my gaudy pants to wipe my face which, due to the fever, was ominously dry. Just then I should have been pouring sweat.

"And still," he said, "Gmilo must be taken. I will capture him."

"I wish you loads of luck."

He then took me by the wrist with a sharp pressure and said, "I would not blame you, Mr. Henderson, for wishing this to be delusion or a hallucination. But for my sake, as you have applied to me for reciprocal truth-telling, I request you to be patient and keep a firm hold."

About a handful of sulfa pills would do me a lot of good, I thought.

"Oh, Mr. Henderson-Sungo," he said, after a long instant of thought, keeping his uncanny pressure on my wrist—there was seldom any abruptness in what he did. "Yes, I easily could understand that—delusion, imagination, dreaming. However, this is not dreaming and sleeping, but waking. Ha, ha! Men of most powerful appetite have always been the ones to doubt reality the most. Those who could not bear that hopes should turn to misery, and loves to hatreds and deaths and silences, and so on. The mind has a right to its reasonable doubts, and with every short life it awakens and sees and understands what so many other minds of equally short life span have left behind. It is natural to refuse belief that so many small spans should have made so glorious one large thing. That human creatures by pondering should be *correct*. This is what makes a fellow gasp. Yes, Sungo, this same temporary creature is a master of imagination. And right now this very valuable possession appears to make him die and not to live. Why? It is astonishing what a fact that is. Oh, what a distressing picture, Henderson," he said. "To come to the upshot, do not doubt me, Dahfu, Itelo's friend, your friend. For you and I have become united as friends and you must give me your confidence."

"That's okay by me, Your Royal Highness," I said. "That suits me down to the ground. I don't understand you yet, but I am willing to go along on suspended judgment. And don't worry too much about the hallucination possibility. When you come right down to it, there aren't many guys who have stuck with real life through thick and thin, like me. It's my most basic loyalty. From time to time I've lost my head, but I've always made a comeback, and by God, it hasn't been easy, either. But I love the stuff. Grun-tu-molani!"

"Yes," he said, "indeed so. This is an attitude which I endorse. Grun-tu-molani. But in what shape and form? Now, Mr. Henderson, I am convinced you are a man of wide and spacious imagination, and that also you need. . . . You particularly *need*."

"Need is on the right track," I said. "The form it actually takes is, *I want, I want*."

Astonished, he asked me, "Why, what is that?"

"There's something in me that keeps that up," I said. "There have been times when it hardly ever let me alone."

This struck him full-on, so to speak, and he sat perfectly still with his hands mounted on his large thighs, and his face with his high-rising mouth and his wide, open-nostriled, polished nose looking at me.

"And you hear this?"

"I used to hear it practically all the time," I said.

In a low tone he said, "What is it? Demanding birthright? How strange! This is a very impressive manifestation. I have no memory of a previous description of it. Has it ever said what it wants?"

"No," I said, "never. I haven't been able to get it to name names."

"So extraordnary," he said, "and terribly painful, eh? But it will persist until you have replied, I gather. I am touched to hear about it. And whatever it is, how hungry it must be. The resemblance is also to a long prison term. But you say it will not declare which want it wants? Nor give specific directions either to live or to die?"

"Well, I have been threatening suicide a lot, Your Highness. Every once in a while something gets into me and I throw my weight around and threaten my wife with blowing my brains out. No, I could never get it to say what it wants, and so far I have provided only what it does not want."

"Oh, death from what we do not want is the most common

of all the causes. Well, this is such a remarkable phenomenon, isn't it, Henderson? How much better I can interpret now why you succeeded with Mummah. Solely on the basis of that imprisoned want."

I cried, "Oh, can you see that now, Your Royal Highness? Really? I'm so grateful, you can't have any idea. Why, I can hardly see straight." And that was a fact. A spirit of love and gratitude was moving and pressing and squeezing unbearably inside me. "You want to know what this experience means to me? Why talk about its being strange or illusion? I know it's no illusion when I can speak straight out and tell you what it has been to hear, *I want, I want,* going on and on. With this to lean on I don't have to worry about hallucinations. I know in my bones that what moves me so is the straight stuff. Before I left home I read in a magazine that there are flowers in the desert (that's the Great American Desert) that bloom maybe once in forty or fifty years. It all depends on the amount of rainfall. Now according to this article, you can take the seeds and put them in a bucket of water, but they won't germinate. No, sir, Your Highness, soaking in water won't do it. It has to be the rain coming through the soil. It has to wash over them for a certain number of days. And then for the first time in fifty or sixty years you see lilies and larkspurs and such. Roses. Wild peaches." I was very much choked up toward the end, and I said hoarsely, "The magazine was the *Scientific American.* I think I told you, Your Highness, my wife subscribes to it. Lily. She has a very lively and curious mi—" Mind was what I wished to say. To speak of Lily also moved me very greatly.

"I understand you, Henderson," he said with gravity. "Well, we have a certain mutual comprehension or entente."

"King, thanks," I said. "All right, we're beginning to get somewhere."

"For a while I request you to reserve the thanks. I have to ask first for your patient confidence. Plus, at the very outset, I request you to believe that I did not leave the world and return to my Wariri with an aim of withdrawal."

I might as well say at this place that he had a hunch about the lions; about the human mind; about the imagination, the intelligence, and the future of the human race. Because, you see, intelligence is free now (he said), and it can start anywhere or go anywhere. And it is possible that he lost his head, and that he was carried away by his ideas. This was because he was no mere dreamer but one of those dreamer-doers, a guy with a program. And when I say that he lost his head, what I mean is not that his judgment abandoned him but that his enthusiasms and visions swept him far out.

Chapter XVII

The King had said that he welcomed my visit because of the opportunity for conversation it gave him, and that was no lie. We talked and talked and talked, and I can't pretend that I completely understood him. I can only say I suspended judgment, listening carefully and bearing in mind how he had warned me that the truth might come in forms for which I was unprepared.

So I will give you a rough summary of his point of view. He had some kind of conviction about the connection between insides and outsides, especially as applied to human beings. And as he had been a zealous student and great reader he had held down the job of janitor in his school library up there in Syria, and sat after closing hours filling his head with out-of-the-way literature. He would say, for instance, "James, *Psychology*, a very attractive book." He had studied his way through a load of such books. And what he was engrossed by was a belief in the transformation of human material, that you could work either way, either from the rind to the core or from the core to the rind; the flesh influencing the mind, the mind influencing the flesh, back again to the mind, back once more to the flesh. The process as he saw it was utterly dynamic. Thinking of mind and flesh as I knew them, I said, "Are you really and truly sure it's like that, Your Highness?"

Sure? He was better than sure. He was triumphantly sure. He reminded me very much of Lily in his convictions. It exalted them both to believe something and they had a tendency to make curious assertions. Dahfu also liked to talk about his father. He told me, for instance, that his late father Gmilo had been a lion type in every respect except the beard and mane. He was too modest to claim a resemblance to lions himself, but I saw it. I had already seen it when he was in the arena leaping and whirling the skulls by the ribbons and catching them. He started with the elementary observation, which many people had made before him, that mountain people were mountainlike, plains people plainlike, water people waterlike, cattle people ("Yes, the Arnewi, your pals, Sungo") cattlelike. "It is a somewhat Montesquieu idea," he said, and thus he went on with endless illustrations. These were things millions of people had noted in their life experience: horse people had bangs and big teeth, large veins, coarse laughter; dogs and masters came to resemble one another; husbands and wives took on a strong similarity. Crouching forward in those green silk pants, I was thinking, "And pigs . . . ?" But the king was saying, "Nature is a deep imitator. And as man is the prince of organisms he is the master of adaptations. He is the artist of suggestions. He himself is his principal work of art, in the body, working in the flesh. What miracle! What triumph! Also, what a disaster! What tears are to be shed!"

"Yes, if you're right, it's mighty saddening," I said.

"Debris of failure fills the tomb and grave," he said, "the dust eats back its own, yet a vital current is still flowing. There is an evolution. We must think of it."

Briefly, he had a full scientific explanation of the way in which people were shaped. For him it was not enough that there might be disorders of the body that originated in the brain. *Everything* originated there. "Although I do not wish to reduce the stature of our discussion," he said, "yet for the sake of example the pimple on a lady's nose may be her own idea, accomplished by a conversion at the solemn command of her psyche; even more fundamentally the nose itself, though part hereditary, is part also her own idea."

My head felt as light as a wicker basket by now, and I said, "A pimple?"

"I mean it as an index to deep desires flaming outward," he said. "But if you are inclined to blame—no! No blame redounds. We are far from so free as to be masters. But just the same the thing is accomplished from within. Disease is a speech of the psyche. That is a permissible metaphor. We say that flowers have the language of love. Lilies for purity. Roses for passion. Daisies won't tell. Ha! I once read this on a cushion embroidery. But, and I am in earnest, the psyche is a polyglot, for if it converts fear into symptoms it also converts hope. There are cheeks or whole faces of hope, feet of respect, hands of justice, brows of serenity, and so forth." He was pleased by the response he read in my face, which must have been a dilly. "Oh?" he said. "I startle you?" He loved that.

In the course of further conferences I told him, "I admit that this idea of yours really hits me where I live—am I so responsible for my own appearance? I admit I have had one hell of a time over my external man. Physically, I am a puzzle to myself."

He said, "The spirit of the person in a sense is the author of his body. I have never seen a face, a nose, like yours. To me that feature alone, from a conversion point of view, is totally a discovery."

"Why, King," I said, "that's the worst news I ever heard, except death in the family. Why should I be responsible, any more than a tree? If I was a willow you wouldn't say such things to me."

"Oh," he said, "you take upon yourself too much." And he went on to explain, citing all kinds of medical evidence and investigations of the brain. He told me, over and over again, that the cortex not only received impressions from the extremities and the senses but sent back orders and directives. And how this really was, and which ventricles regulated which functions, like temperature or hormones, and so on, I really couldn't keep quite clear. He kept talking about vegetal functions, or some such term, and he lost me every other sentence.

Finally he forced on me a whole load of his literature and I had to take it down to my apartment and promise to study it. These books and journals he had carried back from school with him. "How?" I said. And he explained he had come by way of Malindi and bought a donkey there. He had brought nothing else, no clothes (what did he need them for?) or other belongings except a stethoscope and a blood-pressure apparatus. For he really had been a third-year medical student when recalled to his tribe. "That's where I should have gone right after the war—to med school," I said. "Instead of horsing around. Do you think I would have made a good doctor?" He said "Oh?"—he didn't see why not. At first he exhibited a degree of reserve. But after I convinced him of my sincerity he really appeared to see a future for me. He implied that although I might be doing my internship when other men were retiring from active life, after all, it wasn't a question of other men but of me, E. H. Henderson. I had picked up Mummah. Let's not forget that. Anyway a steeple might fall on me and flatten me out, but apart from such unforeseeable causes I was built to last ninety years. So eventually the king came to take a serious view of my ambition, and he would generally say with great gravity, "Yes, this is a very admirable perspective." There was another matter which he treated with equal gravity, and it was that of my duties as the rain king. When I tried to make a joke about it he stopped me short and said, "It is proper to remember, Henderson, you are the Sungo."

So then my program, minus one factor: Every morning the two amazons, Tamba and Bebu, waited on me and offered me a joxi, or trample massage. Never failing to be surprised and disappointed at my refusal, they took the treatment themselves; they administered it to each other. Every morning also I had an interview with Romilayu and tried to reassure him about my conduct. I believe it worried and perplexed him that I was so intimate, frère et cochon, with the king. But I kept telling him, "Romilayu, you've just got to understand. This is a very special king." But he realized from the state I was in that there was more than talk going on between Dahfu and me, there was also an experiment getting under way which I will defer telling you about.

Before lunch, the amazons held a muster. These women with the short vests or jerkins abased themselves before me in the dust. Each moistened her mouth so that the dirt would cling to it, and took my foot and put it on top of her head. There was much pageantry, heat, pressure, solemnity, drumming, and bugling all over the place. And I still had fever. Small fires of disease and eagerness were alight within me. My nose was exceedingly dry even if I was the king of moisture. I stank of lion, too—how noticeably, I can't say. Anyhow, I appeared in the green bloomers with my helmet and my crepe-soled shoes in front of the amazon band. Then they brought up the state umbrellas with their folds like thick eyelids. Women were squeezing bagpipes under their elbows. Amid all this twiddling and screeching the servants opened the bridge chairs and we all sat down to lunch.

Everybody was there, the Bunam, Horko, the Bunam's assistant. It was just as well that this Bunam didn't require much space. For Horko left him very little. Thin and straight, the Bunam looked at me with that everlasting stare of human experience; it took root twistedly between his eyes. His two wives, with bald heads and gay short teeth, both were very sunny. They looked like a pair of real fun-loving girls. Ever and again, Horko smoothed his robe on his belly or gave a touch to the heavy red stones that pulled his earlobes down. A white woolly ball or dumpling was set before me, like farina only coarser and saltier; at least it would do no further harm to my bridgework. I could certainly die of pain before I reached civilization if the metal parts which were anchored on the little stumps of teeth ground down by Mlle. Montecuccoli and Spohr the dentist were to come loose. I reproached myself, for I have a spare and I should never have started without it. Together with the plaster impressions it was in a

box, and that box was in the trunk of my Buick. There was a
spring that held the jack to the spare tire, and for safe-keeping
I had put the box with the extra bridge in the same place. I
could see it. I saw it just as if I were lying in that trunk. It was
a gray cardboard box, filled with pink tissue paper and labeled
"Buffalo Dental Manufacturing Company." Fearing to lose
what remained of the bridgework, I chewed even the salty
dumplings with extreme caution. The Bunam with that
fanatical fold of deep thought ate like everybody else. He and
the black-leather fellow looked very occult; the latter always
seemed about to unfold a pair of wings and take off. He too
was chewing, and as a matter of fact there was a certain
amount of Alice-in-Wonderland jollity in the palace yard.
Even a number of kids, all head and middle, like little black
pumpernickels, were playing a pebble game in the dust.

When Atti roared under the palace, there was no comment.
Just Horko, of all people, gave a wince, but it merged rapidly
again into his low-featured smile. He was always so gleaming,
his very blood must have been like furniture polish. Like the
king he had a rich physical gift, and the same eye tinge, only
his eyes bulged. And I thought that during those years he had
spent in Lamu, while his nephew was away at school in the
north, he must have had himself a ball. He was certainly no
church-goer, if I am any judge.

Well, it was the same every day. After the ceremonies of the
meal I went, attended by the amazons, to Mummah. She had
been brought back to her shrine by six men who had carried
her laid across heavy poles. I witnessed this myself. Her room,
which she shared with Hummat, was in a separate courtyard
of the palace where there were wooden pillars and a stone
tank with some disagreeable water. This was our special
Sungo's supply. My daily visit to Mummah cheered me up.
For one thing, the worst part of the day was over (I shall
explain in due time) and for another I developed a strong
personal attachment to her, due not only to my success but to
some quality in her, either as a work of art or as a divinity.
Ugly as she was, with the stork-nest tresses and unreliable legs

giving under the mass of her body, I attributed benevolent purposes to her. I would say, "Hi-de-do, old lady. Compliments of the season. How's your old man?" For I took Hummat to be married to her, the clumsy old mountain god that Turombo, the champion in the red fez, had lifted up. It looked like a good marriage, and they stood there contented with each other, near the stone tub of rank water. And while I gave Mummah the time of day, Tamba and Bebu filled a couple of gourds and we went through another passage where a considerable troop of the amazons with umbrella and hammock were waiting. Both of these articles were green, like my pants, the Sungo's own color. I was helped into this hammock and lay at the bottom of it, a bursting weight, looking up at the brilliant heaven made still by the force of afternoon heat, and the taut umbrella wheeling, now clockwise, now the other way, with lazy, sleepy fringes. Seldom did we leave the gate of the palace without a rumble from Atti, below, which always made the perspiring, laboring amazons stiffen. The umbrella bearer might waver then and I would catch a straight blow of the sun, one of those buffets of violent fire which made the blood leap into my brain like the coffee in a percolator.

With this reminder of the experiments the king and I were engaged in, pursuing his special aim, we entered the town with one drum following. People came up to Tamba and Bebu with little cups and got a dole of water. Women especially, as the Sungo was also in charge of fertility; you see, it goes together with moisture. This expedition took place every afternoon to the beat of the idle, almost irregular single deep drum. It made a taut and almost failing sound of puncture which, however, was always approximately in rhythm. Out in the sun walked the women coming from their huts with earthenware cups for their drops of tank water. I lay in the shade and listened to the sleepy drum-summons with my fingers heavily linked upon my belly. When we reached the center of town I climbed out. This was the market place. It was also the magistrate's court. Dressed in a red gown, the judge sat on the top of a dunghill.

He was a coarse-featured fellow; I didn't care for his looks. There was always a litigation, and the defendant was tied to a pole and gagged by means of a forked stick which stuck into his palate and pressed down his tongue. The trial would stop for me. The lawyers quit hollering and the crowd yelled, "Sungo! Aki-Sungo" (Great White Sungo). I got out and took a bow. Tamba or Bebu would hand me a perforated gourd like the sprinklers that laundresses used in the old days. No, wait—like the aspergillum the Catholics use in their churches. I would sprinkle them and people would come to me laughing and bowing and offer their backs to the spray, old toothless fellows with grizzled hair in the cleft of their posteriors and maidens whose breasts pointed toward the ground, strong fellows with powerful spines. It didn't escape me altogether that there was some mockery mingled with respect for my strength and my office. Anyway, I always saw to it the prisoner tied to the post got his full share, and added water drops to the perspiration on the poor guy's skin.

Such, roughly, were my rain king's duties, but it was the king's special aim that I have to tell you about, and all the literature that he had given me. This I shunned; after our preliminary conversation I guessed that there might be trouble in it. There were the two books, which looked pretty well used up, and there were scientific reprints, coverless, with shabby top pages. I looked through a few of these. The print was close and black, and the only clearings in the text were filled with diagrams of molecules. Otherwise the words were as thick and heavy as tombstones, and I was very disheartened. It was much like taking the limousine to La Guardia Field and passing those cemeteries in Queens. So heavy. Each of the dead having been mailed away, and those stones like the postage stamps death has licked.

Anyway, it was a hot afternoon and I sat down with the literature to see what I could do with it. I was wearing my costume, those green silk drawers, and the helmet with its nipple on the top, and the shoes with the crepe soles trodden out of shape and curled like sneering lips. So that's how it is.

Illness and fever have made me sleepy. The sun is very
absolute. The stripes of shadow look solid. The air is dreamy
with the heat and the mountains in places are like molasses
candy, yellow, brittle, cellular, cavey, scorched. They look as
if they might be bad for the teeth. And I have this literature.
Dahfu and Horko had loaded it on the donkey when they
came over the mountains from the coast. Afterward the beast
was butchered and fed to the lioness.

Why should I have to read the stuff? I thought. My
resistance to it was great. Firstly I was afraid to find out that
the king might be a crank; I felt it was not right, after I had
come this long way to pierce the spirit's sleep, and picked up
Mummah and become rain king, that Dahfu should turn out
to be just another eccentric. Therefore I stalled. I laid out a
few games of solitaire. After which I felt extremely sleepy and
stared at the sun-fixed colors outside, green as paint, brown as
crust.

I am a nervous and emotional reader. I hold a book up to
my face and it takes only one good sentence to turn my brain
into a volcano; I begin thinking of everything at once and a
regular lava of thought pours down my sides. Lily claims I
have too much mental energy. According to Frances, on the
other hand, I didn't have any brain power at all. All I can
truly say is that when I read in one of my father's books, "The
forgiveness of sin is perpetual," it was just the same as being
hit in the head with a rock. I have told, I think, that my father
used currency for bookmarks and I assume I must have
pocketed the money in that particular book and then forgot
even its title. Maybe I didn't want to hear any more than that
about sin. Just as it was, it was perfect, and I might have been
afraid the guy would spoil it when he went on. Anyway, I am
the inspirational, and not the systematic, type. Besides, if I
wasn't going to abide by that one sentence, what good would
it do to read the entire book?

No, I haven't ever been calm enough to read, and there was
a time when I would have dumped my father's books to the
pigs if I'd thought it might do them good. Such a supply of

books confused me. When I started to read something about France, I realized I didn't know anything about Rome, which came first, and then Greece, and then Egypt, going backward all the time to the primitive abyss. As a matter of fact, I didn't know enough to read one single book. Eventually I found the only things I could enjoy were things like *The Romance of Surgery*, *The Triumph over Pain*, or medical biographies—like Osler, Cushing, Semmelweis, and Metchnikoff. And owing to my attachment to Wilfred Grenfell I became interested in Labrador, Newfoundland, the Arctic Circle, and finally the Eskimos. You would have thought that Lily would have gone along with me on the Eskimos, but she didn't, and I was very disappointed. The Eskimos are stripped down to essentials and I thought they would appeal to her because she is such a basic type.

Well, she is, and then again, she is not. She's not naturally truthful. Look at the way she lied about all her fiancés. And I'm not sure that Hazard did punch her in the eye on the way to the wedding. How can I be? She told me her mother was dead while the old woman was still living. She lied too about the carpet, for it *was* the one on which her father shot himself. I am tempted to say that ideas make people untruthful. Yes, they frequently lead them into lies.

Lily is something of a blackmailer, also. You know I dearly love that big broad, and for my own amusement sometimes I like to think of her part by part. I start with a hand or a foot or even a toe and go to all the limbs and joints. It gives me wonderful satisfaction. One breast is smaller than the other, like junior and senior; her pelvic bones are not well covered, she is a little gaunt there. But her body looks gentle and pretty. Moreover her face blushes white, which touches me more than anything else. Nevertheless she is reckless and a spendthrift and doesn't keep the house clean and is a con artist and exploits me. Before we were married, I wrote about twenty letters for her all over the place, to the State Department and a dozen or so missions. *She used me as a character reference.* She was going to Burma or to Brazil, and the implied threat was that I would never see her again. I was on the spot. I couldn't louse her up to all these people. But when we were married and I wanted to spend our honeymoon camping among the Copper Eskimos, she wouldn't hear of it. Anyway (still on the subject of books) I read Freuchen and Gontran de Poncins and practiced living out of doors in winter. I built an igloo with a knife and during zero weather Lily and I fell out because she wouldn't bring the kids and sleep with me under skins as the Eskimos do. I wanted to try that.

I looked through all the readings Dahfu had given me. I knew they were supposed to have a bearing on lions and yet, page after page, not one single reference to any lion. I felt like groaning, like snoozing, like anything except tackling such hard material on this hot African day when the sky was as blue as grain alcohol is white. The first article, which I picked because the opening paragraph looked easy, was signed Scheminsky, and it was not easy at all. But I fought it until I came across the term Obersteiner's allochiria, and there I broke down. I thought, "Hell! What is it all about! Because I told the king I wanted to be a doctor, he thinks I have medical training. I'd better straighten him out on this." The stuff was just too difficult.

But anyway I gave it the best that was in me. I skipped over Obersteiner's allochiria, and in the end managed to make sense of a paragraph here and there. Most of these articles had to do with the relation between body and brain, and they especially emphasized posture, confusions between right and left, and various exaggerations and deformities of sensation. Thus a fellow with a normal leg might be convinced that he had the leg of an elephant. This was very interesting in itself and a few of the descriptions were absolutely dandy. What I kept thinking was, "I'd better scour, brighten, freshen up the old intelligence, and understand what the man is driving at, for my life may depend on it." It was just my luck to think I had found the conditions of life simplified so I could deal with them—finally!—and then to end up in a ramshackle palace reading these advanced medical publications. I suppose there must be few native princes left who are not educated, and all the polytechnical schools enroll gens de couleur from all over the world, and some of them have made prodigious discoveries already. But I never heard of anyone who was precisely on King Dahfu's track. Of course it was possible that he was in a league all by himself. This suggested again that I might find myself in some really hot water with him, for you can't expect people who are in a class by themselves to be reasonable. Being the only occupant of a certain class, I know this from personal experience.

I was taking a short rest from the article by Scheminsky, playing a game of solitaire and breathing hard as I bent over it, when the king's Uncle Horko, on this particular day of heat, entered my room on the first floor of the palace. Behind him came the Bunam, and with the Bunam there was always his companion or assistant, the black-leather man. These three made way to let a fourth person enter, an elderly woman who had the look of a widow. You can seldom be mistaken about widows. They had fetched her in to see me, and from their way of standing aside it was plain she was the principal visitor. Preparatory to rising, I gave a stagger—space was limited in my room and it was already pretty well occupied by Tamba and Bebu, who were lying down, and Romilayu, who was in the corner. There were eight of us in a room not really big enough to hold me. The bed was fixed and couldn't be moved outside. It was covered with hides and native rags, and the spattered cards over which I had been brooding were laid out in four uneven files—I had pushed aside King Dahfu's literature. And now they brought me this elderly woman in a fringed dress that hung from her shoulders to about the middle of her thighs. They filed in from the burning wilds of the African afternoon and, as I had been fixed with the seeing blindness of a card player on the glossy, dirty reds and blacks, I couldn't focus at first on the woman. But then she came near to me, and I saw that she had a round but not perfectly round

face. On one side of it the symmetry was out. At the jaw, this
was. Her nose was cocked and she had large lips, while the
gentle forward projection of her face made it seem that she
was offering it to you. Her mouth was somewhat lacking in
teeth but I recognized her at once. "Why," I thought, "it's a
relative of Dahfu's. She must be his mother." I saw the
relationship in the slope of her face and in the lips and the red
tinge of her eyes.

"Yasra. Queen," said Horko. "Dahfu mama."

"Ma'am, it's an honor," I said.

She took my hand and placed it on her head, which
was shaved, of course. All the married women had shaven
heads. Her action was facilitated by a difference of almost two
feet in our heights. Horko and I stood over all the rest.
He was wrapped in his red cloth, and the stones in his ears
hung like the two lobes of a rooster when he bent to speak to
her.

I took off my helmet, baring the huge welts and bruises on
my nose and cheeks, left over from the rain ceremony. My
eyes must have been a little crazy with solemnity for they drew
the notice of the black-leather man, who appeared to point at
them and said something to the Bunam. But I put the old
queen's hand on my head respectfully saying, "Lady, Henderson at your service. And I really mean it." Over my shoulder I
said to Romilayu, "Tell her that." His tuft of hair was close
behind me, and under it his forehead was more than usually
wrinkled. I saw the Bunam look at the cards and printed
matter on the bed, and I scooped them all behind me, as I
didn't want the king's property exposed to his scrutiny. Then I
told Romilayu, "Say to the queen that she has a fine son. The
king is a friend of mine and I am just as much his friend. Say I
am proud to know him."

Meantime I thought, "She's in very bad company, ain't
she?" because I knew it was the Bunam's job to take the life of
the failing king; Dahfu had told me that. Actually the Bunam
was her husband's executioner—and now the queen came
with him late in the afternoon to pay a social call? It didn't
seem right.

At home this would have been the cocktail hour. The great wheels and all the sky-marring frames would be slowing, darkening, and the world, with its connivance and invention and its load of striving and desire to transform, would relax its strain.

The old queen may have sensed my thought, for she was sad and troubled. The Bunam was staring at me, evidently meaning to get at me in some way, while Horko, with his low-hung, fleshy face, looked gloomy at first. The purpose of this visit was two-fold—to get me to reveal about the lioness and then also to use any influence I might have with the king. He was in trouble, and very seriously, over Atti.

Horko did most of the talking, mixing up the several languages he had picked up during his stay in Lamu. He used a kind of French as well as English and a little Portuguese. His blood gleamed through his face with a high polish and his ears were dragged down by their ornaments almost to his fat shoulders. He introduced the subject by saying a little about his residence in Lamu—a very up-to-date town, as he described it. Automobiles, café and music, many languages spoken. "Tout le monde très distingué, très chic," he said. I shut off my defective ear with one hand and gave him the full benefit of the other, nodding, and when he saw that I responded to his Lamu Afro-French, he began to liven up. You could see that his heart belonged to that town, and for him the years he had spent there were probably the greatest. It was his Paris. It gave me no trouble to imagine that he had promoted himself a house and servants and girls and spent his days in a café in a seersucker jacket, with a boutonnière maybe, for he was a promoter. He was displeased with his nephew for having gone away and left him there eight or nine years. "Go away Lamu school," he said. "Pas assez bon. Bad, bad, I say. No go away Lamu. We go. He go. Papa King Gmilo die. Moi aller chercher Dahfu. One years." He lifted a stout finger to me over the bald head of Queen Yasra, and from his indignation I took it he must have been held responsible for Dahfu's disappearance. It was his duty to bring back the heir.

But he observed that I didn't like the tone he took, and said, "You friend Dahfu?"

"Damn right I am."

"Oh me, too. Roi neveu. Aime neveu. Sans blague. Danger-ous."

"Come on, what is this all about?" I said.

Seeing me dissatisfied, the Bunam spoke sharply to Horko, and the queen mother, Yasra, gave a cry, "Sasi ai. Ai, sasi, Sungo." Looking upward at me she must have seen the underside of my chin and the mustache and my open nostrils, but not my eyes, so that she didn't know how I was receiving her plea, for that is what it was. She therefore began to kiss my knuckles over and over again, somewhat as Mtalba had done the night before my doomed expedition against the frogs. Once more I was aware of a sensitivity there. These hands have lost shape a good deal as a result of the abuses they have been subjected to. There was, for instance, the forefinger with which I had aimed, in imitation of Pancho Villa, at that cat under the bridge table. "Oh, lady, don't do that," I said. "Romilayu—Romilayu—tell her to quit it," I said. "If I had as many fingers as there are hammers to a piano," I told him, "they'd all be at her service. What does the old queen want? These guys are putting the squeeze on her, I can see it."

"Help son, sah," said Romilayu at my back.

"From what?" I said.

"Lion witch, sah. Oh, very bad lion."

"They've frightened the old mother," I said, glowering at the Bunam and his assistant. "This is the sexton-beetle. Not happy without corpses or putting people away in the grave. I can smell it on you. And look at this leather-winged bat, his side-kick. He could play the Phantom of the Opera. He's got a face like an ant-eater—a soul-eater. You tell them right here and now I think the king is a brilliant and noble man. Make it very strong," I said to Romilayu, "for the old lady's sake."

But I could not change the subject no matter how I praised the king. They had come to brief me about lions. With one single exception, lions contained the souls of sorcerers. The

king had captured Atti and brought her home in place of his
father Gmilo, who was still at large. They took this very hard,
and the Bunam was here to warn me that Dahfu was
implicating me in his witchcraft. "Oh, pooh," I said to these
men. "I never could be a witch. My character is just the
opposite." Between them Horko and Romilayu made me
finally feel the importance and solemnity—the heaviness—of
the situation. I tried to avoid it, but there it was: they laid it on
me like a slab of stone. People were angry. The lioness was
causing mischief. Certain women who had been her enemies
in the previous incarnation were having miscarriages. Also
there was the drought, which I had ended by picking up
Mummah. Consequently I was very popular. (Blushing, I felt
a kind of surly rose color in my face.) "It was nothing," I said.
But then Horko told me how bad it was that I went down into
the den. I was reminded again that Dahfu was not in full
possession of the throne until Gmilo was captured. So the old
king was forced to be out in the bush among bad companions
(the other lions, each and every one a proven evildoer). They
claimed that the lioness was seducing Dahfu, and made him
incapable of doing his duty, and it was she who kept Gmilo
away.

I tried to say to them that other people took a far different
view of lions. I told them that they couldn't be right to
condemn all the lions except one, and there must be a mistake
somewhere. Then I appealed to the Bunam, seeing that he was
obviously the leader of the anti-lion forces. I thought his
wrinkled stare, the stern vein of his forehead, and those
complex fields of skin about his eyes must signify (even here,
where all Africa was burning like oceans of green oil under the
absolute and extended sky) what they would have signified
back in New York, namely, deep thought. "Well, I think you
should go along with the king. He is an exceptional man and
does exceptional things. Sometimes these great men have to go
beyond themselves. Like Caesar or Napoleon or Chaka the
Zulu. In the king's case, the interest happens to be science.
And though I'm no expert I guess he's thinking of mankind as

a whole, which is tired of itself and needs a shot in the arm
from animal nature. You ought to be glad that he's not a
Chaka and won't knock you off. Lucky for you he's not the
type." I thought a threat might be worth trying. It seemed,
however, to have no effect. The old woman still whispered,
holding my fingers, while the Bunam, as Romilayu addressed
him, doing his best to translate my words, was drawn up with
savage stiffness so that only his eyes moved, and they moved
very little, but mainly glittered. And then, when Romilayu was
through, the Bunam signaled to his assistant by snapping his
fingers, and the black-leather man drew from his rag cloak an
object which I mistook at first for a shriveled eggplant. He
held it by the stalk and brought it toward my face. A pair of
dry dead eyes now looked at me, and teeth from a breathless
mouth. From the eyes came a listless and *finished* look. They
saw me from beyond. One of the nostrils of this toy was
flattened down, the other was expanded and the entire face
seemed to bark, this black, dry, childlike or dwarfish mummy
which was gripped by the neck. My breath burned like
mustard, and that voice of inward communication which I
had heard when I picked up the corpse tried to speak but it
could not rise above a whisper. I suppose some people are
more full of death than others. Evidently I happen to have a
great death potential. Anyway, I begin to ask (or perhaps it
was more a plea than a question), why is it always near
me—why! Why can't I get away from it awhile! Why, why!

"Well, what is this thing?" I said.

This was the head of one of the lion-women—a sorceress.
She had gone out and had trysts with lions. She had poisoned
people and bewitched them. The Bunam's assistant had
caught up with her, and she was tried by ordeal and strangled.
But she had come back. These people made no bones about it,
but said she was the very same lioness that Dahfu had
captured. She was Atti. It was a positive identification.

"Ame de lion," said Horko. "En bas."

"I don't know how you can be so sure," I said. I could not
take my eyes from the shriveled head with its finished, listless

look. It spoke to me as that creature had done in Banyules at the aquarium after I had put Lily on the train. I thought as I had then, in the dim watery stony room, "This is it! The end!"

Chapter XVIII

That night Romilayu's praying was more fervent than ever. His lips stretched far forward and the muscles jumped under his skin while his moaning voice rose from the greatest depths. "That's right, Romilayu," I said, "pray. Pour it on. Pray like anything. Give it everything you've got. Come on, Romilayu, pray, I tell you." He didn't seem to me to be putting enough into it, and I flabbergasted him altogether by getting out of bed in the green silk drawers and kneeling beside him on the floor to join him in prayer. If you want to know something, it wasn't the first time in recent years by any means that I had addressed some words to God. Romilayu looked from under that cloud of poodle hair that hung over his low forehead, then sighed and shuddered, but whether with satisfaction at finding I had some religion in me or with terror at hearing my voice suddenly in his channel, or at the sight I made, I couldn't be expected to know. Oh, I got carried away! That withered head and the sight of poor Queen Yasra had got to my deepest feelings. And I prayed and prayed, "Oh, you . . . Something," I said, "you Something because of whom there is not Nothing. Help me to do Thy will. Take off my stupid sins. Untrammel me. Heavenly Father, open up my dumb heart and for Christ's sake preserve me from unreal things. Oh, Thou who tookest me from pigs, let me not be killed over lions. And forgive my crimes and nonsense and let me return to Lily and the kids." Then silent on my heavy knees and palm pressed to palm I went on praying while my weight bowed me nearly to the broad boards.

I was shaken, you see, because I now understood clearly that I was caught between the king and the Bunam's faction.

The king was set upon carrying out his experiment with me. He believed that it was never too late for any man to change, no matter how fully formed. And he took me for an instance, and was determined that I should absorb lion qualities from his lion.

When I asked to see him in the morning after the visit of Yasra, the Bunam, and Horko, I was directed to his private pavilion. It was a garden laid out with some signs of formal design. At the four corners were dwarf orange trees. A flowering vine covered the palace wall like bougainvillaea, and here the king was sitting under one of his unfurled umbrellas. He wore his wide velvet hat with the fringe of human teeth and occupied a cushioned seat, surrounded by wives who kept drying his face with little squares of colored silk. They lit his pipe and handed him drinks, making sure that he was screened by a brocaded cloth whenever he took a sip. Beside one of the orange trees an old fellow was playing a stringed instrument. Very long, only a little shorter than a bass fiddle, rounded at the bottom, it stood on a thick peg and was played with a horse-hair bow. It gave thick rasping notes. The old musician himself was all bone, with knees that bent outward and a long shiny head, tier upon tier of wrinkles. A few white weblike hairs were carried in the air behind him.

"Oh, Henderson-Sungo, good you are here. We shall have entertainments."

"Listen, I've got to talk to you, Your Highness," I said. I kept wiping my face.

"Of course, but we shall have dancing."

"But I've got to tell you something, Your Majesty."

"Yes, of course, but there is dancing first. My ladies are entertaining."

His ladies! I thought, and looked about me at this gathering of naked women. For after he had told me that he would be strangled when he couldn't be of any further service to them, I took kind of a dim view of them. But there were some who looked splendid, the tallest ones moving with a giraffe-like elegance, their small faces ornamented with patterns of scars.

Their hips and breasts suited their bodies better than any costume could have done. As for their features, they were broad but not coarse; on the contrary, their nostrils were very thin and fine, and their eyes were soft. They were painted and ornamented and perfumed with a musk that smelled a little like sweet coal oil. Some wore beads like hollow walnuts of gold, looped two or three times about themselves and hanging down as far as their legs. Others had corals and beads and feathers, and the dancers wore colored scarves which waved flimsily from their shoulders as they sprinted with elegant long legs across the court and the basic scratching of the music went on as the old fellow pushed his bow, rasp, rasp, rasp.

"But there is something I have got to say to you."

"Yes, I suspected so, Henderson-Sungo. However, we must watch the dancing. That is Mupi, she is excellent." The instrument sobbed and groaned and croaked as the old fellow polished on it with his barbarous bow. Mupi, trying out the music, swayed two or three times, then raised her leg stiff-kneed, and when her foot returned slowly to the ground it seemed to be searching for something. And then she began to rock and continued groping with alternate feet and closed her eyes. The thin beaten gold shells, like hollow walnuts, rustled on this Mupi's body. She took the king's pipe from his hand and knocked out the coals on her thigh, pressing down with her hand, and while she burned herself her eyes, which were very fluid with the pain, never stopped looking into his.

The king whispered to me, "This is a good girl—very good girl."

"She's certainly gone on you," I said. The dancing continued to the croaking of the two-stringed instrument. "Your Highness, I've got to talk . . ." The fringe of teeth clicked as he turned his head with the soft, large-brimmed hat. In the shade of this hat his face was more vivid than ever, especially his hollow-bridged nose and his high-swelled lips.

"Your Highness."

"Oh, you are very persistent. Very well. As you claim it is so urgent, let us go where we can talk." He stood up and his

rising caused a great disturbance among the women. They
began to spring back and forth, loping across the little
pavilion, crying out, and making a clatter with their ornaments; some wept with disappointment that the king was
going and some attacked me with shrill voices for taking
Dahfu away while several shrieked, "Sdudu lebah!" Lebah—I
had already picked the word up—was Wariri for lion. They
were warning him about Atti; they were charging him with
desertion. The king with a big gesture waved at them,
laughing. He seemed very affectionate and I guess he was
saying he cared for them all. I was waiting, standing by, huge,
my worried face still stiff from the bruises.

The women were right, for Dahfu did not lead me back to
his apartment again but took me again to the den, below.
When I realized where he was going I hurried after him
saying, "Wait, wait. Let's talk this thing over. Just one single
minute."

"I am sorry, Henderson-Sungo, but we are bound to go to
Atti. I will listen to you down there."

"Well, forgive me for saying it, King, but you're very
stubborn. In case you don't know it you are in a hell of a
position."

"Oh, the divil," he said. "I am aware what they are up to."

"They came and showed me the head of a person they
claimed was the same as Atti in a former existence."

The king stopped. Tatu had just let us through the door and
was standing holding the heavy bolt in her arms, waiting in
the gallery. "That is the well-known fear business. We will
withstand it. Old man, sometimes things cannot be so nice in
cases like this. Do they harass you? It is because I have shown
my fondness about you." He took me by the shoulder.

Owing perhaps to the touch of his hand, I almost broke
down on the threshold of the stairs. "Here," I said, "I am
ready to do almost anything you say. I've taken a lot from life,
but basically it hasn't really scared me, King. I am a soldier.
All my people have been soldiers. They protected the peas-
ants, and they went on the crusades and fought the Moham-

medans. And I had one ancestor on my mother's side—why, General U. S. Grant wouldn't even start an engagement without him. He would say, 'Billy Waters here?' 'Present, sir.' 'Very good. Begin the battle.' Hell's bells, I've got martial blood in me. But Your Highness, you're breaking me down with this lion business. And what about your mother?"

"Oh, divil my mother, Sungo," he said. "Do you think the world is nothing but an egg and we are here to set upon it? First come the phenomena. Utterly above all else. I talk to you about a great discovery and you argue me mothers. I am aware they are working the fear business upon her, as well. My mother has outlived father Gmilo already by half of a decade. Come through the door with me and let Tatu close it. Come, come." I stood. He shouted, "Come, I say!" and I stepped through the doorway. I saw Tatu as she labored to place the great chunk of wood which was the bolt. It fell, the door banged, and we were in darkness. The king was running down the stairs.

Where the light came through the grating in the ceiling, that watery, stone-conditioned yellow light, I caught up with him.

He said, "Why are you blustering at me so with your face? You have a perilous expression."

I said, "King, it's the way I feel. I told you before I am mediumistic. And I feel trouble."

"No doubt, as there is trouble. But I will capture Gmilo and the trouble will entirely cease. No one will dispute or contest me then. There are scouts daily for Gmilo. As a matter of fact reports have come of him. I can assure you of a capture very soon."

I said fervently that I certainly hoped he would catch him and get the thing over with, so we could stop worrying about those two strangling characters, the Bunam and the black-leather man. Then they would stop persecuting his mother. At this second mention of his mother he looked angry. For the first time he subjected me to a long scowl. Then he resumed his way down the stairs. Shaken, I followed him. Well, I reflected, this black king happened to be a genius. Like Pascal

at the age of twelve discovering the thirty-second proposition
of Euclid all by himself.

But why lions?

Because, Mr. Henderson, I replied to myself, you don't
know the meaning of true love if you think it can be
deliberately selected. You just love, that's all. A natural force.
Irresistible. He fell in love with his lioness at first sight—coup
de foudre. I went crashing down the weed-grown part of the
stairway engaged in this dialogue with myself. At the same
time I held my breath as we approached the den. The cloud of
fright about me was even more suffocating than before; it
seemed to give actual resistance to my face and made my
breathing clumsy. My respiration grew thick. Hearing us, the
beast began to roar in her inner room. Dahfu looked through
the grating and said, "It is all right, we may go in."

"Now? You think she's okay? She sounds disturbed to me.
Why don't I wait out here," I said, "till you find out how the
wind blows?"

"No, you must come," said the king. "Don't you understand yet, I am trying to do something for you? A benefit? I
can hardly think of a person who may need this more. Really
the danger of life is negligible. The animal is tame."

"Tame for you, but she doesn't really know me yet. I'm just
as ready to take a reasonable chance as the next guy. But I
can't help it, I am afraid of her."

He paused, and during this pause I thought I was going
down greatly in his estimation, and nothing could have hurt
me more than that. "Oh," he said, and he was particularly
thoughtful. Silently he paused and thought. In this moment he
looked and sounded, again, larger than life. "I think I recall
when we were speaking of blows that there was a lack of the
brave." Then he sighed and said, with his earnest mouth
which even in the shadow of his hat had a very red color,
"Fear is a ruler of mankind. It has the biggest dominion of all.
It makes you white as candles. It splits each eye in half. More
of fear than of any other thing has been created," he said. "As
a molding force it comes second only to Nature itself."

"Then doesn't this apply to you, too?"

He said, with a nod of full agreement, "Oh, certainly. It applies. It applies to everyone. Though nothing may be visible, still it is heard, like radio. It is on almost all the frequencies. And all tremble, and all are wincing, in greater or lesser degree."

"And you think there is a cure?" I said.

"Why, I surely believe there is. Otherwise all the better imagining will have to be surrendered. Anyways, I will not urge you to come in with me and do as I have done. As my father Gmilo did. As Gmilo's father Suffo did. As we all did. No. If it is positively beyond you we may as well exchange good-by and go separate ways."

"Wait a minute now, King, don't be hasty," I said. I was mortified and frightened; nothing could have been more painful than to lose my connection with him. Something had gone off in my breast, my eyes filled, and I said, almost choking, "You wouldn't brush me off like that, would you, King? You know how I feel." He realized how hard I was taking it; nevertheless he repeated that perhaps it would be better if I left, for although we were temperamentally suited as friends and he had deep affection for me, too, and was grateful for the opportunity to know me and also for my services to the Wariri in lifting up Mummah, still, unless I understood about lions, no deepening of the friendship was possible. I simply had to know what this was about. "Wait a minute, King," I said. "I feel tremendously close to you and I'm prepared to believe what you tell me."

"Sungo, thank you," he said. "I also am close to you. It is very mutual. But I require more deep relationship. I desire to be understood and communicated to. We have to develop an underlying similarity which lies within you by connection with the lion. Otherwise, how shall we maintain the truth agreement we made?"

Moved as anything, I said, "Oh, this is hard, King, to be threatened with loss of friendship."

The threat was exceedingly painful also to him. Yes, I saw

that he suffered almost as hard as I did. Almost. Because who can suffer like me? I am to suffering what Gary is to smoke. One of the world's biggest operations.

"I don't understand it," I said.

He took me up to the door and made me look through the grating at Atti the lioness, and in that soft, personal tone peculiar to him which went strangely to the center of the subject, he said, "What a Christian might feel in Saint Sophia's church, which I visited in Turkey as a student, I absorb from lion. When she gives her tail a flex, it strikes against my heart. You ask, what can she do for you? Many things. First she is unavoidable. Test it, and you will find she is unavoidable. And this is what you need, as you are an avoider. Oh, you have accomplished momentous avoidances. But she will change that. She will make consciousness to shine. She will burnish you. She will force the present moment upon you. Second, lions are experiencers. But not in haste. They experience with deliberate luxury. The poet says, 'The tigers of wrath are wiser than the horses of instruction.' Let us embrace lions also in the same view. Moreover, observe Atti. Contemplate her. How does she stride, how does she saunter, how does she lie or gaze or rest or breathe? I stress the respiratory part," he said. "She do not breathe shallow. This freedom of the intercostal muscles and her abdominal flexibility" (her lower belly, which was disclosed to our view, was sheer white) "gives the vital continuity between her parts. It brings those brown jewel eyes their hotness. Then there are more subtle things, as how she leaves hints, or elicits caresses. But I cannot expect you to see this at first. She has much to teach you."

"Teach? You really mean that she might change me."

"Excellent. Precisely. Change. You fled what you were. You did not believe you had to perish. Once more, and a last time, you tried the world. With a hope of alteration. Oh, do not be surprised by such a recognition," he said, seeing how it moved me to discover that my position was understood. "You have told me much. You are frank. This makes you irresistible, as not many are. You have rudiments of high character. You could be noble. Some parts may be so long-buried as to be classed dead. Is there any resurrectibility in them? This is where the change comes in."

"You think there's a chance for me?" I said.

"Not at all impossible if you follow my directions."

The lioness stroked past the door. I heard her low, soft, continuous snarl.

Dahfu now started to go in. My nether half turned very cold. My knees felt like two rocks in a cold Alpine torrent. My mustache stabbed and stung into my lips, which made me realize that I was frowning and grimacing with terror, and I knew that my eyes must be filling with fatal blackness. As before, he took my hand as we entered and I came into the den saying inwardly, "Help me, God! Oh, help!" The odor was blinding, for here, near the door where the air was trapped, it stank radiantly. From this darkness came the face of the lioness, wrinkling, with her whiskers like the thinnest spindles scratched with a diamond on the surface of a glass. She allowed the king to fondle her, but passed by him to examine me, coming round with those clear circles of inhuman wrath, convex, brown, and pure, rings of black light within them. Between her mouth and nostrils a line divided her lip, like the waist of the hourglass, expanding into the muzzle. She sniffed my feet, working her way to the crotch once more and causing my parts to hide in my belly as best they could. She next put her head into my armpit and purred with such tremendous vibration it made my head buzz like a kettle.

Dahfu whispered, "She likes you. Oh, I am glad. I am enthusiastic. I am so proud of both of you. Are you afraid?"

I was bursting. I could only nod.

"Later you will laugh at yourself with amusement. Now it is normal."

"I can't even bring my hands together to wring them," I said.

"Feel paralysis?" he said.

The lioness went away, making a tour of the den along the walls on the thick pads of her feet.

"Can you see?" he said.

"Barely. I can barely see a single thing."

"Let us begin with the walk."

"Behind bars, I'd like that fine. It would be great."

"You are avoiding again, Henderson-Sungo." His eyes were looking at me from under the softly folded velvet brim. "Change does not lie that way. You must form a new habit."

"Oh, King, what can I do? My openings are screwed up tight, both back and front. They may go to the other extreme in a minute. My mouth is all dried out, my scalp is wrinkling up, I feel thick and heavy at the back of my head. I may be passing out."

I remember that he looked at me with keen curiosity, as if wondering about these symptoms from a medical standpoint. "All the resistances are putting forth their utmost," was his comment. It didn't seem possible that the black of his face could be exceeded, and yet his hair, visible at the borders of his hat, was blacker. "Well," he said, "we shall let them come out. I am firmly confident in you."

I said weakly, "I'm glad you think so. If I'm not torn to pieces. If I'm not left down here half-eaten."

"Take my assurance. No such eventuality is possible. Now, watch the way she walks. Beautiful? You said it! Furthermore this is uninstructed, specie-beauty. I believe when the fear has subsided you will be capable of admiring her beauty. I think that part of the beauty emotion does result from an overcoming of fear. When the fear yields, a beauty is disclosed in its place. This is also said of perfect love if I recollect, and it means that ego-emphasis is removed. Oh, Henderson, watch how she is rhythmical in behavior. Did you do the cat in Anatomy One? Watch how she gives her tail a flex. I feel it as if undergoing it personally. Now let us follow her." He began to lead me around after the lioness. I was bent over, and my legs were thick and drunken. The green silk pants no longer floated but were charged with electricity and clung to the back of my thighs. The king did not stop talking, which I was glad of, since his words were the sole support I had. His reasoning I couldn't follow in detail—I wasn't fit to—but gradually I understood that he wanted me to imitate or dramatize the behavior of lions. What is this going to be, I thought, the Stanislavski method? The Moscow Art Theater? My mother took a tour of Russia in 1905. On the eve of the Japanese War she saw the Czar's mistress perform in the ballet.

I said to the king, "And how does Obersteiner's allochiria and all that medical stuff you gave me to read come into this?"

He patiently said, "All the pieces fit properly. It will presently be clear. But first by means of the lion try to distinguish the states that are given and the states that are made. Observe that Atti is all lion. Does not take issue with the inherent. Is one hundred per cent within the given."

But I said in a broken voice, "If she doesn't try to be human, why should I try to act the lion? I'll never make it. If I have to copy someone, why can't it be you?"

"Oh, shush these objections, Henderson-Sungo. *I* copied her. Transfer from lion to man is possible, I know by experience." And then he shouted, "Sakta," which was a cue to the lioness to start running. She trotted, and the king began to bound after her, and I ran too, trying to keep close to him. "Sakta, sakta," he was crying, and she picked up speed. Now she was going fast along the opposite wall. In a few minutes she would come up behind me.

I started to call to him, "King, King, wait, let me go in front of you, for Christ's sake."

"Spring upward," he called back to me. But I was clumping and pounding after him trying to pass him, and sobbing. In the mind's eye I saw blood in great drops, bigger than quarters, spring from my skin as she sank her claws into me, for I was convinced that as I was in motion I was fair game and she would claw me as soon as she was within range. Or perhaps she would break my neck. I thought that might be preferable. One stroke, one dizzy moment, the mind fills with night. Ah, God! No stars in that night. There is nothing.

I could not catch up with the king, and therefore I pretended to stumble and threw myself heavily on the ground, off to the side, and gave a crazy cry. The king when he saw me prostrate on my belly held out his hand to Atti to stop her, shouting, "Tana, tana, Atti." She sprang sideward and began to walk toward the wooden shelf. From the dust I watched her. She gathered herself down upon her haunches and lightly reached the shelf on which she liked to lie. She pointed one leg outward and started to wash herself with her tongue. The king squatted beside her and said, "Are you hurt, Mr. Henderson?"

"No, I just got jolted," I said.

Then he began to explain. "I intend to loosen you up, Sungo, because you are so contracted. This is why we were running. The tendency of your conscious is to isolate self. This makes you extremely contracted and self-recoiled, so next I wish—"

"Next?" I said. "What next? I've had it. I'm humbled to the dust already. What else am I supposed to do, King, for heaven's sake? First I was stuck with a dead body, then thrown into the cattle pond, clobbered by the amazons. Okay. For the rain. Even the Sungo pants and all that. Okay! But now this?"

With much forbearance and sympathy he answered, picking up a pleated corner of his velvet headgear, the color of thick wine, "Patient, Sungo," he said. "Those aforementioned things were for us, for the Wariri. Do not think I am ever ingrate. But this latter is for you."

"That's what you keep saying. But how can this lion routine cure what I've got?"

The forward slope of the king's face suggested, as his mother's did, that it was being offered to you. "Oh," he said, "high conduct, high conduct! There will never be anything but misery without high conduct. I knew that you went out from home in America because of a privation of high conduct. You have met your first opportunities of it well, Henderson-Sungo, but you must go on. Take advantage of the studies I have made, which by chance are available to you."

I licked my hand, for I had scratched it in falling, and then I sat up, brooding. He squatted opposite me with his arms about his knees. He looked steadily at me across his large folded arms while he tried to make me meet his gaze.

"What do you want me to do?"

"As I have done. As Gmilo, Suffo, all the forefathers did. They all acted the lion. Each absorbed lion into himself. If you do as I wish, you too will act the lion."

If this body, if this flesh of mine were only a dream, then there might be some hope of awakening. That was what I thought as I lay there smarting. I lay, so to speak, at the bottom of things. Finally I sighed and started to get up, making one of the greatest efforts I have ever made. At this he said, "Why rise, Sungo, since we have you in a prone position?"

"What do you mean, prone position? Do you want me to crawl?"

"No, naturally not, crawl is for a different order of creature. But be on all the fours. I wish you to assume the posture of a lion." He got on all fours himself, and I had to admit that he looked very much like a lion. Atti, with crossed paws, only occasionally looked at us.

"You see?" he said.

And I answered, "Well, you ought to be able to do it. You were brought up on it. Besides, it's your idea. But I can't." I slumped back on the ground.

"Oh," he said. "Mr. Henderson, Mr. Henderson! Is this the man who spoke of rising from a grave of solitude? Who recited me the poem of the little fly on the green leaf in the setting sun? Who wished to end Becoming? Is this the Henderson who flew half around the world because he had a voice which said *I want?* And now, because his friend Dahfu extends a remedy to him, falls down? You dismiss my relationship?"

"Now, King, that's not true. It's just not true, and you know it. I'd do anything for you."

To prove this, I rose up on my hands and feet and stood

there with knees sagging, trying to look straight ahead and as much like a lion as possible.

"Oh, excellent," he said. "I am so glad. I was sure you had sufficient flexibility in you. Settle on your knees now. Oh, that is better, much better." My paunch came forward between my arms. "Your structure is far from ordinary," he said. "But I offer you sincerest congratulations on laying aside the former attitude of fixity. Now, sir, will you assume a little more limberness? You appear cast in one piece. The midriff dominates. Can you move the different portions? Minus yourself of some of your heavy reluctance of attitude. Why so sad and so earthen? Now you are a lion. Mentally, conceive of the environment. The sky, the sun, and creatures of the bush. You are related to all. The very gnats are your cousins. The sky is your thoughts. The leaves are your insurance, and you need no other. There is no interruption all night to the speech of the stars. Are you with me? I say, Mr. Henderson, have you consumed much amounts of alcohol in your life? The face suggests you have, the nose especially. It is nothing personal. Much can be changed. By no means all, but very very much. You can have a new poise, which will be your own poise. It will resemble the voice of Caruso, which I have heard on records, never tired because the function is as natural as to the birds. However," he said, "it is another animal you strongly remind me of. But of which?"

I wasn't going to tell him anything. My vocal cords, anyway, seemed stuck together like strands of overcooked spaghetti.

"Oh, truly! How very big you are," he said. He went on in this vein.

At last I found my voice and asked him, "How long do you want me to hold this?"

"I have been observing," he said. "It is very important that you feel *something* of a lion on your maiden attempt. Let us start with the roaring."

"It won't excite her, you think?"

"No, no. Now look, Mr. Henderson, I wish you to picture that you are a lion. A literal lion."

I moaned.

"No, sir. Please oblige me. A real roar. We must hear your voice. It tends to be rather choked. I told you the tendency of your conscious is to isolate self. So fancy you are with your kill. You are warning away an intruder. You may begin with a growl."

Having come so far with the guy there was no way to back out. Not one single alternative remained. I had to do it. So I began to make a rumble in my throat. I was in despair.

"More, more," he said impatiently. "Atti has taken no notice, therefore it is far from the thing."

I let the sound grow louder.

"And glare as you do so. Roar, roar, roar, Henderson-Sungo. Do not be afraid. Let go of yourself. Snarl greatly. Feel the lion. Lower on the forepaws. Up with hindquarters. Threaten me. Open those magnificent mixed eyes. Oh, give more sound. Better, better," he said, "though still too much pathos. Give more sound. Now, with your hand—your paw—attack! Cuff! Fall back! Once more—strike, strike, strike, strike! Feel it. Be the beast! You will recover humanity later, but for the moment, be it utterly."

And so I was the beast. I gave myself to it, and all my sorrow came out in the roaring. My lungs supplied the air but the note came from my soul. The roaring scalded my throat and hurt the corners of my mouth and presently I filled the den like a bass organ pipe. This was where my heart had sent me, with its clamor. This is where I ended up. Oh, Nebuchadnezzar! How well I understand that prophecy of Daniel. For I had claws, and hair, and some teeth, and I was bursting with hot noise, but when all this had come forth, there was still a remainder. That last thing of all was my human longing.

As for the king, he was in a state of enthusiasm, praising me, rubbing his hands together, looking into my face. "Oh, good, Mr. Henderson. Good, good. You are the sort of man I took you to be," I heard him say when I stopped to draw breath. I might as well go the whole way, I thought, as I was crouching in the dust and the lion's offal, since I had come so far; therefore I gave it everything I had and roared my head off. Whenever I opened my bulging eyes I saw the king in his hat rejoicing by my side, and the lioness on the trestle staring at me, a creature entirely of gold sitting there.

When I could do no more I fell flat on my face. The king thought I might have passed out, and he felt my pulse and patted my cheeks saying, "Come, come, dear fellow." I opened my eyes and he said, "Ah, are you okay? I worried about you. You went from crimson to black starting from the sternum and rising into the face."

"No, I'm all right. How am I doing?"

"Wonderfully, my brother Henderson. Believe me, it will prove beneficial. I will lead Atti away and let you take rest. We have done enough for the first time."

We were sitting on the trestle together and talking after the king had shut Atti in her inner room. He seemed positive that the lion Gmilo was going to turn up very soon. He had been observed in the vicinity. Then he would release the lioness, he told me, and end the controversy with the Bunam. After this he began to talk again about the connection between the body and the brain. He said, "It is all a matter of having a desirable model in the cortex. For the noble self-conception is everything. For as conception is, so the fellow is. Put differently, you are in the flesh as your soul is. And in the manner described a fellow really is the artist of himself. Body and face are secretly painted by the spirit of man, working through the cortex and brain ventricles three and four, which direct the flow of vital energy all over. And this explains what I am so excited about, Henderson-Sungo." For he was highly excited by now. He was soaring. He was up there with enthusiasm. Trying to keep up with his flight made me dizzy. Also I felt very bitter over some implications of his theory, which I was beginning to understand. For if I was the painter of my own nose and forehead and of such a burly stoop and such arms and fingers, why, it was an out-and-out felony against myself. What had I done! A bungled lump of humanity! Oh, ho, ho, ho, ho! Would death please wash me away and dissolve this giant collection of errors. "It's the pigs," I suddenly realized, "the pigs! Lions for him, pigs for me. I wish I was dead."

"You are pensive, Henderson-Sungo."

I came near holding a grudge against the king at that moment. I should have realized that his brilliance was not a secure gift, but like this ramshackle red palace rested on doubtful underpinnings.

Now he began to give me a new sort of lecture. He said that nature might be a mentality. I wasn't sure quite what he meant by that. He wondered whether even inanimate objects might have a mental existence. He said that Madame Curie had written something about the beta particles issuing like flocks of birds. "Do you remember?" he said. "The great Kepler believed that the whole planet slept and woke and breathed. Was this talking through his hat? In that case the mind of the human may associate with the All-Intelligent to perform certain work. By imagination." And then he began to repeat what a procession of monsters the human imagination had created instead. "I have subsumed them under the types I mentioned," he said, "as the appetite, the agony, the fateful-hysterical, the fighting Lazaruses, the immune elephants, the mad laughers, the hollow genital, and so on. Think of what there could be instead by different imaginations. What gay, brilliant types, what merriment types, what beauties and goodness, what sweet cheeks or noble demeanors. Ah, ah, ah, what we could be! Opportunity calls to rise to summits. You should have been such a summit, Mr. Henderson-Sungo."

"Me?" I said, still dazed by my own roaring. My mental horizon was far from clear, although the clouds on it were not low and dark.

"So you see," said Dahfu, "you came to me speaking of grun-tu-molani. What could be grun-tu-molani upon a background of cows?"

Swine! he might have said to me.

It was vain to curse Nicky Goldstein for this. It was not his fault that he was a Jew, that he had announced he was going to raise minks in the Catskills and that I had told him I was going to raise pigs. Fate is much more complex than that. I must have been committed to pigs long before I laid eyes on Goldstein. Two sows, Hester and Valentina, used to follow me

about with freckled bellies and sour, red, rust-gleaming
bristles, silky in luster, stiff as pins to the touch. "Don't let
them loll in the driveway," said Frances. That was when I
warned her, "You'd better not hurt them. Those animals have
become a part of me."

Well, had those creatures become a part of me? I hesitated
to come clean with Dahfu and to ask him right out bluntly
whether he could see their influence. Secretly investigating
myself, I felt my cheekbones. They stuck out like the
mushrooms that grow from the trunks of trees, those mushrooms which prove to be as white as lard when you break
them open. Under my helmet, my fingers crept toward my
eyelashes. Pigs' eyelashes occur only on the upper lid. I had
some on the lower, but they were sparse and blunt. When a
boy I had practiced to become like Houdini and tried to pick
up needles from the floor with my eyelashes while hanging
upside down from the foot of my bed. He had done it. I never
managed to, but that was not because my eyelashes were too
short. Oh, I had changed all right. Everybody changes.
Change is ordained. Changes must come. But how? The king
would say that they were directed by the master-image. And
now I felt my jowls, my snout; I did not dare to look down at
what had happened to me. Hams. Tripes, a whole caldron full
of them. Trunk, a fat cylinder. It seemed to me that I couldn't
even breathe without grunting. Brother! I put my hand over
my nose and mouth and looked with distressed eyes at the
king. But he heard the guttural vibration of the vocal cords
and said, "What is the peculiar noise you are making,
Henderson-Sungo?"

"What does it sound like, King?"

"I don't know. An animal syllable? Oddly, you look well
after your exertion."

"I don't feel so well. I'm not one of your summits. You
know that as well as I do."

"You show the work of a powerful and original although
blockaded imagination."

"Is that what you see?" I said.

He said, "What I see is greatly mixed. Fantastic elements have fought forth from your body. Excrescences. You are an exceptional amalgam of vehement forces." He sighed and gave a quiet smile; his mood was very quiet just then. He said, "We do not speak in blame terms. So many factors are mediating. Fomenting. Promulgating. Everyone is different. A billion small things unperceived by the object of their influence. True, pure intelligence does the best it can, but who can judge? Negative and positive elements strive, and we can only look at them and wonder or weep. You may sometimes see a clear case of angel and vulture in collision. The eye is of heaven, the nose gives a certain flare. But face and body are the book of the soul, open to the reader of science and sympathy." Grunting, I looked at him.

"Sungo," he said, "listen painstakingly, and I will tell you what I have a strong conviction about." I did as he said, for I thought he might tell me something hopeful about myself. "The career of our specie," he said, "is evidence that one imagination after another grows literal. Not dreams. Not mere dreams. I say not mere dreams because they have a way of growing actual. At school in Malindi I read all of Bulfinch. And I say not mere dream. No. Birds flew, harpies flew, angels flew, Daedalus and son flew. And see here, it is no longer dreaming and story, for literally there is flying. You flew here, into Africa. All human accomplishment has this same origin, identically. Imagination is a force of nature. Is this not enough to make a person full of ecstasy? Imagination, imagination, imagination! It converts to actual. It sustains, it alters, it redeems! You see," he said, "I sit here in Africa and devote myself to this in personal fashion, to my best ability, I am convinced. What Homo sapiens imagines, he may slowly convert himself to. Oh, Henderson, how glad I am that you are here! I have longed for somebody to discuss with. A companion mind. You are a godsend to me."

Chapter XIX

Around the palace was a vegetable and mineral junkyard. The trees were niggardly and grew with gnarls and spikes. Then there were the flowers, which also lay in the Sungo's department. My girls watered them and they thrived in those white hollow stones. The sun made the red blossoms extremely sleek and taut. Daily, I would come up from the den all shaken by my roaring, my throat grated, my head in fever and my eyes like wet soot, weak in the legs, and especially delicate and trembling in the knees. All I needed then was the weight of the sun to make me feel like a convalescent. You know how it is about some people when they convalesce from wasting diseases. They become strangely sensitive; they go around and muse; little sights pierce them, they get sentimental; they see beauty in all the corners. So, watched by all, I would go and bend over those flowers, I would stoop hopelessly with my eyes of damp soot at the bowls of petrified mineral junk filled with soaked humus and sniff the flowers and grunt and sigh with a sort of heavy, beady wretchedness, the Sungo pants sticking to me and the hair on my head, especially at the back, thriving. I was growing black curls, thicker than usual, like a Merino sheep, very black, and they were unseating my helmet. Maybe my mind, beginning to change sponsors, so to speak, was stimulating the growth of a different man.

Everybody knew where I was coming from, and I presume had heard me roaring. If I could hear Atti they could hear me. Watched by all, and watched dangerously by enemies, mine and the king's, I lumbered out into the yard and tried to smell the flowers. Not that they had a smell. They had only the color. But that was enough; it fell on my soul, clamoring, while Romilayu always came up behind to offer support, if needed. ("Romilayu, what do you think of these flowers? They are noisy as hell," I said.) At this time, when I must have seemed contaminated and dangerous due to contact with the lion, he did not shrink from me or seek safety in the background. He did not let me down. And since I love loyalty beyond anything else, I tried to show that I excused him from all his obligations to me. "You're a true pal," I said. "You deserve much more than a jeep from me. I want to add something to it." I patted him on the bushy head—my hand seemed very thick; each of my fingers felt like a yam—and then I grunted all the way back to my apartment. There I lay down to rest. I was all roared out. The very marrow was gone from my bones, so that they felt hollow. I lay on my side, heaving and groaning, with that expanded envelope, my belly. Sometimes I imagined that I was, from the trotters to the helmet, all six feet four inches of me, the picture of that familiar animal, freckled on the belly, with broken tusks and wide cheekbones. True, inside, my heart ran with human feeling, but externally, in the rind if you like, I showed all the strange abuses and malformations of a lifetime.

To tell the truth, I didn't have full confidence in the king's science. Down there in the den, while I went through the utmost hell, he would idle around, calm, easy and almost languid. He would tell me that the lioness made him feel very peaceful. Sometimes as we lay on the trestle after my exercises, all three of us together, he would say, "It is very restful here. Why, I am floating. You must give yourself a chance. You must try. . . ." But I had almost blacked out, before, and I was not yet prepared to start floating.

Everything was black and amber, down there in the den. The stone walls themselves were yellowish. Then straw. Then dung. The dust was sulphur-colored. The skin of the lioness lightened gradually from the dark of the spine, toward the chest a ground-ginger shade, and on the belly white pepper, and under the haunches she became as white as the Arctic. But her small heels were black. Her eyes also were ringed absolutely with black. At times she had a meat flavor on her breath.

"You must try to make more of a lion of yourself," Dahfu insisted, and that I certainly did. Considering my handicaps, the king declared I was making progress. "Your roaring still is choked. Of course it is natural, as you have such a lot to purge," he would say. That was no lie, as everyone knows. I would have hated to witness my own antics and hear my own voice. Romilayu admitted he had heard me roar, and you couldn't blame the rest of the natives for thinking that I was Dahfu's understudy in the black arts, or whatever they accused him of practicing. But what the king called pathos was actually (I couldn't help myself) a cry which summarized my entire course on this earth, from birth to Africa; and certain words crept into my roars, like "God," "Help," "Lord have mercy," only they came out "Hooolp!" "Moooorcy!" It's funny what words sprang forth. "Au secours," which was "Secooooooooor" and also "De profoooooondis," plus snatches from the "Messiah" (He was despised and rejected, a man of sorrows, etcetera). Unbidden, French sometimes comes back to me, the language in which I used to taunt my little friend François about his sister.

So I would roar and the king would sit with his arm about his lioness, as though they were attending an opera performance. She certainly looked very formal in attire. After a dozen or so of these agonizing efforts I would feel dim and dark within the brain and my arms and legs would give out.

Allowing me a short rest, he made me try again and again. Afterward he was very sympathetic. He would say, "I assume now you are feeling better, Mr. Henderson?"

"Yes, better."

"Lighter?"

"Sure, lighter, too, Your Honor."

"More calm?"

Then I would begin to snort. I was all jolted up within. My face was boiling; I was lying in the dust, and I would sit up to look at the two of them.

"How are your emotions?"

"Like a caldron, Your Highness, a regular caldron."

"I see you are laboring with a lifetime accumulation." Then he would say, almost pityingly, "You are still afraid of Atti?"

"Damn right I am. I'd sooner jump out of a plane. I wouldn't be half so scared. I applied for paratroops in the war. Come to think of it, Your Highness, I think I could bail out at fifteen thousand feet in these pants and stand a good chance."

"Your humor is delicious, Sungo."

This man was completely lacking in what we all know as civilized character.

"I am sure that you soon will begin to feel something of what it is to be a lion. I am convinced of your capacity. The old self is resisting?"

"Oh, yes, I feel that old self more than ever," I said. "I feel it all the time. It's got a terrific grip on me." I began to cough and grunt, and I was in despair. "As if I were carrying an eight-hundred-pound load—like a Galápagos turtle. On my back."

"Sometimes a condition must worsen before bettering," he said, and he began to tell me of diseases he had known when he was on the wards as a student, and I tried to picture him as a medical student in white coat and white shoes instead of the velvet hat adorned with human teeth and the satin slippers. He held the lioness by the head; her broth-colored eyes watched me; those whiskers, suggesting diamond scratches, seemed so cruel that her own skin shrank from them at the base. She had an angry nature. What can you do with an angry nature?

This was why, when I returned from the den, I felt as I did in the torrid light of the yard, with its stone junk and the red flowers. Horko's bridge table was set up under the umbrella for lunch, but first I went to rest and get my wind back, and I would think, "Well, maybe every guy has his own Africa. Or if he goes to sea, his own ocean." By which I meant that as I was a turbulent individual, I was having a turbulent Africa. This is not to say, however, that I think the world exists for my sake. No, I really believe in reality. That's a known fact.

Each day I grew more aware that everybody knew where I had spent the morning and feared me for it—I had arrived like a dragon; maybe the king had sent for me to help him defy the

Bunam and overturn the religion of the whole tribe. And I
tried to explain to Romilayu at least that Dahfu and I were
not practicing any evil. "Look, Romilayu," I told him, "the
king just happens to have a very rich nature. He didn't have to
come back and put himself at the mercy of his wives. He did it
because he hopes to benefit the whole world. A fellow may do
many a crazy thing, and as long as he has no theory about it
we forgive him. But if there happens to be a theory behind his
actions everybody is down on him. That's how it is with the
king. But he isn't hurting me, old fellow. It's true it sounds like
it, but don't you believe it. I make that noise of my own free
will. If I don't look well, that's because I haven't been feeling
well; I have a fever, and the inside of my nose and throat are
inflamed. (Rhinitis?) I guess the king would give me something for it if I asked him but I don't feel like telling him."

"I don' blame you, sah."

"Don't get me wrong. The human race needs guys like this
king more than ever. Change must be possible! If not, it's too
damn bad."

"Yes, sah."

"Americans are supposed to be dumb but they are willing
to go into this. It isn't just me. You have to think about white
Protestantism and the Constitution and the Civil War and
capitalism and winning the West. All the major tasks and the
big conquests were done before my time. That left the biggest
problem of all, which was to encounter death. We've just got
to do something about it. It isn't just me. Millions of
Americans have gone forth since the war to redeem the
present and discover the future. I can swear to you, Romilayu,
there are guys exactly like me in India and in China and South
America and all over the place. Just before I left home I saw
an interview in the paper with a piano teacher from Muncie
who became a Buddhist monk in Burma. You see, that's what
I mean. I am a high-spirited kind of guy. And it's the destiny
of my generation of Americans to go out in the world and try
to find the wisdom of life. It just is. Why the hell do you think
I'm out here, anyway?"

"I don' know, sah."

"I wouldn't agree to the death of my soul."

"Me Methdous, sah."

"I know it, but that would never help me, Romilayu. And please don't try to convert me, I'm in trouble enough as it is."

"I no bothah you."

"I know. You are standing by me in my hour of trial, God bless you for it. I also am standing by King Dahfu until he captures his father, Gmilo. When I get to be a friend, Romilayu, I am a devoted friend. I know what it is to lie buried in yourself. One thing I have learned, though I am a hard man to educate. I tell you, the king has a rich nature. I wish I could learn his secret."

Then Romilayu with the scars shining on his wrinkled face (manifestations of his former savagery) but with soft sympathetic eyes which contained a light that didn't come from the air (it could never have penetrated the shade, like an umbrella pine, that grew across his low forehead), wanted to know what secret I was trying to get from Dahfu.

"Why," I said, "there's something about danger that doesn't perplex the guy. Look at all the things he has to fear, and still look at the way he lies on that sofa. You've never seen that. He has an old green sofa upstairs which must have been brought by the elephants a century ago. And the way he lies on it, Romilayu! And the females wait on him. But on the table near him he has those two skulls used at the rain ceremony, one his father's and the other his grandfather's. Are you married, Romilayu?" I asked him.

"Yes, sah, two time. But now got one wife."

"Why, that's just like me. And I have five children, including twin boys about four years old. My wife is very big."

"Me, six children."

"Do you worry about them? It's a wild continent still, no two ways about that. I am all the time worrying lest my two little kids wander off in the woods. We ought to get a dog—a big dog. But we'll be living in town anyway from now on. I am going to go to school. Romilayu, I am going to send a letter to

my wife, and you are going to take it to Baventai and mail it. I
promised you baksheesh, old man, and here are the papers for
the jeep, made over to you. I wish I could take you back to the
States with me, but since you have a family it's not practical."
His face expressed very little pleasure at the gift. It wrinkled
especially hard, and as I knew him by now I said, "Hell, man,
don't be toying with tears all the time. What's to cry over?"

"You in trouble, sah," he said.

"Yes, I know I am. But since I'm a reluctant type of fellow,
life has decided to use strong measures on me. I am a shunner,
Romilayu, and so this serves me right. What's the matter, old
pal, do I look bad?"

"Yes, sah."

"My feelings always did leak into my looks," I said. "That's
the type of constitution I have. Is it that woman's head they
showed us that worries you?"

"Dem kill you, maybe?" said Romilayu.

"Okay, that Bunam is a bad actor. The guy is a scorpion.
But don't forget I am the Sungo. Doesn't Mummah protect
me? I think maybe my person is sacred. Besides, with my
twenty-two neck they'd have to have two guys to strangle me.
Ha, ha! You mustn't worry about me, Romilayu. As soon as
this business with the king is completed and I have helped him
capture his dad, I'll join you in Baventai."

"Please God, 'e mek quick," said Romilayu.

When I mentioned the Bunam to the king, he laughed at
me. "When I possess Gmilo, I am absolute master," he said.

"But that animal is raging and killing out there in the
savanna," I said, "and you act as though you had him safe in
storage already."

"Lions do not often leave a given locale," he said. "Gmilo is
near here. Any day he will be encountered. Go and write the
letter to your missis," Dahfu told me, laughing very low on his
green sofa amid his black troop of nude women.

"I'm going to write to her today," I said.

So I went down to have lunch with the Bunam and Horko.
Horko, the Bunam, and the Bunam's black-leather man were
always waiting for me at the bridge table under the umbrella.

"Gentlemen . . ." "Asi Sungo," said everyone. I was always aware that these people had heard me roaring and probably could smell the odor of the den on me. But I brazened it out. The Bunam, when he did glance my way, which was rarely, was very somber. I thought, "I may get you first. No man can know that and you'd better not push me hard." The behavior of Horko on the other hand was invariably genial, and he hung out his red tongue and leaned over the little table with his knuckles like tree boles until it swayed with his weight. There was an air of intrigue under the transparent silk of the umbrella, while entertainers skipped for us out in the sun and feet flitted in and out of robes as Horko's people danced to amuse us and the old musician played his pendulum viol and others drummed and blew in the palace junkyard with its petrified brains of white stone and the red flowers growing in the humus.

After lunch came the daily water duty. The laboring women, with deep stress marks on the skin of their shoulders from the poles, carried me out into the lanes of the town where the dust of the ruts was reduced to a powder. The lone drum bumped after me; it seemed to warn people to stay away from this Henderson, the lion-contaminated Sungo. People still came to look at me out of curiosity, but not in their previous numbers, nor did they particularly want to be sprinkled by the crazy rain king. So that when we got to the dunghill at the center of town where the court was situated, I made a point of getting on my feet and sprinkling right and left. This was stoically taken. The magistrate in his crimson gown seemed as if he would have stopped me if he had had the power. However, nothing was done. The prisoner with the forked stick in his mouth leaned his face against the post he was tied to. "I hope you win, pal," I said to him and got back into my hammock.

That afternoon I wrote to Lily as follows:
"Honey, you are probably worried about me, but I suppose you have known all along that I was alive."

*Lily claimed she could always tell how I was. She had some
kind of privileged love-intuition.*

"The flight here was spectacular."

Like hovering all the way inside a jewel.

"We are the first generation to see the clouds from both
sides. What a privilege! First people dreamed upward. Now
they dream both upward and downward. This is bound to
change something, somewhere. For me the entire experience
has been similar to a dream. I liked Egypt. Everybody was in
basic white rags. From the air the mouth of the Nile looked
like raveled rope. In some places the valley was green and it
was yellow. The cataracts resembled seltzer. When we landed
in Africa itself and Charlie and I put the show on the road, it
wasn't exactly what I had hoped in leaving home." *As I
discovered a pestilence when I entered the old lady's house and
realized that I must put forth effort or go down in shame.*
"Charlie did not relax in Africa. I was reading R. F. Burton's
First Footsteps in East Africa plus Speke's *Journal*, and we
didn't see eye to eye about any subject. So we parted
company. Burton thought a lot of himself. He was very good
with the épée and saber and he spoke everyone's language. I
picture him as resembling General Douglas MacArthur in
character, very conscious of having a historical role and
thinking of classical Rome and Greece. Personally, I had to
decide to follow a different course, as by any civilized
standard I am done for. However, the geniuses love common
life a great deal."

*When he got back to England, Speke blew his brains out. This
biographical detail I spared Lily. By genius I mean somebody
like Plato or Einstein. Light itself was all Einstein needed. What
could be more common?*

"There was a fellow around named Romilayu, and we
became friends, though at first he was scared of me. I asked
him to show me uncivilized parts of Africa. There are very few
of these left. There are modern governments springing up and
educated classes. I myself have met such educated African
royalty and am the guest right now of a king who is almost an

M.D. Nevertheless, I am off the beaten track, without question, and I have Romilayu (he is a wonderful guy) and Charlie himself, indirectly, to thank for that. To a certain extent it has been terrible, and continues to be. A few times I could have given up my soul as easily as a fish lets out a bubble. You know, Charlie is not a bad egg, at heart. But I shouldn't have come along on a honeymoon trip. I was a fifth wheel. She is one of those Madison Avenue dollies who have their back teeth pulled to produce a fashionable look (sunken cheeks)."

But on further recollection I see that the bride could never in the world forgive me for my behavior at the wedding. I was best man, and it was a formal occasion, and it wasn't only that I didn't kiss her, but that I was somehow alone in the cab with her instead of Charlie on the way down to Gemignano's restaurant after the ceremony. In my inside pocket, rolled up, was a sheet of music—Mozart's "Turkish Rondo" for two violins. I was drunk; how did I get through a violin lesson? At Gemignano's I was very obnoxious. I said, Is this Parmesan cheese or is it Rinso? I spat it out on the tablecloth, and after this I blew my nose in my foulard. Curse my memory for being so complete!

"Did you send a wedding present for me or not? We must send a present. Get some steak knives, for God's sake. I want to tell you that I owe Charlie a lot. Without him I might have gone to the Arctic instead, among the Eskimos. This experience in Africa has been tremendous. It has been tough, it has been perilous, it has been something! But I've matured twenty years in twenty days."

Lily would not sleep in the igloo with me, but I continued my polar experiments anyway. I snared a few rabbits. I practiced spear-throwing. I built a sled, following the descriptions in the books. Four or five coats of frozen urine on the runners and they scooted over the snow like steel. I am positive that I could have arrived at the Pole. But I don't think I would have found what I was looking for there. In that case, I would have overwhelmed the world from the North with my trampling. If I couldn't have my soul it would cost the earth a catastrophe.

"Here they don't know what tourists are, and therefore I'm not a tourist. There was a woman who told her friend, 'Last year we went around the world. This year I think we're going somewhere else.' Ha, ha! Sometimes the mountains here seem very porous, yellow and brown, and remind me of those old molasses sponge candies. I have my own room in the palace. This is a very primitive part of the world. Even the rocks look primitive. From time to time I have a smoldering fever. It feels like one of those coal mines that have been sealed because of combustion. Otherwise I seem to have benefited physically here, except that I have a persistent grunt. I wonder if this is new, or did you ever notice it at home?

"How are the twins and Ricey and Edward? I would like to stop in Switzerland on the way home and see little Alice. I may have my teeth looked after, too, while in Geneva. You might tell Dr. Spohr for me that the bridge broke one morning at breakfast. Send me the spare c/o American Embassy, Cairo. It is in the trunk of the convertible under the wire spring that fastens the jack to the spare tire. I put it there for safekeeping.

"I promised Romilayu a bonus if he would take me off the beaten track. We have made two stops. Humankind has to sway itself more intentionally toward beauty. I met a person who is called The Woman of Bittahness. She looked like a fat old lady, merely, but she had tremendous wisdom and when she took a look at me she thought I was a kind of odd ball, but that didn't faze her, and she said a couple of marvelous things. First she told me that the world was strange to me. It is strange to a child. But I am no child. This gave me pleasure and pain, both."

The Kingdom of Heaven is for children of the spirit. But who is this nosy, gross phantom?

"Of course there's strangeness and strangeness. One kind of strangeness may be a gift, and another kind a punishment. I wanted to tell the old lady that everybody understands life except me—how did she account for it? I seem to be a very vain and foolish, rash person. How did I get so lost? And never mind whose fault it is, how do I get back?"

It is very early in life, and I am out in the grass. The sun flames and swells; the heat it emits is its love, too. I have this self-same vividness in my heart. There are dandelions. I try to gather up this green. I put my love-swollen cheek to the yellow of the dandelions. I try to enter into the green.

"Then she told me I had grun-tu-molani, which is a native term hard to explain but on the whole it indicates that you want to live, not die. I wanted her to tell more about it. Her hair was like fleece and her belly smelled like saffron; she had a cataract in one eye. I'm afraid I will never be able to see her again, because I goofed and we had to get out. I can't go into details. But without Prince Itelo's friendship I might have been in serious trouble. I thought I had lost my opportunity to study my life with the aid of a really wise person, and I was very downcast over it. But I love Dahfu, king of the second tribe we came to. I am with him now and have been given an honorary title, King of the Rain, which is merely standard, I guess, like getting the key to the city from Jimmy Walker used to be. A costume goes with it. But I am not in a position to tell you much more, except in general terms. I am participating in an experiment with the king (almost an M.D., I told you) and this is an ordeal, daily." *The animal's face is pure fire to me. Every day. I have to close my eyes.*

"Lily, I probably haven't said this lately, but I have true feeling for you, baby, which sometimes wrings my heart. You can call it love. Although personally I think that word is full of bluff." *Especially for somebody like me, called from nonexistence into existence: what for? What have I got to do with husbands' love or wives' love? I am too peculiar for that kind of stuff.*

"When Napoleon was out at St. Helena, he talked a lot about morals. It was a little late. A lot he cared for them. So I'm not going to discuss love with you. If you think you are in the clear you can go ahead and talk about it. You said you couldn't live for sun, moon, and stars alone. You said your mother was dead when she wasn't, which was certainly very neurotic of you. You got engaged a hundred times and were always out of breath. You conned me. Is this how love acts? All right, then. But I expected you to help me. This king here is one of the most intelligent people in the world, and I have great faith in him, and he tells me I should move from the states that I myself make into the states which are of themselves. Like if I stopped making such a noise all the time I might hear something nice. I might hear a bird. Are the wrens still nesting in the cornices? I saw the straw sticking out and was amazed that they could get inside." *I could never take after the birds. I would crash all the branches. I would have scared the pterodactyl from the skies.*

"I am giving up the violin. I guess I will never reach my object through it," *to raise my spirit from the earth, to leave the body of this death. I was very stubborn. I wanted to raise myself into another world. My life and deeds were a prison.*

"Well, Lily, everything is going to be different from now on. When I get back I am going to study medicine. My age is against it, but that's just too damn bad, I'm going to do it anyway. You can't imagine how keen I am to get into the laboratory. I can still remember the smell of those places. Formaldehyde. I'll be among a bunch of young kids, I realize, doing chemistry and zoology and physiology and physics and math and anatomy. I expect it to be quite an ordeal, especially dissecting the cadaver." *Once more, Death, you and me.* "However, I have had to have dealings with the dead anyway and haven't made a buck on any of them. I might as well do something in the interests of life, for a change." *What is it, now, this great instrument? Played wrong, why does it suffer so? Right, how can it achieve so much, reaching even God?* "Bones, muscles, glands, organs. Osmosis. I want you to enroll me at Medical Center and give my name as Leo E. Henderson. The reason for that I will tell you when I get home. Aren't you excited? Dearest girl, as a doctor's wife you'll have to be more clean, bathe more often and wash your things. You will have to get used to broken sleep, night calls and all of that. I haven't decided yet where to practice. I guess if I tried it at home I'd scare the neighbors to pieces. If I put my ear against their chests as an M.D., they'd jump out of their skins.

"Therefore, I may apply for missionary work, like Dr. Wilfred Grenfell or Albert Schweitzer. Hey! Axel Munthe—

how about him? Naturally China is out, now. They might catch us and brain-wash us. Ha, ha! But we might try India. I do want to get my hands on the sick. I want to cure them. Healers are sacred." *I have been so bad myself I believe there must be a virtue in me, finally.* "Lily, I'm going to quit knocking myself out."

I don't think the struggles of desire can ever be won. Ages of longing and willing, willing and longing, and how have they ended? In a draw, dust and dust.

"If Medical Center won't let me in, apply first to Johns Hopkins and then to every other joint in the book. Another reason why I want to stop in Switzerland is to look into the medical-school situation. I could talk to people there, explain things, and maybe they would let me in.

"So get busy, dear, with those letters, and another thing: sell the pigs. I want you to sell Kenneth the Tamworth boar and Dilly and Minnie. Get rid of them.

"We are funny creatures. We don't see the stars as they are, so why do we love them? They are not small gold objects but endless fire."

Strange? Why shouldn't it be strange? It is strange. It is all strange.

"I haven't been drinking at all, here, except for a few nips taken while writing this letter. At lunch they serve you a native beer called 'pombo' which is pretty good. They ferment the pineapple. Everybody is very animated here. Folks with feathers, folks with ribbons, with scarf decorations, rings, bracelets, beads, shells, gold walnuts. Some of the harem women walk like giraffes. Their faces slope forward. The king's face has very much of a slope. He is very brilliant and opinionated.

"Sometimes I feel as though I had a whole troop of pygmies jumping up and down inside me, yelling and carrying on. Isn't that odd? Other times I am very calm, calmer than I have ever been.

"The king believes that one should have a suitable image of himself. . . ."

I believe that I tried to explain to Lily what Dahfu's ideas were, but Romilayu lost the last few pages of the letter, and I suppose that it's just as well that he did, for when I wrote them I had had quite a bit to drink. In one I think I said, or maybe I merely thought it, "I had a voice that said, I want! *I* want? I? It should have told me *she* wants, *he* wants, *they* want. And moreover, it's love that makes reality reality. The opposite makes the opposite."

Chapter XX

Romilayu and I said good-by in the morning and when he finally set off with the letter to Lily I had a very unwholesome feeling. My very stomach seemed to drop as his wrinkled face looked through the closing gates of the palace. I believe that he expected at the last minute to be called back by his changeable and irrational employer. But I only stood there in the carapacelike helmet and those pants which made me seem as though I had gotten lost from my troop of Zouaves. The gate shut on Romilayu's scarred and seamed gaze, and I felt unreasonably low. But Tamba and Bebu diverted me from my sadness. As usual they saluted me by lying in the dust and putting my foot on their heads, and then Tamba settled herself on her belly so that Bebu might do the joxi with her feet. She trod her back, spine, neck, and buttocks, which seemed to give Tamba heavenly pleasure. She closed her eyes, groaning and basking. I thought I must try this one day; it must be beneficial, it contented these people so; however, this was not the day for it, I was too sad.

The air was warming quickly but there were still arrears of the stinging cold of night; I felt it through the thin green stuff I wore. The mountain, the one named for Hummat, was yellow; the clouds were white and had great weight. They lay at about the height of Hummat's throat and shoulders, like a collar. Indoors, I sat and waited for the morning to increase in warmth, hands folded, mentally preparing for my daily

exposure to Atti while I earnestly tried to reason: I must
change. I must not live on the past, it will ruin me. The dead
are my boarders, eating me out of house and home. The hogs
were my defiance. I was telling the world that it was a pig. I
must begin to think how to live. I must break Lily from
blackmail and set love on a true course. Because after all Lily
and I were very lucky. But then what could an animal do for
me? In the last analysis? Really? A beast of prey? Even
supposing that an animal enjoys a natural blessing? We had
our share of this creature-blessing until infancy ended. But
now aren't we required to complete something else—project
number two—the second blessing? I couldn't tell such things
to the king, he was so stuck on lions. I have never seen a
person so gone on any creatures. And I couldn't refuse to do
what he wanted owing to the way I felt about him. Yes, in
some ways the fellow was remarkably like a lion, but that
didn't prove lions had made him so. This was more of
Lamarck. In college we had laughed Lamarck right out of the
classroom. I remembered what the teacher said, that this was
a bourgeois idea of the autonomy of the individual mind. All
sons of rich men, we were, or almost all, and yet we laughed at
the bourgeois ideas until we almost split a gut. Well, I
reflected, wrinkling my brow to the limit, missing Romilayu
keenly, this is the payoff of a lifetime of action without
thought. If I had to shoot at that cat, if I had to blow up frogs,
if I had to pick up Mummah without realizing what I was
getting myself into, it was not out of line to crouch on all fours
and roar and act the lion. I might have been learning about
the grun-tu-molani instead, under Willatale. But I will never
regret my feeling toward this man—Dahfu, I mean; I would
have done a great deal more to keep his friendship.

So I was brooding in my palace room when Tatu came in,
wearing the ancient Italian garrison cap. Thinking this was the
daily summons to join the king in the den, I heavily got up,
but she began to tell me by word and gesture that I should
stay where I was and wait for the king. He was coming.

"What's up?" I said. However, nobody could explain, and I

tidied myself a little in anticipation of the king's visit; I had let myself grow filthy and bearded, as it was scarcely suitable to get all cleaned up in order to stand on all fours, roaring and tearing the earth. Today, however, I went to Mummah's cistern and washed my face, my neck, and my ears and let the sun dry me on the threshold of my apartment. It soon did. Meanwhile I regretted that I had sent Romilayu away so soon, for this morning brought to mind more things that I should have told Lily. That wasn't all I had to say, I thought. I love her. By God! I goofed again. But I didn't have much time to spend on regret, for Tatu was coming toward me across the rough yard of the palace, gesturing with both arms and saying, "Dahfu. Dahfu ala-mele." I rose and she led me through the passages of the ground floor to the king's outdoor court. Already he was in his hammock, under the purple shadow of his giant silk umbrella. He held his velvet hat in his fist and beckoned with it, and when he saw me above him his swelled lips opened. He fitted the hat over his raised knee and said, smiling, "I suppose you gather what day it is."

"I figure—"

"Yes, it is the day. Lion day for me."

"This is it, eh?"

"Bait has been eaten by a young male. He fit the description of Gmilo."

"Well, it must be great," I said, "to think you are going to be reunited with a dear parent. I only wish such a thing could happen to me."

"Well, Henderson," he said (this morning he took an exceptional pleasure in my company and conversation), "do you believe in immortality?"

"There's many a soul that would tell you it could never stay another round with life," I said.

"Do you really say so? But you know more of the world than I do. However, Henderson, my good friend, this is a high occasion for me."

"Is there a good chance that it is your dad, the late king? I wish I had known. I wouldn't have sent Romilayu away. He left this morning. Your Highness. Could we send a runner after him?"

The king paid no attention to this, and I figured his excitement was running too high to allow him to consider my practical arrangements. What was Romilayu to him on a day like this?

"You will share the hopo with me," he said, and, although I didn't know what this meant, I of course agreed. My own umbrella approached, this hollow or sheath of green with transverse fibers in the silk transparency which helped to convince me that it was no vision but an object, for why should a vision bother to have such transverse lines? Eh? The pole was held by big female hands. Bearers brought my hammock.

"Do we go after the lion in a hammock?" I said.

"When we reach the bush we will continue on our feet," he said.

So I got into the hammock of the Sungo with one of those heavy utterances of mine, sinking into it. It looked to me as if the two of us were going out barehanded to capture the animal—this lion, that had eaten the old bull, and was sleeping deeply somewhere in the standing grass.

Shaven-headed women flitted near us, shrill and nervous, and a gaudy crowd had collected, just as on the day of the rain ceremony—drummers, men in paint, shells, and feathers, and buglers who blew some practice blasts. The bugles were about a foot long and had big mouths of green oxide metal. They made a devil of a blast, like the taunt of fear, those instruments. So with the bugles and drums and rattles and noisemakers of the beaters' party gathered around us, we were carried through the gates of the palace. The arms of the amazons shook with the strain of lifting me. Various people came and looked at me as we were going into the town; they gazed down into the hammock. Among them were the Bunam and Horko, the latter expecting me, I felt, to say something to him. However, I didn't say a word.

I looked back at them with my huge red face. The beard

had begun to grow out like a broom and the fever, which had
gone up again, affected my eyes and ears. A tremor in the
cheeks occasionally surprised me; I could do nothing about
this, and I reckoned that under the influence of lions the
nerves of my jaws and nose and chin were undergoing an
unsettling change. The Bunam had come in order to communicate with me or warn me; I could see that. I wanted to
demand my H and H Magnum with the scope sights from him
but of course I didn't have the words for "give" and "gun."
The women struggled with my weight and the hammock
bulged out greatly at the bottom and nearly touched the
ground. The poles were almost too much for their shoulders as
they carried the brutal white rain king with his swarthy,
reddened face and dirty helmet and gaudy pants and big,
hairy shins. The people whooped and clapped and leaped up
and down in their rags and hides, flaunting pieces of dyed hair
as pennants, women with babies that swung at their long
spongy breasts and fellows with teeth broken or missing. As
far as I could tell they were not enthusiastic for the king; they
demanded that he bring home Gmilo, the right lion, and get
rid of the sorceress, Atti. Without a sign he passed among
them in his hammock. I knew his face was bathed by the
shadow of the purple umbrella, and he was wearing his large
velvet hat, as attached to it as I was to the helmet. Hat, hair,
and face were in close union under the tinged light of the silk
arch, and he lay and rested with that same sumptuous ease
which I had admired from the beginning. Above him, as
above me, strange hands clasped the ornamented pole of the
umbrella. The sun now shone with power and covered the
mountains and the stones close at hand with shimmering
layers. Near to the ground it was about to materialize into
gold leaf. The huts were holes of darkness and the thatch had
a sick, broken radiance over it.

     Until we got to the town limits I kept saying to myself,
"Reality! Oh, reality! Damn you anyhow, reality!"

     In the bush the women set me down and I stepped from the
hammock onto the blazing ground. This was the hard-packed

white, solar-looking rock. The king, too, was standing. He looked back at the crowd, which had remained near the wall of the town. With the game-beaters was the Bunam, and, following very closely, a white creature, a man completely dyed or calcimined. Under the coat of chalk I recognized him. It was the Bunam's man, the executioner. I identified him by the folds of his narrow face in this white metamorphosis.

"What's the idea of this?" I asked, going up to Dahfu over the packed stone and the stubble of weeds.

"No idea," the king said.

"Is he always like this at a lion hunt?"

"No. Different days, different colors, according to the reading of the omens. White is not the best omen."

"What are they trying to pull off here? They're giving you a bad send-off."

The king behaved as though he could not be bothered. Any human lion would have done as he did. Nevertheless he was irritated if not pierced by this. I made a very heavy half turn to stare at this ill-omened figure that had come to injure the king's self-confidence on the eve of this event, reunion with the soul of his father. "This whitewash is serious?" I said to the king.

Widely separated, his eyes had two separate looks; as I spoke to him they mingled again into one. "They intend it so."

"Sire," I said, "you want me to do something?"

"What thing?"

"You name it. On a day like this to be interfered with is dangerous, isn't it? It ought to be dangerous for them, too."

"Oh? No. What?" he said. "They are living in the old universe. Why not? That is part of my bargain with them, isn't it?" Something of the gold tinge of the stones came into his smile, brilliantly. "Why, this is my great day, Mr. Henderson. I can afford all the omens. After I have captured Gmilo they can say nothing more."

"Sticks and stones will break my bones but this is idle superstition, and so forth. Well, Your Highness, if that's the way you take it, fine, okay." I looked into the rising heat, which borrowed color from the stones and plants. I had expected the king to speak harshly to the Bunam and his follower who was painted with the color of bad omen, but he only made one remark to them. His face appeared very full under that velvet hat with the large brim and the crown full of soft variations. The umbrellas had stayed behind. The women, the king's wives, stood at the low wall of the town at assorted heights; they watched and cried certain (I suppose farewell) things. The stones paled more and more with the force of the heat. The women sent strange cries of love and encouragement or warning or good-by. They waved, they sang, and they signaled with the two umbrellas, which went up and down. The beaters, silent, had not stopped for us but went away with the bugles, spears, drums, and rattles, in a solid body. There were sixty or seventy of them, and they started from us in a mass but gradually dispersed toward the bush. Antlike they began to spread into the golden weeds and boulders of the slope. These boulders, as noted before, were like gross objects combed down from above by an ignorant force.

The departure of the beaters left the Bunam, the Bunam's wizard, the king, and myself, the Sungo, plus three attendants with spears standing about thirty yards from the town.

"What did you tell them?" I asked the king.

"I have said to the Bunam I would accomplish my purpose notwithstanding."

"You should give them each a kick in the tail," I said, scowling at the two guys.

"Come, Henderson, my friend," Dahfu said, and we began to walk. The three men with spears fell in behind us.

"What are these fellows for?"

"To help maneuver in the hopo," he said. "You will see when we come to the small end of the place. That is better than explanation."

As we went down into the high grass of the bush he raised his sloping face with the smooth low-bridged nose and scented the air. I breathed it in, too. Dry and fine, it had an odor like fermented sugar. I began to be aware of the tremble of insects as they played their instruments underneath the stems, down at the very base of the heat.

The king began to go quickly, not so much walking as bounding, and as we followed, the spearmen and I, it occurred to me that the grass was high enough to conceal almost any animal except an elephant and that I didn't have so much as a diaper pin to defend myself with.

"King," I said. "Hisst. Wait a minute." I couldn't raise my voice here; I sensed that this was not the time to make a noise. He probably didn't like this, for he wouldn't stop, but I kept on calling in low tones and finally he waited for me. Greatly worked up, I stared into his eyes at close range, fought a few moments for air, and then said, "Not even a weapon? Just like this? Are you supposed to catch this animal by the tail?"

He decided to be patient with me. I could see the decision being taken. This I would swear to. "The animal, and I hope it is Gmilo, is probably within the area of the hopo. See here, Henderson, I must not be armed. What if I were to wound Gmilo?" He spoke of this possibility with horror. I had failed before (what was the matter with me?) to observe how profoundly excited he was. I had not seen through his cordiality.

"What if?"

"My life would be required as for any harm to a living king."

"And what about me—I'm not supposed to defend myself either?"

He did not answer for a moment. Then he said, "You are with me."

There was nothing I could say after that. I decided that I would do the best I could with my helmet, which would be to strike the animal on the muzzle and confuse it. I grumbled that he would have been better off in Syria or Lebanon as a mere student, and, although I spoke unclearly, he understood me and said, "Oh, no, Henderson-Sungo. I am lucky and you know it." In his close-fitting breeches, he set off again. My trousers hampered me as I rushed over the ground behind him. As for the three men with spears, they gave me very little confidence. Any minute I expected the lion to burst on me like an eruption of fire, to knock me down and tear me into flames of blood. The king mounted on a boulder and drew me up with him. He said, "We are near the north wall of the hopo." He pointed it out. It was built of ragged thorns and dead growths of all sorts, heaped and piled to a thickness of two or three feet. Coarse, croaky-looking flowers grew there; they were red and orange and at the center they were blotted with black, and it gave me a sore throat just to look at them. This hopo was a giant funnel or triangle. At the base it was open, while at the apex or spout was the trap. Only one of the two sides was built by human hands. The other was a natural formation of rock, the bank of an old river, probably, which rose to the height of a cliff. Beside the high wall of brush and thorn was a path which the king's feet found under the spiky yellow grass. We continued toward the small end of the hopo over fallen ribs of branches and twists of vine. From the hips, which were small, his figure broadened or loomed greatly toward the shoulders. He walked with powerful legs and small buttocks.

"You certainly are on fire to come to grips with this animal," I said.

Sometimes I think that pleasure comes only from having your own way, and I couldn't help feeling that this was assimilated by the king from the lions. To have your will, that's what pleasure is, in spite of all the thought that has been done. And he was dragging me along with the power of his personal greatness, because he was so brilliant and had a strong gift of life, manifested in the smoky, bluish trembling of his extra shadow. Because he was bound to have his way. And therefore I lumbered after him without a weapon for protection unless you counted the helmet, unless I could pull down these green pants and bag the animal in them—they might almost have been roomy enough for that.

Then he stopped and turned to me, and said, "You were equally on fire when it came to lifting up the Mummah."

"That's correct, Your Highness," I said. "But did I know what I was doing? No, I didn't."

"But I do."

"Well, okay, King," I said. "It's not for me to question it. I'll do whatever you say. But you told me that the Bunam and the other fellow in the white pigment were from the old universe and I assumed you were out of it."

"No, no. Do you know how to replace the whole thing? It cannot be done. Even if, in supreme moments, there is no old and is no new, but only an essence which can smile at our arrangement—smile even at being human. That is so full of itself," he said. "Nevertheless a play of life has to be allowed. Arrangements must be made." Here his mind was somewhat beyond me, so I didn't interfere with him, and he said, "To Gmilo, the lion Suffo was his father. To me, grandfather. Gmilo, my father. As, if I am going to be the king of the Wariri, it has to be. Otherwise, how am I the king?"

"Okay, I get you," I said. "King," I told him, and I spoke so earnestly it might almost have sounded like a series of threats, "you see these hands? This is your second pair of hands. You see this trunk?" I put my hand on my chest. "It is your reservoir, like. Your Highness, in case anything is going to happen, I want you to understand how I feel." My heart was very much aroused. I began to suffer in the face. In recognition of the fellow's nobleness, I fought to spare him the grossness of my emotions. This was in the shade of the hopo wall, under the embroidery of stiff thorns. The narrow track along the hopo was black and golden, as when grass burns in broad daylight and the heat is visible.

"Thank you, Mr. Henderson. I have understood how you feel." After a quiet hesitation, he said, "Should I guess? Death is on your mind?"

"It's on my mind, all right."

"Oh yes, very much. You are exceptionally given to it."

"Over the years, I've gotten involved with it a lot."

"Exceptionally. Exceptionally," he said as if he were discussing one of my problems with me. "Sometimes I think it is helpful to think of burial in relation to the earth's crust. What is the radius? Four thousand five hundred miles more or less, to the core of the earth. No, graves are not deep but insignificant, a mere few feet from the surface and not far from fearing and desiring. More or less the same fear, more or less the same desire for thousands of generations. Child, father, father, child doing the same. Fear the same. Desire the same. Upon the crust, beneath the crust, again and again and again. Well, Henderson, what are the generations for, please explain to me? Only to repeat fear and desire without a change? This cannot be what the thing is for, over and over and over. Any good man will try to break the cycle. There is no issue from that cycle for a man who do not take things into his hands."

"Oh, King, wait a minute. Once out of the light, it's enough. Does it have to be four thousand five hundred miles to be the grave? How can you talk like that?" But I understood him all the same. All you hear from guys is desire, desire, desire, knocking its way out of the breast, and fear, striking and striking. Enough already! Time for a word of truth. Time for something notable to be heard. Otherwise, accelerating like a stone, you fall from life to death. Exactly like a stone, straight into deafness, and till the last repeating *I want I want I want*, then striking the earth and entering it forever! As a matter of fact, I thought, out in the African sun from which the hooked wall of thorn temporarily cooled me: it's a pleasure when harsh objects like thorns do something for you. Under the black barbs that the bushes had crocheted above us, I thought it out and agreed: the grave was relatively shallow. You couldn't go many miles inside before you found the molten part of the earth. Mainly nickel, I think—nickel, cobalt, pitchblende, or what they call the magma. Almost as it was torn from the sun.

"Let us go," he said. I followed him more willingly after that short talk. He could convince me of almost anything. For his sake I accepted the discipline of being like a lion. Yes, I thought, I believed I could change; I was willing to overcome my old self; yes, to do that a man had to adopt some new standard; he must even force himself into a part; maybe he must deceive himself a while, until it begins to take; his own hand paints again on that much-painted veil. I would never make a lion, I knew that; but I might pick up a small gain here and there in the attempt.

I can't be sure that I have reported accurately all the things the king said. I may have spoiled some of them a little so that I could assimilate them.

Anyway, I followed him empty-handed toward the end of the hopo. Probably the lion had already wakened, for the beaters, about three miles away, had begun to make their noise. It sounded very distant, far out in the golden stripes of the bush. An air-blue, sleepy heat wavered in front of us, and while I squinted against the sprays and flashes of sunlight I saw a sudden elevation in the hopo wall. It was a thatched shelter which sat on a platform, twenty-five or thirty feet in the air. A ladder of vines hung down, and the king took hold of it eagerly, this crude, slack-looking thing. He began to climb it sailor fashion, from the side, pulling himself powerfully and steadily up to the platform. From the dry grass and brown fibers of the doorway he said, "Take hold, Mr. Henderson." He had crouched to hold out the ladder to me and I saw his head, on which was the pleated, tooth-sewn hat, only slightly above his powerful knees. Illness, strangeness, and danger combined and ganged up on me. Instead of an answer, a sob came out of me. It must have been laid down early in my life, for it was stupendous and rose from me like a great sea bubble from the Atlantic floor.

"What is the matter, Mr. Henderson?" Dahfu said.

"God knows."

"Is something wrong with you?"

I kept my head lowered as I shook it. The roaring I had done, I believe, had loosened my whole structure and liberated some things which belonged at the bottom. And this was no time to trouble the king, on his great day of joy.

"I'm coming, Your Highness," I said.

"Take a moment's breath if you need it."

He walked about on the platform under the elevated hut, then came back to the edge again. He looked down from that fragile dome of straw. "Now?" he said.

"Will it bear our weight, up there?"

"Come on, come on, Henderson," he said.

I took hold of the ladder and began climbing, placing both feet on each rung. The spearmen had stood and waited until I (the Sungo) joined the king. Now they passed under the ladder and took up a position around the corner of the hopo. Here, at the end, the construction was primitive but seemed thorough. A barred gate would be dropped to trap the lion after the other game had been driven through, and the men would prod the animal into position with their spears so that the king could effect the capture.

On the fragile ladder, which wavered under my weight, I reached the platform and sat down on the floor of poles lashed together. It was like a heat-borne raft. I began to size up the situation. The whole setup was no deeper than a thimble when compared to the volume offered by a full-grown lion.

"This is it?" I said to the king after I had studied the layout.

"As you see it," he said.

Now on the platform stood this shell of straw, and from the opening on the interior side of the hopo I saw suspended a woven cage weighted with rocks at the bottom. It was bell-shaped and made of semi-rigid vines which were, however, as tough as cables. A vine rope passed through a pulley suspended from a pole which was attached at one end to the roof-tree of the hut and at the other was fixed into the side of the cliff, a width of ten or twelve feet. Below it ran another pole from the floor of the hut; it too was set in the rock at the other end. On this pole or catwalk, no wider than my wrist, if that wide, the king would balance himself with the rope and the bell-shaped net, and when the lion was driven in Dahfu would center the net and let it drop. Releasing his rope, he was supposed to capture the lion.

"This . . . ?"

"What do you think?" he said.

I couldn't bring myself to say much about it, but, hard as I fought my feelings, I couldn't submerge them—not on this particular day. I was visibly struggling with them.

He said, "I captured Atti here."

"Yes, with this same rig?"

"And Gmilo captured Suffo."

I said, "Take the advice of a . . . I know that I'm not much . . . But I think the world of you, Your Highness. Don't . . ."

"Why, what is the matter with your chin, Mr. Henderson? It is moving up and down."

I brought my upper teeth down on my lip. By and by I said, "Your Highness, excuse it. I'd rather cut my throat than demoralize you on a day like this. But does the thing have to be done from up here?"

"It must."

"Can't there be an innovation? I'd do anything, drug the animal . . . give him a Mickey . . ."

"Thank you, Henderson," he said. I think his gentleness with me was more than I deserved. He didn't remind me in so many words that he was king of the Wariri. I soon reminded myself of this fact. He allowed me to be present—his companion. I must not interfere.

"Oh, Your Majesty," I said.

"Yes, Henderson, I know. You are a man of many qualities. I have observed," he said.

"I thought maybe I fitted into one of your bad types," I said.

At this he laughed somewhat. He was sitting cross-legged at the opening of the hut that faced the hopo and the cliff, and he began to enumerate, half musingly, "The agony, the appetite, the immune, the hollow, and all of that. No, I promise you, Henderson, that I have never classified you with a bad group. You are a compound. Maybe a large amount of agony. Maybe a small touch of the Lazarus. But I cannot fully subsume you. No rubric will fully hold you. Maybe because we are friends. One sees much more in a friend. Rubrics will not do with friends."

"I had a little too much business with a certain type of

creature for my own good," I said. "If I had it to do over again, it would be different."

We sat on the shaky platform under the gold straw belfry of thatch. The light was finely grated on the floor. We crouched, waiting under the fibers and straw. The odor of plants came up on the air-blue heat in gusts, and because of my fever I had a feeling that I had found, in midair, a changing point between matter and light. I was watching it being carried from within and thought I saw crying and writhing outside. Not able to stand this sense of things, I got up and stepped on the pole the king was supposed to balance on.

"What are you doing?"

I was trying it out for him. I said, "I am checking on the Bunam."

"You must not stand there, Henderson."

My weight was bowing the wood, but there was no crackling, it was a very hard wood and I was satisfied by the test. I lifted myself back to the platform and we sat together, or crouched, outside the grass wall of the shelter on a narrow projection of the floor, almost within reach of the weighted trap which hung waiting. Opposite us was the cliff of gritty rock, and, following the line of it beyond the end of the hopo, over the heads of the waiting spearmen, I saw a sort of small stone building deep in the ravine. I hadn't noticed it before because in this ravine, or gorge, there was a small forest of cactuses which produced a red bud, or berry, or flower, and this partly blocked it from view.

"Does somebody live there, below?"

"No."

"Is it abandoned? Used? In our part of the country, where farming has gone to hell, you come across old houses everywhere. But that's a crazy place for a residence," I said.

The rope by which the cage or net was slung had been tied to the doorpost, and the king's head was resting against the knot. "It is not for living," he told me without glancing toward the building.

A tomb? I thought. Whose tomb?

"I think they are driving rapidly. Ah! Do you think you can see them? It is getting loud." He stood, and I did too, and shaded my eyes from the glare while I strained my forehead.

"No, I don't see."

"I neither, Henderson. This is the most hard part. I have waited all my life, and we are within the last hour."

"Well, Your Highness," I said, "for you it should be easy. You have known these animals all your life. You are bred for this; you are a pro. If there's anything I love to see, it's a guy who's good at his work. Whether it's a rigger or steeple jack or window-washer or any person who has strong nerves and a skilled body . . . You had me worried when you started that skull dance, but after a minute of it I would have backed you to my last dime." And I took out my wallet, which I kept taped to the inside of the helmet, and to make these moments easier for him, within the rising blare of the horns and the constant running of the drums (while we sat as if marooned in the illuminated air), I said, "Your Highness, did I ever show you these pictures of my wife and children?" I started to look for them in the bulky wallet. I had my passport there, and four one-thousand-dollar bills, taking no chances on traveler's checks in Africa. "Here's my wife. We spent a lot of money on a portrait and had difficulties all through. I begged her not to hang it and almost had a nervous breakdown over it. But this photograph of her is a beauty." In it Lily wore a low-necked dress of polka dots. She looked very amused. It was toward me that she was smiling, for I was at the camera. She was saying affectionately that I was a fool; I probably had been clowning around. Owing to the smile her cheeks were high and full; in the picture you couldn't tell how pure and pale her color was. The king took it from me, and I have to hand it to him that at a moment like this he could contemplate Lily's picture.

"She is a serious person," he said.

"Do you think she looks like a doctor's wife?"

"I think she looks like any serious person's wife."

"But I guess she wouldn't agree about your species idea,

Your Highness, because she decided that I was the only fellow in the world she could marry. One God, one husband, I guess. Well, here are the kids. . . ."

Without comment he looked at Ricey and Edward, little Alice in Switzerland, the twins. "They are not identical, Your Majesty, but they both cut their first tooth on the same day." The next flap of celluloid held a snapshot of myself; I was in the red robe and hunting cap with the violin under my chin and an expression on my face which I had never noticed before. Quickly I turned to my Purple Heart citation.

"Oh? That is so? You are Captain Henderson?"

"I didn't keep the commission. Maybe you'd like to see my scars, Your Highness. The thing happened with a land mine. I didn't get the worst of it. I was thrown about twenty feet. Now here in the thigh you can't see it so well, because it's sunken and the hair has grown over and hidden it. The belly wound was the bad one. My insides started to fall out. I held in my guts and walked bent over to the dressing station."

"You are very pleased about your trouble, Henderson?"

He would always say such things to me and introduce an unforeseen perspective. I have forgotten some of them, but he once asked my opinion about Descartes. "Do you agree with the fellow's proposition that the animal is a soulless machine?" Or, "Do you think that Jesus Christ is still a source of human types, Henderson, as a model-force? I have often thought about my physical types, as the agony, the appetite, and the rest, to be possibly degenerate forms of great originals, as Socrates, Alexander, Moses, Isaiah, Jesus. . . ." This, and the like, was his unforeseen way of conversation.

He observed that I was peculiar about trouble and suffering. And, yes, I knew what he was saying as we sat on those poles beside the lavish bristle of the thatch, this grotesque, dry, hairy, piercing vegetable skeleton. As he waited to achieve his heart's desire, he was telling me that suffering was the closest thing to worship that I knew anything about. Believe me, I knew my man, and strange as he was I understood him. I *was* monstrously proud of my suffering. I thought there was nobody in the world that could suffer quite like me.

But we could not speak quietly to each other any more, for the noise was too near. The sounds of cicadas had been going up in vertical spirals, like columns of thinnest shining wire. Now we could hear none of the minor sounds at all. The spearmen behind the hopo lifted up the barred gate to let through the creatures whom the beaters had flushed. For the grasses of the bush were beginning to quiver, as water will when a fish-filled net approaches the surface.

"Look there," said Dahfu. He pointed to the cliff side of the hopo, where deer with twisted horns were running; whether they were gazelles or elands I couldn't say. A buck was in the lead. He had tall, twisted horns like smoked glass, and he leaped in terror with blasting breath and huge eyes. On one knee, Dahfu was watching the grass for signs, sighting across his forearm so that his nose was almost covered. The small animals were making currents in the grass. Flocks of birds went straight up, like masses of notes; they flew toward the cliffs and down into the ravine. The deer clattered beneath us. I looked below. Those were planks at the bottom. I hadn't noticed that. They were raised six or eight inches from the ground, and the king said, "Yes. After the capture, Henderson, wheels are put under so the animal can be transported." He stooped low to call instructions to the spearmen. When he bent, I wanted to hold on to him, but I had never touched his person. I wasn't sure it would be right.

After the buck and the three does, which squeezed through the narrow opening of the hopo with heart-bursting terror, came a crowd of small beasts; they rushed the opening like immigrants. More cautious, a hyena showed up, and, unlike the other creatures who didn't know we were there, this creature shot a look up at us on the platform and gave its shallow, batlike snarl. I looked for something to throw at it. But there was nothing with us on the platform to throw and I spat down instead.

"Lion is there—lion, lion!" The king stood, pointing, and about a hundred yards away, I saw a slow stirring in the grass, not the throbbing of the smaller animals but a circular, heavy disturbance which a powerful body made.

"Do you think that would be Gmilo? Hey, hey, hey—is he here? You can take him, King. I know you can." I had risen on the narrow stand of floor projecting from beneath the grass wall, and I was thrusting and cranking my arm up and down as I spoke.

"Henderson—do not," he said.

Nevertheless I took a step in his direction, and then he cried out at me; his face was angry. So I squatted down and shut my mouth. My blood was full of fever, as if it flowed open to the glare of the sun.

The king then set foot on the slender pole and took two turns of the cage rope around his arm and began to release the knot against which he had rested his head during our wait. The cage, with its big irregular meshes of vine and the hooflike stone weights, swung from the more rigid part at the bottom. Except for the rocks the thing had almost no substance; it was as near to being air as a Portuguese man-of-war is to being water. The king had thrown off his hat; it would have got in his way; and about his tight-grown hair, which rose barely an eighth of an inch above his scalp, the blue of the atmosphere seemed to condense, as when you light a few sticks in the woods and about these black sticks the blue begins to wrinkle.

The sunlight deformed my face with strain, for I was exposed to it as I hung over the end of the hopo like a gargoyle. The light was hard enough then to leave bruises. And still, in spite of the blasts of the beaters, the cicadas were drilling away, sending up those spirals of theirs. On the cliff side of the hopo the rock was showing its character. It muttered it would let nothing through. All things must wait for it. The small blossoms of the cactus in the ravine, if they were blossoms and not berries, foamed red, and the spines pierced me. Things seemed to speak to me. I inquired in silence about the safety of the king who had a crazy idea that he must capture lions. But I got no reply. This was not the purpose of their speech. They only declared themselves, each according to its law, declaring what it was; nothing at all referred to the king. So I crouched there, sick with heat and dread. My feeling about him had crowded aside everything else within me, which put some pressure on the neighboring organs.

With banging and with horn blasts and whooping and screams, the beaters came on, the ones at the rear leaping up from the grass, which was shoulder high, and blowing depraved notes on those horns of green and russet metal. Shots were fired in the air, maybe with my own scope-sight H and H Magnum. And at the front the spears were stitching and jabbing in disorder.

"Did you see that, Mr. Henderson—a mane?" Dahfu leaned forward on the pole, holding the rope, and the rock weights banged together over his head. I couldn't bear to see him balanced there on a mere kite stick, with that fringe of stones clattering and wheeling inches above him on the circular contraption. Any one of them might have stunned him.

"King, I can't stand this. Be careful, for Christ's sake. This is no machine to horse around with." It was enough, I told myself, that this noble man had to risk his life on that primitive invention; he didn't have to make the thing more dangerous than it was. However, there may have been no safe way to do it. And then he did look very practiced as he balanced on the narrow shaft. The rock weights circled with spasmodic power at the king's pull. This intricate clumsy rig clattered around and around like a merry-go-round, and the netted shadow wheeled on the ground.

For the count of about twenty heartbeats I only partly knew where I was or what was happening. Mainly I kept a fixed watch on the king, ready to hurl myself down if he should fall. Then, at the very doors of consciousness, there was a snarl and I looked down from this straw perch—I was on my knees—into the big, angry, hair-framed face of the lion. It was all wrinkled, contracted; within those wrinkles was the darkness of murder. The lips were drawn away from the gums, and the breath of the animal came over me, hot as oblivion, raw as blood. I started to speak aloud. I said, "Oh my God, whatever You think of me, let me not fall under this butcher shop. Take care of the king. Show him Thy mercy." And to this, as a rider, the thought added itself that this was all mankind needed, to be conditioned into the image of a ferocious animal like the one below. I then tried to tell myself because of the clearness of those enraged eyes that only visions ever got to be so hyperactual. But it was no vision. The snarling of this animal was indeed the voice of death. And I thought how I had boasted to my dear Lily how I loved reality. "I love it more than you do," I had said. But oh, unreality! Unreality, unreality! That has been my scheme for a troubled but eternal life. But now I was blasted away from this practice by the throat of the lion. His voice was like a blow at the back of my head.

The barred door had dropped. Small creatures were still escaping through the gaps in streaks of fur, springing and writhing, frantically coiling. The lion rushed under us and threw his weight against these bars. Was he Gmilo? I had been told that Gmilo's ears had been marked as a cub, before he was released by the Bunam. But of course you had to catch the animal before you could look at his ears. This might well be Gmilo. Behind the barrier the men prodded him with the spears while he fought at the shafts and tried to catch them in his jaws. They were too deft for him. In the front rank forty or fifty spear points feinted and worked toward him, while from the back there flew stones, at which the animal shook his huge face with the yellow corded hair which made his forequarters so huge. His small belly was fringed, and also his forelegs, like a plainsman's buckskins. Compared with this creature Atti was no bigger than a lynx.

Balancing on the pole in his slippers, Dahfu released one turn of the rope from his upper arm; the net bucked, and the motion and the clacking of the stones caught the lion's eye. The beaters screamed up at Dahfu, "Yenitu lebah!" Ignoring them, he held fast to the line and turned around the rim of the net, which was now level with his eyes. Stone battered stone as the contraption spun around; the lion rose on his hind legs and threw a blow at these weights. Foremost among the beaters was the white-painted Bunam's man, who darted in and knocked the animal on the cheek with a spear butt. From top to bottom this fellow was clad in his dirty white, like kid leather, his hair covered with the chalky paste. I now felt the weight of the lion against the posts that held up the platform. They were no thicker than stilts and when he hit them they vibrated. I thought the structure was going to crash, and I clutched the floor, for I expected that I might be carried down like a water tower when a freight train jumps the tracks and crashes it to splinters, with a ton of water gushing in the air. Under Dahfu's feet the pole swayed, but he rode out the shock with rope and net.

"King, for God's sake!" I wanted to cry. "What have we got into?"

Again a thick flock of stones flew forward. Some struck the hopo wall but others found the animal and drove him under the circling weights of that cursed net of vines. God curse all vines and creepers! The king began to sway out as he pushed and maneuvered this bell of knots and stones.

I was freed for one moment from my dumbness. My voice returned and I said to him, "King, take it easy. Mind what you're doing." Then a globe arose in my throat, about the size of a darning egg.

That I could see was almost the only proof I had that life continued. For a time all else was cut off.

The lion, getting up on his back legs, struck again at the dipping net. It was now within reach and he caught his claws in the vines. Before he could pull free the king let fall the trap. The rope streaked down from the pulley, the weights rumbled on the boards like a troop of horses, and the cone fell on the lion's head. I was lying on my belly, with my arm stretched out toward the king, but he came to the edge of the platform unhelped by me and cried, "What do you think! Henderson, what do you think!"

The beaters screamed. The lion should have been carried to the ground by the weight of the stones, but he was still standing nearly upright. He was caught on the head, and his forepaws spread out the vines and he fell, fighting. His hindquarters were not caught in the net. The air seemed to grow dark in the pit of the hopo from his roaring. I lay with my hand still extended to the king, but he didn't take it. He was looking downward at the netted face of the lion, the maned belly and armpits, which brought back to me the road north of Salerno and myself being held by the medics and shaved from head to foot for crabs.

"Does it look like Gmilo? Your Highness, what's your guess?" I said. I didn't understand the situation one bit.

"Oh, it is wrong," the king said.

"What's wrong?"

He was startled by a realization of something I had so far missed. I was stunned by the roars and screams of the capture, and watched the terrible labor of the legs, and the claws black and yellow which issued like thorns from the great pads of the lion's feet.

"You've got him. What the hell. What now?"

But now I understood what was the matter, for nobody could approach the animal to examine his ears; he was able to turn beneath the net, and, his hindquarters being free, you couldn't get near him.

"Rope his legs, somebody," I yelled.

The Bunam was below and signaled upward with his ivory stick. The king pushed off from the edge of the platform and took hold of the rope which had been stopped in the pulley by a knot. The overhead pole was bucking and dancing as he got hold of the frayed tail of the rope. He hauled at it, and the pulley started to scream. The lion was incompletely caught, and the king was going to try to work the net over the animal's hindquarters.

I called to him, "King, think it over once. You can't do it. He weighs half a ton, and he's got a solid grip on the net." I didn't realize that only the king could remedy the situation and no one could come between him and the lion, as the lion might be the late King Gmilo. Thus it was entirely up to the king to complete the capture. The pummeling of the drums and the bugling and stone-throwing had stopped, and from the crowd there was only a shout now and then heard when the lion was not roaring. Individual voices were commenting to the king on the situation, which was a bad one.

I stood up saying, "King, I'll go down and look at his ear, just tell me what to look for. Hold it, King, hold." But I doubt whether he heard me. His legs were wide apart in the center of the pole, which bowed deeply and swung and swayed under the energetic movement of his legs, and the rope and pulley and the block made cries as if resined, and the stone weights clattered on the planks. The lion fought on his back and the whole construction swayed. Again I thought the entire hopo tower would collapse and I gripped the straw behind me. Then I saw some smoke or dust above the king and realized that this came from the fastenings of hide that held the block of the pully to the wood. The king's weight and the pull of the lion had been too much for these fastenings. One had torn, that was the puff I saw. And now the other went.

"King Dahfu!" I yelled out.

He was falling. Block and pulley smashed down on the stone before the fleeing beaters. The king had fallen onto the lion. I saw the convulsion of the animal's hindquarters. The claws tore. Instantly there came blood, before the king could throw himself over. I now hung from the edge of the platform by my fingers, hung and then fell, shouting as I went. I wish this had been the eternal pit. The king had rolled himself from the lion. I pulled him farther away. Through the torn clothing his blood sprang out.

"Oh, King! My friend!" I covered up my face.

The king said, "Wo, Sungo." The surfaces of his eyes were strange. They had thickened.

I took off my green trousers to tie up the wound. These were all I had to hand, and they did no good but were instantly soaked.

"Help him! Help!" I said to the crowd.

"I did not make it, Henderson," the king said to me.

"Why, King, what are you talking about? We'll carry you back to the palace. We'll put some sulfa powder into this and stitch you up. You'll tell me what to do, Your Majesty, being the doctor of us two."

"No, no, they will never take me back. Is it Gmilo?"

I ran and caught the rope and pulley and threw the wooden block like a bolo at the still thrusting legs; I wound the rope around them a dozen times, almost tearing the skin from them and yelling, "You devil! Curse you, you son of a bitch!" He raged back through the net. The Bunam then came and looked at the ears. He reached back and called authoritatively for something. His man in the dirty white paint handed him a musket and he put the muzzle against the lion's temple. When he fired the explosion tore a part of the creature's head away.

"It was not Gmilo," the king said.

He was glad his blood would not be on his father's head.

"Henderson," he said, "you will see no harm comes to Atti."

"Hell, Your Highness, you're still king, you'll take care of her yourself." I began to cry.

"No, no, Henderson," he said. "I cannot be . . . among the wives. I would have to be killed." He was moved over these women. Some of them he must have loved. His belly through the torn clothing looked like a grate of fire and some of the beaters were already giving death shrieks. The Bunam stood apart, he kept away from us.

"Bend close," said Dahfu.

I squatted near his head and turned my good ear toward him, the tears meanwhile running between my fingers, and I said, "Oh, King, King, I am a bad-luck type. I am a jinx, and death hangs around me. The world has sent you just the wrong fellow. I am contagious, like Typhoid Mary. Without me you would have been okay. You are the noblest guy I ever met."

"It's the other way around. The shoe is on the other foot. . . . The first night you were here," he explained as a fellow will under the creeping numbness, "that body was the former,

the Sungo before you. Because he could not lift Mummah . . ." His hand was bloody; he put thumb and forefinger
weakly to his throat.

"They strangled him? My God! And what about that big
fellow Turombo, who couldn't pick her up? Ah, he didn't
want to become the Sungo, it's too dangerous. It was wished
on me. I was the fall guy. I was had."

"Sungo also is my successor," he said, touching my hand.

"I take your place? What are you talking about, Your
Highness!"

Eyes closing, he nodded slowly. "No child of age, makes the
Sungo king."

"Your Highness," I said, and raised my weeping voice,
"what have you pulled on me? I should have been told what I
was getting into. Was this a thing to do to a friend?"

Without reopening his eyes, but smiling in his increasing
weakness the king said, "It was done to me. . . ."

Then I said, "Your Majesty, move over and I'll die beside
you. Or else be me and live; I never knew what to do with life
anyway, and I'll die instead." I began to rub and beat my face
with my knuckles, crouching in the dust between the dead lion
and the dying king. "The spirit's sleep burst too late for me. I
waited too long, and I ruined myself with pigs. I'm a broken
man. And I'll never make out with the wives. How can I? I'll
follow you soon. These guys will kill me. King! King!"

But the king had little life left in him now, and we soon
parted. He was picked up by the beaters, the end of the hopo
was opened and we started to go down the ravine among the
cactuses toward that stone building I had first seen from
the platform at the top of the wall. On the way he died of the
hemorrhage.

This small house built of flat slabs had two wooden doors of
the stockade type which opened into two chambers. His body
was laid down in one of these. Into the other they put me. I
scarcely knew what was happening anyway, and I let them
lead me in and bolt the door.

Chapter XXI

At one time, much earlier in this life of mine, suffering had a certain spice. Later on it started to lose this spice; it became merely dirty, and, as I told my son Edward in California, I couldn't bear it any more. Damn! I was tired of being such a monster of grief. But now, with the king's death, it was no longer a topic and it had no spice at all. It was only terrible. Weeping and mourning I was put into the stone room by the old Bunam and his white-dyed assistant. Though the words came out broken, I repeated the one thing, "It's wasted on dummies." (Life is.) "They give it to dummies and fools." (We are where other men ought to be.) So they led me inside, crying my head off. I was too bereaved to ask any questions. By and by a person rising from the floor startled me. "Who the hell is that?" I asked. Two open, wrinkled hands were raised to caution me. "Who are you?" I said again, and then I recognized a head of hair shaped like an umbrella pine and big dusty feet as deformed as vegetable growths.

"Romilayu!"

"Me here too, sah."

They hadn't let him get off with the letter to Lily, but picked him up just as he was leaving town. So even before the hunt began they had decided that they didn't want my whereabouts to be known to the world.

"Romilayu, the king is dead," I said.

He tried to comfort me.

"That marvelous guy. Dead!"

"Fine gen'a'man, sah."

"He thought he could change me. But I met him too late in life, Romilayu. I was too gross. Too far gone."

All I had left in the way of clothing was shoes and helmet, T-shirt and the jockey shorts, and I sat on the floor, where I bent over double and cried without limit. Romilayu at first could not help me.

But maybe time was invented so that misery might have an

end. So that it shouldn't last forever? There may be something
in this. And bliss, just the opposite, is eternal? There is no time
in bliss. All the clocks were thrown out of heaven.

I never took another death so hard. As I had tried to stop
his bleeding, there was blood all over me and soon it was dry.
I tried to rub it off. Well, I thought, maybe this is a sign that I
should continue his existence? How? To the best of my ability.
But what ability have I got? I can't name three things in my
whole life that I did right. So I broke my heart over this, too.

Thus the day passed and the night passed, too, and in the
morning I felt light, dry and hollow. As if I were drifting, like
an old vat. All the moisture was on the outside. Inside, I was
hollow, dark, and dry; I was sober and empty. And the sky
was pink. I saw it through the bars of the door. The Bunam's
black-leather man, still in his coat of white, was our custodian,
and brought us baked yams and other fruit. Two amazons, but
not Tamba and Bebu, were his staff, and everyone treated me
with peculiar deference. During the day I said to Romilayu,
"Dahfu said that when he died I should be king."

"Dem call you Yassi, sah."

"Does that mean king?" That was what it meant. "Some
king," I said, musing. "It's goofy." Romilayu made no
comment whatever. "I would have to be husband to all those
wives."

"You no like dat, sah?"

"Are you crazy, man?" I said. "How could I even think of
taking over that bunch of females? I have all the wife I need.
Lily is just a marvelous woman. Anyway, the king's death has
hurt me too much. I am stricken, can't you see, Romilayu? I
am stricken down and I can't function at all. This has broken
me."

"You no look so too-bad, sah."

"Oh, you want to make me feel better. But you should see
my heart, Romilayu. I have a punchy heart. It's had more
beating than it can take. They've kicked it around far too
much. Don't let this big carcass of mine fool you. I am far too
sensitive. Anyway, Romilayu, it's true I shouldn't have bet

against the rain on that day. It didn't look like good will on
my part. But the king, God bless the guy, let me walk into a
trap. I wasn't really stronger than that man Turombo. He
could have lifted up Mummah. He just didn't want to become
the Sungo. He faked himself out of it. It's too dangerous a
position. This the king did to me."

"But him dange'ah too," said Romilayu.

"Yes, and so he was. Why should I ask to have it better than
he? You're right, old fellow. Thanks for setting me straight." I
thought a while, then asked him, as a man of proven good
sense, "Don't you think I'd scare those girls?" I grimaced to
illustrate my meaning somewhat. "My face is half the length
of another person's body."

"I don't t'ink so, sah."

"Isn't it?" I touched it. "Well, I won't stay, anyhow. Though
I will never have another chance to become a king, I guess."
And thinking deeply about the great man, just dead, just
settled for good and all into nothing, into dark night, I felt he
had picked me to step into his place. It was up to me, if I
wanted to turn my back on home, where I had been nothing.
He believed that I was royal material, and that I might make
good use of a chance to start life anew. And so I sent my
thanks to him, through the stone wall. But I said to Romilayu,
"No, I'd break my heart here trying to fill his position.
Besides, I have to go home. And anyway, I am no stud. No
use kidding, I am fifty-six, or going on it. I'd shake in my
boots that the wives might turn me in. And I'd have to live
under the shadow of the Bunam and Horko and those people,
and never be able to face old Queen Yasra, the king's mother.
I made her a promise. Oh, Romilayu, as if I had ability to
promise anything on. Let's get out of here. I feel like a lousy
impostor. The only decent thing about me is that I have loved
certain people in my life. Oh, the poor guy is dead. Oh, ho, ho,
ho, ho! It kills me. It could be time we were blown off this
earth. If only we didn't have hearts we wouldn't know how
sad it was. But we carry around these hearts, these spotty
damn mangoes in our breasts, which give us away. And it isn't

only that I'm scared of all those wives, but there'll be nobody to talk to any more. I've gotten to that age where I need human voices and intelligence. That's all that's left. Kindness and love." I fell into mourning again, for this was how I had gone on without intermission since being shut in the tomb, and I kept it up a while longer, as I recall. Then suddenly I said to Romilayu, "Pal, the king's death was no accident."

"Whut you mean, sah?"

"It was no accident. It was a scheme, I begin to be convinced of it. Now they can say he was punished for keeping Atti, having her under the palace. You know they wouldn't hesitate to murder the guy. They thought I'd be more pliable than the king. Would you put this past these guys?"

"No sah."

"You bet, no sah. If I ever get my hands on any of these characters I'll crush them like old beer cans." I ground my hands together to show what I would do, and bared my teeth and growled. Perhaps I had learned from lions after all, and not the grace and power of movement that Dahfu had got out of his rearing among them, but the more cruel aspect of the lion, according to my shorter and shallower experience. When you get right down to it, a fellow can't predict what he will pick up in the form of influence. I think that Romilayu was somewhat upset by this jump from mourning to retribution, but he seemed to realize that I wasn't myself, altogether; he was ready to make allowances for me, being really a very generous and understanding type, and quite a Christian fellow. I said, "We must think of crashing out of here. Let's case the joint. Actually, where are we? And what can we do? And what have we got?"

"We got knife, sah," said Romilayu, and he showed it to me. It was his hunting knife, and he had slipped it into his hair when the Bunam's men came after him on the outskirts of the town.

"Oh, good man," I said, and took the knife from him in a stabbing position.

"Dig, bettah," he said.

"Yes, that makes sense. You're right. I'd like to get hold of the Bunam," I said, "but that would be a luxury. Revenge is a luxury. I've got to be canny. Hold me back, Romilayu. It's up to you to restrain me. You see I'm beside myself, don't you? What's next door?" We began to go over the wall, and after a minute examination we found a chink high up between the slabs of stone and we began to dig at it, taking turns with the knife. Sometimes I held Romilayu up in my arms, and sometimes I let him stand on my back while I was on all fours. For him to stand on my shoulders was impracticable, as the ceiling was too low.

"Yes, somebody tampered with the block and pulley at the hopo," I kept saying.

"Maybe, sah."

"There can't be any maybes about it. And why did the Bunam grab you? Because it was a plot against Dahfu and me. Of course, the king let me in for a lot of trouble, too, by allowing me to move Mummah. That he did."

Romilayu dug, revolving the knife blade in the mortar, and he scraped and scooped out the scrapings with his forefinger. The dust fell over me.

"But the king lived under threat of death himself, and what he lived with I could live with. He was my friend."

"You friend, sah?"

"Well, love may be like this, too, old fellow," I explained. "I suppose my dad wished, I *know* he wished, that I had gotten drowned instead of my brother Dick, up there near Plattsburg. Did this mean he didn't love me? Not at all. I, too, being a son, it tormented the old guy to wish it. Yes, if it had been me instead, he would have wept almost as much. He loved both his sons. But Dick should have lived. He was wild only that one time, Dick was; he may have been smoking a reefer. It was too much of a price to pay for one single reefer. Oh, I don't blame the old guy. Except—it's life; and have we got any business to chide it?"

"Yes, sah," he said. He was keenly digging, and I knew he didn't follow me.

"How can you chide it? It has a right to our respect. It does its stuff, that's all. I told that man next door I had a voice that said, I *want*. What did it want?"

"Yes, sah" (scooping more mortar over me).

"It wanted reality. How much unreality could it stand?"

He dug and dug. I was on all fours, and my words were spoken toward the floor. "We're supposed to think that nobility is unreal. But that's just it. The illusion is on the other foot. They make us think we crave more and more illusions. Why, I don't crave illusions at all. They say, Think big. Well, that's boloney of course, another business slogan. But greatness! That's another thing altogether. Oh, greatness! Oh, God! Romilayu, I don't mean inflated, swollen, false greatness. I don't mean pride or throwing your weight around. But the universe itself being put into us, it calls out for scope. The eternal is bonded onto us. It calls out for its share. This is why guys can't bear to be so cheap. And I had to do something about it. Maybe I should have stayed at home. Maybe I should have learned to kiss the earth." (I did so now.) "But I thought I was going to explode, back there. Oh, Romilayu, I wish I could have opened my heart entirely to that poor guy. I'm all torn up over his death. I've never had it so bad.

"But I will show those schemers, if I ever get the chance," I said.

Quietly, Romilayu chipped and dug, then he put his eye to the hole and said, low, "I see, sah."

"What do you see?"

He was silent and dismounted. I stood, rubbing the grit from my back, and put my eye to the hole. There I saw the figure of the dead king. He was wrapped in a shroud of leather, and his features were invisible, for the flap was down over his face. At the hips and feet the body was tied with thongs. The Bunam's assistant was the death-watcher and sat on a stool by the door, sleeping. It was very hot in both these rooms. Beside him were two baskets of cold baked yams. And to the handle of one of these baskets there was tethered a lion cub, still spotted as very young cubs are. I judged it was two or three weeks old. The fellow's sleep was heavy, though he sat on a backless stool. His arms were slack and pressed between his chest and thighs, the hands with their gorged veins nearly dropped to the ground. With hatred in my heart I said to myself, "You wait, you crook. I'll get around to you." Due to the peculiarities of the light, he appeared as white as satin; only his nostrils and the furrows of his cheeks were black. "I'll fix your wagon," I promised him in silence.

"Well, Romilayu," I said. "This time let's use our heads. We won't do as we did the first night here with the body of the other fellow, the Sungo before me. Let us plot. First, I am in line for the throne. They won't want to hurt me, as I'd be a figurehead in the tribe and they would run the show to please themselves. They've got the lion cub, who is my dead friend, so they are moving along pretty fast and we have to move fast, too. Boy, we've got to move even faster."

"Whut you do, sah?" he said, growing worried at my tone.

"Bust out, naturally. Do you think we can make it back to Baventai as we are?"

He couldn't or wouldn't say what he thought of this, and I asked, "It looks bad, eh?"

"You sick," said Romilayu.

"Hah. I can make it if you can. You know how I am when I get going. Are you kidding? I could walk across Siberia on my hands. And anyway, pal, there's no choice. Absolutely the best in me comes out at times like this. It's the Valley Forge element in me. It'll be tough, all right. We'll pack along those yams. That ought to help. You won't stay behind, will you?"

"Wo, no, sah. Dem kill me."

"Then just resign yourself," I said. "I don't think those amazons sit up all night. This is the twentieth century, and they can't make a king of me if I don't let them. Nobody can call me chicken on account of that harem. But, Romilayu, I think it would be smart to act as if I wanted the position. They wouldn't want any harm to come to me. It would put them in a hell of a fix to hurt me. Besides, they must figure that we'd never be fools enough to go through two or three hundred miles of no man's land without food or a gun."

Seeing me in this mood, Romilayu was frightened. "We have to stick together," I said to him, however. "If they should strangle me after a few weeks—and it's likely; I'm in no condition to boast or make big promises—what would happen to you? They'd kill you, too, to protect their secret. And how much grun-tu-molani do you have? You want to live, kid?"

He had no time to answer then, as Horko came to pay us a visit. He smiled, but his behavior was somewhat more formal than before. He called me Yassi and showed his fat red tongue, which he might have done to cool himself after his long walk through the heat of the bush; however, I thought it signified respect.

"How do you do, Mr. Horko?"

Greatly satisfied, he bowed from the waist while he kept his forefinger above his head. The upper part of him was always much crowded by the tight sheath, his court dress of red, and he was congested in the face. The red jewels in his ears dragged them down, and as he grinned I looked at him, but not openly, with hatred. As there was nothing I could do, however, I converted all this hatred into wiliness, and when he said, "You now king. Roi Henderson. Yassi Henderson," I answered, "Yes, Horko. Very sorry about Dahfu, aren't we?"

"Oh, very sorry. Dommage," he said, for he loved to use the phrases he had picked up in Lamu.

Humankind is still fooling around with hypocrisy, I thought. They don't realize that it's too late even for that.

"No more Sungo. You Yassi."

"Yes, indeed," I said. I instructed Romilayu, "Tell the gentleman I am glad to be Yassi, and it's a great honor. When do we start?"

We had to wait, said Romilayu, interpreting, until the worm came from the king's mouth. And then the worm would become a tiny lion, and this cub, the little lion, would become the Yassi.

"If pigs were in this, I'd become an emperor, not just a bush-league king," I said, and took a bitter relish in my own remark. I wished Dahfu had been alive to hear it. "But tell Mr. Horko" (he inclined his thick face, smiling, while the ear-stones dropped again like sinkers; I could have twisted his head and pulled it off with great satisfaction) "it's a terrific honor. Though the late king was a bigger and better man than I am, I will do the best job I can. I think we have a great future. I ran away from home in the first place because I didn't have enough to do in my own country, and this is the type of opportunity I have hoped for." This was how I spoke, and I glowered, but made the glowers seem sincere. "How long do we have to stay in this death house?"

"Him say just three, fo' days, sah."

"Okay?" said Horko. "Not long. You marry toutes les leddy." He started to throw his fingers to show by tens how many there were. Sixty-seven.

"Don't worry about a thing," I said to him.

And when he had left, with ceremony, showing that he felt I was indeed in the bag, I said to Romilayu, "We're going out of here tonight."

Romilayu looked up at me in silence, his upper lip growing very long with despair.

"Tonight," I repeated. "We have the moon. Last night it was bright enough to read the telephone directory by. Have we been in this town a full month?"

"Yes, sah—Whut we do?"

"You'll start yelling in the night. You'll say I've been bitten by a snake, or something. That leather fellow will come with the two amazons to see what's wrong. If he doesn't open the door we'll have to try another scheme. But suppose the door *is* opened. Then take this stone—you understand?—and jam it in by the hinge so the door won't close. That's all we need. Now where's your knife?"

"Me keep knife, sah."

"I don't need it. Yes, you keep the knife. All right, do you follow me? You'll holler that the Sungo Yassi, or whatever I am to these murderers, is bitten by a snake. My leg is swelling fast. And you must stand by the door ready to jam it." I showed him exactly what I wanted done.

So when night began, I sat plotting, concentrating my ideas

and trying to protect their clarity from my fever, which increased every afternoon and rose far into the night. I had to fight against delirium, as my condition was aggravated by the suffocation of the tomb and the hours of vigil I spent at the chink in the wall straining one eye at a time toward the dead figure of the king. Sometimes I imagined that I could see some of the features under the flap of the cowl. But this was more mental . . . mental deceit; dream. My head was out of order, as I realized even then. I was most aware of it at night, under the influence of fever, when mountains and idols and cattle and lions, and gross black women, the amazons, and the face of the king and the thatch of the hopo visited my mind, coming and going unannounced. However, I held tight and waited for moonrise, the time I had chosen to go into action. Romilayu didn't sleep. From the corner where he lay propped, his gaze was never interrupted. I could find him by his eyes, which were always there.

"You no change you min', sah?" he once or twice asked.

"No, no. No change."

And when I judged the time was right, I took a deep, stiff breath, so that my sternum gave a crack. My ribs were sore. "Go!" I said to Romilayu. The fellow next door was certainly sleeping, for I had heard no stir since nightfall. I picked Romilayu up in my arms and held him to the chink we had dug out. Clutching him, I could feel the tremors that ran through his body, and he began to yell and stammer. I added some groans as if from the background, and then the Bunam's man woke up. I heard his feet. Then he must have stood listening as Romilayu repeated in his quaver, "Yassi k'muti!" K'muti I had heard from the beaters as they carried Dahfu toward the tomb. K'muti—he is dying. It must have been the last word to reach his ears. "Wunnutu zazai k'muti. Yassi k'muti." It's not a hard language; I was picking it up fast.

Then the door of the king's tomb opened and the Bunam's man began to shout.

"Oh," said Romilayu to me, "him call two sojer leddy, sah."

I set him on his feet and lay down on the floor. "The stone

is ready," I said. "Go to the door and do your stuff. If we don't get out we haven't got a month to live."

I saw torchlight through the door, which meant that the amazons had come on the double, and it is the most curious thing of all that it was the murder in my heart which calmed me most. It gave me confidence. It was like a balm to me that if I got my hands on the Bunam's narrow-faced man I would be the death of him. "Him at least I will do in," I kept thinking. So, fully calculating, I made cries of fear and weakness—and I gloated at these sounds of weakness, for I really did feel that my strength was low just then but that it would come back to me as soon as I touched the Bunam's man. A strip of board was removed from the door. By the lifted flare the Bunam's man saw me writhing, clutching my leg. The bolt was dropped, and one of the amazons began to open the door. "The stone," I cried as if in pain, and I saw by the flare that Romilayu had pushed the stone oblong below the hinge exactly as I told him, although the point of a spear held by the amazon was right under his chin. He retreated toward me. This I saw under the great, lapping, torn smoky tissue of the fire. The amazon yelled when I pulled her off her feet. The spear point scraped the wall, and I prayed it hadn't touched Romilayu. I struck the woman's head against the stones. Under the circumstances I couldn't afford to make any allowance for her femininity. The fire had been dashed out and the door swiftly closed, but it stuck on the stone just enough to let me get my fingers on the edge. Both the other amazon and the Bunam's man pulled against me, but I tore the thing open. I worked in silence. I was now covered by the night air, which did me good immediately. First I hit the second amazon only with the edge of my hand, a commando trick. It was enough. It lamed her, and she fell to the ground. All this was still in silence, for they made no more noise than I did. Then I went after the man, who was escaping to the other side of the mausoleum. Three strides and I caught him by the hair. I lifted him straight up at arm's length so that he could see my face by the almost risen moon. I snarled. All the skin of his face was drawn upward by the force of my clutch, so that his eyes slanted. As I took him by the throat and began to choke him, Romilayu ran up to me yelling, "No, no, sah."

"I'm going to strangle him."

"No kill him, sah."

"Don't interfere," I yelled, and shook the Bunam's man up and down by the hair. "*He* is the killer. That man inside is dead because of him." But I had stopped choking the Bunam's wizard. I swung his whitened body by the head. No sound came forth.

"You no kill him," said Romilayu earnestly, "Bunam no chase us."

"There's murder in my heart, Romilayu," I said.

"You be my friend, sah?"

"I'll break some of his bones, then. I'll make a deal with you," I said. "You have a right to make a claim on me. Yes, you're my friend. But what about Dahfu? Wasn't he my friend, too? All right, I won't break bones. I'll beat him."

But I didn't beat him, either. I flung the man into the room we had been locked in, and the two amazons with him. Romilayu took away their spears, and we bolted the door. We then went into the other chamber. The moon had now risen and every object was visible. Romilayu picked up the basket of yams, while I walked over to the king.

"Now we go, sah?"

I looked under the cowl. The face was swelled and lumpy, very much distorted. Owing to the effects of the heat, despite the love I felt for him I was obliged to turn away. "Good-by, King," I said. I left him.

But then I had an impulse as we were going. The tethered cub was spitting at us and I picked him up.

"Whut you do?"

"This animal is coming with us," I said.

Chapter XXII

Romilayu started to protest, but I held the creature to me, hearing its tiny snarl and pricked in the chest by its claws. "The king would want me to take it along," I said. "Look, he's got to survive in some form. Can't you see?" The moonlit horizon was extremely clear. It had the effect of making me feel logical. Light was released over us from the summits of the mountains. Thirty miles of terrain opened before us, the path of our flight. I suppose that Romilayu could have pointed out to me that this animal was the child of my enemy who had deprived me of Dahfu. "Well, so look," I said, "I didn't kill that guy. So if I spared him . . . Romilayu, let's not stand here and gab. I can't leave the animal behind and I won't. Look," I said, "I can carry it in my helmet. I don't need it at night." As a matter of fact the night breeze was doing my fever good.

Romilayu gave in to me, and we started our flight, leaping through the shadows of the moon up the side of the ravine. We put the hopo between ourselves and the town, and headed into the mountains, on a straight course for Baventai. I ran behind with the cub, and all that night we did double time, so that by sunrise we had about twenty miles behind us.

Without Romilayu I couldn't have lasted two of the ten days that it took to reach Baventai. He knew where the water was and which roots and insects we could eat. After the yams gave out, as they did on the fourth day, we had to forage for grubs and worms. "You could be a survival instructor for the Air Force," I told him. "You'd be a jewel to them," I also said to him. "So at last I'm living on locusts, like Saint John. 'The voice of one that crieth in the wilderness.'" But we had this lion, which had to be fed and cared for. I doubt whether any such handicap was ever seen before. I had to mince grubs and worms with the knife in my palm and make a paste, and I fed the little creature by hand. During the day, when I had to have the helmet, I carried the cub under my arm, and sometimes I led him on the leash. He slept in the helmet, too, with my wallet and passport, teething on the leather and in the end devouring most of it. I then carried my documents and the four one-thousand-dollar bills inside my jockey shorts.

From gaunt cheeks, my whiskers grew in various colors, and during most of the trek I was demented and raving. I would sit and play with the cub, whom I named Dahfu, while Romilayu foraged. I was too simple in the head to help him. Nevertheless, in many essential matters my mind was very clear and even fine or delicate. As I ate the cocoons and the larvae and ants, crouching in the jockey shorts with the lion lying under me for shade, I spoke oracles and sang—yes, I remembered many songs from nursery and school, like "Fais do-do," "Pierrot," "Malbrouck s'en va-t'en guerre," "Nut Brown Maiden," and "The Spanish Guitar," while I fondled the animal, which had made a wonderful adjustment to me. He rolled between my feet and scratched my legs. Although on a diet of worms and grubs he could not have been very healthy. I feared and Romilayu hoped that the animal would die. But we were lucky. We had the spears and Romilayu killed a few birds. I am pretty sure we killed a bird of prey that had got too near and that we feasted on it.

And on the tenth day (as Romilayu told me afterward, for I had lost count) we came to Baventai. Sitting parched on its rocks, the town was not so parched as we were. The walls were white as eggs, and the brown Arabs in their clothes and muffles watched us arise from the sterile road, myself greeting everyone with two fingers for victory, like Churchill, and giving a cracked, crying, black-throated laugh of survival, holding out the cub Dahfu by the scruff to all those head-swathed and silent men, and the women who revealed only eyes, and the black herdsmen with sunny fat melting from their hair. "Get the band. Get the music," I was saying to them all.

Pretty soon I folded, but I made Romilayu promise to look out for the little animal. "This is Dahfu to me," I said. "Don't let anything happen, please, Romilayu. It would ruin me now. I can't threaten you, old fellow," I said. "I'm too weak, and I can only beg."

Romilayu said I shouldn't worry. At least he told me, "Wo-kay, sah."

"I can beg," I said to him. "I'm not what I thought I was.

"One thing, Romilayu . . ." I was in a native house and lying on a bed while he, squatting beside me, took the animal from my arms. "Is it promised? Between the beginning and the end, is it promised?"

"Whut promise, sah?"

"Well, I mean something *clear*. Isn't it promised? Romilayu, I suppose I mean the reason—*the* reason. It may be postponed until the last breath. But there is justice. I believe there is justice, and that much is promised. Though I am not what I thought."

Romilayu was about to console me, but I said to him, "You don't have to give me consolation. Because the sleep is burst, and I've come to myself. It wasn't the singing of boys that did it," I said. "What I'd like to know is why this has to be fought by everybody, for there is nothing that's struggled against so hard as coming-to. We grow these sores instead. Burning sores, fertile sores." I held the lion on my breast, the child of our murderous enemy. Because of my weakness and fatigue, I was reduced to grimacing at Romilayu. "Don't let me down, old pal," was what I tried to say.

Then I let him take the animal from me and I slept for a while and had dreams, or I didn't sleep but lay on the cot in somebody's house, and those were not dreams but hallucinations. One thing however I kept saying to myself and telling Romilayu, and this was that I had to get back to Lily and the children; I would never feel right until I saw them, and especially Lily herself. I developed a bad case of homesickness. For I said, What's the universe? Big. And what are we? Little. I therefore might as well be at home where my wife loves me. And even if she only seemed to love me, that too was better than nothing. Either way, I had tender feelings toward her. I remembered her in a variety of ways; some of her sayings came back to me, like one should live for this and not for that; not evil but good, not death but life, and all the rest of her theories. But I suppose it made no difference what she said, I wouldn't be kept from loving her even by her preaching. Frequently Romilayu came up to me, and in the worst of my delirium his black face seemed to me like shatter-proof glass to which everything had been done that glass can endure.

"Oh, you can't get away from rhythm, Romilayu," I recall saying many times to him. "You just can't get away from it. The left hand shakes with the right hand, the inhale follows the exhale, the systole talks back to the diastole, the hands play patty-cake, and the feet dance with each other. And the seasons. And the stars, and all of that. And the tides, and all that junk. You've got to live at peace with it, because if it's going to worry you, you'll lose. You can't win against it. It keeps on and on and on. Hell, we'll never get away from rhythm, Romilayu. I wish my dead days would quit bothering me and leave me alone. The bad stuff keeps coming back, and it's the worst rhythm there is. The repetition of a man's bad self, that's the worst suffering that's ever been known. But you can't get away from regularity. But the king said I should change. I shouldn't be an agony type. Or a Lazarus type. The grass should be my cousins. Hey, Romilayu, not even Death knows how many dead there are. He could never run a census. But these dead should go. They *make* us think of them. That is their immortality. In us. But my back is breaking. I'm loaded down. It isn't fair—what about the grun-tu-molani?"

He showed me the little creature. It had survived all the hardships and was thriving like anything.

So after several weeks in Baventai, beginning to recover, I said to my guide, "Well, kid, I suppose I'd better get moving while the cub is still small. I can't wait till he grows into a lion, can I? It will be a job to get him back to the States even if he's half grown."

"No, no. You too sick, sah."

And I said, "Yes, the flesh is not in such hot shape. But I will beat this rap. It's merely some disease. Otherwise, I'm well."

Romilayu was much opposed but I made him take me in
the end to Baktale. There I bought a pair of pants and the
missionary let me have some sulfa until my dysentery was
under control. That took a few days. After this I slept in the
back of the jeep with the lion cub under a khaki blanket, while
Romilayu drove us to Harar, Ethiopia. That took six days.
And in Harar I made Romilayu a few hundred dollars' worth
of presents, I filled the jeep with all sorts of stuff.

"I was going to stop over in Switzerland and visit my little
daughter Alice," I said. "My youngest girl. But I guess I don't
look well, and there's no use frightening the kid. I'd better do
it another time. Besides, there's the cub."

"You tek him home?"

"Where I go he goes," I said. "And Romilayu, you and I
will get together again one day. The world is not so loose any
more. You can locate a man, provided he stays alive. You
have my address. Write to me. Don't take it so hard. Next
time we meet I may be wearing a white coat. You'll be proud
of me. I'll treat you for nothing."

"Oh, you too weak to go, sah," said Romilayu. "I 'fraid to
leave you go."

I took it every bit as hard as he did.

"Listen to me, Romilayu, I'm unkillable. Nature has tried
everything. It has thrown the book at me. And here I am."

He saw, however, that I was feeble. You could have tied me
up with a ribbon of haze.

And after we had said good-by, finally, for good, I realized
that he still dogged my steps and kept an eye on me from a
distance as I went around Harar with the cub. My legs
quaked, my beard was like the purple sage, and I was
sight-seeing in front of old King Menelik's palace, accompanied by the lion, while bushy Romilayu, fear and anxiety in
his face, watched from around the corner to make sure I
didn't collapse. For his own good I paid no attention to him.
When I boarded the plane he still was observing me. It was
the Khartoum flight and the lion was in a wicker basket. The
jeep was beside the airstrip and Romilayu was in it, praying at

the wheel. He held together his hands like giant crayfish and I knew he was doing his utmost to obtain safety and well-being for me. I cried, "Romilayu!" and stood up. Several of the passengers seemed to think I was about to overturn the small plane. "That black fellow saved my life," I said to them.

However, we were now in the air, flying over the shadows of the heat. I then sat down and brought out the lion, holding him in my lap.

In Khartoum I had a hassle with the consular people about arrangements. There was quite a squawk about the lion. They said there were people who were in the business of selling zoo animals in the States, and they told me if I didn't go about it in the right way the lion would have to be in quarantine. I said I was willing to go to a vet and get some shots, but I told them, "I'm in a hurry to get home. I've been sick and I can't stand any delay." The guys said they could see for themselves that I had been through quite a bit. They tried to pump me about my trip, and asked how I had lost all my stuff. "It's none of your lousy business," I said. "My passport is okay, isn't it? And I've got dough. My great-grandfather was head of your crummy outfit, and he was no cold-storage, Ivy League, button-down, broken-hipped civilian like you. All you fellows are just the same. You think U.S. citizens are dummies and morons. Listen, all I want from you is to expedite— Yes, I saw a few things in the interior. Yes, I did. I have had a look into some of the fundamentals, but don't expect me to tickle your idle curiosity. I wouldn't talk even to the ambassador, if he asked me."

They didn't like this. I had the staggers in their office. The lion was on the fellows' desk and knocked down their stapler and nipped them through the clothes. They got rid of me the fastest way they could, and I flew into Cairo that same evening. There I called Lily on the transatlantic phone. "It's me, baby," I cried. "I'm coming home Sunday." I knew she must be pale and going paler, purer and purer in the face as she always did under great excitement, and that her lips must have moved five or six times before she could get out a word.

"Baby, I'm coming home," I said. "Speak clearly, don't mumble now." "Gene!" I heard, and after that the waves of half the world, the air, the water, the earth's vascular system, came in between. "Honey, I aim to do better, can you hear? I've had it now." Of what she said I could make out no more than two or three words. Space with its weird cries came between. I knew she was speaking about love; her voice thrilled, and I guessed she was moralizing and calling me back. "For a big broad you sound very tiny," I kept saying. She could hear me all right. "Sunday, Idlewild. Bring Donovan," I said. This Donovan is an old lawyer who was a trustee of my father's estate. He must be eighty now. I thought I might need his legal help on account of the lion.

This was Wednesday. On Thursday we flew to Athens. I thought I should see the Acropolis. So I hired a car and a guide, but I was too ill and in too much confusion to take in very much of it. The lion was with us, on a leash, and except for the suntans I had bought in Baktale I was dressed as in Africa—same helmet, same desert boots. My beard had grown out considerably; on one side it gushed out half white but with many streaks of blond, red, black, and purple. The embassy people had suggested a shave to make identification easier from the passport. But I did not take their advice. As far as the Acropolis went, I saw something on the heights, which was yellow, bonelike, rose-colored. I realized it must be very beautiful. But I couldn't get out of the automobile, and the guide didn't even suggest it. Altogether he said very little, almost nothing; however, his eyes showed what he thought. "There are reasons for it all," I said to him.

On Friday I got to Rome. I bought a corduroy outfit, burgundy colored, and an alpine hat with Bersagliere feathers, plus a shirt and underpants. Except to buy this stuff I didn't leave my room. I wasn't eager to make a show of myself on the Via Veneto walking the cub on a leash.

On Saturday we flew again by way of Paris and London, which was the only arrangement I could make. To see either place again I had no curiosity. Or any other place, for that matter. For me the best part of the flight was over water. I couldn't seem to get enough of it, as if I had been dehydrated —the water, combing along, endless, the Atlantic, deep. But the depth made me happy. I sat by the window, in the clouds. The sea was thickened by the late, awful, air-blind, sea-blanched sun. We were carried over the calm swarm of the water, the lead-sealed but expanding water, the heart of the water.

Other passengers were reading. Personally, I can't see that. How can you sit in a plane and be so indifferent? Of course, they weren't coming from mid-Africa like me; they weren't discontinuous with civilization. They arose from Paris and London into the skies with their books. But I, Henderson, with my glowering face, with corduroy and Bersagliere feathers—the helmet was inside the wicker basket with the cub, as I figured he needed a familiar object to calm him on this novel, exciting trip—I couldn't get enough of the water, and of these upside-down sierras of the clouds. Like courts of eternal heaven. (Only they aren't eternal, that's the whole thing; they are seen once and never seen again, being figures and not abiding realities; Dahfu will never be seen again, and presently I will never be seen again; but everyone is given the components to see: the water, the sun, the air, the earth.)

The stewardess offered me a magazine to calm me down, seeing how overwrought I was. She was aware that I had the lion cub Dahfu in the baggage compartment, as I had ordered chops and milk for him, and there was a certain inconvenience about my going back and forth constantly and prowling around the rear of the plane. She was an understanding girl, and finally I told her what it was all about, that the lion cub was important to me, and that I was bringing him home to my wife and children. "It's a souvenir of a very dear friend," I said. It was also an enigmatic form of that friend, I might have tried to explain to this girl. She was from Rockford, Illinois. Every twenty years or so the earth renews itself in young maidens. You know what I mean? Her cheeks had the perfect form that belongs to the young; her hair was kinky gold. Her teeth were white and posted on every approach. She was all sweet corn and milk. Blessings on her hips. Blessings on her thighs. Blessings on her soft little fingers which were somewhat covered by the cuffs of her uniform. Blessings on that rough gold. A wonderful little thing; her attitude was that of a pal or playmate, as is common with Midwestern young women. I said, "You make me think of my wife. I haven't seen her in months."

"Oh? How many months?" she said.

That I couldn't tell her, for I didn't know the date. "Is it about September?" I asked.

Astonished, she said, "Honestly, don't you know? It'll be Thanksgiving next week."

"So late! I missed out on enrollment. I'll have to wait until next semester. You see, I got sick in Africa and had a delirium and lost count of time. When you go in deep you run that risk, you know that, don't you, kid?"

She was amused that I called her kid.

"Do you go to school?"

"Instead of coming to ourselves," I said, "we grow all kinds of deformities and enormities. At least something can be done for those. You know? While we wait for the day?"

"Which day, Mr. Henderson?" she said, laughing at me.

"Haven't you ever heard the song?" I said. "Listen, and I'll sing you a little of it." We were back at the rear of the plane where I was feeding the animal Dahfu. I sang, "And who shall abide the day of His coming (the day of His coming)? And who shall stand when He appeareth (when He appeareth)?"

"That is Handel?" she said. "That's from Rockford College."

"Correct," I said. "You are a sensible young woman. Now I have a son, Edward, whose wits were swamped by all that cool jazz. . . . I slept through my youth," I went on as I was feeding the lion his cooked meat. "I slept and slept like our first-class passenger." Note: I must explain that we were on one of those stratocruisers with a regular stateroom, and I had noticed the stewardess going in there with steak and champagne. The fellow never came out. She told me he was a famous diplomat. "I guess he just has to sleep, it's costing so much," I commented. "If he has insomnia it'll be a terrible let-down to a man in his position. You know why I'm impatient to see my wife, Miss? I'm eager to know how it will be now that the sleep is burst. And the children, too. I love them very much—I think."

"Why do you say think?"

"Yes, I think. We'll have to see. You know we're a very funny family for picking up companions. My son Edward had a chimpanzee who was dressed in a cowboy suit. Then in California he and I nearly took a little seal into our lives. Then my daughter brought home a baby. Of course we had to take it away from her. I hope she will consider this lion as a replacement. I hope I can persuade her."

"There's a little kid on the plane," said the stewardess. "He'd probably adore the lion cub. He looks pretty sad."

And I said, "Who is it?"

"Well, his parents were Americans. There's a letter around his neck that tells the story. This kid doesn't speak English at all. Only Persian."

"Go on," I said to her.

"The father worked for oil people in Persia. The kid was raised by Persian servants. Now he's an orphan and going to live with grandparents in Carson City, Nevada. At Idlewild I'm supposed to turn him over to somebody."

"Poor little bastard," I said. "Why don't you bring him, and we'll show him the lion."

So she fetched the boy. He was very white and wore short pants with strap garters and a little dark green sweater. He was a black-haired boy, like my own. This kid went to my heart. You know how it is when your heart drops. Like a fall-bruised apple in the cold morning of autumn. "Come here, little boy," I said, and reached for the child's hand. "It's a bad business," I told the stewardess, "to ship a little kid around the world alone." I took the cub Dahfu and gave it to him. "I don't think he knows what it is—he probably imagines it's a kitty."

"But he likes it."

As a matter of fact the animal did lighten the boy's melancholy, and so we let them play. And when we went back to our seats I kept him with me and tried to show him pictures in the magazine. I gave him his dinner, and at night he fell asleep in my lap, and I had to ask the girl to keep her eye on the lion for me—I couldn't move now. She said he was asleep, too.

And during this leg of the flight, my memory did me a great favor. Yes, I was granted certain recollections and they had made a sizable difference to me. And after all, it's not all to the bad to have had a long life. Something of benefit can be found in the past. First I was thinking, Take potatoes. They actually belong to the deadly nightshade family. Next I thought, Actually, pigs don't have a monopoly on grunting, either.

This reflection made me remember that after my brother Dick's death I went away from home, being already a big boy of about sixteen, with a mustache, a college freshman. The reason why I left was that I couldn't bear to see the old man mourn. We have a beautiful house, a regular work of art. The foundations are of stone and three feet thick; the ceilings are eighteen feet. The windows are twelve, and start at the floor, so that the light fills everything through that kind of marred old-fashioned glass. There's a peace that even I haven't been able to destroy, in those old rooms. Only one thing is wrong: the joint isn't modern. It's not like the rest of life at all, and therefore it's misleading. And as far as I was concerned, Dick could have had it. But the old man, gushing white beard from all his face, he made me feel our family line had ended with Dick up in the Adirondacks, when he shot at the pen and plugged the Greek's coffee urn. Dick also was a curly-headed man with broad shoulders, like the rest of us. He was drowned in the wild mountains, and now my dad looked at me and despaired.

An old man, disappointed, of failing strength, may try to reinvigorate himself by means of anger. Now I understand it. But I couldn't see it at sixteen, when we had a falling out. I was working that summer wrecking old cars, cutting them up for junk with the torch. I was lord and master of the wrecked cars, at a place about three miles from home. It did me good to work in this wrecking yard. That summer I did nothing but dismantle cars. I was grease and rust all over and scalded and dazzled with the cutting torch, and I made mountains of fenders and axles and car innards. On the day of Dick's funeral, I went to work, too. And in the evening, when I washed myself in the back of the house under the garden hose, I was gasping as the chill water rushed over my head, and the old man came out on the back porch, in the dark green of the vines. By the side was a neglected orchard which later I cut down. The water blurted over me. It was cold as outer space. Fiercely, the old man started to yell at me. The hose bubbled on my head while inside I was hotter than the cutting torch that I took to all those old death cars from the highway. My father in his grief swore at me. I knew he meant it because he put aside his customary elegance of words. He cursed, I guess, because I didn't comfort him.

So I went away. I hitchhiked to Niagara Falls. I reached Niagara and stood looking in. I was entranced by the crash of the water. Water can be very healing. I went on the *Maid of the Mists*, the old one, since burned, and through the Cave of the Winds, and the rest of it. And then I went on up to Ontario and picked up a job in an amusement park. This was most of all what I recalled on the plane, with the head of the American-Persian child on my lap, the North Atlantic leading its black life beneath us as the four propellers were fanning us homeward.

It was Ontario, then, though I don't remember which part of the province. The park was a fairground, too, and Hanson, the guy in charge, slept me in the stables. There the rats jumped back and forth over my legs at night, and fed on oats, and the watering of the horses began at daybreak, in the blue light that occurs at the end of darkness in the high latitudes. The Negroes came to the horses at this blue time of the night, when the damp was heavy.

I worked with Smolak. I almost had forgotten this animal, Smolak, an old brown bear whose trainer (also Smolak; he

had been named for him) had beat it with the rest of the
troupe and left him on Hanson's hands. There was no need of
a trainer. Smolak was too old and his master had dusted him
off. This ditched old creature was almost green with time and
down to his last teeth, like the pits of dates. For this shabby
animal Hanson had thought up a use. He had been trained to
ride a bike, but now he was too old. Now he could feed from a
dish with a rabbit; after which, in a cap and bib, he drank
from a baby bottle while he stood on his hind legs. But there
was one more thing, and this was where I came in. There was
a month yet to the end of the season, and every day of this
month Smolak and I rode on a roller coaster together before
large crowds. This poor broken ruined creature and I, alone,
took the high rides twice a day. And while we climbed and
dipped and swooped and swerved and rose again higher than
the Ferris wheels and fell, we held on to each other. By a
common bond of despair we embraced, cheek to cheek, as all
support seemed to leave us and we started down the perpen-
dicular drop. I was pressed into his long-suffering, age-worn,
tragic, and discolored coat as he grunted and cried to me. At
times the animal would wet himself. But he was apparently
aware I was his friend and he did not claw me. I took a pistol
with blanks in case of an assault; it never was needed. I said to
Hanson, as I recall, "We're two of a kind. Smolak was cast off
and I am an Ishmael, too." As I lay in the stable, I would
think about Dick's death and about my father. But most of the
time I lived not with horses but with Smolak, and this poor
creature and I were very close. So before pigs ever came on
my horizon, I received a deep impression from a bear. So if
corporeal things are an image of the spiritual and visible
objects are renderings of invisible ones, and if Smolak and I
were outcasts together, two humorists before the crowd, but
brothers in our souls—I enbeared by him, and he probably
humanized by me—I didn't come to the pigs as a tabula rasa.
It only stands to reason. Something deep already was in-
scribed on me. In the end, I wonder if Dahfu would have
found this out for himself.

Once more. Whatever gains I ever made were always due to

love and nothing else. And as Smolak (mossy like a forest elm) and I rode together, and as he cried out at the top, beginning the bottomless rush over those skimpy yellow supports, and up once more against eternity's blue (oh, the stuff that has been done within this envelope of color, this subtle bag of life-giving gases!) while the Canadian hicks were rejoicing underneath with red faces, all the nubble-fingered rubes, we hugged each other, the bear and I, with something greater than terror and flew in those gilded cars. I shut my eyes in his wretched, time-abused fur. He held me in his arms and gave me comfort. And the great thing is that he didn't blame me. He had seen too much of life, and somewhere in his huge head he had worked it out that for creatures there is nothing that ever runs unmingled.

Lily will have to sit up with me if it takes all night, I was thinking, while I tell her all about this.

As for this kid resting against me, bound for Nevada with nothing but a Persian vocabulary—why, he was still trailing his cloud of glory. God knows, I dragged mine on as long as I could till it got dingy, mere tatters of gray fog. However, I always knew what it was.

"Well, look at you two," said the hostess, meaning that the kid also was awake. Two smoothly gray eyes moved at me, greatly expanded into the whites—new to life altogether. They had that new luster. With it they had ancient power, too. You could never convince me that *this was for the first time.*

"We are going to land for a while," said the young woman.

"The hell you say. Have we crept up on New York so soon? I told my wife to meet me in the afternoon."

"No, it's Newfoundland, for fuel," she said. "It's getting on toward daylight. You can see that, can't you?"

"Oh, I'm dying to breathe some of this cold stuff we've been flying through," I said. "After so many months in the Torrid Zone. You get what I mean?"

"I guess you'll have an opportunity," said the girl.

"Well, let me have a blanket for this child. I'll give him a breath of fresh air, too."

We started to slope and to go in, at which time there was a

piercing red from the side of the sun into the clouds near the
sea's surface. It was only a flash, and next gray light returned,
and cliffs in an ice armor met with the green movement of the
water, and we entered the lower air, which lay white and dry
under the gray of the sky.

"I'm going to take a walk. Will you come with me?" I said
to the kid. He answered me in Persian. "Well, it's okay," I
said. I held out the blanket, and he stood on the seat and
entered it. Wrapping him, I took him in my arms. The
stewardess was going in to that invisible first-class passenger
with coffee.

"All set? Why, where's your coat?" she asked me.

"That lion is all the baggage that I have," I said. "But that's
all right. I'm country bred. I'm rugged."

So we were let out, this kid and I, and I carried him down
from the ship and over the frozen ground of almost eternal
winter, drawing breaths so deep they shook me, pure happiness, while the cold smote me from all sides through the stiff
Italian corduroy with its broad wales, and the hairs of my
beard turned spiky as the mosture of my breath froze
instantly. Slipping, I ran over the ice in those same suede
desert boots. The socks were rotting within and crumbled, as I
had never got around to changing them. I told the kid,
"Inhale. Your face is too white from your orphan's troubles.
Breathe in this air, kid, and get a little color." I held him close
to my chest. He didn't seem to be afraid that I would fall with
him. While to me he was like medicine applied, and the air,
too; it also was a remedy. Plus the happiness that I expected
at Idlewild from meeting Lily. And the lion? He was in it, too.
Laps and laps I galloped around the shining and riveted body
of the plane, behind the fuel trucks. Dark faces were looking
from within. The great, beautiful propellers were still, all four
of them. I guess I felt it was my turn now to move, and so
went running—leaping, leaping, pounding, and tingling over
the pure white lining of the gray Arctic silence.

From

Herzog:

A Visit to Ramona

Time to clean up. He turned from the desk
and the deepening light of the afternoon and dropping the
robe entered the bathroom and turned on the water in the
basin. He drank, in the obscurity of the cool tiled room. New
York has the sweetest water in the world, for a metropolis.
Then he began to soap his face. He could look forward to a
good dinner. Ramona knew how to cook, and how to set a
table. There would be candles, linen napkins, flowers. Perhaps
the flowers were being rushed from the shop now, in evening
traffic. On the windowsill of Ramona's dining room pigeons
roosted. You heard wings flapping in the airshaft. As for the
menu, on a summer evening like this she'd probably prepare
vichyssoise, then shrimp Arnaud—New Orleans style. White
asparagus. A cool dessert. Rum-flavored ice cream with
raisins? Brie and cold-water biscuits? He was judging by
previous dinners. Coffee. Brandy. And, all the time, Egyptian
music on the phonograph in the adjoining room—Mohammad al Bakkar playing "Port Said" with zithers, drums, and
tambourines. In that room was a Chinese rug, the light of the
green lamp deep and quiet. Here also she had fresh flowers. If
I had to work all day in a flower shop, I wouldn't want to be
pursued by the smell of flowers at night. On the coffee table
she had art books and international magazines. Paris, Rio,
Rome, all were represented. Invariably, also, the latest presents from Ramona's admirers were displayed. Herzog always

read the little cards. For what other reason did she leave them? George Hoberly for whom she was cooking shrimp Arnaud last spring still sent her gloves, books, theater tickets, opera glasses. You could trace his love-crazed wanderings up and down New York by the labels. Ramona said he didn't know what he was doing. Herzog was sorry for him.

The bluish-green carpet, the Moorish knickknacks and arabesques, the wide comfortable sofa-bed, the Tiffany lamp with glass like plumage, the deep armchairs by the windows, the downtown view of Broadway and Columbus Circle. And after dinner, when they were settling down here with coffee and brandy, Ramona would ask whether he wouldn't like to take off his shoes. Why not? A free foot on a summer night eases the heart. And by and by, going by precedents, she'd ask why he was so abstracted—was he thinking of his children? Then he'd say . . . he was shaving now, scarcely glancing in the mirror, finding the stubble with his fingertips . . . he'd say that he was no longer so worried about Marco. The boy had a firm character. He was one of the more stable breed of Herzogs. Ramona then would give him level-headed advice about his little daughter. Moses would say how could he abandon her to those psychopaths? Could she doubt that they were psychopaths? Did she want to look again at the letter from Geraldine—the frightful letter that told what they were doing? And there would follow another discussion of Madeleine, Zelda, Valentine Gersbach, Sandor Himmelstein, the Monsignor, Dr. Edvig, Phoebe Gersbach. Against his will, like an addict struggling to kick the habit, he would tell again how he was swindled, conned, manipulated, his savings taken, driven into debt, his trust betrayed by wife, friend, physician. If ever Herzog knew the loathsomeness of a *particular* existence, knew that the *whole* was required to redeem every separate spirit, it was then, in his terrible passion, which he tried, impossibly, to share, telling his story. Then, in the midst of it, the realization would come over him that he had no right to tell, to inflict it, that his craving for confirmation, for help, for justification, was useless. Worse, it was unclean. (For some

reason the French word suited him better, and he said
"Immonde!" and again, more loudly, *"C'est immonde!"*)
However, Ramona would tenderly sympathize with him. No
doubt she genuinely pitied him, though the injured are, for
primitive reasons, unattractive and even ludicrous. In a
spiritually confused age, however, a man who could feel as he
did might claim a certain distinction. He was beginning to see
that his particular brand of short-sightedness, lack of realism,
and apparent ingenuousness conferred a high status on him.
For Ramona it evidently surrounded him with glamour. And
provided that he remain *macho* she would listen with glistening eyes, with more sympathy, and more, and more. She
transformed his miseries into sexual excitements and, to give
credit where it was due, turned his grief in a useful direction.
Cannot agree with Hobbes that where there is no overawing
power men have no pleasure (*voluptas*) in keeping company
but instead (*molestia*) a great deal of grief. There is always an
overawing power, namely, one's terror. To set aside these
theoretical considerations, however, when he was done, having drunk four or five glasses of Armagnac from the Venetian
decanter, far above the Puerto Rican disorders of the street, it
would be Ramona's turn. You treat me right, I treat you right.

He continued shaving, like a blind man, by touch and by
sound, the sound of bristle and blade.

Ramona was highly experienced at entertaining gentlemen.
The shrimp, wine, flowers, lights, perfumes, the rituals of
undressing, the Egyptian music whining and clanging, be-
spoke practice, and he regretted that she'd had to live this
way, but it flattered him, also. Ramona was astonished that
any woman should find fault with Moses. He told her that he
was often a flat failure with Madeleine. It might be the release
of his angry feeling against Mady that improved his performance. At this Ramona looked severe.

"I don't know—it might be *me*—have you considered that?"
she said. "Poor Moses—unless you're having a bad time with
a woman you can't believe you're being serious."

Moses rinsed his face with pleasant witch hazel, a brimming handful, and blew upon his cheeks from the corners of his mouth. He tuned in Polish dance music on the small transistor radio on the glass shelf over the sink, and powdered his feet. Then he gave in for a while to the impulse to dance and leap on the soiled tiles, some of which came free from the grout and had to be kicked under the tub. It was one of his oddities in solitude to break out in song and dance, to do queer things out of keeping with his customary earnestness. He danced out the number until the Polish commercial—"Ochyne-pynch-ochyne, Pynch Avenue, Flushing." He mimicked the announcer in the ivory yellow gloom of the tile bathroom—the water closet, as he anachronistically called it. He was ready to go for another polka when he discovered, breathing hard, that the sweat was rolling down his sides, and that another dance would make a shower necessary. He didn't have the time or patience for that. He couldn't bear the thought of drying himself—one of those killing chores he had always hated.

He put on clean drawers, socks. In stocking feet he trod the toes of his shoes to bring out a dull shine. Ramona did not like his taste in shoes. Before the window of the Bally shop on Madison Avenue she pointed at a pair of ankle-high Spanish boots and said, "That's what you need—those vicious-looking black things." Smiling, she looked upward so that he was confronted by the brightness of her eyes. She had marvelous, slightly curved white teeth. Her lips would part and close over these significant teeth, and she had a short, curved, French nose, small and fine; hazel eyes; thick vivid black hair. The weight of her face was mainly in the lower part. A slight defect, in Herzog's view. Nothing serious.

"You want me to dress up like a flamenco dancer?" said Herzog.

"You ought to use a little imagination about clothes—encourage certain aspects of your character."

You would think—Herzog smiled broadly—he was a piece of human capital badly invested. To her surprise, perhaps, he

agreed with her. Almost cheerfully, he agreed. Strength,
intelligence, feeling, opportunity had been wasted on him.
What he could not see, however, was that such Spanish
shoes—which, by the way, greatly appealed to his childish
taste—would improve his character. And we must improve.
Must!

He put on trousers. Not the Italian pants: they'd be
uncomfortable after dinner. One of the new poplin shirts was
next. He removed all the pins. Then he put on the madras
jacket. He bent down to see what he could see of the harbor
through the small opening of the bathroom window. Nothing
in particular. Only a sense of water bounding the overbuilt
island. It was a movement of orientation that he was making,
like the glance at his watch which did not tell him the time.
And next came his specific self, an apparition in the square
mirror. How did he look? Oh, terrific—you look exquisite,
Moses! Smashing! The primitive self-attachment of the
human creature, that sweet instinct for the self, so deep, so old
it may have a cellular origin. As he breathed, he was aware of
it, quiet but far-reaching, all through his system, a pleasing
hunger in his remotest nerves. *Dear Professor Haldane . . .*
No, that was not Herzog's man at this moment. *Dear Father
Teilhard de Chardin, I have tried to understand your notion of
the inward aspect of the elements. That sense organs, even
rudimentary sense organs, could not evolve from molecules
described by mechanists as inert. Thus matter itself should
perhaps be studied as evolving consciousness . . . is the carbon
molecule lined with thought?*

His shaven face, muttering in the mirror—great shadows
under the eyes. That's okay, he thought; if the light's not too
bright, you're still a grand-looking man. For a while yet, you
can get women. All but that bitch, Madeleine, whose face
looks either beautiful or haggy. Go, then—Ramona will feed
you, give you wine, remove your shoes, flatter you, smooth
down your hackles, kiss you, pinch your lip with her teeth.
Then uncover the bed, turn down the lights, and go into the
essentials. . . .

He was half elegant, half slovenly. That had always been his
style. If he knotted his tie with care, his shoelaces dragged. His
brother Shura, immaculate in his tailored clothes, manicured
and barbered at the Palmer House, said this was done on
purpose. Once it had perhaps been his boyish defiance, but by
now it was an established part of the daily comedy of Moses
E. Herzog. . . .

He stirred. He'd better be on his way. It was growing late.
He was expected uptown. But he was not yet ready to leave.
He took a new sheet of paper and wrote *Dear Sono.*

She had gone back to Japan long ago. When was it? He
turned his eyes upward as he tried to calculate the length of
time, and he saw the white clouds rolling above Wall Street
and the harbor. *I don't blame you for going home.* She was a
person of means. She owned a house in the country, too.
Herzog had seen the colored photographs—an Oriental
countryside with rabbits, hens, piglets, her own hot spring in
which she bathed. She had a picture of the village blind man
who came to massage her. She loved massages, believed in
them. She had often massaged Moses, and he had massaged
her.

*You were right about Madeleine, Sono. I shouldn't have
married her. I should have married you.*

But Sono had never really learned to speak English. For
two years, she and Moses had conversed in French—*petit
nègre.* He wrote, *Ma chère, Ma vie est devenue un cauchemar
affreux. Si tu savais!* At McKinley High School, from a
forbidding spinster, Miss Miloradovitch, he had learned his
French. *The most useful course I took.*

Sono had seen Madeleine only once, but once was enough.
She warned me as I sat in her broken Morris chair. "Moso,
méfie-toi. Prends garde, Moso."

She had a tender heart, and Herzog knew that if he wrote
her of the sadness of his life, she would certainly cry.
Instantaneous tears. They had a way of appearing without the

usual Western preliminaries. Her black eyes rose from the
surface of her cheeks in the same way that her breasts rose
from the surface of her body. No, he would not write her sad
news of any sort, he decided. Instead, he allowed himself to
picture her as she might be now (it was morning in Japan),
bathing in her steaming spring, her small mouth open, singing.
She bathed often, and sang as she washed, her eyes upcast and
her lips dainty and tremulous. The songs were sweet and odd,
narrow, steep, at times with catlike sounds.

During the trouble time when he was being divorced from
Daisy and he came to visit Sono in her West Side apartment,
she would immediately run the little tub and fill it with Macy's
bath salts. She unbuttoned Moses' shirt, took off his clothes,
and when she had him settled ("Easy now, it's hot") in the
swirling, foaming, perfumed water she let drop her petticoat
and got in behind him, singing that vertical music of hers.

> "Chin-chin
> Je te lave le dos
> Mon Mo-so."

As a young girl she had gone to live in Paris, and she was
caught there by the War. She was down with pneumonia when
the American troops entered and was still sick when she was
repatriated via the Trans-Siberian Railroad. She no longer
cared for Japan, she said; the West had spoiled her for life in
Tokyo, and her rich father allowed her to study design in New
York.

She told Herzog that she was not sure she believed in God,
but that if he did she would also try to have faith. If on the
other hand he was a Communist she was prepared to become
one, too. Because "Les Japonaises sont très fidèles. Elles ne
sont pas comme les Américaines. Bah!" Still, American
women also amused her. She often entertained the Baptist
ladies who were her sponsors with the Immigration Department. She prepared shrimp or raw fish for them or treated
them to the tea ceremony. Moses sometimes sat waiting on

the stoop of the brownstone opposite when the ladies were slow to leave. Sono with great enjoyment—she was greedy for intrigue (the abysses of female secrecy!)—would come to the window and give him the high sign, pretending to water her plants. She grew little ginkgo trees and cactuses in yoghurt containers.

On the West Side, she occupied three rooms with high ceilings; at the back there grew an ailanthus tree, and one of the front windows contained a giant air-conditioner; it must have weighed a ton. Fourteenth Street bargains filled the apartment—an overstuffed chesterfield, bronze screens, lamps, nylon drapes, masses of wax flowers, articles of wrought iron and twisted wire and glass. Here Sono went back and forth busily on bare feet, coming down on her heels sturdily. Her lovely body was covered unbecomingly in knee-length bargain negligees bought on the stands near Seventh Avenue. Every purchase involved her in a battle with the other bargain hunters. Excitedly holding her soft throat she would tell Herzog with sharp cries what had happened. "Chéri! J'avais déjà choisi mon tablier. Cette femme s'est foncée sur moi. Woo! Elle était noire! Moooan dieu! Et grande! Derrière immense. Immense poitrine. Et sans soutien-gorge. Tout à fait comme Niagara Fall. En chair noire." Sono puffed out her cheeks and crooked her arms as though suffocating with fat, thrusting out her belly, then displaying her rump. "Je disais, 'No, no, leddy. I here first.' Elle avait les bras comme ça—enflés. Et quelle gorge! Il y avait du monde au balcon. 'No!' je disais. 'No, no, leddy.' " Proudly Sono showed her nostrils, made her eyes heavy and dangerous. She set a hand on her hip. Herzog in the broken Morris chair from the Catholic Salvage said, "That's the stuff, Sono. They can't push the Samurai around on Fourteenth Street."

Abed, he had touched Sono's eyelids experimentally, as she lay smiling. Those strange, complex, soft, pale lids would keep the imprint of a touch for quite a while. *To tell the truth, I never had it so good,* he wrote. *But I lacked the strength of character to bear such joy.* That was hardly a joke. When a

man's breast feels like a cage from which all the dark birds
have flown—he is free, he is light. And he longs to have his
vultures back again. He wants his customary struggles, his
nameless, empty works, his anger, his afflictions and his sins.
In this parlor of Oriental luxury, making a principled quest—
principled, mind you—for life-giving pleasure, solving for
Moses E. Herzog the puzzle of the body (curing himself of the
fatal disorder of worldliness which rejects worldly happiness,
this Western plague, this mental leprosy), he seemed to have
found his object. But often he sat morose, depressed, in the
Morris chair. Well, curse such sadness! But she liked even
that. She saw me with the eyes of love, and she said, "Ah! T'es
mélancolique—c'est très beau!" It may be that guilt and
sadness made me look Oriental. A morose, angry eye, a long
upper lip—what people used to call the Chinese Gleep. It was
beau to her. And no wonder she thought I might be a
Communist. The world should love lovers; but not theoreticians. Never theoreticians! Show them the door. Ladies, throw
out these gloomy bastards! Hence, loathéd melancholy! In
dark Cimmerian desart ever dwell.

Sono's three tall rooms in the brownstone apartment were
hung with transparent bargain curtains, like the Far East in
the movies. There were many interiors. The inmost was the
bed, with sheets of spearmint green, or washed-out chloro-
phyll, unmade, everything in disorder. After the bath, Herzog's body was red. When she had dried and powdered him,
she dressed him in a kimono, her pleased but still slightly
unwilling Caucasian doll. The stiff cloth cramped him under
the arms as he sat on the pillows. She brought him tea in her
best cups. He listened to her talk. She would tell him the latest
scandals of the Tokyo press. A woman had mutilated her
unfaithful lover and was found with the missing parts in her
obi. A locomotive engineer slept through a signal and killed a
hundred and fifty-four people. Her father's concubine was
now driving a Volkswagen. She parked at the gate of the
house, for she was not allowed into the yard. And Herzog
thought . . . is this really possible? Have all the traditions,

passions, renunciations, virtues, gems, and masterpieces of
Hebrew discipline and all the rest of it—rhetoric, a lot of it,
but containing true facts—brought me to these untidy green
sheets, and this rippled mattress? As if anyone cared what he
was doing here. As if it affected the fate of the world in any
way. It was his own business. "I got a right," Herzog
whispered, though his face neither changed nor moved. Very
good. The Jews were strange to the world for a great length of
time, and now the world is being strange to them in return.
Sono brought out a bottle and spiked his tea with cognac or
Chivas Regal. When she had taken a few nips herself she gave
a playful growl. Herzog could not help laughing. Sono then
brought out her scrolls. Fat merchants made love to slender
girls who looked away comically as they submitted. Moses
and Sono sat cross-legged on the bed. She pointed to things,
winking and exclaiming and pressing her round face to
his.

Something was always frying or brewing in her kitchen, a
dark closet rank with fish and soy sauce, seaweed vermicelli,
old tea leaves. The plumbing was often out of order. She
wanted Herzog to have a talk with the Negro janitor, who
would only laugh at her when she demanded service. Sono
kept two cats; their pan was never clean. When Herzog was in
the subway, coming to see her, he already began to smell those
odors of her apartment. Their darkness passed through his
heart. He violently desired Sono, and just as violently did not
want to go. Even now he felt the fever, remembered the smells,
experienced the difficulty. He shivered when he rang her bell.
The chain rattled, she pulled open the large door and threw
her arms about his neck. Her face was elaborately made up,
and she smelled of musk. The cats tried to make an escape.
She captured them, and then she cried out—always the same
cry—

"Moso! Je viens de rentrer!"

She was breathless. She had run to meet him and beat him
home by seconds. Why? Why did she always have to be just
under the wire? Perhaps to show that she had an independent

and active life; she did not sit waiting. The tall door with the curved top admitted him. Sono secured it again with bolt and chain (precautions of a woman living alone; but she said the super tried to let himself in without knocking). Herzog with a beating heart but composed face entered, looked around with pale-faced dignity at the hangings (sienna, crimson, green) and the fireplace stuffed with the wrappings of her latest purchases, the draftsman's table where she did her homework and where the cats perched. He smiled at eager Sono, and sat down in the Morris chair. "Mauvais temps, eh chéri?" she said, and she began at once to cheer him. She took off his miserable shoes, telling him where she had been. Some lovely Christian Science ladies had invited her to a concert at the Cloisters. She had seen a double feature at the Thalia—Danielle Darrieux, Simone Signoret, Jean Gabin, et Harry Bow-wow. The Nippon-America Society invited her to the United Nations building, where she presented flowers to the Nizam of Hyderabad. Through a Japanese trade mission she also met Mr. Nasser and Mr. Sukarno and the Secretary of State and the President. Tonight she had to go to a night club with the foreign minister of Venezuela. Moses had learned not to doubt her. She always produced a night-club photograph in which she sat beautiful and laughing in a low-cut gown. She had Mendès-France's autograph on a menu. She would never ask Herzog to take her to the Copacabana. This was a mark of her respect for his deep gravity. "T'es philosophe. O mon philosophe, mon professeur d'amour. T'es très important. Je le sais." She rated him higher than kings and presidents.

As she put the kettle on for Herzog's tea, she never failed to describe the events of her day from the kitchen at the top of her voice. She saw a three-legged dog which made a truck swerve into a pushcart. A cabdriver wanted to give her his parrot, but the cats would kill it. She could not accept such a responsibility. A panhandling old woman—vieille mendiante —got her to buy a copy of the *Times* for her. That was all the old creature wanted, this morning's *Times*. A policeman said he would give Sono a ticket for jay-walking. A man had exposed himself behind a subway pillar. "Ooooh, c'était honteux—quelle chose!" She measured with her hands from her own body. "One foots, Moso. Très laide."

"Ça t'a plu," Moses said smiling.

"Oh no! Moso, no! Elle était vilain." She was, however, delightfully excited. Moses looked at her gently, suspiciously as well, perhaps, lying back elegantly in the broken reclining chair. The fever he had felt as he was coming had now begun to subside. Even the smells were never quite so bad as he had anticipated. The cats were less jealous of him. They came to be petted. He grew used to their Siamese mewing, more passionate and hungry than that of American cats.

Then she said, "Et cette blouse—combien j'ai payé? Dis-moi."

"You paid—let me see—you paid three bucks for it."

"No, no," she cried, "sixty sen'. Solde!"

"Impossible. Why, that thing is worth five bucks. You must be the greatest shopper in New York."

Gratified, she gave him a brilliant wink and took off his socks, chafing his feet. She brought him tea and poured a double shot of Chivas Regal into it. For him she kept the best of everything. "Veux-tu scrombled eggs, chéri-koko. As-tu faim?" A cold rain was killing desolate New York with its green icy spikes. *When I pass Northwest Orient Airlines, I always mean to price a ticket to Tokyo.* She put soy sauce on the eggs. Herzog ate and drank. All the food was salty. He swallowed a great deal of tea. "We take bath," said Sono, and began to unbutton his shirt. "Tu veux?"

Teas and baths—the steam of boiling water loosened the wallpaper from the green plaster behind. The great console radio through a cloth-of-gold speaker played the music of Brahms. The cats were cuffing shrimp shells under the chairs.

"Oui—je veux bien," he said.

She went to run the water. He heard her singing as she sprinkled the lilac salts and bubble-bath powder.

I wonder who's scrubbing her now.

Sono asked for no great sacrifices. She did not want me to work for her, to furnish her house, support her children, to be regular at meals or to open charge accounts in luxury shops; she asked only that I should be with her from time to time. But some people are at war with the best things of life and pervert them into fantasies and dreams. The Yiddish French we spoke was funny but innocent. She told me no such broken truths and dirty lies as I heard in my own language, and my simple declarative sentences couldn't do her much harm. Other men have forsaken the West, looking for just this. It was delivered to me in New York City.

The bath was not without its occasional trials. At times, Sono examined Herzog's body for signs that he was unfaithful. Lovemaking, she was strongly convinced, turned men lean. "Ah!" she would say. "Tu as maigri. Tu fais amour?" He denied it but she shook her head, continuing to smile, though her face became puffy and bitter. She refused to believe him. But she would forgive him, at last. Her good humor returning, she put him in the tub, climbing in behind him. Singing, or growling mock orders at him in military Japanese. But peace had come. They bathed. She put her feet forward for him to soap. She dipped water in a plastic dish and poured it over his head. Draining the tub at last, she turned on the shower to rinse away the suds, and they stood together smiling under the spray. "Tu seras bien propre, chéri-koko."

Yes, she kept me very clean. With amusement and with sorrow, Herzog recalled it all.

They dried themselves with Turkish towels from Fourteenth Street. She dressed him in the kimono, kissing his chest. He kissed the palms of her hands. Her eyes were tender, shrewd, they showed a thrifty light at times; she knew where to invest her sensuality and how to increase it. She sat him on the bed, and there she served him tea. Her concubine. They sat cross-legged, sipping from the small cups, looking at the scrolls. The door was bolted, the telephone off the hook. Tremulous, Sono's face came near, and she touched his cheek with her chub lips. They helped each other out of the Oriental garments. "Doucement, chéri. Oh, lentement. Oh!" Turning up her eyes so that he saw only the whites.

She tried to explain to me once that earth and the planets

were sucked from the sun by a passing star. As if a dog should trot by a bush and set free worlds. And in those worlds life appeared, and within that life such as we—souls. And even stranger creatures than we, she said. I liked to hear this, but I didn't understand her well. I know I kept her from returning to Japan. For my sake, she disobeyed her father. Her mother died, and Sono did not mention it for weeks. And once she said, "Je ne crains pas la mort. Mais tu me fais souffrir, Moso." I hadn't called her in a month. She had had pneumonia again. No one had come to see her. She was weak and pale, and she cried and said, "Je souffre trop." But she did not let him comfort her; she had heard that he was seeing Madeleine Pontritter.

She did, however, say, "Elle est méchante, Moso. Je suis pas jalouse. Je ferai amour avec un autre. Tu m'as laissée. Mais elle a les yeux très, très froids."

He wrote, *Sono, you were right. I thought you might like to know. Her eyes are very cold.* Still, they are her eyes, and what is she to do about them? It would not be practical for her to hate herself. Luckily, God sends a substitute, a husband.

Ah, in the midst of such realizations, a man needs some comfort. Herzog once more set off on his visit to Ramona. As he stood at the door with the long metal shank of the police lock in his hand, his memory sought a certain song title. Was it "Just One More Kiss"? Not that. Nor "The Curse of an Aching Heart." "Kiss Me Again." That was it. It struck him very funny, and laughter made him clumsy as he set up the complicated lock to protect his worldly goods. Three thousand million human beings exist, each with *some* possessions, each a microcosmos, each infinitely precious, each with a peculiar treasure. There is a distant garden where curious objects grow, and there, in a lovely dusk of green, the heart of Moses E. Herzog hangs like a peach.

I need this outing like a hole in the head, he thought as he turned the key. Still, he was going, wasn't he. He was pocketing the key. And now ringing for the elevator. He

listened to the sound of the power, the cables threshing. He
went down alone, humming "Kiss Me," and trying to capture,
as if it were an elusive fragile thread, the reason why these old
songs were running through his head. Not the obvious reason.
(He had an aching heart, was going forth to be kissed.) The
recondite reason (if that was worth finding). He was glad to
reach the open air, to breathe. He dried the sweatband of the
straw hat with his handkerchief—it was hot in the shaft. And
who wore such a hat, such a blazer? Why, Lou Holtz, of
course, the old vaudeville comic. He sang, "I picked a lemon
in the garden of love, where they say only *peaches* grow."
Herzog's face again quickened with a smile. The old Oriental
Theatre in Chicago. Three hours of entertainment for two bits.

At the corner he paused to watch the work of the wrecking
crew. The great metal ball swung at the walls, passed easily
through brick, and entered the rooms, the lazy weight
browsing on kitchens and parlors. Everything it touched
wavered and burst, spilled down. There rose a white tranquil
cloud of plaster dust. The afternoon was ending, and in the
widening area of demolition was a fire, fed by the wreckage.
Moses heard the air, softly pulled toward the flames, felt the
heat. The workmen, heaping the bonfire with wood, threw
strips of molding like javelins. Paint and varnish smoked like
incense. The old flooring burned gratefully—the funeral of
exhausted objects. Scaffolds walled with pink, white, green
doors quivered as the six-wheeled trucks carried off fallen
brick. The sun, now leaving for New Jersey and the west, was
surrounded by a dazzling broth of atmospheric gases. Herzog
observed that people were spattered with red stains, and that
he himself was flecked on the arms and chest. He crossed
Seventh Avenue and entered the subway.

Out of the burning, the dust, down the stairs he hurried
underground, listening for a train, fingers examining the coins
in his pocket, seeking a subway token. He inhaled the odors of
stone, of urine, bitterly tonic, the smells of rust and of
lubricants, felt the presence of a current of urgency, speed,
of infinite desire, possibly related to the drive within himself,

his own streaming nervous vitality. (Passion? Perhaps hyste-
ria? Ramona might relieve him by sexual means.) He took a
long breath, inhaling the musty damp air endlessly, on and on,
stabbed in both shoulders as his chest expanded, but continuing. Then he let the air out slowly, very slowly, down, down,
into his belly. He did it again, again, and felt better for it. He
dropped his fare in the slot where he saw a whole series of
tokens lighted from within and magnified by the glass.
Innumerable millions of passengers had polished the wood of
the turnstile with their hips. From this arose a feeling of
communion—brotherhood in one of its cheapest forms. This
was serious, thought Herzog as he passed through. The more
individuals are destroyed (by processes such as I know) the
worse their yearning for collectivity. Worse, because they
return to the mass agitated, made fervent by their failure. Not
as brethren, but as degenerates. Experiencing a raging con-
sumption of potato love. Thus occurs a second distortion of
the divine image, already so blurred, wavering, struggling. The
real question! He stood looking down at the tracks. The most
real question!

Rush hour was just ended. Almost empty local cars were
scenes of rest and peace, conductors reading the papers.
Waiting for his uptown express, Herzog made a tour of the
platform, looking at the mutilated posters—blacked-out teeth
and scribbled whiskers, comical genitals like rockets, ridiculous copulations, slogans and exhortations. *Moslems, the
enemy is White. Hell with Goldwater, Jews! Spicks eat* SHIT.
Phone, I will go down on you if I like the sound of your voice.
And by a clever cynic, *If they smite you, turn the other face.*
Filth, quarrelsome madness, the prayers and wit of the crowd.
Minor works of Death. Trans-descendence—that was the new
fashionable term for it. Herzog carefully examined all such
writings, taking his own public-opinion poll. He assumed the
unknown artists were adolescents. Taunting authority. Imma-
turity, a new political category. Problems connected with the
increasing mental emancipation of untrained unemployables.
Better the Beatles. Further occupying the idle moment,

Herzog looked at the penny scale. The mirror was wired—could not be smashed except by an ingenious maniac. The benches were bolted down, the candy-vending machines padlocked.

A note to Willie the Actor, the famous bank robber now serving a life sentence. *Dear Mr. Sutton, The study of locks.* Mechanical devices and Yankee genius . . . He began again, *Second only to Houdini,* Willie never carried a gun. In Queens, once, he used a toy pistol. Disguised as a Western Union messenger, he entered the bank and took it over with his cap gun. The challenge was irresistible. Not the money, really, but the problem of getting in, and the companion problem of escape. Narrow-shouldered, with sunk cheeks and the mothy, dapper mustache, blue baggy eyes above, Willie lay thinking of banks. On his inadoor bed in Brooklyn, sucking a cigarette, wearing his hat and a pair of pointed shoes, he had visions of roofs leading to roofs, of power lines, sewer connections, vaults. All locks opened at his touch. Genius cannot let the world be. He had buried his loot in Flushing Meadows, in tin cans. He might have retired. But he took a walk, he saw a bank, a creative opportunity. This time he was caught and went to prison. But he planned a great getaway, made an elaborate mental survey and drew a master plan, crawled through pipes, dug under walls. He almost had it made. The stars were in view. But the screws were waiting when he broke through the earth. They carried him back—this insignificant person, the escape artist; one of the greatest, *and not very far behind Houdini, either. Motive: The power and completeness of all human systems must be continually tested, outwitted, at the risk of freedom, of life.* Now he is a lifer. They say he owns a set of the Great Books, corresponds with Bishop Sheen. . . .

Dear Dr. Schrodinger, In What Is Life? *you say that in all of nature only man hesitates to cause pain. As destruction is the master-method by which evolution produces new types, the reluctance to cause pain may express a human will to obstruct natural law. Christianity and its parent religion, a few short millennia, with frightful reverses . . .* The train had stopped, the door was already shutting when Herzog roused himself and squeezed through. He caught a strap. The express flew uptown. It emptied and refilled at Times Square, but he did not sit down. It was too hard to fight your way out again from a seat. Now, where were we? *In your remarks on entropy . . . How the organism maintains itself against death—in your words, against thermodynamic equilibrium . . . Being an unstable organization of matter, the body threatens to rush away from us. It leaves. It is real. It! Not we! Not I! This organism, while it has the power to hold its own form and suck what it needs from its environment, attracting a negative stream of entropy, the being of other things which it uses, returning the residue to the world in simpler form. Dung. Nitrogenous wastes. Ammonia. But reluctance to cause pain coupled with the necessity to devour . . . a peculiar human trick is the result, which consists in admitting and denying evils at the same time. To have a human life, and also an inhuman life. In fact, to have everything, to combine all elements with immense ingenuity and greed. To bite, to swallow. At the same time to pity your food. To have sentiment. At the same time to behave brutally. It has been suggested (and why not!) that reluctance to cause pain is actually an extreme form, a delicious form of sensuality, and that we increase the luxuries of pain by the injection of a moral pathos. Thus 'working both sides of the street. Nevertheless, there are moral realities,* Herzog assured the entire world as he held his strap in the speeding car, *as surely as there are molecular and atomic ones. However, it is necessary today to entertain the very worst possibilities openly. In fact we have no choice as to that. . . .*

This was his station, and he ran up the stairs. The revolving gates rattled their multiple bars and ratchets behind him. He hastened by the change booth where a man sat in a light the color of strong tea, and up the two flights of stairs. In the mouth of the exit he stopped to catch his breath. Above him the flowering glass, wired and gray, and Broadway heavy and blue in the dusk, almost tropical; at the foot of the downhill Eighties lay the Hudson, as dense as mercury. On the points of radio towers in New Jersey red lights like small hearts beat or tingled. In midstreet, on the benches, old people: on faces, on heads, the strong marks of decay: the big legs of women and blotted eyes of men, sunken mouths and inky nostrils. It was the normal hour for bats swooping raggedly (Ludeyville), or pieces of paper (New York) to remind Herzog of bats. An escaped balloon was fleeing like a sperm, black and quick into the orange dust of the west. He crossed the street, making a detour to avoid a fog of grilled chicken and sausage. The crowd was traipsing over the broad sidewalk. Moses took a keen interest in the uptown public, its theatrical spirit, its performers—the transvestite homosexuals painted with great originality, the wigged women, the lesbians looking so male you had to wait for them to pass and see them from behind to determine their true sex, hair dyes of every shade. Signs in almost every passing face of a deeper comment or interpretation of destiny—eyes that held metaphysical statements. And even pious old women who trod the path of ancient duty, still, buying kosher meat.

Herzog had several times seen George Hoberly, Ramona's friend before him, following him with his eyes from one or another of these doorways. He was thin, tall, younger than Herzog, correctly dressed in Ivy League Madison Avenue clothes, dark glasses on his lean, sad face. Ramona, with the accent on "nothing," said she felt nothing but pity for him. His two attempted suicides probably made her realize how indifferent she was to him. Moses had learned from Madeleine that when a woman was done with a man she was done with him utterly. But tonight it occurred to him that, since Ramona was keen on men's styles and often tried to guide his choices, Hoberly might be wearing the clothes she had picked for him. He is vainly appealing, in the trappings of his former happiness and love, like the trained mouse in the frustration experiment. Even being phoned by the police and running to Bellevue in the middle of the night to be by his side now bores Ramona. The whole feeling-and-sensation market has shot up—shock, scandal priced out of range for the average man. You have to do more than take a little gas, or slash the wrists.

Pot? Zero! Daisy chains? Nothing! Debauchery? A museum word from prelibidinous times! The day is fast approaching— Herzog in his editorial state—when only proof that you are despairing will entitle you to the vote, instead of the means test, the poll tax, the literacy exam. You must be forlorn. Former vices now health measures. Everything changing. Public confession of each deep wound which at one time was borne as if nothing were amiss. A good subject: the history of composure in Calvinistic societies. When each man, feeling fearful damnation, had to behave as one of the elect. All such historic terrors—every agony of spirit—must at last be released. Herzog began to be almost eager to see Hoberly, to have another look at that face wasted by suffering, insomnia, nights of pills and drink, of prayer—his dark glasses, his almost brimless fedora. Unrequited love. Nowadays called hysterical dependency. There were times when Ramona spoke of Hoberly with great sympathy. She said she had been crying over one of his letters or gifts. He kept sending her purses and perfumes, and long extracts from his journal. He had even sent her a large sum in cash. This she turned over to Aunt Tamara. The old lady opened a savings account for him. Let the money gather a little interest, at least. Hoberly was attached to the old woman. Moses, too, was fond of her.

He rang Ramona's bell and the buzzer opened the lobby door at once. She was considerate that way. One more delicate attention. The arrival of her lover was never routine. The elevator let people out—a fellow with a heavy front, one eye shut, smoking a strong cigar; a woman with two chihuahuas, red nail polish matching the harness of the dogs. And perhaps in the whirling fumes of the street, through two glass doors, his rival watched him. Moses rode up. On the fifteenth floor Ramona had the door ajar, on the chain. She didn't want to be surprised by the wrong man. When she saw Moses, she unbolted and took his hand, drawing him to her side. She offered her face to him. Herzog found it full, and very hot. Her perfume sprang out at him. She wore a white satin blouse, cut to suggest the wrapping of a shawl and showing her bust. Her

face was flushed; she did not need the added color of rouge.
"I'm glad to see you, Ramona. I'm very glad," he said. He
hugged her, discovering in himself a sudden eagerness, a
hunger for contact. He kissed her.

"So—you're glad to see me?"

"I am! I am!"

She smiled and shut the door, bolting it again. She led
Herzog by the hand along the uncarpeted hall where her heels
made a military clatter. It excited him. "Now," she said, "let's
have a look at Moses in his finery." They stopped before the
gilt, ornate mirror. "You have a great straw hat. And what a
coat—Joseph's coat of stripes."

"You approve?"

"I certainly do. It's a beautiful jacket. You look Indian in it,
with your dark coloring."

"I may join the Bhave group."

"Which is that?"

"Sharing large estates among the poor. I'll give away
Ludeyville."

"You'd better consult me before you start another give-
away program. Shall we have a drink? Perhaps you'd like to
wash up while I get the drinks."

"I shaved before leaving the house."

"You look hot, as if you've been running, and you've got
soot on your face."

He must have leaned against a subway pillar. Or perhaps it
was a smudge from the wreckage bonfire. "Yes, I see."

"I'll get you a towel, dear," said Ramona.

In the bathroom, Herzog turned his tie to the back of his
neck to keep it from drooping into the basin. This was a
luxurious little room, with indirect lighting (kindness to
haggard faces). The long tap glittered, the water rushed forth.
He sniffed the soap. *Muguet.* The water felt very cold on his
nails. He recalled the old Jewish ritual of nail water, and the
word in the Haggadah, *Rachatz!* "Thou shalt wash." It was
obligatory also to wash when you returned from the cemetery
(*Beth Olam*—the Dwelling of the Multitude). But why think of

cemeteries, of funerals, now? Unless . . . the old joke about
the Shakespearean actor in the brothel. When he took off his
pants, the whore in bed gave a whistle. He said, "Madam, we
come to bury Caesar, not to praise him." How schoolboy
jokes clung to you!

He opened his mouth under the tap and let the current run
also into his shut eyes, gasping with satisfaction. Broad disks
of iridescent brightness swam under his lids. He wrote to
Spinoza, *Thoughts not causally connected were said by you to
cause pain. I find that is indeed the case. Random association,
when the intellect is passive, is a form of bondage. Or rather,
every form of bondage is possible then. It may interest you to
know that in the twentieth century random association is believed
to yield up the deepest secrets of the psyche.* He realized he was
writing to the dead. To bring the shades of great philosophers
up to date. But then why shouldn't he write to the dead? He
lived with them as much as with the living—perhaps more;
and besides, his letters to the living were increasingly mental,
and anyway, to the Unconscious, what was death? Dreams
did not recognize it. *Believing that reason can make steady
progress from disorder to harmony and that the conquest of chaos
need not be begun anew every day.* How I wish it! How I wish it
were so! How Moses prayed for this!

As for his relation to the dead, it was very bad indeed. He
really believed in letting the dead bury their own dead. And
that life was life only when it was understood clearly as dying.
He opened the large medicine chest. They used to build on the
grand scale, in old New York. Fascinated, he studied Ramona's bottles—skin freshener, estrogenic deep-tissue lotion,
Bonnie Belle antiperspirant. Then this crimson prescription—
twice daily for upset stomach. He smelled it and thought it
must contain belladonna—calming for the stomach, mydriatic
in the eyes. Made of deadly nightshade. There were also pills
for menstrual cramp. Somehow, he didn't think Ramona was
the type. Madeleine used to scream. He had to take her in a
taxi to St. Vincent's where she cried for a Demerol injection.
These forceps-looking things he thought must be for curling
the eyelashes. They looked like the snail tongs in a French

restaurant. He sniffed the scouring mitten. Especially for the elbows and heels, he thought, to rub away the bumps. He pressed the toilet lever with his foot; it flushed with silent power; the toilets of the poor always made noise. He applied a little brilliantine to the dry ends of his hair. His shirt was damp, of course, but she was wearing perfume enough for them both. And how was he otherwise? All things considered, not too bad. Ruin comes to beauty, inevitably. The space-time continuum reclaims its elements, taking you away bit by bit, and then again comes the void. But better the void than the torment and boredom of an incorrigible character, doing always the same stunts, repeating the same disgraces. But these instants of disgrace and pain could seem eternal, so that if a man could capture the eternity of these painful moments and give them a different content, he would achieve a revolution. How about that!

Wrapping the palm of his hand tightly in the towel, like a barber, Herzog wiped the drops of moisture at his hairline. Next he thought he would weigh himself. He used the toilet first, to make himself a little lighter, and stripped off his shoes without bending, climbing on the scale with an elderly sigh. Between his toes, the pointer swept past the 170 mark. He was regaining the weight he had lost in Europe. He forced his feet into the shoes again, treading down the backs, and returned to Ramona's sitting room—her sitting and sleeping room. She was waiting with two glasses of Campari. Its taste was bittersweet and its odor a little gassy—from the gas main. But all the world was drinking it, and Herzog drank it too. Ramona had chilled the glasses in the freezer.

"*Salud.*"

"*Sdrutch!*" he said.

"Your necktie is hanging down your back."

"Is it?" He pulled it to the front again. "Forgetful. I once tucked my jacket into the back of my trousers, coming from the gentlemen's room, and walked in to teach a class."

Ramona seemed astonished that he would tell such a story on himself. "Wasn't that dreadful?"

"Not too good. But it should have been very liberating for

the students. Teacher is mortal. Besides, the humiliation didn't destroy him. This should have been more valuable than the course itself. In fact, one of the young ladies told me later I was very human—such a relief to us all. . . ."

"What is funny is how completely you answer any question. You are a funny man." Engagingly affectionate; her fine large teeth, tender dark eyes, enriched by black lines, smiled upon him. "It's the way you try to sound rough or reckless, though—like a guy from Chicago—that's even more amusing."

"Why amusing?"

"It's an act. Swagger. It's not really you." She refilled his glass and stood up to go to the kitchen. "I've got to look after the rice. I'll put on some Egyptian music to keep you cheerful." A wide patent-leather belt set off her waist. She bent over the phonograph.

"The food smells delicious."

Mohammad al Bakkar and his band began with drums and tambourines, and then a clatter of wires and braying wind instruments. A guttural pimping voice began to sing, "Mi Port Said . . ." Herzog, alone, looked at the books and theater programs, magazines and pictures. A photograph of Ramona as a little girl stood in a Tiffany frame—seven years old, a wise child leaning on a bank of plush, her finger pressing on her temple. He remembered the pose. A generation ago it used to get them. Little Einsteins. Prodigious wisdom in children. Pierced ears, a locket, a kiss-me curl, and the kind of early sensuality in tiny girls which he recalled very well.

Aunt Tamara's clock began to chime. He went into her parlor to look at its old-fashioned porcelain face with long gilt lines, like cat whiskers, and listened to the bright quick notes. Beneath it was the key. To own a clock like this you had to have regular habits—a permanent residence. Raising the window shade of this little European parlor with its framed scenes of Venice and friendly Dutch porcelain inanities, you saw the Empire State Building, the Hudson, the green, silver evening, half of New York lighting up. Thoughtful, he pulled

the shade down again. This—this asylum was his for the
asking, he believed. Then why didn't he ask? Because today's
asylum might be the dungeon of tomorrow. To listen to
Ramona, it was all very simple. She said she understood his
needs better than he, and she might well be right. Ramona
never hesitated to express herself fully, and there was something unreserved, positively operatic about some of her
speeches. Opera. Heraldry. She said her feelings for him had
depth and maturity and that she had an enormous desire to
help him. She told Herzog that he was a better man than he
knew—a deep man, beautiful (he could not help wincing when
she said this), but sad, unable to take what his heart really
desired, a man tempted by God, longing for grace, but
escaping headlong from his salvation, often close at hand.
This Herzog, this man of many blessings, for some reason had
endured a frigid, middlebrow, castrating female in his bed,
given her his name and made her the instrument of creation,
and Madeleine had treated him with contempt and cruelty as
if to punish him for lowering and cheapening himself, for lying
himself into love with her and betraying the promise of his
soul. What he really must do, she went on, in this same
operatic style—unashamed to be so fluent; he marveled at
this—was to pay his debt for the great gifts he had received,
his intelligence, his charm, his education, and free himself to
pursue the meaning of life, not by disintegration, where he
would never find it, but humbly and yet proudly continuing
his learned studies. She, Ramona, wanted to add riches to his
life and give him what he pursued in the wrong places. This
she could do by the art of love, she said—the art of love which
was one of the sublime achievements of the spirit. It was love
she meant by riches. What he had to learn from her—while
there was time; while he was still virile, his powers substan-
tially intact—was how to renew the spirit through the flesh (a
precious vessel in which the spirit rested). Ramona—bless
her!—was as florid in these sermons as in her looks. Oh, what
a sweet orator she was! But where were we? Ah, yes, he was to
continue his studies, aiming at the meaning of life. He,

Herzog, overtake life's meaning! He laughed into his hands, covering his face.

But (sobering) he knew that he elicited these speeches by his airs. Why did little Sono cry, "O mon philosophe—mon professeur d'amour!"? Because Herzog behaved like a philosophe who cared only about the very highest things—creative reason, how to render good for evil, and all the wisdom of old books. Because he thought and cared about belief. (Without which, human life is simply the raw material of technological transformation, of fashion, salesmanship, industry, politics, finance, experiment, automatism, et cetera, et cetera. The whole inventory of disgraces which one is glad to terminate in death.) Yes, he looked like, behaved like, Sono's philosophe.

And after all, why was he here? He was here because Ramona also took him seriously. She thought she could restore order and sanity to his life, and if she did that it would be logical to marry her. Or, in her style, he would desire to be united with her. And it would be a union that really unified. Tables, beds, parlors, money, laundry and automobile, culture and sex knit into one web. Everything would at last make sense, was what she meant. Happiness was an absurd and even harmful idea, unless it was really comprehensive; but in this exceptional and lucky case where each had experienced the worst sorts of morbidity and come through by a miracle, by an instinct for survival and delight which was positively religious—there was simply no other way to talk about her life, said Ramona, except in terms of Magdalene Christianity —comprehensive happiness was possible. In that case, it was a duty; to refuse to answer the accusations against happiness (that it was a monstrous and selfish delusion, an absurdity) was cowardly, a surrender to malignancy, capitulating to the death instinct. Here was a man, Herzog, who knew what it was to rise from the dead. And she, Ramona, she knew the bitterness of death and nullity, too. Yes, she too! But with him she experienced a real Easter. She knew what Resurrection was. He might look down his conscious nose at sensual delight, but with her, when their clothes were off, he knew what it was. No amount of sublimation could replace that erotic happiness, that knowledge.

Not even tempted to smile, Moses listened earnestly, bowing his head. Some of it was current university or paperback chatter and some was propaganda for marriage, but, after such debits were entered against her, she was genuine. He sympathized with her, respected her. It was all real enough. She had something genuine at heart.

When he jeered in private at the Dionysiac revival it was himself he made fun of. Herzog! A prince of the erotic Renaissance, in his *macho* garments! And what about the kids? How would they like a new stepmother? And Ramona, would she take Junie to see Santa Claus?

"Ah, this is where you are," said Ramona. "Aunt Tamara would be flattered if she knew you were interested in her Czarist museum."

"These old-time interiors," said Herzog.

"Isn't it touching?"

"They drugged you with schmaltz."

"The old woman is so fond of you."

"I like her, too."

"She says you brighten up the house."

"That *I* . . ." He smiled.

"Why not? You have a tender trusting face. You can't bear to hear that, can you. Why not?"

"I put the old woman out when I come," he said.

"You're wrong. She loves these trips. She puts on a hat, and gets dressed up. It's such a thing for her to go to the railroad station. Anyway . . ." Ramona's tone changed. "She needs to get away from George Hoberly. He's become her problem now." For a brief instant she was downcast.

". . . Sorry," said Herzog. "Has it been bad lately?"

"Poor man . . . I feel so sorry for him. But come, Moses, dinner is all ready and I want you to open the wine." In the dining room she handed him the bottle—Pouilly Fuissé, well chilled—and the French corkscrew. With competent hands and strong purpose, his neck reddening as he exerted himself, he pulled the cork. Ramona had lighted the candles. The table was decorated with spiky red gladiolas in a long dish. On the windowsill the pigeons stirred and grumbled; they fluttered and went to sleep again. "Let me help you to this rice," said Ramona. She took the plate, good bone china with a cobalt rim (the steady spread of luxury into all ranks of society since the fifteenth century, noted by the famous Sombart, inter alia). But Herzog was hungry, and the dinner was delicious. (He would become austere hereafter.) Tears of curious, mixed origin came into his eyes as he tasted the shrimp remoulade. "Awfully good—my God, how good!" he said.

"Haven't you eaten all day?" said Ramona.

"I haven't seen food like this for some time. Prosciutto and Persian melon. What's this? Watercress salad. Good Christ!"

She was pleased. "Well, eat," she said.

After the shrimp Arnaud and salad, she offered cheese and cold-water biscuits, rum-flavored ice cream, plums from Georgia, and early green grapes. Then brandy and coffee. In the next room, Mohammad al Bakkar kept singing his winding, nasal, insinuating songs to the sounds of wire coathangers moved back and forth, and drums, tambourines and mandolins and bagpipes.

"What have you been doing?" said Ramona.

"Me? Oh, all kinds of things. . . ."

"Where did you go on the train? Were you running away from me?"

"Not from you. But I suppose I was running."

"You're still a little afraid of me, aren't you."

"I wouldn't say that. . . . Confused. Trying to be careful."

"You're used to difficult women. To struggle. Perhaps you like it when they give you a bad time."

"Every treasure is guarded by dragons. That's how you can tell it's valuable. . . . Do you mind if I unbutton my collar? It seems to be pressing on an artery."

"But you came right back. Perhaps that was because of me."

Moses was strongly tempted to lie to her, to say, "Yes,

Ramona, it was you." Strict and literal truthfulness was a
trivial game and might even be a disagreeable neurotic
affliction. Ramona had Moses' complete sympathy—a woman
in her thirties, successful in business, independent, but still
giving such suppers to gentlemen friends. But in times like
these, how should a woman steer her heart to fulfillment? In
emancipated New York, man and woman, gaudily disguised,
like two savages belonging to hostile tribes, confront each
other. The man wants to deceive, and then to disengage
himself; the woman's strategy is to disarm and detain him.
And this is Ramona, a woman who knows how to look after
herself. Think how it is with some young thing, raising
mascara-ringed eyes to heaven, praying, "Oh, Lord, let no bad
man come unto my chubbiness."

Besides which, Herzog realized that to eat Ramona's shrimp
and drink her wine, and then sit in her parlor listening to the
straggling lustfulness of Mohammad al Bakkar and his Port
Said specialists, thinking such thoughts, was not exactly
commendable. *And Monsignor Hilton, what is priestly celibacy?
A more terrible discipline is to go about and visit women, to see
what the modern world has made of carnality. How little
relevance certain ancient ideas have. . . .*

But at least one thing became clear. To look for fulfillment
in another, in interpersonal relationships, was a feminine
game. And the man who shops from woman to woman,
though his heart aches with idealism, with the desire for pure
love, has entered the female realm. After Napoleon fell, the
ambitious young man carried his power drive into the
boudoir. And there the women took command. As Madeleine
had done, as Wanda might as easily have done. And what
about Ramona? And Herzog, formerly a silly young thing,
now becoming a silly old thing, by accepting the design of a
private life (approved by those in authority) turned himself
into something resembling a concubine. Sono made this
entirely clear, with her Oriental ways. He had even joked
about it with her, trying to explain how unprofitable his visits
to her appeared to him at last. *"Je bêche, je sème, mais je ne*

récolte point." He joked—but no, he was no concubine, not at all. He was a difficult, aggressive man. As for Sono, she was trying to instruct him, to show how a man should treat a woman. The pride of the peacock, the lust of the goat, and the wrath of the lion are the glory and wisdom of God.

"Wherever you were going, with your valise, your fundamentally healthy instincts brought you back. They're wiser than you," said Ramona.

Herzog Writes
His Last Letters

Dear Marco. I've come up to the old home-stead to look things over and relax a bit. The place is in pretty good shape, considering. Perhaps you'd like to spend some time here with me, only the two of us—roughing it—after camp. We'll talk about it Parents' Day. I'm looking forward to that, eagerly. Your little sister whom I saw in Chicago yesterday is very lively and as pretty as ever. She received your postcard.

Do you remember the talks we had about Scott's Antarctic Expedition, and how poor Scott was beaten to the Pole by Amundsen? You seemed interested. This is a thing that always gets me. There was a man in Scott's party who went out and lost himself to give the others a chance to survive. He was ailing, footsore, couldn't keep up any longer. And do you remember how by chance they found a mound of frozen blood, the blood of one of their slaughtered ponies, and how thankful they were to thaw and drink it? The success of Amundsen was due to his use of dogs instead of ponies. The weaker were butchered and fed to the stronger. Otherwise the expedition would have failed. I have often wondered at one thing. Hungry as they were, the dogs would sniff at the flesh of their own and back away. The skin had to be removed before they would eat it.

Maybe you and I could take a trip at Xmas to Canada just to get the feel of genuine cold. I am a Canadian, too, you know. We could visit Ste. Agathe, in the Laurentians. Expect me on the 16th, bright and early.

Dear Luke—Be so kind as to post these enclosures. I hope to

497

*hear your depression is over. I think your visions of the aunt being
rescued by the fireman and of the broads playing piggy-move-up
are signs of psychological resiliency. I predict your recovery. As
for me. . . .* As for you, thought Herzog, you will not tell him
how you feel now, all this overflow! It wouldn't make him
happier. Keep it to yourself if you feel exalted. Anyway, he
may think you've simply gone off your nut.

But if I am out of my mind, it's all right with me.

*My dear Professor Mermelstein. I want to congratulate you on
a splendid book. In some matters you scooped me, you know, and
I felt like hell about it—hated you one whole day for making a
good deal of my work superfluous (Wallace and Darwin?).
However, I well know what labor and patience went into such a
work—so much digging, learning, synthesizing, and I'm all
admiration. When you are ready to print a revised edition—or
perhaps another book—it would be a great pleasure to talk over
some of these questions. There are parts of my projected book I'll
never return to. You may do what you like with those materials.
In my earlier book (to which you were kind enough to refer) I
devoted one section to Heaven and Hell in apocalyptic Romanticism. I may not have done it to your taste, but you ought not to
have overlooked it completely. You ought to have a look at the
monograph by that fat natty brute Egbert Shapiro, "From Luther
to Lenin, A History of Revolutionary Psychology." His* fat
cheeks give him a great resemblance to Gibbon. *It is a
valuable piece of work. I was greatly impressed by the section
called Millenarianism and Paranoia. It should not be ignored
that modern power systems do offer a resemblance to this
psychosis. A gruesome and crazy book on this has been written by
a man named Banowitch. Fairly inhuman, and filled with vile
paranoid hypotheses such as that crowds are fundamentally
cannibalistic, that people standing secretly terrify the sitting, that
smiling teeth are the weapons of hunger, that the tyrant is mad for
the sight of (possibly edible?) corpses about him. It seems quite
true that the making of corpses has been the most dramatic
achievement of modern dictators and their followers (Hitler,
Stalin, etc.).* Just to see—Herzog tried this on, experimenting

—whether Mermelstein didn't have a vestige of old Stalinism about him. *But this fellow Shapiro is something of an eccentric, and I mention him as an extreme case. How we all love extreme cases and apocalypses, fires, drownings, stranglings, and the rest of it. The bigger our mild, basically ethical, safe middle classes grow the more radical excitement is in demand. Mild or moderate truthfulness or accuracy seems to have no pull at all. Just what we need now!* ("When a dog is drowning, you offer him a cup of water," Papa used to say, bitterly.) *In any case, if you had read that chapter of mine on apocalypse and Romanticism you might have looked a little straighter at that Russian you admire so much—Isvolsky? The man who sees the souls of monads as the legions of the damned, simply atomized and pulverized, a dust storm in Hell; and warns that Lucifer must take charge of collectivized mankind, devoid of spiritual character and true personality. I don't deny this makes some sense, here and there, though I do worry that such ideas, because of the bit of suggestive truth in them, may land us in the same old suffocating churches and synagogues. I was somewhat bothered by borrowings and references which I considered "hit and run," or the use of other writers' serious beliefs as mere metaphors. For instance, I liked the section called "Interpretations of Suffering" and also the one called "Toward a Theory of Boredom." This was an excellent piece of research. But then I thought the treatment you gave Kierkegaard was fairly frivolous. I venture to say Kierkegaard meant that truth has lost its force with us and horrible pain and evil must teach it to us again, the eternal punishments of Hell will have to regain their reality before mankind turns serious once more. I do not see this. Let us set aside the fact that such convictions in the mouths of safe, comfortable people playing at crisis, alienation, apocalypse, and desperation, make me sick. We must get it out of our heads that this is a doomed time, that we are waiting for the end, and the rest of it, mere junk from fashionable magazines. Things are grim enough without these shivery games. People frightening one another—a poor sort of moral exercise. But, to get to the main point, the advocacy and praise of suffering take us in the wrong direction and those of us*

*who remain loyal to civilization must not go for it. You have to
have the power to employ pain, to repent, to be illuminated, you
must have the opportunity and even the time. With the religious,
the love of suffering is a form of gratitude to experience or an
opportunity to experience evil and change it into good. They
believe the spiritual cycle can and will be completed in a man's
existence and he will somehow make use of his suffering, if only
in the last moments of his life, when the mercy of God will reward
him with a vision of the truth, and he will die transfigured. But
this is a special exercise. More commonly suffering breaks people,
crushes them, and is simply unilluminating. You see how
gruesomely human beings are destroyed by pain, when they have
the added torment of losing their humanity first, so that their
death is a total defeat, and then you write about "modern forms
of Orphism" and about "people who are not afraid of suffering"
and throw in other such cocktail-party expressions. Why not say
rather that people of powerful imagination, given to dreaming
deeply and to raising up marvelous and self-sufficient fictions,
turn to suffering sometimes to cut into their bliss, as people pinch
themselves to feel awake. I know that my suffering, if I may
speak of it, has often been like that, a more extended form of life,
a striving for true wakefulness and an antidote to illusion, and
therefore I can take no moral credit for it. I am willing without
further exercise in pain to open my heart. And this needs no
doctrine or theology of suffering. We love apocalypses too much,
and crisis ethics and florid extremism with its thrilling language.
Excuse me, no. I've had all the monstrosity I want. We've
reached an age in the history of mankind when we can ask about
certain persons, "What is this Thing?" No more of that for
me—no, no! I am simply a human being, more or less. I am even
willing to leave the more or less in your hands. You may decide
about me. You have a taste for metaphors. Your otherwise
admirable work is marred by them. I'm sure you can come up
with a grand metaphor for me. But don't forget to say that I will
never expound suffering for anyone or call for Hell to make us
serious and truthful. I even think man's perception of pain may
have grown too refined. But that is another subject for lengthy
treatment.*

Very good, Mermelstein. Go, and sin no more. And Herzog, perhaps somewhat sheepish over this strange diatribe, rose from the mattress (the sun was moving away) and went downstairs again. He ate several slices of bread, and baked beans—a cold bean sandwich, and afterward carried outside his hammock and two lawn chairs.

Thus began his final week of letters. He wandered over his twenty acres of hillside and woodlot, composing his messages, none of which he mailed. He was not ready to pedal to the post office and answer questions in the village about Mrs. Herzog and little June. As he knew well, the grotesque facts of the entire Herzog scandal had been overheard on the party line and become the meat and drink of Ludeyville's fantasy life. He had never restrained himself on the telephone; he was too agitated. And Madeleine was far too patrician to care what the hicks were overhearing. Anyway, she had been throwing him out. It reflected no discredit on her.

Dear Madeleine—You are a terrific one, you are! Bless you! What a creature! To put on lipstick, after dinner in a restaurant, she would look at her reflection in a knife blade. He recalled this with delight. *And you, Gersbach, you're welcome to Madeleine. Enjoy her—rejoice in her. You will not reach me through her, however. I know you sought me in her flesh. But I am no longer there.*

Dear Sirs, The size and number of the rats in Panama City, when I passed through, truly astonished me. I saw one of them sunning himself beside a swimming pool. And another was looking at me from the wainscoting of a restaurant as I was eating fruit salad. Also, on an electric wire which slanted upward into a banana tree, I saw a whole rat-troupe go back and forth, harvesting. They ran the wire twenty times or more without a single collision. My suggestion is that you put birth-control chemicals in the baits. Poisons will never work (for Malthusian reasons; reduce the population somewhat and it only increases more vigorously). But several years of contraception may eliminate your rat problem.

Dear Herr Nietzsche—My dear sir, May I ask a question from the floor? You speak of the power of the Dionysian spirit to

*endure the sight of the Terrible, the Questionable, to allow itself
the luxury of Destruction, to witness Decomposition, Hideousness, Evil. All this the Dionysian spirit can do because it has the
same power of recovery as Nature itself. Some of these expressions, I must tell you, have a very Germanic ring. A phrase like
the "luxury of Destruction" is positively Wagnerian, and I know
how you came to despise all that sickly Wagnerian idiocy and
bombast. Now we've seen enough destruction to test the power of
the Dionysian spirit amply, and where are the heroes who have
recovered from it? Nature (itself) and I are alone together, in the
Berkshires, and this is my chance to understand. I am lying in a
hammock, chin on breast, hands clasped, mind jammed with
thoughts, agitated, yes, but also cheerful, and I know you value
cheerfulness—true cheerfulness, not the seeming sanguinity of
Epicureans, nor the strategic buoyancy of the heartbroken. I also
know you think that deep pain is ennobling, pain which burns
slow, like green wood, and there you have me with you, somewhat.
But for this higher education survival is necessary. You must
outlive the pain.* Herzog! you must stop this quarrelsomeness
and baiting of great men. *No, really, Herr Nietzsche, I have
great admiration for you. Sympathy. You want to make us able to
live with the void. Not lie ourselves into good-naturedness, trust,
ordinary middling human considerations, but to question as has
never been questioned before, relentlessly, with iron determination, into evil, through evil, past evil, accepting no abject comfort.
The most absolute, the most piercing questions. Rejecting
mankind as it is, that ordinary, practical, thieving, stinking,
unilluminated, sodden rabble, not only the laboring rabble, but
even worse the "educated" rabble with its books and concerts and
lectures, its liberalism and its romantic theatrical "loves" and
"passions"—it all deserves to die, it will die. Okay. Still, your
extremists must survive. No survival, no* Amor Fati. *Your
immoralists also eat meat. They ride the bus. They are only the
most bus-sick travelers. Humankind lives mainly upon perverted
ideas. Perverted, your ideas are no better than those of the
Christianity you condemn. Any philosopher who wants to keep his
contact with mankind should pervert his own system in advance to*

*see how it will really look a few decades after adoption. I send
you greetings from this mere border of grassy temporal light, and
wish you happiness, wherever you are. Yours, under the veil of
Maya, M.E.H.*

Dear Dr. Morgenfruh. Dead for some time now. *This is
Herzog, Moses E.* Discover yourself. *We played billiards in
Madison, Wisconsin.* Tell him more. *Until Willie Hoppe arrived
to demonstrate, and put us to shame.* The great billiard artist got
absolute obedience from those three balls; as if he whispered
to them, stroked them a little with his cue, and they would
part and kiss again. And old Morgenfruh with his bald head
and fine, humorous, curved nose and foreign charm, applauding, getting up all his breath to exclaim "Bravo." Morgenfruh
played the piano and made himself weep. Helen played
Schumann better but she had less at stake. She frowned at the
music as if to show that it was dangerous, but that she could
tame it. Morgenfruh, however, groaned, sitting at the keys in
his fur coat. Next he sang along, and last he cried—it
overcame him. He was a splendid old man, only partly
fraudulent, and what more can you ask of anyone? *Dear Dr.
Morgenfruh, Latest intelligence from the Olduvai Gorge in East
Africa gives grounds to suppose that man did not descend from a
peaceful arboreal ape, but from a carnivorous, terrestrial type,
a beast that hunted in packs and crushed the skulls of prey with a
club or femoral bone. It sounds bad, Morgenfruh, for the
optimists, for the lenient hopeful view of human nature. The work
of Sir Solly Zuckerman on the apes in the London Zoo, of which
you spoke so often, has been superseded. Apes in their own
habitat are less sexually driven than those in captivity. It must be
that captivity, boredom, breeds lustfulness. And it may also be
that the territorial instinct is stronger than the sexual. Abide in
light, Morgenfruh. I will keep you posted from time to time.*

Despite the hours he spent in the open he believed he still
looked pale. Perhaps this was because the mirror of the
bathroom door into which he stared in the morning reflected
the massed green of the trees. No, he did not look well. His
excitement must be a great drain on his strength, he thought.

And then there was the persistently medicinal smell of the tapes on his chest to remind him that he was not quite well. After the second or third day he stopped sleeping on the second floor. He didn't want to drive the owls out of the house and leave a brood to die in the old fixture with the triple brass chain. It was bad enough to have those tiny skeletons in the toilet bowl. He moved downstairs, taking with him a few useful articles, an old trench coat and rain hat, his boots ordered from Gokey's in St. Paul—marvelous, flexible, handsome snakeproof boots; he had forgotten that he had them. In the storeroom he made other interesting discoveries, photographs of the "happy days," boxes of clothing, Madeleine's letters, bundles of canceled checks, elaborately engraved wedding announcements, and a recipe book belonging to Phoebe Gersbach. The photographs were all of him. Madeleine had left those behind, taking the others. Interesting—her attitude. Among the abandoned dresses were her expensive maternity outfits. The checks were for large sums, and many of these were paid to Cash. Had she secretly been saving? He wouldn't put it past her. The announcements made him laugh; Mr and Mrs Pontritter were giving their daughter in marriage to Mr Moses E Herzog Ph D.

In one of the closets he found a dozen or so Russian books under a stiff painter's drop cloth. Shestov, Rozanov—he rather liked Rozanov, who was, luckily, in English. He read a few pages of *Solitaria*. Then he looked over the paint situation—old brushes, thinners, evaporated, crusted buckets. There were several cans of enamel, and Herzog thought, What if I should paint up the little piano? I could send it out to Chicago, to Junie. The kid is really highly musical. As for Madeleine, she'll have to take it in, the bitch, when it's delivered, paid for. She can't send it back. The green enamel seemed to him exactly right, and he wasted no time but found the most usable brushes and set himself to work, full of eagerness, in the parlor. *Dear Rozanov.* He painted the lid of the piano with absorption; the green was light, beautiful, like summer apples. *A stupendous truth you say, heard from none of*

the prophets, is that private life is above everything. More
universal than religion. Truth is higher than the sun. The soul is
passion. "I am the fire that consumeth." It is joy to be choked
with thought. A good man can bear to listen to another talk about
himself. You can't trust the people who are bored by such talk.
God has gilded me all over. I like that, God has gilded me all
over. Very touching, this man, though extremely coarse at
times, and stuffed with violent prejudices. The enamel covered
well but it would probably need a second coat, and he might
not have enough paint for that. Putting down the brush he
gave the piano lid time to dry, considering how to get the
instrument out of here. He couldn't expect one of the giant
interstate vans to climb this hill. He would have to hire Tuttle
from the village to come in his pick-up truck. The cost would
amount to something like a hundred dollars, but he must do
everything possible for the child, and he had no serious
problems about money. Will had offered him as much as he
needed to get through the summer. *A curious result of the*
increase of historical consciousness is that people think explana-
tion is a necessity of survival. They have to explain their
condition. And if the unexplained life is not worth living, the
explained life is unbearable, too. "Synthesize or perish!" Is that
the new law? But when you see what strange notions, hallucina-
tions, projections, issue from the human mind you begin to believe
in Providence again. To survive these idiocies . . . Anyway the
intellectual has been a Separatist. And what kind of synthesis is a
Separatist likely to come up with? Luckily for me, I didn't have
the means to get too far away from our common life. I am
glad of that. I mean to share with other human beings as far as
possible and not destroy my remaining years in the same way.
Herzog felt a deep, dizzy eagerness to *begin.*

He had to get water from the cistern; the pump was too
rusty; he had primed it and worked the handle but only tired
himself. The cistern was full. He raised the iron lid with a pry
bar and put down a bucket. It made a good sound, dropping,
and you couldn't get softer water anywhere, but it had to be
boiled. There was always a chipmunk or two, a rat, dead at

the bottom though it looked pure enough when you drew it up, pure, green water.

He went to sit under the trees. *His* trees. He was amused, resting here on his American estate, twenty thousand dollars' worth of country solitude and privacy. He did not feel an owner. As for the twenty grand, the place was certainly not worth more than three or four. Nobody wanted these old-fashioned houses on the fringes of the Berkshires, not the fashionable section where there were music festivals and modern dancing, riding to hounds or other kinds of snobbery. You couldn't even ski on these slopes. No one came here. He had only gentle, dotty old neighbors, Jukes and Kallikaks, rocking themselves to death on their porches, watching television, the nineteenth century quietly dying in this remote green hole. Well, this was his own, his hearth; these were *his* birches, catalpas, horse chestnuts. His rotten dreams of peace. The patrimony of his children—a sunken corner of Massachusetts for Marco, the little piano for June painted a loving green by her solicitous father. That, too, like most other things he would probably botch. But at least he would not die here, as he had once feared. In former summers, when cutting the grass, he would sometimes lean on the mower, overheated, and think, What if I were to die suddenly, of a heart attack? Where will they put me? Maybe I should pick my own spot. Under the spruce? That's too close to the house. Now he reflected that Madeleine would have had him cremated. *And these explanations are unbearable, but they have to be made. In the seventeenth century the passionate search for absolute truth stopped so that mankind might transform the world. Something practical was done with thought. The mental became also the real. Relief from the pursuit of absolutes made life pleasant. Only a small class of fanatical intellectuals, professionals, still chased after these absolutes. But our revolutions, including nuclear terror, return the metaphysical dimension to us. All practical activity has reached this culmination: everything may go now, civilization, history, meaning, nature. Everything! Now to recall Mr. Kierkegaard's question . . .*

*To Dr. Waldemar Zozo: You, Sir, were the Navy psychiatrist
who examined me in Norfolk, Va., about 1942, and told me I was
unusually immature. I knew that, but professional confirmation
caused me deep anguish. In anguish I was not immature. I could
call upon ages of experience. I took it all very seriously then.
Anyway, I was subsequently discharged for asthma, not childish-
ness. I fell in love with the Atlantic.* O the great reticulated,
mountain-bottomed sea! *But the sea fog paralyzed my voice,
and for a communications officer it was the end. However, in your
cubicle, as I sat naked, pale, listened to the sailors at drill in the
dust, heard what you told me about my character, felt the
Southern heat, it was unsuitable that I should wring my hands. I
kept them lying on my thighs.*

*From hatred at first, but later because I became objectively
interested, I followed your career in the journals. Your article
"Existential Unrest in the Unconscious" recently beguiled me. It
was really quite a classy piece of work. You don't mind if I speak
to you in this way, I hope. I am really in an unusually free
condition of mind. "In paths untrodden," as Walt Whitman
marvelously put it. "Escaped from the life that exhibits itself. . . ." Oh, that's a plague, the life that exhibits itself, a real
plague! There comes a time when every ridiculous son of Adam
wishes to arise before the rest, with all his quirks and twitches and
tics, all the glory of his self-adored ugliness, his grinning teeth, his
sharp nose, his madly twisted reason, saying to the rest—in an
overflow of narcissism which he interprets as benevolence—"I am
here to witness. I am come to be your exemplar." Poor dizzy
spook! . . . Escaped, anyway, as Whitman says, from the life
that exhibits itself and "talked to by tongues aromatic." . . . But
here is a further interesting fact. I recognized you last spring in
the Primitive Art Museum on 54th Street.* How my feet ached! I
had to ask Ramona to sit down. *I said to the lady I had come
with, "Isn't that Dr. Waldemar Zozo?" She happened also to
know you, and brought me up to date: You were quite rich, a
collector of African antiquities, your daughter a folk singer, and
much else. I realized sharply how I still loathed you. I thought I
had forgiven you, too. Isn't that interesting? Seeing you, your*

*white turtle neck shirt and dinner jacket, your Edwardian
mustache, your damp lips, the back hair trained over your bald
spot, your barren paunch, apish buttocks* (chemically old!) *I
recognized with joy how I abhorred you. It sprang fresh from my
heart after 22 years!*

His mind took one of its odd jumps. He opened a clean
page in his grimy notebook, and in the twig-divided shade of a
wild cherry, infested with tent caterpillars, he began to make
notes for a poem. He was going to try an Insect Iliad for Junie.
She couldn't read, but maybe Madeleine would allow Luke
Asphalter to take the child to Jackson Park and read the
installments to her as he received them. Luke knew a lot of
natural history. It would do him good, too. Moses, pale with
this heartfelt nonsense, stared at the ground with brown eyes,
standing round-shouldered, the notebook held behind him as
he thought it over. He could make the Trojans ants. The
Argives might be water-skaters. Luke might find them for her
along the edge of the lagoon, where those stupid caryatides
were posted. The water-skaters, therefore, with long velvet
hairs beaded with glittering oxygen. Helen, a beautiful wasp.
Old Priam a cicada, sucking sap from the roots and with his
trowel-shaped belly plastering the tunnels. And Achilles a
stag-beetle with sharp spikes and terrible strength, but
doomed to a brief life though half a god. At the edge of the
water he cried out to his mother

> *Thus spoke Achilles
> And Thetis heard him in the ooze,
> Sitting beside her ancient father
> In glorious debris, enough for all.*

But this project was quickly abandoned. It wasn't a good
idea, really not. For one thing, he wasn't stable enough, he
could never keep his mind at it. His state was too strange, this
mixture of clairvoyance and spleen, *esprit de l'escalier*, noble
inspirations, poetry and nonsense, ideas, hyperesthesia—wandering about like this, hearing forceful but indefinite music

within, seeing things, violet fringes about the clearest objects.
His mind was like that cistern, soft pure water sealed under
the iron lid but not entirely safe to drink. No, he was better
occupied painting the piano for the child. Go! let the fiery
claw of imagination take up the green brush. Go! But the first
coat was not dry yet, and he wandered out to the woods,
eating a piece of bread from the package he carried in his
trench-coat pocket. He was aware that his brother might now
show up at any time. Will had been disturbed by his
appearance. It was unmistakable. And I had better look out,
thought Herzog, people do get put away, and seem even to
intend it. I have wanted to be cared for. I devoutly hoped
Emmerich would find me sick. But I have no intention of
doing that—I am responsible, responsible to reason. This is
simply temporary excitement. Responsible to the children. He
walked quietly into the woods, the many leaves, living and
fallen, green and tan, going between rotted stumps, moss,
fungus disks; he found a hunters' path, also a deer trail. He
felt quite well here, and calmer. The silence sustained him,
and the brilliant weather, the feeling that he was easily
contained by everything about him *Within the hollowness of
God*, as he noted, *and deaf to the final multiplicity of facts,* as
well as *blind to ultimate distances. Two billion light-years out.
Supernovae.*

> *Daily radiance, trodden here*
> *Within the hollowness of God*

To God he jotted several lines.
*How my mind has struggled to make coherent sense. I have not
been too good at it. But have desired to do your unknowable will,
taking it, and you, without symbols. Everything of intensest
significance. Especially if divested of me.*
Returning once more to practical considerations, he must
be very careful with Will and talk to him only in the most
concrete terms about concrete matters, like this property, and
look as ordinary as possible. If you wear a wise look, he

warned himself, you'll be in trouble, and fast. No one can bear
such looks any longer, not even your brother. Therefore,
watch your face! Certain expressions burn people up, and
especially the expression of wisdom, which can lead you
straight to the loony bin. You will have earned it!

He lay down near the locust trees. They bloomed with a
light, tiny but delicious flower—he was sorry to have missed
that. He recognized that with his arms behind him and his legs
extended any way, he was lying as he had lain less than a week
ago on his dirty little sofa in New York. But was it only a
week—five days? Unbelievable! How different he felt! Confident, even happy in his excitement, stable. The bitter cup
would come round again, by and by. This rest and well-being
were only a momentary difference in the strange lining or
variable silk between life and void. *The life you gave me has
been curious,* he wanted to say to his mother, *and perhaps the
death I must inherit will turn out to be even more profoundly
curious. I have sometimes wished it would hurry up, longed for it
to come soon. But I am still on the same side of eternity as ever.
It's just as well, for I have certain things still to do. And without
noise, I hope. Some of my oldest aims seem to have slid away.*
But I have others. *Life on this earth can't be simply a picture.*
And terrible forces in me, including the force of admiration or
praise, powers, including loving powers, very damaging,
making me almost an idiot because I lacked the capacity to
manage them. *I may turn out to be not such a terrible hopeless
fool as everyone, as you, as I myself suspected.* Meantime, to lay
off certain persistent torments. To surrender the hyperactivity
of this hyperactive face. But just to put it out instead to the
radiance of the sun. *I want to send you, and others, the most
loving wish I have in my heart. This is the only way I have to
reach out—out where it is incomprehensible. I can only pray
toward it. So . . . Peace!*

From

Mr. Sammler's Planet:

Introducing Mr. Sammler

> *Shortly after dawn, or what would have been*
dawn in a normal sky, Mr. Artur Sammler with his bushy eye
took in the books and papers of his West Side bedroom and
suspected strongly that they were the wrong books, the wrong
papers. In a way it did not matter much to a man of
seventy-plus, and at leisure. You had to be a crank to insist on
being right. Being right was largely a matter of explanations.
Intellectual man had become an explaining creature. Fathers
to children, wives to husbands, lecturers to listeners, experts to
laymen, colleagues to colleagues, doctors to patients, man to
his own soul, explained. The roots of this, the causes of the
other, the source of events, the history, the structure, the
reasons why. For the most part, in one ear out the other. The
soul wanted what it wanted. It had its own natural knowledge.
It sat unhappily on superstructures of explanation, poor bird,
not knowing which way to fly.

The eye closed briefly. A Dutch drudgery, it occurred to
Sammler, pumping and pumping to keep a few acres of dry
ground. The invading sea being a metaphor for the multiplication of facts and sensations. The earth being an earth of ideas.

He thought, since he had no job to wake up to, that he
might give sleep a second chance to resolve certain difficulties
imaginatively for himself, and pulled up the disconnected
electric blanket with its internal sinews and lumps. The satin
binding was nice to the finger tips. He was still drowsy, but
not really inclined to sleep. Time to be conscious.

He sat and plugged in the electric coil. Water had been prepared at bedtime. He liked to watch the changes of the ashen wires. They came to life with fury, throwing tiny sparks and sinking into red ridigity under the Pyrex laboratory flask. Deeper. Blenching. He had only one good eye. The left distinguished only light and shade. But the good eye was dark-bright, full of observation through the overhanging hairs of the brow as in some breeds of dog. For his height he had a small face. The combination made him conspicuous.

His conspicuousness was on his mind; it worried him. For several days, Mr. Sammler returning on the customary bus late afternoons from the Forty-second Street Library had been watching a pickpocket at work. The man got on at Columbus Circle. The job, the crime, was done by Seventy-second Street. Mr. Sammler if he had not been a tall straphanger would not with his one good eye have seen these things happening. But now he wondered whether he had not drawn too close, whether he had also been seen seeing. He wore smoked glasses, at all times protecting his vision, but he couldn't be taken for a blind man. He didn't have the white cane, only a furled umbrella, British-style. Moreover, he didn't have the look of blindness. The pickpocket himself wore dark shades. He was a powerful Negro in a camel's-hair coat, dressed with extraordinary elegance, as if by Mr. Fish of the West End, or Turnbull and Asser of Jermyn Street. (Mr. Sammler knew his London.) The Negro's perfect circles of gentian violet banded with lovely gold turned toward Sammler, but the face showed the effrontery of a big animal. Sammler was not timid, but he had had as much trouble in life as he wanted. A good deal of this, waiting for assimilation, would never be accommodated. He suspected the criminal was aware that a tall old white man (passing as blind?) had observed, had seen the minutest details of his crimes. Staring down. As if watching open-heart surgery. And though he dissembled, deciding not to turn aside when the thief looked at him, his elderly, his compact, civilized face colored strongly, the short hairs bristled, the lips and gums were stinging. He felt a constriction, a clutch of sickness at the base of the skull where the nerves, muscles, blood vessels were tightly interlaced. The breath of wartime Poland passing over the damaged tissues—that nerve-spaghetti, as he thought of it.

Buses were bearable, subways were killing. Must he give up the bus? He had not minded his own business as a man of seventy in New York should do. It was always Mr. Sammler's problem that he didn't know his proper age, didn't appreciate his situation, unprotected here by position, by privileges of remoteness made possible by an income of fifty thousand dollars in New York—club membership, taxis, doormen, guarded approaches. For him it was the buses, or the grinding subway, lunch at the automat. No cause for grave complaint, but his years as an "Englishman," two decades in London as correspondent for Warsaw papers and journals, had left him with attitudes not especially useful to a refugee in Manhattan. He had developed expressions suited to an Oxford common room; he had the face of a British Museum reader. Sammler as a schoolboy in Cracow before World War I fell in love with England. Most of that nonsense had been knocked out of him. He had reconsidered the whole question of Anglophilia, thinking skeptically about Salvador de Madariaga, Mario Praz, André Maurois and Colonel Bramble. He knew the phenomenon. Still, confronted by the elegant brute in the bus he had seen picking a purse—the purse still hung open—he adopted an English tone. A dry, a neat, a prim face declared that one had not crossed anyone's boundary; one was satisfied with one's own business. But under the high armpits Mr. Sammler was intensely hot, wet; hanging on his strap, sealed in by bodies, receiving their weight and laying his own on them as the fat tires took the giant curve at Seventy-second Street with a growl of flabby power.

He didn't in fact appear to know his age, or at what point of life he stood. You could see that in his way of walking. On the streets, he was tense, quick, erratically light and reckless, the elderly hair stirring on the back of his head. Crossing, he lifted the rolled umbrella high and pointed to show cars, buses, speeding trucks, and cabs bearing down on him the way he intended to go. They might run him over, but he could not help his style of striding blind.

With the pickpocket we were in an adjoining region of recklessness. He knew the man was working the Riverside bus. He had seen him picking purses, and he had reported it to the police. The police were not greatly interested in the report. It had made Sammler feel like a fool to go immediately to a phone booth on Riverside Drive. Of course the phone was smashed. Most outdoor telephones were smashed, crippled. They were urinals, also. New York was getting worse than Naples or Salonika. It was like an Asian, an African town, from this standpoint. The opulent sections of the city were not immune. You opened a jeweled door into degradation, from hypercivilized Byzantine luxury straight into the state of nature, the barbarous world of color erupting from beneath. It might well be barbarous on either side of the jeweled door. Sexually, for example. The thing evidently, as Mr. Sammler was beginning to grasp, consisted in obtaining the privileges, and the free ways of barbarism, under the protection of civilized order, property rights, refined technological organization, and so on. Yes, that must be it.

Mr. Sammler ground his coffee in a square box, cranking counterclockwise between long knees. To commonplace actions he brought a special pedantic awkwardness. In Poland, France, England, students, young gentlemen of his time, had been unacquainted with kitchens. Now he did things that cooks and maids had once done. He did them with a certain priestly stiffness. Acknowledgment of social descent. Historical ruin. Transformation of society. It was beyond personal humbling. He had gotten over those ideas during the war in Poland—utterly gotten over all that, especially the idiotic pain of losing class privileges. As well as he could with one eye, he darned his own socks, sewed his buttons, scrubbed his own sink, winter-treated his woolens in the spring with a spray can. Of course there were ladies, his daughter, Shula, his niece (by marriage), Margotte Arkin, in whose apartment he lived. They did for him, when they thought of it. Sometimes they did a great deal, but not dependably, routinely. The routines he did himself. It was conceivably even part of his youthfulness—youthfulness sustained with certain tremors. Sammler knew these tremors. It was amusing—Sammler noted in old women wearing textured tights, in old sexual men, this quiver of vivacity with which they obeyed the sovereign youth-style. The powers are the powers—overlords, kings, gods. And of course no one knew when to quit. No one made sober decent terms with death.

The grounds in the little drawer of the mill he held above the flask. The red coil went deeper, whiter, white. The kinks had tantrums. Beads of water flashed up. Individually, the pioneers gracefully went to the surface. Then they all seethed together. He poured in the grounds. In his cup, a lump of sugar, a dusty spoonful of Pream. In the night table he kept a bag of onion rolls from Zabar's. They were in plastic, a transparent uterine bag fastened with a white plastic clip. The night table, copper-lined, formerly a humidor, kept things fresh. It had belonged to Margotte's husband, Ussher Arkin. Arkin, killed three years ago in a plane crash, a good man, was missed, was regretted, mourned by Sammler. When he was invited by the widow to occupy a bedroom in the large apartment on West Ninetieth Street, Sammler asked to have Arkin's humidor in his room. Sentimental herself, Margotte said, "Of course, Uncle. What a nice thought. You did love Ussher." Margotte was German, romantic. Sammler was something else. He was not even her uncle. She was the niece of his wife, who had died in Poland in 1940. His late wife. The widow's late aunt. Wherever you looked, or tried to look, there were the late. It took some getting used to.

Grapefruit juice he drank from a can with two triangular punctures kept on the window sill. The curtain parted as he reached and he looked out. Brownstones, balustrades, bay windows, wrought-iron. Like stamps in an album—the dun rose of buildings canceled by the heavy black of grilles, of corrugated rainspouts. How very heavy human life was here, in forms of bourgeois solidity. Attempted permanence was sad. We were now flying to the moon. Did one have a right to private expectations, being like those bubbles in the flask? But then also people exaggerated the tragic accents of their condition. They stressed too hard the disintegrated assurances; what formerly was believed, trusted, was now bitterly circled in black irony. The rejected bourgeois black of stability thus translated. That too was improper, incorrect. People justifying idleness, silliness, shallowness, distemper, lust—turning former respectability inside out.

Such was Sammler's eastward view, a soft asphalt belly rising, in which lay steaming sewer navels. Spalled sidewalks with clusters of ash cans. Brownstones. The yellow brick of elevator buildings like his own. Little copses of television antennas. Whiplike, graceful thrilling metal dendrites drawing images from the air, bringing brotherhood, communion to immured apartment people. Westward the Hudson came between Sammler and the great Spry industries of New Jersey. These flashed their electric message through intervening night. SPRY. But then he was half blind.

In the bus he had been seeing well enough. He saw a crime committed. He reported it to the cops. They were not greatly shaken. He might then have stayed away from that particular bus, but instead he tried hard to repeat the experience. He went to Columbus Circle and hung about until he saw his man again. Four fascinating times he had watched the thing done, the crime, the first afternoon staring down at the masculine hand that came from behind lifting the clasp and tipping the pocketbook lightly to make it fall open. Sammler saw a polished Negro forefinger without haste, with no criminal tremor, turning aside a plastic folder with Social Security or credit cards, emery sticks, a lipstick capsule, coral paper tissues, nipping open the catch of a change purse—and there lay the green of money. Still at the same rate, the fingers took out the dollars. Then with the touch of a doctor on a patient's belly the Negro moved back the slope leather, turned the gilded scallop catch. Sammler, feeling his head small, shrunk

with strain, the teeth tensed, still was looking at the patent-
leather bag riding, picked, on the woman's hip, finding that he
was irritated with her. That she felt nothing. What an idiot!
Going around with some kind of stupid mold in her skull.
Zero instincts, no grasp of New York. While the man turned
from her, broad-shouldered in the camel's-hair coat. The dark
glasses, the original design by Christian Dior, a powerful
throat banded by a tab collar and a cherry silk necktie
spouting out. Under the African nose, a cropped mustache.
Ever so slightly inclining toward him, Sammler believed he
could smell French perfume from the breast of the camel's-
hair coat. Had the man noticed him then? Had he perhaps
followed him home? Of this Sammler was not sure.

He didn't give a damn for the glamour, the style, the art of
criminals. They were no social heroes to him. He had had
some talks on this very matter with one of his younger
relations, Angela Gruner, the daughter of Dr. Arnold Gruner
in New Rochelle, who had brought him over to the States in
1947, digging him out of the DP camp in Salzburg. Because
Arnold (Elya) Gruner had Old World family feelings. And
studying the lists of refugees in the Yiddish papers, he had
found the names Artur and Shula Sammler. Angela, who was
in Sammler's neighborhood several times a week because her
psychiatrist was just around the corner, often stopped in for a
visit. She was one of those handsome, passionate, rich girls
who were always an important social and human category. A
bad education. In literature, mostly French. At Sarah Lawrence College. And Mr. Sammler had to try hard to remember
the Balzac he had read in Cracow in 1913. Vautrin the
escaped criminal. From the hulks. *Trompe-la-mort*. No, he
didn't have much use for the romance of the outlaw. Angela
sent money to defense funds for black murderers and rapists.
That was her business of course.

However, Mr. Sammler had to admit that once he had seen
the pickpocket at work he wanted very much to see the thing
again. He didn't know why. It was a powerful event, and
illicitly—that is, against his own stable principles—he craved

a repetition. One detail of old readings he recalled without effort—the moment in *Crime and Punishment* at which Raskolnikov brought down the ax on the bare head of the old woman, her thin gray-streaked grease-smeared hair, the rat's-tail braid fastened by a broken horn comb on her neck. That is to say that horror, crime, murder, did vivify all the phenomena, the most ordinary details of experience. In evil as in art there was illumination. It was, of course, like the tale by Charles Lamb, burning down a house to roast a pig. Was a general conflagration necessary? All you needed was a controlled fire in the right place. Still, to ask everyone to refrain from setting fires until the thing could be done in the right place, in a higher manner, was possibly too much. And while Sammler, getting off the bus, intended to phone the police, he nevertheless received from the crime the benefit of an enlarged vision. The air was brighter—late afternoon, daylight-saving time. The world, Riverside Drive, was wickedly lighted up. Wicked because the clear light made all objects so explicit, and this explicitness taunted Mr. Minutely-Observant Artur Sammler. All metaphysicians please note. Here is how it is. You will never see more clearly. And what do you make of it? This phone booth has a metal floor; smooth-hinged the folding green doors, but the floor is smarting with dry urine, the plastic telephone instrument is smashed, and a stump is hanging at the end of the cord.

Not in three blocks did he find a phone he could safely put a dime into, and so he went home. In his lobby the building management had set up a television screen so that the doorman could watch for criminals. But the doorman was always off somewhere. The buzzing rectangle of electronic radiance was vacant. Underfoot was the respectable carpet, brown as gravy. The inner gate of the elevator, supple brass diamonds folding, grimy and gleaming. Sammler went into the apartment and sat on the sofa in the foyer, which Margotte had covered with large squares of Woolworth bandannas, tied at the corners and pinned to the old cushions. He dialed the police and said, "I want to report a crime."

"What kind of crime?"

"A pickpocket."

"Just a minute, I'll connect you."

There was a long buzz. A voice toneless with indifference or fatigue said, "Yes."

Mr. Sammler in his foreign Polish Oxonian English tried to be as compressed, direct, and factual as possible. To save time. To avoid complicated interrogation, needless detail.

"I wish to report a pickpocket on the Riverside bus."

"O.K."

"Sir?"

"O.K. I said O.K., report."

"A Negro, about six feet tall, about two hundred pounds, about thirty-five years old, very good-looking, very well-dressed."

"O.K."

"I thought I should call in."

"O.K."

"Are you going to do anything?"

"We're supposed to, aren't we? What's your name?"

"Artur Sammler."

"All right, Art. Where do you live?"

"Dear sir, I will tell you, but I am asking what you intend to do about this man."

"What do you think we should do?"

"Arrest him."

"We have to catch him first."

"You should put a man on the bus."

"We haven't got a man to put on the bus. There are lots of buses, Art, and not enough men. Lots of conventions, banquets, and so on we have to cover, Art. VIPs and Brass. There are lots of ladies shopping at Lord and Taylor, Bonwit's, and Saks', leaving purses on chairs while they go to feel the goods."

"I understand. You don't have the personnel, and there are priorities, political pressures. But I could point out the man."

"Some other time."

"You don't want him pointed out?"

"Sure, but we have a waiting list."

"I have to get on *your* list?"

"That's right, Abe."

"Artur."

"Arthur."

Tensely sitting forward in bright lamplight, Artur Sammler like a motorcyclist who has been struck in the forehead by a pebble from the road, trivially stung, smiled with long lips. America! (he was speaking to himself). Advertised throughout the universe as *the* most desirable, most exemplary of all nations.

"Let me make sure I understand you, officer—mister detective. This man is going to rob more people, but you aren't going to do anything about it. Is that right?"

It was right—confirmed by silence, though no ordinary silence. Mr. Sammler said, "Good-by, sir."

After this, when Sammler should have shunned the bus, he rode it oftener than ever. The thief had a regular route, and he dressed for the ride, for his work. Always gorgeously garbed. Mr. Sammler was struck once, but not astonished, to see that he wore a single gold earring. This was too much to keep to himself, and for the first time he then mentioned to Margotte, his niece and landlady, to Shula, his daughter, that this handsome, this striking, arrogant pickpocket, this African prince or great black beast was seeking whom he might devour between Columbus Circle and Verdi Square.

To Margotte it was fascinating. Anything fascinating she was prepared to discuss all day, from every point of view with full German pedantry. Who was this black? What were his origins, his class or racial attitudes, his psychological views, his true emotions, his aesthetic, his political ideas? Was he a revolutionary? Would he be for black guerrilla warfare? Unless Sammler had private thoughts to occupy him, he couldn't sit through these talks with Margotte. She was sweet but on the theoretical side very tedious, and when she settled down to an earnest theme, one was lost. This was why he

ground his own coffee, boiled water in his flask, kept onion
rolls in the humidor, even urinated in the washbasin (rising on
his toes to a meditation on the inherent melancholy of animal
nature, continually in travail, according to Aristotle). Because
mornings could disappear while Margotte in her goodness
speculated. He had learned his lesson one week when she
wished to analyze Hannah Arendt's phrase The Banality of
Evil, and kept him in the living room, sitting on a sofa (made
of foam rubber, laid on plywood supported by two-inch
sections of pipe, backed by trapezoids of cushion all covered
in dark-gray denim). He couldn't bring himself to say what he
thought. For one thing, she seldom stopped to listen. For
another, he doubted that he could make himself clear.
Moreover, most of her family had been destroyed by the
Nazis like his own, though she herself had gotten out in 1937.
Not he. The war had caught him, with Shula and his late wife,
in Poland. They had gone there to liquidate his father-in-law's
estate. Lawyers should have attended to this, but it was
important to Antonina to supervise it in person. She was killed
in 1940, and her father's optical-instrument factory (a small
one) was dismantled and sent to Austria. No postwar indemnity was paid. Margotte received payment from the West
German government for her family's property in Frankfurt.
Arkin hadn't left her much; she needed this German money.
You didn't argue with people in such circumstances. Of course
he had circumstances of his own, as she recognized. He had
actually gone through it, lost his wife, lost an eye. Still, on the
theoretical side, they could discuss the question. Purely as a
question. Uncle Artur, sitting, knees high in the sling chair, his
pale-tufted eyes shaded by tinted glasses, the forked veins
coming down from the swells of his forehead and the big
mouth determined to be silent.

"The idea being," said Margotte, "that here is no great
spirit of evil. Those people were too insignificant, Uncle. They
were just ordinary lower-class people, administrators, small
bureaucrats, or Lumpenproletariat. A mass society does not
produce great criminals. It's because of the division of labor

all over society which broke up the whole idea of general
responsibility. Piecework did it. It's like instead of a forest
with enormous trees, you have to think of small plants with
shallow roots. Modern civilization doesn't create great individual phenomena any more."

The late Arkin, generally affectionate and indulgent, knew
how to make Margotte shut up. He was a tall, splendid,
half-bald, mustached man with a good subtle brain in his
head. Political theory had been his field. He taught at Hunter
College—taught women. Charming, idiotic, nonsensical girls,
he used to say. Now and then, a powerful female intelligence,
but very angry, very complaining, too much sex-ideology,
poor things. It was when he was on his way to Cincinnati to
lecture at some Hebrew college that his plane crashed.
Sammler noticed how his widow tended now to impersonate
him. She had become the political theorist. She spoke in his
name, as presumably he would have done, and there was no
one to protect his ideas. The common fate also of Socrates
and Jesus. Up to a point, Arkin had enjoyed Margotte's
tormenting conversation, it must be admitted. Her nonsense
pleased him, and under the mustache he would grin to
himself, long arms reaching to the ends of the trapezoidal
cushions, and his stockinged feet set upon each other (he took
off his shoes the instant he sat down). But after she had gone
on a while, he would say, "Enough, enough of this Weimar
schmaltz. Cut it, Margotte!" That big virile interruption would
never be heard again in this cockeyed living room.

Margotte was short, round, full. Her legs in black net
stockings, especially the underthighs, were attractively heavy.
Seated, she put out one foot like a dancer, instep curved
forward. She set her strong little fist on her haunch. Arkin
once said to Uncle Sammler that she was a first-class device as
long as someone aimed her in the right direction. She was a
good soul, he told him, but the energetic goodness could be
tremendously misapplied. Sammler saw this for himself. She
couldn't wash a tomato without getting her sleeves wet. The
place was burglarized because she raised the window to

admire a sunset and forgot to lock it. The burglars entered the dining room from the rooftop just below. The sentimental value of her lockets, chains, rings, heirlooms was not appreciated by the insurance company. The windows were now nailed shut and draped. Meals were eaten by candlelight. Just enough glow to see the framed reproductions from the Museum of Modern Art, and across the table, Margotte serving, spattering the tablecloth; her lovely grin, dark and tender, with clean, imperfect small teeth, and eyes dark blue and devoid of wickedness. A bothersome creature, willing, cheerful, purposeful, maladroit. The cups and tableware were greasy. She forgot to flush the toilet. But all that one could easily live with. It was her earnestness that gave the trouble—considering everything under the sun with such German wrongheadedness. As though to be Jewish weren't trouble enough, the poor woman was German too.

"So. And what is your opinion, dear Uncle Sammler?" At last she asked. "I know you have thought a lot about this. You experienced so much. And you and Ussher had such conversations about that crazy old fellow—King Rumkowski. The man from Lodz. . . . What do you think?"

Uncle Sammler had compact cheeks, his color was good for a man in his seventies, and he was not greatly wrinkled. There were, however, on the left side, the blind side, thin long lines like the lines in a cracked glass or within a cake of ice.

To answer was not useful. It would produce more discussion, more explanation. Nevertheless, he was addressed by another human being. He was old-fashioned. The courtesy of some reply was necessary.

"The idea of making the century's great crime look dull is not banal. Politically, psychologically, the Germans had an idea of genius. The banality was only camouflage. What better way to get the curse out of murder than to make it look ordinary, boring, or trite? With horrible political insight they found a way to disguise the thing. Intellectuals do not understand. They get their notions about matters like this from literature. They expect a wicked hero like Richard III.

But do you think the Nazis didn't know what murder was? Everybody (except certain blue-stockings) knows what murder is. That is very old human knowledge. The best and purest human beings, from the beginning of time, have understood that life is sacred. To defy that old understanding is not banality. There was a conspiracy against the sacredness of life. Banality is the adopted disguise of a very powerful will to abolish conscience. Is such a project trivial? Only if human life is trivial. This woman professor's enemy is modern civilization itself. She is only using the Germans to attack the twentieth century—to denounce it in terms invented by Germans. Making use of a tragic history to promote the foolish ideas of Weimar intellectuals."

Arguments! Explanations! thought Sammler. All will explain everything to all, until the next, the new common version is ready. This version, a residue of what people for a century or so say to one another, will be, like the old, a fiction. More elements of reality perhaps will be incorporated in the new version. But the important consideration was that life should recover its plenitude, its normal contented turgidity. All the old fusty stuff had to be blown away, of course, so we might be nearer to nature. To be nearer to nature was necessary in order to keep in balance the achievements of modern Method. The Germans had been the giants of this Method in industry and war. To relax from rationality and calculation, machinery, planning, technics, they had romance, mythomania, peculiar aesthetic fanaticism. These, too, were like machines—the aesthetic machine, the philosophic machine, the mythomanic machine, the culture machine. Machines in the sense of being systematic. System demands mediocrity, not greatness. System is based on labor. Labor connected to art is banality. Hence the sensitivity of cultivated Germans to everything banal. It exposed the rule, the might of Method, and their submission to Method. Sammler had it all figured out. Alert to the peril and disgrace of explanations, he was himself no mean explainer. And even in the old days, in the days when he was "British," in the lovely twenties and thirties when he lived in Great Russell Street, when he was acquainted with Maynard Keynes, Lytton Strachey, and H. G. Wells and loved "British" views, before the great squeeze, the human physics of the war, with its volumes, its vacuums, its voids (that period of dynamics and direct action upon the individual, comparable biologically to birth), he had never much trusted his judgment where Germans were concerned. The Weimar Republic was not attractive to him in any way. No, there was an exception—he had admired its Plancks and Einsteins. Hardly anyone else.

In any case, he was not going to be one of those kindly European uncles with whom the Margottes of this world could have day-long high-level discussions. She would have liked him trailing after her through the apartment while, for two hours, she unpacked the groceries, hunting for lunch a salami which was already on the shelf; while she slapped and smoothed the bed with short strong arms (she kept the bedroom piously unchanged, after the death of Ussher—his swivel chair, his footstool, his Hobbes, Vico, Hume, and Marx underlined), discussing things. He found that even if he could get a word in edgewise it was encircled and cut off right away. Margotte swept on, enormously desirous of doing good. And really she was good (that was the point), she was boundlessly, achingly, hopelessly on the right side, the best side, of every big human question: for creativity, for the young, for the black, the poor, the oppressed, for victims, for sinners, for the hungry.

A significant remark by Ussher Arkin, giving much to think of after his death, was that he had learned to do the good thing as if practicing a vice. He must have been thinking of his wife as a sexual partner. She had probably driven him to erotic invention, and made monogamy a fascinating challenge. Margotte, continually recalling Ussher, spoke of him always, Germanically, as her Man. "When my Man was alive . . . my Man used to say." Sammler was sorry for his widowed niece. You could criticize her endlessly. High-minded, she bored you, she made cruel inroads into your time,

your thought, your patience. She talked junk, she gathered
waste and junk in the flat, she bred junk. Look, for instance, at
these plants she was trying to raise. She planted avocado pits,
lemon seeds, peas, potatoes. Was there anything ever so
mangy, trashy, as these potted objects? Shrubs and vines
dragged on the ground, tried to rise on grocer's string
hopefully stapled fanwise to the ceiling. The stems of the
avocados looked like the sticks of fireworks falling back after
the flash, and produced a few rusty, spiky, anthrax-damaged,
nitty leaves. This botanical ugliness, the product of so much
fork-digging, watering, so much breast and arm, heart and
hope, told you something, didn't it? First of all, it told you
that the individual facts were filled with messages and
meanings, but you couldn't be sure what the messages meant.
She wanted a bower in her living room, a screen of glossy
leaves, flowers, a garden, blessings of freshness and beauty—
something to foster as woman the germinatrix, the matriarch
of reservoirs and gardens. Humankind, crazy for symbols,
trying to utter what it doesn't know itself. Meantime the
spreading fanlike featherless quills: no peacock purple, no
sweet blue, no true green, but only spots before your eyes.
Redeemed by a feeling of ready and available human
warmth? No, you couldn't be sure. The strain of unrelenting
analytical effort gave Mr. Sammler a headache. The worst of it
was that these frazzled plants would not, could not respond.
There was not enough light. Too much clutter.

But when it came to clutter, his daughter, Shula, was much
worse. He had lived with Shula for several years, just east of
Broadway. She had too many oddities for her old father. She
passionately collected things. In plainer words, she was a
scavenger. More than once, he had seen her hunting through
Broadway trash baskets (or, as he still called them, dustbins).
She wasn't old, not bad looking, not even too badly dressed,
item by item. The full effect would have been no worse than
vulgar if she had not been obviously a nut. She turned up in a
miniskirt of billiard-table green, revealing legs sensual in
outline but without inner sensuality; at the waist a broad

leather belt; over shoulders, bust, a coarse strong Guatemalan embroidered shirt; on her head a wig such as a female impersonator might put on at a convention of salesmen. Her own hair had a small curl, a minute distortion. It put her in a rage. She cried out that it was thin, she had masculine hair. Thin it evidently was, but not the other. She had it straight from Sammler's mother, a hysterical woman, certainly, and anything but masculine. But who knew how many sexual difficulties and complications were associated with Shula's hair? And, from the troubled widow's peak, following an imaginary line of illumination over the nose, originally fine but distorted by restless movement, over the ridiculous comment of the lips (swelling, painted dark red), and down between the breasts to the middle of the body—what problems there must be! Sammler kept hearing how she had taken her wig to a good hairdresser to have it set, and how the hairdresser exclaimed, please! to take the thing away, it was too cheap for him to work on! Sammler did not know whether this was an isolated incident involving one homosexual stylist, or whether it had happened on several separate occasions. He saw many open elements in his daughter. Things that ought but failed actually to connect. Wigs for instance suggested Orthodoxy; Shula in fact had Jewish connections. She seemed to know lots of rabbis in famous temples and synagogues on Central Park West and on the East Side. She went to sermons and free lectures everywhere. Where she found the patience for this Sammler could not say. He could bear no lecture for more than ten minutes. But she, with loony, clever, large eyes, the face full of white comment and skin thickened with concentration, sat on her rucked-up skirt, the shopping bag with salvage, loot, coupons, and throwaway literature between her knees. Afterward she was the first to ask questions. She became well acquainted with the rabbi, the rabbi's wife and family—involved in Dadaist discussions about faith, ritual, Zionism, Masada, the Arabs. But she had Christian periods as well. Hidden in a Polish convent for four years, she had been called Slawa, and now there were times when she answered

only to that name. Almost always at Easter she was a
Catholic. Ash Wednesday was observed, and it was with a
smudge between the eyes that she often came into clear focus
for the old gentleman. With the little Jewish twists of kinky
hair descending from the wig beside the ears and the florid lips
dark red, skeptical, accusing, affirming something substantive
about her life-claim, her right to be whatever—whatever it all
came to. Full of comment always, the mouth completing the
premises stated from an insane angle by the merging dark
eyes. Not altogether crazy, perhaps. But she would come in
saying that she had been run down by mounted policemen in
Central Park. They were trying to recapture a deer escaped
from the zoo, and she was absorbed, reading an article in
Look, and they knocked her over. She was, however, quite
cheerful. She was far too cheerful for Sammler. At night she
typed. She sang at her typewriter. She was employed by cousin
Gruner, the doctor, who had this work invented for her.
Gruner had saved her (it amounted to that) from her equally
crazy husband, Eisen, in Israel, sending Sammler ten years
ago to bring Shula-Slawa to New York.

That had been Sammler's first journey to Israel. Brief. On a
family matter.

Unusually handsome, brilliant-looking, Eisen had been
wounded at Stalingrad. With other mutilated veterans in
Rumania, later, he had been thrown from a moving train.
Apparently because he was a Jew. Eisen had frozen his feet;
his toes were amputated. "Oh, they were drunk," said Eisen in
Haifa. "Good fellows—*tovarischni*. But you know what Russians are when they have a few glasses of vodka." He grinned
at Sammler. Black curls, a handsome Roman nose, shining
sharp senseless saliva-moist teeth. The trouble was that he
kicked and beat Shula-Slawa quite often, even as a newlywed.
Old Sammler in the cramped, stone-smelling, whitewashed
apartment in Haifa considered the palm branches at the
window in a warm, clear atmosphere. Shula was cooking for
them out of a Mexican cookbook, making bitter chocolate
sauce, grating coconuts over chicken breasts, complaining that

you could not buy chutney in Haifa. "When I was thrown out," said Eisen cheerfully, "I thought I would go and see the Pope. I took a stick and walked to Italy. The stick was my crutch, you see."

"I see."

"I went to Castel Gandolfo. The Pope was very nice to us."

After three days Mr. Sammler saw that he would have to remove his daughter.

He could not stay long in Israel. He was unwilling to spend Elya Gruner's money. But he did visit Nazareth and took a taxi to Galilee, for the historical interest of the thing, as long as he was in the vicinity. On a sandy road, he found a gaucho. Under a platter hat fastened beneath the large chin, in Argentinian bloomers tucked into boots, with a Douglas Fairbanks mustache, he was mixing feed for small creatures racing about him in a chicken-wire enclosure. Water from a hose ran clear and pleasant in the sun over the yellow meal or mash and stained it orange. The little animals though fat were lithe; they were heavy, their coats shone, opulent and dense. These were nutrias. Their fur made hats worn in cold climates. Coats for ladies. Mr. Sammler, feeling red-faced in the Galilean sunlight, interrogated this man. In his bass voice of a distinguished traveler—a cigarette held between his hairy knuckles, smoke escaping past his hairy ears—he put questions to the gaucho. Neither spoke Hebrew. Nor the language of Jesus. Mr. Sammler fell back on Italian, which the nutria breeder in Argentine gloom comprehended, his heavy handsome face considering the greedy beasts about his boots. He was Bessarabian-Syrian-South American—a Spanish-speaking Israeli cowpuncher from the pampas.

Did he butcher the little animals himself? Sammler wished to know. His Italian had never been good. *"Uccidere?"* *"Ammazzare?"* The gaucho understood. When the time came, he killed them himself. He struck them on the head with a stick.

Didn't he mind doing this to his little flock? Hadn't he known them from infancy—was there no tenderness for

individuals—were there no favorites? The gaucho denied it all.
He shook his handsome head. He said that nutrias were very
stupid.

"Son muy tontos."

"Arrivederci," said Sammler.

"Adios. Shalom."

Mr. Sammler's hired car took him to Capernaum, where
Jesus had preached in the synagogue. From afar, he saw the
Mount of the Beatitudes. Two eyes would have been inade-
quate to the heaviness and smoothness of the color, parted
with difficulty by fishing boats—the blue water, unusually
dense, heavy, seemed sunk under the naked Syrian heights.
Mr. Sammler's heart was very much torn by feelings as he
stood under the short, leaf-streaming banana trees.

> And did those feet in ancient time
> Walk upon . . .

But those were England's mountains green. The mountains
opposite, in serpentine nakedness, were not at all green; they
were ruddy, with smoky cavities and mysteries of inhuman
power flaming above them.

The many impressions and experiences of life seemed no
longer to occur each in its own proper space, in sequence,
each with its recognizable religious or aesthetic importance,
but human beings suffered the humiliations of inconsequence,
of confused styles, of a long life containing several separate
lives. In fact the whole experience of mankind was now
covering each separate life in its flood. Making all the ages of
history simultaneous. Compelling the frail person to receive,
to register, depriving him because of volume, of mass, of the
power to impart design.

Well, that was Sammler's first visit to the Holy Land. A
decade later, for another purpose, he went again.

Shula had returned with Sammler to America. Rescued
from Eisen, who walloped her, he said, because she went to
Catholic priests, because she was a liar (lies infuriated him;

paranoiacs, Sammler concluded, are more passionate for pure
truth than other madmen), Shula-Slawa set up housekeeping
in New York. Creating, that is, a great clutter-center in the
New World. Mr. Sammler, a polite Slim-Jim (the nickname
Dr. Gruner had given him), a considerate father, muttering
appreciation of each piece of rubbish as presented to him, was
in certain moods explosive, under provocation more violent
than other people. In fact, his claim for indemnity from the
Bonn government was based upon damage to his nervous
system as well as his eye. Fits of rage, very rare but shattering,
laid him up with intense migraines, put him in a postepileptic
condition. Then he lay most of a week in a dark room, rigid,
hands gripped on his chest, bruised, aching, incapable of an
answer when spoken to. With Shula-Slawa, he had a series of
such attacks. First of all, he couldn't bear the building Gruner
had put them into, with its stone stoop slumping to one side,
into the cellar stairway of the Chinese laundry adjoining. The
lobby made him ill, tiles like yellow teeth set in desperate
grime, and the stinking elevator shaft. The bathroom where
Shula kept an Easter chick from Kresge's until it turned into a
hen that squawked on the edge of the tub. The Christmas
decorations which lasted into spring. The rooms themselves
were like those dusty red paper Christmas bells, folds within
folds. The hen with yellow legs in his room on his documents
and books was too much one day. He was aware that the sun
shone brightly, the sky was blue, but the big swell of the
apartment house, heavyweight vaselike baroque, made him
feel that the twelfth-story room was like a china cabinet into
which he was locked, and the satanic hen-legs of wrinkled
yellow clawing his papers made him scream out.

Shula-Slawa then agreed that he should move. She told
everyone that her father's lifework, his memoir of H. G. Wells,
made him too tense to live with. She had H. G. Wells on the
brain, the large formation of a lifetime. H. G. Wells was the
most august human being she knew of. She had been a small
girl when the Sammlers lived in Woburn Square, Bloomsbury,
and with childish genius accurately read the passions of her

parents—their pride in high connections, their snobbery, how
contented they were with the cultural best of England. Old
Sammler thinking of his wife in prewar Bloomsbury days
interpreted a certain quiet, bosomful way she had of conveying with a downward stroke of the hand, so delicate you had
to know her well to identify it as a vaunting gesture: we have
the most distinguished intimacy with the finest people in
Britain. A small vice—almost nutritive, digestive—which gave
Antonina softer cheeks, smoother hair, deeper color. If a little
social-climbing made her handsomer (plumper between the
legs—the thought rushed in and Sammler had stopped trying
to repel these mental rushes), it had its feminine justification.
Love *is* the most potent cosmetic, but there are others. And
the little girl may actually have observed that the very
mention of Wells had a combined social-erotic influence on
her mother. Judging not, and recalling Wells always with
respect, Sammler knew that he had been a horny man of
labyrinthine extraordinary sensuality. As a biologist, as a
social thinker concerned with power and world projects, the
molding of a universal order, as a furnisher of interpretation
and opinion to the educated masses—as all of these he
appeared to need a great amount of copulation. Nowadays
Sammler would recall him as a little lower-class Limey, and as
an aging man of declining ability and appeal. And in the
agony of parting with the breasts, the mouths, and the
precious sexual fluids of women, poor Wells, the natural
teacher, the sex emancipator, the explainer, the humane
blesser of mankind, could in the end only blast and curse
everyone. Of course he wrote such things in his final sickness,
horribly depressed by World War II.

What Shula-Slawa said came back amusingly to Sammler
through Angela Gruner. Shula visited Angela in the East
Sixties, where her cousin had the beautiful, free, and wealthy
young woman's ideal New York apartment. Shula admired
this. Apparently without envy, without self-consciousness,
Shula with wig and shopping bag, her white face puckering
with continual inspiration (receiving and transmitting wild

messages), sat as awkwardly as possible in the super comfort of Angela's upholstery, blobbing china and forks with lipstick. In Shula's version of things her father had had conversations with H. G. Wells lasting several years. He took his notes to Poland in 1939, expecting to have spare time for the memoir. Just then the country exploded. In the geyser that rose a mile or two into the skies were Papa's notes. But (with *his* memory!) he knew it all by heart, and all you had to do was ask what Wells had said to him about Lenin, Stalin, Mussolini, Hitler, world peace, atomic energy, the Open Conspiracy, the colonization of the planets. Whole passages came back to Papa. He had to concentrate of course. Thus she turned about his moving in with Margotte until it became her idea. He had moved away to concentrate better. He said he didn't have much time left. But obviously he exaggerated. He looked so well. He was such a handsome person. Elderly widows were always asking her about him. The mother of Rabbi Ipsheimer. The grandmother of Ipsheimer, more likely. Anyway (Angela still reporting), Wells had communicated things to Sammler that the world didn't know. When finally published they would astonish everybody. The book would take the form of dialogues like those with A. N. Whitehead which Sammler admired so much.

Low-voiced, husky, a hint of joking brass in her tone, Angela (*just* this side of coarseness, a beautiful woman) said, "Her Wells routine is *so* great. Were you that close to H. G., Uncle?"

"We were well acquainted."

"But chums? Were you bosom buddies?"

"Oh? My dear girl, in spite of my years, I am a man of the modern age. You do not find David and Jonathan, Roland and Olivier bosom buddies in these days. The man's company was very pleasant. He seemed also to enjoy conversation with me. As for his views, he was just a mass of intelligent views. He expressed as many as he could, and at all times. Everything he said I found eventually in written form. He was like Voltaire, a graphomaniac. His mind was unusually active, he thought he should explain everything, and he actually said some things very well. Like 'Science is the mind of the race.' That's true, you know. It's a better thing to emphasize than other collective facts, like disease or sin. And when I see the wing of a jet plane I don't only see metal, but metal tempered by the agreement of many minds which know the pressure and velocity and weight, calculating on their slide rules whether they are Hindus or Chinamen or from the Congo or Brazil. Yes, on the whole he was a sensible intelligent person, certainly on the right side of many questions."

"And you used to be interested."

"Yes, I used to be interested."

"But she says you're composing that great work a mile a minute."

She laughed. Not merely laughed, but laughed brilliantly. In Angela you confronted sensual womanhood without remission. You smelled it, too. She wore the odd stylish things which Sammler noted with detached and purified dryness, as if from a different part of the universe. What were those, white-kid buskins? What were those tights—sheer, opaque? Where did they lead? That effect of the hair called frosting, that color under the lioness's muzzle, that swagger to enhance the natural power of the bust! Her plastic coat inspired by cubists or Mondrian, geometrical black and white forms; her trousers by Courrèges and Pucci. Sammler followed these jet phenomena in the *Times*, and in the women's magazines sent by Angela herself. Not too closely. He did not read too much of this. Careful to guard his eyesight, he passed pages rapidly back and forth before his eye, the large forehead registering the stimulus to his mind. The damaged left eye seemed to turn in another direction, to be preoccupied separately with different matters. Thus Sammler knew, through many rapid changes, Warhol, Baby Jane Holzer while she lasted, the Living Theater, the outbursts of nude display more and more revolutionary, Dionysus '69, copulation on the stage, the philosophy of the Beatles; and in the art world, electric shows and minimal painting. Angela was in her thirties now,

independently wealthy, with ruddy skin, gold-whitish hair, big
lips. She was afraid of obesity. She either fasted or ate like a
stevedore. She trained in a fashionable gym. He knew her
problems—he had to know, for she came and discussed them
in detail. She did not know *his* problems. He seldom talked
and she seldom asked. Moreover, he and Shula were her
father's pensioners, dependents—call it what you like. So after
psychiatric sessions, Angela came to Uncle Sammler to hold a
seminar and analyze the preceding hour. Thus the old man
knew what she did and with whom and how it felt. All that she
knew how to say he had to hear. He could not choose but.

Sammler in his *Gymnasium* days once translated from Saint
Augustine: "The Devil hath established his cities in the
North." He thought of this often. In Cracow before World
War I he had had another version of it—desperate darkness,
the dreary liquid yellow mud to a depth of two inches over
cobblestones in the Jewish streets. People needed their candles, their lamps and their copper kettles, their slices of lemon
in the image of the sun. This was the conquest of grimness
with the aid always of Mediterranean symbols. Dark environ-
ments overcome by imported religious signs and local domestic amenities. Without the power of the North, its mines, its
industries, the world would never have reached its astonishing
modern form. And regardless of Augustine, Sammler had
always loved his Northern cities, especially London, the
blessings of its gloom, of coal smoke, gray rains, and the
mental and human opportunities of a dark muffled environment. There one came to terms with obscurity, with low tones,
one did not demand full clarity of mind or motive. But now
Augustine's odd statement required a new interpretation.
Listening to Angela carefully, Sammler perceived different
developments. The labor of Puritanism now was ending. The
dark satanic mills changing into light satanic mills. The
reprobates converted into children of joy, the sexual ways of
the seraglio and of the Congo bush adopted by the emancipated masses of New York, Amsterdam, London. Old
Sammler with his screwy visions! He saw the increasing

triumph of Enlightenment—Liberty, Fraternity, Equality, Adultery! Enlightenment, universal education, universal suffrage, the rights of the majority acknowledged by all governments, the rights of women, the rights of children, the rights of criminals, the unity of the different races affirmed, Social Security, public health, the dignity of the person, the right to justice—the struggles of three revolutionary centuries being won while the feudal bonds of Church and Family weakened and the privileges of aristocracy (without any duties) spread wide, democratized, especially the libidinous privileges, the right to be uninhibited, spontaneous, urinating, defecating, belching, coupling in all positions, tripling, quadrupling, polymorphous, noble in being natural, primitive, combining the leisure and luxurious inventiveness of Versailles with the hibiscus-covered erotic ease of Samoa. Dark romanticism now took hold. As old at least as the strange Orientalism of the Knights Templar, and since then filled up with Lady Stanhopes, Baudelaires, de Nervals, Stevensons, and Gauguins—those South-loving barbarians. Oh, yes, the Templars. They had adored the Muslims. One hair from the head of a Saracen was more precious than the whole body of a Christian. Such crazy fervor! And now all the racism, all the strange erotic persuasions, the tourism and local color, the exotics of it had broken up but the mental masses, inheriting everything in a debased state, had formed an idea of the corrupting disease of being white and of the healing power of black. The dreams of nineteenth-century poets polluted the psychic atmosphere of the great boroughs and suburbs of New York. Add to this the dangerous lunging staggering crazy violence of fanatics, and the trouble was very deep. Like many people who had seen the world collapse once, Mr. Sammler entertained the possibility it might collapse twice. He did not agree with refugee friends that this doom was inevitable, but liberal beliefs did not seem capable of self-defense, and you could smell decay. You could see the suicidal impulses of civilization pushing strongly. You wondered whether this Western culture could survive universal dissemination—whether only its science and technology or administrative practices would travel, be adopted by other societies. Or whether the worst enemies of civilization might not prove to be its petted intellectuals who attacked it at its weakest moments—attacked it in the name of proletarian revolution, in the name of reason, and in the name of irrationality, in the name of visceral depth, in the name of sex, in the name of perfect instantaneous freedom. For what it amounted to was limitless demand—insatiability, refusal of the doomed creature (death being sure and final) to go away from this earth unsatisfied. A full bill of demand and complaint was therefore presented by each individual. Non-negotiable. Recognizing no scarcity of supply in any human department. Enlightenment? Marvelous! But out of hand, wasn't it?

Sammler saw this in Shula-Slawa. She came to do his room. He had to sit in his beret and coat, for she needed fresh air. She arrived with cleaning materials in the shopping bag—ammonia, shelf paper, Windex, floor wax, rags. She sat out on the sill to wash the windows, lowering the sash to her thighs. Her little shoe soles were inside the room. On her lips—a burst of crimson asymmetrical skeptical fleshy business-and-dream sensuality—the cigarette scorching away at the tip. There was the wig, too, mixed yak and baboon hair and synthetic fibers. Shula, like all the ladies perhaps, was needy—needed gratification of numerous instincts, needed the warmth and pressure of men, needed a child for sucking and nurture, needed female emancipation, needed the exercise of the mind, needed continuity, needed interest—*interest!*—needed flattery, needed triumph, power, needed rabbis, needed priests, needed fuel for all that was perverse and crazy, needed noble action of the intellect, needed culture, demanded the sublime. No scarcity was acknowledged. If you tried to deal with all these immediate needs you were a lost man. Even to consider it all the way she did, spraying cold froth on the panes, swabbing it away, left-handed with a leftward swing of the bust (*ohne Büstenhalter*), was neither affection for her, nor preservation for her father. When she arrived and opened windows and doors the personal atmosphere Mr. Sammler had accumulated and stored blew away, it seemed. His back door opened to the service staircase, where a hot smell of incineration rushed from the chute, charred paper, chicken entrails, and burnt feathers. The Puerto Rican sweepers carried transistors playing Latin music. As if supplied with this jazz from a universal unfailing source, like cosmic rays.

"Well, Father, how is it going?"

"What is going?"

"The work. H. G. Wells?"

"As usual."

"People take up too much of your time. You don't get enough reading done. I know you have to protect your eyesight. But is it going all right?"

"Tremendous."

"I wish you wouldn't make jokes about it."

"Why, is it too important for jokes?"

"Well, it is important."

Yes. O.K. He was sipping his morning coffee. Today, this very afternoon, he was going to speak at Columbia University. One of his young Columbia friends had persuaded him. Also, he must call up about his nephew. Dr. Gruner. It seemed the doctor himself was in the hospital. Had had, so Sammler was told, minor surgery. Cutting in the neck. One could do without that seminar today. It was a mistake. Could he back out, beg off? No, probably not.

Shula had hired university students to read to him, to spare his eyes. She herself had tried it, but her voice made him nod off. Half an hour of her reading, and the blood left his brain. She told Angela that her father tried to fence her out of his higher activities. As if they had to be protected from the very person who believed most in them! It was a very sad paradox. But for four or five years she had found student-readers. Some had graduated, now were in professions or business but still came back to visit Sammler. "He is like their guru," said Shula-Slawa. More recent readers were student activists. Mr. Sammler was quite interested in the radical movement. To judge by their reading ability, the young people had had a meager education. Their presence sometimes induced (or deepened) a long, still smile which had the effect more than anything else of blindness. Hairy, dirty, without style, levelers, ignorant. He found after they had read to him for a few hours that he had to teach them the subject, explain the terms, do etymologies for them as though they were twelve-year-olds. "*Janua*—a door. Janitor—one who minds the door." "*Lapis,* a stone. Dilapidate, take apart the stones. One cannot say it of a person." But if one could, one would say it of these young persons. Some of the poor girls had a bad smell. Bohemian protest did them the most harm. It was elementary among the tasks and problems of civilization, thought Mr. Sammler, that some parts of nature demanded more control than others. Females were naturally more prone to grossness, had more smells, needed more washing, clipping, binding, pruning, grooming, perfuming, and training. These poor kids may have resolved to stink together in defiance of a corrupt tradition built on neurosis and falsehood, but Mr. Sammler thought that an unforeseen result of their way of life was loss of femininity, of self-esteem. In their revulsion from authority they would respect no persons. Not even their own persons.

Anyhow, he no longer wanted these readers with the big dirty boots and the helpless vital pathos of young dogs with their first red erections, and pimples sprung to the cheeks from foaming beards, laboring in his room with hard words and thoughts that had to be explained, stumbling through Toynbee, Freud, Burckhardt, Spengler. For he had been reading historians of civilization—Karl Marx, Max Weber, Max Scheler, Franz Oppenheimer. Side excursions into Adorno, Marcuse, Norman O. Brown, whom he found to be worthless fellows. Together with these he took on *Doktor Faustus, Les Noyers de l'Altenburg*, Ortega, Valéry's essays on history and politics. But after four or five years of this diet, he wished to read only certain religious writers of the thirteenth century— Suso, Tauler, and Meister Eckhart. In his seventies he was interested in little more than Meister Eckhart and the Bible.

For this he needed no readers. He read Eckhart's Latin at the public library from microfilm. He read the Sermons and the Talks of Instruction—a few sentences at a time—a paragraph of Old German—presented to his good eye at close range. While Margotte ran the carpet sweeper through the rooms. Evidently getting most of the lint on her skirts. And singing. She loved Schubert lieder. Why she had to mingle them with the zoom of the vacuum eluded his powers of explanation. But then he could not explain a liking for certain combinations: for instance, sandwiches of sturgeon, Swiss cheese, tongue, steak tartare, and Russian dressing in layers—such things as one saw on fancy delicatessen menus. Yet customers seemed to order them. No matter where you picked it up, humankind, knotted and tangled, supplied more oddities than you could keep up with.

A combined oddity, for instance, which drew him today into the middle of things: One of his ex-readers, young Lionel Feffer, had asked him to address a seminar at Columbia University on the British Scene in the Thirties. For some reason this attracted Sammler. He was fond of Feffer. An ingenious operator, less student than promoter. With his florid color, brown beaver beard, long black eyes, big belly, smooth hair, pink awkward large hands, loud interrupting voice, hasty energy, he was charming to Sammler. Not trustworthy. Only charming. That is, it sometimes gave Sammler great pleasure to see Lionel Feffer working out in his peculiar manner, to hear the fizzing of his vital gas, his fuel.

Sammler didn't know what seminar this was. Not always attentive, he failed to understand clearly; perhaps there was nothing clear to understand; but it seemed that he had promised, although he couldn't remember promising. But Feffer confused him. There were so many projects, such cross references, so many confidences and requests for secrecy, so many scandals, frauds, spiritual communications—a continual flow backward, forward, lateral, above, below; like any page of Joyce's *Ulysses*, always *in medias res*. Anyway, Sammler had apparently agreed to give this talk for a student project to help backward black pupils with their reading problems.

"You must come and talk to these fellows, it's of the utmost importance. They have never heard a point of view like yours," said Feffer. The pink oxford-cloth shirt increased the color of his face. The beard, the straight large sensual nose made him look like François Premier. A bustling, affectionate, urgent, eruptive, enterprising character. He had money in the stock market. He was vice-president of a Guatemalan insurance company covering railroad workers. His field at the university was diplomatic history. He belonged to a corresponding society called the Foreign Ministers' Club. Its members took up a question like the Crimean War or the Boxer Rebellion and did it all again, writing one another letters as the foreign ministers of France, England, Germany, Russia. They obtained very different results. In addition, Feffer was a busy seducer, especially, it seemed, of young wives. But he found time as well to hustle on behalf of handicapped children. He got them free toys and signed photographs of hockey stars; he found time to visit them in the hospital. He "found time." To Sammler this was a highly significant American fact. Feffer led a high-energy American life to the point of anarchy and breakdown. And yet devotedly. And of course he was in psychiatric treatment. They all were. They could always say that they were sick. Nothing was omitted.

"The British Scene in the Thirties—you must. For my seminar."

"*That* old stuff?"

"Exactly. Just what we need."

"Bloomsbury? All of that? But why? And for whom?"

Feffer called for Sammler in a taxi. They went uptown in style. Feffer stressed the style of it. He said the driver must wait while Sammler gave his talk. The driver, a Negro, refused. Feffer raised his voice. He said this was a legal matter. Sammler persuaded him to drop it as he was about to call the police. "There is no need to have a taxi waiting for me," said Sammler.

"Go get lost then," said Feffer to the cabbie. "And no tip."

"Don't abuse him," Sammler said.

"I won't make any distinction because he's black," said Lionel. "I hear from Margotte that you've been running into a black pickpocket, by the way."

"Where do we go, Lionel? Now that I'm about to speak, I have misgivings. I feel unclear. What, really, am I supposed to say? The topic is so vast."

"You know it better than anyone."

"I know it, yes. But I am uneasy—somewhat shaky."

"You'll be great."

Then Feffer led him into a large room. He had expected a small one, a seminar room. He had come to reminisce, for a handful of interested students, about R. H. Tawney, Harold Laski, John Strachey, George Orwell, H. G. Wells. But this was a mass meeting of some sort. His obstructed vision took in a large, spreading, shaggy, composite human bloom. It was malodorous, peculiarly rancid, sulphurous. The amphitheater was filled. Standing room only. Was Feffer running one of his rackets? Was he going to pocket the admission money? Sammler mastered and dismissed this suspicion, ascribing it to surprise and nervousness. For he was surprised, frightened. But he pulled himself together. He tried to begin humorously by recalling the lecturer who had addressed incurable alcoholics under the impression that they were the Browning Society. But there was no laughter, and he had to remember that Browning Societies had been extinct for a long time. A microphone was hung on his chest. He began to speak of the mental atmosphere of England before the Second World War. The Mussolini adventure in East Africa. Spain in 1936. The Great Purges in Russia. Stalinism in France and Britain. Blum, Daladier, the People's Front, Oswald Mosley. The mood of English intellectuals. For this he needed no notes, he could easily recall what people had said or written.

"I assume," he said, "you are acquainted with the background, the events of nineteen seventeen. You know of the mutinous armies, the February Revolution in Russia, the disasters that befell authority. In all European countries the old leaders were discredited by Verdun, Flanders Field, and

Tannenberg. Perhaps I could begin with the fall of Kerensky. Maybe with Brest-Litovsk."

Doubly foreign, Polish-Oxonian, with his outrushing white back hair, the wrinkles streaming below the smoked glasses, he pulled the handkerchief from the breast pocket, unfolded and refolded it, touched his face, wiped his palms with thin elderly delicacy. Without pleasure in performance, without the encouragement of attention (there was a good deal of noise), the little satisfaction he did feel was the meager ghost of the pride he and his wife had once taken in their British successes. In his success, a Polish Jew so well acquainted, so handsomely acknowledged by the nobs, by H. G. Wells. Included, for instance, with Gerald Heard and Olaf Stapledon in the *Cosmopolis* project for a World State, Sammler had written articles for *News of Progress*, for the other publication, *The World Citizen*. As he explained in a voice that still contained Polish sibilants and nasals, though impressively low, the project was based on the propagation of the sciences of biology, history, and sociology and the effective application of scientific principles to the enlargement of human life; the building of a planned, orderly, and beautiful world society: abolishing national sovereignty, outlawing war; subjecting money and credit, production, distribution, transport, population, arms manufacture, et cetera, to world-wide collective control, offering free universal education, personal freedom (compatible with community welfare) to the utmost degree; a service society based on a rational scientific attitude toward life. Sammler, with growing interest and confidence recalling all this, lectured on *Cosmopolis* for half an hour, feeling what a kind-hearted, ingenuous, stupid scheme it had been. Telling this into the lighted restless hole of the amphitheater with the soiled dome and caged electric fixtures, until he was interrupted by a clear loud voice. He was being questioned. He was being shouted at.

"Hey!"

He tried to continue. "Such attempts to draw intellectuals away from Marxism met with small success. . . ."

A man in Levi's, thick-bearded but possibly young, a figure of compact distortion, was standing shouting at him.

"Hey! Old Man!"

In the silence, Mr. Sammler drew down his tinted spectacles, seeing this person with his effective eye.

"Old Man! You quoted Orwell before."

"Yes?"

"You quoted him to say that British radicals were all protected by the Royal Navy? Did Orwell say that British radicals were protected by the Royal Navy?"

"Yes, I believe he did say that."

"That's a lot of shit."

Sammler could not speak.

"Orwell was a fink. He was a sick counterrevolutionary. It's good he died when he did. And what you are saying is shit." Turning to the audience, extending violent arms and raising his palms like a Greek dancer, he said, "Why do you listen to this effete old shit? What has he got to tell you? His balls are dry. He's dead. He can't come."

Sammler later thought that voices had been raised on his side. Someone had said, "Shame. Exhibitionist."

But no one really tried to defend him. Most of the young people seemed to be against him. The shouting sounded hostile. Feffer was gone, had been called away to the telephone. Sammler, turning from the lectern, found his umbrella, trench coat, and hat behind him and left the platform, guided by a young girl who had rushed up to express indignation and sympathy, saying it was a scandal to break up such a good lecture. She showed him through a door, down several stairs, and he was on Broadway at 116th Street.

Abruptly out of the university.

Back in the city.

And he was not so much personally offended by the event as struck by the will to offend. What a passion to be *real*. But *real* was also brutal. And the acceptance of excrement as a standard? How extraordinary! Youth? Together with the idea of sexual potency? All this confused sex-excrement-militancy,

explosiveness, abusiveness, tooth-showing, Barbary ape howling. Or like the spider monkeys in the trees, as Sammler once
had read, defecating into their hands, and shrieking, pelting
the explorers below.

He was not sorry to have met the facts, however saddening,
regrettable the facts. But the effect was that Mr. Sammler did
feel somewhat separated from the rest of his species, if not in
some fashion severed—severed not so much by age as by
preoccupations too different and remote, disproportionate on
the side of the spiritual, Platonic, Augustinian, thirteenth-cen-
tury. As the traffic poured, the wind poured, and the sun,
relatively bright for Manhattan—shining and pouring through
openings in his substance, through his gaps. As if he had been
cast by Henry Moore. With holes, lacunae. Again, as after
seeing the pickpocket, he was obliged to events for a
difference, an intensification of vision. A delivery man with a
floral cross filling both arms, a bald head dented, seemed to be
drunk, fighting the wind, tacking. His dull boots small, and his
short wide pants blowing like a woman's skirts. Gardenias,
camellias, calla lilies, sailing above him under light transparent plastic. At the Riverside bus stop Mr. Sammler noted
the proximity of a waiting student, used his eye-power to
observe that he wore wide-wale corduroy pants of urinous
green, a tweed coat of a carrot color with burls of blue wool;
that sideburns stood like powerful bushy pillars to the head;
that civilized tortoise-shell shafts intersected these; that he
had hair thinning at the front; a Jew nose, a heavy all-savor-
ing, all-rejecting lip. Oh, this was an artistic diversion of the
streets for Mr. Sammler when he was roused to it by some
shock. He was studious, he was bookish, and had been trained
by the best writers to divert himself with perceptions. When he
went out, life was not empty. Meanwhile the purposive,
aggressive, business-bent, conative people did as mankind
normally did. If the majority walked about as if under a spell,
sleepwalkers, circumscribed by, in the grip of, minor neurotic
trifling aims, individuals like Sammler were only one stage
forward, awakened not to purpose but to aesthetic consump-

tion of the environment. Even if insulted, pained, somewhere bleeding, not broadly expressing any anger, not crying out with sadness, but translating heartache into delicate, even piercing observation. Particles in the bright wind, flinging downtown, acted like emery on the face. The sun shone as if there were no death. For a full minute, while the bus approached, squirting air, it was like that. Then Mr. Sammler got on, moving like a good citizen toward the rear, hoping he would not be pushed past the back door, for he had only fifteen blocks to go, and there was a thick crowd. The usual smell of long-seated bottoms, of sour shoes, of tobacco muck, of stogies, cologne, face powder. And yet along the river, early spring, the first khaki—a few weeks of sun, of heat, and Manhattan would (briefly) join the North American continent in a day of old-time green, the plush luxury, the polish of the season, shining, nitid, the dogwood white, pink, blooming crabapple. Then people's feet would swell with the warmth, and at Rockefeller Center strollers would sit on the polished stone slabs beside the planted tulips and tritons and the water, all in a spirit of pregnancy. Human creatures under the warm shadows of skyscrapers feeling the heavy pleasure of their nature, and yielding. Sammler too would enjoy spring—one of those penultimate springs. Of course he was upset. Very. Of course all that stuff about Brest-Litovsk, all that old news about revolutionary intellectuals versus the German brass was in this context downright funny. Inconsequent. Of course those students were comical, too. And what was the worst of it (apart from the rudeness)? There were appropriate ways of putting down an old bore. He might well be, especially in a public manifestation, lecturing on *Cosmopolis*, an old bore. The worst of it, from the point of view of the young people themselves, was that they acted without dignity. They had no view of the nobility of being intellectuals and judges of the social order. What a pity! old Sammler thought. A human being, valuing himself for the right reasons, has and restores order, authority. When the internal parts are in order. They must be in order. But what was it to be arrested in the stage of toilet training! What was it to be entrapped by a psychiatric standard (Sammler blamed the Germans and their psycho-analysis for this)! Who had raised the diaper flag? Who had made shit a sacrament? What literary and psychological movement was that? Mr. Sammler, with bitter angry mind, held the top rail of his jammed bus, riding downtown, a short journey.

He certainly had no thought of his black pickpocket. Him he connected with Columbus Circle. He always went uptown, not down. But at the rear, in his camel's-hair coat, filling up a corner with his huge body, he was standing. Sammler against strong internal resistance saw him. He resisted because at this swaying difficult moment he had no wish to see him. Lord! not now! Inside, Sammler felt an immediate descent; his heart sinking. As sure as fate, as a law of nature, a stone falling, a gas rising. He knew the thief did not ride the bus for transportation. To meet a woman, to go home—however he diverted himself—he unquestionably took cabs. He could afford them. But now Mr. Sammler was looking down at his shoulder, the tallest man in the bus, except for the thief himself. He saw that in the long rear seat he had cornered someone. Powerfully bent, the wide back concealed the victim from the other passengers. Only Sammler, because of his height, could see. Nothing to be grateful to height or vision for. The cornered man was old, was weak; poor eyes, watering with terror; white lashes, red lids, and a sea-mucus blue, his eyes, the mouth open with false teeth dropping from the upper gums. Coat and jacket were open also, the shirt pulled forward like detached green wallpaper, and the lining of the jacket ragged. The thief tugged his clothes like a doctor with a clinic patient. Pushing aside tie and scarf, he took out the wallet. His own homburg he then eased back (an animal movement, simply) slightly from his forehead, furrowed but not with anxiety. The wallet was long—leatherette, plastic. Open, it yielded a few dollar bills. There were cards. The thief put them in his palm. Read them with a tilted head. Let them drop. Examined a green federal-looking check, probably Social

Security. Mr. Sammler in his goggles was troubled in focusing.
Too much adrenalin was passing with light, thin, frightening
rapidity through his heart. He himself was not frightened, but
his heart seemed to record fear, it had a seizure. He
recognized it—knew what name to apply: tachycardia.
Breathing was hard. He could not fetch in enough air. He
wondered whether he might not faint away. Whether worse
might not happen. The check the black man put into his own
pocket. Snapshots like the cards fell from his fingers. Finished,
he then dropped the wallet back into the gray, worn, shattered
lining, flipped back the old man's muffler. In ironic calm,
thumb and forefinger took the knot of the necktie and yanked
it approximately, but only approximately, into place. It was at
this moment that, in a quick turn of the head, he saw Mr.
Sammler. Mr. Sammler seen seeing was still in rapid currents
with his heart. Like an escaping creature racing away from
him. His throat ached, up to the root of the tongue. There was
a pang in the bad eye. But he had some presence of mind.
Gripping the overhead chrome rail, he stooped forward as if
to see what street was coming up. Ninety-sixth. In other
words, he avoided a gaze that might be held, or any
interlocking of looks. He acknowledged nothing, and now
began to work his way toward the rear exit, gently urgent,
stooping door-ward. He reached, found the cord, pulled, made
it to the step, squeezed through the door, and stood on the
sidewalk holding the umbrella by the fabric, at the button.

The tachycardia now running itself out, he was able to walk,
though not at the usual rate. His stratagem was to cross
Riverside Drive and enter the first building, as if he lived
there. He had beaten the pickpocket to the door. Maybe
effrontery would dismiss him as too negligible to pursue. The
man did not seem to feel threatened by anyone. Took the
slackness, the cowardice of the world for granted. Sammler,
with effort, opened a big glass black-grilled door and found
himself in an empty lobby. Avoiding the elevator, he located
the staircase, trudged the first flight, and sat down on the
landing. A few minutes of rest, and he recovered his oxygen
level, although something within felt attenuated. Simply

thinned out. Before returning to the street (there was no rear exit), he took the umbrella inside the coat, hooking it in the armhole and belting it up, more or less securely. He also made an effort to change the shape of his hat, punching it out. He went past West End to Broadway, entering the first hamburger joint, sitting in the rear, and ordering tea. He drank to the bottom of the heavy cup, to the tannic taste, squeezing the sopping bag and asking the counterman for more water, feeling parched. Through the window his thief did not appear. By now Sammler's greatest need was for his bed. But he knew something about lying low. He had learned in Poland, in the war, in forests, cellars, passageways, cemeteries. Things he had passed through once which had abolished a certain margin or leeway ordinarily taken for granted. Taking for granted that one will not be shot stepping into the street, nor clubbed to death as one stoops to relieve oneself, nor hunted in an alley like a rat. This civil margin once removed, Mr. Sammler would never trust the restoration totally. He had had little occasion to practice the arts of hiding and escape in New York. But now, although his bones ached for the bed and his skull was famished for the pillow, he sat at the counter with his tea. He could not use buses any more. From now on it was the subway. The subway was an abomination.

But Mr. Sammler had not shaken the pickpocket. The man obviously could move fast. He might have forced his way out of the bus in midblock and sprinted back, heavy but swift in homburg and camel's-hair coat. Much more likely, the thief had observed him earlier, had once before shadowed him, had followed him home. Yes, that must have been the case. For when Mr. Sammler entered the lobby of his building the man came up behind him quickly, and not simply behind but pressing him bodily, belly to back. He did not lift his hands to Sammler but pushed. There was no building employee. The doormen, also running the elevator, spent much of their time in the cellar.

"What is the matter? What do you want?" said Mr. Sammler.

He was never to hear the black man's voice. He no more

spoke than a puma would. What he did was to force Sammler
into a corner beside the long blackish carved table, a sort of
Renaissance piece, a thing which added to the lobby melancholy, by the buckling canvas of the old wall, by the red-eyed
lights of the brass double fixture. There the man held Sammler
against the wall with his forearm. The umbrella fell to the
floor with a sharp crack of the ferrule on the tile. It was
ignored. The pickpocket unbuttoned himself. Sammler heard
the zipper descend. Then the smoked glasses were removed
from Sammler's face and dropped on the table. He was
directed, silently, to look downward. The black man had
opened his fly and taken out his penis. It was displayed to
Sammler with great oval testicles, a large tan-and-purple
uncircumcised thing—a tube, a snake; metallic hairs bristled
at the thick base and the tip curled beyond the supporting,
demonstrating hand, suggesting the fleshly mobility of an
elephant's trunk, though the skin was somewhat iridescent
rather than thick or rough. Over the forearm and fist that held
him Sammler was required to gaze at this organ. No compulsion would have been necessary. He would in any case have
looked.

The interval was long. The man's expression was not
directly menacing but oddly, serenely masterful. The thing
was shown with mystifying certitude. Lordliness. Then it was
returned to the trousers. *Quod erat demonstrandum.* Sammler
was .released. The fly was closed, the coat buttoned, the
marvelous streaming silk salmon necktie smoothed with a
powerful hand on the powerful chest. The black eyes with a
light of super candor moved softly, concluding the session, the
lesson, the warning, the encounter, the transmission. He
picked up Sammler's dark glasses and returned them to his
nose. He then unfolded and mounted his own, circular, of
gentian violet gently banded with the lovely Dior gold.

Then he departed. The elevator, with a bump, returning
from the cellar opened simultaneously with the street door.
Retrieving the fallen umbrella, lamely stooping, Sammler rode
up. The doorman offered no small talk. For this sad unsocia-

bility one was grateful. Better yet, he didn't bump into Margotte. Best of all, he dropped and stretched on his bed, just as he was, with smarting feet, thin respiration, pain at the heart, stunned mind and—oh!—a temporary blankness of spirit. Like the television screen in the lobby, white and gray, buzzing without image. Between head and pillow, a hard rectangle was interposed, the marbled cardboard of a note-book, sea-green. A slip of paper was attached with Scotch tape. Drawing it into light, passing it near the eye, and with lips spelling mutely, bitterly, he forced himself to read the separate letters. The note was from S (either Shula or Slawa).

"Daddy: These lectures on the moon by Doctor V. Govinda Lal are on short loan. They connect with the Memoir." Wells of course, writing on the moon circa 1900. "This is the very latest. Fascinating. Daddy—you have to read it. A must! Eyes or no eyes. And soon, please! as Doctor Lal is guest-lecturing up at Columbia. He needs it back." Frowning terribly, patience, forbearance all gone, he was filled with revulsion at his daughter's single-minded, persistent, prosecuting, horrible-comical obsession. He drew a long, lung-racking, body-straightening breath.

Then, bending open the notebook, he read, in sepia, in rust-gilt ink, *The Future of the Moon*. "How long," went the first sentence, "will this earth remain the only home of Man?"

How long? Oh, Lord, you·bet! Wasn't it the time—the very hour to go? For every purpose under heaven. A time to gather stones together, a time to cast away stones. Considering the earth itself not as a stone cast but as something to cast oneself from—to be divested of. To blow this great blue, white, green planet, or to be blown from it.

Three
Stories

The following stories have been selected from
Mosby's Memoirs and Other Stories

Leaving the
Yellow House

The Neighbors—there were in all six white
people who lived at Sego Desert Lake—told one another that
old Hattie could no longer make it alone. The desert life, even
with a forced-air furnace in the house and butane gas brought
from town in a truck, was still too difficult for her. There were
women even older than Hattie in the county. Twenty miles
away was Amy Walters, the gold miner's widow. But she was
a hardier old girl. Every day of the year she took a bath in the
icy lake. And Amy was crazy about money and knew how to
manage it, as Hattie did not. Hattie was not exactly a
drunkard, but she hit the bottle pretty hard, and now she was
in trouble and there was a limit to the help she could expect
from even the best of neighbors.

They were fond of her, though. You couldn't help being
fond of Hattie. She was big and cheerful, puffy, comic,
boastful, with a big round back and stiff, rather long legs.
Before the century began she had graduated from finishing
school and studied the organ in Paris. But now she didn't
know a note from a skillet. She had tantrums when she played
canasta. And all that remained of her fine fair hair was frizzled
along her forehead in small gray curls. Her forehead was not
much wrinkled, but the skin was bluish, the color of skim
milk. She walked with long strides in spite of the heaviness of
her hips, pushing on, round-backed, with her shoulders and
showing the flat rubber bottoms of her shoes.

Once a week, in the same cheerful, plugging but absent way,

she took off her short skirt and the dirty aviator's jacket with
the wool collar and put on a girdle, a dress, and high-heeled
shoes. When she stood on these heels her fat old body
trembled. She wore a big brown Rembrandt-like tam with a
ten-cent-store brooch, eyelike, carefully centered. She drew a
straight line with lipstick on her mouth, leaving part of the
upper lip pale. At the wheel of her old turret-shaped car, she
drove, seemingly methodical but speeding dangerously, across
forty miles of mountainous desert to buy frozen meat pies and
whisky. She went to the laundromat and the hairdresser, and
then had lunch with two martinis at the Arlington. Afterward
she would often visit Marian Nabot's Silvermine Hotel at
Miller Street near skid row and pass the rest of the day
gossiping and drinking with her cronies, old divorcees like
herself who had settled in the West. Hattie never gambled any
more and she didn't care for the movies. And at five o'clock
she drove back at the same speed, calmly, partly blinded by
the smoke of her cigarette. The fixed cigarette gave her a
watering eye.

The Rolfes and the Paces were her only white neighbors at
Sego Desert Lake. There was Sam Jervis too, but he was only
an old gandy walker who did odd jobs in her garden, and she
did not count him. Nor did she count among her neighbors
Darly, the dudes' cowboy who worked for the Paces, nor
Swede, the telegrapher. Pace had a guest ranch, and Rolfe and
his wife were rich and had retired. Thus there were three good
houses at the lake, Hattie's yellow house, Pace's, and the
Rolfes'. All the rest of the population—Sam, Swede, Watchtah
the section foreman, and the Mexicans and Indians and
Negroes—lived in shacks and boxcars. There were very few
trees, cottonwoods and box elders. Everything else, down to
the shores, was sagebrush and juniper. The lake was what
remained of an old sea that had covered the volcanic
mountains. To the north there were some tungsten mines; to
the south, fifteen miles, was an Indian village—shacks built of
plywood or railroad ties.

In this barren place Hattie had lived for more than twenty

years. Her first summer was spent not in a house but in an Indian wickiup on the shore. She used to say that she had watched the stars from this almost roofless shelter. After her divorce she took up with a cowboy named Wicks. Neither of them had any money—it was the Depression—and they had lived on the range, trapping coyotes for a living. Once a month they would come into town and rent a room and go on a bender. Hattie told this sadly, but also gloatingly, and with many trimmings. A thing no sooner happened to her than it was transformed into something else. "We were caught in a storm," she said, "and we rode hard, down to the lake and knocked on the door of the yellow house"—now her house. "Alice Parmenter took us in and let us sleep on the floor." What had actually happened was that the wind was blowing—there had been no storm—and they were not far from the house anyway; and Alice Parmenter, who knew that Hattie and Wicks were not married, offered them separate beds; but Hattie, swaggering, had said in a loud voice, "Why get two sets of sheets dirty?" And she and her cowboy had slept in Alice's bed while Alice had taken the sofa.

Then Wicks went away. There was never anybody like him in the sack; he was brought up in a whorehouse and the girls had taught him everything, said Hattie. She didn't really understand what she was saying but believed that she was being Western. More than anything else she wanted to be thought of as a rough, experienced woman of the West. Still, she was a lady, too. She had good silver and good china and engraved stationery, but she kept canned beans and A-1 sauce and tuna fish and bottles of catsup and fruit salad on the library shelves of her living room. On her night table was the Bible her pious brother Angus—the other brother was a heller—had given her; but behind the little door of the commode was a bottle of bourbon. When she awoke in the night she tippled herself back to sleep. In the glove compartment of her old car she kept little sample bottles for emergencies on the road. Old Darly found them after her accident.

The accident did not happen far out in the desert as she had always feared, but very near home. She had had a few martinis with the Rolfes one evening, and as she was driving home over the railroad crossing she lost control of the car and veered off the crossing onto the tracks. The explanation she gave was that she had sneezed, and the sneeze had blinded her and made her twist the wheel. The motor was killed and all four wheels of the car sat smack on the rails. Hattie crept down from the door, high off the roadbed. A great fear took hold of her—for the car, for the future, and not only for the future but spreading back into the past—and she began to hurry on stiff legs through the sagebrush to Pace's ranch.

Now the Paces were away on a hunting trip and had left Darly in charge; he was tending bar in the old cabin that went back to the days of the pony express, when Hattie burst in. There were two customers, a tungsten miner and his girl.

"Darly, I'm in trouble. Help me. I've had an accident," said Hattie.

How the face of a man will alter when a woman has bad news to tell him! It happened now to lean old Darly; his eyes went flat and looked unwilling, his jaw moved in and out, his wrinkled cheeks began to flush, and he said, "What's the matter—what's happened to you now?"

"I'm stuck on the tracks. I sneezed. I lost control of the car. Tow me off, Darly. With the pickup. Before the train comes."

Darly threw down his towel and stamped his high-heeled boots. "Now what have you gone and done?" he said. "I told you to stay home after dark."

"Where's Pace? Ring the fire bell and fetch Pace."

"There's nobody on the property except me," said the lean old man. "And I'm not supposed to close the bar and you know it as well as I do."

"Please, Darly. I can't leave my car on the tracks."

"Too bad!" he said. Nevertheless he moved from behind the bar. "How did you say it happened?"

"I told you, I sneezed," said Hattie.

Everyone, as she later told it, was as drunk as sixteen thousand dollars: Darly, the miner, and the miner's girl.

Darly was limping as he locked the door of the bar. A year before, a kick from one of Pace's mares had broken his ribs as he was loading her into the trailer, and he hadn't recovered from it. He was too old. But he dissembled the pain. The high-heeled narrow boots helped, and his painful bending looked like the ordinary stooping posture of a cowboy. However, Darly was not a genuine cowboy, like Pace who had grown up in the saddle. He was a late-comer from the East and until the age of forty had never been on horseback. In this respect he and Hattie were alike. They were not genuine Westerners.

Hattie hurried after him through the ranch yard.

"Damn you!" he said to her. "I got thirty bucks out of that sucker and I would have skinned him out of his whole pay check if you minded your business. Pace is going to be sore as hell."

"You've got to help me. We're neighbors," said Hattie.

"You're not fit to be living out here. You can't do it any more. Besides, you're swacked all the time."

Hattie couldn't afford to talk back. The thought of her car on the tracks made her frantic. If a freight came now and smashed it, her life at Sego Desert Lake would be finished. And where would she go then? She was not fit to live in this place. She had never made the grade at all, only seemed to have made it. And Darly—why did he say such hurtful things to her? Because he himself was sixty-eight years old, and he had no other place to go, either; he took bad treatment from Pace besides. Darly stayed because his only alternative was to go to the soldiers' home. Moreover, the dude women would still crawl into his sack. They wanted a cowboy and they thought he was one. Why, he couldn't even raise himself out of his bunk in the morning. And where else would he get women? "After the dude season," she wanted to say to him, "you always have to go to the Veterans' Hospital to get fixed up again." But she didn't dare offend him now.

The moon was due to rise. It appeared as they drove over the ungraded dirt road toward the crossing where Hattie's turret-shaped car was sitting on the rails. Driving very fast,

Darly wheeled the pickup around, spraying dirt on the miner
and his girl, who had followed in their car.

"You get behind the wheel and steer," Darly told Hattie.

She climbed into the seat. Waiting at the wheel, she lifted
up her face and said, "Please, God, I didn't bend the axle or
crack the oil pan."

When Darly crawled under the bumper of Hattie's car the
pain in his ribs suddenly cut off his breath, so instead of
doubling the tow chain he fastened it at full length. He rose
and trotted back to the truck on the tight boots. Motion
seemed the only remedy for the pain; not even booze did the
trick any more. He put the pickup into towing gear and began
to pull. One side of Hattie's car dropped into the roadbed with
a heave of springs. She sat with a stormy, frightened,
conscience-stricken face, racing the motor until she flooded it.

The tungsten miner yelled, "Your chain's too long."

Hattie was raised high in the air by the pitch of the wheels.
She had to roll down the window to let herself out because the
door handle had been jammed from inside for years. Hattie
struggled out on the uplifted side crying, "I better call the
Swede. I better have him signal. There's a train due."

"Go on, then," said Darly. "You're no good here."

"Darly, be careful with my car. Be careful."

The ancient sea bed at this place was flat and low, and the
lights of her car and of the truck and of the tungsten miner's
Chevrolet were bright and big at twenty miles. Hattie was too
frightened to think of this. All she could think was that she
was a procrastinating old woman, she had lived by delays; she
had meant to stop drinking, she had put off the time, and now
she had smashed her car—a terrible end, a terrible judgment
on her. She got to the ground and, drawing up her skirt, she
started to get over the tow chain. To prove that the chain
didn't have to be shortened, and to get the whole thing over
with, Darly threw the pickup forward again. The chain jerked
up and struck Hattie in the knee and she fell forward and
broke her arm.

She cried, "Darly, Darly, I'm hurt. I fell."

"The old lady tripped on the chain," said the miner. "Back up here and I'll double it for you. You're getting nowheres."

Drunkenly the miner lay down on his back in the dark, soft red cinders of the roadbed. Darly had backed up to slacken the chain.

Darly hurt the miner, too. He tore some skin from his fingers by racing ahead before the chain was secure. Without complaining, the miner wrapped his hand in his shirttail saying, "She'll do it now." The old car came down from the tracks and stood on the shoulder of the road.

"There's your goddamn car," said Darly to Hattie.

"Is it all right?" she said. Her left side was covered with dirt, but she managed to pick herself up and stand, round-backed and heavy, on her stiff legs. "I'm hurt, Darly." She tried to convince him of it.

"Hell if you are," he said. He believed she was putting on an act to escape blame. The pain in his ribs made him especially impatient with her. "Christ, if you can't look after yourself any more you've got no business out here."

"You're old yourself," she said. "Look what you did to me. You can't hold your liquor."

This offended him greatly. He said, "I'll take you to the Rolfes. They let you booze it up in the first place, so let them worry about you. I'm tired of your bunk, Hattie."

He raced uphill. Chains, spade, and crowbar clashed on the sides of the pickup. She was frightened and held her arm and cried. Rolfe's dogs jumped at her to lick her when she went through the gate. She shrank from them crying, "Down, down."

"Darly," she cried in the darkness, "take care of my car. Don't leave it standing there on the road. Darly, take care of it, please."

But Darly in his ten-gallon hat, his chin-bent face wrinkled, small and angry, a furious pain in his ribs, tore away at high speed.

"Oh, God, what will I do," she said.

The Rolfes were having a last drink before dinner, sitting at

their fire of pitchy railroad ties, when Hattie opened the door.
Her knee was bleeding, her eyes were tiny with shock, her face
gray with dust.

"I'm hurt," she said desperately. "I had an accident. I
sneezed and lost control of the wheel. Jerry, look after the car.
It's on the road."

They bandaged her knee and took her home and put her to
bed. Helen Rolfe wrapped a heating pad around her arm.

"I can't have the pad," Hattie complained. "The switch
goes on and off, and every time it does it starts my generator
and uses up the gas."

"Ah, now, Hattie," Rolfe said, "this is not the time to be
stingy. We'll take you to town in the morning and have you
looked over. Helen will phone Dr. Stroud."

Hattie wanted to say, "Stingy! Why you're the stingy ones. I
just haven't got anything. You and Helen are ready to hit each
other over two bits in canasta." But the Rolfes were good to
her; they were her only real friends here. Darly would have let
her lie in the yard all night, and Pace would have sold her to
the bone man. He'd give her to the knacker for a buck.

So she didn't talk back to the Rolfes, but as soon as they left
the yellow house and walked through the super-clear moonlight under the great skirt of box-elder shadows to their new
station wagon, Hattie turned off the switch, and the heavy
swirling and battering of the generator stopped. Presently she
became aware of real pain, deeper pain, in her arm, and she
sat rigid, warming the injured place with her hand. It seemed
to her that she could feel the bone sticking out. Before leaving,
Helen Rolfe had thrown over her a comforter that had
belonged to Hattie's dead friend India, from whom she had
inherited the small house and everything in it. Had the
comforter lain on India's bed the night she died? Hattie tried
to remember, but her thoughts were mixed up. She was fairly
sure the deathbed pillow was in the loft, and she believed she
had put the death bedding in a trunk. Then how had this
comforter got out? She couldn't do anything about it now but
draw it away from contact with her skin. It kept her legs
warm. This she accepted, but she didn't want it any nearer.

More and more Hattie saw her own life as though, from birth to the present, every moment had been filmed. Her fancy was that when she died she would see the film in the next world. Then she would know how she had appeared from the back, watering the plants, in the bathroom, asleep, playing the organ, embracing—everything, even tonight, in pain, almost the last pain, perhaps, for she couldn't take much more. How many twists and angles had life to show her yet? There couldn't be much film left. To lie awake and think such thoughts was the worst thing in the world. Better death than insomnia. Hattie not only loved sleep, she believed in it.

The first attempt to set the bone was not successful. "Look what they've done to me," said Hattie and showed visitors the discolored breast. After the second operation her mind wandered. The sides of her bed had to be raised, for in her delirium she roamed the wards. She cursed at the nurses when they shut her in. "You can't make people prisoners in a democracy without a trial, you bitches." She had learned from Wicks how to swear. "*He* was profane," she used to say. "I picked it up unconsciously."

For several weeks her mind was not clear. Asleep, her face was lifeless; her cheeks were puffed out and her mouth, no longer wide and grinning, was drawn round and small. Helen sighed when she saw her.

"Shall we get in touch with her family?" Helen asked the doctor. His skin was white and thick. He had chestnut hair, abundant but very dry. He sometimes explained to his patients, "I had a tropical disease during the war."

He asked, "Is there a family?"

"Old brothers. Cousins' children," said Helen. She tried to think who would be called to her own bedside (she was old enough for that). Rolfe would see that she was cared for. He would hire private nurses. Hattie could not afford that. She had already gone beyond her means. A trust company in Philadelphia paid her eighty dollars a month. She had a small savings account.

"I suppose it'll be up to us to get her out of hock," said

Rolfe. "Unless the brother down in Mexico comes across. We may have to phone one of those old guys."

In the end, no relations had to be called. Hattie began to recover. At last she could recognize visitors, though her mind was still in disorder. Much that had happened she couldn't recall.

"How many quarts of blood did they have to give me?" she kept asking. "I seem to remember five, six, eight different transfusions. Daylight, electric light . . ." She tried to smile, but she couldn't make a pleasant face as yet. "How am I going to pay?" she said. "At twenty-five bucks a quart. My little bit of money is just about wiped out."

Blood became her constant topic, her preoccupation. She told everyone who came to see her, "—have to replace all that blood. They poured gallons into me. Gallons. I hope it was all good." And, though very weak, she began to grin and laugh again. There was more hissing in her laughter than formerly; the illness had affected her chest.

"No cigarettes, no booze," the doctor told Helen.

"Doctor," Helen asked him, "do you expect her to change?"

"All the same, I am obliged to say it."

"Life sober may not be much of a temptation to her," said Helen.

Her husband laughed. When Rolfe's laughter was intense it blinded one of his eyes. His short Irish face turned red; on the bridge of his small, sharp nose the skin whitened. "Hattie's like me," he said. "She'll be in business till she's cleaned out. And if Sego Lake turned to whisky she'd use her last strength to knock her old yellow house down to build a raft of it. She'd float away on whisky. So why talk temperance?"

Hattie recognized the similarity between them. When he came to see her she said, "Jerry, you're the only one I can really talk to about my troubles. What am I going to do for money? I have Hotchkiss Insurance. I paid eight dollars a month."

"That won't do you much good, Hat. No Blue Cross?"

"I let it drop ten years ago. Maybe I could sell some of my valuables."

"What valuables have you got?" he said. His eye began to droop with laughter.

"Why," she said defiantly, "there's plenty. First there's the beautiful, precious Persian rug that India left me."

"Coals from the fireplace have been burning it for years, Hat!"

"The rug is in *perfect* condition," she said with an angry sway of the shoulders. "A beautiful object like that never loses its value. And the oak table from the Spanish monastery is three hundred years old."

"With luck you could get twenty bucks for it. It would cost fifty to haul it out of here. It's the house you ought to sell."

"The house?" she said. Yes, that had been in her mind. "I'd have to get twenty thousand for it."

"Eight is a fair price."

"Fifteen. . . ." She was offended, and her voice recovered its strength. "India put eight into it in two years. And don't forget that Sego Lake is one of the most beautiful places in the world."

"But where is it? Five hundred and some miles to San Francisco and two hundred to Salt Lake City. Who wants to live way out here but a few eccentrics like you and India? And me?"

"There are things you can't put a price tag on. Beautiful things."

"Oh, bull, Hattie! You don't know squat about beautiful things. Any more than I do. I live here because it figures for me, and you because India left you the house. And just in the nick of time, too. Without it you wouldn't have had a pot of your own."

His words offended Hattie; more than that, they frightened her. She was silent and then grew thoughtful, for she was fond of Jerry Rolfe and he of her. He had good sense and moreover he only expressed her own thoughts. He spoke no more than the truth about India's death and the house. But she told herself, He doesn't know everything. You'd have to pay a San Francisco architect ten thousand just to *think* of such a house. Before he drew a line.

"Jerry," the old woman said, "what am I going to do about replacing the blood in the blood bank?"

"Do you want a quart from me, Hat?" His eye began to fall shut.

"You won't do. You had that tumor, two years ago. I think Darly ought to give some."

"The old man?" Rolfe laughed at her. "You want to kill him?"

"Why!" said Hattie with anger, lifting up her massive face. Fever and perspiration had frayed the fringe of curls; at the back of the head the hair had knotted and matted so that it had to be shaved. "Darly almost killed me. It's his fault that I'm in this condition. He must have *some* blood in him. He runs after all the chicks—all of them—young and old."

"Come, you were drunk, too," said Rolfe.

"I've driven drunk for forty years. It was the sneeze. Oh, Jerry, I feel wrung out," said Hattie, haggard, sitting forward in bed. But her face was cleft by her nonsensically happy grin. She was not one to be miserable for long; she had the expression of a perennial survivor.

Every other day she went to the therapist. The young woman worked her arm for her; it was a pleasure and a comfort to Hattie, who would have been glad to leave the whole cure to her. However, she was given other exercises to do, and these were not so easy. They rigged a pulley for her and Hattie had to hold both ends of a rope and saw it back and forth through the scraping little wheel. She bent heavily from the hips and coughed over her cigarette. But the most important exercise of all she shirked. This required her to put the flat of her hand to the wall at the level of her hips and, by working her finger tips slowly, to make the hand ascend to the height of her shoulder. That was painful; she often forgot to do it, although the doctor warned her, "Hattie, you don't want adhesions, do you?"

A light of despair crossed Hattie's eyes. Then she said, "Oh, Dr. Stroud, buy my house from me."

"I'm a bachelor. What would I do with a house?"

"I know just the girl for you—my cousin's daughter. Perfectly charming and very brainy. Just about got her Ph.D."

"You must get quite a few proposals yourself," said the doctor.

"From crazy desert rats. They chase me. But," she said, "after I pay my bills I'll be in pretty punk shape. If at least I could replace that blood in the blood bank I'd feel easier."

"If you don't do as the therapist tells you, Hattie, you'll need another operation. Do you know what adhesions are?"

She knew. But Hattie thought, *How long must I go on taking care of myself?* It made her angry to hear him speak of another operation. She had a moment of panic, but she covered it up. With him, this young man whose skin was already as thick as buttermilk and whose chestnut hair was as dry as death, she always assumed the part of a child. In a small voice she said, "Yes, doctor." But her heart was in a fury.

Night and day, however, she repeated, "I was in the Valley of the Shadow. But I'm alive." She was weak, she was old, she couldn't follow a train of thought very easily, she felt faint in the head. But she was still here; here was her body, it filled space, a great body. And though she had worries and perplexities, and once in a while her arm felt as though it were about to give her the last stab of all; and though her hair was scrappy and old, like onion roots, and scattered like nothing under the comb, yet she sat and amused herself with visitors; her great grin split her face; her heart warmed with every kind word.

And she thought, People will help me out. It never did me any good to worry. At the last minute something turned up, when I wasn't looking for it. Marian loves me. Helen and Jerry love me. Half Pint loves me. They would never let me go to the ground. And I love them. If it were the other way around, I'd never let them go down.

Above the horizon, in a baggy vastness which Hattie by herself occasionally visited, the features of India, her *shade*, sometimes rose. India was indignant and scolding. Not mean. Not really mean. Few people had ever been really mean to Hattie. But India was annoyed with her. "The garden is going to hell, Hattie," she said. "Those lilac bushes are all shriveled."

"But what can I do? The hose is rotten. It broke. It won't reach."

"Then dig a trench," said the phantom of India. "Have old Sam dig a trench. But save the bushes."

Am I thy servant still? said Hattie to herself. *No,* she thought, *let the dead bury their dead.*

But she didn't defy India now any more than she had done when they lived together. Hattie was supposed to keep India off the bottle, but often both of them began to get drunk after breakfast. They forgot to dress, and in their slips the two of them wandered drunkenly around the house and blundered into each other, and they were in despair at having been so weak. Late in the afternoon they would be sitting in the living room, waiting for the sun to set. It shrank, burning itself out on the crumbling edges of the mountains. When the sun passed, the fury of the daylight ended and the mountain surfaces were more blue, broken, like cliffs of coal. They no longer suggested faces. The east began to look simple, and the lake less inhuman and haughty. At last India would say, "Hattie—it's time for the lights." And Hattie would pull the switch chains of the lamps, several of them, to give the generator a good shove. She would turn on some of the wobbling eighteenth-century-style lamps whose shades stood out from their slender bodies like dragonflies' wings. The little engine in the shed would shuffle, then spit, then charge and bang, and the first weak light would rise unevenly in the bulbs.

"Hettie!" cried India. After she drank she was penitent, but her penitence too was a hardship to Hattie, and the worse her temper the more British her accent became. *"Where the hell ah you Het-tie!"* After India's death Hattie found some poems she had written in which she, Hattie, was affectionately and even touchingly mentioned. That was a good thing—Litera-

ture. Education. Breeding. But Hattie's interest in ideas was
very small, whereas India had been all over the world. India
was used to brilliant society. India wanted her to discuss
Eastern religion, Bergson and Proust, and Hattie had no head
for this, and so India blamed her drinking on Hattie. "I can't
talk to you," she would say. "You don't understand religion or
culture. And I'm here because I'm not fit to be anywhere else.
I can't live in New York any more. It's too dangerous for a
woman my age to be drunk in the street at night."

And Hattie, talking to her Western friends about India,
would say, "She is a lady" (implying that they made a pair).
"She is a creative person" (this was why they found each other
so congenial). "But helpless? Completely. Why she can't even
get her own girdle on."

"Hettie! Come here. Het-tie! Do you know what sloth is?"

Undressed, India sat on her bed and with the cigarette in
her drunken, wrinkled, ringed hand she burned holes in the
blankets. On Hattie's pride she left many small scars, too. She
treated her like a servant.

Weeping, India begged Hattie afterward to forgive her.
*"Hattie, please don't condemn me in your heart. Forgive me,
dear, I know I am bad. But I hurt myself more in my evil than I
hurt you."*

Hattie would keep a stiff bearing. She would lift up her face
with its incurved nose and puffy eyes and say, "I am a
Christian person. I never bear a grudge." And by repeating
this she actually brought herself to forgive India.

But of course Hattie had no husband, no child, no skill, no
savings. And what she would have done if India had not died
and left her the yellow house nobody knows.

Jerry Rolfe said privately to Marian, "Hattie can't do
anything for herself. If I hadn't been around during the
forty-four blizzard she and India both would have starved.
She's always been careless and lazy and now she can't even
chase a cow out of the yard. She's too feeble. The thing for her
to do is to go East to her damn brother. Hattie would have
ended at the poor farm if it hadn't been for India. But besides

the damn house India should have left her some dough. She didn't use her goddamn head."

When Hattie returned to the lake she stayed with the Rolfes. "Well, old shellback," said Jerry, "there's a little more life in you now."

Indeed, with joyous eyes, the cigarette in her mouth and her hair newly frizzed and overhanging her forehead, she seemed to have triumphed again. She was pale, but she grinned, she chuckled, and she held a bourbon old-fashioned with a cherry and a slice of orange in it. She was on rations; the Rolfes allowed her two a day. Her back, Helen noted, was more bent than before. Her knees went outward a little weakly; her feet, however came close together at the ankles.

"Oh, Helen dear and Jerry dear, I am so thankful, so glad to be back at the lake. I can look after my place again, and I'm here to see the spring. It's more gorgeous than ever."

Heavy rains had fallen while Hattie was away. The sego lilies, which bloomed only after a wet winter, came up from the loose dust, especially around the marl pit; but even on the burnt granite they seemed to grow. Desert peach was beginning to appear, and in Hattie's yard the rosebushes were filling out. The roses were yellow and abundant, and the odor they gave off was like that of damp tea leaves.

"Before it gets hot enough for the rattlesnakes," said Hattie to Helen, "we ought to drive up to Marky's ranch and gather watercress."

Hattie was going to attend to lots of things, but the heat came early that year and, as there was no television to keep her awake, she slept most of the day. She was now able to dress herself, though there was little more that she could do. Sam Jervis rigged the pulley for her on the porch and she remembered once in a while to use it. Mornings when she had her strength she rambled over to her own house, examining things, being important and giving orders to Sam Jervis and Wanda Gingham. At ninety, Wanda, a Shoshone, was still an excellent seamstress and housecleaner.

Hattie looked over the car, which was parked under a cottonwood tree. She tested the engine. Yes, the old pot would still go. Proudly, happily, she listened to the noise of tappets; the dry old pipe shook as the smoke went out at the rear. She tried to work the shift, turn the wheel. That, as yet, she couldn't do. But it would come soon, she was confident.

At the back of the house the soil had caved in a little over the cesspool and a few of the old railroad ties over the top had rotted. Otherwise things were in good shape. Sam had looked after the garden. He had fixed a new catch for the gate after Pace's horses—maybe because he could never afford to keep them in hay—had broken in and Sam found them grazing and drove them out. Luckily, they hadn't damaged many of her plants. Hattie felt a moment of wild rage against Pace. He had brought the horses into her garden for a free feed, she was sure. But her anger didn't last long. It was reabsorbed into the feeling of golden pleasure that enveloped her. She had little strength, but all that she had was a pleasure to her. So she forgave even Pace, who would have liked to do her out of the house, who had always used her, embarrassed her, cheated her at cards, swindled her. All that he did he did for the sake of his quarter horses. He was a fool about horses. They were ruining him. Racing horses was a millionaire's amusement.

She saw his animals in the distance, feeding. Unsaddled, the mares appeared undressed; they reminded her of naked women walking with their glossy flanks in the sego lilies which curled on the ground. The flowers were yellowish, like winter wool, but fragrant; the mares, naked and gentle, walked through them. Their strolling, their perfect beauty, the sound of their hoofs on stone touched a deep place in Hattie's nature. Her love for horses, birds, and dogs was well known. Dogs led the list. And now a piece cut from a green blanket reminded Hattie of her dog Richie. The blanket was one he had torn, and she had cut it into strips and placed them under the doors to keep out the drafts. In the house she found more traces of him: hair he had shed on the furniture. Hattie was going to borrow Helen's vacuum cleaner, but there wasn't really enough current to make it pull as it should. On the doorknob of India's room hung the dog collar.

Hattie had decided that she would have herself moved into India's bed when it was time to die. Why should there be two deathbeds? A perilous look came into her eyes, her lips were pressed together forbiddingly. *I follow,* she said, speaking to India with an inner voice, *so never mind.* Presently—before long—she would have to leave the yellow house in her turn. And as she went into the parlor, thinking of the will, she sighed. Pretty soon she would have to attend to it. India's lawyer, Claiborne, helped her with such things. She had phoned him in town, while she was staying with Marian, and talked matters over with him. He had promised to try to sell the house for her. Fifteen thousand was her bottom price, she said. If he couldn't find a buyer, perhaps he could find a tenant. Two hundred dollars a month was the rental she set. Rolfe laughed. Hattie turned toward him one of those proud, dulled looks she always took on when he angered her. Haughtily she said, "For summer on Sego Lake? That's reasonable."

"You're competing with Pace's ranch."

"Why, the food is stinking down there. And he cheats the dudes," said Hattie. "He really cheats them at cards. You'll never catch me playing blackjack with him again."

And what would she do, thought Hattie, if Claiborne could neither rent nor sell the house? This question she shook off as regularly as it returned. *I don't have to be a burden on anybody,* thought Hattie. *It's looked bad many a time before, but when push came to shove, I made it. Somehow I got by.* But she argued with herself: *How many times? How long, O God—an old thing, feeble, no use to anyone?* Who said she had any right to own property?

She was sitting on her sofa, which was very old—India's sofa—eight feet long, kidney-shaped, puffy, and bald. An underlying pink shone through the green; the upholstered tufts were like the pads of dogs' paws; between them rose bunches of hair. Here Hattie slouched, resting, with knees wide apart and a cigarette in her mouth, eyes half-shut but farseeing. The mountains seemed not fifteen miles but fifteen hundred feet away, the lake a blue band; the tealike odor of the roses, though they were still unopened, was already in the air, for Sam was watering them in the heat. Gratefully Hattie yelled, "Sam!"

Sam was very old, and all shanks. His feet looked big. His old railroad jacket was made tight across the back by his stoop. A crooked finger with its great broad nail over the mouth of the hose made the water spray and sparkle. Happy to see Hattie, he turned his long jaw, empty of teeth, and his long blue eyes, which seemed to bend back to penetrate into his temples (it was his face that turned, not his body), and he said, "Oh, there, Hattie. You've made it home today? Welcome, Hattie."

"Have a beer, Sam. Come around the kitchen door and I'll give you a beer."

She never had Sam in the house, owing to his skin disease. There were raw patches on his chin and behind his ears. Hattie feared infection from his touch, having decided that he had impetigo. She gave him the beer can, never a glass, and she put on gloves before she used the garden tools. Since he would take no money from her—Wanda Gingham charged a dollar a day—she got Marian to find old clothes for him in town and she left food for him at the door of the damp-wood-smelling boxcar where he lived.

"How's the old wing, Hat?" he said.

"It's coming. I'll be driving the car again before you know it," she told him. "By the first of May I'll be driving again." Every week she moved the date forward. "By Decoration Day I expect to be on my own again," she said.

In mid-June, however, she was still unable to drive. Helen Rolfe said to her, "Hattie, Jerry and I are due in Seattle the first week of July."

"Why, you never told me that," said Hattie.

"You don't mean to tell me this is the first you heard of it," said Helen. "You've known about it from the first—since Christmas."

It wasn't easy for Hattie to meet her eyes. She presently put her head down. Her face became very dry, especially the lips. "Well, don't you worry about me. I'll be all right here," she said.

"Who's going to look after you?" said Jerry. He evaded nothing himself and tolerated no evasion in others. Except that, as Hattie knew, he made every possible allowance for her. But who would help her? She couldn't count on her friend Half Pint, she couldn't really count on Marian either. She had had only the Rolfes to turn to. Helen, trying to be steady, gazed at her and made sad, involuntary movements with her head, sometimes nodding, sometimes seeming as if she disagreed. Hattie, with her inner voice, swore at her: *Bitch-eyes. I can't make it the way she does because I'm old. Is that fair?* And yet she admired Helen's eyes. Even the skin about them, slightly wrinkled, heavy underneath, was touching, beautiful. There was a heaviness in her bust that went, as if by attachment, with the heaviness of her eyes. Her head, her hands and feet should have taken a more slender body. Helen, said Hattie, was the nearest thing she had on earth to a sister. But there was no reason to go to Seattle—no genuine business. Why the hell Seattle? It was only idleness, only a holiday. The only reason was Hattie herself; this was their way of telling her that there was a limit to what she could expect them to do for her. Helen's nervous head wavered, but her thoughts were steady. She knew what was passing through Hattie's mind. Like Hattie, she was an idle woman. Why was her right to idleness better?

Because of money? thought Hattie. Because of age? Because she has a husband? Because she had a daughter in Swarthmore College? But an interesting thing occurred to her. Helen disliked being idle, whereas Hattie herself had never made any bones about it: an idle life was all she was good for. But for her it had been uphill all the way, because when Waggoner divorced her she didn't have a cent. She even had to support Wicks for seven or eight years. Except with horses, Wicks had no sense. And then she had had to take tons of dirt from India. *I am the one,* Hattie asserted to herself. *I would know*

*what to do with Helen's advantages. She only suffers from them.
And if she wants to stop being an idle woman why can't she start
with me, her neighbor?* Hattie's skin, for all its puffiness, burned
with anger. She said to Rolfe and Helen, "Don't worry. I'll
make out. But if I have to leave the lake you'll be ten times
more lonely than before. Now I'm going back to my house."

She lifted up her broad old face, and her lips were childlike
with suffering. She would never take back what she had said.

But the trouble was no ordinary trouble. Hattie was herself
aware that she rambled, forgot names, and answered when no
one spoke.

"We can't just take charge of her," Rolfe said. "What's
more, she ought to be near a doctor. She keeps her shotgun
loaded so she can fire it if anything happens to her in the
house. But who knows what she'll shoot? I don't believe it was
Jacamares who killed that Doberman of hers."

Rolfe drove into the yard the day after she moved back to
the yellow house and said, "I'm going into town. I can bring
you some chow if you like."

She couldn't afford to refuse his offer, angry though she
was, and she said, "Yes, bring me some stuff from the
Mountain Street Market. Charge it." She had only some
frozen shrimp and a few cans of beer in the icebox. When
Rolfe had gone she put out the package of shrimp to thaw.

People really used to stick by one another in the West.
Hattie now saw herself as one of the pioneers. The modern
breed had come later. After all, she had lived on the range like
an old-timer. Wicks had had to shoot their Christmas dinner
and she had cooked it—venison. He killed it on the reserva-
tion, and if the Indians had caught them, there would have
been hell to pay.

The weather was hot, the clouds were heavy and calm in a
large sky. The horizon was so huge that in it the lake must
have seemed like a saucer of milk. *Some milk!* Hattie thought.
Two thousand feet down in the middle, so deep no corpse
could ever be recovered. A body, they said, went around with
the currents. And there were rocks like eyeteeth, and hot

springs, and colorless fish at the bottom which were never caught. Now that the white pelicans were nesting they patrolled the rocks for snakes and other egg thieves. They were so big and flew so slow you might imagine they were angels. Hattie no longer visited the lake shore; the walk exhausted her. She saved her strength to go to Pace's bar in the afternoon.

She took off her shoes and stockings and walked on bare feet from one end of her house to the other. On the land side she saw Wanda Gingham sitting near the tracks while her great-grandson played in the soft red gravel. Wanda wore a large purple shawl and her brown head was bare. All about her was—was nothing, Hattie thought; for she had taken a drink, breaking her rule. Nothing but mountains, thrust out like men's bodies; the sagebrush was the hair on their chests.

The warm wind blew dust from the marl pit. This white powder made her sky less blue. On the water side were the pelicans, pure as spirits, slow as angels, blessing the air as they flew with great wings.

Should she or should she not have Sam do something about the vine on the chimney? Sparrows nested in it, and she was glad of that. But all summer long the king snakes were after them and she was afraid to walk in the garden. When the sparrows scratched the ground for seed they took a funny bound; they held their legs stiff and flung back the dust with both feet. Hattie sat down at her old Spanish monastery table, watching them in the cloudy warmth of the day, clasping her hands, chuckling and sad. The bushes were crowded with yellow roses, half of them now rotted. The lizards scrambled from shadow to shadow. The water was smooth as air, gaudy as silk. The mountains succumbed, falling asleep in the heat. Drowsy, Hattie lay down on her sofa, its pads to her always like dogs' paws. She gave in to sleep and when she woke it was midnight; she did not want to alarm the Rolfes by putting on her lights so she took advantage of the moon to eat a few thawed shrimps and go to the bathroom. She undressed and lifted herself into bed and lay there feeling her sore arm. Now

she knew how much she missed her dog. The whole matter of
the dog weighed heavily on her soul. She came close to tears,
thinking about him, and she went to sleep oppressed by her
secret.

I suppose I had better try to pull myself together a little,
thought Hattie nervously in the morning. *I can't just sleep my
way through.* She knew what her difficulty was. Before any
serious question her mind gave way. It scattered or diffused.
She said to herself, *I can see bright, but I feel dim. I guess I'm
not so lively any more. Maybe I'm becoming a little touched in
the head, as Mother was.* But she was not so old as her mother
was when she did those strange things. At eighty-five, her
mother had to be kept from going naked in the street. *I'm not
as bad as that yet. Thank God! Yes, I walked into the men's
wards, but that was when I had a fever, and my nightie was on.*

She drank a cup of Nescafé and it strengthened her
determination to do something for herself. In all the world she
had only her brother Angus to go to. Her brother Will had led
a rough life; he was an old heller, and now he drove everyone
away. He was too crabby, thought Hattie. Besides he was
angry because she had lived so long with Wicks. Angus would
forgive her. But then he and his wife were not her kind. With
them she couldn't drink, she couldn't smoke, she had to make
herself small-mouthed, and she would have to wait while they
read a chapter of the Bible before breakfast. Hattie could not
bear to sit at table waiting for meals. Besides, she had a house
of her own at last. Why should she have to leave it? She had
never owned a thing before. And now she was not allowed to
enjoy her yellow house. *But I'll keep it*, she said to herself
rebelliously. *I swear to God I'll keep it. Why, I barely just got it.
I haven't had time.* And she went out on the porch to work the
pulley and do something about the adhesions in her arm. She
was sure now that they were there. *And what will I do?* she
cried to herself. *What will I do? Why did I ever go to Rolfe's that
night—and why did I lose control on the crossing?* She couldn't
say, now, "I sneezed." She couldn't even remember what had
happened, except that she saw the boulders and the twisting

blue rails and Darly. It was Darly's fault. He was sick and old
himself. *He* couldn't make it. He envied her the house, and her
woman's peaceful life. Since she returned from the hospital he
hadn't even come to visit her. He only said, "Hell, I'm sorry
for her, but it was her fault." What hurt him most was that she
had said he couldn't hold his liquor.

Fierceness, swearing to God did no good. She was still the
same procrastinating old woman. She had a letter to answer
from Hotchkiss Insurance and it drifted out of sight. She was
going to phone Claiborne the lawyer, but it slipped her mind.
One morning she announced to Helen that she believed she
would apply to an institution in Los Angeles that took over
the property of old people and managed it for them. They
gave you an apartment right on the ocean, and your meals
and medical care. You had to sign over half of your estate.
"It's fair enough," said Hattie. "They take a gamble. I may
live to be a hundred."

"I wouldn't be surprised," said Helen.

However, Hattie never got around to sending to Los
Angeles for the brochure. But Jerry Rolfe took it on himself to
write a letter to her brother Angus about her condition. And
he drove over also to have a talk with Amy Walters, the gold
miner's widow at Fort Walters—as the ancient woman called
it. The Fort was an old tar paper building over the mine. The
shaft made a cesspool unnecessary. Since the death of her
second husband no one had dug for gold. On a heap of stones
near the road a crimson sign FORT WALTERS was placed.
Behind it was a flagpole. The American flag was raised every
day.

Amy was working in the garden in one of dead Bill's shirts.
Bill had brought water down from the mountains for her in a
homemade aqueduct so she could raise her own peaches and
vegetables.

"Amy," Rolfe said, "Hattie's back from the hospital and
living all alone. You have no folks and neither has she. Not to
beat around the bush about it, why don't you live together?"

Amy's face had great delicacy. Her winter baths in the lake, her vegetable soups, the waltzes she played for herself alone on the grand piano that stood beside her wood stove, the murder stories she read till darkness obliged her to close the book—this life of hers had made her remote. She looked delicate, yet there was no way to affect her composure, she couldn't be touched. It was very strange.

"Hattie and me have different habits, Jerry," said Amy. "And Hattie wouldn't like my company. I can't drink with her. I'm a teetotaller."

"That's true," said Rolfe, recalling that Hattie referred to Amy as if she were a ghost. He couldn't speak to Amy of the solitary death in store for her. There was not a cloud in the arid sky today, and there was no shadow of death on Amy. She was tranquil, she seemed to be supplied with a sort of pure fluid that would feed her life slowly for years to come.

He said, "All kinds of things could happen to a woman like Hattie in that yellow house, and nobody would know."

"That's a fact. She doesn't know how to take care of herself."

"She can't. Her arm hasn't healed."

Amy didn't say that she was sorry to hear it. In the place of those words came a silence which might have meant that. Then she said, "I might go over there a few hours a day, but she would have to pay me."

"Now, Amy, you must know as well as I do that Hattie has no money—not much more than her pension. Just the house."

At once Amy said, no pause coming between his words and hers, "I would take care of her if she'd agree to leave the house to me."

"Leave it in your hands, you mean?" said Rolfe. "To manage?"

"In her will. To belong to me."

"Why, Amy, what would you do with Hattie's house?" he said.

"It would be my property, that's all. I'd have it."

"Maybe you would leave Fort Walters to her in your will," he said.

"Oh, no," she said. "Why should I? I'm not asking Hattie for her help. I don't need it. Hattie is a city woman."

Rolfe could not carry this proposal back to Hattie. He was too wise ever to mention her will to her.

But Pace was not so careful of her feelings. By mid-June Hattie had begun to visit his bar regularly. She had so many things to think about she couldn't stay at home. When Pace came in from the yard one day—he had been packing the wheels of his horse-trailer and was wiping grease from his fingers—he said with his usual bluntness, "How would you like it if I paid you fifty bucks a month for the rest of your life, Hat?"

Hattie was holding her second old-fashioned of the day. At the bar she made it appear that she observed the limit; but she had started drinking at home. One before lunch, one during, one after lunch. She began to grin, expecting Pace to make one of his jokes. But he was wearing his scoop-shaped Western hat as level as a Quaker, and he had drawn down his chin, a sign that he was not fooling. She said, "That would be nice, but what's the catch?"

"No catch," he said. "This is what we'd do. I'd give you five hundred dollars cash, and fifty bucks a month for life, and you let me sleep some dudes in the yellow house, and you'd leave the house to me in your will."

"What kind of a deal is that?" said Hattie, her look changing. "I thought we were friends."

"It's the best deal you'll ever get," he said.

The weather was sultry, but Hattie till now had thought that it was nice. She had been dreamy but comfortable, about to begin to enjoy the cool of the day; but now she felt that such cruelty and injustice had been waiting to attack her, that it would have been better to die in the hospital than be so disillusioned.

She cried, "Everybody wants to push me out. You're a cheater, Pace. God! I know you. Pick on somebody else. Why do you have to pick on me? Just because I happen to be around?"

"Why, no, Hattie," he said, trying now to be careful. "It was just a business offer."

"Why don't you give me some blood for the bank if you're such a friend of mine?"

"Well, Hattie, you drink too much and you oughtn't to have been driving anyway."

"I sneezed, and you know it. The whole thing happened because I sneezed. Everybody knows that. I wouldn't sell you my house. I'd give it away to the lepers first. You'd let me go away and never send me a cent. You never pay anybody. You can't even buy wholesale in town any more because nobody trusts you. I'm stuck, that's all, just stuck. I keep on saying that this is my only home in all the world, this is where my friends are, and the weather is always perfect and the lake is beautiful. But I wish the whole damn empty old place were in Hell. It's not human and neither are you. But I'll be here the day the sheriff takes away your horses—you never mind! I'll be clapping and applauding!"

He told her then that she was drunk again, and so she was, but she was more than that, and though her head was spinning she decided to go back to the house at once and take care of some things she had been putting off. This very day she was going to write to the lawyer, Claiborne, and make sure that Pace never got her property. She wouldn't put it past him to swear in court that India had promised him the yellow house.

She sat at the table with pen and paper, trying to think how to put it.

"I want this on record," she wrote. "I could kick myself in the head when I think of how he's led me on. I have been his patsy ten thousand times. As when that drunk crashed his Cub plane on the lake shore. At the coroner's jury he let me take the whole blame. He said he had instructed me when I was working for him never to take in any drunks. And this flier was drunk. He had nothing on but a T shirt and Bermuda shorts and he was flying from Sacramento to Salt Lake City. At the inquest Pace said I had disobeyed his instructions. The same was true when the cook went haywire. She was a tramp. He never hires decent help. He cheated her on the bar bill and

blamed me and she went after me with a meat cleaver. She
disliked me because I criticized her for drinking at the bar in
her one-piece white bathing suit with the dude guests. But he
turned her loose on me. He hints that he did certain services
for India. She would never have let him touch one single
finger. He was too common for her. It can never be said about
India that she was not a lady in every way. He thinks he is the
greatest sack-artist in the world. He only loves horses, as a
fact. He has no claims at all, oral or written, on this yellow
house. I want you to have this over my signature. He was cruel
to Pickle-Tits who was his first wife, and he's no better to the
charming woman who is his present one. I don't know why
she takes it. It must be despair." Hattie said to herself, *I don't
suppose I'd better send that.*

She was still angry. Her heart was knocking within; the
deep pulses, as after a hot bath, beat at the back of her thighs.
The air outside was dotted with transparent particles. The
mountains were as red as furnace clinkers. The iris leaves were
fan sticks—they stuck out like Jiggs's hair.

She always ended by looking out of the window at the
desert and lake. *They drew you from yourself. But after they had
drawn you, what did they do with you? It was too late to find out.
I'll never know. I wasn't meant to. I'm not the type,* Hattie
reflected. *Maybe something too cruel for women, young or old.*

So she stood up and, rising, she had the sensation that she
had gradually become a container for herself. You get old,
your heart, your liver, your lungs seem to expand in size, and
the walls of the body give way outward, swelling, she thought,
and you take the shape of an old jug, wider and wider toward
the top. You swell up with tears and fat. She no longer even
smelled to herself like a woman. Her face with its much-slept-
upon skin was only faintly like her own—like a cloud that has
changed. It was a face. It became a ball of yarn. It had drifted
open. It had scattered.

I was never one single thing anyway, she thought. *Never my
own. I was only loaned to myself.*

But the thing wasn't over yet. And in fact she didn't know

for certain that it was ever going to be over. You only had
other people's word for it that death was such-and-such. How
do I know? she asked herself challengingly. Her anger had
sobered her for a little while. Now she was again drunk. . . . *It
was strange. It is strange. It may continue being strange.* She
further thought, *I used to wish for death more than I do now.
Because I didn't have anything at all. I changed when I got a roof
of my own over me. And now? Do I have to go? I thought Marian
loved me, but she already has a sister. And I thought Helen and
Jerry would never desert me, but they've beat it. And now Pace
has insulted me. They think I'm not going to make it.*

She went to the cupboard—she kept the bourbon bottle
there; she drank less if each time she had to rise and open the
cupboard door. And, as if she were being watched, she poured
a drink and swallowed it.

The notion that in this emptiness someone saw her was
connected with the other notion that she was being filmed
from birth to death. That this was done for everyone. And
afterward you could view your life. A hereafter movie.

Hattie wanted to see some of it now, and she sat down on
the dogs'-paw cushions of her sofa and, with her knees far
apart and a smile of yearning and of fright, she bent her round
back, burned a cigarette at the corner of her mouth and
saw—the Church of Saint Sulpice in Paris where her organ
teacher used to bring her. It looked like country walls of stone,
but rising high and leaning outward were towers. She was very
young. She knew music. How she could ever have been so
clever was beyond her. But she did know it. She could read all
those notes. The sky was gray. After this she saw some
entertaining things she liked to tell people about. She was a
young wife. She was in Aix-les-Bains with her mother-in-law,
and they played bridge in a mud bath with a British general
and his aide. There were artificial waves in the swimming
pool. She lost her bathing suit because it was a size too big.
How did she get out? Ah, you got out of everything.

She saw her husband, James John Waggoner IV. They were
snow-bound together in New Hampshire. "Jimmy, Jimmy,

how can you fling a wife away?" she asked him. "Have you
forgotten love? Did I drink too much—did I bore you?" He
had married again and had two children. He had gotten tired
of her. And though he was a vain man with nothing to be vain
about—no looks, not too much intelligence, nothing but an
old Philadelphia family—she had loved him. She too had been
a snob about her Philadelphia connections. Give up the name
of Waggoner? How could she? For this reason she had never
married Wicks. "How dare you," she had said to Wicks,
"come without a shave in a dirty shirt and muck on you, come
and ask me to marry! If you want to propose, go and clean up
first." But his dirt was only a pretext.

Trade Waggoner for Wicks? she asked herself again with a
swing of her shoulders. She wouldn't think of it. Wicks was an
excellent man. But he was a cowboy. Socially nothing. He
couldn't even read. But she saw this on her film. They were in
Athens Canyon, in a cratelike house, and she was reading
aloud to him from *The Count of Monte Cristo*. He wouldn't let
her stop. While walking to stretch her legs, she read, and he
followed her about to catch each word. After all, he was very
dear to her. Such a man! Now she saw him jump from his
horse. They were living on the range, trapping coyotes. It was
just the second gray of evening, cloudy, moments after the sun
had gone down. There was an animal in the trap, and he went
toward it to kill it. He wouldn't waste a bullet on the creatures
but killed them with a kick, with his boot. And then Hattie
saw that this coyote was all white—snarling teeth, white scruff.
"Wicks, he's white! White as a polar bear. You're not going to
kill him, are you?" The animal flattened to the ground. He
snarled and cried. He couldn't pull away because of the heavy
trap. And Wicks killed him. What else could he have done?
The white beast lay dead. The dust of Wicks's boots hardly
showed on its head and jaws. Blood ran from the muzzle.

And now came something on Hattie's film she tried to shun.
It was she herself who had killed her dog, Richie. Just as Rolfe
and Pace had warned her, he was vicious, his brain was

turned. She, because she was on the side of all dumb
creatures, defended him when he bit the trashy woman
Jacamares was living with. Perhaps if she had had Richie from
a puppy he wouldn't have turned on her. When she got him he
was already a year and a half old and she couldn't break him
of his habits. But she thought that only she understood him.
And Rolfe had warned her, "You'll be sued, do you know
that? The dog will take out after somebody smarter than that
Jacamares's woman, and you'll be in for it."

Hattie saw herself as she swayed her shoulders and said,
"Nonsense."

But what fear she had felt when the dog went for her on the
porch. Suddenly she could see, by his skull, by his eyes, that
he was evil. She screamed at him, "Richie!" And what had she
done to him? He had lain under the gas range all day growling
and wouldn't come out. She tried to urge him out with the
broom, and he snatched it in his teeth. She pulled him out,
and he left the stick and tore at her. Now, as the spectator of
this, her eyes opened, beyond the pregnant curtain and the
air-wave of marl dust, summer's snow, drifting over the water.
"Oh, my God! Richie!" Her thigh was snatched by his jaws.
His teeth went through her skirt. She felt she would fall.
Would she go down? Then the dog would rush at her
throat—then black night, bad-odored mouth, the blood pouring from her neck, from torn veins. Her heart shriveled as the
teeth went into her thigh, and she couldn't delay another
second but took her kindling hatchet from the nail, strengthened her grip on the smooth wood, and hit the dog. She saw
the blow. She saw him die at once. And then in fear and
shame she hid the body. And at night she buried him in the
yard. Next day she accused Jacamares. On him she laid the
blame for the disappearance of her dog.

She stood up; she spoke to herself in silence, as was her
habit. *God, what shall I do? I have taken life. I have lied. I have
borne false witness. I have stalled. And now what shall I do?
Nobody will help me.*

And suddenly she made up her mind that she should go and

do what she had been putting off for weeks, namely, test herself with the car, and she slipped on her shoes and went outside. Lizards ran before her in the thirsty dust. She opened the hot, broad door of the car. She lifted her lame hand onto the wheel. With her right hand she reached far to the left and turned the wheel with all her might. Then she started the motor and tried to drive out of the yard. But she could not release the emergency brake with its rasplike rod. She reached with her good hand, the right, under the steering wheel and pressed her bosom on it and strained. No, she could not shift the gears and steer. She couldn't even reach down to the hand brake. The sweat broke out on her skin. Her efforts were too much. She was deeply wounded by the pain in her arm. The door of the car fell open again and she turned from the wheel and with her stiff legs hanging from the door she wept. What could she do now? And when she had wept over the ruin of her life she got out of the old car and went back to the house. She took the bourbon from the cupboard and picked up the ink bottle and a pad of paper and sat down to write her will.

"My Will," she wrote, and sobbed to herself.

Since the death of India she had numberless times asked the question, To Whom? Who will get this when I die? She had unconsciously put people to the test to find out whether they were worthy. It made her more severe than before.

Now she wrote, "I Harriet Simmons Waggoner, being of sound mind and not knowing what may be in store for me at the age of seventy-two (born 1885), living alone at Sego Desert Lake, instruct my lawyer, Harold Claiborne, Paiute County Court Building, to draw my last will and testament upon the following terms."

She sat perfectly still now to hear from within who would be the lucky one, who would inherit the yellow house. For which she had waited. Yes, waited for India's death, choking on her bread because she was a rich woman's servant and whipping girl. But who had done for her, Hattie, what she had done for India? And who, apart from India, had ever held out a hand to her? Kindness, yes. Here and there people had been kind. But the word in her head was not kindness, it was succor. And who had given her that? *Succor?* Only India. If at least, next best after succor, someone had given her a shake and said, "Stop stalling. Don't be such a slow, old, procrastinating sit-stiller." Again, it was only India who had done her good. She had offered her succor. "Het-tie!" said that drunken mask. "Do you know what sloth is? Demn you! poky old demned thing!"

But I was waiting, Hattie realized. *I was waiting, thinking, "Youth is terrible, frightening. I will wait it out. And men? Men are cruel and strong. They want things I haven't got to give."* There were no kids in me, thought Hattie. *Not that I wouldn't have loved them, but such my nature was. And who can blame me for having it? My nature?*

She drank from an old-fashioned glass. There was no orange in it, no ice, no bitters or sugar, only the stinging, clear bourbon.

So then, she continued, looking at the dry sun-stamped dust and the last freckled flowers of red wild peach, *to live with Angus and his wife? And to have to hear a chapter from the Bible before breakfast? Once more in the house—not of a stranger, perhaps, but not far from it either?* In other houses, in someone else's house, to wait for mealtimes was her lifelong punishment. She always felt it in the throat and stomach. And so she would again, and to the very end. However, she must think of someone to leave the house to.

And first of all she wanted to do right by her family. None of them had ever dreamed that she, Hattie, would ever have something to bequeath. Until a few years ago it had certainly looked as if she would die a pauper. So now she could keep her head up with the proudest of them. And, as this occurred to her, she actually lifted up her face with its broad nose and victorious eyes; if her hair had become shabby as onion roots, if, at the back, her head was round and bald as a newel post, what did that matter? Her heart experienced a childish glory, not yet tired of it after seventy-two years. She, too, had

amounted to something. *I'll do some good by going*, she
thought. *Now I believe I should leave it to, to* . . . She returned
to the old point of struggle. She had decided many times and
many times changed her mind. She tried to think, *Who would
get the most out of this yellow house?* It was a tearing thing to go
through. If it had not been the house but, instead, some brittle
thing she could hold in her hand, then her last action would be
to throw and smash it, and so the thing and she herself would
be demolished together. But it was vain to think such
thoughts. To whom should she leave it? Her brothers? Not
they. Nephews? One was a submarine commander. The other
was a bachelor in the State Department. Then began the roll
call of cousins. Merton? He owned an estate in Connecticut.
Anna? She had a face like a hot-water bottle. That left Joyce,
the orphaned daughter of her cousin Wilfred. Joyce was the
most likely heiress. Hattie had already written to her and had
her out to the lake at Thanksgiving, two years ago. But this
Joyce was another odd one; over thirty, good, yes, but placid,
running to fat, a scholar—ten years in Eugene, Oregon,
working for her degree. In Hattie's opinion this was only
another form of sloth. Nevertheless, Joyce yet hoped to marry.
Whom? Not Dr. Stroud. He wouldn't. And still Joyce had
vague hopes. Hattie knew how that could be. At least have a
man she could argue with.

She was now more drunk than at any time since her
accident. Again she filled her glass. *Have ye eyes and see not?
Sleepers awake!*

Knees wide apart she sat in the twilight, thinking. Marian?
Marian didn't need another house. Half Pint? She wouldn't
know what to do with it. Brother Louis came up for
consideration next. He was an old actor who had a church for
the Indians at Athens Canyon. Hollywood stars of the silent
days sent him their negligees; he altered them and wore them
in the pulpit. The Indians loved his show. But when Billy
Shawah blew his brains out after his two-week bender, they
still tore his shack down and turned the boards inside out to
get rid of his ghost. They had their old religion. No, not
Brother Louis. He'd show movies in the yellow house to the

tribe or make a nursery out of it for the Indian brats.

And now she began to consider Wicks. When last heard from he was south of Bishop, California, a handy man in a saloon off toward Death Valley. It wasn't she who heard from him but Pace. Herself, she hadn't actually seen Wicks since—how low she had sunk then!—she had kept the hamburger stand on Route 158. The little lunchroom had supported them both. Wicks hung around on the end stool, rolling cigarettes (she saw it on the film). Then there was a quarrel. Things had been going from bad to worse. He'd begun to grouse now about this and now about that. He beefed about the food, at last. She saw and heard him. "Hat," he said, "I'm good and tired of hamburger." "Well, what do you think I eat?" she said with that round, defiant movement of her shoulders which she herself recognized as characteristic (*me all over*, she thought). But he opened the cash register and took out thirty cents and crossed the street to the butcher's and brought back a steak. He threw it on the griddle. "Fry it," he said. She did, and watched him eat.

And when he was through she could bear her rage no longer. "Now," she said, "you've had your meat. Get out. Never come back." She kept a pistol under the counter. She picked it up, cocked it, pointed it at his heart. "If you ever come in that door again, I'll kill you," she said.

She saw it all. *I couldn't bear to fall so low*, she thought, *to be slave to a shiftless cowboy.*

Wicks said, "Don't do that, Hat. Guess I went too far. You're right."

"You'll never have a chance to make it up," she cried. "Get out!"

On that cry he disappeared, and since then she had never seen him.

"Wicks, dear," she said. "Please! I'm sorry. Don't condemn me in your heart. Forgive me. I hurt myself in my evil. I always had a thick idiot head. I was born with a thick head."

Again she wept, for Wicks. She was too proud. A snob. Now they might have lived together in this house, old friends, simple and plain.

She thought, *He really was my good friend.*

But what would Wicks do with a house like this, alone, if he was alive and survived her? He was too wiry for soft beds or easy chairs.

And she was the one who had said stiffly to India, "I'm a Christian person. I do not bear a grudge."

Ah yes, she said to herself. *I have caught myself out too often. How long can this go on?* And she began to think, or try to think, of Joyce, her cousin's daughter. Joyce was like herself, a woman alone, getting on in years, clumsy. Probably never been laid. Too bad. She would have given much, now, to succor Joyce.

But it seemed to her now that that too, the succor, had been a story. First you heard the pure story. Then you heard the impure story. Both stories. She had paid out years, now to one shadow, now to another shadow.

Joyce would come here to the house. She had a little income and could manage. She would live as Hattie had lived, alone. Here she would rot, start to drink, maybe, and day after day read, day after day sleep. See how beautiful it was here? It burned you out. How empty! It turned you into ash.

How can I doom a younger person to the same life? asked Hattie. It's for somebody like me. When I was younger it wasn't right. But now it is, exactly. Only I fit in here. It was made for my old age, to spend my last years peacefully. If I hadn't let Jerry make me drunk that night—if I hadn't sneezed! Because of this arm, I'll have to live with Angus. My heart will break there away from my only home.

She was now very drunk, and she said to herself, *Take what God brings. He gives no gifts unmixed. He makes loans.*

She resumed her letter of instructions to lawyer Claiborne: "Upon the following terms," she wrote a second time. "Because I have suffered much. Because I only lately received what I have to give away, I can't bear it." The drunken blood was soaring to her head. But her hand was clear enough. She wrote, "It is too soon! Too soon! Because I do not find it in my heart to care for anyone as I would wish. Being cast off and lonely, and doing no harm where I am. Why should it be? This breaks my heart. In addition to everything else, why must I worry about this, which I must leave? I am tormented out of my mind. Even though by my own fault I have put myself into this position. And I am not ready to give up on this. No, not yet. And so I'll tell you what, I leave this property, land, house, garden, and water rights, to Hattie Simmons Waggoner. Me! I realize this is bad and wrong. Not possible. Yet it is the only thing I really wish to do, so may God have mercy on my soul."

How could that happen? She studied what she had written and finally she acknowledged that she was drunk. "I'm drunk," she said, "and don't know what I'm doing. I'll die, and end. Like India. Dead as that lilac bush."

Then she thought that there was a beginning, and a middle. She shrank from the last term. She began once more—a beginning. After that, there was the early middle, then middle middle, late middle middle, quite late middle. In fact the middle is all I know. The rest is just a rumor.

Only tonight I can't give the house away. I'm drunk and so I need it. And tomorrow, she promised herself, I'll think again. I'll work it out, for sure.

Mosby's
Memoirs

The birds chirped away. Fweet, Fweet, Boot-
chee-Fweet. Doing all the things naturalists say they do.
Expressing abysmal depths of aggression, which only Man—
Stupid Man—heard as innocence. We feel everything is so
innocent—because our wickedness is so fearful. Oh, very
fearful!

Mr. Willis Mosby, after his siesta, gazing down-mountain at
the town of Oaxaca where all were snoozing still—mouths,
rumps, long black Indian hair, the antique beauty photo-
graphically celebrated by Eisenstein in *Thunder over Mexico*.
Mr. Mosby—Dr. Mosby really; erudite, maybe even profound; thought much, accomplished much—had made some
of the most interesting mistakes a man could make in the
twentieth century. He was in Oaxaca now to write his
memoirs. He had a grant for the purpose, from the Guggenheim Foundation. And why not?

Bougainvillaea poured down the hillside, and the humming-
birds were spinning. Mosby felt ill with all this whirling, these
colors, fragrances, ready to topple on him. Liveliness, beauty,
seemed very dangerous. Mortal danger. Maybe he had drunk
too much mescal at lunch (beer, also). Behind the green and
red of Nature, dull black seemed to be thickly laid like mirror
backing.

Mosby did not feel quite well; his teeth, gripped tight, made
the muscles stand out in his handsome, elderly tanned jaws.
He had fine blue eyes, light-pained, direct, intelligent, disbe-

lieving; hair still thick, parted in the middle; and strong vertical grooves between the brows, beneath the nostrils, and at the back of the neck.

The time had come to put some humor into the memoirs. So far it had been: Fundamentalist family in Missouri—Father the successful builder—Early schooling—The State University—Rhodes Scholarship—Intellectual friendships—What I learned from Professor Collingwood—Empire and the mental vigor of Britain—My unorthodox interpretation of John Locke—I work for William Randolph Hearst in Spain—The personality of General Franco—Radical friendships in New York—Wartime service with the O.S.S.—The limited vision of Franklin D. Roosevelt—Comte, Proudhon, and Marx revisited—de Tocqueville once again.

Nothing very funny here. And yet thousands of students and others would tell you, "Mosby had a great sense of humor." Would tell their children, "This Mosby in the O.S.S.," or "Willis Mosby, who was in Toledo with me when the Alcázar fell, made me die laughing." "I shall never forget Mosby's observations on Harold Laski." "On packing the Supreme Court." "On the Russian purge trials." "On Hitler." So it was certainly high time to do something. He had given it some consideration. He would say, when they sent down his ice from the hotel bar (he was in a cottage below the main building, flowers heaped upon it; envying a little the unencumbered mountains of the Sierra Madre) and when he had chilled his mescal—warm, it tasted rotten—he would write that in 1947, when he was living in Paris, he knew any number of singular people. He knew the Comte de la Mine-Crevée, who sheltered Gary Davis the World Citizen after the World Citizen had burnt his passport publicly. He knew Mr. Julian Huxley at UNESCO. He discussed social theory with Mr. Lévi-Straus but was not invited to dinner—they ate at the Musée de l'Homme. Sartre refused to meet with him; he thought all Americans, Negroes excepted, were secret agents. Mosby for his part suspected all Russians abroad of working for the G.P.U. Mosby knew French well; extremely fluent in

Spanish; quite good in German. But the French cannot identify originality in foreigners. That is the curse of an old civilization. It is a heavier planet. Its best minds must double their horsepower to overcome the gravitational field of tradition. Only a few will ever fly. To fly away from Descartes. To fly away from the political anachronisms of left, center, and right persisting since 1789. Mosby found these French exceedingly banal. These French found him lean and tight. In well-tailored clothes, elegant and dry, his good Western skin, pale eyes, strong nose, handsome mouth, and virile creases. *Un type sec.*

Both sides—Mosby and the French, that is—with highly developed attitudes. Both, he was lately beginning to concede, quite wrong. Possibly equidistant from the truth, but lying in different sectors of error. The French were worse off because their errors were collective. Mine, Mosby believed, were at least peculiar. The French were furious over the collapse in 1940 of *La France Pourrie,* their lack of military will, the extensive collaboration, the massive deportations unopposed (the Danes, even the *Bulgarians* resisted Jewish deportations), and, finally, over the humiliation of liberation by the Allies. Mosby, in the O.S.S., had information to support such views. Within the State Department, too, he had university colleagues—former students and old acquaintances. He had expected a high postwar appointment, for which, as director of counter-espionage in Latin America, he was ideally qualified. But Dean Acheson personally disliked him. Nor did Dulles approve. Mosby, a fanatic about *ideas,* displeased the institutional gentry. He had said that the Foreign Service was staffed by rejects of the power structure. Young gentlemen from good Eastern colleges who couldn't make it as Wall Street lawyers were allowed to interpret the alleged interests of their class in the State Department bureaucracy. In foreign consulates they could be rude to D.P.s and indulge their country-club anti-Semitism, which was dying out even in the country clubs. Besides, Mosby had sympathized with the Burnham position on managerialism, declaring, during

the war, that the Nazis were winning because they had made
their managerial revolution first. No Allied combination could
conquer, with its obsolete industrialism, a nation which had
reached a new state of history and tapped the power of the
inevitable, etc. And then Mosby, holding forth in Washington,
among the elite Scotch drinkers, stated absolutely that however deplorable the concentration camps had been, they
showed at least the rationality of German political ideas. The
Americans had no such ideas. They didn't know what they
were doing. No design existed. The British were not much
better. The Hamburg fire-bombing, he argued in his clipped
style, in full declarative phrases, betrayed the idiotic emptiness
and planlessness of Western leadership. Finally, he said that
when Acheson blew his nose there were maggots in his
handkerchief.

Among the defeated French, Mosby admitted that he had a
galled spirit. (His jokes were not too bad.) And of course he
drank a lot. He worked on Marx and Tocqueville, and he
drank. He would not cease from mental strife. The Comte de
la Mine-Crevée (Mosby's own improvisation on a noble and
ancient name) kept him in PX booze and exchanged his
money on the black market for him. He described his swindles
and was very entertaining.

Mosby now wished to say, in the vein of Sir Harold
Nicolson or Santayana or Bertrand Russell, writers for whose
memoirs he had the greatest admiration, that Paris in 1947,
like half a Noah's Ark, was waiting for the second of each
kind to arrive. There was one of everything. Something of this
sort. Especially among Americans. The city was very bitter,
grim; the Seine looked and smelled like medicine. At an
American party, a former student of French from Minnesota,
now running a shady enterprise, an agency which specialized
in bribery, private undercover investigations, and procuring
broads for V.I.P.s, said something highly emotional about the
City of Man, about the meaning of Europe for Americans, the
American failure to preserve human scale. Not omitting to
work in Man the Measure. And every other tag he could bring

back from Randall's *Making of the Modern Mind* or *Readings
in the Intellectual History of Europe*. "I was tempted," Mosby
meant to say (the ice arrived in a glass jar with tongs; the
natives no longer wore the dirty white drawers of the past).
"Tempted . . ." He rubbed his forehead, which projected like
the back of an observation car. "To tell this sententious little
drunkard and gyp artist, formerly a pacifist and vegetarian,
follower of Gandhi at the University of Minnesota, now
driving a very handsome Bentley to the Tour d'Argent to eat
duck *à l'orange*. Tempted to say, 'Yes, but we come here
across the Atlantic to relax a bit in the past. To recall what
Ezra Pound had once said. That we would make another
Venice, just for the hell of it, in the Jersey marshes any time
we liked. Toying. To divert ourselves in the time of colossal
mastery to come. Reproducing anything, for fun. Baboons
trained to row will bring us in gondolas to discussions of
astrophysics. Where folks burn garbage now, and fatten pigs
and junk their old machines, we will debark to hear a
concert.' "

Mosby the thinker, like other busy men, never had time for
music. Poetry was not his cup of tea. Members of Congress,
Cabinet officers, Organization Men, Pentagon planners, Party
leaders, Presidents had no such interests. They could not be
what they were and read Eliot, hear Vivaldi, Cimarosa. But
they planned that others might enjoy these things and benefit
by their power. Mosby perhaps had more in common with
political leaders and Joint Chiefs and Presidents. At least, they
were in his thoughts more often than Cimarosa and Eliot.
With hate, he pondered their mistakes, their shallowness.
Lectured on Locke to show them up. Except by the will of the
majority, unambiguously expressed, there was no legitimate
power. The only absolute democrat in America (perhaps in
the world—although who can know what there is in the world,
among so many billions of minds and souls) was Willis
Mosby. Notwithstanding his terse, dry, intolerant style of
conversation (more precisely, examination), his lank dignity of
person, his aristocratic bones. Dark long nostrils hinting at the

afflictions that needed the strength you could see in his jaws.
And, finally, the light-pained eyes.

A most peculiar, ingenious, hungry, aspiring, and heartbroken animal, who, by calling himself Man, thinks he can
escape being what he really is. Not a matter of his definition,
in the last analysis, but of his being. Let him say what he likes.

> Kingdoms are clay: our dungy earth alike
> Feeds beast as man; the nobleness of life
> Is to do thus.

Thus being love. Or any other sublime option. (Mosby knew
his Shakespeare anyway. *There* was a difference from the
President. And of the Vice-President he said, "I wouldn't trust
him to make me a pill. A has-been druggist!")

With sober lips he sipped the mescal, the servant in the
coarse orange shirt enriched by metal buttons reminding him
that the car was coming at four o'clock to take him to Mitla,
to visit the ruins.

"*Yo mismo soy una ruina,*" Mosby joked.

The stout Indian, giving only so much of a smile—no
more—withdrew with quiet courtesy. Perhaps I was fishing,
Mosby considered. Wanted him to say I was *not* a ruin. But
how could he? Seeing that for him I *am* one.

Perhaps Mosby did not have a light touch. Still, he thought
he did have an eye for certain kinds of comedy. And he *must*
find a way to relieve the rigor of this account of his mental
wars. Besides, he could really remember that in Paris at that
time people, one after another, revealed themselves in a comic
light. He was then seeing things that way. Rue Jacob, Rue
Bonaparte, Rue du Bac, Rue de Verneuil, Hôtel de l'Uni-
versité—filled with funny people.

He began by setting down a name: Lustgarten. Yes, there
was the man he wanted. Hymen Lustgarten, a Marxist, or
former Marxist, from New Jersey. From Newark, I think. He
had been a shoe salesman, and belonged to any number of
heretical, fanatical, bolshevistic groups. He had been a

Leninist, a Trotskyist, then a follower of Hugo Oehler, then of Thomas Stamm, and finally of an Italian named Salemme who gave up politics to become a painter, an abstractionist. Lustgarten also gave up politics. He wanted now to be successful in business—rich. Believing that the nights he had spent poring over *Das Kapital* and Lenin's *State and Revolution* would give him an edge in business dealings. We were staying in the same hotel. I couldn't at first make out what he and his wife were doing. Presently I understood. The black market. This was not then reprehensible. Postwar Europe was like that. Refugees, adventurers, G.I.s. Even the Comte de la M.-C. Europe still shuddering from the blows it had received. Governments new, uncertain, infirm. No reason to respect their authority. American soldiers led the way. Flamboyant business schemes. Machines, whole factories, stolen, treasures shipped home. An American colonel in the lumber business started to saw up the Black Forest and send it to Wisconsin. And, of course, Nazis concealing their concentration-camp loot. Jewels sunk in Austrian lakes. Art works hidden. Gold extracted from teeth in extermination camps, melted into ingots and mortared like bricks into the walls of houses. Incredibly huge fortunes to be made, and Lustgarten intended to make one of them. Unfortunately, he was incompetent.

You could see at once that there was no harm in him. Despite the bold revolutionary associations, and fierceness of doctrine. Theoretical willingness to slay class enemies. But Lustgarten could not even hold his own with pushy people in a *pissoir*. Strangely meek, stout, swarthy, kindly, grinning with mulberry lips, a froggy, curving mouth which produced wrinkles like gills between the ears and the grin. And perhaps, Mosby thought, he comes to mind in Mexico because of his Toltec, Mixtec, Zapotec look, squat and black-haired, the tip of his nose turned downward and the black nostrils shyly widening when his friendly smile was accepted. And a bit sick with the wickedness, the awfulness of life but, respectfully persistent, bound to get his share. Efficiency was his style— action, determination, but a traitorous incompetence trembled within. Wrong calling. Wrong choice. A bad mistake. But he was persistent.

His conversation amused me, in the dining room. He was proud of his revolutionary activities, which had consisted mainly of cranking the mimeograph machine. Internal Bulletins. Thousands of pages of recondite examination of fine points of doctrine for the membership. Whether the American working class should give *material* aid to the Loyalist Government of Spain, controlled as that was by Stalinists and other class enemies and traitors. You had to fight Franco, and you had to fight Stalin as well. There was, of course, no material aid to give. But *had* there been any, *should* it have been given? This purely theoretical problem caused splits and expulsions. I always kept myself informed of these curious agonies of sectarianism, Mosby wrote. The single effort made by Spanish Republicans to purchase arms in the United States was thwarted by that friend of liberty Franklin Delano Roosevelt, who allowed one ship, the *Mar Cantábrico*, to be loaded but set the Coast Guard after it to turn it back to port. It was, I believe, that *genius* of diplomacy, Mr. Cordell Hull, who was responsible, but the decision, of course, was referred to F.D.R., whom Huey Long amusingly called Franklin de la *No!* But perhaps the most refined of these internal discussions left of left, the documents for which were turned out on the machine by that Jimmy Higgins, the tubby devoted party-worker Mr. Lustgarten, had to do with the Finnish War. Here the painful point of doctrine to be resolved was whether a Workers' State like the Soviet Union, even if it was a *degenerate* Workers' State, a product of the Thermidorian Reaction following the glorious Proletarian Revolution of 1917, could wage an Imperialistic War. For only the *bourgeoisie* could be Imperialistic. Technically, Stalinism could not be Imperialism. By definition. What then should a Revolutionary Party say to the Finns? Should they resist Russia or not? The Russians were monsters but they would expropriate the Mannerheim White-Guardist landowners and move, painful though it might be, in the correct historical direction. This, as a sect-watcher, I greatly relished. But it was too foreign a subtlety for many of the sectarians. Who were, after all, Americans. Pragmatists at heart. It was *too* far out for Lustgarten. He decided, after the war, to become (it shouldn't be hard) a rich man. Took his savings and, I believe his wife said, his mother's savings, and went abroad to build a fortune.

Within a year he had lost it all. He was cheated. By a German partner, in particular. But also he was caught smuggling by Belgian authorities.

When Mosby met him (Mosby speaking of himself in the third person as Henry Adams had done in *The Education of Henry Adams*)—when Mosby met him, Lustgarten was working for the American Army, employed by Graves Registration. Something to do with the procurement of crosses. Or with supervision of the lawns. Official employment gave Lustgarten PX privileges. He was rebuilding his financial foundations by the illegal sale of cigarettes. He dealt also in gas-ration coupons which the French Government, anxious to obtain dollars, would give you if you exchanged your money at the legal rate. The gas coupons were sold on the black market. The Lustgartens, husband and wife, persuaded Mosby to do this once. For them, he cashed his dollars at the bank, not with la Mine-Crevée. The occasion seemed important. Mosby gathered that Lustgarten had to drive at once to Munich. He had gone into the dental-supply business there with a German dentist who now denied that they had ever been partners.

Many consultations between Lustgarten (in his international intriguer's trenchcoat, ill-fitting; head, neck, and shoulders sloping backward in a froggy curve) and his wife, a young woman in an eyelet-lace blouse and black velveteen skirt, a velveteen ribbon tied on her round, healthy neck. Lustgarten, on the circular floor of the bank, explaining as they stood apart. And sweating blood; being reasonable with Trudy, detail by tortuous detail. It grated away poor Lustgarten's patience. Hands feebly remonstrating. For she asked female questions or raised objections which gave him agonies of

patient rationality. Only there was nothing rational to begin
with. That is, he had had no legal right to go into business
with the German. All such arrangements had to be licensed by
the Military Government. It was a black-market partnership
and when it began to show a profit, the German threw
Lustgarten out. With what they call impunity. Germany as a
whole having discerned the limits of all civilized systems of
punishment as compared with the unbounded possibilities of
crime. The bank in Paris, where these explanations between
Lustgarten and Trudy were taking place, had an interior of
some sort of red porphyry. Like raw meat. A color which
bourgeois France seemed to have vested with ideas of
potency, mettle, and grandeur. In the Invalides also, Napoleon's sarcophagus was of polished red stone, a great, swooping,
polished cradle containing the little green corpse. (We have
the testimony of M. Rideau, the Bonapartist historian, as to
the color.) As for the living Bonaparte, Mosby felt, with
Auguste Comte, that he had been an anachronism. The
Revolution was historically necessary. It was socially justified.
Politically, economically, it was a move toward industrial
democracy. But the Napoleonic drama itself belonged to an
archaic category of personal ambitions, feudal ideas of war.
Older than feudalism. Older than Rome. The commander at
the head of armies—nothing rational to recommend it.
Society, increasingly rational in its organization, did not need
it. But humankind evidently desired it. War is a luxurious
pleasure. Grant the first premise of hedonism and you must
accept the rest also. Rational foundations of modernity are
cunningly accepted by man as the launching platform of ever
wilder irrationalities.

Mosby, writing these reflections in a blue-green color of ink
which might have been extracted from the landscape. As his
liquor had been extracted from the green spikes of the mescal,
the curious sharp, dark-green fleshy limbs of the plant
covering the fields.

The dollars, the francs, the gas rations, the bank like the
beefsteak mine in which W. C. Fields invested, and shrinking

but persistent dark Lustgarten getting into his little car on the sodden Parisian street. There were few cars then in Paris. Plenty of parking space. And the streets were so yellow, gray, wrinkled, dismal. But the French were even then ferociously telling the world that they had the *savoir-vivre*, the *gai savoir*. Especially Americans, haunted by their Protestant Ethic, had to hear this. My God—sit down, sip wine, taste cheese, break bread, hear music, know love, stop running, and learn ancient life-wisdom from Europe. At any rate, Lustgarten buckled up his trenchcoat, pulled down his big hoodlum's fedora. He was bunched up in the seat. Small brown hands holding the steering wheel of the Simca Huit, and the grinning despair with which he waved.

"*Bon voyage,* Lustgarten."

His Zapotec nose, his teeth like white pomegranate seeds. With a sob of the gears he took off for devastated Germany.

Reconstruction is big business. You demolish a society, you decrease the population, and off you go again. New fortunes. Lustgarten may have felt, *qua* Jew, that he had a right to grow rich in the German boom. That all Jews had natural claims beyond the Rhine. On land enriched by Jewish ashes. And you never could be sure, seated on a sofa, that it was not stuffed or upholstered with Jewish hair. And he would not use German soap. He washed his hands, Trudy told Mosby, with Lifebuoy from the PX.

Trudy, a graduate of Montclair Teachers' College in New Jersey, knew French, studied composition, had hoped to work with someone like Nadia Boulanger, but was obliged to settle for less. From the bank, as Lustgarten drove away in a kind of doomed, latently tearful daring in the rain-drenched street, Trudy invited Mosby to the Salle Pleyel, to hear a Czech pianist performing Schönberg. This man, with muscular baldness, worked very hard upon the keys. The difficulty of his enterprise alone came through—the labor of culture, the trouble it took to preserve art in tragic Europe, the devoted drill. Trudy had a nice face for concerts. Her odor was agreeable. She shone. In the left half of her countenance, one eye kept wandering. Stone-hearted Mosby, making fun of flesh and blood, of these little humanities with their short inventories of bad and good. The poor Czech in his blazer with chased buttons and the muscles of his forehead rising in protest against *tabula rasa*—the bare skull.

Mosby could abstract himself on such occasions. Shut out the piano. Continue thinking about Comte. Begone, old priests and feudal soldiers! Go, with Theology and Metaphysics! And in the Positive Epoch Enlightened Woman would begin to play her part, vigilant, preventing the managers of the new society from abusing their powers. Over Labor, the Supreme Good.

Embroidering the trees, the birds of Mexico, looking at Mosby, and the hummingbird, so neat in its lust, vibrating tinily, and the lizard on the soil drinking heat with its belly. To bless small creatures is supposed to be real good.

Yes, this Lustgarten was a funny man. Cheated in Germany, licked by the partner, and impatient with his slow progress in Graves Registration, he decided to import a Cadillac. Among the new postwar millionaires of Europe there was a big demand for Cadillacs. The French Government, moving slowly, had not yet taken measures against such imports for rapid resale. In 1947, no tax prevented such transactions. Lustgarten got his family in Newark to ship a new Cadillac. Something like four thousand dollars was raised by his brother, his mother, his mother's brother for the purpose. The car was sent. The customer was waiting. A down payment had already been given. A double profit was expected. Only, on the day the car was unloaded at Le Havre new regulations went into effect. The Cadillac could not be sold. Lustgarten was stuck with it. He couldn't even afford to buy gas. The Lustgartens were seen one day moving out of the hotel, into the car. Mrs. Lustgarten went to live with musical friends. Mosby offered Lustgarten the use of his sink for washing and shaving. Weary Lustgarten, defeated, depressed, frightened at last by his own plunging, scraped at his bristles, mornings, with a modest cricket noise, while sighing. All that money—mother's savings, brother's pension. No wonder his eyelids turned blue. And his smile, like a spinster's sachet, the last fragrance ebbed out long ago in the trousseau never used. But the long batrachian lips continued smiling.

Mosby realized that compassion should be felt. But passing in the night the locked, gleaming car, and seeing huddled Lustgarten, sleeping, covered with two coats, on the majestic seat, like Jonah inside Leviathan, Mosby could not say in candor that what he experienced was sympathy. Rather he reflected that this shoe salesman, in America attached to foreign doctrines, who could not relinquish Europe in the New World, was now, in Paris, sleeping in the Cadillac, encased in this gorgeous Fisher Body from Detroit. At home exotic, in Europe a Yankee. His timing was off. He recognized this himself. But believed, in general, that he was too early. A pioneer. For instance, he said, in a voice that creaked with shy assertiveness, the French were only now beginning to be Marxians. He had gone through it all years ago. What did these people know! Ask them about the Shakhty Engineers! About Lenin's Democratic Centralism! About the Moscow Trials! About "Social Fascism"! They were ignorant. The Revolution having been totally betrayed, these Europeans suddenly discovered Marx and Lenin. "Eureka!" he said in a high voice. And it was the Cold War, beneath it all. For should America lose, the French intellectuals were preparing to collaborate with Russia. And should America win they could still be free, defiant radicals under American protection.

"You sound like a patriot," said Mosby.

"Well, in a way I am," said Lustgarten. "But I am getting to be objective. Sometimes I say to myself, 'If you were outside the world, if you, Lustgarten, didn't exist as a man, what would your opinion be of this or that?'"

"Disembodied truth."

"I guess that's what it is."

"And what are you going to do about the Cadillac?" said Mosby.

"I'm sending it to Spain. We can sell it in Barcelona."

"But you have to get it there."

"Through Andorra. It's all arranged. Klonsky is driving it."

Klonsky was a Polish Belgian in the hotel. One of Lustgarten's associates, congenitally dishonest, Mosby thought. Kinky hair, wrinkled eyes like Greek olives, and a cat nose and cat lips. He wore Russian boots.

But no sooner had Klonsky departed for Andorra than Lustgarten received a marvelous offer for the car. A capitalist in Utrecht wanted it at once and would take care of all excise problems. He had all the necessary *tuyaux,* unlimited drag. Lustgarten wired Klonsky in Andorra to stop. He raced down on the night train, recovered the Cadillac, and started driving back at once. There was no time to lose. But after sitting up all night on the *rapide,* Lustgarten was drowsy in the warmth of the Pyrenees and fell asleep at the wheel. He was lucky, he later said, for the car went down a mountainside and might have missed the stone wall that stopped it. He was only a foot or two from death when he was awakened by the crash. The car was destroyed. It was not insured.

Still faintly smiling, Lustgarten, with his sling and cane, came to Mosby's café table on the Boulevard Saint-Germain. Sat down. Removed his hat from dazzling black hair. Asked permission to rest his injured foot on a chair. "Is this a private conversation?" he said.

Mosby had been chatting with Alfred Ruskin, an American poet. Ruskin, though some of his front teeth were missing, spoke very clearly and swiftly. A perfectly charming man. Inveterately theoretical. He had been saying, for instance, that France had shot its collaborationist poets. America, which had no poets to spare, put Ezra Pound in Saint Elizabeth's. He then went on to say, barely acknowledging Lustgarten, that America had had no history, was not a historical society. His proof was from Hegel. According to Hegel, history was the history of wars and revolutions. The United States had had only one revolution and very few wars. Therefore it was historically empty. Practically a vacuum.

Ruskin also used Mosby's conveniences at the hotel, being too fastidious for his own latrine in the Algerian back streets of the Left Bank. And when he emerged from the bathroom he invariably had a topic sentence.

"I have discovered the main defect of Kierkegaard."

Or, "Pascal was terrified by universal emptiness, but Valéry says the difference between empty space and space in a bottle is only quantitative, and there is nothing intrinsically terrifying about quantity. What is your view?"

We do not live in bottles—Mosby's reply.

Lustgarten said when Ruskin left us, "Who is that fellow? He mooched you for the coffee."

"Ruskin," said Mosby.

"*That* is Ruskin?"

"Yes, why?"

"I hear my wife was going out with Ruskin while I was in the hospital."

"Oh, I wouldn't believe such rumors," said Mosby. "A cup of coffee, an apéritif together, maybe."

"When a man is down on his luck," said Lustgarten, "it's the rare woman who won't give him hell in addition."

"Sorry to hear it," Mosby replied.

And then, as Mosby in Oaxaca recalled, shifting his seat from the sun—for he was already far too red, and his face, bones, eyes, seemed curiously thirsty—Lustgarten had said, "It's been a terrible experience."

"Undoubtedly so, Lustgarten. It must have been frightening."

"What crashed was my last stake. It involved family. Too bad in a way that I wasn't killed. My insurance would at least have covered my kid brother's loss. And my mother and uncle."

Mosby had no wish to see a man in tears. He did not care to sit through these moments of suffering. Such unmastered emotion was abhorrent. Though perhaps the violence of this abomination might have told Mosby something about his own moral constitution. Perhaps Lustgarten did not want his face

to be working. Or tried to subdue his agitation, seeing from
Mosby's austere, though not unkind, silence that this was not
his way. Mosby was by taste a Senecan. At least he admired
Spanish masculinity—the *varonil* of Lorca. The *clavel varonil,*
the manly red carnation, the clear classic hardness of honora-
ble control.

"You sold the wreck for junk, I assume?"

"Klonksy took care of it. Now look, Mosby. I'm through
with that. I was reading, thinking, in the hospital. I came over
to make a pile. Like the gold rush. I really don't know what
got into me. Trudy and I were just sitting around during the
war. I was too old for the draft. And we both wanted action.
She in music. Or life. Excitement. You know, dreaming at
Montclair Teachers' College of the Big Time. I wanted to
make it possible for her. Keep up with the world, or
something. But really—in my hospital bed I realized—I was
right the first time. I am a socialist. A natural idealist. Reading
about Attlee, I felt at home again. It became clear that I am
still a political animal."

Mosby wished to say, "No, Lustgarten. You're a dandler of
swarthy little babies. You're a piggyback man—a giddyap
horsie. You're a sweet old Jewish Daddy." But he said
nothing.

"And I also read," said Lustgarten, "about Tito. Maybe the
Tito alternative is the real one. Perhaps there is hope for
socialism somewhere between the Labour Party and the
Yugoslav type of leadership. I feel it my duty," Lustgarten
told Mosby, "to investigate. I'm thinking of going to Belgrade."

"As what?"

"As a matter of fact, that's where you could come in," said
Lustgarten. "If you would be so kind. You're not *just* a
scholar. You wrote a book on Plato, I've been told."

"On the *Laws.*"

"And other books. But in addition you know the Movement. Lots of people. More connections than a switch-
board. . . ."

The slang of the forties.

"You know people at the *New Leader*?"

"Not my type of paper," said Mosby. "I'm actually a political conservative. Not what you would call a Rotten Liberal but an out-and-out conservative. I shook Franco's hand, you know."

"Did you?"

"This very hand shook the hand of the Caudillo. Would you like to touch it for yourself?"

"Why should I?"

"Go on," said Mosby. "It may mean something. Shake the hand that shook the hand."

Very strangely, then, Lustgarten extended padded, swarthy fingers. He looked partly subtle, partly ill. Grinning, he said, "Now I've made contact with real politics at last. But I'm serious about the *New Leader*. You probably know Bohn. I need credentials for Yugoslavia."

"Have you ever written for the papers?"

"For the *Militant*."

"What did you write?"

Guilty Lustgarten did not lie well. It was heartless of Mosby to amuse himself in this way.

"I have a scrapbook somewhere," said Lustgarten.

But it was not necessary to write to the *New Leader*. Lustgarten, encountered two days later on the Boulevard, near the pork butcher, had taken off the sling and scarcely needed the cane. He said, "I'm going to Yugoslavia. I've been invited."

"By whom?"

"Tito. The Government. They're asking interested people to come as guests to tour the country and see how they're building socialism. Oh, I know," he quickly said, anticipating standard doctrinal objection, "you don't build socialism in one country, but it's no longer the same situation. And I really believe Tito may redeem Marxism by actually transforming the dictatorship of the proletariat. This brings me back to my first love—the radical movement. I was never meant to be an entrepreneur."

"Probably not."

"I feel some hope," Lustgarten shyly said. "And then also, it's getting to be spring." He was wearing his heavy moose-colored bristling hat, and bore many other signs of interminable winter. A candidate for resurrection. An opportunity for the grace of life to reveal itself. But perhaps, Mosby thought, a man like Lustgarten would never, except with supernatural aid, exist in a suitable form.

"Also," said Lustgarten touchingly, "this will give Trudy time to reconsider."

"Is that the way things are with you two? I'm sorry."

"I wish I could take her with me, but I can't swing that with the Yugoslavs. It's sort of a V.I.P. deal. I guess they want to affect foreign radicals. There'll be seminars in dialectics, and so on. I love it. But it's not Trudy's dish."

Steady-handed, Mosby on his patio took ice with tongs, and poured more mescal flavored with *gusano de maguey*—a worm or slug of delicate flavor. These notes on Lustgarten pleased him. It was essential, at this point in his memoirs, to disclose new depths. The preceding chapters had been heavy. Many unconventional things were said about the state of political theory. The weakness of conservative doctrine, the lack, in America, of conservative alternatives, of resistance to the prevailing liberalism. As one who had personally tried to create a more rigorous environment for slovenly intellectuals, to force them to do their homework, to harden the categories of political thought, he was aware that on the right as on the left the results were barren. Absurdly, the college-bred dunces of America had longed for a true left-wing movement on the European model. They still dreamed of it. No less absurd were the right-wing idiots. You cannot grow a rose in a coal mine. Mosby's own right-wing graduate students had disappointed him. Just a lot of television actors. Bad guys for the Susskind interview programs. They had transformed the master's manner of acid elegance, logical tightness, factual punctiliousness, and merciless laceration in debate into a sort of shallow Noël Coward style. The real, the original Mosby approach brought Mosby hatred, got Mosby fired. Princeton University had offered Mosby a lump sum to retire seven years early. One hundred and forty thousand dollars. Because his mode of discourse was so upsetting to the academic community. Mosby was invited to no television programs. He was like the Guerrilla Mosby of the Civil War. When he galloped in, all were slaughtered.

Most carefully, Mosby had studied the memoirs of Santayana, Malraux, Sartre, Lord Russell, and others. Unfortunately, no one was reliably or consistently great. Men whose lives had been devoted to thought, who had tried mightily to govern the disorder of public life, to put it under some sort of intellectual authority, to get ideas to save mankind or to offer it mental aid in saving itself, would suddenly turn into gruesome idiots. Wanting to kill everyone. For instance, Sartre calling for the Russians to drop A-bombs on American bases in the Pacific because America was now presumably monstrous. And exhorting the blacks to butcher the whites. This moral philosopher! Or Russell, the Pacifist of World War I, urging the West to annihilate Russia after World War II. And sometimes, in his memoirs—perhaps he was gaga—strangely illogical. When, over London, a Zeppelin was shot down, the bodies of Germans were seen to fall, and the brutal men in the street horribly cheered, Russell wept, and had there not been a beautiful woman to console him in bed that night, this heartlessness of mankind would have broken him utterly. What was omitted was the fact that these same Germans who fell from the Zeppelin had come to bomb the city. They were going to blow up the brutes in the street, explode the lovers. This Mosby saw.

It was earnestly to be hoped—this was the mescal attempting to invade his language—that Mosby would avoid the common fate of intellectuals. The Lustgarten digression should help. The correction of pride by laughter.

There were twenty minutes yet before the chauffeur came to take the party to Mitla, to the ruins. Mosby had time to continue. To say that in September the Lustgarten who reappeared looked frightful. He had lost no less than fifty

pounds. Sun-blackened, creased, in a filthy stained suit, his
eyes infected. He said he had had diarrhea all summer.

"What did they feed their foreign V.I.P.s?"

And Lustgarten shyly bitter—the lean face and inflamed
eyes materializing from a spiritual region very different from
any heretofore associated with Lustgarten by Mosby—said,
"It was just a chain gang. It was hard labor. I didn't
understand the deal. I thought we were invited, as I told you.
But we turned out to be foreign volunteers-of-construction. A
labor brigade. And up in the mountains. Never saw the
Dalmatian coast. Hardly even shelter for the night. We slept
on the ground and ate shit fried in rancid oil."

"Why didn't you run away?" asked Mosby.

"How? Where?"

"Back to Belgrade. To the American Embassy at least?"

"How could I? I was a guest. Came at their expense. They
held the return ticket."

"And no money?"

"Are you kidding? Dead, broke. In Macedonia. Near
Skoplje. Bug-stung, starved, and running to the latrine all
night. Laboring on the roads all day, with pus in my eyes,
too."

"No first aid?"

"They may have had the first, but they didn't have the
second."

Mosby thought it best to say nothing of Trudy. She had
divorced Lustgarten.

Commiseration, of course.

Mosby shaking his head.

Lustgarten with a certain skinny dignity walking away. He
himself seemed amused by his encounters with Capitalism and
Socialism.

The end? Not quite. There was a coda: The thing had quite
good form.

Lustgarten and Mosby met again. Five years later. Mosby
enters an elevator in New York. Express to the forty-seventh
floor, the executive dining room of the Rangeley Foundation.

There is one other passenger, and it is Lustgarten. Grinning. He is himself again, filled out once more.

"Lustgarten!"

"Willis Mosby!"

"How are you, Lustgarten?"

"I'm great. Things are completely different. I'm happy. Successful. Married. Children."

"In New York?"

"Wouldn't live in the U.S. again. It's godawful. Inhuman. I'm visiting."

Without a blink in its brilliancy, without a hitch in its smooth, regulated power, the elevator containing only the two of us was going up. The same Lustgarten. Strong words, vocal insufficiency, the Zapotec nose, and under it the frog smile, the kindly gills.

"Where are you going now?"

"Up to *Fortune*," said Lustgarten. "I want to sell them a story."

He was on the wrong elevator. This one was not going to *Fortune*. I told him so. Perhaps I had not changed either. A voice which for many years had informed people of their errors said, "You'll have to go down again. The other bank of elevators."

At the forty-seventh floor we emerged together.

"Where are you settled now?"

"In Algiers," said Lustgarten. "We have a laundromat there."

"We?"

"Klonsky and I. You remember Klonsky?"

They had gone legitimate. They were washing burnooses. He was married to Klonsky's sister. I saw her picture. The image of Klonsky, a cat-faced woman, head ferociously encased in kinky hair, Picasso eyes at different levels, sharp teeth. If fish, dozing in the reefs, had nightmares, they would be of such teeth. The children also were young Klonskys. Lustgarten had the snapshots in his wallet of North African leather. As he beamed, Mosby recognized that pride in his success was Lustgarten's opiate, his artificial paradise.

"I thought," said Lustgarten, "that *Fortune* might like a piece on how we made it in North Africa."

We then shook hands again. Mine the hand that had shaken Franco's hand—his that had slept on the wheel of the Cadillac. The lighted case opened for him. He entered in. It shut.

Thereafter, of course, the Algerians threw out the French, expelled the Jews. And Jewish-Daddy-Lustgarten must have moved on. Passionate fatherhood. He loved those children. For Plato this child-breeding is the lowest level of creativity.

Still, Mosby thought, under the influence of mescal, my parents begot me like a committee of two.

From a feeling of remotion, though he realized that the car for Mitla had arrived, a shining conveyance waited, he noted the following as he gazed at the afternoon mountains:

> Until he was some years old
> People took care of him
> Cooled his soup, sang, chirked,
> Drew on his long stockings,
> Carried him upstairs sleeping.
> He recalls at the green lakeside
> His father's solemn navel,
> Nipples like dog's eyes in the hair
> Mother's thigh with wisteria of blue veins.
>
> After they retired to death,
> He conducted his own business
> Not too modestly, not too well.
> But here he is, smoking in Mexico
> Considering the brown mountains
> Whose fat laps are rolling
> On the skulls of whole families.

Two Welsh women were his companions. One was very ancient, lank. The Wellington of lady travelers. Or like C. Aubrey Smith, the actor who used to command Gurkha regiments in movies about India. A great nose, a gaunt jaw, a

pleated lip, a considerable mustache. The other was younger.
She had a small dewlap, but her cheeks were round and dark
eyes witty. A very satisfactory pair. Decent was the word.
English traits. Like many Americans, Mosby desired such
traits for himself. Yes, he was pleased with the Welsh ladies.
Though the guide was unsuitable. Overweening. His fat
cheeks a red pottery color. And he drove too fast.

The first stop was at Tule. They got out to inspect the
celebrated Tule tree in the churchyard. This monument of
vegetation, intricately and densely convolved, a green cypress,
more than two thousand years old, roots in a vanished lake
bottom, older than the religion of this little heap of white and
gloom, this charming peasant church. In the comfortable dust,
a dog slept. Disrespectful. But unconscious. The old lady,
quietly dauntless, tied on a scarf and entered the church. Her
stiff genuflection had real quality. She must be Christian.
Mosby looked into the depths of the Tule. A world in itself! It
could contain communities. In fact, if he recalled his Gerald
Heard, there was supposed to be a primal tree occupied by
early ancestors, the human horde housed in such appealing,
dappled, commodious, altogether beautiful organisms. The
facts seemed not to support this golden myth of an encom-
passing paradise. Earliest man probably ran about on the
ground, horribly violent, killing everything. Still, this dream of
gentleness, this aspiration for arboreal peace was no small
achievement for the descendants of so many killers. For his
religion, this tree would do, thought Mosby. No church for
him.

He was sorry to go. *He* could have lived up there. On top, of
course. The excrements would drop on you below. But the
Welsh ladies were already in the car, and the bossy guide
began to toot the horn. Waiting was hot.

The road to Mitla was empty. The heat made the landscape
beautifully crooked. The driver knew geology, archaeology.
He was quite ugly with his information. The War Table, the
Caverns, the Triassic Period. Inform me no further! Vex not
my soul with more detail. I cannot use what I have! And now
Mitla appeared. The right fork continued to Tehuantepec. The

left brought you to the Town of Souls. Old Mrs. Parsons (Elsie
Clews Parsons, as Mosby's mental retrieval system told him)
had done ethnography here, studied the Indians in these
baked streets of adobe and fruit garbage. In the shade, a dark
urinous tang. A long-legged pig struggling on a tether. A sow.
From behind, observant Mosby identified its pink small
female opening. The dungy earth feeding beast as man.

But here were the fascinating temples, almost intact. This
place the Spanish priests had not destroyed. All others they
had razed, building churches on the same sites, using the same
stones.

A tourist market. Coarse cotton dresses, Indian embroidery,
hung under flour-white tarpaulins, the dust settling on the
pottery of the region, black saxophones, black trays of glazed
clay.

Following the British travelers and the guide, Mosby was
going once more through an odd and complex fantasy. It was
that he was dead. He had died. He continued, however, to
live. His doom was to live life to the end as Mosby. In the
fantasy, he considered this his purgatory. And when had
death occurred? In a collision years ago. He had thought it a
near thing then. The cars were demolished. The actual Mosby
was killed. But another Mosby was pulled from the car. A
trooper asked, "You okay?"

Yes, he was okay. Walked away from the wreck. But he still
had the whole thing to do, step by step, moment by moment.
And now he heard a parrot blabbing, and children panhandled him and women made their pitch, and he was getting his
shoes covered with dust. He had been working at his memoirs
and had provided a diverting recollection of a funny man—
Lustgarten. In the manner of Sir Harold Nicolson. Much less
polished, admittedly, but in accordance with a certain protocol, the language of diplomacy, of mandarin irony. However
certain facts had been omitted. Mosby had arranged, for
instance, that Trudy should be seen with Alfred Ruskin. For
when Lustgarten was crossing the Rhine, Mosby was embracing Trudy in bed. Unlike Lord Russell's beautiful friend, she
did not comfort Mosby for the disasters he had (by intellec-

tual commitment) to confront. But Mosby had not advised her about leaving Lustgarten. He did not mean to interfere. However, his vision of Lustgarten as a funny man was transmitted to Trudy. She could not be the wife of such a funny man. But he *was,* he *was* a funny man! He was, like Napoleon in the eyes of Comte, an anachronism. Inept, he wished to be a colossus, something of a Napoleon himself, make millions, conquer Europe, retrieve from Hitler's fall a colossal fortune. Poorly imagined, unoriginal, the rerun of old ideas, and so inefficient. Lustgarten didn't have to happen. And so he *was* funny. Trudy too was funny, however. What a large belly she had. Since individuals are sometimes born from a twin impregnation, the organism carrying the undeveloped brother or sister in vestigial form—at times no more than an extra organ, a rudimentary eye buried in the leg, or a kidney or the beginnings of an ear somewhere in the back—Mosby often thought that Trudy had a little sister inside her. And to him she was a clown. This need not mean contempt. No, he liked her. The eye seemed to wander in one hemisphere. She did not know how to use perfume. Her atonal compositions were foolish.

At this time, Mosby had been making fun of people.

"Why?"

"Because he had needed to."

"Why?"

"Because!"

The guide explained that the buildings were raised without mortar. The mathematical calculations of the priests had been perfect. The precision of the cut stone was absolute. After centuries you could not find a chink, you could not insert a razor blade anywhere. These geometrical masses were balanced by their own weight. Here the priests lived. The walls had been dyed. The cochineal or cactus louse provided the dye. Here were the altars. Spectators sat where you are standing. The priests used obsidian knives. The beautiful youths played on flutes. Then the flutes were broken. The bloody knife was wiped on the head of the executioner. Hair must have been clotted. And here, the tombs of the nobles. Stairs leading down. The Zapotecs, late in the day, had practiced this form of sacrifice, under Aztec influence.

How game this Welsh crone was. She was beautiful. Getting in and out of these pits, she required no assistance.

Of course you cannot make yourself an agreeable, desirable person. You can't will yourself into it without regard to the things to be done. Imperative tasks. Imperative comprehensions, monstrous compulsions of duty which deform. Men will grow ugly under such necessities. This one a director of espionage. That one a killer.

Mosby had evoked, to lighten the dense texture of his memoirs, a Lustgarten whose doom was this gaping comedy. A Lustgarten who didn't have to happen. But himself, Mosby, also a separate creation, a finished product, standing under the sun on large blocks of stone, on the stairs descending into this pit, he was complete. He had completed himself in this cogitating, unlaughing, stone, iron, nonsensical form.

Having disposed of all things human, he should have encountered God.

Would this occur?

But having so disposed, what God was there to encounter?

But they had now been led below, into the tomb. There was a heavy grille, the gate. The stones were huge. The vault was close. He was oppressed. He was afraid. It was very damp. On the elaborately zigzag-carved walls were thin, thin pipings of fluorescent light. Flat boxes of ground lime were here to absorb moisture. His heart was paralyzed. His lungs would not draw. Jesus! I cannot catch my breath! To be shut in here! To be dead here! Suppose one were! Not as in accidents which ended, but did not quite end, existence. *Dead*-dead. Stooping, he looked for daylight. Yes, it was there. The light was there. The grace of life still there. Or, if not grace, air. Go while you can.

"I must get out," he told the guide. "Ladies, I find it very hard to breathe."

The Old
System

It was a thoughtful day for Dr. Braun.
Winter. Saturday. The short end of December. He was alone
in his apartment and woke late, lying in bed until noon, in the
room kept very dark, working with a thought—a feeling: Now
you see it, now you don't. Now a content, now a vacancy.
Now an important individual, a force, a necessary existence;
suddenly nothing. A frame without a picture, a mirror with
missing glass. The feeling of necessary existence might be the
aggressive, instinctive vitality we share with a dog or an ape.
The difference being in the power of the mind or spirit to
declare *I am.* Plus the inevitable inference *I am not.* Dr. Braun
was no more pleased with being than with its opposite. For
him an age of equilibrium seemed to be coming in. How nice!
Anyway, he had no project for putting the world in rational
order, and for no special reason he got up. Washed his
wrinkled but not elderly face with freezing tap water, which
changed the nighttime white to a more agreeable color. He
brushed his teeth. Standing upright, scrubbing the teeth as if
he were looking after an idol. He then ran the big old-fashioned tub to sponge himself, backing into the thick stream of
the Roman faucet, soaping beneath with the same cake of
soap he would apply later to his beard. Under the swell of his
belly, the tip of his parts, somewhere between his heels. His
heels needed scrubbing. He dried himself with yesterday's
shirt, an economy. It was going to the laundry anyway. Yes,
with the self-respecting expression human beings inherit from
ancestors for whom bathing was a solemnity. A sadness.

But every civilized man today cultivated an unhealthy self-detachment. Had learned from art the art of amusing self-observation and objectivity. Which, since there had to be something amusing to watch, required art in one's conduct. Existence for the sake of such practices did not seem worth while. Mankind was in a confusing, uncomfortable, disagreeable stage in the evolution of its consciousness. Dr. Braun (Samuel) did not like it. It made him sad to feel that the thought, art, belief of great traditions should be so misemployed. Elevation? Beauty? Torn into shreds, into ribbons for girls' costumes, or trailed like the tail of a kite at Happenings. Plato and the Buddha raided by looters. The tombs of Pharaohs broken into by desert rabble. And so on, thought Dr. Braun as he passed into his neat kitchen. He was well pleased by the blue-and-white Dutch dishes, cups hanging, saucers standing in slots.

He opened a fresh can of coffee, much enjoyed the fragrance from the punctured can. Only an instant, but not to be missed. Next he sliced bread for the toaster, got out the butter, chewed an orange; and he was admiring long icicles on the huge red, circular roof tank of the laundry across the alley, the clear sky, when he discovered that a sentiment was approaching. It was said of him, occasionally, that he did not love anyone. This was not true. He did not love anyone steadily. But unsteadily he loved, he guessed, at an average rate.

The sentiment, as he drank his coffee, was for two cousins in upstate New York, the Mohawk Valley. They were dead. Isaac Braun and his sister Tina. Tina was first to go. Two years later, Isaac died. Braun now discovered that he and Cousin Isaac had loved each other. For whatever use or meaning this fact might have within the peculiar system of light, movement, contact, and perishing in which he tried to find stability. Toward Tina, Dr. Braun's feelings were less clear. More passionate once, but at present more detached.

Isaac's wife, after he died, had told Braun, "He was proud of you. He said, 'Sammy has been written up in *Time*, in all the papers, for his research. But he never says a word about his scientific reputation!' "

"I see. Well, computers do the work, actually."

"But you have to know what to put into these computers."

This was more or less the case. But Braun had not continued the conversation. He did not care much for being *first* in his field. People were boastful in America. Matthew Arnold, a not entirely appetizing figure himself, had correctly observed this in the U.S. Dr. Braun thought this native American boastfulness had aggravated a certain weakness in Jewish immigrants. But a proportionate reaction of self-effacement was not praiseworthy. Dr. Braun did not want to be interested in this question at all. However, his cousin Isaac's opinions had some value for him.

In Schenectady there were two more Brauns of the same family, living. Did Dr. Braun, drinking his coffee this afternoon, love them, too? They did not elicit such feelings. Then did he love Isaac more because Isaac was dead? There one might have something.

But in childhood, Isaac had shown him great kindness. The others, not very much.

Now Braun remembered certain things. A sycamore tree beside the Mohawk River. Then the river couldn't have been so foul. Its color, anyhow, was green, and it was powerful and dark, an easy, level force—crimped, green, blackish, glassy. A huge tree like a complicated event, with much splitting and thick chalky extensions. It must have dominated an acre, brown and white. And well away from the leaves, on a dead branch, sat a gray-and-blue fish hawk. Isaac and his little cousin Braun passed in the wagon—the old coarse-tailed horse walking, the steady head, in blinders, working onward. Braun, seven years old, wore a gray shirt with large bone buttons and had a short summer haircut. Isaac was dressed in work clothes, for in those days the Brauns were in the secondhand business—furniture, carpets, stoves, beds. His senior by fifteen years, Isaac had a mature business face. Born to be a man, in the direct Old Testament sense, as that bird on the sycamore was born to fish in water. Isaac, when he had come to America, was still a child. Nevertheless his old-country Jewish dignity was very firm and strong. He had the outlook of ancient generations on the New World. Tents and kine and wives and maidservants and manservants. Isaac was handsome, Braun thought—dark face, black eyes, vigorous hair, and a long scar on the cheek. Because, he told his scientific cousin, his mother had given him milk from a tubercular cow in the old country. While his father was serving in the Russo-Japanese War. Far away. In the Yiddish metaphor, on the lid of hell. As though hell were a caldron, a covered pot. How those old-time Jews despised the goy wars, their vainglory and obstinate *Dummheit*. Conscription, mustering, marching, shooting, leaving the corpses everywhere. Buried, unburied. Army against army. Gog and Magog. The czar, that weak, whiskered arbitrary and woman-ridden man, decreed that Uncle Braun would be swept away to Sakhalin. So by irrational decree, as in *The Arabian Nights*, Uncle Braun, with his greatcoat and short humiliated legs, little beard, and great eyes, left wife and child to eat maggoty pork. And when the War was lost Uncle Braun escaped through Manchuria. Came to Vancouver on a Swedish ship. Labored on the railroad. He did not look so strong, as Braun remembered him in Schenectady. His chest was deep and his arms long, but the legs like felt, too yielding, as if the escape from Sakhalin and trudging in Manchuria had been too much. However, in the Mohawk Valley, monarch of used stoves and fumigated mattresses—dear Uncle Braun! He had a small, pointed beard, like George V, like Nick of Russia. Like Lenin, for that matter. But large, patient eyes in his wizened face, filling all of the space reserved for eyes.

A vision of mankind Braun was having as he sat over his coffee Saturday afternoon. Beginning with those Jews of 1920.

Braun as a young child was protected by the especial affection of his cousin Isaac, who stroked his head and took him on the wagon, later the truck, into the countryside. When

Braun's mother had gone into labor with him, it was Isaac whom Aunt Rose sent running for the doctor. He found the doctor in the saloon. Faltering, drunken Jones, who practiced among Jewish immigrants before those immigrants had educated their own doctors. He had Isaac crank the Model T. And they drove. Arriving, Jones tied Mother Braun's hands to the bedposts, a custom of the times.

Having worked as a science student in laboratories and kennels, Dr. Braun had himself delivered cats and dogs. Man, he knew, entered life like these other creatures, in a transparent bag or caul. Lying in a bag filled with transparent fluid, a purplish water. A color to mystify the most rational philosopher. What is this creature that struggles for birth in its membrane and clear fluid? Any puppy in its sac, in the blind terror of its emergence, any mouse breaking into the external world from this shining, innocent-seeming blue-tinged transparency!

Dr. Braun was born in a small wooden house. They washed him and covered him with mosquito netting. He lay at the foot of his mother's bed. Tough Cousin Isaac dearly loved Braun's mother. He had great pity for her. In intervals of his dealing, of being a Jewish businessman, there fell these moving reflections of those who were dear to him.

Aunt Rose was Dr. Braun's godmother, held him at his circumcision. Bearded, nearsighted old Krieger, fingers stained with chicken slaughter, cut away the foreskin.

Aunt Rose, Braun felt, was the original dura mater—the primal hard mother. She was not a big woman. She had a large bust, wide hips, and old-fashioned thighs of those corrupted shapes that belong to history. Which hampered her walk. Together with poor feet, broken by the excessive female weight she carried. In old boots approaching the knee. Her face was red, her hair powerful, black. She had a straight sharp nose. To cut mercy like a cotton thread. In the light of her eyes Braun recognized the joy she took in her hardness. Hardness of reckoning, hardness of tactics, hardness of dealing and of speech. She was building a kingdom with the labor of Uncle Braun and the strength of her obedient sons.

They had their shop, they had real estate. They had a hideous synagogue of such red brick as seemed to grow in upstate New York by the will of the demon spirit charged with the ugliness of America in that epoch, which saw to it that a particular comic ugliness should influence the soul of man. In Schenectady, in Troy, in Gloversville, Mechanicville, as far west as Buffalo. There was a sour paper mustiness in this synagogue. Uncle Braun not only had money, he also had some learning and he was respected. But it was a quarrelsome congregation. Every question was disputed. There was rivalry, there were rages; slaps were given, families stopped speaking. Pariahs, thought Braun, with the dignity of princes among themselves.

Silent, with silent eyes crossing and recrossing the red water tank bound by twisted cables, from which ragged ice hung down and white vapor rose, Dr. Braun extracted a moment four decades gone in which Cousin Isaac had said, with one of those archaic looks he had, that the Brauns were descended from the tribe of Naphtali.

"How do we know?"

"People—families—*know*."

Braun was reluctant, even at the age of ten, to believe such things. But Isaac, with the authority of a senior, almost an uncle, said, "You'd better not forget it."

As a rule, he was gay with young Braun. Laughing against the tension of the scar that forced his mouth to one side. His eyes black, soft, and flaming. Off his breath, a bitter fragrance that translated itself to Braun as masculine earnestness and gloom. All the sons in the family had the same sort of laugh. They sat on the open porch. Sundays, laughing, while Uncle Braun read aloud the Yiddish matrimonial advertisements. "Attractive widow, 35, dark-favored, owning her own dry-goods business in Hudson, excellent cook, Orthodox, well-bred, refined. Plays the piano. Two intelligent, well-behaved children, eight and six."

All but Tina, the obese sister, took part in this satirical Sunday pleasure. Behind the screen door, she stood in the kitchen. Below, the yard, where crude flowers grew—zinnias, plantain lilies, trumpet vine on the chicken shed.

Now the country cottage appeared to Braun, in the Adirondacks. A stream. So beautiful! Trees, full of great strength. Wild strawberries, but you must be careful about the poison ivy. In the drainage ditches, polliwogs. Braun slept in the attic with Cousin Mutt. Mutt danced in his undershirt in the morning, naked beneath, and sang an obscene song:

> "I stuck my nose up a nanny goat's ass
> And the smell was enough to blind me."

He was leaping on bare feet, and his thing bounded from thigh to thigh. Going into saloons to collect empty bottles, he had learned this. A ditty from the stokehold. Origin, Liverpool or Tyneside. Art of the laboring class in the machine age.

An old mill. A pasture with clover flowers. Braun, seven years old, tried to make a clover wreath, pinching out a hole in the stems for other stems to pass through. He meant the wreath for fat Tina. To put it on her thick savory head, her smoky black harsh hair. Then in the pasture, little Braun overturned a rotten stump with his foot. Hornets pursued and bit him. He screamed. He had painful crimson lumps all over his body. Aunt Rose put him to bed and Tina came huge into the attic to console him. An angry fat face, black eyes, and the dilated nose breathing at him. Little Braun, stung and burning. She lifted her dress and petticoat to cool him with her body. The belly and thighs swelled before him. Braun felt too small and frail for this ecstasy. By the bedside was a chair, and she sat. Under the dizzy heat of the shingled roof, she rested her legs upon him, spread them wider, wider. He saw the barbarous and coaly hair. He saw the red within. She parted the folds with her fingers. Parting, her dark nostrils opened, the eyes looked white in her head. She motioned that he should press his child's genital against her fat-flattened thighs. Which, with agonies of incapacity and pleasure, he did. All was silent. Summer silence. Her sexual odor. The flies and gnats stimulated by delicious heat or the fragrance. He heard a mass of flies tear themselves from the windowpane. A sound of detached adhesive. Tina did not kiss, did not embrace. Her face was menacing. She was defying. She was drawing him—taking him somewhere with her. But she promised nothing, told him nothing.

When he recovered from his bites, playing once more in the yard, Braun saw Isaac with his fiancée, Clara Sternberg, walking among the trees, embracing very sweetly. Braun tried to go with them, but Cousin Isaac sent him away. When he still followed, Cousin Isaac turned him roughly toward the cottage. Little Braun then tried to kill his cousin. He wanted with all his heart to club Isaac with a piece of wood. He was still struck by the incomparable happiness, the luxury of that pure murderousness. Rushing toward Isaac, who took him by the back of the neck, twisted his head, held him under the pump. He then decreed that little Braun must go home, to Albany. He was far too wild. Must be taught a lesson. Cousin Tina said in private, "Good for *you,* Sam. I hate him, too." She took Braun with her dimpled, inept hand and walked down the road with him in the Adirondack dust. Her gingham-fitted bulk. Her shoulders curved, banked, like the earth of the hill-cut road. And her feet turned outward by the terrifying weight and deformity of her legs.

Later she dieted. Became for a while thinner, more civilized. Everyone was more civilized. Little Braun became a docile, bookish child. Did very well at school.

All clear? Quite clear to the adult Braun, considering his fate no more than the fate of others. Before his tranquil look, the facts arranged themselves—rose, took a new arrangement. Remained awhile in the settled state and then changed again. We were getting somewhere.

Uncle Braun died angry with Aunt Rose. He turned his face to the wall with his last breath to rebuke her hardness. All the men, his sons, burst out weeping. The tears of the women were different. Later, too, their passion took other forms. They bargained for more property. And Aunt Rose defied Uncle Braun's will. She collected rents in the slums of Albany and Schenectady from properties he had left to his sons. She dressed herself in the old fashion, calling on nigger tenants or the Jewish rabble of tailors and cobblers. To her the old Jewish words for these trades—*Schneider, Schuster*—were terms of contempt. Rents belonging mainly to Isaac she banked in her own name. Riding ancient streetcars in the factory slums. She did not need to buy widow's clothes. She had always worn suits, they had always been black. Her hat was three-cornered, like the town crier's. She let the black braid hang behind, as though she were in her own kitchen. She had trouble with bladder and arteries, but ailments did not keep her at home and she had no use for doctoring and drugs. She blamed Uncle Braun's death on Bromo-Seltzer, which, she said, had enlarged his heart.

Isaac did not marry Clara Sternberg. Though he was a manufacturer, her father turned out on inquiry to have started as a cutter and have married a housemaid. Aunt Rose would not tolerate such a connection. She took long trips to make genealogical investigations. And she vetoed all the young women, her judgments severe without limit. "A false dog." "Candied poison." "An open ditch. A sewer. A born whore!"

The woman Isaac eventually married was pleasant, mild, round, respectable, the daughter of a Jewish farmer.

Aunt Rose said, "Ignorant. A common man."

"He's honest, a hard worker on the land," said Isaac. "He recites the Psalms even when he's driving. He keeps them under his wagon seat."

"I don't believe it. A son of Ham like that. A cattle dealer. He stinks of manure." And she said to the bride in Yiddish, "Be so good as to wash thy father before bringing him to the synagogue. Get a bucket and scalding water, and 20 Mule Team Borax and ammonia, and a horse brush. The filth is ingrained. Be sure to scrub his hands."

The rigid madness of the Orthodox. Their haughty, spinning, crazy spirit.

Tina did not bring her young man from New York to be examined by Aunt Rose. Anyway, he was neither young, nor handsome, nor rich. Aunt Rose said he was a minor hoodlum, a slugger. She had gone to Coney Island to inspect his family—a father who sold pretzels and chestnuts from a cart, a mother who cooked for banquets. And the groom himself—so thick, so bald, so grim, she said, his hands so common and his back and chest like fur, a fell. He was a beast, she told young Sammy Braun. Braun was a student then at Rensselaer Polytechnic and came to see his aunt in her old kitchen—the great black-and-nickel stove, the round table on its oak pedestal, the dark-blue-and-white check of the oilcloth, a still life of peaches and cherries salvaged from the secondhand shop. And Aunt Rose, more feminine with her corset off and a gaudy wrapper over her thick Victorian undervests, camisoles, bloomers. Her silk stockings were gartered below the knee and the wide upper portions, fashioned for thighs, drooped down flimsy, nearly to her slippers.

Tina was then handsome, if not pretty. In high school she took off eighty pounds. Then she went to New York City without getting her diploma. What did *she* care for such things! said Rose. And how did she get to Coney Island by herself? Because she was perverse. Her instinct was for freaks. And there she met this beast. This hired killer, this second Lepke of Murder, Inc. Upstate, the old woman read the melodramas of the Yiddish press, which she embroidered with her own ideas of wickedness.

But when Tina brought her husband to Schenectady, installing him in her father's secondhand shop, he turned out to be a big innocent man. If he had ever had guile, he lost it with his hair. His baldness was total, like a purge. He had a sentimental, dependent look. Tina protected him. Here Dr. Braun had sexual thoughts, about himself as a child and about her childish bridegroom. And scowling, smoldering Tina, her angry tenderness in the Adirondacks, and how she was beneath, how hard she breathed in the attic, and the violent strength and obstinacy of her crinkled, sooty hair.

Nobody could sway Tina. That, thought Braun, was probably the secret of it. She had consulted her own will, kept her own counsel for so long, that she could accept no outer guidance. Anyone who listened to others seemed to her weak.

When Aunt Rose lay dead, Tina took from her hand the ring Isaac had given her many years ago. Braun did not remember the entire history of that ring, only that Isaac had loaned money to an immigrant who disappeared, leaving this jewel, which was assumed to be worthless but turned out to be valuable. Braun could not recall whether it was ruby or emerald; nor the setting. But it was the one feminine adornment Aunt Rose wore. And it was supposed to go to Isaac's wife, Sylvia, who wanted it badly. Tina took it from the corpse and put it on her own finger.

"Tina, give that ring to me. Give it here," said Isaac.

"No. It was hers. Now it's mine."

"It was not Mama's. You know that. Give it back."

She outfaced him over the body of Aunt Rose. She knew he would not quarrel at the deathbed. Sylvia was enraged. She did what she could. That is, she whispered, "Make her!" But it was no use. He knew he could not recover it. Besides, there were too many other property disputes. His rents in Aunt Rose's savings bank.

But only Isaac became a millionaire. The others simply hoarded, old immigrant style. He never sat waiting for his legacy. By the time Aunt Rose died, Isaac was already worth a great deal of money. He had put up an ugly apartment building in Albany. To him, an achievement. He was out with his men at dawn. Having prayed aloud while his wife, in curlers, pretty but puffy with sleepiness, sleepy but obedient, was in the kitchen fixing breakfast. Isaac's Orthodoxy only increased with his wealth. He soon became an old-fashioned Jewish paterfamilias. With his family he spoke a Yiddish unusually thick in old Slavic and Hebrew expressions. Instead of "important people, leading citizens," he said *"Anshe ha-ir,"* Men of the City. He, too, kept the Psalms near. As active, worldly Jews for centuries had done. One copy lay in the glove compartment of his Cadillac. To which his great gloomy sister referred with a twist of the face—she had become obese again, wider and taller, since those Adirondack days. She said, "He reads the Tehillim aloud in his air-conditioned Caddy when there's a long freight train at the crossing. That crook! He'd pick God's pocket!"

One could not help thinking what fertility of metaphor there was in all of these Brauns. Dr. Braun himself was no exception. And what the explanation might be, despite twenty-five years of specialization in the chemistry of heredity, he couldn't say. How a protein molecule might carry such propensities of ingenuity, and creative malice and negative power. Originating in an invisible ferment. Capable of printing a talent or a vice upon a billion hearts. No wonder Isaac Braun cried out to his God when he sat seated in his great black car and the freights rumbled in the polluted shimmering of this once-beautiful valley

> Answer me when I call, O God of my
> righteousness.

"But what do you think?" said Tina. "Does he remember his brothers when there is a deal going? Does he give his only a sister a chance to come in?"

Not that there was any great need. Cousin Mutt, after he was wounded at Iwo Jima, returned to the appliance business. Cousin Aaron was a C.P.A. Tina's husband, bald Fenster, branched into housewares in his secondhand shop. Tina was back of that, of course. No one was poor. What irritated Tina was that Isaac would not carry the family into real estate, where the tax advantages were greatest. The big depreciation allowances, which she understood as legally sanctioned graft. She had her money in savings accounts at a disgraceful two and a half percent, taxed at the full rate. She did not trust the stock market.

Isaac had tried, in fact, to include the Brauns when he built the shopping center at Robbstown. At a risky moment, they abandoned him. A desperate moment, when the law had to be broken. At a family meeting, each of the Brauns had agreed to put up $25,000, the entire amount to be given under the table to Ilkington. Old Ilkington headed the board of directors of the Robbstown Country Club. Surrounded by factories, the club was moving farther into the country. Isaac had learned this from the old caddie master when he gave him a lift, one morning of fog. Mutt Braun had caddied at Robbstown in the early twenties, had carried Ilkington's clubs. Isaac knew Ilkington, too, and had a private talk with him. The old goy, now seventy, retiring to the British West Indies, had said to Isaac, "Off the record. One hundred thousand. And I don't want to bother about Internal Revenue." He was a long, austere man with a marbled face. Cornell 1910 or so. Cold but plain. And, in Isaac's opinion, fair. Developed as a shopping center, properly planned, the Robbstown golf course was worth half a million apiece to the Brauns. The city in the postwar boom was spreading fast. Isaac had a friend on the zoning board who would clear everything for five grand. As for the contracting, he offered to do it all on his own. Tina insisted that a separate corporation be formed by the Brauns to make sure the building profits were shared equally. To this Isaac agreed. As head of the family, he took the burden upon himself. He would have to organize it all. Only Aaron the C.P.A. could help him, setting up the books. The meeting, in Aaron's office, lasted from noon to three P.M. All the difficult problems were examined. Four players, specialists in the harsh music of money, studying a score. In the end, they agreed to perform.

But when the time came, ten A.M. on a Friday, Aaron balked. He would not do it. And Tina and Mutt also reneged. Isaac told Dr. Braun the story. As arranged, he came to Aaron's office carrying the $25,000 for Ilkington in an old briefcase. Aaron, now forty, smooth, shrewd, and dark, had the habit of writing tiny neat numbers on his memo pad as he spoke to you. Dark fingers quickly consulting the latest tax publications. He dropped his voice very low to the secretary on the intercom. He wore white-on-white shirts and silk-brocade ties, signed "Countess Mara." Of them all, he looked most like Uncle Braun. But without the beard, without the kingly pariah derby, without the gold thread in his brown eye. In many externals, thought scientific Braun, Aaron and Uncle Braun were drawn from the same genetic pool. Chemically, he was the younger brother of his father. The differences within were due possibly to heredity. Or perhaps to the influence of business America.

"Well?" said Isaac, standing in the carpeted office. The grandiose desk was superbly clean.

"How do you know Ilkington can be trusted?"

"I think he can."

"*You* think. He could take the money and say he never heard of you in all his life."

"Yes, he might. But we talked that over. We have to gamble."

Probably on his instructions, Aaron's secretary buzzed him. He bent over the instrument and out of the corner of his mouth he spoke to her very deliberately and low.

"Well, Aaron," said Isaac. "You want me to guarantee your investment? Well? Speak up."

Aaron had long ago subdued his thin tones and spoke in the gruff style of a man always sure of himself. But the sharp breaks, mastered twenty-five years ago, were still there. He stood up with both fists on the glass of his desk, trying to control his voice.

He said through clenched teeth, "I haven't slept!"

"Where is the money?"

"I don't have that kind of cash."

"No?"

"You know damn well. I'm licensed. I'm a certified accountant. I'm in no position . . ."

"And what about Tina—Mutt?"

"I don't know anything about them."

"Talked them out of it, didn't you? I have to meet Ilkington at noon. Sharp. Why didn't you tell me sooner?"

Aaron said nothing.

Isaac dialed Tina's number and let the phone ring. Certain that she was there, gigantically listening to the steely, beady drilling of the telephone. He let it ring, he said, about five minutes. He made no effort to call Mutt. Mutt would do as Tina did.

"I have an hour to raise this dough."

"In my bracket," Aaron said, "the twenty-five would cost me more than fifty."

"You could have told me this yesterday. Knowing what it means to me."

"You'll turn over a hundred thousand to a man you don't know? Without a receipt? Blind? Don't do it."

But Isaac had decided. In our generation, Dr. Braun thought, a sort of playboy capitalist has emerged. He gaily takes a flier in rebuilt office machinery for Brazil, motels in East Africa, high-fidelity components in Thailand. A hundred thousand means little. He jets down with a chick to see the scene. The governor of a province is waiting in his Thunderbird to take the guests on jungle expressways built by graft and peons to a surf-and-champagne weekend where the executive, youthful at fifty, closes the deal. But Cousin Isaac had put his stake together penny by penny, old style, starting with rags and bottles as a boy; then fire-salvaged goods; then used cars; then learning the building trades. Earth moving, foundations, concrete, sewage, wiring, roofing, heating systems. He got his money the hard way. And now he went to the bank and borrowed $75,000, at full interest. Without security, he gave it to Ilkington in Ilkington's parlor. Furnished in old goy taste and disseminating an old goy odor of tiresome, silly, respectable things. Of which Ilkington was clearly so proud. The applewood, the cherry, the wing tables and cabinets, the upholstery with a flavor of dry paste, the pork-pale colors of gentility. Ilkington did not touch Isaac's briefcase. He did not intend, evidently, to count the bills, nor even to look. He offered Isaac a martini. Isaac, not a drinker, drank the clear gin. At noon. Like something distilled in outer space. Having no color. He sat there sturdily, but felt lost—lost to his people, his family, lost to God, lost in the void of America. Ilkington drank a shaker of cocktails, gentlemanly, stony, like a high slab of something generically human, but with few human traits familiar to Isaac. At the door he did not say he would keep his word. He simply shook hands with Isaac, saw him to the car. Isaac drove home and sat in the den of his bungalow. Two whole days. Then on Monday, Ilkington phoned to say that the Robbstown directors had decided to accept his offer for the property. A pause. Then Ilkington added that no written instrument could replace trust and decency between gentlemen.

Isaac took possession of the country club and filled it with a shopping center. All such places are ugly. Dr. Braun could not say why this one struck him as especially brutal in its ugliness. Perhaps because he remembered the Robbstown Club. Restricted, of course. But Jews could look at it from the road. And the elms had been lovely—a century or older. The light, delicate. And the Coolidge-era sedans turning in, with small curtains at the rear window, and holders for artificial flowers. Hudsons, Auburns, Bearcats. Only machinery. Nothing to feel nostalgic about.

Still, Braun was startled to see what Isaac had done. Perhaps in an unconscious assertion of triumph—in the vividness of victory. The green acres reserved, it was true, for mild idleness, for hitting a little ball with a stick, were now paralyzed by parking for five hundred cars. Supermarket, pizza joint, chop suey, laundromat, Robert Hall clothes, a dime store.

And this was only the beginning. Isaac became a millionaire. He filled the Mohawk Valley with housing developments. And he began to speak of "my people," meaning those who lived in the buildings he had raised. He was stingy with land, he built too densely, it was true, but he built with benevolence. At six in the morning, he was out with his crews. He lived very simply. Walked humbly with his God, as the rabbi said. A Madison Avenue rabbi, by this time. The little synagogue was wiped out. It was as dead as the Dutch painters who would have appreciated its dimness and its shaggy old peddlers. Now there was a *temple* like a World's Fair pavilion. Isaac was president, having beaten out the father of a famous hoodlum, once executioner for the Mob in the Northeast. The worldly rabbi with his trained voice and tailored suits, like a Christian minister except for the play of Jewish cleverness in his face, hinted to the old-fashioned part of the congregation that he had to pour it on for the sake of the young people. America. Extraordinary times. If you wanted the young women to bless Sabbath candles, you had to start their rabbi at $20,000, and add a house and a Jaguar.

Cousin Isaac, meantime, grew more old-fashioned. His car was ten years old. But he was a strong sort of man. Self-assured, a dark head scarcely thinning at the top. Upstate women said he gave out the positive male energy they were beginning to miss in men. He had it. It was in the manner with which he picked up a fork at the table, the way he poured from a bottle. Of course, the world had done for him exactly what he had demanded. That meant he had made the right demand and in the right place. It meant his reading of life was metaphysically true. Or that the Old Testament, the Talmud, and Polish Ashkenazi Orthodoxy were irresistible.

But that wouldn't altogether do, thought Dr. Braun. There was more there than piety. He recalled his cousin's white teeth and scar-twisted smile when he was joking. "I fought on many fronts," Cousin Isaac said, meaning women's bellies. He often had a sound American way of putting things. Had known the back stairs in Schenectady that led to the sheets, the gripping arms and spreading thighs of workingwomen. The Model T was parked below. Earlier, the horse waited in harness. He got great pleasure from masculine reminiscences. Recalling Dvorah the greenhorn, on her knees, hiding her head in pillows while her buttocks soared, a burst of kinky hair from the walls of whiteness, and her feeble voice crying, "*Nein.*" But she did not mean it.

Cousin Mutt had no such anecdotes. Shot in the head at Iwo Jima, he came back from a year in the hospital to sell Zenith, Motorola, and Westinghouse appliances. He married a respectable girl and went on quietly amid a bewildering expansion and transformation of his birthplace. A computer center taking over the bush-league park where a scout had him spotted before the war as material for the majors. On most important matters, Mutt went to Tina. She told him what to do. And Isaac looked out for him, whenever possible buying appliances through Mutt for his housing developments. But Mutt took his problems to Tina. For instance, his wife and her sister played the horses. Every chance they got, they drove to Saratoga, to the trotting races. Probably no great harm in this. The two sisters with gay lipstick and charming dresses. And laughing continually with their pretty jutting teeth. And putting down the top of the convertible.

Tina took a mild view of this. Why shouldn't they go to the track? Her fierceness was concentrated, all of it, on Braun the millionaire.

"That whoremaster!" she said.

"Oh, no. Not in years and years," said Mutt.

"Come, Mutt. I know whom he's been balling. I keep an eye on the Orthodox. Believe me, I do. And now the governor has put him on a commission. Which is it?"

"Pollution."

"Water pollution, that's right. Rockefeller's buddy."

"Well, you shouldn't, Tina. He's our brother."

"He feels for *you*."

"Yes, he does."

"A multimillionaire—lets you go on drudging in a little business? He's heartless. A heartless man."

"It's not true."

"What? He never had a tear in his eye unless the wind was blowing," said Tina.

Hyperbole was Tina's greatest weakness. They were all like that. The mother had bred it in them.

Otherwise, she was simply a gloomy, obese woman, sternly combed, the hair tugged back from her forehead, tight, so that the hairline was a fighting barrier. She had a totalitarian air. And not only toward others. Toward herself, also. Absorbed in the dictatorship of her huge person. In a white dress, and with the ring on her finger she had seized from her dead mother. By a *putsch* in the bedroom.

In her generation—Dr. Braun had given up his afternoon to the hopeless pleasure of thinking affectionately about his dead—in her generation, Tina was also old-fashioned for all her modern slang. People of her sort, and not only the women, cultivated charm. But Tina willed consistently to appeal for nothing, to have no charm. Absolutely none. She never tried to please. Her aim must have been majesty. Based on what? She had no great thoughts. She built on her own nature. On a primordial idea, hugely blown up. Somewhat as her flesh in its dress of white silk, as last seen by Cousin Braun some years ago, was blown up. Some sub-suboffice of the personality, behind a little door of the brain where the restless spirit never left its work, had ordered this tremendous female form, all of it, to become manifest, with dark hair on the forearms, conspicuous nostrils in the white face, and black eyes staring. The eyes had an affronted expression; sometimes a look of sulphur; a clever look—they had all the looks, even the look of kindness that came from Uncle Braun. The old man's sweetness. Those who try to interpret humankind through its eyes are in for much strangeness—perplexity.

The quarrel between Tina and Isaac lasted for years. She accused him of shaking off the family when the main chance came. He had refused to cut them in. He said that they had all deserted him at the zero hour. Eventually the brothers made it up. Not Tina. She wanted nothing to do with Isaac. In the first phase of enmity she saw to it that he should know exactly what she thought of him. Brothers, aunts, and old friends reported what she was saying about him. He was a crook. Mama had lent him money; he would not repay; that was why she had collected those rents. Also, Isaac had been a silent partner of Zaikas, the Greek, the racketeer from Troy. She said that Zaikas had covered for Isaac, who was implicated in the state-hospital scandal. Zaikas took the fall, but Isaac had to put $50,000 in Zaikas's box at the bank. The Stuyvesant Bank, that was. Tina said she even knew the box number.

Isaac said little to these slanders, and after a time they stopped.

And it was when they stopped that Isaac actually began to feel the anger of his sister. He felt it as head of the family, the oldest living Braun. After he had not seen his sister for two or three years, he began to remind himself of Uncle Braun's affection for Tina. The only daughter. The youngest. Our baby sister. Thoughts of the old days touched his heart. Having gotten what he wanted, Tina said to Mutt, he could redo the past in sentimental colors. Isaac would remember that in 1920 Aunt Rose wanted fresh milk, and the Brauns kept a cow in the pasture by the river. What a beautiful place. And how delicious it was to crank the Model T and drive at dusk to milk the cow beside the green water. Driving, they sang songs. Tina, then ten years old, must have weighed two hundred pounds, but the shape of her mouth was very sweet, womanly—perhaps the pressure of the fat, hastening her maturity. Somehow she was more feminine in childhood than later. It was true that at nine or ten she sat on a kitten in the rocker, unaware, and smothered it. Aunt Rose found it dead when her daughter stood up. "You huge thing," she said to her daughter, "you animal." But even this Isaac recollected with amused sadness. And since he belonged to no societies, never played cards, never spent an evening drinking, never went to Florida, never went to Europe, never went to see the State of Israel, Isaac had plenty of time for reminiscences. Respectable elms about his house sighed with him for the past. The squirrels were orthodox. They dug and saved. Mrs. Isaac Braun wore no cosmetics. Except a touch of lipstick when going out in public. No mink coats. A comfortable Hudson seal, yes. With a large fur button on the belly. To keep her, as he liked her, warm. Fair, pale, round, with a steady innocent look, and hair worn short and symmetrical. Light brown, with kinks of gold. One gray eye, perhaps, expressed or came near expressing slyness. It must have been purely involuntary. At least there was not the slightest sign of conscious criticism or opposition. Isaac was master. Cooking, baking, laundry, all housekeeping, had to meet his standard. If he didn't like the smell of the cleaning woman, she was sent away. It was an ample plain old-fashioned respectable domestic life on an East European model completely destroyed in 1939 by Hitler and Stalin. Those two saw to the eradication of the old conditions, made sure that certain modern concepts became social realities. Maybe the slightest troubling ambiguity in one of Cousin Sylvia's eyes was the effect of a suppressed historical comment. As a woman, Dr. Braun considered, she had more than a glimmering of this modern transformation. Her husband was a multimillionaire. Where was the life this might have bought? The houses, servants, clothes, and cars? On the farm she had operated machines. As his wife, she was obliged to forget how to drive. She was a docile, darling woman, and she was in the kitchen baking spongecake and chopping liver, as Isaac's mother had done. Or should have done. Without the flaming face, the stern meeting brows, the rigorous nose, and the club of powerful braid lying on her spine. Without Aunt Rose's curses.

In America, the abuses of the Old World were righted. It was appointed to be the land of historical redress. However, Dr. Braun reflected, new uproars filled the soul. Material details were of the greatest importance. But still the largest strokes were made by the spirit. Had to be! People who said this were right.

Cousin Isaac's thoughts: a web of computations, of front-ages, elevations, drainage, mortgages, turn-around money. And since, in addition, he had been a strong, raunchy young man, and this had never entirely left him (it remained only as witty comment), his piety really did appear to be put on. Superadded. The Psalm-saying at building sites. *When I consider the heavens, the work of Thy fingers . . . what is Man that Thou art mindful of him?* But he evidently meant it all. He took off whole afternoons before high holidays. While his fair-faced wife, flushed with baking, noted with the slightly Biblical air he expected of her that he was bathing, changing upstairs. He had visited the graves of his parents. Announcing, "I've been to the cemetery."

"Oh," she said with sympathy, the one beautiful eye full of candor. The other fluttering with a minute quantity of slyness.

The parents, stifled in the clay. Two crates, side by side. Grass of burning green sweeping over them, and Isaac repeating a prayer to the God of Mercy. And in Hebrew with a Baltic accent at which modern Israelis scoffed. September trees, yellow after an icy night or two, now that the sky was blue and warm, gave light instead of shadow. Isaac was concerned about his parents. Down there, how were they? The wet, the cold, above all the worms worried him. In frost, his heart shrank for Aunt Rose and Uncle Braun, though as a builder he knew they were beneath the frost line. But a human power, his love, affected his practical judgment. It flew off. Perhaps as a builder and housing expert (on two of the governor's commissions, not one) he especially felt his dead to be unsheltered. But Tina—they were her dead, too—felt he was still exploiting Papa and Mama and that he would have exploited her, too, if she had let him.

For several years, at the same season, there was a scene between them. The pious thing before the Day of Atonement was to visit the dead and to forgive the living—forgive and ask forgiveness. Accordingly, Isaac went annually to the old home. Parked his Cadillac. Rang the bell, his heart beating hard. He waited at the foot of the long, enclosed staircase. The small brick building, already old in 1915 when Uncle Braun had bought it, passed to Tina, who tried to make it modern. Her ideas came out of *House Beautiful*. The paper with which she covered the slanted walls of the staircase was unsuitable. It did not matter. Tina, above, opened the door, saw the masculine figure and scarred face of her brother and said, "What do you want?"

"Tina! For God's sake, I've come to make peace."

"What peace! You swindled us out of a fortune."

"The others don't agree. Now, Tina, we are brother and sister. Remember Father and Mother. Remember . . ."

She cried down at him, "You son of a bitch, I *do* remember! Now get the hell out of here."

Banging the door, she dialed her brother Aaron, lighting

one of her long cigarettes. "He's been here again," she said. "What shit! He's not going to practice his goddamn religion on me."

She said she hated his Orthodox cringe. She could take him straight. In a deal. Or a swindle. But she couldn't bear his sentiment.

As for herself, she might smell like a woman, but she acted like a man. And in her dress, while swooning music came from the radio, she smoked her cigarette after he was gone, thundering inside with great flashes of feeling. For which, otherwise, there was no occasion. She might curse him, thought Dr. Braun, but she owed him much. Aunt Rose, who had been such a harsh poet of money, had left her daughter needs—such needs! Quiet middle-age domestic decency (husband, daughter, furnishings) did nothing for needs like hers.

So when Isaac Braun told his wife that he had visited the family graves, she knew that he had gone again to see Tina. The thing had been repeated. Isaac, with a voice and gesture that belonged to history and had no place or parallel in upstate industrial New York, appealed to his sister in the eyes of God, and in the name of souls departed, to end her anger. But she cried from the top of the stairs, "Never! You son of a bitch, never!" and he went away.

He went home for consolation, and walked to the synagogue later with an injured heart. A leader of the congregation, weighted with grief. Striking breast with fist in old-fashioned penitence. The new way was the way of understatement. Anglo-Saxon restraint. The rabbi, with his Madison Avenue public-relations airs, did not go for these European Judaic, operatic fist-clenchings. Tears. He made the cantor tone it down. But Isaac Braun, covered by his father's prayer shawl with its black stripes and shedding fringes, ground his teeth and wept near the ark.

These annual visits to Tina continued until she became sick. When she went into the hospital, Isaac phoned Dr. Braun and asked him to find out how things really stood.

"But I'm not a medical doctor."

"You're a scientist. You'll understand it better."

Anyone might have understood. She was dying of cancer of the liver. Cobalt radiation was tried. Chemotherapy. Both made her very sick. Dr. Braun told Isaac, "There is no hope."

"I know."

"Have you seen her?"

"No. I hear from Mutt."

Isaac sent word through Mutt that he wanted to come to her bedside.

Tina refused to see him.

And Mutt, with his dark sloping face, unhandsome but gentle, dog-eyed, softly urged her, "You should, Tina."

But Tina said, "No. Why should I? A Jewish deathbed scene, that's what he wants. No."

"Come, Tina."

"No," she said, even firmer. Then she added, "I hate him." As though explaining that Mutt should not expect her to give up the support of this feeling. And a little later she added, in a lower voice, as though speaking generally, "I can't help him."

But Isaac phoned Mutt daily, saying, "I have to see my sister."

"I can't get her to do it."

"You've got to explain it to her. She doesn't know what's right."

Isaac even telephoned Fenster, though, as everyone was aware, he had a low opinion of Fenster's intelligence. And Fenster answered, "She says you did us all dirt."

"I? She got scared and backed out. I had to go it alone."

"You shook us off."

Quite simple-mindedly, with the directness of the Biblical fool (this was how Isaac saw him, and Fenster knew it), he said, "You wanted it all for yourself, Isaac."

That they should let him, ungrudgingly, enjoy his great wealth, Isaac told Dr. Braun, was too much to expect. Of human beings. And he was very rich. He did not say how much money he had. This was a mystery in the family. The old people said, "He himself doesn't know."

Isaac confessed to Dr. Braun, "I never understood her." He was much moved, even then, a year later.

Cousin Tina had discovered that one need not be bound by the old rules. That, Isaac's painful longing to see his sister's face being denied, everything was put into a different sphere of advanced understanding, painful but truer than the old. From her bed she appeared to be directing this research.

"You ought to let him come," said Mutt.

"Because I'm dying?"

Mutt, plain and dark, stared at her, his black eyes momentarily vacant as he chose an answer. "People recover," he said.

But she said, with peculiar indifference to the fact, "Not this time." She had already become gaunt in the face and high in the belly. Her ankles were swelling. She had seen this in others and understood the signs.

"He calls every day," said Mutt.

She had had her nails done. A dark-red, almost maroon color. One of those odd twists of need or desire. The ring she had taken from her mother was now loose on the finger. And, reclining on the raised bed, as if she had found a moment of ease, she folded her arms and said, pressing the lace of the bed jacket with her finger tips, "Then give Isaac my message, Mutt. I'll see him, yes, but it'll cost him money."

"Money?"

"If he pays me twenty thousand dollars."

"Tina, that's not right."

"Why not! For my daughter. She'll need it."

"No, she doesn't need that kind of dough." He knew what Aunt Rose had left. "There's plenty and you know it."

"If he's got to come, that's the price of admission," she said. "Only a fraction of what he did us out of."

Mutt said simply, "He never did me out of anything." Curiously, the shrewdness of the Brauns was in his face, but he never practiced it. This was not because he had been wounded in the Pacific. He had always been like that. He sent Tina's message to Isaac on a piece of business stationery, BRAUN APPLIANCES, 42 CLINTON. Like a contract bid. No word of comment, not even a signature.

For 20 grand cash Tina says yes otherwise no.

In Dr. Braun's opinion, his Cousin Tina had seized upon the force of death to create a situation of opera. Which at the same time was a situation of parody. As he stated it to himself, there was a feedback of mockery. Death the horrid bridegroom, waiting with a consummation life had never offered. Life, accordingly, she devalued, filling up the clear light remaining (which should be reserved for beauty, miracle, nobility) with obese monstrosity, rancor, failure, self-torture.

Isaac, on the day he received Tina's terms, was scheduled to go out on the river with the governor's commission on pollution. A boat was sent by the Fish and Game Department to take the five members out on the Hudson. They would go south as far as Germantown. Where the river, with mountains on the west, seems a mile wide. And back again to Albany. Isaac would have canceled this inspection, he had so much thinking to do, was so full of things. "Overthronged" was the odd term Braun chose for it, which seemed to render Isaac's state best. But Isaac could not get out of this official excursion. His wife made him take his Panama hat and wear a light suit. He bent over the side of the boat, hands clasped tight on the dark-red, brass-jointed rail. He breathed through his teeth. At the back of his legs, in his neck, his pulses beating; and in the head an arterial swell through which he was aware, one-sidedly, of the air streaming, and gorgeous water. Two young professors from Rensselaer lectured on the geology and wildlife of the upper Hudson and on the industrial and community problems of the region. The towns were dumping raw sewage into the Mohawk and the Hudson. You could watch the flow from giant pipes. Cloacae, said the professor with his red beard and ruined teeth. Much dark metal in his mouth, pewter ridges instead of bone. And a pipe with which he pointed to the turds yellowing the river. The cities, spilling their filth. How dispose of it? Methods were discussed—treatment plants. Atomic power. And finally he presented an ingenious engineering project for sending all waste into the interior of the earth, far under the crust, thousands of feet into deeper strata. But even if pollution were stopped today, it would take fifty years to restore the river. The fish had persisted but at last abandoned their old spawning grounds. Only a savage scavenger eel dominated the water. The river great and blue in spite of the dung pools and the twisting of the eels.

One member of the governor's commission had a face remotely familiar, long and high, the mouth like a latch, cheeks hollow, the bone warped in the nose, and hair fading. Gentle. A thin person. His thoughts on Tina, Isaac had missed his name. But looking at the printed pages prepared by the staff, he saw that it was Ilkington Junior. This quiet, likable man examining him with such meaning from the white bulkhead, long trousers curling in the breeze as he held the metal rail behind him.

Evidently he knew about the $100,000.

"I think I was acquainted with your father," Isaac said, his voice very low.

"You were, indeed," said Ilkington. He was frail for his height; his skin was pulled tight, glistening on the temples, and a reddish blood lichen spread on his cheekbones. Capillaries. "The old man is well."

"Well. I'm glad."

"Yes. He's well. Very feeble. He had a bad time, you know."

"I never heard."

"Oh, yes, he invested in hotel construction in Nassau and lost his money."

"All of it?" said Isaac.

"All his legitimate money."

"I'm very sorry."

"Lucky he had a little something to fall back on."

"He did?"

"He certainly did."

"Yes, I see. That *was* lucky."

"It'll last him."

Isaac was glad to know and appreciated the kindness of

Ilkington's son in telling him. Also the man knew what the Robbstown Country Club had been worth to him, but did not grudge him, behaved with courtesy. For which Isaac, filled with thankfulness, would have liked to show gratitude. But what you showed, among these people, you showed with silence. Of which, it seemed to Isaac, he was now beginning to appreciate the wisdom. The native, different wisdom of gentiles, who had much to say but refrained. What was this Ilkington Junior? He looked into the pages again and found a paragraph of biography. Insurance executive. Various government commissions. Probably Isaac could have discussed Tina with such a man. Yes, in heaven. On earth they would never discuss a thing. Silent impressions would have to do. Incommunicable diversities, kindly but silent contact. The more they had in their heads, the less people seemed to know how to tell it.

"When you write to your father, remember me to him."

Communities along the river, said the professor, would not pay for any sort of sewage-treatment plants. The Federal Government would have to arrange it. Only fair, Isaac considered, since Internal Revenue took away to Washington billions in taxes and left small change for the locals. So they pumped the excrements into the waterways. Isaac, building along the Mohawk, had always taken this for granted. Building squalid settlements of which he was so proud. . . . Had been proud.

He stepped onto the dock when the boat tied up. The State Game Commissioner had taken an eel from the water to show the inspection party. It was writhing toward the river in swift, powerful loops, tearing its skin on the planks, its crest of fin standing. *Treph!* And slimy black, the perishing mouth open.

The breeze had dropped and the wide water stank. Isaac drove home, turning on the air conditioner of his Cadillac. His wife said, "What was it like?"

He had no answer to give.

"What are you doing about Tina?"

Again, he said nothing.

But knowing Isaac, seeing how agitated he was, she predicted that he would go down to New York City for advice. She told this later to Dr. Braun, and he saw no reason to doubt it. Clever wives can foretell. A fortunate husband will be forgiven his predictability.

Isaac had a rabbi in Williamsburg. He was Orthodox enough for that. And he did not fly. He took a compartment on the Twentieth Century when it left Albany just before daybreak. With just enough light through the dripping gray to see the river. But not the west shore. A tanker covered by smoke and cloud divided the bituminous water. Presently the mountains emerged.

They wanted to take the old crack train out of service. The carpets were filthy, the toilets stank. Slovenly waiters in the dining car. Isaac took toast and coffee, rejecting the odors of ham and bacon by expelling breath. Eating with his hat on. Racially distinct, as Dr. Braun well knew. A blood group characteristically eastern Mediterranean. The very fingerprints belonging to a distinctive family of patterns. The nose, the eyes long and full, the skin dark, slashed near the mouth by a Russian doctor in the old days. And looking out as they rushed past Rhinecliff, Isaac saw, with the familiarity of hundreds of journeys, the grand water, the thick trees—illuminated space. In the compartment, in captive leisure, shut up with the foul upholstery, the rattling door. The old arsenal, Bannerman's Island, the playful castle, yellow-green willows around it, and the water sparkling, as green as he remembered it in 1910—one of the forty million foreigners coming to America. The steel rails, as they were then, the twisting currents and the mountain round at the top, the wall of rock curving steeply into the expanding river.

From Grand Central, carrying a briefcase with all he needed in it, Isaac took the subway to his appointment. He waited in the anteroom, where the rabbi's bearded followers went in and out in long coats. Dressed in business clothes, Isaac, however, seemed no less archaic than the rest. A bare floor. Wooden seats, white stippled walls. But the windows were smeared, as though the outside did not matter. Of these

people, many were survivors of the German holocaust. The
rabbi himself had been through it as a boy. After the war, he
had lived in Holland and Belgium and studied sciences in
France. At Montpellier. Biochemistry. But he had been
called—summoned—to these spiritual duties in New York;
Isaac was not certain how this had happened. And now he
wore the full beard. In his office, sitting at a little table with a
green blotting pad, and a pen and note paper. The conversation was in the *jargón*—in Yiddish.

"Rabbi, my name is Isaac Braun."

"From Albany. Yes, I remember."

"I am the eldest of four—my sister, the youngest, the
muzínka, is dying."

"Are you sure of this?"

"Of cancer of the liver, and with a lot of pain."

"Then she is. Yes, she is dying." From the very white, full
face, the rabbi's beard grew straight and thick in rich bristles.
He was a strong, youthful man, his stout body buttoned
tightly, straining in the shiny black cloth.

"A certain thing happened soon after the war. An opportunity to buy a valuable piece of land for building. I invited my
brothers and my sister to invest with me, Rabbi. But on the
day . . ."

The rabbi listened, his white face lifted toward a corner of
the ceiling, but fully attentive, his hands pressed to the ribs,
above the waist.

"I understand. You tried to reach them that day. And you
felt abandoned."

"They deserted me, Rabbi, yes."

"But that was also your good luck. They turned their faces
from you, and this made you rich. You didn't have to share."

Isaac admitted this but added, "If it hadn't been one deal, it
would have been another."

"You were destined to be rich?"

"I was sure to be. And there were so many opportunities."

"Your sister, poor thing, is very harsh. She is wrong. She has
no ground for complaint against you."

"I am glad to hear that," said Isaac. "Glad," however, was only a word, for he was suffering.

"She is not a poor woman, your sister?"

"No, she inherited property. And her husband does pretty well. Though I suppose the long sickness costs."

"Yes, a wasting disease. But the living can only will to live. I am speaking of Jews. They wanted to annihilate us. To give our consent would have been to turn from God. But about your problem: Have you thought of your brother Aaron? He advised the others not to take the risk."

"I know."

"It was to his interest that she should be angry with you, and not with him."

"I realize that."

"He is guilty. He is sinning against you. Your other brother is a good man."

"Mutt? Yes, I know. He is decent. He barely survived the war. He was shot in the head."

"But is he still himself?"

"Yes, I believe so."

"Sometimes it takes something like that. A bullet through the head." The rabbi paused and turned his round face, the black quill beard bent on the folds of shiny cloth. And then, as Isaac told him how he went to Tina before the high holidays, he looked impatient, moving his head forward, but his eyes turning sideward. "Yes. Yes." He was certain that Isaac had done the right things. "Yes. You have the money. She grudged you. Unreasonable. But that's how it seems to her. You are a man. She is only a woman. You are a rich man."

"But, Rabbi," said Isaac, "now she is on her deathbed, and I have asked to see her."

"Yes? Well?"

"She wants money for it."

"Ah? Does she? Money?"

"Twenty thousand dollars. So that I can be let into the room."

The burly rabbi was motionless, white fingers on the

armrests of the wooden chair. "She knows she is dying, I suppose?" he said.

"Yes."

"Yes. Our Jews love deathbed jokes. I know many. Well. America has not changed everything, has it? People assume that God has a sense of humor. Such jokes made by the dying in anguish show a strong and brave soul, but skeptical. What sort of woman is your sister?"

"Stout. Large."

"I see. A fat woman. A chunk of flesh with two eyes, as they used to say. Staring at the lucky ones. Like an animal in a cage, perhaps. Separated. By sensual greed and despair. A fat child like that—people sometimes behave as though they were alone when such a child is present. So those little monster souls have a strange fate. They see people as people are when no one is looking. A gloomy vision of mankind."

Isaac respected the rabbi. Revered him, thought Dr. Braun. But perhaps he was not old-fashioned enough for him, notwithstanding the hat and beard and gabardine. He had the old tones, the manner, the burly poise, the universal calm judgment of the Jewish moral genius. Enough to satisfy anyone. But there was also something foreign about him. That is, contemporary. Now and then there was a sign of the science student, the biochemist from the south of France, from Montpellier. He would probably have spoken English with a French accent, whereas Cousin Isaac spoke like anyone else from upstate. In Yiddish they had the same dialect— White Russian. The Minsk region. The Pripet Marshes, thought Dr. Braun. And then returned to the fish hawk on the brown and chalky sycamore beside the Mohawk. Yes. Perhaps. Among these recent birds, finches, thrushes, there was Cousin Isaac with more scale than feather in his wings. A more antique type. The ruddy brown eye, the tough muscles of the jaw working under the skin. Even the scar was precious to Dr. Braun. He knew the man. Or rather, he had the longing of having known. For these people were dead. A useless love.

"You can afford the money?" the rabbi asked. And when

Isaac hesitated, he said, "I don't ask you for the figure of your fortune. It is not my concern. But could you give her the twenty thousand?"

And Isaac, looking greatly tried, said, "If I had to."

"It wouldn't make a great difference in your fortune?"

"No."

"In that case, why shouldn't you pay?"

"You think I should?"

"It's not for me to tell you to give away so much money. But you gave—you gambled—you trusted the man, the goy."

"Ilkington? That was a business risk. But Tina? So you believe I should pay?"

"Give in. I would say, judging the sister by the brother, there is no other way."

Then Isaac thanked him for his time and his opinion. He went out into the broad daylight of the street, which smelled of muck. The tedious mortar of tenements, settled out of line, the buildings sway-backed, with grime on grime, as if built of castoff shoes, not brick. The contractor observing. The ferment of sugar and roasting coffee was strong, but the summer air moved quickly in the damp under the huge machine-trampled bridge. Looking about for the subway entrance, Isaac saw instead a yellow cab with a yellow light on the crest. He first told the driver, "Grand Central," but changed his mind at the first corner and said, "Take me to the West Side Air Terminal." There was no fast train to Albany before late afternoon. He could not wait on Forty-second Street. Not today. He must have known all along that he would have to pay the money. He had come to get strength by consulting the rabbi. Old laws and wisdom on his side. But Tina from the deathbed had made too strong a move. If he refused to come across, no one could blame him. But he would feel greatly damaged. How would he live with himself? Because he made these sums easily now. Buying and selling a few city lots. Had the price been $50,000, Tina would have been saying that he would never see her again. But $20,000— the figure was a shrewd choice. And Orthodoxy had no remedy. It was entirely up to him.

Having decided to capitulate, he felt a kind of deadly recklessness. He had never been in the air before. But perhaps it was high time to fly. Everyone had lived enough. And anyway, as the cab crept through the summer lunch-time crowds on Twenty-third Street, there seemed plenty of humankind already.

On the airport bus, he opened his father's copy of the Psalms. The black Hebrew letters only gaped at him like open mouths with tongues hanging down, pointing upward, flaming but dumb. He tried—forcing. It did no good. The tunnel, the swamps, the auto skeletons, machine entrails, dumps, gulls, sketchy Newark trembling in fiery summer, held his attention minutely. As though he were not Isaac Braun but a man who took pictures. Then in the plane running with concentrated fury to take off—the power to pull away from the magnetic earth; and more: When he saw the ground tilt backward, the machine rising from the runway, he said to himself in clear internal words, "*Shema Yisroel*," Hear, O Israel, God alone is God! On the right, New York leaned gigantically seaward, and the plane with a jolt of retracted wheels turned toward the river. The Hudson green within green, and rough with tide and wind. Isaac released the breath he had been holding, but sat belted tight. Above the marvelous bridges, over clouds, sailing in atmosphere, you know better than ever that you are no angel.

The flight was short. From Albany airport, Isaac phoned his bank. He told Spinwall, with whom he did business there, that he needed $20,000 in cash. "No problem," said Spinwall. "We have it."

Isaac explained to Dr. Braun, "I have passbooks for my savings accounts in my safe-deposit box."

Probably in individual accounts of $10,000, protected by federal deposit insurance. He must have had bundles of these.

He went through the round entrance of the vault, the mammoth delicate door, circular, like the approaching moon seen by space navigators. A taxi waited as he drew the money and took him, the dollars in his briefcase, to the hospital. Then at the hospital, the hopeless flesh and melancholy festering and drug odors, the splashy flowers and wrinkled garments. In the large cage elevator that could take in whole beds, pulmotors, and laboratory machines, his eyes were fixed on the silent, beautiful Negro woman dreaming at the control as they moved slowly from lobby to mezzanine, from mezzanine to first. The two were alone, and since there was no going faster, he found himself observing her strong, handsome legs, her bust, the gold wire and glitter of her glasses, and the sensual bulge in her throat, just under the chin. In spite of himself, struck by these as he slowly rose to his sister's deathbed.

At the elevator, as the gate opened, was his brother Mutt.

"Isaac!"

"How is she?"

"Very bad."

"Well, I'm here. With the money."

Confused, Mutt did not know how to face him. He seemed frightened. Tina's power over Mutt had always been great. Though he was three or four years her senior. Isaac somewhat understood what moved him and said, "That's all right, Mutt, if I have to pay. I'm ready. On her terms."

"She may not even know."

"Take it. Say I'm here. I want to see my sister, Mutt."

Unable to look at Isaac, Mutt received the briefcase and went in to Tina. Isaac moved away from her door without glancing through the slot. Because he could not stand still, he moved down the corridor, hands clasped behind his back. Past the rank of empty wheelchairs. Repelled by these things which were made for weakness. He hated such objects, hated the stink of hospitals. He was sixty years old. He knew the route he, too, must go, and soon. But only knew, did not yet feel it. Death still was at a distance. As for handing over the money, about which Mutt was ashamed, taking part unwillingly in something unjust, grotesque—yes, it was farfetched, like things women imagined they wanted in pregnancy, hungry for peaches, or beer, or eating plaster from the walls. But as for himself, as soon as he handed over the money, he felt no more concern for it. It was nothing. He was glad to be rid of it. He could hardly understand this about himself. Once the money was given, the torment stopped. Nothing at all. The thing was done to punish, to characterize him, to convict him of something, to put him in a category. But the effect was just the opposite. What category? Where was it? If she thought it made him suffer, it did not. If she thought she understood his soul better than anyone—his poor dying sister; no, she did not.

And Dr. Braun, feeling with them this work of wit and despair, this last attempt to exchange significance, rose, stood, looking at the shafts of ice, the tatters of vapor in winter blue.

Then Tina's private nurse opened the door and beckoned to Isaac. He hurried in and stopped with a suffocated look. Her upper body was wasted and yellow. Her belly was huge with the growth, and her legs, her ankles were swollen. Her distorted feet had freed themselves from the cover. The soles like clay. The skin was tight on her skull. The hair was white. An intravenous tube was taped to her arm, and other tubes from her body into excretory jars beneath the bed. Mutt had laid the briefcase before her. It had not been unstrapped. Fleshless, hair coarse, and the meaning of her black eyes impossible to understand, she was looking at Isaac.

"Tina!"

"I wondered," she said.

"It's all there."

But she swept the briefcase from her and in a choked voice said, "No. Take it." He went to kiss her. Her free arm was lifted and tried to embrace him. She was too feeble, too drugged. He felt the bones of his obese sister. Death. The end. The grave. They were weeping. And Mutt, turning away at the foot of the bed, his mouth twisted open and the tears running from his eyes. Tina's tears were much thicker and slower.

The ring she had taken from Aunt Rose was tied to Tina's wasted finger with dental floss. She held out her hand to the nurse. It was all prearranged. The nurse cut the thread. Tina said to Isaac, "Not the money. I don't want it. You take Mama's ring."

And Dr. Braun, bitterly moved, tried to grasp what emotions were. What good were they! What were they for! And no one wanted them now. Perhaps the cold eye was better. On life, on death. But, again, the cold of the eye would be proportional to the degree of heat within. But once humankind had grasped its own idea, that it was human and human through such passions, it began to exploit, to play, to disturb for the sake of exciting disturbance, to make an uproar, a crude circus of feelings. So the Brauns wept for Tina's death. Isaac held his mother's ring in his hand. Dr. Braun, too, had tears in his eyes. Oh, these Jews—these Jews! Their feelings, their hearts! Dr. Braun often wanted nothing more than to stop all this. For what came of it? One after another you gave over your dying. One by one they went. You went. Childhood, family, friendship, love were stifled in the grave. And these tears! When you wept them from the heart, you felt you justified something, understood something. But what did you understand? Again, *nothing!* It was only an intimation of understanding. A promise that mankind might —*might*, mind you—eventually, through its gift which might— *might* again!—be a divine gift, comprehend why it lived. Why life, why death.

And again, why these particular forms—these Isaacs and these Tinas? When Dr. Braun closed his eyes, he saw, red on black, something like molecular processes—the only true heraldry of being. As later, in the close black darkness when the short day ended, he went to the dark kitchen window to have a look at stars. These things cast outward by a great begetting spasm billions of years ago.

Some other books published by Penguin
are described on the following page.

For a complete list of books available
from Penguin in the United States,
write to Dept. DG, Penguin Books,
299 Murray Hill Parkway,
East Rutherford, N.J. 07073.

In Canada for a complete list of Penguin
Books write to Penguin Books Canada Limited,
2801 John Street, Markham, Ontario, Canada L3R 1B4.

Some other volumes in The Viking
Portable Library